Cynthia Harrod-Eagles is the author of the contemporary Bill Slider Mystery series as well as the Morland Dynasty novels. Her passions are music, wine, horses, architecture and the English countryside.

Visit the author's website at www.cynthiaharrodeagles.com

The Morland Dynasty series:

DYNASTY

29

The Burning Roses

Cynthia Harrod-Eagles

sphere

SPHERE

First published in Great Britain in 2006 by Sphere
This paperback edition published in 2007 by Sphere
Reprinted 2008, 2011, 2012, 2013

Copyright © 2006 Cynthia Harrod-Eagles

The moral right of the author has been asserted.

*All characters and events in this publication, other than those
clearly in the public domain, are fictitious and any resemblance
to real persons, living or dead, is purely coincidental.*

A CIP catalogue record for this book
is available from the British Library.

ISBN 978-0-7515-3346-0

Typeset in Plantin by Palimpsest Book Production Limited,
Grangemouth, Stirlingshire
Printed and bound in Great Britain by
Clays Ltd, St Ives plc

Papers used by Sphere are from well-managed forests
and other responsible sources.

AUTHOR'S NOTE

After some consideration, I decided it might cause complications if my fictional characters joined real regiments. So while the various military actions described in this book really happened, the West Herts and South Kents are my invention. The York Commericials likewise never existed, but they are based on genuine 'Pals' units.

THE MORLANDS OF MORLAND PLACE

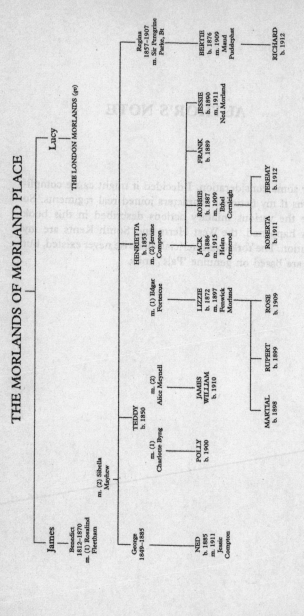

THE LONDON MORLANDS

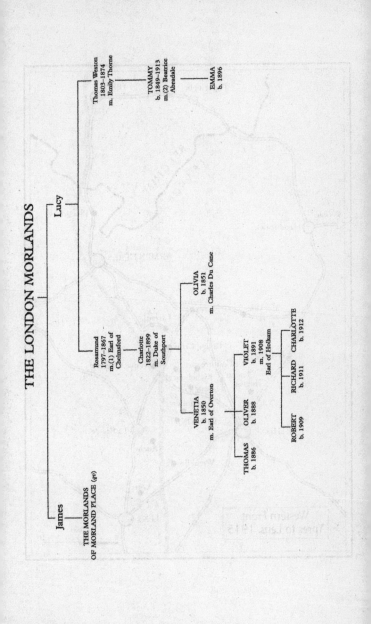

James — Lucy

THE MORLANDS
OF MORLAND PLACE (qv)

Rosamund
1797–1867
m (1) Earl of
Chelmsford

Thomas Weston
1803–1874
m. Emily Thorne

Charlotte
1822–1899
m. Duke of
Southport

TOMMY
b. 1849–1913
m.(2) Beatrice
Abradale

EMMA
b. 1896

VENETIA
b. 1850
m. Earl of Overton

OLIVIA
b. 1851
m. Charles Du Cane

THOMAS
b. 1886

OLIVER
b. 1888

VIOLET
b. 1891
m. 1908
Earl of Holkam

ROBERT
b. 1909

RICHARD
b. 1911

CHARLOTTE
b. 1912

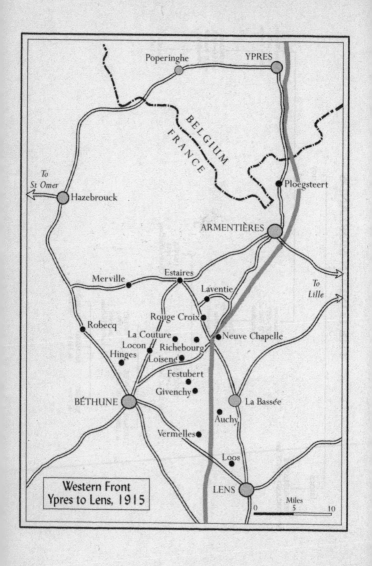

Poperinghe

YPRES

BELGIUM
FRANCE

Ploegsteert

To
St Omer

Hazebrouck

ARMENTIÈRES

To
Lille

Merville

Estaires

Laventie

Rouge Croix

Robecq

La Couture

Neuve Chapelle

Locon
Hinges

Richebourg
Loisene

Festubert

Givenchy

BÉTHUNE

La Bassée

Auchy

Vermelles

Loos

**Western Front
Ypres to Lens, 1915**

LENS

Miles
0   5   10

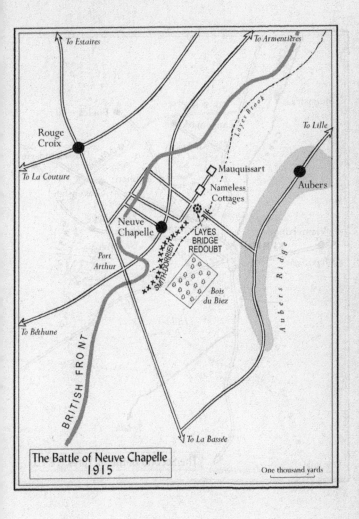

To Estaires

To Armentières

Layes Brook

Rouge Croix

To La Couture

To Lille

Mauquissart

Nameless Cottages

Aubers

Neuve Chapelle

LAYES BRIDGE REDOUBT

SMITH-DORRIEN

Port Arthur

Bois du Biez

Aubers Ridge

To Béthune

BRITISH FRONT

To La Bassée

The Battle of Neuve Chapelle
1915

One thousand yards

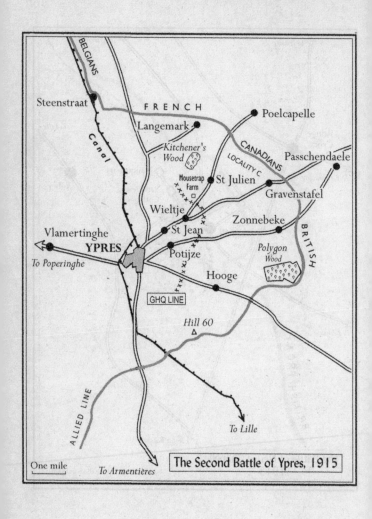

The Second Battle of Ypres, 1915

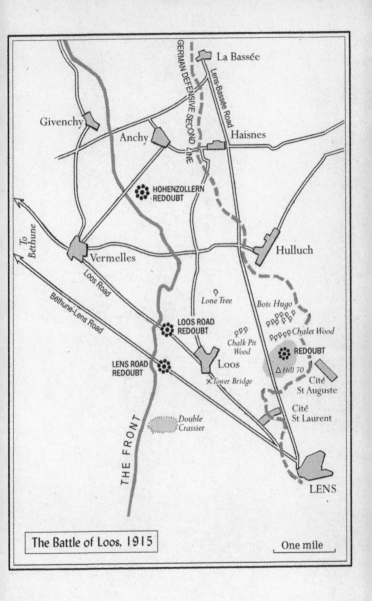

GERMAN DEFENSIVE SECOND LINE

La Bassée

Lens-Bassée Road

Givenchy

Anchy

Haisnes

HOHENZOLLERN REDOUBT

To Béthune

Vermelles

Hulluch

Loos Road

Lone Tree

Bois Hugo

Béthune-Lens Road

LOOS ROAD REDOUBT

Chalk Pit Wood

Chalet Wood

REDOUBT

Hill 70

LENS ROAD REDOUBT

Loos

Tower Bridge

Cité St Auguste

THE FRONT

Double Crassier

Cité St Laurent

LENS

The Battle of Loos, 1915

One mile

BOOK ONE

Embarkation

The gorse upon the twilit down,
The English loam so sunset brown,
The bowed pines and the sheep-bells' clamour,
The wet, lit lane and the yellow-hammer,
The orchard and the chaffinch song
Only to the Brave belong.
And he shall lose their joy for aye
If their price he cannot pay.
Who shall find them dearer far
Enriched by blood after long war

Robert Nichols, 'At the Wars'

BOOK ONE

CHAPTER ONE

February, 1915

Jessie could see that the concert was not going well. The soldiers in their suits of 'hospital blue' welcomed any diversion to ease the tedium (and often pain) of their convalescence; but glancing around the hall from her vantage-point at the side of the piano, where she was page-turner, she had noted the looks of bemusement, and the slight, uncontrollable fidgetings.

The performers who had volunteered their services were well-meaning, but their choice of material took no account of the audience's taste: their experience so far in the war had been confined to wounded officers. Besides, even if it had occurred to people like Mr Morrison and Mrs Bickersteth that the Tommies would like something different, they would not have thought they ought to get it. There was a strong element of 'improvement' in the afternoon's choice of material.

Jessie was anxious for the occasion to go well, both for the soldiers' sake and because she had invested so much of her own time and effort in it. It was the amply named Clifton Ladies' Committee for the Relief of Soldiers' Families and the Comfort of the Wounded – known for convenience as the Relief Committee – that had mooted the idea. The convalescents, lately arrived in the newly erected huts in the grounds of Clifton Hospital, plainly deserved some diversion. The idea was probably not unconnected with the fact that the rival Bootham Ladies'

3

Committee had announced that they were holding an entertainment for *their* convalescent soldiers at Bootham Park.

Mrs Upton-Haye had offered the use of Clifton Grange for the event, on condition that it was called a concert rather than an entertainment, and on the unspoken condition that it would outshine the Bootham event in every respect. This involved, to begin with, choosing a date before Bootham's, which had meant all the preparations had to be crammed into an inadequate amount of time.

Jessie's uncle Teddy – Mr Edward Morland of Morland Place, one of York's leading citizens – had been applied to, as he was for every charitable activity. With his usual willingness he had paid for the timber and supplied his estate carpenters to erect a platform at one end of the ballroom at the Grange. This was then draped and decorated with strings of Union Jacks and the red, white and blue bunting left over from the Coronation.

Jessie had been busy all morning, helping to set out Mrs Upton-Haye's rout chairs (gilded and spindly – she looked alarmed at every creak as the soldiers shifted on them) in the ballroom, and the trestles for tea in the Marble Hall. She had then ferried large quantities of food, prepared by Uncle Teddy's cook, from Morland Place, and finally helped transport the convalescents from the hospital to the concert, driving back and forth several times. It made her glad that she still had the big Arno. Her husband, Ned, absent in training camp with his Pals battalion, had wanted to change it for a little car, which he thought more suitable for Jessie than the heavy motor, but he had not yet got round to it.

Jessie was happy to be busy, not only for the worthy cause, but because it helped to keep her mind off her own troubles. She was less sure about her personal participation in the concert: Mrs Upton-Haye had persuaded her to play some Chopin, and was giving over the whole second half of the concert to it. Jessie was to be the leaven in the lump. '*So* good for the men to be exposed to something truly *cultural* for a change,' Mrs Upton-Haye had said.

4

Well, perhaps it might be good for them, but would they enjoy it? Wasn't the purpose of the concert to give the poor fellows a little pleasure?

Perhaps she was the only one who thought so. Up on the platform, Mrs Bickersteth, with seismic vibrato, had given them 'All in the April Evening' and 'Lo Hear the Gen-tel La-hark', and had finished off with 'Una Voce Poco Fa', to which her voice was sadly not equal – definitely *una voce* too far, Jessie thought to herself.

Mr Morrison, who fancied himself a tenor, had given a selection of sentimental folk songs from forty years ago, featuring young ladies with names like Pretty Peggy, Sweet Polly and Dainty Maud, who had a propensity to intense virtue and early death, which seemed somehow interlinked. He sang with an *embarras* of feeling, pressing his hands to his breast, rolling his eyes tragically and dragging out the mournful parts to such lengths that Miss Trevor from the church, accompanying him on the piano, was at a loss how to fill in the time until they joined forces again and had to insert a lot of superfluous runs and trills.

Little Billy Watts, who was only seven, gave a violin recital. Jessie had no idea what he had played, and guessed that the enthusiastic applause at the end was a tribute to the fact that he had stopped doing it.

Mr Belfield gave them 'Full Fathom Five', and then 'In the De-he-hepths of the Dee-hee-heep', a *basso profundo* song which went so low that even the most vigorous bending of his knees could not get him down far enough and he had disconcertingly to jump up the octave to finish.

Mingled with this musical cornucopia there had been a number of poetical recitals and monologues of an uplifting and deeply patriotic nature. And old Mr Wicksteed, who had been wounded as a young lieutenant at Balaclava, gave his well-known account of the Charge of the Light Brigade, made confusing for those who had not heard it before by the fact that, like Lord Raglan before him, Mr Wicksteed continually referred to the enemy as 'the French'. As he was very deaf and almost blind, it was impossible to stop him once he'd started, and he rambled on at length, his voice descending at several points to an incoherent mumble as, eyes closed, he relived those days of his glory in the privacy of his own memory.

It was no wonder, Jessie thought, that she had noted more sighs than smiles among the audience. But at last it was time for the tea interval. The men rose and rushed as fast as their various injuries would allow into the grand entrance hall where, behind the trestle tables, the Relief Committee presided over huge teapots, pitchers of milk and lemonade, mountains of sandwiches and plates of home-made cakes, buns and biscuits. There was no danger that this part of the entertainment would fail to please: hospital food was ample but dull. The Committee, in their best hats, beamed, and the men were able to thank them with honest fervour.

Those whose injuries made it hard for them to stand were accommodated on benches around the walls, and Jessie was ferrying tea and cake to them when Mrs Major Wycherley, her particular friend, arrived. Mrs Upton-Haye, who was standing near the door with her hands lightly clasped before her, surveying the fruits of her benevolence with a gracious smile, buttonholed her, and it was some moments before Mrs Wycherley could prise herself away and hurry to Jessie's side.

'Oh dear, I'm sorry I'm so late. One of the young officers had a telegram about his brother, and there was no-one but me for him to talk to. In the circumstances I could hardly rush away. I'm glad I'm in time to turn for you. But to miss the whole first half was shocking of me. How did it go?'

Jessie searched for words. 'It was – memorable.'

'Oh dear, was it that bad? Who are these two cups for?'

'There are four men over in the corner who haven't got anything. Take some cake, too. I'll bring the other two.'

'I'll wait for you,' said Mrs Wycherley. 'Wouldn't it have been easier for us and for the soldiers if they had been mugs?' She watched the wielding of a vast enamel teapot, which needed two hands to lift it. 'What enormous teapots, though. Where did they come from?'

'They're the ones we use at Morland Place when we have

6

the summer fête there. Uncle Teddy lent them. There are enamel mugs that go with them, but Mrs Upton-Haye wouldn't have them. She said that outdoor events were one thing but she couldn't bear tin mugs in the house. She insisted on cups and saucers.'

'Oh, well,' said Mrs Wycherley, who had more experience than Jessie of the vagaries of volunteers, 'it was nice of her to offer the house for the concert. And at least the saucer gives you somewhere to put the cake. That fruit cake looks nice – shall we take some of that? I expect they'd like something substantial.'

'It might take their minds off cigarettes. Mrs Upton-Haye won't let them smoke, either. Next time,' Jessie vowed, 'we hold it in the Scout Hall or the Working Men's Institute. Then they can smoke all they like.'

Mrs Wycherley laughed. 'I dare say they are glad of the change, anyway. You know how bored convalescents get, and it must be worse for the men than for the officers.' She and Jessie had been visiting wounded Belgian officers since the war began.

'But I didn't want this concert to be in the "better than nothing" category,' Jessie said, as they carried the cups over to the last four soldiers. 'Mrs Upton-Haye is going to make some closing remarks. She has a speech written out – pages of it – all about duty and sacrifice and the noble calling and so on. I'm not sure it isn't too high a price to pay for an afternoon away from the hospital. Oh, please don't get up,' she added, as they reached the men, who naturally tried to rise at the approach of ladies. 'You've just got settled. We've brought you tea and cake.'

'Can you manage?' said Mrs Wycherley. 'Let me put your stick down here for you. That's better. I'm so sorry you can't smoke.'

'Don't worry yourself, ma'am,' said one of them, looking embarrassed at being apologised to by high-ups. 'We're all right as we are.'

'It's right kind of you to lay all this on for us, mum,' said another with his leg in a cast.

7

'It's our pleasure,' said Mrs Wycherley, seriously, 'and it's very little in return for all you men are doing for us over there. Where were you injured?'

She questioned them expertly and they were soon at ease and telling their stories, even venturing a little joke or two.

'I'm afraid the concert is rather dull for you,' Jessie said at last.

'Oh, no, mum. It's ever such a nice change,' said the soldier whose left foot was missing, and whose face was drawn in lines of suffering. 'We like a bit o' music, don't we, lads?'

The others murmured agreement as fervently as natural honesty allowed.

'You were down the front, by the pianny, weren't you, miss?' said another. 'Thought I saw you.'

'Mrs Morland is going to play for you after tea,' said Mrs Wycherley, as though offering a great treat. Jessie made a face at her, more sure than ever that the Tommies wouldn't enjoy it.

'That'll be nice, mum,' said the soldier in the cast. 'What'll you be playing, if I might ask?'

'Chopin,' said Jessie, shortly.

'I don't know that one,' he said. 'Is it a song?'

'A song? No, it's—' Her face suddenly grew thoughtful. 'Excuse me one moment.' She pulled Mrs Wycherley aside and said, in an urgent undertone, 'I have to do something. Can you take over for me?'

'With the tea? Certainly.'

'I may be a little while.'

Mrs Wycherley raised her eyebrows. 'Not too long, I hope. You know I can't play the piano.'

'Oh, no, I'll be back to do my piece. But if I'm not quite in time, can you stall them?'

Mrs Wycherley asked no more questions. 'Of course, dear. I'll think of something. You'd better try to get out without Mrs Upton-Haye seeing you, though, or she might bar the door.'

Jessie gave her a distracted smile and hurried away.

8

She had not returned by the time the men filed back into the ballroom, and Mrs Wycherley drifted down to the front to be ready to intervene if necessary. But fortunately Mrs Upton-Haye opened the second half with a lengthy list of individual thanks to those who had made the occasion possible, and then asked the vicar to make a few remarks. He was still making them when Jessie came tiptoeing down the side aisle with a folder of music under her arm.

Reaching Mrs Wycherley, she whispered, 'Am I late?'

'No. Nothing but the vicar has happened yet. I think he's attempting to give the longest sermon in history.'

Fortunately the sight of two ladies whispering made him lose his thread, and he was forced to go early to his concluding prayer. At the 'amen' Jessie headed for the piano, and Mrs Wycherley stood beside her to turn. Jessie put the folder on the top, selected a piece of music, put it on the stand, and as Mrs Wycherley's eyebrows went up in surprise, she faced the audience, now politely hushed, and said, 'I have an announcement to make. I was asked to play you some music by Chopin, but during the tea interval I had second thoughts about it, and I decided you might enjoy this more.'

She sat down, and began to play 'Tipperary'. Because she was reading the music she didn't see, as Mrs Wycherley did, the instant brightening of faces all over the room, but she heard the enthusiasm with which the men joined in the chorus, and there was no doubt about the storm of applause that broke when the song was ended. Mrs Upton-Haye, sitting in the front row beside the vicar, glared and fidgeted, but as the vicar himself joined in the last chorus, she did not feel she could go over and remonstrate; nor could she take Mrs Ned Morland off, since there was nothing else arranged that could take her place. Seething inwardly, she was forced to smile coldly and let her continue.

Jessie played more popular 'numbers', like 'Boys in Khaki, Boys in Blue' and 'Sister Susie Sewing Shirts for Soldiers'. Her voice, though true, was too small to fill a hall; but fortunately Mrs Wycherley could sing, and had a strong voice.

She took over the verses, facing the audience so that she could encourage the men to roar the choruses. Later, in a spirit of pure mischief, Jessie put up 'Aba Daba Honeymoon', which the men adored but which made Mrs Upton-Haye reel in shock at the vulgarity, then 'Ragtime Soldier Man', and as a finale thumped out 'I Like Pickled Onions', which almost made the hostess faint dead away. The men enjoyed that one so much they roared through it twice and then applauded, stamped and whistled their approval. At Mrs Wycherley's urging, Jessie stood, pink-faced with pleasure, to take a bow.

Mrs Upton-Haye hurried up onto the platform to terminate the proceedings before they could plumb any greater depths, and in her agitation quite forgot her speech, so the afternoon ended for the men without a damper.

'You sly thing!' said Mrs Wycherley as Jessie put the music back in the folder. 'Where did you get all this?'

'I drove back to Morland Place for it. My sister-in-law, Ethel, has all the new songs. My brother Robbie buys her everything as soon as it comes out. I couldn't bear the idea of making those poor men sit through Chopin.'

'They might have liked it,' Mrs Wycherley suggested.

'Not the way I play it,' Jessie laughed.

'Oh, Lord, Mrs Upton-Haye is trying to come this way. Fortunately the vicar has her pinned. We'd better hurry, before she can wriggle free.'

They walked quickly up the aisle, threading through the departing soldiers, who gladly made way for them, with grateful grins and nods when they saw who it was. 'Was she very annoyed?' Jessie asked.

'I thought she would explode in "Ragtime Soldier Man", when we got to the bit that says, "As long as I can run/They'll never find me/They'll be behind me". It didn't really fit in with the patriotic tone of the entertainment. And then, my dear, the *vulgarity* of the pickled-onion song!'

Jessie grinned. 'It's a pity she didn't let me do some encores. I have "Snookey Ookums" in here, and "Monkey Doodle Doo". I'd have loved her to hear those.'

10

'And I'd have loved to see her face,' Mrs Wycherley said, laughing.

Jessie left the hall elated, but reaction set in as she drove the short distance home to Maystone Villa, her nice little square stone house on the Clifton Road. Darkness had long fallen and the dank February chill made the bare trees that loomed into her headlights look dreary. The wind pressing past the motor's windows bothered her. In the first days after she had lost the baby, while she was being cared for by her mother at Morland Place, she had been haunted by a sound like a baby crying. Sometimes, since she had come back to Maystone, she heard it again, at nights, when the wind was in the chimney. The sound made her ache with a misery like a physical pain. Her baby had never cried. It had been dead in her womb, Dr Hasty said, which was why she had miscarried. She shivered. Even inside the motor, her heavy coat wasn't enough to keep out the deadly cold. It looked and smelt to her as though it might snow tonight or tomorrow.

Home at last. As she crunched over the gravel Gladding, the stableman/gardener, emerged unwillingly to put the motor away – the only task concerning it that he would undertake. Jessie even had to get a Boy Scout to clean it, for Gladding said he only groomed horses: 'Ah don't 'ave to do wi' them smelly things. The devil's work, they are, and Ah'll not encourage 'em.' He even grumbled under his breath now as he held the door for her; but then the front door of the house opened and a warm body dashed out and flung itself at her with a gladness that raised her spirits. Brach, her Morland hound bitch, always behaved as if every parting, however short, had been a lifetime long.

Jessie caressed the big, harsh-haired body as it revolved round her with cat-like fluidity, and winced as the iron bar of a tail lashed at her knees. 'Oh, foolish, foolish girl. Yes, I missed you too!'

In the yellow slice of light at the doorway Tomlinson had appeared and was smiling a welcome. Tomlinson had been

11

her lady's maid, and was now effectively housekeeper in the depleted household, but after so many years she was a friend, too.

'Did it go well, madam?' she asked, as Jessie came towards her with Brach still twirling and trying to trip her up.

'It got better towards the end,' Jessie said. 'I think the men enjoyed it.'

'Supper's ready any time you want it,' said Tomlinson, studying her face. 'You look tired. A glass of wine would do you good.'

'That would be nice,' Jessie agreed. 'But first I must go and see the horses. Will you take this in?' She handed her the folder of music. 'And remind me to take it back to Mrs Robert tomorrow.'

Tomlinson looked a mild query. 'Take the music back to Mrs Robert?'

'I didn't play the Chopin after all.' And she turned away towards the stable.

Tomlinson opened the folder and looked at the first sheet. 'Ragtime,' she murmured, and smiled. It was good to see her lady getting back a bit of spirit. But she did look tired. It was easy to overdo things when you'd recently had a miscarriage. She must make sure she rested properly tomorrow – even if she had to tie her to the sofa.

Jessie stopped on the way in the feed-room to pick up a couple of handfuls of horse-nuts, and then went into the stable. There were only four horses in residence at the moment, and until two weeks ago there hadn't been any, which hadn't made Gladding complain any less about his work. Jessie had stopped riding altogether while she was pregnant – not that it had mattered in the end, she thought bitterly. She might just as well have enjoyed herself for all the difference it made. During that time her darling Hotspur, the black gelding who had been given to her by her beloved late father, had been turned out – though she had gone to visit him in his field most days. He came forward eagerly now to greet her, knuckering softly and lowering his head for her caresses.

'I'm sorry I haven't been able to take you out today,

darling,' she told him. He lipped up the nuts from her palm and nodded appreciatively. 'I hope Gladding exercised you properly.' Hotspur made another deep chuckling sound and stamped a foot. It often seemed to Jessie that he tried to join in conversations with her. 'We'll have a long ride tomorrow, I promise.' He nuzzled her hair, and then lowered his nose to blow at Brach, who licked his muzzle in response. They were old friends.

The other occupied boxes contained the two Bhutia mares, Mouse and Minna – Jessie had broken them to harness and they pulled the phaeton and the trap – and the new young mare she had brought up to school. Vesper was a two-year-old, and Jessie was bringing her on as an eventual replacement for Hotspur when he grew too old. That was assuming the army did not take her, as they had taken Jessie's hunters. Gladding was strictly forbidden to ride Vesper, and gave her led exercise only, when Jessie was too busy to take her out. It was not a satisfactory arrangement, and another reason why Jessie hated the mean old man whose delight seemed to be to make everyone around him miserable. Why couldn't she have a nice groom, and one who wouldn't spoil young horses?

She stayed a long time with the horses – so long that Brach lay down in the straw and set her nose on her paws – conscious of an unwillingness to go back to the house. It seemed so empty now, with Ned away (and no new baby in the room Tomlinson had been going to make into the nursery). She did not, of course, entertain without him, so it hardly mattered that she was down to only three indoor staff: Tomlinson, and the housemaids, Peggy and Susie. She hadn't even had a cook since Mrs Peck left – but Peggy could cook well enough for her alone.

But a house without a man in it seemed an oddly disjointed thing, an entity that had lost its purpose. It made her realise how often, not only at Maystone but in all the households she knew, things were always done a certain way, or never done at all, because 'the master liked it that way'. Mealtimes were set for his convenience; the choice of menu

13

reflected his tastes; the routines, the cleaning rotas, the lighting of fires, the very placing of the ornaments and which side of the door the umbrella stand was sited – all the details of daily life were arranged round the man of the house.

Ned was at training camp up on Black Brow with the York Commercials – the Pals battalion Uncle Teddy had helped to bring into being – and when the battalion was ready, it would go overseas, perhaps to France; so he would not occupy his house, except for brief periods of leave, until the war was over. And how long would that be? Her cousin Bertie had said from the beginning that it would not 'all be over by Christmas', as people had claimed. Bertie had said it would be three or four years, and though that had seemed impossible in the heady excitement of August 1914, it was beginning now to seem horribly likely. The terrible weeks-long battle of Ypres had been a victory, but with nothing gained, except that the line had not been broken. The German attack had been repulsed; but the price had been so dreadfully high. The British Expeditionary Force had virtually ceased to exist. Bertie's battalion, which had gone to France twelve hundred strong, had been reduced to 108 men and three officers.

No, it seemed likely now that it would not soon be over. Women like her – thousands, all over the country – would have to get used to living without men in their households. They would have to find other things to fill their days, and other ways to organise their routines.

Brach suddenly sat up, ears pricked, and whined. Then she stood and stared up at Jessie with urgency, pawing her leg. Her kind could not bark, but she had her own ways of communicating. 'What is it, girl?' Jessie asked, and turned her head to listen. The sound of tyres on the gravel. Not motor tyres, but the thin tandem sound of bicycle wheels. Her mind flew to the obvious conclusion – a telegram? But who would contact her urgently at this time of night? It couldn't be Morland Place, because they would have telephoned. She had a husband, two brothers and two cousins all in uniform, but Ned, brother Frank and cousin Lenny

14

Manning were all still in training, and Jack, her favourite brother, who was in the RFC, had been shot down in November and his injuries would prevent his return to active service for some months yet. Only Bertie was at the front. But an 'official' telegram about Bertie would not come to her, it would go to his wife, Maud; and Maud would not telegraph her.

While she was thinking these things she had been hurrying out of the stables and towards the house, and was in time to see the telegraph boy climbing back onto his bicycle out in the road. Tomlinson was standing at the front door holding the envelope; Peggy and Susie lurked behind her at the end of the hall. Already, in a manless household, a telegram had become an event.

'Oh, madam, I was just going to come and find you.'

'It's all right, I heard the wheels.'

'It's addressed to you, not the master,' Tomlinson said, handing over the envelope.

She opened it where she stood, unable to bear even the delay of going indoors, however undignified that might seem to the servants. Then she smiled.

'Coming home short leave Tuesday stop,' she read aloud. 'Please meet 5.55 p.m. train stop. Signed, E. Morland.'

'But it's after six now,' Tomlinson said. She looked over her shoulder at the hall clock. 'It's nearly half past!'

'This was sent this morning,' Jessie said. 'It must have got mislaid.'

'It's a disgrace,' Tomlinson said indignantly. 'You pay enough for a telegram! Something should be said to that postmaster.'

'Yes, but not this minute. I shall have to go to the station as I am. Run and tell Gladding to get the motor out again, will you?'

But even as she said it there was the sound of an engine out in the road and a taxi-cab clattered into the drive and pulled up. Brach flattened her ears and sang, almost dancing on the spot in her excitement, as the door opened and a figure muffled in army greatcoat and cap stepped out.

'He must have got tired of waiting,' Jessie said.

The master had come home.

It seemed to Jessie that the house had come alive again. There was movement, bustle; there were lights all over the house, the sound of men's voices – Ned had brought his servant Daltry, who had been his manservant before the war and had followed him into the army. Daltry seemed to be everywhere: taking Ned's bag to his dressing-room, supervising the lighting of the dining-room fire – Susie was on her knees before it with a sheet of newspaper – laughing in the kitchen with the maids as they hurried to transform Jessie's supper into a proper dinner, fetching up wine to go with it. He had taken off his khaki jacket right away and donned his black apron, and now was rubbing up the silver and laying the table. His presence had had a visible effect on the female servants, in the way they held themselves, moved, the way they turned their heads, laughed. The men meant extra work for them, but they didn't mind. It had given them purpose again.

Brach trotted busily back and forth, from room to room, from person to person, the ticking sound of her nails on the hall floor each time she crossed a small poignant background that Jessie heard out of all proportion to its volume or importance, as at times of great emotion one will notice tiny irrelevant details. Brach thrust her nose into everything, stared up into faces, smiled, waved her tail, trying to understand, trying to fit these new, familiar people into their old places in her mind's pattern.

Jessie thought she knew how the dog felt. She herself was bemused, seemed to be standing outside herself, watching, though she heard her own voice from time to time answering questions and commenting. Daltry had stepped back into his former role as manservant/footman/butler so easily that even his uniform breeches and puttees under his apron did not make him seem strange – only, as the maids' flutterings attested, a little more exciting.

But Ned had become a stranger, and not only to her

16

but also, obviously, to himself. He seemed ill at ease in his own house, kept starting to do something and then distracting himself. He spoke to Jessie disjointedly: his mind was evidently still at camp, for he began to talk about things concerned with it, as if he were talking to Daltry, and then remembered: 'Oh, but of course you won't know about that,' or 'Foolish of me – that won't mean anything to you.'

She bore with it patiently, following him about so as to be there to be spoken to. She stared and stared at him, trying, like Brach, to rediscover him. But he seemed nothing like the nice Cousin Ned she had grown up with, still less like the husband he had later become. He *looked* different: too clearly drawn, all hard edges and sharp definitions. Passing the dining-room at one moment she had seen Daltry draw off the baize table-cover and reveal the hard and shining wood underneath. It was like that with Ned, as though all his life so far he had worn a soft, muffling cover that had now been stripped away. She did not know this man, his look, his voice; she did not know what he might be thinking. When she had kissed him on arrival he even smelt different. A stranger had walked into her house masquerading as her husband, and she did not know how to react to him – except, like Brach, to keep smiling and wagging her tail. She stared at him to try to rediscover him, but when he looked at her she found her eyes sliding away from direct contact, with an odd kind of shyness.

Daltry rounded them up and drove them gently into the drawing-room to serve them sherry. The fire was bright here, for it had been lit earlier, for her evening alone. On the small oval table at the end the single cover had been laid for her supper, and Daltry whisked across with a tut to remove it. Ned's eyes followed the movement, then returned enquiringly to Jessie.

'I've been eating in here,' she said. 'It saves on lighting fires – and the dining-room is too big for one to eat alone.'

'Oh, Jessie, I'm sorry,' he said. He seemed unduly troubled by this.

'Why should you be? The war isn't your fault. Goodness, I expect it's much worse up at Black Brow. You must have had to give up all sorts of things.'

'Well, not really. As far as the mess goes, we're pretty comfortable. There's an excellent cook, a good cellar, fine cigars, port and brandy, all the newspapers. The colonel saw to all that.'

'Dear old Colonel Hound!' Jessie exclaimed eagerly, glad of a point of contact, of something she actually knew about. Colonel Bassett, fondly known as Hound, was an old friend of Major and Mrs Wycherley.

'He says, "Any fool can be uncomfortable." And he says, "Good food fuels a good campaign." He has lots of sayings like that. He likes mess standards to be kept up, too. We have to dress and so on – no shoddiness.'

'I haven't been dressing,' she said apologetically. She was still in her daytime suit from the concert. 'Should I—?'

'Oh! No – really – it doesn't matter. I can't change anyway. I've only a clean shirt for the morning with me.' Their eyes met at last and he smiled stiffly. 'You look beautiful to me in anything.'

She couldn't sustain the contact and stared down at her sherry glass. 'What's it like up there? Cold, I expect.'

'Terribly cold,' he said. Brach came and laid her head on his knee and he stroked it. A dog could be a great comfort at moments of awkwardness. There was never any difficulty about showing your love to a dog. 'But we're getting hardened to it. It doesn't trouble us as much as it did at first, and it wasn't nearly as cold then. The men are snug enough, with those wood-burning stoves in the huts. Better off than us, really – our bedroom fireplaces are so small they hardly have any effect. I don't suppose when the mining company built the bungalows they ever thought people would stay there in the middle of winter.'

'Has it snowed yet?'

'Only a sprinkling or two. But if we get anything heavy, Hound says we may have to move. Already it's getting too hard to dig.'

18

'Dig?'

'It's what we do most of. Digging trenches and marching. Lots of marching. The men are getting awfully fed up. But they're good fellows. They just want to be off to the war. Once we get our rifles, they'll be happy. That will be the sign that we're really on our way. They're afraid the whole show will be over before they've had a chance to have a biff at the Bosch.'

He spoke differently, too, she thought – used different language. 'Awfully fed up'; 'show'; 'biff'. It didn't sound like him. But, of course, his language would have to have changed, since his whole life had changed. 'Where will you be sent?' she asked.

'Oh, goodness knows. There's a new rumour every week – practically every day. Egypt, Malta, the Sudan, France. The men all hope for France, of course. But nothing can happen until we get our rifles. They're supposed to be arriving every week, but they never turn up.'

He lapsed into silence, his eyes on the flames, deep in thought. His stroking hand stopped, and Brach sighed and took her great head over to Jessie's lap instead.

Daltry came in to announce that dinner was ready. So he had known, Jessie thought, that they would not be changing. She met his eyes as she went past. That was easy, compared with Ned. Daltry was only more like himself: himself emphasised. One of his eyebrows flickered in some kind of message to her, but she could not think what it might be – except that it seemed sympathetic, and comforted her a little.

Safely separated by the dining-table – Daltry had put them face to face at one end – and with eating and drinking to occupy them, it was easier to talk. Ned came at last to the point of his visit.

'You haven't asked why I'm here,' he said, spooning soup. It was pea, the same that Jessie had had at luncheon the day before – probably what she would have had tomorrow, too – but made more interesting by the addition of shavings of ham and little marrow balls.

19

'I – I hadn't thought about it,' Jessie said, dragging her mind back. 'It was all so sudden. Your telegram said you had leave.'

'Yes, but didn't you think it was odd I should have leave again so soon?'

He had been home for a week in December when she lost the baby. She didn't like to be reminded of that. She looked at her plate and said, 'It didn't occur to me. I don't understand the ways of the army.'

'And you an officer's wife!' he chided, trying for a joke. 'You'll have to learn about the ways of the army sooner or later.'

'I suppose so.' Ned and Bertie and Frank and Lenny – Jack too. Did he think he needed to tell her that?

Ned finished his soup and laid down his spoon. He had thought coming home would be easy; he had not expected to feel so out of place, so much an alien. The shapes and sizes of everything were all wrong to his eyes, used to the wild open space of Black Brow, the huts, the bungalows. The house seemed cramped and confining; the silence behind everything, when he was used to being in shouting distance of a thousand men with their continuous bustle, was disconcerting. He had dreamt of Jessie and longed for her, but he could not get hold of her now she was here. She wasn't in khaki, she wasn't a soldier, square and hard and brown: she was soft and pale and silent and mysterious. He had longed for this every day since he had left, and now all he wanted was to run away back to camp.

Daltry removed the plates and brought the fish. It was tinned herrings, with pickled French beans from the store-cupboard, decorated with radishes cut into roses. Jessie was amused at the ingenuity, and looked forward to the rest of the meal with intellectual interest, if not with appetite.

Ned drank some wine and began to eat, hardly noticing what was on his fork. As a soldier he was hungrier and less discriminating than before the war. 'At all events,' he tried again, 'this is a special leave, which the Hound granted me for a special purpose.'

20

Jessie said nothing. She was unwilling to ask him what the special purpose was, in case it turned out to be her.

Ned was forced to go on unencouraged. 'The thing is – Jessie—' He said her name to make her look at him. 'The thing is that the government is taking over the factory.'

'The mill?' she said in surprise.

'Yes. They're requisitioning it. And as there will be a lot of things to arrange, the Hound allowed me special leave.'

'But what does it mean, requisitioning it?'

'Much the same as when they requisitioned your horses, except, of course, that I'll get the mill back eventually. In the mean time, they'll pay me a small amount for the use of it.'

'How small?' she asked sharply, beginning to realise what might be coming.

'Small enough. You remember when they took your hunters, and paid you seventy-five pounds each for them?'

'Yes – and if I'd ever wanted to sell them, which I didn't, I'd have got three hundred and fifty at least.'

'Well, there you are, then,' said Ned. He made as if to eat a radish, then put down his knife and fork. 'It's going to mean a difference to us. It's going to mean we're less well off than before.'

'You mean we'll be poor?'

'Not poor, exactly, but there won't be anything spare for luxuries. It won't matter to me, because I shall be in the army until the war is over, so I'm – provided for, if you like.'

'Three meals a day and a roof over your head,' she said, with a faint smile.

'Exactly. Of course, there's uniform, and mess bills, and other things to pay for, but I shall have the essentials, and the luxuries I can cut down on if I have to. But for you – well, I don't want you to have to alter your way of life. I don't want you to have to do without.'

'I dare say everyone will have to give up something. Why should I be any different?'

'Because you're my wife, and it's my duty to keep you in

21

the style to which you are accustomed.' He chewed his lip, as if coming to the hard part. 'This house, Jess – it's expensive to keep up. And, really, don't you think it's too big for you? Apart from saving money, if you moved into something smaller you might be more comfortable – don't you think?'

She scanned his face. 'Just be honest with me. We can't afford this house any more, and we have to give it up – is that what you're saying?'

He nodded unwillingly. 'I wish it could be otherwise. I know it's your home—'

'*Our* home.'

'Our home, that's what I meant. But if we give it up I can still support you decently. I don't want you to have to scrimp. If I can install you in a small place for the rest of the war, then when it's over, when I come home, we can find a proper house. We might even be able to get this one back again.'

'Do you think you can get rid of the lease?'

'Pickering's sure he can. I think he has someone in mind.' Pickering was his father Teddy's land agent at Morland Place.

'You've already talked about it?'

'I made enquiries. Naturally.'

'Naturally,' she said. She was, naturally, the last to know. That was how the world was arranged. 'What about the servants?'

'If you move to a smaller place, I can afford Tomlinson and one of the maids. Whoever does your cooking, I suppose.'

'That's Peggy.'

'The other one will easily get a place. Everyone's short of servants.'

'And Gladding?'

'I will personally take great pleasure in giving Gladding his notice,' said Ned, grimly – oh, this was a new, forceful Ned! 'You can keep your horses at Twelvetrees. And I'll sell the Arno and buy you a little car to run around in. I wouldn't want you to have to give up your hospital visiting and such-like. Hoggett at the garage thinks he knows someone who'd like the Arno, and he'll easily get a little thing that will do for you.'

'You've spoken to Hoggett, too,' she said, staring into her glass.

'I've tried to think of everything,' he said, part proud, part anxious. He studied her, trying to gauge her reaction. Daltry drifted in and removed the fish plates, glancing under his eyebrows at their faces. He brought in the entrée – just cold beef, Jessie noticed, from Monday night's joint (she had been at Morland Place on Sunday) but there was hot gravy sauce with it, and potatoes, leeks, stewed mushrooms (dried, from the storecupboard again) with onions, and purple broccoli. Peggy and Tomlinson handed the vegetables – wartime had already meant that the old Morland rule of only male servants waiting at table had had to be modified – and then they all withdrew and left Ned and Jessie alone.

'So,' Ned said, as soon as the door closed, eager now to have it done, 'what do you think?'

'It doesn't sound as though I have a choice,' she said; and then, thinking that sounded petulant, added, 'Everyone has to make sacrifices in wartime.'

'There is an alternative,' said Ned. She looked up, and saw it in his face before he said it. 'You could go back to Morland Place. Father would be more than glad to have you.'

'Yes,' said Jessie. It was not just a form of words, as she knew: Uncle Teddy loved nothing more than to have his family around him. Her brother Rob and his wife and children lived there, as well as Jessie's mother, and Uncle Teddy had almost broken his heart when Jessie and Ned had told him they wanted their own house when they got married. He would be delighted to have Jessie back.

'It's what I'd prefer for you,' Ned said anxiously, 'if you don't mind it. I'd like to think of you there, with company around you, and people to look after you, rather than all

23

alone in a strange house. It makes more sense to me. I can come to you there if – when – I have leave. And meanwhile you'll be with the family.'

'Yes,' said Jessie. She'd be able to keep an eye on her mother, too – she had thought she looked tired lately, and was sure she was doing too much. She could have her horses there, and be just as convenient for everything in and around York if she had a little car. And Uncle Teddy's chauffeur, Simmonds, would be on hand to look after it, which was a distinct advantage. 'It does seem more sensible than keeping up a separate place when you're away.'

'As long as – well, as long as you can bear it.'

'Bear it?'

'All the children – babies – you know.'

Ah, yes, there was that. Ethel was heavily pregnant now, due to deliver in a few weeks. And up in the nursery there were Ethel and Robbie's other children, Roberta and Jeremy, and Uncle Teddy's little boy James. So much fecundity, so many reproaches to Jessie's failure! She and Ned had been married four years, but she had managed only one false alarm and two miscarriages. And he so wanted children. She closed her face to him, pushed down the feelings. 'Why should I mind it?' she said lightly. 'I love the children. They make the house lively.'

He looked both doubtful and relieved. 'When the war's over,' he said, 'and things are back to normal, we'll have a fine house, I promise you.'

So it was decided, she thought. He had decided that way before he ever opened the subject – hers was simply to agree. But perhaps the financial situation was worse than he wanted her to know. And it *did* make more sense than running a separate establishment.

He talked on about other arrangements – storing furniture, selling things they didn't want, moving house, the servants – while they finished the beef and were served apple pie with thick Morland Place cream, and toyed with cheese and port. Then they retired to the drawing-room and Daltry brought them coffee, and Ned, in response to Jessie's

24

prompting, told stories about life in camp and the 'other fellows', which, while they sometimes started out with promise, all descended into pointlessness because of their esoteric nature. He fell back on describing inter-company football and rugby matches and officers' shooting competitions. And then it was time for bed.

As soon as Tomlinson had undone her, Jessie sent her away and hurried into her nightdress and dressing-gown before Ned could come back from his dressing-room. He found her brushing her hair at the dressing-table, a ceremony he had always loved to watch. It had often been an erotic forerunner of passion. But as he approached her from behind to put out a hand to her hair, her eyes flinched away from his in the glass and she got up quickly and moved to the bed.

'I'm very tired,' she said. 'And you must be too. Put the light out and come to bed.'

For the life of him, he didn't know if this was an invitation or a rejection. With her back to him she shed her dressing-gown and climbed up into the bed, pulling the covers up to her neck. He turned out the lights and felt his way to bed in the darkness; then lay on his back, not touching her, listening to her breathing, trying to gauge her thoughts. Up at Black Brow, in his narrow, cold bed in his bare, chilly room, he had thought of her every night. He had imagined her, soft, curved, warm, curled in the downy nest of their bed at home, imagined himself with her, drawing her to him, lying folded in sleep with her in their ship of the night, sailing the dark waters together. In his dreams, in his imaginings, there was no difficulty anywhere, no difference between them, no distance; they came together with the ease of familiarity and the warmth of love.

But now he felt himself a stranger in her bed. What did she want of him? Should he touch her or not? He had last seen her just after the miscarriage, when she had been inconsolable and he – well, it made him hot with shame to think of it, but in his grief and anxiety for her he had been angry;

25

he feared he had blamed her, accused her. Did she remember that? Did she bear a grudge? How unhappy was she still? Could he comfort her, or only make things worse? What was the state of her body? *Was it too soon?* He had thought, marrying Jessie, that everything after that would be easy. Winning her was the hard part: once she had said yes, they would fly through life effortlessly, arms linked, happy, of one mind. So he had imagined. He had not suspected there could be such agonies of doubt and incomprehension.

Jessie lay rigid, staring at the ceiling, wondering what was to happen. She had got into bed with a stranger, and she was afraid. In their marriage they had frequently pulled in opposite directions, had often argued and sometimes quarrelled, but in bed they had always met in passion, and its clean fire had burnt away all difficulties. She had always loved being made love to by him, loved the feeling of his body and the touch of his lips, gloried in his desire for her, which brought him to trembling in her arms.

But not now. Now her body had turned traitor. It was cold and empty. Her senses seemed numb. She could find no spark of desire in herself for him. She didn't want him to touch her, especially in *that* way. The thought of his entering her filled her with dread. Was it just the miscarriage? Was it just a temporary trouble? Or had something broken inside her, so that she would never feel that way again? She knew that he wanted her – she could feel the heat and hardness of his arousal even though it was not touching her. She felt that as a good wife, a soldier's wife, she should give him what he wanted, especially as there was so little time and she did not know when she might see him again. But she didn't want him to do it. She felt frightened and repelled, and lonely and lost.

He turned on his side, facing her, and laid a hand on her shoulder, feeling her flinch at the touch. He removed the hand. 'There's something else I have to tell you,' he said.

It was a long time before her voice came out of the darkness, faint as though she were a long way off. 'What is it?'

'I might be leaving the battalion.'

The words made no sort of sense to her in her rigid state of fear, and she could only say, 'Oh?'

'They're so short of officers, you see, that they are talking about taking officers from the Kitchener battalions that aren't ready, and attaching them to the units that are going to the Front. The Hound talked to me last week and asked if I'd be willing to go, if they wanted me. Well, of course, you have to go where you're sent in the army, but he said all the service battalion COs had been asked to put forward names of officers they thought suitable, who would be willing to transfer. He said a lot of COs were sending returns saying none of their officers was suitable, so as not to lose them, but he didn't think that was right. We've a war to fight, after all. And – well – I said I would go. So you see, I may be sent to the Front sooner than we thought.'

'To the Front?' She sounded a thousand miles away.

'I'm glad, really. This waiting gets on everyone's nerves. All the fellows want to go, but even when we finally get our rifles, the chances are we'll be sent to Egypt or the Sudan, on garrison duty to release the regulars. I shall miss the fellows, but this way I'll get to serve where it will really make a difference. You do see?'

'Yes, I do see,' she whispered. His hand, hot and heavy, touched her shoulder again, and she forced herself not to shrink away. He stroked her neck with a finger for a moment, and then caressed her hair, but when the hand drifted towards her breast she cried out, 'I can't! Oh, please, I can't!'

He had felt how rigid she was, had hoped that his hand might soothe her. Now he withdrew it, and said, 'It's all right.'

'I'm sorry,' she said, and her voice sounded like a sob.

'No, I'm sorry. It's too soon. I shouldn't have. I'm a selfish beast – oh, Jess, don't cry. I didn't mean to make you cry.'

'I'm not crying,' she gasped, and it was true. She was shaking and trembling with reaction – rather like those shivering fits she had had after the miscarriage. 'I'm cold. So cold,' she whimpered.

27

'Let me hold you,' he said softly. 'Just that. I promise, I promise I won't do anything. Just let me hold you and make you warm.' Slowly, carefully, he gathered her against him, and held her softly and in silence until the shaking stopped and he felt her begin to relax. 'Jess, I'm sorry. I didn't think. It's much too soon. Forgive me.'

'There's nothing to forgive,' she said, muffled by his chest.

He pressed her a little closer. 'I love you so,' he whispered.

After a long time, she said, 'Yes.' But that was all.

They rose early the next morning, unrested, both of them sad. He had to go to the mill, to make arrangements for the requisition. 'I shall be there, and at the solicitor's, all day. I wish I could spend more time with you, but it just isn't possible. And I shall have to go back to camp tonight, so I shan't see you again. I'm so sorry.'

'I'm sorry too,' she said. 'It was – such a short visit.'

'It was Hound's kindness that we even had this time. It could have been just to York and back in the day, and then I wouldn't have seen you at all.'

She dressed quickly while he was in the bathroom and went down to arrange breakfast. 'You didn't have to get up with me,' he said.

'I want to drive you in to York,' she said. 'Please let me.'

'If you want to – I'd like it,' he said, almost shyly.

She forced a smile. 'You've hardly ever let me drive you. "The Arno's too heavy for a woman,"' she quoted him.

'We'll get you a little car. I'll write to Hoggett.'

'Don't bother, I can speak to him myself.'

But he had not been gone long enough to allow that. 'I'll do it, dear. You shouldn't be bothered with things like that.'

Outside it was horribly cold, the sky like an iron lid over the earth, the first fine specks of snow already sifting down. Daltry, with grim enjoyment, had forced Gladding to get the motor out, start the engine and scrape off the ice, so it was ready for them when it was time to leave. It was a short drive to Layerthorpe, and they didn't speak. Jessie drove carefully, thinking Ned was watching her, but it was not her driving he was watching. He was memorising every curve of her face, every lock of hair, for when he was back in camp.

'Drop me at the gates,' he said, when they arrived. 'Then you won't have to turn round.'

She turned to him, offering her lips, guilty at how little comfort she had given him, regretful now he was going away; but he would not kiss her here, in the street where anyone, where his employees, might see them. He kissed her cheek formally, and said, 'I'll write to you all about the arrangements. And I'll telephone Father today from my office.'

She could have done that, too. She would make her own arrangements with Uncle Teddy, she thought, and was suddenly impatient for him to go. He was a stranger again, irrelevant in her life. She didn't know what to do with him or how to think of him.

The snow was coming down faster as he stepped out of the motor. 'Drive back carefully,' he said. 'I should have taken a cab.'

It was only his care for her, but it felt as if he was throwing her gesture back in her face. 'Goodbye,' she said. He turned away, and she drove off.

Leaving the city, coming out onto the Clifton Road, she found a world bleached of colour. The snow was beginning to lie, the sky was white, the trees were veiled and only sketchily grey, like pencil strokes against it. She wanted to weep, but she didn't know precisely why, or for whom. She tried to distract her mind by thinking of what she had to do today, but her mind was as blank as the world around her.

She turned in at the sweep of the little grey stone house, and stopped the motor. Her married home, she thought, her first home of her own – soon to be home no longer. It seemed empty and lonely again, now its man had gone. Ned had gone, would soon be off to the Front. It seemed like the end of something more than Maystone Villa. He had

29

said they might get it back at the end of the war, but she felt it was not possible. They would never live there again. She wondered, for a frightened, lucid moment, if they would ever live anywhere together again.

CHAPTER TWO

The casualties sustained in 1914 had staggered the War Council, and finally convinced them that the war would not speedily be brought to an end. It was true that from the beginning Lord Kitchener had opined it would 'last three years, not three months'. But still the ingrained trust in the might of the British Army had persuaded the politicians otherwise. They had believed in the short war – until nine-tenths of the BEF had fallen victim to German shells and machine-guns.

At the end of 1914 the Council had seriously considered withdrawing from France altogether. The Western Front presented an intractable problem. The line stretched unbroken from Switzerland to the Channel, and all along it the Germans had the advantage of higher – and drier – ground. They had dug themselves deep and impregnable bunkers. Their trenches were of hotel luxury compared with the sodden scrapes the Allied soldiers shivered in, and were protected by forests of barbed wire. Manoeuvre was impossible, there was no flank that could be turned, and frontal attack had already proved murderous. Lord Kitchener had pronounced that the German line was 'a fortress which cannot be taken by assault'.

Yet something had to be done, that was plain; something other than – as Lord Overton, a military member of the Council, said to his wife Venetia – 'sitting tight and waiting for a miracle'.

Later in 1915 the new volunteer battalions – the Kitchener units, as they were referred to – would begin to be ready. The question was, what to do with them.

'It's plain Kitchener himself has no idea what to do next,' Overton said. 'When the Cabinet asks, he simply waffles.'

'I can't imagine him waffling,' Venetia said. 'He was always so clipped and to-the-point.'

'Ah, you knew him when he was younger – and in the field he was never at a loss. He was an excellent soldier, but he's not a strategist. The large-scale movement of armies is not his forte.'

'Especially when they *don't* move?' Venetia suggested.

'Precisely.'

Sir John French, the Commander-in-Chief in France, favoured the plan of his French counterpart, General Joffre, which was to launch a series of attacks on the German line where it bulged in a huge salient deep into French sovereign territory. By attacking from three angles Joffre hoped to squeeze the salient, break through the line and so cut the German supply chain at the point where it was at its longest and most vulnerable. Without supplies the German offensive would wither and die.

Joffre had been eloquent in his desire for British support for the plan, and Sir John felt it was so important that he travelled to London in person to urge it on the War Council, at their meeting on the 13th of January.

'I had a talk with him in the lobby before we went into the meeting,' Overton said that night. 'He's quite bitter about the Council's failings.'

'And what are they?' Venetia asked. They were having a late supper in her sitting-room. Overton's War Office work and her medical duties meant they were both very busy people: to eat together at all often required meals at odd times and in odd places.

'Sir John says we're starving him of men. Well, we're doing what we can about that. It takes time to train and equip soldiers, and our standing army was very small. But worse, he says, we're handing out ammunition, particularly shells,

32

with a teaspoon. The Germans have ten times, a hundred times, as much.'

'That is a serious failing,' said Venetia.

Overton refilled her wine glass – at these late suppers they dismissed the servants and fended for themselves. 'The peacetime War Office was equipped to supply a small army. The whole Army Contracts Department has only twenty clerks to do everything, and the munitions manufacturers have more orders than they can cope with.'

'Can't more manufacturers be used?' Venetia asked.

'Kitchener's against it. He says only experienced firms can make shells of the right quality and, since he's virtually dictator as far as the war's concerned, his word is law.'

'So it's Kitchener's fault?'

'He's not a bad chap,' Overton protested, for he was fond of the great man. 'But he's stubborn, and rather limited in vision. It does slow us down, having to pass every decision through him.'

'Can't you get rid of him?'

'Not possible. He's so hugely popular in the country. It would cause a terrible crisis of confidence to sack him: the people feel that as long as he's leading us we can't lose the war.'

'I suppose that's true,' Venetia sighed.

'The worst of it is,' said Overton, 'that his dithering encourages bumptious amateurs like Churchill and Lloyd George to think they know better and come up with their own ideas.'

Venetia had been long enough a soldier's wife to know what happened when laymen devised military strategy. 'I take it they didn't care for Sir John's plan,' she anticipated.

Overton shook his head. 'They hardly listened. I'm afraid the Cabinet ministers all want an attack in the east, on Turkey. They're desperate to avoid more heavy casualties in France, and want to open up a new theatre. And now that Turkey has entered the war on Germany's side, the whole region is unstable. Bulgaria is wavering, and the government's keen for a show of strength that will bring the Bulgars in on our side.'

33

'What does the War Office think about it?'

'Kitchener quite likes the idea. Because of his long service out east, he's inclined to think everything important happens there.'

'But would an attack on Turkey be likely to make much difference?'

'It would be a way to take a victory without much loss of life, which is a political objective.'

'Simply to have a few good headlines in the newspapers?' Venetia said in disgust. 'How paltry!'

'Politics is no longer a gentlemen's occupation, now the newspapers have so much influence,' said Overton. 'The public want action, and the Western Front is at stalemate. I'm afraid it's rather a case of "We must do something; this is something; let's do it."'

'My father must be turning in his grave,' said Venetia. 'Will you have a little cheese?'

'Just a morsel. Thank you. Oh, I suppose on the face of it the Easterners do have some reasoning behind them. Russia is desperately hard-pressed, and Churchill's idea – to take Constantinople and open up the Black Sea to supply ships – might give them some relief.'

'Politicians always want to take Constantinople,' said Venetia. 'And even if the route were opened, what supplies do we have to send? We've barely enough for ourselves – *not* enough, in the case of munitions.'

'It's such a pleasure to talk to someone who has a grasp of the facts,' Overton said. 'Someone who isn't swayed by sentiment and rhetoric. I wish you were on the War Council.'

'A *woman*?' Venetia said, in mock horror. 'Never.'

'It will come one day. Remember, it's not so long ago that people would have said, "A woman surgeon – never!" And yet here you are.'

'Ah, but war more than anything is men's work. They'll never let us take their favourite toy away from them.'

'I suppose if women were in charge there would *be* no war,' Overton teased.

34

But Venetia said, 'Germany attacked first. We couldn't let them get away with it. So, the plan is to attack Turkey and take Constantinople – and the Council has agreed?'

'All but me and one other. Well, you know what Churchill's like in full flood. As well try to resist the Victoria Falls! He's put it up as a purely naval expedition, so Fisher, the First Sea Lord, is grudgingly with him.'

'I'd have thought Lloyd George would be against a plan he didn't think of.'

Overton smiled at her estimation of the chancellor of the exchequer. 'Actually, he's attached himself firmly to it. He means to take the credit.'

'*If* it succeeds.'

'That's the beauty of a purely naval attack. If it doesn't succeed, they can claim it was just a show of strength to remind the region of our power to strike.'

'A plan without a drawback,' Venetia said drily. 'What did Sir John French think?'

'Churchill's eloquence won him over, once he was assured they wouldn't be taking any of his troops. But he didn't get the support he wanted for his joint action with Joffre.'

'Poor Sir John! You should have invited him back to dinner, Beauty.'

'He promised to dine with us next time he's in England. He said he had to hurry back to St Omer tonight. I suspect he has one of his beautiful women waiting for him,' Overton added with a smile, for French had more than once been criticised by the stiffer part of society for his succession of well-connected mistresses.

Venetia laughed. 'I sincerely hope he has. It must be hard enough for him out there, without denying him his comforts. He's too sensitive for a soldier – that's the reality. He feels the men's deaths too much.'

'I shouldn't want a commander who did *not* feel them.'

'Perhaps that's true. So when does Churchill's plan go into action?'

'At once,' said Overton. 'A fleet of warships is to go in by way of the Dardanelles and bombard the Turkish forts on the strait. Constantinople, they believe, will fall of its own accord as soon as the ships appear.'

'But what then? You need troops to hold a place once you've taken it.'

'I tried to get that point across, but no-one was listening. The politicians loved the plan. You know how they always like multiple objectives: attack Germany's ally, encourage Bulgaria to join us, and open the sea route to Russia. They have to be seen to be doing *something* for the Russians. Grand Duke Nicholas has been sending increasingly urgent appeals for weeks.'

Venetia knew that. Their elder son, Thomas, was a military attaché to the Court of St Petersburg, and his letters had been full of bad war news. 'But this scheme won't divert German troops away from the Russian front,' she said. 'Allies or not, the Germans hate the Turks: they won't hurry to help them.'

'That's what I said. But my colleagues assured me that securing the Black Sea will open the back door into Germany through the Danube. They all got terribly excited about that, as if the war was all but won.'

'It's a long march from the Black Sea to Germany,' Venetia pointed out.

'You can't expect politicians to know that – they don't read maps.'

'And we haven't an army to send anyway.' He only grunted in reply, frowning in thought. Venetia eyed her husband with sympathy. 'You look tired, Beauty. All this is too much for you.'

At these words he straightened up and smiled. 'I'm not ready to babble of green fields yet, my love. And the country needs men of experience. Don't you know there's a war on? But I've been thinking that *you* were looking rather tired, lately,' he counter-attacked cunningly, 'what with all these committees of yours, and your work at the hospital.'

'Nonsense,' Venetia said, rising to his bait. 'I'm sixty-five, not eighty-five – and when I'm eighty-five I shall still back myself to out-operate any youngster you care to put up against me.' She stretched out her hands and flexed them. 'As long as these remain steady, and arthritis doesn't strike. Thank God it's not in the family.'

Overton smiled, rose, and held out his hand. 'Excellent. Then since we've established that neither of us is in the least tired, shall we go to bed?'

One day in the middle of February Venetia was at home, busy reviewing case notes; but she put them aside gladly on the arrival of her daughter Violet, Lady Holkam.

Violet had been the loveliest débutante of her year, with her dark hair, flawless skin and violet-blue eyes: at twenty-three, having had three children, she was, to her mother, even more beautiful. Her father, Lord Overton, had been so handsome in his youth he had been known as 'Beauty' Winchmore, and Venetia was glad Violet had inherited his looks rather than hers.

In character Violet was also more like her father, being easy-tempered, charming, and fond of company and comfort. She had never had the violent ambition and fierce opinions that had made Venetia's life so stormy – and ultimately so satisfying. It sometimes seemed odd to her that her daughter's aim in life had always been to get married, have children and be châtelaine of a nice house; but then her own sister, Olivia, had been just the same. Beauty said the fact was that it was she, Venetia, who was the odd one out. Perhaps she was a throwback to her great-grandmother Lucy, whose wild exploits had included running away dressed as a boy to join the navy, and racing a curricle from London to Brighton.

Venetia rose to meet her daughter as she came in, and said, 'Darling, you look good enough to eat!'

Violet's day dress of beige foulard clung to her softly all the way down, in the slender style of current high fashion: the over-tunic ended mid-thigh, with a broad sash of black silk round the hips, and the narrow skirt stopped just on the ankle, revealing a glimpse of high-heeled black ankle boots. She was wearing her large sable wrap, against which the alabaster skin of her face seemed to glow as if lit from within; her hat was close-fitting, black with an enormous black ostrich spray fixed to it with a diamond brooch. She carried a silky Pekingese dog in each arm: she dropped them to the floor as she crossed to embrace her mother, and they rushed round the room sniffing everything, their small coral tongues bright semicircles in their black velvet faces.

'This is a nice surprise,' Venetia said, hugging her. 'Hmm, you smell good too.'

'Do I? It must be me – I haven't put anything on,' said Violet, returning her mother's embrace with enthusiasm.

'And is that a new hat?'

'Newish. I had it for the State Opening. Nothing I had would do – hats are going to be small this year.'

'How annoying of them,' Venetia sympathised, and turned to Violet's companion, who had followed her in. 'Emma, dear.'

Emma Weston was a cousin of sorts, an orphan who made her home with Violet to avoid having to live with her guardian in a remote and unpleasantly damp part of Scotland. She was nineteen, very pretty, and extremely rich – or would be when she came of age. Venetia kept a distant eye on her, to see that she didn't make any unsuitable connections.

Emma kissed her, and said, 'I can't see that it matters about hats when there's a war on. I shan't worry about changing mine. Goodness, everything's so exciting!'

'Except that all the young men keep going away?' Venetia suggested.

'But they come back again on leave,' Emma explained, with a grin, 'and then they're keener than ever on dancing, after the Front.'

Violet sat on the sofa, let her fur slip off and began pulling off her gloves. 'We met Lady Dawnay coming out of Selfridges' library, and she said Kit was coming home next week. And Freddie said he thought he saw Peter Hargrave in Whitehall.'

Venetia looked at Emma, who blushed, but only a little. She had had a preference for Peter Hargrave last year, but at her age absence, when accompanied by the excitements of London, tended to make the heart grow forgetful. 'I expect he was mistaken,' she said. 'You know how Freddie is.'

Sir Freddie Copthall was Violet's most constant attendant. Lord Holkam rarely escorted her to parties.

'All the same,' Violet said, 'I thought of giving a small dance next week, for Kit Dawnay and any of the others who are home. I know the Season hasn't properly started yet, but so many people stayed up this winter because of the war. And then I can take a collection for my Indian Soldiers' Fund.'

'That's a new one, isn't it?' Venetia asked. Her daughter was much in demand for committees.

'Well, yes, but I couldn't resist when I was asked. The poor Indians are suffering so much at the Front. Imagine going from the burning heat of India to Flanders in winter! They're tremendously brave and fight like tigers, and it's wonderful to see the loyalty of the Empire troops. But apart from the cold and wet, which they're not used to, they have special requirements about diet. They can't eat our biscuit – and of course they hate anything to do with pigs, so bacon won't do either.'

'You seem remarkably well informed on the subject,' Venetia said.

'We had a talk on Monday by a major from the Secunderabad Cavalry – most interesting,' said Violet, her eyes bright with animation.

'He was home from the Front, wounded,' Emma added. 'Goodness, he was handsome! I was so glad it wasn't a bad wound. Anyway, he said that the Indians would sooner starve to death than eat the wrong food – isn't that strange? And they have all sorts of odd superstitions and religious bans, which make it hard for the army to cater for them. So the fund was set up to get them things like chapatti flour for their biscuit, and extra warm clothes.'

'And we're trying to get the Brighton Pavilion for a hospital for them,' Violet went on, 'because we thought the poor things would feel so much more at home there. So, you see, it's a very good cause. Would you and Papa come next week?'

'To a dance?' Venetia protested; and then, at Violet's melting look, which she found hard to resist, 'Well, I suppose we might drop in around supper-time.'

'Oh, *do*, please. It will make such a difference if the papers say you were there, because people always send money afterwards when they read about it.'

'Very well, darling. Would you like me to see if I can persuade the King to look in as well, on his way to something or other?'

'Oh, you're so kind! But I really rather hoped you might get him *and* the Queen to come to my big hospital ball in May. I don't want to wear them out.'

Venetia smiled. 'Very well, I shall keep back the big guns for later. But you'd better give me the date of your ball as soon as possible, because Their Majesties will have their diaries filled, even in wartime.'

'Especially in wartime,' Emma said. 'It seems to me there are more people in London, having more fun than *ever*. The shops and restaurants are always full, and you can hardly get a ticket for anything. And *everyone* is having parties and dinners and luncheons. One would hardly know there was a war at all, if it weren't for the young men in uniform.'

'And the recruitment offices, all hung with Union Jacks,' Violet added, 'and the recruiting sergeants standing on street corners.'

'And the public houses being shut in the afternoons.'

'And flag-sellers everywhere, and people with collecting-boxes.'

'And the women handing out white feathers,' Venetia put in. 'I saw one yesterday on my way to the hospital. The poor fellow she had cornered was desperately embarrassed, and really quite angry because he was a munitions worker so, of course, he was needed at home and couldn't volunteer, but the woman wouldn't listen, and I could see he quite wanted to strike her, except that he was too much a natural

40

gentleman. I wanted to strike her myself. It's time something was done to protect essential workers.'

'The funny thing is,' said Violet, 'that it's so often the former suffragettes who do it. They've become so passionate about the war.'

'I suppose they feel the need of a cause,' said Venetia. 'Now they've suspended their activities for the duration, it must leave a hole in their lives.'

'I saw that woman who was such a friend of Cousin Anne's the other day,' Violet said. 'Miss Whatever-it-was? Miss Polk, that was it.'

'Oh, really?' said Venetia coolly. Vera Polk had behaved most insultingly to Venetia while she was the companion of Lady Anne Farraline. Anne, a militant campaigner, had died in a motor accident almost a year ago, and Venetia had hoped never to hear Miss Polk's name again.

'Oh, was that the woman you pointed out to me?' Emma said, and turned to Venetia. 'She was in a FANY uniform, and, goodness, it looked smart! I must say one quite longs for something like that. The men have all the fun in the war, the uniforms and everything. Do you think Uncle Bruce would let me join the FANYs?'

'I should think he'd have a fit,' said Venetia. 'You're too young, in any case.'

'I see. Very well,' said Emma, meekly – too meekly, Venetia thought, narrowing her eyes. But her intention to probe Emma's ambitions further was diverted by the door opening. Lord Overton appeared, followed by the butler, Burton, and the footman with the tea things.

Her husband, she thought, looked tired and cross, but the sight of his daughter instantly cheered him. By the time he had ingested two cups of tea and several buttered teacakes, and listened to the light chatter of the happy young women for half an hour, he was almost relaxed. Venetia thought she would forbear to ask him anything about his day until later, but Violet, without a wife's sensibilities, suddenly asked, 'Where have you just come from, Papa? Was it something interesting or important?'

And so the frown came back to Lord Overton's face, and though he passed off the question lightly, his pleasure in the moment was spoiled and he soon excused himself. Not long afterwards the young women went home to dress for dinner, and Venetia went to look for him. She found him, as she expected, in the library, at his favourite desk, under one of the long windows onto Manchester Square, writing.

'What is it?' she asked. 'By your expression it's something of a bombshell.'

'Yes, and dropped by the Admiralty,' said Overton. 'This Dardanelles business – it seems now that Fisher was unhappy with the plan all along, but allowed himself to be swayed by his political master—'

'Churchill.'

'Precisely. Now the Admiralty has sent a memorandum saying that a naval bombardment cannot succeed alone, and that there must be a strong military force to follow up and take occupation of the forts as they are silenced.'

'That's what you said,' Venetia pointed out.

'I did, but I didn't advocate it. The only benefit of the initial plan was that it would be quite easy to pull back from, if things went wrong. Committing troops to a landing on the Gallipoli Peninsula, about which virtually nothing is known, and without any intelligence about the strength of the Turkish forces there, seems madness to me. We haven't even any modern maps, and the few we have show no detail of the terrain.'

'I didn't think we had any troops to send, in any case,' said Venetia.

'There's the Twenty-ninth Division. They've just come back from India, and Sir John French was expecting to have them for his spring offensive. Now Churchill wants them for Gallipoli, and Kitchener's wavering.'

'I shouldn't have thought K would want to waste them on the Straits.'

'Equally, he doesn't want to pitch them into the slaughter-house in France, given that his beloved BEF has disappeared without trace. The Twenty-ninth is his last division of

42

seasoned regulars. I think he'll agree in the end. The Horseguards' pride will rear up – the old rivalry with the Admiralty. I heard him say, "If the Fleet can't get through the Straits unaided, the Army will have to see the business through."'

'Can't you persuade him?'

'I'll try – but he's keen on doing something "in the east".' He sighed and passed a weary hand over his brow. 'The worst of it is, they're not going to postpone the naval operation.'

Venetia was startled. 'But it will take a month for the army to get there, won't it?'

'At least that,' Overton agreed. 'But the government wants an immediate strike in the area, to stop the Bulgars allying with the Germans. They hope to bring Greece and Rumania over to us as well. They feel there's no time to be wasted.'

They were silent a moment in thought. If the naval attempt to force the Straits were successful, there would be no troops on hand to occupy the forts that had been taken. If it were unsuccessful, the enemy would have plenty of time to improve his defences before the army arrived. And either way, the alert would have been given as to where the Allies meant to strike.

Venetia went over to her husband's side and stroked his hair, and he let his head rest against her a moment. 'Perhaps it will all go well,' she said. 'Turks are no match for our men; and the British navy is the finest in the world.'

He straightened up. 'Of course. And if the navy forces the Straits, the Turks will lose heart and may just give up.'

'In any case, there's nothing you can do about it, except give your opinion,' she concluded.

'Quite so,' he said; but he did not look as though that was of any comfort to him.

As Jessie had expected, Uncle Teddy was more than delighted that she was to 'come back home', as he put it. He had never seen the point of young married people taking on all the expense of setting up a separate establishment when there was room at Morland Place for all. He would have undertaken all the trouble of the removal himself, too, had it not been that his presence was required in Manchester, where the industrial unrest that was plaguing the country had spread to his factories.

Just the previous October, he had been elated to be awarded a government contract for producing khaki cloth for uniforms. With the sudden increase in recruitment, thousands of volunteer soldiers had been parading and training in their civilian clothes, or at best in uniforms made up of spare blue serge. Huge quantities of khaki were wanted, and the existing suppliers had no hope of meeting demand. While the war lasted, there would be a continuous requirement for replacements, and to clad new drafts of soldiers. So it was an immensely lucrative contract to have landed.

He also had the contract for the third of White Star's 'Olympic' liners. The ship had originally been intended to be named *Gigantic*, but that was now thought to sound too much like *Titanic*, so at her launch in February 1914 she had been given the name *Britannic*. She was still in dock, for wartime shortages had delayed her completion, and fitting out would not be finished for months yet; but of course Teddy had to have his plans in place. He had lost his contract with Cunard for linens, which had caused short-term problems for him; but the war had brought a huge increase in demand for sheet cotton, both for hospitals and convalescent homes, and for use as shrouds, and enough of the new business had come his way. So Teddy's factories were working full-out; and since plenty of work meant plenty of pay for the hands, everything ought to have been going smoothly.

However, the unions were not happy even with this buoyant state. They were resisting the replacement of the skilled men who had volunteered with unskilled labour, even where the jobs required no special training. The process, known as dilution, was held to be a threat that would undermine the rights they had fought so hard for, and sweep away their jobs. And they believed that owners were making huge

44

profits at the workers' expense, and that while prices were rising, as they always did in wartime, wages were not.

At Teddy's mills, the trouble had started with the engineers, who were refusing to allow an unskilled worker to perform any job previously done by a member of the Amalgamated Society of Engineers. Since a quarter of them had left to join the army, this had led to a slowing of production, as there were not enough ASE men left to fill three shifts. The engineers were threatening to strike if the management brought in non-union hands to operate the idle machines. Now the unrest had spread to the other workers, who were demanding a rise in pay, and hinting at a strike if they didn't get it.

Teddy was furiously indignant that his employees should take up such an attitude in wartime, when everyone was supposed to be pulling together. It was downright unpatriotic – practically treason. He hurried over to Manchester where he interviewed his managers, then the section leaders and the union representatives and gradually, as the days passed, hammered out a compromise. The non-engineering workers were easier to placate. They were getting plenty of overtime, and going on strike did not appeal to the rank-and-file as it did to the union leaders. At his managers' suggestion he had a leaflet printed and circulated about the importance of the war effort, the patriotic duty of everyone to do his bit and work hard to supply the brave Tommies who were risking their lives for England's freedom. Simultaneously he had a rumour circulated that there would be a bonus at the end of the year just before Christmas if certain targets were met; and he brought forward plans he had been formulating to build a workers' canteen to provide the employees with a hot dinner at a subsidised price. There was a new government initiative that would allow the cost of such a canteen to be offset against taxes, so it would not be too expensive; and as far as the employees were concerned, the food would be so cheap it would be the equivalent of a pay rise.

The engineers were harder to settle, and calls to their patriotism had limited effect. They had trained for seven years on an apprentice pittance to qualify as tradesmen, and while many of the jobs they performed did not require much skill, still they were *their* jobs. Teddy and his managers had some long, hard arguing to do to reach an agreement. Certain tasks were to remain exclusively ASE jobs, but on other tasks they would take non-union men alongside them, a limited number to a section, with the ASE men supervising in return for a rise in wages. It was a clumsy arrangement, certain to cause delays, but it was better than a strike, and at least it would mean they could reinstate three shifts, spreading the union men among them.

While he was away in Manchester, Jessie had to manage her removal alone. She did the packing herself, helped by the servants (though not, of course, Gladding), and, at the weekends by Polly, Uncle Teddy's daughter by his first wife. Polly was almost fifteen and in her last term at school, where she was a weekly boarder. She was thrilled that Jessie was coming back to live at Morland Place: 'Just at the right time, when I shall be home all day. We can go riding together, and all sorts of things.'

'I shall have my hospital work to do, and the stables at Twelvetrees to run,' Jessie pointed out.

'I can help with those, too,' said Polly, and added pathetically, 'I shall be *terribly* lonely, you know, after having all my friends around me at school, just being the only girl in the house.'

Jessie laughed. 'You minx! You know you're longing to be done with school.'

'Oh, I am and I'm not, at the same time. Didn't you like school?'

'Not a bit.'

'Well, I like some things. We have jolly romps in the dorm sometimes. And some of the girls are topping. But nowhere can ever be as nice as Morland Place, can it? Except,' she said, looking round the drawing-room, where they were wrapping and packing ornaments, 'that this is such a sweet house, and it will be rather sad to see it go. Are you *very* attached to it?'

46

'I've been happy here,' Jessie said. 'Oh, not that one, I shall want that with me.'

'What about these horrid vases?'

'They're not horrid. They're very valuable.'

'They're a horrid colour. And those nasty flowers.'

'It's called *famille noire* and it's French, and they were given to Ned and me for our wedding by Lady Olivia Du Cane – Cousin Venetia's sister, you know.'

Polly grinned. 'I bet some fusty old aunt gave them to her for *her* wedding and she'd been longing to get rid of them ever since.'

'Polly, you are naughty! But wrap them really carefully, darling,' said Jessie, 'because I plan to give them to you for yours.'

'Thanks for warning me. Shall I drop them and be done with it?'

'Absolutely not! Oh dear, look at the time! We should have finished all this by now.'

Tomlinson came in just then and said, 'I've finished the linen cupboard, madam.' She looked around quickly, taking in the situation. 'Would you like me to finish off here while you and Miss Polly have luncheon? I've laid it in the morning-room.'

'Oh, would you? Have you? You really are a brick,' Jessie said gratefully. 'I *have* to go to Heworth Park this afternoon because I promised Captain Destoits I'd go on with reading *Great Expectations*. It's so sad – they haven't told him yet he'll never see again, but I think he's beginning to guess.'

After living a bivouac kind of life for a week, as gradually more and more of the house was packed up, the moving began. The horses went first, to the stables at Morland Place, led over by Gladding and Thwaite, one of Uncle Teddy's grooms, and followed by a cart carrying the tack and stable gear. Then went the boxes of linen, china, ornaments and kitchen equipment that would not be needed, to be stored in one of Morland Place's endless attics. Most of the furniture would also not be needed: some was to be stored at Morland Place, one or two items Jessie would keep about

47

her, and the rest was collected by an auction house to be sold. These removals were done by a professional removals firm – Ned had insisted on that, saying his father should not be troubled with it. Finally Jessie's clothes and personal effects, and Ned's things, together with a few pieces of furniture, ornaments and paintings, were collected by Pickford's men and taken to Morland Place, with Peggy and Susie travelling in the van.

Jessie and Tomlinson checked everything one last time and then locked up. For a moment they stood looking at the silent house, its shutters fastened; grey stone and slate against a low grey sky. It seemed to have closed its eyes, shut away its face from them, as one who keeps his thoughts from those he no longer loves.

'It's the end of an era, madam,' said Tomlinson.

Jessie roused herself. It was cold: even through her gloves her fingers were numb. 'All things come to an end. We must move on.'

They were to drive over to Morland Place in the new little car Hoggett had found her, a neat four-year-old Austin with cream paintwork and black trim. It was standing ready for them, the engine running, the fine snowflakes that were falling again melting to steam on its bonnet. It had been brought out of its shed unwillingly by Gladding, who was standing nearby, morosely hunched against the snow, a fine powdering on his shoulders and cap. Jessie walked over to hand him the house keys. The agent, Pickering, had found new tenants, but they would not be moving in for a month, and it had been arranged that Gladding would stay on for that time as caretaker.

Jessie would have liked to find a kind word to say goodbye, but in all fairness she was glad to be rid of him. Since Ned had given him his notice he had been increasingly surly, and over the packing and moving he had surpassed himself in unhelpfulness, refusing to lift or carry anything, presumably on the understanding that he could not be dismissed twice.

'Here are the keys,' she said. 'No doubt Mr Pickering will

be in touch with you. I'll send a man later this week for any mail that arrives.'

The cold did not make Gladding rosy. His face was grey, the end of his nose blue, and he looked like an image of a man, made in stone. Stone images don't speak. He took the keys, and walked away. Jessie heard Tomlinson draw in her breath at the rudeness, but only shook her head, and went back to the car. Uncle Teddy had been generosity itself over the servants, and said he would take them all; he'd even offered a place for Gladding, but Jessie and Ned had both shuddered at the idea, imagining how he'd upset the Morland Place staff.

Tomlinson was to continue as Jessie's maid, and had suggested that she maided Polly, too, when she was home, to help guide her through the transition from schoolroom miss to young lady.

'Nobody could do it better than you, dear Mary,' Jessie said, with a fond look. 'I remember how you shaped me when I was a girl.'

'Thank you, madam,' said Tomlinson, 'but you shouldn't call me "Mary" if we're to set Miss Polly straight from the beginning.'

'You're very proper,' Jessie laughed. 'Well, I shall only do so when we're alone. You must allow me that.'

Peggy and Susie would both be housemaids. With several of the men having already volunteered, the female servants were having to take over more of the work, and extra hands were needed. But Jessie knew Uncle Teddy would have taken them even if they weren't needed, for her sake.

'I hope the girls will be happy at Morland Place,' she said to Tomlinson. 'They've never worked in a big place before, have they?'

'I'll keep an eye on them, madam,' said Tomlinson. 'I'm sure they'll settle in. They're sensible girls, and Morland Place always was a happy house.'

With regard to accommodation, Henrietta had insisted on moving into the East Bedroom so as to give the Blue Room to Jessie and Ned. 'It's bigger and nicer, and you'll want space to have your bits and pieces around you,' she said; and when Jessie protested, 'I don't need that big room any more. In fact, I've been thinking of moving anyway. It feels too big to me now – too empty – and it reminds me too much of your father. I shall be cosier in a smaller room.'

Jessie was sure she was just saying that to persuade, and said so.

'Truly, darling,' Henrietta said, with a limpid look. 'Besides, it will encourage me to start getting rid of a lot of things I don't need any more. I've clothes in the wardrobe I haven't worn in years. I've been meaning to clear out all my cupboards and drawers, but I'm too lazy to begin. This will be the spur.'

Jessie was still suspicious, but could not put her finger on a flaw in the argument. 'Well, you must let Tomlinson help you, then,' she said finally.

'That's very sweet of you. Don't look like that, my Jessie. I shall be very happy in East, I promise you, and I shall like to think of you and Ned enjoying the Blue Room when he's home. Perhaps you'll be so comfortable there you'll never go away again, which would make your uncle happy.'

It was true that the Blue Room was much nicer, not only larger but lighter and sunnier, with its attractive blue and white wallpaper and Chinese carpet, and the deep blue drapes on bed and window. There would be plenty of room for the furniture Jessie wanted to keep about her, including Ned's desk, which she would have had difficulty in fitting into the East Bedroom, owing to the position of the window. But it had always been her mother and father's room, and there was something about the transaction that made her feel slightly uneasy.

'I shall be glad to be able to keep an eye on Mother, at any rate,' she said aloud, as the car crunched over Maystone's gravel for the last time. 'She does too much. She looks tired.'

'If you like, madam, I can help her with running the house, take over some of her tasks for her. I'm accustomed to housekeeping here, now. I'm sure there are lots of little ways I can lighten the burden,' said Tomlinson.

50

'Thank you, Mary,' Jessie said, and rested her hand on her maid's for an instant in gratitude. They reached the end of the drive and she stopped to check it was clear, took one glance back at the house, and then drove forward into the fine snow, along the wet black road, a dark ribbon between the snowy verges and the bare hedges and trees, laced and crusted with white. There was a lump in her throat to be leaving, and her eyes were damp; but she was going *home*, she told herself fiercely. At the end of this journey there would be her mother – and someone else equally pleased to see her: Brach, left at Morland Place for the past week so that the emptying of the house would not upset her. Brach was always happy at Morland Place, where she had grown up, but she would be beside herself with joy at the sight of her mistress.

If only Papa could have been there as well. Still – going home! She thought briefly, almost guiltily, of Ned up at the camp on Black Brow, wondering when the call would come to go to France. Maystone had been his house, too – more, really, than it had been Jessie's, since it had meant more to him. The house was gone and soon Ned would be gone and she would be back where she had started in her maiden home. It was almost, Jessie thought, as if the past three and a half years, the whole of her marriage, had been a diversion, a side-stream going round in a loop, now to be cut off. An ox-bow: her marriage was an ox-bow, she thought. And when she resumed it, it would be far downstream from here.

CHAPTER THREE

Ethel's baby was born in the last week of February, in the North Bedroom at Morland Place, without difficulty and after a short labour. Robbie had just gone off to work at the bank in York when her pains began, and the telephone message was sent to him shortly after noon that he was the father of another fine girl. Mrs Cornleigh, Ethel's mother, had just had time to get there – the Cornleighs did not have the telephone so a boy had had to be sent with a message – but Ethel had Henrietta with her all the time, as well as Emma, the Morland Place nanny, who had been with Henrietta for years and had helped with the delivery of all her children. The women agreed between them that Ethel was getting on so well there was no need for the expense of a doctor, and Mrs Cornleigh, when she arrived, confirmed their opinion, and added vaguely that, 'after all, there was a war on,' the logic of which, in the exciting circumstances, no-one questioned.

Alice, Uncle Teddy's wife, who had lost her second child and now could not have any more, asked Jessie to take her for a drive in the phaeton as soon as the business began. She said she was thinking of learning to handle the reins herself, so she could drive to her morning calls, wartime petrol being so expensive. Jessie saw through the fiction – Aunt Alice's dainty hands were used to nothing harsher than embroidery thread – but she went along with it. Her courage was not yet quite equal to hearing any of the confinement-chamber sounds. And what if something should go wrong? Ethel had had no difficulty in producing little Roberta and Jeremy, but Jessie felt almost superstitious, as if her presence in the house might actually cause the unthinkable. So she dashed out as soon as Aunt Alice asked her and harnessed Mouse and Minna herself. She spent the whole morning driving her around, conscientiously instructing her in the handling of reins, whip and brake, until the ringing of the house bell, heard from a distance, told them that it was all over and that Morland Place had a new soul under its roof.

Teddy was at home, and had spent the morning pacing up and down the business-room dictating letters to Hopkins, his new secretary – who afterwards had extensively to recompose them, since in places (whenever there were sounds from above) they became less than coherent. As soon as Henrietta came downstairs to say it was all safely over, Teddy had ordered the house bell rung, and when Ethel was sitting up and ready to receive the family, he was the first to bring her congratulations, and the all-important champagne to give her strength after her ordeal.

Alice soon joined him, and was in time to see the new resident being presented to the other nursery inmates, Roberta and Jeremy, and Teddy and Alice's son James. Jeremy, not quite three, and Roberta, not quite four, had nothing to say, only stared in amazement, but James, who was nearly five, remarked that the baby was very red and very ugly and he liked puppies better – could he have a puppy of his own, please, Farver?

Jessie had hung back in the stables, doing quite unnecessary things for the Bhutias, to the patient puzzlement of Thwaite, whom she had thus made redundant; but at last she had to face up to it. She went in and marched straight-backed up to North. There was quite a throng in the room, and a babble of conversation, but it fell quiet as she appeared. The bodies parted for her. Her mother touched her arm as she passed, Teddy nodded encouragingly to her, and Alice looked her sympathy.

Ethel was sitting up in a very fetching blue bedjacket with the white bundle in her arms, gazing down proudly and happily into its face. Jessie felt a lump come into her throat. Ethel looked up at the sudden hush and, seeing Jessie, smiled, and instantly and wordlessly held out the baby to her.

Jessie took it, feeling that her arms must tremble, afraid they would be weak. But, strangely, the tiny, light bundle (so very light – she had forgotten how little newborn babies were) felt quite natural in her hands, and she settled it without thought in the crook of her arm. The small, rather squashed, very red face was sealed in sleep, though the eyes moved back and forth under the delicately sheened lids, and the miniature fingers twitched a little as if grasping after something lost. After the first sharp pain, Jessie felt a kind of peace come over her. It was all right. It wasn't that this baby could replace the one she had lost, or could comfort her for her own shortcomings; but it said that life was life, and it was strong, and it went on. The dead baby Jessie had borne was not the end, just a rock in the stream: the river of existence poured past it and went rushing on. It was all right.

'She's lovely,' Jessie said, and though her voice creaked a little, something in it reassured the waiting family, and there was almost an audible sigh of relief. 'What are you going to call her?'

'I can't decide until Robbie comes home,' said Ethel dutifully. 'We only discussed boys' names – we didn't think it would be a girl.'

She held out her arms for the baby, but Jessie said, 'Oh, let me hold her just a little longer.'

Sawry, the butler, appeared at the door with more glasses and a second bottle of champagne, and hemmed softly so that Teddy, who was blocking his path, would make way.

'The servants' hall wishes its heartiest congratulations to be conveyed to Mrs Robert, if you please, madam,' he said to Henrietta. 'And, indeed, to you and the master.'

'Tell them thank you from me, Sawry,' Ethel said.

'And tell them there'll be something special with their supper tonight, to wet the baby's head,' said Teddy.

'Thank you, sir.'

By the time Robbie got home, his wife and new child had both had a good, long sleep, and were entertaining a succession of visitors. Nanny Emma had decreed that Mrs Robert should have no more than two people in the room at once or her milk would never come in. The rest were drinking more champagne in the drawing-room, and the party had been joined by more of Ethel's family: her father, her married sister Angela with her husband John Fulbright; her nineteen-year-old sister Ada with her fiancé Bobby Deakes, and her youngest brother Arthur, who was eighteen.

Her brothers Seb and Peter were both away at camp, having volunteered. Arthur was going as soon as he had his nineteenth birthday, and Bobby Deakes was already in uniform, waiting to be summoned by the new unit he had joined. Robbie, who had been twitted by Polly for not volunteering, was grateful for John Fulbright's resolutely unmilitary presence. The Fulbrights had two children and would have been surprised at any suggestion that he should go, which had been Robbie's annoyed response to Polly, but she had a way of getting under a chap's skin.

But this evening was Robbie's evening, and his hand was shaken and his shoulder clapped and his cheek pattered with kisses; and after he had been up to see Ethel he brought the baby down to parade it round the drawing-room for more admiration.

'But, Rob, what *are* you going to call her?' Jessie finally spoke up for everyone.

'I just had a word with Ethel,' Robbie said, looking self-conscious. 'We hadn't thought of any girls' names, but now – what do you all think of Harriet?'

There was a moment of mulling silence, and then Jessie said, 'Harriet Compton. I like it. It sounds like a respected lady novelist.'

'Or the headmistress of a girls' school,' Henrietta joined in.

'Or how about the first lady Member of Parliament?' Uncle Teddy cried boisterously, and they all laughed. 'To Harriet Compton,' he said, raising his glass, and they all drank the toast with blessings.

The excitement of the week was not over, for on the Wednesday evening Jessie's brother Frank arrived home on embarkation leave. He was the closest to her in age, and as children they had often been the ones to play together, though Jack had always been her particular favourite. Frank had been mad about soldiers as a little boy, though as he grew up and his academic abilities made themselves known, he had turned to the more cerebral fascinations of mathematics and physics. The war had interrupted his tenure of a prestigious readership at University College, London. Everyone had been very surprised that the detached and bookish Frank had even noticed the war had begun, let alone dashed off and volunteered for the Rifles.

And now he was off to Malta.

'I thought you said, back in December, that you were being sent to Egypt,' Robbie objected, as they all sat round in the small dining-room, watching him enjoy a late supper. The army seemed to have done something extraordinary to his appetite, and with the speed and precision of a man who has learned not to waste opportunity, he demolished cold beef with fried potatoes, and apple pie with Wensleydale cheese, in large quantities.

'So we thought,' he answered, 'but it turned out to be just a rumour. They fly around all the time – you have no idea! Only two weeks ago it was "known for certain" that we'd be going to India. I'm glad *that* turned out not to be true. They say that once you're sent to India you never get away – though, of course,' he added, with a small smile, 'that may be just another rumour.'

'But this time it's true? It is Malta?' Henrietta asked, watching her handsome son with a sense of wonder. Of all her children he was the one who most resembled his father, her much loved and lost Jerome. In uniform he looked older and taller and much more solid around the shoulders than the scholarly boy she had last seen in 'civvies'. His face was lean and his eyes clear and more direct – the dreamy, half-elsewhere expression he had always worn had gone. She remembered how he had written to her, when he volunteered, of his desire to fight for his country and the seriousness of his patriotic resolve, and tried for his sake not to be glad that it was Malta rather than France.

'Yes. We're taking over the garrison, to release the Terriers who are holding it, so that they can go to the Front. Of course, they're in a better state of readiness than we are, but we're rather disappointed not to be bound for the Front ourselves. There won't be much going on in Malta, from all accounts. We just hold the fort in case of a German invasion – which isn't very likely – and keep watch for submarines. But our colonel promises us we'll be training hard, so as to be ready when the call comes.'

'*If* it comes,' Robbie corrected. 'I read in one of the papers that, what with the new offensive this spring and the new front opening up in the east, we should see the Germans off by the end of the year.'

Frank didn't argue. He merely gave his brother a side-long glance from his bright blue eyes – which looked even brighter now that his face was tanned – and changed the subject. 'So, I've a new little niece? I can't wait to see her.'

Rob was turned. 'Oh, she's not much to look at just yet,' he said airily. 'You know how it is with babies. But Ethel thinks she'll grow up to be a beauty. She has my nose, it seems, and Ethel's eyes – and Nanny Emma says her hair is sure to curl.'

So the evening passed in pleasant family talk. The next morning, after breakfast, Frank asked Jessie if she would go riding with him. 'If there's a horse to carry me? I haven't had any riding for ages, and I'd like to see round the old place before I go off to foreign climes.'

'You can have my Warrior,' said Teddy. 'I shan't want him today.'

'Thanks, Uncle. Will you come, Jess?'

'Of course. I was going over to Twelvetrees anyway. You

won't mind stopping there for ten minutes while I attend to some things?'

'I'll be interested to see what you're doing there,' Frank said. He smiled. 'My little sister, a businesswoman, running her own affairs!'

She smiled back. 'But I always *was* bossy – that's what you'll say next.'

'I shouldn't be so rude. You managed our play, that's true.'

'When you boys would let me play. You were always trying to keep me out.'

Later, when they walked out to the stables together, he asked, 'Have you heard from Jack recently?'

'I had a letter last week, with a page from Helen. They've moved to the Antelope – the inn at Upavon – and they're still looking for a place to rent, but of course they're hard to find with so many new people coming into the area because of the RFC. It's lovely there, he says, on the edge of the downs, high up, with wide open skies.'

'And what is he doing? The last I heard it wasn't decided yet.'

'Oh, the factory and the flying school are still fighting over him, so Helen says, and he *will* try to satisfy both. He can't drive yet, so she has to drive him, from Upavon to Netheravon and back, from the hotel to the factory to the school. It must be torture for him,' she added reflectively, 'to be surrounded by people flying and not to be able to fly himself. I'd have thought he'd do better to work at the factory rather than teach at the school – less to remind him.'

'But he'll be flying again soon, won't he?' said Frank. 'His ankle *will* heal up eventually – there's no doubt about that, surely?'

'I hope not,' said Jessie. 'Helen doesn't say specifically, which is a bit worrying. Poor Jackie, it would be a terrible price to pay for having been shot down, if he weren't to be able ever to go up again.'

'He's alive,' said Frank, quietly.

She threw him a quick glance. 'Yes, of course. We must all be grateful for that.'

The horses were ready for them, tacked up and standing in the yard, held by Thwaite and one of the boys, Wickes. Hotspur knuckered to Jessie eagerly as soon as she appeared, longing to go out. Uncle Teddy's Warrior was a large-boned fleabitten grey, his dead white coat freckled all over with flecks of black and brown and ginger. He had a rather gaunt-looking head, and a reputation for being mean in the stable, but he was a very comfortable ride.

He laid his ears back and showed his teeth as Frank approached, and Thwaite growled at him, 'Get off it, you old fool! Would ye?' To Frank he said, 'Don't mind 'im, sir. He's grand once you're in t'saddle.'

While Thwaite saw Jessie up and settled, Wickes threw Frank up, and was soundly nipped by Warrior as he bent to tighten the girth. He stood away, rubbing his behind ruefully, but as soon as Frank gave the office, the grey's ears shot forward and he walked on politely, mouthing his bit and looking as eager and well-behaved as Hotspur.

'Treacle wouldn't melt in his mouth,' Frank observed to Jessie.

'We think he must have been ill-treated in stable before Uncle got him,' she answered. 'Poor chap. But he's only six, so there's time for him to forget and learn our Morland ways.'

The snow had gone, but it was a cold day, with a dull and pewter sky threatening more rain. February Fill-dyke, Frank thought. He looked about him eagerly as they trotted along the track towards Twelvetrees. He hadn't been home for a long time – and who knew when he would be back again? He and Jessie, Jack and Rob had not been born at Morland Place, but they had grown up here, and it was home to them. Jack had been ten and Jessie six when, with their older half-sister Lizzie, they had first come to Morland Place. The house had been virtually empty and part derelict, and the contrast with their restrained and tidy first years in Kensington could not have been greater. How they had run wild about the great old house – up one staircase and down another, from attic to cellar and back, their young feet echoing in the vast empty rooms! How they had roamed the unfettered countryside – they who had been used to a regulated daily walk with Nanny along the paths of an urban park. It was like being let out of a cage. No wonder the old Place had taken such a hold of their hearts.

The house had been restored since then, of course, the land brought back from the wilderness, and now it was a tidy and productive estate. He looked at the neat hedges, well-cared-for barns and buildings, the healthy stock, the sprouting crops; he smelt the good earth and the damp grass, and felt the clean air on his face, and he knew that deep and wordless sense of belonging, of oneness with the land, that every Morland felt sooner or later for the place that bred him. And beyond Morland Place were the green rolling hills and fertile fields, the purple moors and bare, windy uplands, the winding rivers, the snug villages and ancient towns of England, which were Morland Place writ large. That love he had for his home, and his sense of being of one substance with it, was the same thing as his deep love – like that of every Englishman – for his country. It was a thing beyond patriotism; it had a holiness to it.

Now he looked sideways at his sister and said quietly, 'It's worth fighting for – all this.'

She said in a rush, as though it were something she had been waiting to say, 'Oh, yes! I'm so glad you feel it. The war – the fighting – people being killed – it's hateful; but however bad it is, it has to be done. For this. To keep England safe. I do understand! And if I were a man . . .'

'You'd go, too. I know,' said Frank. 'I'm glad that you understand. I wanted you to know that it wasn't for the fun of playing soldiers.'

'But it *is* fun?'

'Tremendous fun,' he grinned. 'But though we laugh and joke and never say serious things about it, we all feel it, Jess – every one of us is there for the same reason. And we *will* win.'

She nodded, thinking how handsome he looked just then, his face firm with resolve. How lucky she was to have such brothers!

At Twelvetrees she attended to her business, while Frank inspected the occupants of the stables and chatted to the grooms. The new batch of two-year-olds – the yearlings of 1914, which was all the army requisition officer had left her – had recently been brought up and were learning their trade, to be handled in stable, to be tacked and untacked, led and groomed. 'If all that sort of thing is done properly and thoroughly,' Jessie told him, 'we don't have a tenth as much trouble when we back them – though,' she added, with a smile, 'it can still be quite a lively time.'

'You don't do that sort of thing yourself?' he said, alarmed. He remembered the time as a child she had tried to ride her father's unbroken stallion and almost got herself killed.

'Oh, I like to keep my hand in,' she said, enjoying his expression. 'Come on, I've finished here for now. Let's go and have a gallop on Marston Moor.'

Later they rode home, the horses stretched and happy, walking contentedly on a loose rein. The sky had lifted a little, the threat of rain postponed, blown away by the rising of a brisk little wind that turned the horses' manes over and ruffled their riders' bare heads. There were primroses under the hedges, and purple and white violets, and here and there on the bank tops the wild daffodils bent and rose on their short stems in a gleeful dance.

Frank said, 'There was something in particular I wanted to say to you, Jessie.'

'I thought so,' she said. 'What is it?'

'You remember last year, when I got my readership, how I told you that there were no females in my life and not likely to be?'

Jessie needed no more clue than that. 'Oh, Frank! How exciting – you have a young lady?'

'Well, I don't know that I *have* her, precisely, but—'

'Who is she? What's she like? Tell me everything.'

He had hoped for the invitation. 'Her name is Maria,' he said. 'Maria Stanhope.'

* * *

It was her hands he had noticed first. He was often in the college library, of course, ordering and collecting books, asking for things to be looked up, discussing where he might find this or that piece of information; but it had always been the librarian, Mr Benson, who had dealt with his needs. One day he went in to find Benson's desk empty, and Benson nowhere to be found. He was aware, of course, that the assistant librarian was quiet little Miss Stanhope, but he had never spoken to her. Now, however, seeing her in a far dark corner, he approached with his question.

She was sitting on the short library steps, a small pile of heavy books on her lap, her dark clothing and dark bent head blending into the shadowy background of deep brown wood and leather. But her long white hands with their delicate fingers seemed to shine by comparison, moving and flickering like marsh lights as she ran them through the pages. He stared at them, fascinated, for several seconds before she sensed his presence and looked up.

Her pale little face shone, too, white amid all the brown, punctuated by large dark eyes. 'Oh!' she breathed, a little, startled note; her eyes met his, and the faint stain of a blush came into her cheeks. 'I'm sorry. I didn't see you.'

'No, *I*'m sorry,' he said quickly. 'I didn't mean to startle you.' He felt he ought to remove his gaze, but it seemed strangely difficult. 'I was looking for Mr Benson.'

'He was called away, suddenly,' she said, her voice sounding slightly breathless. 'I don't know when he'll be back. Can I help you?'

'Oh – well – I don't know,' he began doubtfully, and saw at once that he had offended her. A spark came into her eyes.

'I have worked here for three years, Mr Compton. I know every book in the catalogue.'

'You know my name?' he said, intrigued.

'Of course,' she said simply. She stood up, putting the books on the top step, and brushed down her skirt in an automatic, but to him fetchingly graceful, gesture. 'What is it that you want? Try me, and I think you'll find I can help you just as well.'

He didn't answer at once: he was being washed through with unprecedented sensations. He had never before been aware of a woman as a woman. His mother, his sisters, the servants, his landladies, all those females with whom he had had intimate contact – he had known, of course, that they were women, but they were just themselves, and neatly contained in their categories. Beyond them there was a world of females – half the human race, indeed – with whom he had nothing to do at all. They did not impinge on him in any way. They were part of the world's furniture, along with all the men he did not know.

But now, suddenly, this small creature with her white skin and dark curly hair, her determined chin and bright, sparking eyes, her breathy voice and her expressive hands had burst into the bubble that surrounded him, and was making him notice her in a completely different way. He observed the slenderness of her neck where it disappeared into the collar of her dark blouse; the rise and fall of her small bosom beneath the fabric; the elegant curve of her skirt over her hips and the way it fell to an inch above the ground, where the pointed toe of her little shoe could be seen. He was aware of a faint scent coming from her, which he could not identify – something vaguely floral. Most of all, he was simply aware of *her*, as though some essence were being radiated from her, which he was suddenly able to pick up – strong, firm signals of her identity, which were unique and disturbing and which he would never again be able to ignore or mistake. He felt that if he walked into a completely dark room now, he would know if she was in it.

He saw her foot give an impatient tap, and dragged himself together. 'Yes, of course. I'm sure you can help me. What I wanted was this . . .'

She dealt with his requirements quickly and efficiently, with an air of briskness and faint rebuke that he found enchanting.

After that he tried always to take his requests to her rather than to Benson – who watched matters developing with a grim look that said this was exactly why he had not wanted

63

a female assistant in the first place. Miss Stanhope seemed also to be watching developments, but warily. She tried to be businesslike with Frank, and for some time his efforts to be friendly and to ask her about herself were rebuffed, though with a tactful skill, which, had he appreciated it, would have told him she had been propositioned in this library by other males before him.

One day he went into the library just before one o'clock and, slipping past Benson, who was reading at his desk, approached Miss Stanhope, who was balanced on top of the library steps getting down a large book from the top shelf. Whether his approach had distracted her he didn't know, but she stepped down a rung clumsily and began to overbalance. He caught the hand she had flung out and steadied her while she descended to floor level, the book clasped against her chest with the other. And then she turned to him and looked up.

It was like a lightning bolt. As their eyes met, it seemed that all barriers had dissolved between them, and what was Frank and what was Miss Stanhope touched and communicated, raw and undiluted. It lasted only a second, but at the end of it he still had hold of her hand, and he heard himself saying, 'Would you care to have luncheon with me?'

She said, 'I always bring sandwiches from home, and eat them in Russell Square Gardens.'

And a Frank he didn't know, a cunning, quick-witted Frank who was able to think ahead in situations such as this, said, 'Oh, I have sandwiches too. Do you think I might join you, and eat them with you?'

As a man who rarely ate luncheon of any sort, had never had to buy a sandwich in his life and had no idea how to go about it, he had a small problem to overcome, which meant that it was half an hour before he could join her in the garden. She was sitting on a bench under a great plane tree reading a book, and he hurried to her like a man hurrying home on a cold day. She made no comment about his lateness or about his badly wrapped sandwich (he had had to beg – and bribe – one of the refectory workers to make it for him), but greeted him without preamble with a question about Hume, showing him the book she was reading.

So began their friendship. As often as he could, he joined her in the park at lunchtime, and gradually learnt a little about her. Her name was Maria, she was twenty, and she lived in Wimbledon, one of those railway suburbs of London with street after street of identical little houses, all very respectable but not the sort of place that normally came in his way. Her father was a retired schoolmaster, and a great deal older than her mother. Her mother was an army officer's daughter. They were respectable, even – through her maternal grandfather – genteel; but there was no money in the family, which was why Maria had had to get a job. She was intelligent, and had been well educated at a good girls' school. If there had been any money, she could have gone to university herself. Instead, she had done the next best thing and, having to go out to work, had attached herself to an academic institution.

In the park he found her very different from the quiet Miss Stanhope who blended into the background in the library. She was wonderful to talk to – quick and witty, with an enquiring mind, and an ability instantly to understand and absorb, which told him, as nothing else could, how hard it must have been for her to accept the limit to her intellectual ambition imposed by lack of money. Their conversations were mostly academic and impersonal. Of herself she revealed as little as possible, telling him bare facts without commenting on them. Later he realised that she must have known what a social gulf there was between them and was treading warily. But hers was the only caution. He was so beguiled by her, he cared nothing for any other implications.

Their talks in the park – and occasionally his walking with her to the Underground station in the evening to catch her train – were not nearly enough for him. One day when they were talking about literature she let slip that she had never been to the theatre, and he asked her at once if he

65

might take her one evening. She withdrew a little and looked grave, and said she would not be allowed, and he bumped his nose against the rules of chaperonage, and another area of sensitivity. In spite of the fact that she had a job, in spite of the fact that she travelled alone on the train to and from work every day – or indeed, perhaps, *because* of those facts – her parents kept a very strict standard of chaperonage over her at other times. Since Frank had never been interested in women, it was something he had not come across before, though in the back of his mind he knew it existed. If he wanted to talk privately to a male colleague, he simply arranged the time and place to suit them both. He had been mentally classing Miss Stanhope with his male colleagues – sign of the esteem in which he held her intellect. Miss Stanhope had been offended, however, taking it as a slight on her status as a working woman.

He apologised, explained, said that he was stupid not to have thought of it. There was a short, difficult silence between them, at the end of which, diffidently, she asked if he would like to come to her home one Sunday and meet her parents.

All the way down in the train his hands were damp, and he fidgeted in his seat, wondering what on earth he had let himself in for. He had no idea what to expect. It was rather like being summoned to the headmaster's study, not knowing which of his sins had been discovered. Maria had given him instructions on how to get to the house from the station, but he had misunderstood or forgotten something, for he got lost straight away. He wandered in increasing alarm and apprehension. Every street looked exactly the same, row upon row of neat, identical, semi-detached 'villas', in red brick with white trim and a grey slate roof, a tiny front garden and a path of tiles in terracotta and blue diamonds leading up to the front door. Every house was shut up tight and there was no-one at all in the streets to ask the way. It was like a strange dream: the whole town seemed deserted, not so much as a dog trotting by. In London proper there was never this emptiness and silence.

He found Ruskin Avenue at last by accident, and rang the doorbell in a state of perturbation. It was opened by a thin, undersized servant with bedraggled hair slipping out of its pins, who breathed through her mouth and stared at him without speaking.

'Mr Stanhope?' Frank said. 'My name is Compton.'

She didn't precisely announce him, but she did show him into the drawing-room before backing away and disappearing. It was a small room of dark aspect with heavy red wallpaper and drapes, crowded with stiff furniture and a plethora of ornaments and pictures, in the taste of thirty years before. Mr and Mrs Stanhope were seated on either side of the unlit fire, Maria on the shiny black horsehair sofa, and all rose as he came in. The introductions were made by Maria, and they all sat again. Frank sat on the sofa too, but at a respectable distance from his object.

Mr Stanhope was elderly, with sparse hair and heavy spectacles, and an old-fashioned moustache and the whiskers that had used to be called 'Dundrearies'. His face seemed to have collapsed into a kind of hopelessness and his voice was faint and indeterminate. Mrs Stanhope was small and dark like Maria but fat, her round figure straining tautly against her clothing so that she looked like an india-rubber ball. Her voice was sharp and clipped, but perhaps seeming more so because of the contrast with her husband's. Far from sternly examining Frank and testing his worthiness, as he had expected of this first meeting, Maria's parents had seemed almost in awe of him. They appeared uncomfortably anxious to please him, and it was Maria who, in a quiet but skilful way, ordered the occasion and kept things going.

They had luncheon, the four of them, in a small, stiff dining-room. Maria helped the single, rather useless maid, to serve. She made no fuss about it, and Frank, with his new sensitivity to her, understood that it was her pride not to care that he saw her going back and forth to the kitchen because they could not afford more servants. He guessed that she had had to take a hand in the cooking, too. The quality of the food was uncertain. The soup had an unpleasant, metallic flavour (could it have been tinned soup? he wondered), but it was succeeded by a piece of cod with a delicate parsley sauce. The meat was overdone and the vegetables underdone, but the apricot tart was delicious, to be followed by tinned sardines on dry toast. Maria ate with a red spot of vexation on her cheeks at every shortcoming, and he longed to tell her it didn't matter. He was used to much worse food at his lodgings – when he noticed it at all: he normally read while he ate.

As a social occasion, the whole thing took on an air of the bizarre in his memory. He and the Stanhopes were from different worlds, and had nothing in common. Conversation was stilted, except when he and Maria spoke to each other. After the meal he was invited to walk round the small back garden with Mr Stanhope, who offered him a cigarette, pointed out various unremarkable shrubs, and then talked about what had been in the newspapers during the week – an easy topic to get them by. They rejoined Mrs Stanhope and Maria in the drawing-room and tea was drunk, while Mrs Stanhope asked him about his family, and he tried to answer without making the Morlands and Morland Place sound any different from the Stanhopes and Ruskin Avenue, Wimbledon.

And then at last a nod from Maria told him he might take his leave. He and the Stanhope parents parted with warm words but probably equal relief on both sides. He felt like a released prisoner going back to the normality and bustle of London. He could not see anything in either parent that could have given rise to the wonder that was Maria, and wished he could have known them when they were younger, before making-do and maintaining respectability had crushed the life out of them.

But after that, with the proprieties having been undergone and a relationship established, he was able to see Maria sometimes outside work. He invited her, with her mother, to the theatre one evening – her father rarely stirred from the house any more. One Saturday afternoon he met her and her mother in Oxford Street, where they had gone on a shopping expedition, and took them to tea at Selfridges. On another occasion he took her to an art exhibition one evening after work – the chaperon that time was an elderly cousin of Mrs Stanhope's who lived in a dim sort of way in a flat in Hammersmith. And, at the other end of the District Railway, Frank was invited twice to partner Maria at tennis parties at a local tennis club, and once to join an expedition to Hampton Court by motor, with some acquaintances of the Stanhope parents, their son and daughter and two friends.

Frank tried to describe these strained circumstances to Jessie without going into too much detail – the restrictions and the frustrations, his position and her job, the long hours each of them worked and the impossibility of ever being alone together, unless you called sitting in a public park in the middle of the day 'alone'. Jessie nodded with sympathy, thinking how odd and difficult it all sounded. Before her marriage, genial Uncle Teddy had arranged parties and dances and outings so that she could meet young men, and in Morland Place, its gardens and grounds, there was always plenty of space where young people could be easy and talk, with chaperonage at its most discreet. She had not appreciated before how difficult life must be for middle-class girls with no money.

'So this has been going on for months?' she said at last, when Frank had come to the end of his narrative. 'You sly thing, never to mention a word about it!'

'It all seemed too difficult to talk about, especially in a letter.'

'But you love her? It's serious?'

They had checked their horses by the big elm tree, having run out of ride before they ran out of subject. The horses had eased their reins until they could graze, and their riders were so preoccupied they had not noticed this breach of equine manners.

'It's serious, all right,' Frank said. 'I've never felt anything like this before. Maria's so – she's – oh, I can't explain it, but I can't imagine life without her.'

69

'I'm so pleased for you,' Jessie said warmly. 'I never thought you would fall in love.'

'Neither did I. I suppose that's what it is – being in love?'

'It sounds like it to me. Have you spoken about marriage?'

He shook his head. 'No.'

'Frankie!'

'I've *thought* about it,' he said. It had come upon him gradually, as he grew used to being in love with her, that marriage was where love tended, being the only way of completely and permanently securing her person to his. But the most casual thinking about marriage had revealed new and insuperable problems. 'I couldn't possibly afford an establishment, on my salary,' he said dully.

'No hope of a raise?'

'Not as things stand. When my present tenure is over, I could apply for a more lucrative post, probably at another university. A chair, perhaps, if I could publish another successful paper in the next couple of years – and then I'd be able to propose to her. I'd got as far as that in my thinking when the war came.'

'Was it partly because of her that you volunteered?'

He was surprised. 'How did you guess?'

'A lot of things about you have changed.'

He looked away. 'I had to do my duty. I have to keep the world safe for her. Do you understand? I wouldn't be worthy of her if I shirked that.'

'Of course I understand. I think it's wonderful of you,' Jessie said, laying an impulsive hand on his. 'But hadn't you at least better get engaged to her before you go away?'

'I can't ask her to commit herself, Jess. I may be away for years. Anything might happen.'

'You mean, you might be—?'

'I don't think I shall be killed, if that's what you mean. I have a very strong feeling that I shall come through all right. I may be wounded, but that's all. But if the war goes on for years, she might not want to wait that long. Someone else might come along who could marry her sooner. It wouldn't be fair to tie her up with nothing definite at the end of it.'

70

'Well, if it was me,' Jessie said, 'I'd sooner be tied than not. But I suppose you must know best. Poor girl. Does she know you're going away?'

'I'm going to tell her tomorrow. I've arranged to see her at home.'

'Are you going to tell here?' She jerked her head towards Morland Place.

'No,' he said. 'I decided not, in the end. I wasn't sure – well, that they'd approve. I know I personally have no money, but Uncle Teddy is frightfully rich and we're landed gentry on both sides, so I wasn't sure how they'd view a girl who goes to work.'

'Oh, phooey! Mother and Uncle Teddy don't care about things like that.'

'Hm. I'm not so sure. At any rate, I don't want to risk it. I couldn't bear it if anyone said anything slighting about her.'

'I'm sure no-one would,' Jessie said, though she did wonder for a moment about Polly, whose tongue was unregulated, and Rob, who did think a lot about the family's image. And, of course, the servants were very strict about keeping up standards, because their status depended on that of their employers, and they had their ways of letting you know what they thought about anything important.

'I'm not going to tell, anyway,' said Frank. 'There's no point as things stand, and it's too complicated. I couldn't go through it all again, the way I've told you. But I wanted you to know. I've told Maria about you, and I hoped that perhaps while I'm away you and she could write to each other. That way she and I could get news of each other, and you could – keep an eye on her, I suppose, at a distance.'

'If you got engaged you could write to her yourself.'

'No, I can't do that. It wouldn't be fair on her. But will you write to her?'

'Of course. If I go to London this year I could even visit her.'

'Bless you. You're a brick.'

'Though if she's such a bluestocking, she'll think me an absolute fool,' Jessie added.

'She's not a bluestocking. She's just clever and witty and quite wonderful.'

'Poor Frank. You really are in love! And poor Maria. I hope the war's over quickly, for both your sakes.'

CHAPTER FOUR

Polly was a weekly boarder at a school in Ripon. When she came home on Friday afternoon she was furious that she had missed both Frank's visit and the arrival of Ethel's baby. She had hoped that this time she might be allowed to watch, or at least get close enough to learn something about the process. All the girls at school were fascinated by childbirth but none of them really *knew* anything, and were forced to rely on old wives' tales and the more sensational kind of literature: 'Sweat poured from my every pore as I heard the hideous screams of my poor wife, audible even through the closed bedchamber door' etc.

So on Saturday morning Jessie took pity on her and set aside her work to go out for an early ride with her. They rode out through Ten Thorn Gap to the Whin and made a large circuit by Rufforth and White House Farm, where they paused to talk to Mrs Bellerby, who was by the gate. She begged them to come in for milk and cake. Jessie was summoning up an excuse when she saw almost the same longing for company and variety on Polly's face as on Mrs Bellerby's, and so she gave in. They left the horses in the yard and the dogs – Brach and Polly's hound Bell – in the scullery, and spent half an hour at the kitchen table eating Mrs Bellerby's delectable Fat Rascals. Polly played with the kittens that had been born six weeks ago in a box in the corner by the range, and Mrs Bellerby pumped Jessie for news. Jessie asked about the two eldest Bellerby sons, Joe and Tom, who had volunteered straight off, to their mother's enormous pride. They were in the same battalion as Lenny Manning, the Morlands' American cousin, which gave Polly a chance to talk about *him*, so all in all, Jessie thought, it was a very charitable visit. She even remembered to ask to see – again – the photograph of the two boys in their uniform, taken before they went off to camp.

'O' course, joining the Terriers they got their uniform straight off, while the Kitchener boys had to drill for months in their civvies,' Mrs Bellerby said, stroking the photograph fondly with a thumb. 'They look champion, don't you think so, Mrs Morland? As handsome two lads as any in Yorkshire, though I says it as shouldn't.'

'They look splendid,' Jessie concurred, and indeed they did, being tall and well set-up from a lifetime of work in the open air. 'You must be very proud.'

'I am that – and so's their dad, though it's made things very hard for him around the farm. Dad's longing for them to get out to France and get in the fighting, which the boys are too. They say once they get out there, the war'll be as good as over. It's just their fun, you understand,' she said, smiling up at Jessie, but it was plain she believed it too. *Get some Yorkshire lads on t'job*, Jessie paraphrased inside her mind, *and get t'job done right!*

They took their leave, mounting from the old block in the stableyard.

'Four Fat Rascals and two glasses of milk,' Jessie said, 'and you had an enormous breakfast. I don't know where you put it all.'

'School food all week,' Polly reminded her. 'You can't think! Do you suppose Daddy would let me have one of those kittens?'

They rode on, skirting Askham Bryan, and pausing at Eastfield to deliver a message for Uncle Teddy. Here, not all Mrs Pike's blandishments or Polly's melting looks could persuade Jessie to come in for tea and parkin, but there were polite enquiries to be made after family members on both sides before they could continue. They had a last canter

74

across Acomb moor, and then Jessie insisted that they must walk the last half-mile to bring the horses in cool.

They were just approaching the track that crossed Hob Moor, running from the South Road to Morland Place, when they saw a man walking up it towards them. A man in uniform – even from a distance the Sam Browne said he was an officer. The horses turned their heads and pricked their ears, the dogs froze a moment, then bounded off towards him joyfully, and Polly shouted, 'It's Ned!' and kicked Cobweb into a most unladylike gallop.

Jessie turned Hotspur and walked down towards him, everything inside her holding its breath. When she reached him he looked up at her, through Polly's excited chatter, fending off the dogs who were revolving and gazing and lashing his legs with their hard tails. Her eyes asked the question, and he answered with an infinitesimal nod. This was it, then, she thought. Embarkation leave.

'Why didn't you tell us you were coming?' she asked, in lieu of greeting.

'I sent a telegram, but when I found there was no-one waiting to meet me at the station, I realised I must have sent it to Maystone without thinking.'

'But they'd have told you if it wasn't delivered.'

'I suppose Gladding must have taken it in and not told anyone.'

'That's so like him,' Jessie said. 'You could have taken a taxi.'

'I wanted the walk.'

'Oh, what does it matter how he came? He's here!' Polly said, beaming at her brother. 'How long can you stay?'

'I have to be back tomorrow night. Where were you two going?'

'Home. We've just finished our ride,' said Jessie.

'You can have Cobweb, if you like,' said Polly. 'I can ride behind Jessie.'

'I'm too heavy for Cobweb,' Ned said, with a smile.

'Well, let me carry your bag, then.'

'It isn't heavy.'

75

'But let me – do.'

He yielded it, and they walked along together. Ned kept Polly chattering with deft questions. He could not talk to Jessie as he wanted to until they were alone. In the yard at Morland Place Polly was out of the saddle in an instant, grabbed Ned's hand and towed him into the house, wanting to be the one to announce his arrival. The dogs rushed in his wake, glued to him by excitement. Left alone, Jessie dismounted, handed over the reins, gave the grooms their instructions and walked into the house. By then the first exclamations and hugs were over, though Teddy, summoned from the business-room, was still patting Ned as though he could not get enough of touching him, and Henrietta, brought out from the kitchen, was still saying how well and strong he looked, and swearing he had got taller as well as broader.

'It's the uniform,' Jessie said. 'Frank looked taller, too.'

Ned turned as if grateful for the excuse to look at her. 'Was Frank here?'

'On Wednesday. Embarkation leave. His battalion's going to Malta.'

Polly at last made the connection. 'Is that what this is? Are you going overseas?'

'Not the York Commercials – just me. I've been transferred to a Terrier unit that was short of officers. I have to join them in London, on their way to France.'

'To France!' Polly cried. 'You're going to the Front? Oh, you lucky thing!' She hung on his arm affectionately. 'I'm so glad you're going. It was awful having only Bertie there, and everybody else stuck here in England. I bet you're excited!'

'I'm not sure excited is the word,' Ned said. 'I'm glad to be going, though. Everyone in the battalion would have liked to go. We all want to have a crack at the enemy.'

'Well, this *is* good news, my son,' Teddy said, putting an arm round his shoulders. 'I knew Colonel Bassett had recommended you, but I didn't think anything would happen this quickly. Of course, there's the new offensive

76

everyone's expecting. I wonder if you'll be involved in that?' He turned away, taking Ned with him, towards the drawing-room, and the others followed, Henrietta merely pausing to tell the hovering Sawry to send in refreshments and have Ned's bag taken up to the Blue Room.

There was so much to be said on all sides that it was almost lunchtime before Ned was able to excuse himself. 'I must wash the smuts off before we eat,' he said, rising. But before he got any further Nanny Emma appeared with the new baby in her arms: she had waited ever since she heard of his arrival for the visit to her nursery, and had run out of patience. Ned admired baby Harriet and said all the right things, then recollected that he must call in to see Ethel and congratulate her. So by the time he and Jessie got to the Blue Room, the luncheon bell was on the point of being rung.

He closed the bedroom door behind them and walked straight to his wife, taking her in his arms. Jessie closed her eyes, feeling the rough khaki under her fingers, and his cheek against her hair. She felt all the old complex of affections for him as the cousin she had grown up with: the playmate of her childhood, the kind older brother who had defended her and danced with her in her adolescence. But under-neath, where once she had taken for granted the feelings of wifeliness, there was an emptiness. When she had lost the baby, something had broken that was not yet mended. She wondered if it ever would be. Worse, she was afraid of him – not that he would ever harm her, but that he was going to want something of her she couldn't give him. She didn't want him to touch her body; the thought of intimacy with him sickened her; and she felt a surge of despair because she was going to spend the rest of her life married to him, and if these feelings never changed, what a hell that might be.

He drew back from her now, looked long and carefully into her face, kissed her lightly on the lips and said, 'I really must wash before luncheon. I wonder when we're going to have time to be alone together?'

'Not today, that's for sure. While you were talking to Mother I overheard Uncle Teddy telling Aunt Alice who he wants to invite to dinner tonight. He means to give you a right royal send-off, that's for sure. And if I know him he's already telephoning friends and neighbours so they can drop in this afternoon.'

Ned said, 'I could almost wish he weren't so proud of me.'

'We're all proud of you,' she said.

He paused, on his way to the washstand, and said seriously, 'Are *you*?'

'Of course,' she said nervously, wondering what was coming next.

But the luncheon bell sounded. He stared a moment longer and then said, 'I hope the water's still warm. We were rather a long time in Ethel's room.'

'You were very sweet to her,' Jessie said, more relaxed now he had his back to her.

He poured water from the jug into the bowl, took off his jacket and rolled up his sleeves, washed his hands and face. She handed him the towel and he emerged from its folds to say, 'It's a dear little baby. Did you mind terribly, Jess? I wish I could have been here to support you. I felt so bad about it.'

'You needn't,' she said. 'I was all right. I *have* to be all right. I can't expect other people not to have babies just because—' She didn't finish the sentence.

Ned put aside the towel and stepped closer. 'We'll have others,' he said, and she recoiled inwardly from the tenderness of his voice and the look in his eyes.

She picked up his jacket and pushed it at him, an object to put between them. 'The bell went ages ago. We'd better hurry.'

On Saturday Rob worked at the bank only in the morning, so he was home for luncheon, and had brought with him Ethel's elder brother, David, who was a solicitor in York and a great friend of his. David had been one of Jessie's suitors when she came out and, since he had reached the age of twenty-eight unmarried, Polly liked to claim romantically that he 'had a broken heart' and 'would never love another woman'. Whatever the truth of it, he sat at Jessie's side and engaged her in amusing chat, which relieved her, on this occasion, of thinking too much about Ned. She glanced across at him from time to time through the protracted meal, and thought how handsome he looked, how very grown-up and manly in his uniform, how interesting, how – yes, how attractive. Paradoxically, with the width of the table between them and his attention elsewhere than on her, she was able to find him attractive again. And when she thought of him in France, at the Front, commanding men in the heat of battle, she felt the faintest tremor of her old feelings. The further he was from her, the more she liked him – and what did that make her? she asked herself, with sour reproach.

She had been right about Uncle Teddy. All the time they were upstairs he had been telephoning to tell people his son was home on embarkation leave, on the way to the Front, and all afternoon people were dropping in to see Ned, shake his hand, and congratulate Teddy and Alice. And at dinner they sat down sixteen at the table, with more people expected afterwards for the evening. It was like old times, as Henrietta whispered to Jessie.

Polly dined down, to her great delight, and in the drawing-room afterwards she could not be detached from her brother's side. Jessie was sitting at the piano – usually it was Alice or Ethel who played, but Ethel was still confined, and Alice had been bracketed and immobilised by her old friends Mrs Winnington and Mrs Spindlow. Jessie played automatically and looked from face to face, always coming back to Ned: Ned, politely amused, patiently answering questions, smiling at people's jokes, listening courteously to older people, and with affection to his little sister's babbling; Ned at the heart of this evening, the centre of attention, always responding but rarely initiating anything of his own. She realised again that she did not know what he thought or how he felt about anything. He was opaque to her. He was the perfect stranger she had married. She knew he loved

79

her, but what did that *mean*, exactly? What did it feel like to be inside him looking out? If she could somehow, by magic, experience his feelings, would she recognise them as anything she had a name for? Would what he felt about her be what she thought of as love?

He lifted his eyes just then and met hers in a searing moment of contact, and there was no mistaking, at least, his look of longing. In that instant she made up her mind. He was a soldier going away to the war, and it was her duty as his wife to send him away happy, knowing that she cared for him. It was only one night. She must give him what he wanted, and hide her own feelings. She was afraid – afraid for so many reasons – but she owed it to him, not only as his lawfully wedded wife, but in the name of the affection she bore him, and the kindness there had been between them.

So when the evening finally ended and they walked upstairs together, she slipped her hand under his arm, and when he looked down at her she smiled up at him. She was trembling so much he must have felt it, but of course that did her no discredit with him, no harm at all.

What with breakfast, then visiting the nursery and playing with the children, church, luncheon and a walk round with his father, Ned's Sunday was used up desperately quickly. Before he had drawn breath, it seemed, it was time for tea, after which he would have to leave to get his train. Ethel, tired of missing everything, came carefully down to tea, and was petted and praised, cosseted and warned not to stay up too long, and then everything everyone else had already heard had to be told all over again for her. Henrietta had not needed to urge Mrs Stark to lay on a special spread. She had been baking at intervals ever since Ned arrived, so that he should have a 'proper Yorkshire tea'. He protested that he had only just had a proper Yorkshire luncheon, but he managed to do himself credit all the same and go a reasonable way to trying everything, saying to his father that he was likely to remember this meal with longing in days to come.

He was half in a daze all day, remembering the night before. He would not have forced himself on Jessie, but she had turned to him in bed, making it clear she wanted him, and his heart had lifted. But, oh, how she had trembled! Her body, which he remembered as wonderfully yielding, shaping itself to his, was stiff with apprehension; and no wonder, he thought, given what she had gone through. He had been as gentle as he could with her, in tenderness for her physical condition, though his own passion had been hard to contain. He was afraid that he might have hurt her. At all events, it was not like before. He felt there had been no pleasure in it for her, as there had always used to be. He could not warm her; she was doing it for him, and it left him unsatisfied, feeling selfish and bad, as though he had used her. It left him feeling less a man – and with her he had always been a king.

He had half expected her to cry afterwards. But she had not wept, only sighed – such a sigh! He did not know what it meant, only that it was not a happy sound; but she had curled in his arms afterwards, as they had used to lie, and he had fallen quickly asleep. Waking beside her had been wonderful, after the months of waking in his cold, narrow cot up at Black Brow; almost wonderful enough to wipe out the sadness of last night's failure. She had smiled at him as she woke, and when he said he loved her, she had answered that she loved him, too. Knowing that he was going away, for he did not know how long, he had watched her all day, whatever she did, whoever she spoke to, observing every movement of her hand, every expression of her face, with the greed of one facing a long starvation. The night's sadness blended into the sadness of leaving, so that he was able to convince himself at last that that was all it was.

Time ran out, and he had to go. 'Will you drive me to the station?' he asked her.

'Oh, let me come!' Polly cried urgently, but Henrietta caught her hand and drew her back, and Alice shook her head at her. Polly pouted, but desisted. His few things were packed in his valise, extravagant farewells were said all round, and Henrietta pressed on him a packet of sandwiches 'for the journey', which he took with thanks and an embrace, not mentioning that the journey was too short for him to need nourishment. But, of course, she must have known that. Everyone wanted to give him something. Even Brach brought him an extremely chewed object that turned out to be someone's glove, and when they walked out into the yard she bustled past them and jumped into the back of the car, determined not to be left behind.

'Oh, let her come,' said Ned.

'I wish I had a present for you,' Jessie said, as she drove down the track in the Austin, bumping wildly over the ruts which Uncle Teddy's big Benz made nothing of. 'We should have gone into York yesterday, then I could have bought you something. If only Uncle Teddy hadn't invited the whole neighbourhood!'

'Never mind,' said Ned, pushing Brach off his shoulder and wiping his ear. 'You still can give me a present, if you really want to. You can post it on to me. There's something I'd like very much.'

'What's that?'

'A photograph of you, small enough to carry in my pocket book. Would you have one taken?'

'Of course, if you like,' she said. 'But that's not what I'd call a present. A proper present is something like—'

'A packet of roast-beef sandwiches?' She laughed. 'A photograph is what I'd really like.'

'Then I'll send you one.' She drove on for a while, then, 'Do you think you'll be in this new offensive Uncle Teddy was talking about?'

'I don't know. They haven't told me anything, except that I'm to join the South Kent Rifles on their way to France. But the talk in the mess is that they need every man they can get, what with having to send a force out to the Dardanelles, and being short of troops in any case. So I should think it's likely.'

Jessie was silent a moment, and then said quietly, 'Shall you be scared? If it comes to battle?'

82

'I don't know. How can I know that?' He looked side-long at her. 'What does Bertie say? He must have written about it, or talked to you about it in the old days.'

'He always said when the time comes there's too much to do to be scared.'

'I can believe that might be true.' Another silence, and he had no idea where her thoughts were. She drove steadily, her eyes on the road, her profile to him, strong and womanly, her hands capable and quiet on the wheel as they were always capable and quiet on the reins when she rode. The faint scar down her cheek showed pale in this light. She was so beautiful. 'Scared or not,' he said, 'I hope I will do my duty.'

'I know you will,' she said, almost absently.

At the station he said, 'Don't come in. If this war goes on long, there will be too many goodbyes. Standing about on platforms waiting for trains to pull out is dreary work.'

'Very well,' she said dutifully, and he felt a perverse pang that she had not protested, even a little.

He kissed her. 'I'll write. You'll write to me?'

'Of course.' He climbed down and reached back in for his valise. 'Oh – your sandwiches!'

'Mustn't forget those,' he said, with a difficult smile. 'Well, goodbye.'

He walked away, and she called after him, 'Take care of yourself!' He lifted a hand in acknowledgement, but he did not look back, having set himself, she thought, not to.

If and when the York Commercials marched out, there would be a fine sending-off, crowds and music, cheering and flags; but one officer leaving for the Front made no ripple in the early-morning routine of the camp. Transport was there to take him and his servant Daltry to the station with their bags, but no-one turned out to wave goodbye. There was a thick white fog hiding all but the nearest buildings and pine trees; its condensation dripped from twigs and eaves, and made an unnatural silence, through which came the occasional yark of a crow, and the sound of the sheep on the high moor bleating.

Once on the train, it was a slow journey, with all the unexplained delays of the wartime railway, and nothing to do but read, smoke and stare out of the window. Outside, as they crept south, it grew wet and cold, with gusty rain slapping the carriage windows from a low, grey sky – depressing weather for a man leaving his beloved wife, and with no colleagues to emphasise the excitement of the occasion. There were so many stops on the way down, with the train being shunted onto side lines to allow other, more favoured, traffic through, that he was afraid he would miss his connection; but after Doncaster it picked up speed, and having crossed London in a taxi he reached Waterloo with ten minutes to spare.

The battalion was still in process of embarking, and from the number of people and the amount of baggage still to be got aboard, it was evident the train would not be leaving on time. Ned found the commanding officer, Colonel Lindsay, standing near the barrier in conversation with another officer, and went to report to him.

'Ah, yes, Mr Morland. Glad you could make it,' said the colonel, returning his salute and then shaking his hand cordially. 'This is the adjutant, Dickie Apthorpe.'

'How d'ye do?' Apthorpe looked him over with keen, photographing eyes.

'Desperately short of officers,' Lindsay went on. 'Had to poach a couple of chaps from Maidstone – well, they were only going to India, by all accounts. Our need was greater. And then two more chaps like yourself were draughted in. Up to strength now, but it was touch and go.'

'Sir,' said Ned, 'will the men know that I'm – well, where I came from?'

'Worried about your lack of experience? Don't be,' Lindsay said kindly. 'Your colonel spoke highly of you. You'll soon settle down.'

'We're all in the same boat, more or less,' said Apthorpe. 'Very few of us have battle experience. One in five of the men only joined last August – practically raw recruits.'

'This is a friendly regiment,' Lindsay concluded. 'The

man who does his duty has nothing to fear. I've put you in D Company. Dickie, take Mr Morland along and introduce him to the other subs.'

By the time the train pulled out – only half an hour late – Ned was well settled into the compartment he was sharing with seven other subalterns. All were cheerful young men in the prime of youth. The youngest, Brown, looked around nineteen or twenty. The oldest, Arthurs, was perhaps a year or so older than Ned himself, and two of the others, Cheddy and Singer, perhaps in a spirit of irony, called him 'Uncle'. They received Ned warmly with a minimum of questions and, oddly, he was at once very much at home with them. With the other officers of the York Commercials he had always felt himself an outsider; with these complete strangers he felt comfortable.

As the slow journey wound onward across the country to Southampton, it transpired that some of the complete strangers were not quite as unknown as he had thought. Nugent said shyly that his brother had known Ned from Eton, where he had been in the same house – Jourdelay's – but a couple of years above him. Ned admitted he had been at Eton and remembered Johnny Nugent; and then Wharton and Knatchbull, who seemed to be friends, exclaimed that they had been at Eton too, and after some discussion decided they had *thought* there was something familiar about Ned. They had been two years below him, and in a different house, but once the confusion had been cleared up about his having had a different name back then, before Teddy had adopted him, they remembered that his sporting prowess had made him something of a hero to them. 'I shall never forget that wonderful fifty you made against Harrow,' said Knatchbull.

'Nor shall I,' Ned laughed. 'I never did anything like it again.'

'You used to go about with Thomas Winchmore and Eddie Vibart, didn't you?' said Wharton.

'My cousins,' Ned admitted.

And then it transpired that Arthurs had met Eddie, and

knew Thomas's name because his father was in the Diplomatic, and suddenly Ned had an entire compartment full of old friends. It was all so natural and easy that he saw the point of having been sent to Eton all those years ago.

The train pottered on, and darkness was falling by the time they reached Southampton. Here there was a long delay, and one of the captains, Richardson, stuck his head round the door to say that their ship was not ready for them, and that the colonel said they could go off in batches to get some dinner.

As Ned climbed down from the train with Wharton, Nugent, Knatchbull and Singer, he said, 'Won't the men get anything to eat?'

'They were issued rations this morning – enough for two days,' Wharton said.

Singer laughed. 'Trouble is, nine-tenths of 'em will have eaten the lot already. Just like children! You can never trust a Tommy to carry his own food.'

'Don't let your heart bleed, however,' said Nugent. 'Even as we speak, help is at hand – look there.'

Along the platform several trolleys were trundling at speed, loaded with coffee, buns, sausage rolls, sandwiches, cake, chocolate and cigarettes, by which means some local entrepreneurs were intending to separate the British Army from its pay.

The five young men walked out from the station to the nearest hotel and dined well enough on sardines, chicken with fried potatoes, and mushrooms on toast, washed down with a fairly decent burgundy. They walked back, pleasantly full, smoking an after-dinner cigarette, and talking about what the food and wine in France would be like. Only Nugent had ever been abroad, having been taken on a family holiday to Biarritz when he was ten. For the others, France was as much a land of legend as Araby, and they aired their quaintest preconceptions for the amusement of each other.

It was pitch dark when the battalion finally marched to the dockside through a blowy, wet black evening, and embarked up a gangway that jerked and heaved with the restless movements of the tethered vessel. For the men, few of whom had ever been outside his county, let alone his country, the novelty of being on a ship raised them to a pitch of excitement. They chattered like a roost of starlings, staring, pointing, laughing, and it took a long time to get them settled. Ned located some of his own platoon, introduced himself and made a start on learning the names. They were in high spirits, every face creased in a grin, and there were jokes and laughter and dozens of questions, most of which he couldn't answer. When he left them, he heard them already beginning a sing-song, to the wail of someone's mouth organ:

> Send out the boys of the Old Brigade,
> Who kept old England free,
> Send out me brother, me sister and me mother,
> But for Gawd's sake don't send me!

The officers had a lounge to themselves, and settled to reading, conversation or staking out a corner in which to doze. It wasn't until after midnight that they sailed. Ned went out on deck to see the casting-off and stood watching the dock fall behind as the tugs hauled the ship out into the sailing channel. The rain had stopped for a while, though it was still breezy and the air was damp and salty. He stayed there at the rail for a long time, looking at the myriad lights of the shore and their broken reflections in the Solent, watching the fingers of searchlights sweeping the sky for aircraft and the sea for submarines.

Someone came up to the rail beside him; a glance, and he moved to make room for Arthurs. Arthurs offered his cigarette case, and lit for them both. The shape and lights of the land fell slowly behind. They cleared the last bulk of the Isle of Wight and the choppiness of the Channel lifted them suddenly and made them stagger; and now they were out in the darkness of the open sea, with only the stars and the dark shapes of the two escorting destroyers, plunging along to either side of them, for company.

Arthurs drew the last from his cigarette and threw the glowing butt over the side. 'Listen to 'em,' he said. The men had let out whoops of surprise and perhaps dismay when the action of the ship changed; but now they had got used to it and resumed their sing-songs and their loud chat and laughter. 'You'd think they were going on holiday – a day trip to Southend.'

'I suppose it is a holiday to them,' Ned said. 'Different from anything they've done before. Plenty of company, enough to eat and nothing to worry about.'

'You're a funny one,' Arthurs said, not unkindly. 'Noticing. You don't say much, but you listen all the time.' A raucous splurge of laughter and voices came from the nearest deck-house. Arthurs shook his head and gestured back to where England had disappeared into the darkness. 'How many of 'em will ever see that again?'

'It doesn't do to think that way,' said Ned.

'You're right. Too much imagination is not a good quality in a soldier.' He pushed himself off the rail. 'How about a nightcap? I've some brandy in my haversack.'

'Delighted,' said Ned.

They reached Boulogne in the early hours of a bitterly cold, misty morning. A breakfast ration was issued to everyone of cold bacon, bread and butter and tea, and they disembarked at six thirty. Setting their boots for the first time on the surface of France, the men discovered, as other units had before them, the disadvantage of slippery French cobblestones, and the impossibility of marching over them with an even swing. Their exclamations of interest at being in a foreign country and of exasperation with what was underfoot were equally quashed by the NCOs, who wanted the battalion to show its most disciplined face to whatever Frenchies were there to see them.

The people of Boulogne had by now seen more troops passing through than they could count, but they managed a cheer or two and a friendly wave as the battalion marched to the railway station. The men exclaimed all over again when they discovered they were to travel in cattle-wagons, with straw on the floor and *40 Hommes, 8 Chevaux* stencilled on the sides. Some waggish soldiers who had used the wagons before them had chalked up an alternative message *Caution: Do not lean out of the Window*. The men, who were in high spirits, made a number of suggestions for other inscriptions, and it was probably fortunate for international relations that no-one had any chalk.

It took a very long time to entrain, and the journey across France was even slower than the one across England. Outside, the bitter sky lowered, and towards noon a thin snow began swirling down on the creeping train. The officers had the luxury of compartments to travel in, but the heating pipes had been disconnected, and it was horribly cold: the men, crowded together and with cosy straw to bury their feet in, were probably better off. There were no conveniences, either, the carriages not having corridors, so they had to urinate out of the window, a delicate operation that required good balance and, since everyone else had to do the same, careful timing. But at least their ration luncheon of bread, cheese and bully beef was still intact, and they supplemented it with their own butter, chocolate, biscuits, tinned sardines and bottles of beer and wine.

It was not until three p.m. that they finally drew into a station with a steamy sigh from the engine that suggested they had reached their destination. Cheddy rubbed the condensation from the window and read the station name. 'St Omer,' he said. 'Do you think this is it, at last?'

'That's where General Headquarters is,' said Knatchbull.

'St Omer?' said Arthurs. 'That's only thirty or forty miles from Boulogne, and it's taken us five hours to get here. We could almost have walked it quicker.'

'There's the colonel getting down,' Cheddy said, his head out of the window. 'This must be it.'

'Whether or not, I'm getting out,' Wharton said. 'I need to stretch my legs.'

'What wouldn't I give for a decent cup of tea?' said Singer.

Suddenly the adjutant was there, looking bandbox smart,

despite the long journey and having had to shave in cold water that morning. Ned felt grubby and rumpled at the sight of him.

'Right, chaps. We're detraining here. We'll parade in the station yard, and march off to our billet, which I'm told is about three miles away.'

'That'll stretch your legs for you,' Knatchbull murmured to Wharton.

'Just far enough to work up an appetite,' said Brown.

'Once everyone's been allocated his billet,' Apthorpe went on, 'there will be a hot meal for the men. You can tell them that – it'll cheer them up on the march. Those damned French cobbles are beyond a joke.'

'Are we going up to the Front, sir?' Brown asked.

'I can't answer that,' said Apthorpe. 'I'm afraid I don't know yet where we're bound. I expect orders will arrive tonight or tomorrow.'

When he had walked on, Arthurs said, 'We're not far from the Front, anyway.'

'How far?' Brown asked.

'Oh, I should say not more than thirty or forty miles.'

Wharton laughed. 'That sounds far enough to me, given it's taken us two days to get this far.'

Detraining everyone and everything seemed to take hours, but then they paraded and marched off, over the awkward, slippery cobbles that stubbed the men's toes and twisted their ankles. Ned at least was riding, his horse having been shipped to the Kents' barracks ahead of him. He could tell Compass Rose didn't like what was underfoot: she slipped and tripped and sweated at the uncertainty. The fine snow was still drifting down, but hardly settling – just a faint rime along the tops of hedges and a faint powdering on roofs. The low sky was bringing on an early dark. So this was France, he thought. It didn't look much different from England, except that it was flatter and emptier. There were hedges and copses, open fields, the occasional farm building; but no people, except in uniform, and no traffic but army vehicles.

It took them well over an hour to march to the village where they were billeting – a desolate, empty place, most of the residents long gone, signs of neglect about most of the houses, rubbish everywhere, the gardens overgrown with weeds and brambles. Ned could see that the sight sobered his men somewhat, perhaps reminding them of why they were here. They halted in the road while they were told off company by company and then platoon by platoon and shown to their billets. Ned's and Wharton's platoons were put together in a barn. Ned was glad to see it had a sound roof and was quite dry inside, and still full of straw, which meant they'd be able to bed down comfortably. They were still filing inside when the Service Corps lorry arrived with the promised hot meal: stew with boiled potatoes, together with a ration of cheese, bread, and tea. Faces lit up at the thought of hot food after two days of picnicking, and Ned and Wharton left them to the NCOs and walked off to find their own lodgings.

The junior officers were all together in a large farmhouse, and one of the company cooks, aided by the officers' servants, had managed to get the kitchen range going so there was a hot dinner for them, too, and hot water for washing.

'Hot water for shaving in the morning, with any luck,' said Arthurs, stretching with pleasure.

Coffee was served, and everyone lit cigarettes, except Singer, who smoked thin cigarillos. Ned finished his coffee quickly. He was tired from the long journey but he felt restless. 'I think I'll take a turn outside,' he said. 'Breath of fresh air. Anyone coming?'

'We just had two hours of that,' said Cheddy. 'Marching from the station – or had you forgotten?'

'I'm just getting comfortable at last,' said Arthurs.

'Me for bed any minute,' said Wharton, yawning.

'I'll come,' said Brown. 'Just five minutes, though.'

They went out through the kitchen door and into what had once been a garden, but was now trampled into a wasteland. It had stopped snowing, and the wind had dropped, but in the stillness it was even colder than before. They walked away from the lighted windows into the darkness, their breath rising in clouds before them. At the end of the garden was a hedge and beyond it the vegetable patch. There was not much left, only a few pigeon-bitten cabbages, some gaunt stems of Brussels sprouts, almost picked out, the ghostly dried vines of last autumn's beans. A thin moon was just rising, gleaming on the fine film of snow that decorated an abandoned and rusty cultivator on the far side.

'Not exactly an entrancing landscape,' said Brown. 'It's bloody cold out here, Morland. I think I'm going back in.'

'Wait,' said Ned, catching his arm as he turned. 'What's that?'

They listened. 'Sounds like thunder,' said Brown. But even as he said it, he knew it wasn't, and he met Ned's eyes with a shine of excitement.

'It's not thunder, it's guns,' said Ned. 'Artillery.' The rumbling and the intermittent thud-thud-thud were coming from the east. From the Front. Suddenly thirty miles did not seem so far away. They had arrived at last. This was the war, the real thing.

'I wonder if it's our guns or theirs,' said Brown.

'What does it matter?' Ned said, with a grin.

They were moved up the next day to a village called La Couture, just a couple of miles from the line. The whole area was seething with troops, well scattered in their billets to avoid being spotted by enemy aircraft. Within hours there wasn't a soldier in the battalion who did not know what the plan was. Their object was a village called Neuve Chapelle, which was in German hands. Behind it was a piece of high ground called Aubers Ridge, which gave the Germans both the advantage of height, and a screen behind which to move troops, out of sight of the British Army. Beyond Aubers Ridge lay an open plain and, no more than nine miles away, the city of Lille – the industrial heart of Flanders – crying out to be liberated.

The line in front of Neuve Chapelle formed a shallow

salient, curving out towards the British, which would make it harder for the Germans to defend.

'We have reliable intelligence,' Colonel Lindsay told the officers at the briefing, 'that this part of the line is very thinly held. The Germans have been withdrawing large numbers of men to reinforce the Russian front. We now believe that there are only two German divisions facing us. As you probably know, there are now six British divisions here, ready to oppose them. For the first time in this war, gentlemen, it will be the Germans who are outnumbered.'

This was the plan that Sir John French had urged on the war committee: a determined assault on this part of the line, which would take Neuve Chapelle, and from there carry Aubers Ridge. Knock the Germans off their high ground, and the way was open to retake Lille. Such a blow would be devastating to the Germans' morale, and it would sever their vital supply line. 'This could be the battle that will end the war, gentlemen. It is of vital importance that it succeeds – and it *will* succeed. We have everything on our side.'

The attack would have three prongs. In the centre the immediate object was Neuve Chapelle itself; on the left the Moated Grange and the village of Mauquissart, and on the right the German trenches to the south of Neuve Chapelle and the Bois du Biez. Having taken those, the three forces would converge together on Aubers Ridge.

'Our guns will lay down an extremely heavy artillery barrage at the beginning of the action that will tear open the enemy barbed wire and pound their trenches, knocking the fight out of them. Then the first wave goes in. This battalion will not be in the first wave,' the colonel said, with evident regret. 'The first wave will take the German trenches before Neuve Chapelle, the second wave will then advance through them and take the village. Those will all be regular troops. Then we will advance and take over the trenches, allowing the first wave to pass through the village and take the trenches beyond. We will be the first Territorial troops into action, and I hope you appreciate, gentlemen, what an honour it is, and what an opportunity to prove our worth.'

It certainly struck the men that way, and whenever Ned was near any of them he heard them talking about it. They were excited and eager for the battle, ready to show what Terriers were made of. The regulars called them 'Saturday-night soldiers', and they wanted only the chance to wash out the insult in German blood. Not one of them doubted that the battle would be won. The Germans – everybody knew this – would not stand having their line broken. They would crumple as soon as things didn't go their way. The whole line would be rolled up, and total victory would be within grasp. And the South Kents were the men to do it. Very well, so a fifth of them were raw recruits with only six months' training: nevertheless they were all volunteers, which made them worth two of any German conscript, and eager for a fight. They would prove their worth in the best way possible – not with words but with deeds – and show that Terriers were every bit as good as Regulars when it came to the pinch.

Preparations for the battle had already been going for several days when they reached La Couture, but there was plenty more hard work to be done. The area on both sides of the Front was lacerated with trenches. They meandered up and down as the contours of the land dictated, dog-legging to take in the corner of a wood or a defensible structure, leaving a variable gap between the British and German lines, but nowhere more than a hundred yards wide. The whole area was a mess of smashed buildings, derelict farms and splintered trees, cut through by streams and drainage ditches. Remarkably, Neuve Chapelle was still intact, and from its stout walls German snipers made the lives of the front-line troops a misery by day and night.

The terrible weather through the winter had rendered many of the trenches on the British side waterlogged and unusable, but recently they had begun to dry out and the ground to firm up. So now the preparatory work of the troops was to repair and drain old trenches and dig new ones. There was also a number of waterways crossing the battlefield, from small rivers down to drainage ditches and culverts, and it was necessary to make bridges over them. There were gun platforms to build, miles of telephone wires to be laid, and tons and tons of equipment to be brought up to dumps close to the line, to serve the army as it advanced.

All this work could only be done at night, which greatly increased the labour and difficulty. Ned, beginning to know the names and faces of his men, learnt a great deal about their character in these trying circumstances. Night after night, throughout the hours of darkness, they laboured like beasts of burden, carrying boxes of ammunition, bombs and shells, boxes of rations, reels of barbed wire, planks, sand-bags, tools; carrying them across waterlogged fields and along paths that were now morasses, stumbling and cursing in the darkness, tripping on wire, sliding in mud, falling into culverts and dragging themselves out mired and frozen. It was heartbreaking labour, made more difficult because they had always to be carrying rifle and ammunition, in case of attack, which hampered them dreadfully. Yet they never sulked or shirked, and Ned noticed that even while they were labouring they were always looking round, trying to get an idea of the terrain and fix landmarks in their minds, so that they could fight more intelligently when the time came.

At the end of every night they crawled wearily back to their billets, to be faced still with the chore of cleaning themselves and their kit before morning parade; but having cursed until they ran out of curses, they were aware of a warm feeling of achievement, of being important to the plan; and always that low current of excitement that the battle was coming, and they were going to be at the heart of it. Ned heard them talking about it. The action was to take place on the 10th of March; often he heard them say that they would be eating their supper in Lille that night.

On the 8th of March they were still at La Couture. But on the morning of Tuesday the 9th, when they got back from

95

their night's labours, orders came from Headquarters that they were to go up to the line in the early hours of the 10th.

'Leaving it to the last minute as usual,' Wharton grumbled to Ned, as they walked back to their billet.

'Maybe it's better not to have too much time waiting in the trenches,' said Ned. 'It's bound to be pretty uncomfortable.'

'I suppose you're right. Last in, first out – isn't that what they say?'

It had been a hard night and they were all exhausted. They turned in until called for breakfast and parade, and the day was spent packing up superfluous kit and storing it, and making a series of last-minute inspections. When they went up tomorrow the men would only take rations, greatcoat, a spare pair of socks, and twenty rounds of ammunition. The officers, too, had to pack away all their comforts into their haversacks, not to be accessible again until the battle was over.

The atmosphere in the mess that night was quietly elated, though nobody lingered much over the meal: they had to turn in early, since they would be called at half past one in the morning. Ned walked outside for a last cigarette, and Wharton and Knatchbull went with him. They strolled a few yards up the road and stopped to look at the stars.

'Well, tomorrow's the day,' said Knatchbull.

'I wonder what it'll be like?' Wharton said. 'Do you think one will be scared?'

'My cousin says there's always too much to do to think about it,' said Ned. 'But I suppose it's a thing one can never know about oneself until the moment comes.'

'My pater says that you can't be brave *unless* you're scared,' said Knatchbull.

'That's a good thought,' said Wharton. 'I'm looking forward to it, anyway. A chance to *do* something at last.'

Ned's mind was a tired tumble of orders and plans and the faces of his men, his fellow officers, his recent journeyings. The bitter cold and the black, starry sky reminded him of Black Brow and his training, and Colonel Bassett who believed in him. And always in the background of his thoughts was Morland Place, home, his family, and Jessie. For them, and for England, he would do his utmost tomorrow, to the last fibre of his body and mind.

'A chance to make them proud of us,' he said aloud, and he didn't need to elaborate to his companions. They knew who 'them' meant.

CHAPTER FIVE

Daltry woke him at half past one, and he jerked awake, with
the sense of oppression of coming up too quickly from the
depths, to face a day of unknown responsibilities. But Daltry,
bless him, had a mug of hot coffee right there in his hand,
which at once made the moment seem less daunting.

'Black as the ace of spades out there, sir, and icy cold,
but it's dry for now. A little misty.'

Ned didn't need to be told it was cold: the condensation
of his breath, which had rolled down the tiny window, had
formed icicles hanging from the windowsill. They were at
eye level to him as he sat up and wrapped his hands round
the hot mug. Here at the Front there were no camp beds
for the officers. He had been sleeping on the bare floorboards, wrapped only in his blankets – though Daltry had
folded his greatcoat together and put it under him as a
mattress. Even so, there wasn't a bit of him that didn't ache,
and his hip bone, on which he had been lying, was quite
numb.

Daltry went on, 'Hot water in ten minutes, sir, for your
shave, and there'll be breakfast at two. The men get theirs
at two as well.'

'Thank you,' Ned said and, setting his mug aside, hauled
himself to his feet. The room he had been allocated, up
under the roof, must either have been an under-servant's
bedroom or a box-room. It was tiny, about six feet by seven,
with a sloping ceiling on which he now banged his head.

98

Daltry grinned sympathetically, stooping to pick up the blankets and fold them. The window was in the end wall of the house, and Ned rubbed a pane with his hand – there was a thin film of ice over it – and looked out, but there was nothing to see except blackness. He felt a kind of shaky emptiness at the thought of the day ahead. He would be going into battle. What would it be like? Would he do the right things, make the right decisions? Men's lives would depend on him. He knew what his orders were, but when the time came, would he know how to carry them out? He had a weak moment of wishing himself back home, at Maystone, of wishing he had never volunteered. There had been no need, after all: he was a married man, excuse enough for many, as he knew.

Then Daltry came back in with the can of hot water, and he shook away these despicable thoughts. England needed him. He had his duty to do, and he would do it and trust to God that it would be enough.

His man laid out his shaving gear on a towel, as he always did at home – a wonderful little piece of normality in a newly mad world. 'I can manage now, Daltry,' Ned said. 'You'd better go and get yourself ready. Make sure you have something to eat. You'll need it later. I can dress myself.'

'If you're sure, sir.'

'Yes, I'm sure. Run along.' Their eyes met. Daltry had been his servant in peacetime, and at Maystone he had not only acted as valet but butler and footman, handyman sometimes, occasional secretary, and father to the maids. He was a great deal more than a gentleman's gentleman, though he was superlative in that role. Today, like most of the 'supernumeraries', he would be acting as a stretcher-bearer. Ned had one of his platoon as his runner, because Daltry, like him, was too new to the battalion to know all the names. So they would not see each other again until the battle was over. 'Good luck today,' he said.

'Thank you, sir. Best of luck to you, too.'

They clasped hands briefly; and Daltry was gone.

Having shaved carefully and washed, Ned dressed, then

brushed and oiled down his hair, taking care that no strand was out of place. The Kents demanded the highest standards of smartness of their officers, but also he demanded it of himself, on this day most of all. He must look his best for the battle. Words from his schooldays came into his mind – the Oracle at Delphi, to Philip of Macedon: 'The bull is garlanded. All is done. The sacrifice is ready.' He put on his jacket, buttoned it, brushed it smooth. No Sam Browne worn at the Front – no sword now, either, which seemed rather a shame. Officers had been issued with a pistol instead – which they had had to pay for. It was more practical, but left something lacking to the heroic ideal.

Daltry had buffed his boots to a fine gleam – when had he had the time? He must have been up at midnight – and rubbed up his buttons and cap badge. Ned looked at himself in the scrap of mirror and saw nothing else to do. He would go polished and garlanded like a sacrifice to the battle. He would do his duty.

The battalion paraded at three a.m. Looking round his own men, Ned saw that they were ready and eager, every face cheerful and alert, like hounds on a hunting morning. The black night seemed still and silent, but when he listened more closely it was invested with a sort of whispery busyness you could feel rather than hear, made up of a host of tiny sounds just below the level of hearing, the sounds of an army on the move.

The command came and they marched off down the road towards Rouge Croix, crunching the silence to shards with the sound of their boots on the pavement. It was bitterly cold. The air was hard to breathe, and Ned could taste the frost and feel it prickling the skin of his face. There were so many units on the move that there were delays at every crossroads as they were halted to let another party cross. He heard excited whispers passed back by the men.

'That's the Black Watch.'

'Look, a machine-gun company!'

'Those are the Londons – they're Terriers too!'

Guides were stationed all along the road and at every junction, to ensure everyone got to the right place. Finally the Kents were directed off the road into an orchard where they halted. The groom took Compass Rose from Ned and led her away, and they were directed company by company into the reserve trenches. The drying-out process had not been complete, and there was still water in the bottom of them. Planks had been put down, but under the weight of traffic as the men shuffled along into position, they gradually sank in the mud and the water came up over them.

Now there was nothing to do but wait. With immobility the cold became terrible, creeping into the feet first, and then upwards towards the heart. In the black stillness, time seemed to drag unnaturally. It felt as though it would never be dawn. The men leant together for warmth and some of them managed to doze standing up, like horses, but mostly they were too uncomfortable and too excited. At a quarter to six orders came for them to move into trenches further forward, which troops destined for the first line had just vacated. Ned marvelled at the planning that must have gone into manoeuvring so many men, crammed together in such a small area, in such a short period and in the dark. They clambered out awkwardly, their feet too cold to feel, and stumbled over the rough ground. It was hard now, frozen solid with the frost – a definite improvement on the slimy, clinging mud of the previous six nights.

Though called a trench, their new shelter was not below ground at all, but rather a breastwork of sandbags. It had the advantage, at least, of being dry underfoot. They huddled down below it, the men pressing close together for warmth. At last it was beginning to get light, and Ned could see his platoon and the others beyond it, a long line of khaki against the muddy bulwark. He peered over the breastwork at the scene that would be the battlefield. The village was ahead and to the right – he could see a huddle of buildings and a church spire, with a line of German trenches in front of it, distinguished by its prickly hedge of barbed wire. And that long, raised line of trees on the horizon was Aubers

101

Ridge – not much of an elevation, but in this flat country enough to be both a landmark and a prize. The trees stood out not only because of the high ground, but because they were whole and undamaged. Elsewhere on the field, trees were nothing but stumps with frayed and splintered tops – though here and there a few small pollarded willows, marking the line of a stream, had survived intact because they were so low-growing and on low ground.

In such flat country you could see a long way, and as the light grew he could distinguish, here and there across the battlefield, other clumps of half-ruined buildings, and away on the left wing, sticking up noticeably, a gigantic mill. Of course, with the advantage of Aubers Ridge, the Germans would be able to see even further. Had they observed all the preparations on this side of the line?

It no longer mattered. Promptly at seven thirty, when it was full daylight, the British guns opened up. The first crash was tremendous, and it would have taken a deaf man not to start. One or two of the Kents ducked in alarm and put their fingers in their ears for a moment, before straightening up and trying to look insouciant. Across their heads Ned met the eyes of Wharton, in command of the next platoon, and they grinned at each other. It begins, Ned thought. But the noise of the guns was terrible, unimaginable. It was not just a bang, as he would have imagined it would be, but a terrible clashing, crashing, jangling din, like a billion saucepans being smashed and crushed by some immense machine. The pitch of it was unendurable. He felt as though his head were being split by the noise. There was a battery not far behind them and the shells were shrieking right over them; he could feel the thundering of the guns transmitted through the earth to his feet; the very air seemed to tremble and dither with the violence of the explosions.

Captain Richardson was coming along the line now. He put his mouth up to Ned's ear – the only way to be heard – and bawled, 'Don't grit your teeth like that. Relax your jaw and open your mouth a little and it won't hurt so much. Tell your men.'

Ned tried it and found it was true – something to do with equalising the air pressure inside and out, perhaps, he thought. Once the message had passed down his men he saw that they looked a little more comfortable, and none of them seemed to mind the awful noise of the barrage as he did. On the contrary, they seemed pleased and excited at the thought of *their* guns giving Fritz hell. You could see the line of the German trenches now by the cloud of dust and smoke that hung above it all the way along. There would be the flash of shell-burst, and then a huge volume of earth and debris would shoot up into the air like a black fountain. Sometimes you could see the small starfish shapes of bodies hurtling high into the air along with the smoke and clods and planks and sandbags, and the men would grin at each other in excited triumph – *that was the stuff to give 'em*! Away to the left he watched a building – a farmhouse, he supposed – being hit by shells. It seemed almost to melt away under fire, sinking down into a puddle of debris in a matter of minutes, as though it were dissolving.

Suddenly there was a pause. Ned shook his head and pressed his ears to stop them ringing, and looked at his watch. Just after eight o'clock. The elevation of the guns was being changed – the barrage was being lifted to allow the first wave of troops to go in. He did not hear the whistles, but suddenly the men appeared, scrambling up out of the trenches in a long line and trotting forward into the battered land. The engineers had been out in the hours of darkness and cut wide passages through their own wire, and the barrage should have seen to the German wire. He still could not hear anything, but there must have been firing from the German trenches, because he could see men falling down. One man whirled round on the spot and Ned thought for an awful moment that he was going to run away, but it was a bullet that had spun him: he fell face forward and moved no more.

The artillery behind them resumed their beating din.

★ ★ ★

Things were going well. The barrage had evidently done its work for the first wave of troops took the German trenches almost without opposition, and soon coloured flags were being waved from various points, the agreed signal that the trenches were secure for the second wave to advance through them towards Neuve Chapelle. The barrage lifted again, aiming for the German trenches on the far side of the village. In particular there were trenches called the Smith-Dorrien line, which, as the name suggested, had first been dug when the British held the area. They lay between Neuve Chapelle and the Bois du Biez, running for quite a distance in a sinuous curve, and were to be the jumping-off point for the attack on Aubers Ridge. The second wave went at Neuve Chapelle with such determination that they carried it at a run. Everything was happening to plan. The excitement along the line was almost palpable. *Supper in Lille tonight* was the light in many an eye. The burghers of Lille, for so long frustratingly close to the Front yet helpless under the German heel, would surely give their liberators a welcome to be remembered. Wine and beer would flow like water!

Now the stretcher-bearers were going out into the first part of the battlefield. And there were groups of figures coming back towards the British line, along the battered remains of a road. As the first of them drew nearer, a cheer went up from Ned's men as it was seen that they were not in decent British khaki but hateful German grey: German prisoners, who had flung up their hands in the first trenches as the British came over, were being brought back under escort. Each group had a grinning Tommy in charge, who was cheered by every unit he passed. The Germans, Ned thought, looked bewildered at the speed of events, but perhaps also somewhat relieved at being safely away from that hideous shelling.

One sight that caused particular delight among the Kents was that of half a dozen tall, blond Huns with their hands up, being prodded along by a tiny Gurkha soldier half their size. He was beaming with satisfaction, and when the Kents cheered him, he looked round to acknowledge the tribute, and waved at them the thing he was carrying in his other hand: a German head. He was gripping it by the hair, and Ned had time to notice that its eyes were open, as if in great surprise. It was well known that, as well as their rifles and bayonets, the Gurkhas always carried a long, wickedly sharp knife – the *kukri*. Their favourite method of despatch was to decapitate the enemy with one stroke.

Ned remembered a story Arthurs had told in the mess one night, when they had first learnt that they were to have Gurkhas fighting on their right: a Gurkha sentry met a German sentry, both out on patrol in no man's land. Before the German could aim his rifle, the Gurkha gave a lightning-swift sideways slash with his knife at the German's neck.

'Ha ha, Gurkha!' said the German. 'You missed!'

'Ha ha, German!' said the Gurkha. 'You just try to nod head!'

At last, at half past ten the order came to advance. Neuve Chapelle had been secured, and the Kents were to move up to take over the first line of German trenches. The moment had come! Ned saw the men exchange glances as the order filtered through to stand ready, and every face seemed like to split in two with a grin of delight. Ned felt a huge pride in them, and a fierce determination never to let them down. His mouth was dry, and his heart was pounding, but it was from excitement. There was no room in him for any other emotion. They were going 'over the top'!

'On my command,' he shouted, his arm up. His eyes were fixed along the line to where he could see Wharton with his arm up, and further along Knatchbull, and others beyond him. His body seemed coiled like a spring under him. The arms he could see went down, passing the command, in a ripple that took less than a second. His own arm came down, and he blew his whistle. 'Advance!' he yelled, as he dropped it from his mouth, and in the same instant he was up, scrambling awkwardly over the sandbags, propelled by his madly thrusting legs, out into the open.

He had thought he would feel exposed, leaving the shelter

105

of the trench, but he had never felt less alone in his life. To either side of him was a long line of khaki, and he and they were no longer individuals but one body, armed with a bristling hedge of rifles with bayonets fixed, pointing forwards, seeking out the enemy. Away from the breastwork the noise of the battery was instantly less, and a few yards on it was possible to hear again. Ned thought his ears were still ringing from the noise, but when he glanced up he saw that there was a skylark, hanging above the battlefield, singing as though the air around it were not being torn by explosives. It was the strangest thing he had ever seen, and the one thing above all others he remembered about that day.

But he could not spare more than a glance, for he had to watch his step. The ground they were crossing was littered with bodies, many dead, some still moving; and it was pocked with shell-holes. Some of them were still smoking, and from them came the most terrible stench, the vile and bitter smell of lyddite, which made his nostrils sting and his eyes burn.

They were not advancing unchallenged. The enemy were shelling the area, though the shells were far apart and seemed almost random. Still, he saw one strike twenty yards to his right, saw men fall and men disappear in the smoke. Another burst some way in front of him, and he heard shards of deadly shrapnel scream past him, saw one of his own men drop, even heard his cry. The two men nearest the fallen man hesitated, wanting to help him. Ned yelled fiercely, 'Come on!' and saw the section corporal shove one of the two with the flat of his hand.

Avoiding the shell-holes, picking his way forward, finding the nearest plank or bridge crossing of the many culverts that lay in their way kept his mind occupied so that he did not notice how far they had gone or had still to go. In any case, with the dust and smoke from the shellfire mingling with the mist of the day, it was hard to see very far ahead or to either side. And then he came to the ditch.

He had seen it marked on the map because it lay in his part of the line and he had to take his men over a bridge there. But looking up and down the line he could see no bridge, not even a plank. Wait – yes, a little way down to his left there was a place where the bank of the ditch had a huge piece bitten out, and there was some matchwood debris scattered about. A shell must have hit it. The men were coming up behind him now, looking to him for instructions. The ditch was a culvert filled with muddy water, too deep and steep-sided to ford. But just there to his right, where it changed direction, bending round the corner of a field, it seemed to be narrower. They ought to be able to jump it. Well, they had no choice!

'This way!' he shouted. 'Single file. Follow me.' A shell burst on the other side of the ditch and he was pelted with earth and stones. One of his men, Eades, fell down backwards and sat stupidly looking at the place where his leg had been, taken off at the knee by a whirling knife of shrapnel. Yes, he thought, the ditch could be jumped. He took a run up, launched himself and cleared it, not easily, but sufficiently.

He turned back to his men. 'Come on, come on!' he shouted. He picked out a man whose name he knew. 'You, Winfield. Jump!'

The corporal prodded Winfield into action and he ran and jumped. Acres, behind him, didn't need prodding, and flung himself across. Several others now jumped in turn. The next man hesitated. 'Come on, man! Hurry up!' Ned shouted.

As if to underline the urgency there was a crack of rifle fire, and a bullet threw up a spurt of earth on the ditch's rim.

The corporal now took his turn, and came up beside Ned.

'Someone's firing at us, sir,' he shouted. Another bullet whined past and splashed into the water.

'It came from the village,' Ned shouted back. 'Must be a sniper, got left behind.'

They both glanced towards the village, which still looked a long way off. Another bullet smacked the earth a few feet to Ned's left. He felt no fear, only anger. 'He's got the range of us,' he said. 'Take these men forward.' More men made

107

the jump and he gestured to them to trot on after the corporal. The next man, Purser, hesitated.

'Come *on*!' Ned screamed at him. 'Don't look, just jump!'

Purser flung himself wildly, and the crack of the rifle shot sounded simultaneously. It seemed the sniper had got his aim and was going to pick them off comfortably one by one as they jumped. Purser fell forward, and someone behind him cried out, but he wasn't hit, only hadn't jumped far enough. He landed on the ditch's rim, sprawling, from his waist down in the water. The last man over, Morton, went to him, and with his help he hauled himself up, wet and muddy.

The next in line jumped, and at the rifle's crack Ned saw a spurt of khaki and red spray up from his shoulder. He stumbled on landing and clapped his hand to it, but ran on without pausing. The next man ran at the ditch, took his jump fast, and was missed. The next, Pratt, jumped, the rifle cracked, and he flew sideways, falling, hit the bank and tumbled back into the ditch, lying supine in the water, his eyes open and fixed in death. The sergeant, a tall man, went next, his long legs making nothing of the jump, and was missed. 'You go on, sir,' he shouted. 'I'll see the rest across.'

Ned nodded and turned away, hearing the rifle crack and someone behind him scream. He did not look back. He saw his men ahead of him, going into the smoke, and he knew they were casting too far to the right. He ran after them, more men following him, avoiding the stinking shell-holes, towards the trenches they were to occupy. Ahead and to his right a shell burst and Purser bent backwards as though he were going to perform an acrobatic feat, then collapsed. Hit by shrapnel, Ned's mind told him. He knew it was Purser by his muddy legs.

In the centre the battle had gone well. The first wave had carried the German trenches, and Neuve Chapelle had been taken by the second; but on the wings there had been problems. On the left wing the barrage had not touched the

German trenches or torn a gap in their barbed wire, and when the troops advanced they were mown down by machine-gun fire. On their immediate right some advance had been made, but the men who had managed to make ground were now ahead of the line and dangerously isolated – 'in the air' was the expression. On the far right flank, the mist and the loss of landmarks after the barrage had caused confusion and the troops had gone the wrong way, too far to the right, so that although they had captured a length of German trench, they too were 'in the air', and between them and the next troops on their left was a section of untouched and well-armed enemy trench, which was sweeping the ground with machine-gun fire.

The plan, for wings and centre to join and advance on the high ground of Aubers Ridge together, was for the present unworkable. All over the battlefield were groups of men fighting for their own piece of ground, with little idea of where anyone else was, or how to join up with them. Communication with Headquarters had broken down, for German shellfire had cut the telephone wires in numerous places, and all the efforts of the signallers could not keep up with repairs. Commanders were reduced to the old method of sending runners, but on such a battle-field, even if the runners got through, by the time they reached Headquarters the news they brought was out of date. And when they tried to return to their units, either they could not find them because they had had to move on, or the orders they brought no longer had any rele-vance. Officers had to do the best they could to interpret the situation for themselves, and advance, dig in or retreat as seemed appropriate.

When the Kents reached the German trenches, there were dead men in grey everywhere and, amid the debris, bloody rags of uniform and scraps of flesh. One of the men picked up a severed arm, not knowing what it was, and stood staring at it – not, Ned noted, with horror so much as intense interest. Well, boys are naturally ghoulish, and mostly

109

untroubled by gruesome things. Some of his nearest companions laughed at the soldier and he grinned and pretended to hit them with it. Ned was glad the corporal stepped in, told him to 'chuck that bloody thing out' and 'stop messing about'.

Ned went along his section, getting them into position in case of a counter-attack, making sure everyone restocked with ammunition, checking on wounds and counting losses. He had lost ten of his platoon, four definitely dead, the rest perhaps only injured. He took down the names in his pocket book, with a note of who had seen them fall. There were a dozen minor injuries among the rest, most of them sustained at the culvert, and he directed one of the corporals to see they were all looked to, using their own field-dressings.

The sergeant came up to him to say that there was a churn of water in one of the dugouts, and ask if he could give the men a drink. At the very mention of water Ned's tongue seemed to shrivel in his mouth, reminding him that none of them had had anything to drink since breakfast at two a.m. He had a moment to wonder whether the Germans might have poisoned it, but then reasoned that it had all happened so fast they would not have had time. 'Yes, carry on, Sergeant,' he said.

He reached the end of his line and met Wharton, having been on the same mission. They grinned at each other.

'I say, what a lark!' Wharton said.

'It was a bit hot at times. I didn't like that ditch.'

'How's that?'

Ned explained.

'I say, bad luck. We managed to get across all right. There was a place further up where a shell had flattened the whole thing so we could ford it. Here, want some of this?' He displayed a flat, square tin, containing a block of chocolate, and broke off a couple of squares to hand to Ned.

'Did you bring that with you? I wish I'd thought of it,' Ned said.

Wharton snapped the tin shut and showed him the elegantly painted lid. 'German,' he said. 'There was a dead

Hun in the trench where I jumped in. He was in the way, so I told some men to heave him over the side, and this fell out of his pocket. Shame to waste it, I thought. I say, were you scared at any point?'

Ned shook his head, bemused. 'No. Funny thing, I never really thought about it.'

'Me neither. Oh, better go – I see my sergeant wants me.'

The chocolate helped to lubricate Ned's mouth until he was able to get a drink of water, which was after all his men had had one and there were only a few drops left in the churn. But they did not stay put for long. Soon a runner came up with new orders, that they were to advance through Neuve Chapelle and occupy the Smith-Dorrien line of trenches. They got through the village without difficulty, except that of picking their way over the ruins, and across the shell-pocked area beyond. But when they reached Smith-Dorrien, they found the trenches full of water and un-inhabitable. There was no sign that the Germans had ever used them, so presumably they had been waterlogged all winter.

The Kents halted while the captains consulted with Colonel Lindsay, and Ned watched the group, trying to guess what they were saying. There was some gesturing both forward and back. Ned hoped they would go forward. It would be too tame to retreat now. But while they were still in consultation some German troops had crept back down through the woods up ahead of them, and now opened fire.

There was no cover, and the Smith-Dorrien trenches plainly could give no shelter. The order came swiftly back from Colonel Lindsay to retire fifty yards and start building themselves a protective bulwark out of the bricks and rubble of the ruined buildings behind them. It was desperate work, especially as they were being fired on. One platoon per company was told off to take position and fire back, but with rifles alone against field guns the best they could hope for was to slow the firing down. Ned's platoon was the one for his company. He and his men took what shelter they could from blocks of rubble, or just lay down flat, and fired away at the muzzle flashes that were all that could be seen of the enemy position. Behind them men laboured and cursed as they tore their hands on rough bricks and chunks of coping stone; far over to the left there was the cheering sound of British artillery pounding away. No-one knew how the battle was going, or what they were to do next. Colonel Lindsay had sent off a runner with details of the new situation, but it was a long way to Headquarters, and who knew if he would ever get there, let alone bring orders back?

The Bosch had brought up a machine-gun on some sort of mobile mounting, and were touring up and down the road that ran along the edge of the wood, raking the area with fire. There were lots of men down, now, laying the dust with their blood. Ned had been hit by a piece of flying brick, thrown up by a shell-burst: it had cut his forehead and dazed him for a moment, and the blood, which was running freely, kept dripping into his eyes and blinding him. He called to his men, encouraging them, and kept up fire of his own with the rifle of one of the dead. He had quite a good piece of cover, part of a fallen factory chimney, but there was no doubt things were getting hotter.

He had sent his messenger, Blean, to the colonel to say that his men were running out of ammunition; now Blean came dashing back, jinking like a rabbit, to fling himself down in the dust and gasp, 'Sir, Colonel Lindsay says to fall back.'

Ned glanced back and saw that a breastwork of sorts now existed. But there was open ground to be covered before they could get on the right side of it. He looked along his line, and saw crumpled figures; others still firing but bloodied. He must have lost a dozen of his platoon now, he thought. And even as he looked, another man jumped as though stung by a wasp, and fell motionless.

As if they knew the defenders were preparing to fall back, the enemy increased their fire. Ned's little piece of shelter was being knocked away brick by brick, but still it felt wonderfully safe compared with the open space that had to be crossed.

'Platoon, on my command, fall back to the breastworks. At the double. Go!'

The men peeled themselves away and ran, heads down and determined. One or two delayed to fire off a few more rounds, creating an impromptu rearguard; Ned waited until they, too, had taken to their heels, then got up and ran. He heard the whine of machine-gun bullets and the explosion of a shell but he had no idea if anything had come close to him. His whole mind was fixed on the breastworks and the shrinking distance between him and them. He ran so fast he was in danger of overtaking some of his own men. In front of him one of them stumbled and fell to his hands and knees, and as he reached him Ned stuck out an arm, scooped him to his feet and lugged him along as he half ran, half limped. When they tumbled down into safety he discovered it was Camber he was clutching.

'Thank you, sir, thank you, sir,' he panted. 'Me ankle went on me. Must've twisted it.' He reached down to take hold of it, and swore with pain, then swore again as his hands came away bloody. Ned crouched to look: the man's puttee was bloody, and the foot was at an unnatural angle. The ankle must have been struck by a bullet – probably shattered. How in hell had he managed to put any weight on it at all over those last, desperate yards? It showed how 'the heat of the moment' could give men miraculous powers.

'Don't try and stand on it. I think it's broken,' he said. 'You must get yourself to the aid station. Eastry! See if you can find a bit of timber he can use as a crutch.'

He and his platoon got themselves in among the other defenders, and took position to hold the line and fire at anything in range. The machine-gun could not reach them here, but now the Germans were shelling along the line of the breastwork. The shells screamed and burst in a roar and a fountain of earth and bricks and, as Ned watched, each one seemed to strike ten yards further along, coming nearer and nearer his position. There was nothing in the world to be done about it: one could only wait and take what came. Another shell screamed and blasted; then another. He heard

113

the cries of the men who were hit by that one. And the next one's ours, he thought calmly. He heard Blean, standing near him, say softly, 'Bloody hell, now we're for it.'

'Get down, everyone,' Ned yelled, and flung himself down, folding his arms over his head. The scream of the shell was like a voice out of hell, but there was utter stillness inside him as he waited for death. The earth lifted under him and there was a tremendous roar, and a pelting shower of earth and stones hit his back and legs. After a moment he raised his head. It had missed them by yards. He could see the dust and smoke where it had struck, and smell the reek of its exhaust. He sat up, shaking and brushing the debris off himself. His left arm was bruised and his left hand cut from stones that had hit it. Around him his men were cautiously moving, sitting up, looking round, grinning at each other. Ned found he wanted to laugh, and controlled himself. He ordered his men to their firing positions again. Now the moment had passed, he found that, oddly, he also wanted to cry. He had wondered many times in the past week how he would face death if it came, and what his last thoughts would be. He had imagined they would be of Jessie. But in fact, as he waited for the shell, he hadn't thought of anything at all. It seemed a terrible waste.

They dug in, improving their temporary shelter, firing when any suitable target presented itself, and otherwise simply enduring. Then suddenly the firing stopped. The Germans had melted away, withdrawing back into the woods whence they had come. Colonel Lindsay sent off a runner with the information about the new situation, then walked up and down, growling with frustration. The ground in front of them was open, and if they advanced now and took the woods, they would have the upper hand. The Bois du Biez was a key point on the battlefield. But it was four thirty before a reply came back from Headquarters. The Kents were to move to their left and join up with the 7th and 8th Divisions which, as soon as all were in place, would advance on Aubers Ridge.

Clouds had been gathering for some time since, and now

were heavy and iron-grey, not only threatening rain but bringing on an early dusk. In semi-darkness the battalion stumbled over the horrible terrain, pitted with shell-holes, slashed with drainage ditches, over mired and rutted paths, through ragged hedges, past ruined buildings and blasted trees. The rain began, obscuring visibility still further. Aubers Ridge itself was lost in the low cloud that was like hanging fog; and when they reached their rendezvous position, there was no sign of either of the divisions they were meant to join. In the encroaching gloom the Kents crouched down and sheltered as best they could while runners were sent out to look for the 7th and 8th – and for the enemy.

Soaked and hungry, Ned went in search of Wharton, to see if he had any chocolate left. He found him talking to Knatchbull, who had had conversation with a wounded lieutenant who had been making his painful way back to a dressing station. The lieutenant had said he had heard Sir Henry Rawlinson, commander of IV Corps, saying earlier that afternoon that he believed the Germans had a redoubt right in the centre of the line, perhaps in the orchard near Mauquissart, and that, unless it was captured, it would make the advance on Aubers Ridge impossible.

'This fellow,' said Knatchbull, 'thought Sir Henry was right, and that the Bosch might even have dug themselves a second line in front of the ridge. If so, we'll have a merry time of it when we advance.'

Ned noted he was almost rubbing his hands with relish at the thought of it.

'I don't mind how many lines and redoubts the jolly old Hun has,' Wharton said, 'as long as we get to take a crack at him. I'm worn out with waiting around. What do we need the Seventh and Eighth for? I wish the Old Man would just give the order and let us go on our own.'

'More than his neck's worth,' said Knatchbull. 'A lowly colonel has to take orders, don't you know. Might spoil the pretty pattern the red-tabs have worked out.'

'It's getting dark,' Ned said, looking round the horizon. 'I don't think we'll be eating supper in Lille tonight.'

'As long as we eat it on Aubers Ridge,' said Wharton, 'we can always make it "Lille for luncheon". Sounds all right, doesn't it? Ought to be a song.'

The confusion was finally sorted out after much to-ing and fro-ing of messengers: the 8th Division was waiting for the 7th to arrive before moving forward, while the 7th had already moved forward and was waiting for the 8th to come up to it. When everyone was finally in position it was well after half past five, raining heavily and almost dark.

As soon as they began to advance, they discovered that the unknown lieutenant had been right: there was another German line in front of the ridge. Most of it had not been dug yet, but there were three stout and well-fortified redoubts marking where it would be: one on the left at Mauquissart, one in the middle at a group of buildings, marked Nameless Cottages on the British maps, and one on the right at the crossing of a small road over the Layes brook. Each was invested with machine-guns, which between them could pretty well sweep the whole line.

'We have to take them,' said Captain Richardson, relaying the information and orders from the colonel. 'It's imperative to the whole battle. Our objective is the Layes Bridge Redoubt. Once that's taken we'll have a jumping-off point for the ridge tomorrow.'

The lieutenants went back to their platoons and passed on the good news that at last they were to attack the Germans full on and, tired and hungry as they were, the men cheered. They had waited all day for this. The whistles sounded and they started forward. It was no more than a few yards before the impetuous charge slowed to a walk. The ground was as treacherous as any they had crossed to get there, with the added difficulty of near darkness and teeming rain. Half-buried objects caught at their feet, ditches suddenly appeared before them; the rain turned the mud into a skating rink. Ned was soon out of touch with any but his own men, unable to see more than a few yards in any direction. But there was no doubt about the direction they were to go. The Germans opened up, and raked them with a hail of fire,

116

showing their position by the orange flashes from their gun muzzles. In the dark the enemy must have had difficulty in aiming but, then, they hardly needed to: simply swinging their fire back and forth across the area was enough to be sure they would hit the mass of the advancing troops.

Sweating, panting, the Kents struggled on. Ned couldn't believe he had ever been cold. The mud sucked at his feet and in the darkness the countryside seemed to have come to malevolent life, siding with the enemy in its desire to hamper his movement. And the darkness itself was thick with bullets, whining like mosquitoes, each a hard, hot little package of death. Men were going down on all sides. It was, he thought vaguely, sheer murder – vaguely, because his whole attention was gripped with the need to stay on his feet and go forward.

Something struck his leg and he fell. Death whined past over his head, and he gave a short bark of laughter – *missed me, Fritz!* The men just behind him had stopped and were reaching for him. He must not let them falter – and he must stay ahead of them. He got to his feet and staggered forward – staggered because his leg was not right. He felt no pain from it, but it kept buckling under him. 'Come on!' he yelled. 'Follow me!' One of the two men just behind him sank down gracefully into the mud; the other jerked his head aside as if avoiding a blow, and carried on.

Then something hit him a vicious blow on the thigh and he went down flat. The firing seemed, impossibly, to intensify. Machine-gun bullets were as thick as a hornet swarm. He heard someone behind him – his sergeant, he thought – shout, 'Get down! Get down, lads!' He tried to struggle up again to countermand that order, but his legs would not obey him, and now there was a hand on his shoulder, firmly pressing him down. His sergeant had crawled up and was beside him. 'No, sir, no, sir, you stay put. It's no use, sir. The ground's dead. It's just murder to go on.'

'We have to take that redoubt, Sergeant,' Ned said, trying to sound stern, though his voice sounded faint and far away to him.

117

'Yessir, but not right this minute, sir. You're wounded.'

'Am I?'

'Here, sir, let me feel.' Blunt, capable hands moved about him. Ned still felt no pain, but his whole leg had become numb, and when he tried to move it, it wouldn't. 'One in the calf and one in the thigh, sir, seems to me. You can't go on, anyway.'

'Then you must lead them,' Ned said.

'Everyone's stopped, sir. The ground's dead.' The sergeant looked around, and gave a grimace. 'Can't go on and can't go back. Have to make ourselves comfortable here.'

There was a hedge not far in front of them, which gave them a very minimum of shelter. The sergeant gave the order for the platoon to dig itself in, and the men got out their entrenching tools and dug themselves scrapes, while Blean went off in the dark to find the colonel. He returned at last to say that the attack had been halted, and orders were to dig in and wait for further instructions. 'Colonel says we're likely to be here all night, sir,' Blean said. He dropped his voice and became confidential. 'Ever such a lot's killed, sir. Captain Richardson's gone, sir, and Captain Houseman said there's only half of us left.'

'The guns have stopped,' said the sergeant. In the sudden silence, they could hear the rain, pattering on the top of the hedge and drip-dripping off the bottom. But in case the British should think of trying to sneak up in the dark, the Germans fired a warning burst every ten or fifteen minutes, raking the night with random death.

The feeling began to return to Ned's leg, in the form of burning pain. 'Sergeant,' he said, through gritted teeth, 'help me have a look at this blasted leg. I've got a pocket torch here.'

It was not easy to do in the dark and the rain, and with movement restricted by the necessity of keeping low, but they managed it. The bullet to the calf had only sliced through the outer rim, mercifully missing the bone and leaving a bloody trench to mark its passage. The bullet to the thigh had lodged in the muscle, but it must have been

118

almost spent when it struck him, for it was only just under the surface.

'I've got a pen-knife here, sir,' said the sergeant. 'Would you like me to dig it out for you? Won't do so much harm out as in.'

Ned blenched at the thought, even while he was admiring the sergeant's calm and courage in proposing such a service. But he said, 'Let me have the knife. I'll do it myself.'

It's no different from taking out a splinter, he told himself; but his hands shook shamefully at his first attempt. He had to stop and breathe deeply, then focus all his attention on the point of the knife. *It will hurt worse if you do it later, when the numbness has really passed. Get on with it, you damned coward.* The feeling of the knife's point scratching the bullet, metal on metal, set his teeth on edge and he faltered, feeling sick. He saw the sergeant's hand twitch in his longing to take over, and braced himself. He must not show weakness before his men. He dug into the flinching flesh, into the shriek of agony that was his own leg, and the bullet flipped out with a disgusting wet sound. Now he could not help it – he had to lie down or he would faint.

'That's right, sir,' said the sergeant's voice, from far away. 'I'll get a dressing on it, and you'll feel much better in two ticks.'

Another voice – Wharton's, thank God! He had come crawling along the line of the hedge to see how many were left. Ned could not rouse himself to speak for the moment, and the sergeant explained everything.

'I've got a flask here,' Wharton said.

'Right, sir.' The sergeant took it, and splashed a little into the wound, which made Ned gasp and sit up. He grasped the offered flask, tipped a gulp down his throat and felt stronger.

'Glad you made it,' Wharton said. 'This is a fine do, isn't it? Stuck here in the dark. That damned redoubt! But we'll get 'em tomorrow.'

'How many of us left?' Ned managed to ask.

'Hard to say in the dark, but we've lost a lot. The colonel's

119

sent off a report, asking for fresh orders, but Lord knows when they'll come. Better make yourself comfortable.'

The brandy had done him good, and after resting for a while Ned was able, limping heavily, to make the round of his men, to see that they were properly dug in and attending to any minor wounds. And then there was nothing to do but wait. He made himself as comfortable as possible and dozed on and off, waking every few minutes from blackness into blackness, wondering where he was and what had happened. The jangling pain of his leg dulled to a pounding throb. He wondered if he would be able to walk tomorrow. It would be damnable if he had to leave his men and miss the end of the show. He slept again, and was woken at two in the morning when, by a miracle, supplies reached them: cans of stew and tea, which, by a further miracle, were still warm.

CHAPTER SIX

In the early hours of the morning orders came through that
the Kents were to stand fast and consolidate the line, until
they were relieved at five a.m., when they would fall back
into reserve. A new bombardment would take place at six
forty-five, which would specifically target the redoubts. At
seven a.m., the whole front line would advance and take
Aubers Ridge.

The orders arrived at half past four, but they had been
long on their way: the runner had been looking for them in
the wrong place. It seemed, therefore, unlikely that whoever
was to relieve them would know where they were. Colonel
Lindsay sent the runner back, and reinforced him with one
of his own, explaining the position and demanding fresh
orders.

All this was related to the D Company subalterns by
Arthurs, now acting company commander in Richardson's
place. 'Better let the men have their breakfast now. Might
not get another chance.'

'They've only just had their dinner,' said Knatchbull.

Arthurs smiled. 'Did you ever know a Tommy not be able
to manage a meal?' When the meeting broke up, he called
Ned back. 'I hear you were injured. How's the leg?'

'Not too bad, thanks,' Ned answered. 'A bit stiff, but it'll
do.'

'You can carry on?'

'Oh, yes. It was only a scratch.' He did not want to be

separated from his men now. His leg was stiff and throbbing, but he had tried it and it would take his weight. He was determined to go on.

He went back to his scrape and forced himself to eat some breakfast. The boxes of cold bacon and bread had come up at the same time as the stew. It made strange eating at half past four in the morning, and he longed for hot coffee, but he had already appreciated one of the cardinal rules of army life, that you ate food when it was there, because there was a good chance no more would appear for a long time.

Five o'clock came and went, but there was no sign of their relief. Some of the men grumbled, but others seemed pleased rather than otherwise, thinking that if they were not relieved, they would be part of the attack. Six o'clock came, and there was no sign of dawn, either. A thick fog lay over the marshy flats of the battlefield, and by six thirty, when it should have been daylight, it was still murky grey, with poor visibility. The bombardment began at six forty-five promptly, but it was evident that the gunners would have little chance of spotting their target in the prevailing conditions.

'Not only that,' said Wharton, as he and Ned shared a cigarette in an old shell-hole, 'but they'll be worried about hitting any of us, not knowing where we are, so they're bound to fire too far ahead. I mean, wouldn't you?'

At seven the firing stopped, then resumed a few minutes later when the gunners had raised the elevation and lengthened the range. This was the signal for attack, but the Kents had no new orders and, to their frustration, had to stay put. It was obvious at once that the barrage had not knocked out the redoubts. There was ferocious machine-gun fire, and now the Germans replied to the barrage with one of their own, high-explosive and shrapnel shells howling over and pounding the British line. The Kents crouched in their scrapes and waited; fretting, not at all comforted by assurances that no-one could advance through that weight of fire.

★   ★   ★

122

Arthurs returned from Battalion Headquarters – a ruined cottage just behind the trenches, which had a serviceable cellar – at around nine o'clock, having gone to see if there were any more orders.

'We're not the only ones to be fed up,' he said. 'There was a red-tab from the Indian Corps on our right having a confab with our colonel. They were supposed to attack as soon as the Eighth Division moved, but we're the end of the Eighth's line, and we've been told to stay put. So they couldn't go. General fed-upness all round.'

'What about the rest of the Eighth?' Wharton asked. 'Didn't they advance?'

'Oh, yes, but they couldn't get more than a few yards against that sort of inferno. Very heavy casualties. Nothing to do but wait until it stops, or the fog lifts.'

'What about us? Are we still going to be relieved?' asked Ned.

'Not very likely. The colonel says the Germans will probably launch an attack after their barrage, and you can't have troops changing over at a time like that.'

'Good,' said Knatchbull. 'Then we'll be in the thick of it.'

The German barrage went on for three hours, and during that time news came back that, in the centre, the Worcesters and Sherwood Foresters had managed to advance a short way with heavy loss of life but were now pinned down. On the right wing, the Germans had come back through the Bois du Biez during the night and dug themselves in between the wood and the Layes Brook, holding down that wing; and on the left wing where the Middlesex had been cut to pieces the day before, the Northamptonshires had suffered a similar fate that morning.

At last the shelling died away, to be replaced by sporadic bursts of gunfire. The Kents braced themselves for a German attack, but nothing happened, and those officers with field-glasses could see that there was no sign of movement at all on the German line.

'Why don't we go?' Blean appealed to the sergeant,

fidgeting from foot to foot in his frustration. 'We could take 'em now, easy, couldn't we, Sarge?'

'Orders, son,' said the sergeant. 'The last lot we had was to stay put, and stay put we will until the brass says different.' But he cast Ned a beseeching glance as he said it. Ned took the hint and went over towards Headquarters to see if he could find out anything.

He met Nugent from C Company on the same mission, with a bandage, tied roughly round his head under his cap, that looked like a white silk muffler.

'Hullo. Been getting yourself knocked about?' Nugent said, seeing Ned was limping.

'Oh, it's nothing. What about you?'

'Just a scalp wound. Spoiled my scarf, though, that's the worst of it. Blood never comes out, so Mother says.' He drew closer and lowered his voice. 'I say, poor Singer's had it. Shrapnel burst right beside him, took the side of his head right off. I ran over to him, but I could see he was in a bad way – part of his brain was exposed. They carried him back, but I don't think he'll survive.'

'What rotten luck,' Ned said.

'I've known him for years,' Nugent said. 'Joined the Kents at the same time as him. Oh, look, here comes Arthurs.' He had just emerged from the cellar stairs. 'I say, Uncle, any news?'

Arthurs changed direction and the three of them huddled in the shelter of the ruin.

'It's all a bit of a muddle. There's to be a new barrage at two o'clock and an attack at two fifteen, but our orders are still to stay put and consolidate, and to consider ourselves in reserve unless the Germans counter-attack.'

'That doesn't make any sense,' Nugent said indignantly.

'Never mind, sonny,' said Arthurs, trying to sound stern. 'Orders is orders. But the Old Man's sent off a pretty sharp message saying there's no sign of a counter-attack and we want to go now and take the Layes Bridge Redoubt – which he's sure we can. The trouble is that the signallers still can't get anything to work so it all has to be done by runner.'

'Which means it'll be hours before we get a reply,' Nugent grumbled.

'Ah, well, at least the fog's lifting a bit,' Ned said. 'Perhaps this time our guns will be able to see what they're firing at.'

The barrage began on time, but though the fog had thinned somewhat, it was clear from what little they could see that the gunners were still firing blind and that the shells were mostly falling behind German lines where they did no harm. At two fifteen it was lifted, and to their left the Kents could hear whistles and gunfire as the 8th Division advanced. But the Kents' last instructions had been to stay put; and because they could not advance, the attack on their right, where the Indian Corps had the same orders as before, had to be called off. It was nearly three o'clock before the Kents' new orders came, and they were from General Haig himself, direct and specific. They were to attack as soon as the barrage lifted, and take the Layes Bridge Redoubt. The attack *must* go in.

But by now the Germans were well prepared. There were five hundred yards to cover, the last hundred and fifty over open ground with not so much as a tree stump for shelter.

Ned was glad to have his sergeant at his side. Sergeant Johnson, he felt, was the best soldier in the company, and not only a good disciplinarian but a likeable man too. His solid bulk and absolute calm seemed to spread about him in waves. 'Well, this is it, Sergeant,' he said, as they waited for the signal. It was a foolish thing to say, and as soon as he'd said it he wished he hadn't, in case it sounded as though he was afraid. And he wasn't – just tense with anticipation.

But the sergeant glanced at him kindly and said, 'It's what we come for, sir. We'll show those Hun bastards what we're made of.'

And there was the signal. Ned blew his whistle, flung up his arm and shouted, 'Come on!'

Yelling their excitement like a battle cry, the platoon surged forward.

* * *

125

It was like running through a fierce hailstorm, with gale-force winds, except that the hail was deadly. The Germans were prepared all right. Shells came over thick and fast, and the machine-guns raked a continuous fire. It was not just from the redoubts but from the whole line, and they were not firing blind. Ned saw cheerful young Morton blown to pieces by a shell – he simply disappeared. Dorrington stopped dead and fell backwards like a stone, shot through the head. Wendell was ripped almost in half by a line of machine-gun fire across the chest. Ned had no idea how he survived when so many were falling all around him. He felt no pain from his leg as he staggered and stumbled on over the rough ground, and no fear – only a fierce determination that was like joy. But they could not go on like this. So much fire was falling round them that the ground was, in the parlance, 'dead' – and going back was clearly impossible, as well as unthinkable. There was a ditch of some sort about fifty yards in front of the German line. They must get to it somehow and shelter. He waved his arm in a signal to his men, flung himself down in the mud, and crawled forward on his stomach, pulling and pushing with his feet and elbows. The crawl seemed to go on for ever – he even wondered at one point whether he was going in the wrong direction – but then suddenly the ground fell away before him and he tumbled gratefully into the ditch.

It was about four feet deep, so kneeling or sitting down he was below the rim, though waist deep in water. Safe, for the time being. Other bodies tumbled in to either side of him. He caught his breath and looked around. He counted about a dozen of his own men, and beyond them perhaps a dozen more of Wharton's platoon, which had been next along the line – there was no sign of Wharton.

'That was 'ot work, sir,' said Blean, who had clung close to his heels the whole way. His eyes showed wide and white in his grimy, muddy face. 'I thought we'd 'ad it.'

'I got a bullet right through me pack,' said Acres, sitting in the water, poking a wondering finger into the hole. 'I bet it saved me life.'

126

'That's nothing, I got one through me cap,' said Gade. 'Dunno 'ow it missed me 'ead.'

'There's not many of us, sir,' said Eastry. 'Not many of us made it.'

'Can't go back, eever.' Falmer, just beyond him, had lifted his head to look out over the rim in the direction they had come. He ducked violently as shots whistled past overhead.

'Keep down!' Ned shouted, made angry by the near miss. 'For God's sake, what do you think this is? An exercise on Blackheath?'

'Sorry, sir.'

'There's nothing more we can do now except keep our heads down and wait. No heroics.'

But further along the ditch Piggot had also risked a look, and he called to Ned: 'Sir, it's the sarge, sir. Sar'nt Johnson. He's out there, wounded. He's not dead, sir.'

'I said keep down!' Ned ordered. Carefully, carefully, he eased himself round and raised his head, fraction by fraction, wondering why God had seen fit to put the eyes so far down the human face. Machine-gun fire rattled over him and he quailed, but it was well above – two feet above his head, he thought.

There was the sergeant, lying prone, about thirty feet away. As Ned looked, he moved his head, turning his face towards the ditch, and his hand, flung out before him, clenched as he tried to get a grip on the earth and pull himself forward. A shell screamed over and burst some yards away, pelting him with clods of earth and stones. Ned remembered the feeling, and flinched for him. It was only a matter of time, he thought, before a shell struck closer, close enough to kill him.

Even as he thought it, the sergeant's eyes met his own, and the older man shook his head slightly and mouthed something that Ned could not catch.

Ned drew his head back and turned to his men. 'I'm going to get Sergeant Johnson,' he said. 'Your orders are to stay here and keep down until someone comes. Those are orders, do you understand?'

127

They all looked at him, white eyes in black faces – he thought irreverently of hard boiled eggs, and knew that he was suffering from shock of a sort. But it made no difference. He could not leave the sergeant there.

Blean said, 'Let me go, sir. I could get him, easy.'

Ned looked at his messenger's scrawny little body and almost smiled. He'd never be able to shift the sergeant's bulk. 'We need you for the running, Blean,' he said. 'That's what you're good at. Stay down, all of you.'

And he turned away before any of the others could offer, and began to ease himself out of the ditch, oozing flat like a snake over the rim, elbows and toes and fingernails digging into the mud. He raised his head to get the exact position of the sergeant, and saw the man shaking his head with increasing emphasis; but Ned just gave him a grim smile, before putting his own head down for the crawl.

As long as he kept down, he reckoned, the machine-guns would not get him – not unless they aimed at him specifically, and why would they do that? No, it was the shells he had to worry about – and where they struck was so random, there was nothing to be done about it. He wriggled forward as quickly as he could, glancing up to check the position, then pressing his cheek to the mud again. Now he felt his leg aching, the muscles trembling, and he wondered belatedly if they would take the strain. But they had to, that was all. A stray bullet struck the ground actually between his legs – an inch further over and it would have shattered his knee. Another glance, and he was within reach of the sergeant's hand.

The sergeant was looking at him, his face drawn with urgency. 'I told you no, sir,' he cried hoarsely. 'Go back. Go back.'

'Not without you.'

'I'm a goner. Save yourself.'

'Save your breath,' Ned retorted. 'Can you move at all?'

'I'm hurt pretty bad,' the sergeant croaked. 'But you'll never shift me, a man of my size. It's no use, sir. Leave me.'

'Shut up, Sergeant, and that's an order,' said Ned. He

128

was tall and strong – he had passed his medical examination A1. And he wasn't leaving the sergeant there for any consideration. He inched forward until he could grasp the man by his shoulders. 'Grab my shoulders,' he instructed, 'and try to push yourself with your feet.'

Johnson croaked agreement, then closed his eyes.

It was the hardest thing Ned had ever done. The man was big, and a dead weight, and could help himself only a little. Before they had gone a few feet, Ned's arms and shoulders were screaming, his wounded leg flaring. But what it cost the sergeant in pain, he thought, made his efforts pale into insignificance. Not long afterwards, a shell landed almost exactly where Johnson had been lying – close enough, anyway, to have killed him.

Ned crawled on, hitching himself backwards, then dragging the sergeant towards him, his mind a blank, a singing emptiness in the howling wilderness of the battle. Every moment he felt he could not move another inch, and still had to find it in himself to do so. And then he felt hands on his ankles, and his reaching toes went over the edge of the ditch into emptiness. Two of his men, lying flat over the rim of the ditch with their legs down inside it, grasped bits of the sergeant's clothing and added their strength to Ned's failing muscles. Ned backed into the ditch and slumped down gratefully as the others hauled and eased the wounded man down into safety.

'Bloody 'ell! Well done, sir!'

'You did it, sir!'

'Are you all right, Sarge?'

'Where are you hurt, Sarge?'

Ned pulled himself together with an effort and sat up. 'Try to make him comfortable,' he said. 'Keep your *heads* down! Has anyone got a field-dressing? I've used mine. Here, give him a drink of water,' and he handed over his water bottle.

They propped the sergeant against the side of the ditch with his legs stretched out in the water, covered him with a greatcoat and put someone's pack behind his head. Even under the mud and dirt, his face looked drawn with extreme pain. He met Ned's eyes again, and managed to mouth *thank you*, though he could not speak.

'Not much of an improvement, I'm afraid,' Ned said, 'but it's shelter of a sort.'

In the afternoon the British guns at last got the range of the German line, and began pounding it with shells. It gave relief to the isolated forward units, who were able to begin to fall back to greater safety. At sunset the order went out to all units to retire to their positions of that morning. The message did not get as far as Ned, but as soon as it was dark, on his own authority, he got his survivors out of the ditch to begin making their way back. They rigged up a stretcher with greatcoats and rifles, bound together with puttees, and got the sergeant onto it, carrying him between them. It was not a very secure contraption and they had to go slowly for fear of dropping him, so it took a long time, stumbling over the rough ground in the darkness, to get back to the ruined cottage that had been the Kents' head-quarters that morning.

There they found the remnant of the battalion, back in the morning's trenches, under the command of the adjutant – the colonel and the second-in-command both having been killed. Ned had brought in thirty men, including the sergeant, and the whole battalion now numbered about four hundred and fifty. The stretcher-bearers were out, beginning to bring in the wounded, and around fifty walking wounded had gone back already to the first-aid post. Of Ned's company officers, only Arthurs was there. It was not known yet whether the others were wounded, dead or otherwise missing.

The men lay down where they had stopped and fell asleep like logs on the bare ground. Ned and Arthurs went to look at the wounded who had crawled or been brought in by survivors, and were laid out some yards behind the cottage waiting to be taken back to the aid post. There was not much that could be done for them, except give them water and comfort them, but Arthurs had some morphia tablets, which they gave to the worst wounded. Ned begged one for Sergeant Johnson, but when he went over to him, he found he was too late. The sergeant's eyes were open, but fixed. Ned knelt in the mud beside him, unable to believe the ill luck of it, that he had survived so much and then died at the last hurdle. As he knelt there, Arthurs came up behind him and laid a hand on his shoulder.

'Rotten luck, old man,' he said. 'I heard what you did. You've nothing to reproach yourself for.' Ned made a vague sound in his throat, unable to speak for a moment. And Arthurs went on, 'As he won't need that morphia, can I have it back? Someone else wants it.'

Ned pulled himself together, and got up. Arthurs was right – it was the still-living who demanded their attention.

At half past two in the morning the order came for the Kents to retire. The relief they had been promised that morning had finally arrived. The remaining officers shook the men awake and formed them up, shivering in the bleak cold of the early hours, and they marched back across the shattered land to La Couture. It took them two hours to get there, and everyone was grey with weariness by the time they reached it, but there was hot tea and ration food waiting for them, which made everyone feel better; and there was a barn full of straw for them to sleep in.

Ned, Nugent and Arthurs found a corner for themselves, and shared a cigarette before turning in.

'How's the leg?' Arthurs asked Ned. 'Is that your blood soaking through your trousers, or someone else's?'

Ned looked down in vague surprise, and only then as he realised his wound was bleeding did he finally notice how much it was hurting. When he inspected it, the field-dressing was soaked through, but Nugent still had his, having used his scarf for his head, and Ned put it on. 'It's the marching started it off again,' he said, when he had done. 'It'll be all right with a rest.'

Arthurs yawned hugely. 'Better take it while you can, then. I heard that Haig himself was out doing the rounds after

131

sunset, looking at the position, and there's going to be an all-out push tomorrow. They're going to bring the guns much further up, right up to the line, practically; and to make sure they can see what they're aiming at, the barrage is not going to start until ten thirty in the morning. We'll definitely do it tomorrow. Supper in Lille tomorrow night!'

'What a day,' Nugent said, settling himself back into the straw. Then he sat up again, his eyes alight. 'I say, Uncle, they can't call us Saturday-night soldiers any more, can they? Not after today.'

'Certainly not,' said Arthurs. 'We were magnificent. I heard the adj say that no regular battalion could have done better, and many wouldn't have done as well.'

'And the adj is a regular,' said Nugent, softly, to himself in pleasure, 'so he should know.'

The first news of the battle came in, and was received in England with huge rejoicing. The German line had been broken! Neuve Chapelle captured! The apparently invincible German 'army machine' that the Bosch had boasted about and poured money into for a generation had been beaten! Everyone drank in the details with feverish delight. German machine-guns had been captured, unnumbered Germans killed, a thousand prisoners taken!

Later, news of the third day of the battle arrived, and was no less exciting. The Germans had counter-attacked at first light, but had been repulsed with huge losses. Thereafter the British had attacked again and again all day, but once more the fog had prevented the artillery from breaking down the defences and only small advances had been made. By nightfall it was clear that nothing further could be achieved, so the men had consolidated their position and dug in. The battle was over.

Still, the British line had been advanced by a thousand yards, trenches along a front of two miles had been captured, six thousand Germans altogether had been killed and two thousand taken prisoner. The Germans had been taught a lesson they would never forget. And it was only by the

132

narrowest of margins that the victory had not been even greater. If it had not been for the fog, the British Army would have swept through and recaptured Lille, and the war would have been as good as over.

Then the casualty lists began to come in, and the nation paused in its rejoicing. They were surprisingly heavy. As day followed day, they became shockingly large. The cost of the victory at Neuve Chapelle had been enormous. The Middlesex, the Northamptonshires, the Worcesters, the Seaforths – battalions reduced to a handful of survivors. The Kents, too, had been heavily hit.

Now at Morland Place they waited only for news of Ned. Everyone went about his usual routines and tried to be cheerful, for the sake of the servants, but more especially for Jessie, pretending each day was just another normal day, carrying on mundane conversations at meals about the weather and crops and neighbours and local events. Her mother's sympathetic looks – silent, loving, understanding – were all the comfort that could reach Jessie. She felt numb inside, unable to think or feel. Work was the only thing that seemed real to her.

On Monday, the 15th of March, when there was no letter or news, she went out to Woodhouse Farm to see how old Ezra Banks was getting on with the two Bhutia ponies she had broken for him. It was a beautiful spring day of soft sunshine, the buds were fattening, the trees were beginning to mist with green, and the birds were racketing about in the hedges. As she rode into the farmyard little Rosie Banks came running out, to stop and stare wide-eyed, her grubby thumb going at once into her mouth, her rag doll, clutched by one foot, dragging in the dust. Her mother followed her out from the kitchen, wiping her hands on her apron; and young Jimmy emerged from the cow house with a pitchfork in his hand, to silence the yard dogs, who were barking at Brach.

When they were quiet he joined his mother and sister, and began to say, 'Is there any—?'

But Mrs Banks, having squinted up against the sunshine

133

at Jessie's face, silenced him with a covert slap to the wrist. 'Morning, Miss Jessie. A fine one it is, an' all. Did you want our dad? He's out with the sheep.'

'No, thanks, I came to see how Ezra's getting on with the Bhutias.'

'He's liking 'em right well, miss. He's out ploughing with 'em this minute. Says they pull twice their size, and as quick to learn as our old Boxer and Duke. He can send 'em on, and right and left, with a word. He's right grateful to you, miss, for lending 'em. We all are.'

'Well, I'd like to see them in action. It would be useful to know how they perform, if I'm going to school more of them for farm work.'

'Aye, we'll need more like them if this war goes on.' Mrs Banks bit her lip, as the treacherous subject crept in again. 'Grandad's up at Six Acres, Miss Jessie. But won't you step in for a minute, and have something? A nice glass of milk – and I've a veal an' ham pie in cut.'

Jessie imagined how stilted the conversation would be as they tried to avoid the subject, and said, 'Thank you, but no. I'll be getting on.'

Old Ezra was much more soothing company. The field was half done, raked into smooth brown furrows, perfect parallels curving with the swell of the land. The little grey-brown ponies with their bushy forelocks were coming down the incline towards her, pulling the adapted plough, with old Ezra walking behind, the long reins loose in his hands, his short clay pipe jutting out sideways from his jaw. The rich earth curled over to either side of the gleaming blade, like the sea parting to a ship's forefoot, and behind the man a cloud of rooks rose and resettled, picking out the insects from the broken soil.

Ezra was quite willing to take a rest. He called to the ponies to halt as they reached the end of the field where Jessie stood. They pricked their ears at Hotspur, and fluttered their nostrils and whickered softly with interest, remembering him and Jessie both. Ezra's dog, a little brown and white terrier called Bandy, who was a fine ratter, came

134

out from under the hedge to meet them, and stood quiveringly nose to nose with Brach, ears cocked and stumpy tail wildly wagging.

'Now then, Miss Jessie,' Ezra greeted her, looping the reins and taking out his handkerchief to wipe his brow.

'Ezra.' Jessie jumped down, hitched Hotspur's reins over the gatepost, and went to caress the ponies, slipping a palmful of horse-nuts under each soft, questing muzzle – she never went anywhere without a pocketful: she had once embarrassed herself at Clifton Church, reaching in for her collection money and sending them rolling and scattering across the tiles. The ponies cleared her palms, then blew in them hopefully and nibbled at her sleeves. 'Are you pleased with them?'

'I am that,' Ezra said emphatically. He pulled out his tobacco pouch, knocked out the dottle against his boot, and began to refill his pipe. 'Tha'd nivver think to look at 'em, but they're that strong Ah soomtimes forget they're ponies and not 'osses.' He tamped the tobacco down with a great brown thumb. 'And right 'andsome little workers they are, too. Nivvershirk, nor sulk, allus pull together, an' sweeter baists in t' stable tha couldn't wish for.'

'I'm very glad to hear it,' Jessie said, blinking a little at this encomium. Yorkshire men were usually sparing with their praise, and older ones, like Ezra, could hardly be brought to part with a 'not bad, mebbe' without the sort of effort that accompanies the pulling of a tooth.

Ezra forgot his pipe and came down to the ponies' heads, stroked their faces, and lovingly rearranged their forelocks, while they nudged him affectionately. Jessie noted that he had plaited ribbon down the centre section, blue for one and red for the other. He had obviously taken a very strong fancy to the Bhutias – perhaps the more so because he had so mourned the loss of his big horses, which had been taken by the army. 'Aye,' he said softly, more to the ponies than Jessie, 'they're right little beauties, are these. If people were more like 'em, the world'd be a better place.' He looked up, his faded eyes suddenly sharp under the overhang of his brows. 'Astow 'eard anything o' Mr Ned?'

The directness of the question took any hurt from it. 'No, we're still waiting. I suppose in a way it's a good thing we've heard nothing. I expect bad news would have come more quickly.'

Ezra nodded. 'That's right, tha's got to stay cheerful. Life goes on, whatever 'appens. He'll coom through all right if it's God's will – an' if it isn't, there's nowt to be done about it, and tha'll 'ave to carry on, and not snivel.'

'I know,' Jessie said meekly.

'Aye, tha doos – and tha nivver was a whiner, Miss Jessie, Ah'll say that for thi. Remember that time tha fell out o' t' barn in mah farmyard? All t' skin gone from thi knees an' 'ands, an' tha were that determined not to cry!' He chuckled. 'Shoulda been a boy by rights – but then, Ah dessay women 'ave more to bear than men when it comes to it, and more need o' determination.'

Jessie knew he was offering her sympathy in his brusque way for the lost baby, and she shook her head. 'When I read in the papers what our boys are suffering over there, I know I'd never make a man.'

'You tek what's 'anded out, man or woman,' he said gravely, and then changed the subject. 'See ma little tyke Bandy fettlin' oop to thy bitch! Got ideas above 'is station, 'e 'as, since 'e won t' championship last Sat'd'y neet.'

'Did he really? I didn't know.'

'Aye, Sat'd'y neet down Bellerby's barn. 'Ighest score ever in rattin' 'istory. 'Ad to get 'im out o' t' pit wi' a noose on a stick, 'e were that roused up.'

'Well, congratulations,' Jessie said, looking in amazement at the little, short-legged dog, who was prancing round Brach like a puppy, wagging and play-bowing, as sweet and cheerful as a children's pet. He didn't look as though he would kill a fly. 'What was the prize?'

'The cup, o' course. I keep that to stand on't dresser for a year. An' a pound o' baccy for me, an' a big beefsteak for 'im,' said Ezra. He paused to light his pipe at last, and then continued, 'Mind you, Ah didn't give 'im t' beefsteak. We 'ad that in a pie, Sunday. No point in wastin' good steak

136

on a dog 'at doesn't knaw any different. He had his usual bowl o' lights an' glad of 'em.'

Jessie laughed, refreshed by his comical mixture of sentiment and practicality: ribbons for the ponies, but no steak wasted on a dog, however good a ratter he was. Bandy looked across at her laughter, and came running up to her, standing on his hind legs and paddling his front paws in the air until she reached down and caressed his surprisingly silky head. There were several healing rat bites on his white flanks, she noted. 'Well, I'd better get on and let you get back to work,' she said, feeling much better for this exchange about nothing in particular.

'Aye, best tek advantage o' t' fine weather,' he said squinting up at the sky. 'A fair mornin' at this time o' year soon turns off.' She unhitched Hotspur and Ezra came over to throw her up into the saddle. He watched her settle herself and find her stirrup, then laid his hand the merest instant on her bootcap. 'Divn't tha worry about Mr Ned,' he said. 'God knaws what He's doing, however it turns out.'

She rode away, thinking that his words ought to have been no comfort at all, and yet comfort they were.

The rest billets were in a village called Robecq. The men were in two big barns, and all the officers were together in a gentleman's house, which stood in its own small grounds, behind a high wall with a gate that opened onto the main village road. As there were only eight of them left in the battalion, they fitted in nicely and were very comfortable. On the Sunday morning everyone had to get up early to get cleaned up for kit and rifle inspection and then Battalion Church Parade, but after that the officers were free to wander back to their billet where the senior cook had prepared a feast for them. On the march from La Couture he had come across an unfortunate pig, which had been killed by a shrapnel shell, and had negotiated with its owner for it, leaving it, with one of his underlings to guard it, to be picked up and brought on by the transport, which had got hopelessly snarled up in traffic somewhere behind them. The

137

more damaged parts of the animal had gone into a vast stew for the men, but the officers were treated to a Sunday luncheon of roast leg of pork with baked potatoes, washed down with some agreeably rough red wine purchased in the village. It did a great deal to restore spirits, though it did not quite induce hilarity. The empty places round the table, which each of them could people with remembered faces, prevented that. In particular, Ned thought of the young men with whom he had shared the railway carriage: Knatchbull, Brown, Singer, all dead; Wharton and Cheddy, badly injured, on their way even now to the military hospital at Étaples. He remembered the cheerful conversation and laughter of the journey, the eagerness with which they had all looked forward to the adventure. It had been a short adventure for some. They had been in France a little more than a week.

After luncheon it seemed natural for the eight survivors to wander apart, each seeking the solace of his own company. Ned found his writing-pad and pen and took them out into the garden, and in a sheltered spot, sitting with his back to the sun-warmed wall on a large coping stone that had apparently fallen from the top of it, he settled down to write to Jessie.

Dearest Jessie,
I hope this letter is not long delayed in reaching you, or if it is that you will have had news already to say that I am alive and well. We were relieved in the early hours of Friday morning after two days in the fight at Neuve Chapelle, so we missed the third day, but heard most of it, as clogged roads prevented our getting further back to our rest billets, so we were in earshot of the guns. I believe there was very heavy fighting and our fellows made some gains but at the end of the day had to fall back and consolidate the morning's line. Yesterday – Saturday – started with a thick yellow fog, most unpleasant, but at least it allowed our stretcher-bearers to go out and bring in more of the wounded. Once it lifted, the Germans put up a heavy bombardment, and

we learnt that the army was digging in where it was. Having had what was effectively a day of rest – out of the line, even though we had not left our forward billets – we thought we might have to go back into the line for a time to relieve some fellows who had been in the fighting all three days. But in the event word came that a fresh unit had come up and we were able to go back into rest. It took all of Saturday to march back here as the roads were jammed with troops going up and ambulances coming down and we seemed to be halted every few yards. It was after six when we got in and we were all very tired but a good meal bucked us up, and we have had a good dinner today. There are so few of us now we cannot eat all the food the company cooks prepare. It is now Sunday and a fine day. We have had Church Parade and now the men are resting, writing home, and swapping 'souvenirs' – they are all loaded with German helmets etc.

Daltry came up to him just then with a mug of tea, and he realised how long he had been sitting there: the sun had gone round and he was in the shadow of a tall plane tree, just coming into leaf. The warmth was going out of the air, and the birds were beginning their late-afternoon chorus.

'Sorry, I didn't mean to disturb you, sir. I thought you might be getting thirsty.'

'Thanks – yes, I am,' said Ned.

'I've managed to get the mud out of your jacket, sir, but the trousers are too far gone, what with the bullet hole and the blood. I'm afraid you'll have to replace them.'

'I'll write to my tailor later,' he said. 'You haven't spent all day working, have you? It's supposed to be a day of rest for you as well, you know.'

'I'm all right, sir. I'd sooner keep busy,' Daltry said bleakly. 'Keeps my mind off a bit.'

Ned nodded, understanding. In many ways, he thought, Daltry must have had the worst of it.

When his man had gone he read through what he had

written. He sighed, thinking how flat and uninteresting it was. He had never been a brilliant scholar, had never been any good at all at expressing himself with feeling. His talents, such as they were, lay elsewhere. But what would Jessie think, receiving this dull epistle after a long and probably anxious wait? He chewed the end of the pen for a while, seeking inspiration, and then went on:

I was extremely pleased to be reunited with Daltry, who was carrying stretchers for two days without rest. He said he could not count how many men he helped carry, but when he was relieved he had to be issued with a new uniform as his own was soaked through with the blood of the wounded. I have never seen anyone look so tired. I would like to write more, but I still have very many letters to write to the people of my men who didn't make it. I must thank my stars I was not one of them. Please give my respectful regards to Father, Aunt Alice, Aunt Hen and everyone at Morland Place, and my warmest wishes, of course, to you. I think of you often.

He read it through again, sighed, and signed it,

Your affectionate husband,
Ned Morland

After a moment he added,

P.S. I hope soon to receive the photograph we talked about before I left.

And then,

P.P.S. Could you please send out some morphia tablets with your next?

The letter came on Tuesday afternoon. Jessie read it with a sigh not unlike Ned's own. She had grown used to his letters since he first went up to Black Brow, so formal and un-descriptive, so lacking in anything she really wanted to know that they were as much a frustration as a pleasure. The only revealing part of the letter was the bit about Daltry. How bloody did a uniform have to be to become unwearable? It suddenly brought home to her the reality of those casualty lists, and she felt a brief spasm of annoyance with Ned that he could not write more vividly of what he had been through.

Uncle Teddy, it had to be said, found nothing lacking in the letter, and asked her permission to show it to other people. He was already boasting about 'my son at the Front' and 'my boy Ned at Neuve Chapelle', and probably saw the letter through a rosy haze of paternal pride. But Jessie's mother could have told her that Teddy had never been much of a correspondent himself; and he came of a generation who never unbent in letters, seeing them as something in the public domain and therefore to be carefully formulated along acceptable, respectable lines.

As if to emphasise the contrast with what might be done with pen and paper, later the same week Jessie had a letter from Bertie, who was at Ploegsteert Wood – universally known among the soldiery as 'Plug Street Wood' – which was a 'quiet sector'.

Even in a quiet sector [he wrote] there are about a thousand deaths a week. Opposite us at the moment are the Saxons, who are very civilised fellows and don't care to kill us any more than we want to kill them. There is an 'agreement' between us – very much un-official and severely frowned on by the brass – that we lay off each other at breakfast time, and that no-one is to be shot or shelled while in the latrines – a most humane thought! But appearances have to be kept up – they have their own brass to placate – so they have to fire at us from time to time. They are very cour-teous in letting off a few rounds into the air before they begin shelling, to give us time to get our heads down, but a shell is a shell after all, and people get hurt. And then there are the snipers. I don't know what it is about becoming a sniper, and I'm sure they were all once somebody's sons and probably kind to their mothers, but once trained they are a law to themselves and show no quarter, night or day. The men are beginning to learn that they will aim at the tiniest flicker of light and that striking a match for a cigarette is not a good idea after dark. Young Reger was shot through the head only last night, as he paused to light a cigarette while passing along the trench to fetch tea. Poor boy, he was half German by blood, though his father had lived in England most of his life. I'm sure he would have seen the irony, had he been in any condition to care. It gives a whole new meaning to the expression, 'dying for a fag'.

We are quiet here but right now over in the French sector I can hear the guns pounding away. Even at a distance it is the most terrible sound, each individual thump blending into one long, dull roar. It is a fine day, the sort of day for seeking a pleasant corner of the woods with some baccy and a book in one's pocket. But the sound of the guns makes one restless and jittery, as though the pounding were a vibration in one's own body.

Here in the wood the violets are out, sweetly scented, and bees are grazing on them, and in the field behind our trench there is a skylark. It seems a pity to be killing people on a day like this, but some people need killing, and that seems always to have been the way the world is arranged. I remember the skylark we watched the day you drove me home after I was thrown and sprained my ankle. If that was the real world, then what can this be? It must be a dream, which makes me a phantom, or ghost – something of the sort. But I would sooner that than believe that *this* is the real world, for if this is real I'm afraid I will discover that *you* are not. Did I imagine you, and Morland Place, and all my life before? If so, I have a finer imagination than ever I gave myself credit for!

142

Excuse my rambling. We hear they had a hot time of it at Neuve Chapelle, but managed to break the German line, which may mean little on the ground but means everything to morale, stuck in this stalemate as we are. It was obviously the right thing to do, and the right place to do it. The tactics were correct, and had the weather not been against us we might have rolled up the line. I hope the people at home won't be put off by the 'cost'. There's not a man here who did not volunteer, or who does not know what might be asked of him – and not one who would not pay up when the time came. But it must be harder for you all, back in England, to accept that. Here things are simplified, sometimes brutally so. Tell them at home never to doubt we are doing the right thing. I know that *you* won't – you have the heart of a lion. And you have been through one war with me already. It comforts me to know there is someone back there who understands what I'm saying and thinking. Write and tell me all the little details of your life, your work, what you do and think and say. I want to be able to imagine you going about your ordinary life at Morland Place. In the end, that is why we are here – to preserve all that.

Your loving cousin,
Bertie.

To add to her worry about Ned's being in the battle, she had another preoccupation, which she could not share with anyone, not even her mother – perhaps least of all her mother, who might understand with her head but never would with her heart. She waited daily for news from her own body, and was ashamed of herself that what she hoped was not what Ned – or indeed anyone in the family – would want. But she was afraid of pregnancy. After the last time, she did not think she could bear to go through it again, knowing all along that she might lose the child. She could not regret that she had given Ned the love he wanted on the eve of departure, but she dreaded the consequences.

And when, two days after his letter arrived, she discovered that she was not pregnant after all, her relief was overwhelming. Yet it was sharply mingled with shame and, oddly, a kind of regret. She had not wanted to be pregnant, but still it was bitter that she was not. Once again her body had proved inhospitable to new life. Nothing, apparently, could grow in her, and that was a matter for sorrow, wasn't it? She had failed Ned as a wife, failed as a woman.

The confusion of her thoughts, of feeling such contradictory things, could not be borne for long – nor the worries about what would happen after the war, when he came back and their married life resumed. She hated herself for dreading the prospect but she did not see how they could ever go back to the pleasant ignorance of the early days. She had to shut her mind to all these things in order to survive; and so, resolutely, she refused to think of them, and threw herself instead into her work.

CHAPTER SEVEN

Up on the edge of Salisbury Plain, the bright spring weather was no less bright but considerably less warm. A brisk March wind came bowling across the open downland, bending trees and rattling windows; sunshine came in sudden gleams like laughter, as large high clouds rushed headlong across the bright blue sky. Emerging from the motor at the end of a narrow lane that led from the village of Urchfont to nowhere, Jack staggered under the pressure of the wind and had to grab for Helen.

'Undignified,' he said, as she steadied him with a large, capable hand.

'There's no-one but me to see you,' she said reasonably.

'You're the one I care about,' he said, with a grin. He stood on one leg, holding on to her with one hand while with the other he reached into the motor for his crutches, and manoeuvred them under his armpits. Rug leapt out and dashed between his legs to fling himself desperately at the nearest hedge, as was his way, as if he had been shut up in the car all day rather than half an hour.

'Well,' Jack said, when he had got himself balanced again, and had a chance to look around, 'it's certainly out of the way.'

'Too much so,' Helen said. They had passed several other houses since leaving the main road, but they had all been clustered in the first hundred yards or so nearest the village. There hadn't been another dwelling of any sort for the last two miles. 'It's too far from anywhere.'

'But what a situation!' said Jack. The house was not in itself picturesque – no thatched cottage, this, with roses round the door, but a squarish red-brick house of no-nonsense aspect, with a flat face, green-painted door and window-frames, and a slate roof fitted down firmly on top, like a hat worn by a stickler for tidiness. There was no front garden. The lane petered out into a wide, beaten-earth space in front of it, useful for access and parking the car but without visual charm. There was a stone pot on either side of the front doorstep, but nothing had been planted in them since last year's pansies, and they held only a few ghostly stems and seed heads, and some defiant grass. Beside the door a square wooden plate had been screwed to the wall; its faded and peeling paint announced it as Spakeley's Farm. There were no farm buildings, however. They had been demolished long since, during the great agricultural depression; the fields had been sold off to a neighbouring landowner and nothing remained of the farm but this rather plain farmhouse.

'It looks as if it'll be dark inside,' Helen said. 'And cramped. Do you still want to go in?'

'Of course. We've come this far,' said Jack. He cast his wife a quick look. 'Don't you?'

She sighed. 'I don't want to be disappointed all over again. I've seen so many unsuitable places. The agent didn't think this would do – he only suggested it because it has the bath-room downstairs, which suits us but puts most people off. That's probably why it's still empty.'

'You've already told me all that,' said Jack. 'Darling, you don't have to feel responsible. I'm the guilty party in this. I ought to provide you with a home, not vice versa.'

Now Helen grinned, her urchin expression, which he loved and her mother deplored. 'Yes, Lochinvar, and you should have carried me off in front of your saddle, but that's another story. Shall we stick to reality?'

'You're so unromantic,' he complained. 'Let's go in and get out of the wind.' He called to Rug, who had his nose deep in the grass verge, ecstatically drinking up smells, and limped forward.

146

Helen opened the front door – 'Stiff! Must be damp' – and walked in ahead of him, sniffing cautiously.

Jack manoeuvred himself through the door into the narrow hall, which was only just wide enough for him and his crutches without scraping his elbows on the walls. He sniffed too. 'It doesn't smell damp.'

'No, that's one point in its favour. No smell at all.' She had been to see cottages that had reeked of damp, of drains, of cabbage, of dogs, of wet rot – and one, recently inhabited by a mad old woman and her pets, spectacularly of tom-cat. This house only had a smell of dry emptiness. Jack's crutches thudded on the bare floorboards as they looked into the rooms on either side of the passage. One was a small parlour, or morning room, with a very ugly modern tiled fireplace. The wind hooned in the chimney, and in the silence, as they looked round to gauge the room's size, they could hear a number of other sounds generated by it, little creaks and groans and clicks, and the sharp rattle of a window-pane somewhere.

'I rather like it,' Jack said. 'We thought we were coming in out of the wind, but it's in here with us. Like a friendly dog.'

Their own friendly dog was trotting busily about investigating every corner. He made a clittering sound with his nails, interspersed with brisk sneezes as his energetic nose found dust pockets.

The room on the other side of the passage was the kitchen. 'Oh dear,' said Helen. It was dark and the walls were grimy. There was an ancient coal range encrusted with ancient spillings, and on the mantelpiece above it were half a dozen candle stumps, dribbled down their sides and stuck in pools of their own wax. A pile of yellowed newspapers had been abandoned in a corner. There was a stone sink with a wooden draining-board, and a wooden table split down the centre with age.

'Not very handsome,' Jack admitted mildly. 'What about the rest?'

The stairs were steep and narrow. 'The agent thought you

could use one of the downstairs rooms for a bedroom temporarily,' said Helen.

'You mean "we could",' Jack corrected. 'The only benefit of a servantless existence is that you can live a Bohemian life of sharing everything, instead of being proper. And,' he added, with a grin, 'I have to confess I do like being improper with you.'

'Jack Compton! Spare my blushes, please.'

The passage took a right-angled turn, and there was another room, with its window on the side of the house, looking out onto a high laurel hedge. 'Too small and dark for a bedroom.'

'I suppose it might have been meant to be the maid's room,' Helen said, 'when this was a farmhouse.'

The passage turned again, Helen opened a door, and they stepped into a different world. This room was at the back of the house, a featureless oblong with bare floorboards, another ugly fireplace and pinkish-brown wallpaper patterned with a tiny ochre sprig. But directly in front of them was an enormous bay window, which looked out onto the small back garden, and beyond it, separated only by a low, wind-beaten hedge, the downs. They walked across together and stood silent in the bay, gazing out. Green and brown and cloud-dappled, the great upland plain rolled away to the horizon, mile upon open mile. The primordial emptiness of it was like a brooding presence, a reminder that man was a mere upstart, a Johnny-come-lately to this ancient landscape, and could be shrugged off as easily as a mastodon might shrug off a fly. Where were you, the bare land demanded, when I laid down the rocks? Only the wind rollicked heedlessly over it, combing its rough pelt with chilly fingers as it ran.

'Oh, Jack,' Helen breathed.

He freed one hand from a crutch to take hers, and held it. Wilsford Down, Charlton Down, Ensford Down: peopled only with a scattering of sheep here and there, white on green like fallen petals of apple blossom on a lawn; stretching all the way to Upavon and Netheravon, where they could just see the shapes of aeroplanes doing bumps and circuits, so tiny against the background of the great bareback plain they hardly seemed to be above the earth at all. The only other thing that moved was the occasional spark from a window or a motor-car as the clouds rushed across the sky, hiding and revealing the sun.

'We should look at the rest of it,' Helen said at last, trying to remain practical.

At one end the long room opened onto a smaller, square one with a modified version of the same view. 'Bedroom?' said Jack. And at the other end was the bathroom, with a small frosted window onto the side of the house. It held a bath with rust-streaks running down from the taps, and a small hand-basin with a dead spider in it.

'It's hopeless,' said Helen.

'Yes,' said Jack, his face seraphic.

'The you-know-what's down the garden.'

'I bet that has a terrific view, too.'

'You'd never manage the path on crutches.'

'I'd learn to hop.'

'The house is dirty and dark.'

'It can be cleaned. And painted.'

'It's miles from anywhere.'

'Hooray!'

'But what if anything happened?'

'What if it didn't?'

'Jack, be serious,' she pleaded, pressing his arm. 'Suppose one of us needed help?'

'Tactful,' he said, smiling at her. 'You mean what if *I* needed help. But people have lived here in the past and survived. We'll have the telephone put in. We'd need to anyway, for my job.'

'The lines are there,' she admitted. 'They only need joining up again. The previous owner had telephone.'

They walked back as though drawn to the bay window. 'Awfully impractical, that window,' Jack said, as it banged loosely against the frame in the wind. 'Draughty as hell, I bet, in the winter.'

'Yes,' Helen agreed. 'Shall we take it?'

He looked at her quickly. 'You're serious?'

Now she smiled. 'I don't think I can part with this view.'

'I'm glad,' he said. 'It's a funny, ugly old house, but I don't think I can, either.' And she stepped closer to him, and they kissed: it seemed like putting the seal on one of the great landmarks of marriage.

They walked about a bit more, looking into the rooms again. 'We can live entirely down here until my foot's healed,' Jack said. 'I don't know what the upstairs is like—'

'Pretty much like the downstairs, I imagine,' Helen said. 'But if there's another bay-windowed room above the other, it will make a wonderful bedroom to wake up in. Four bedrooms upstairs, the agent said, and two attic rooms, so enough to have people to stay. And one might be turned into a bathroom, perhaps, one day.'

Something about her voice made him look at her. She seemed flushed with love. She met his eyes and gave a little, guilty laugh. 'I didn't tell you, because I didn't think it would matter, as we weren't going to like it; and then when I did, it mattered too much, until I found out if you did too.'

'Didn't tell me what?' he asked, picking through her syntax.

'It isn't for rent, it's for sale.' He was silent. 'I know, I know we were never going to buy, but it's very cheap, because of being empty so long, and being miles from anywhere, and because of the bathroom and so on. It doesn't matter, does it, if we buy instead of renting?'

'We might not always be living here,' he said gently.

'Well, then, we can sell it again. I know it isn't very handsome now, but we could make it nice, and then if we sold it we'd get more for it.' She turned again towards the window. 'If we owned it, it would be our home, not just lodgings. I want to have a home with you, even if it's only for a little time.'

'Would you want to stay here if I went back to France?' he asked, curious.

150

'I'd feel close to you here,' she said. 'It's practically *in* the sky, after all.'

He put his arm round her, and she rested her head on his shoulder, and they watched the wind dancing with the clouds, and the bright flowing light over the downs. Even Rug got up on his short hind legs to rest his forepaws on the windowsill and gaze out.

'Spakeley's Farm?' Jack said at length. 'We'll have to change that.'

'It does rather lack,' she said. She thought. 'How about Downview House?'

'How about Compton's Folly?' he said, laughing.

The Overtons were dressing for the opera – or at least Venetia was: Lord Overton had just come into her room fully clad and was easing a rueful finger inside his collar.

'Either the laundry has shrunk my collars or I'm putting on weight,' he said plaintively. 'And considering the number of meals I've missed recently it can't be the latter.'

'You look just as trim as ever to me,' Venetia said, raising her eyes to his image in the glass. She was in her under-clothes and her new maid Carless was powdering her upper back.

'You look—' Overton began with automatic gallantry to frame a compliment, but the sight of his wife in corset and shift, yet sporting a full diamond parure and hair piled up for the evening left him at a loss. To him she was both beautiful and desirable (perhaps even more so in her shift) but it was hard to find the right words to say so, especially in front of a servant. 'You're not ready,' he said at last, and drew out his watch to give himself something else to look at.

'I'm all done but for my gown,' Venetia said serenely. 'You had much better worry about Oliver.'

'I heard him in the bathroom, scrubbing,' said Overton. 'I wonder he has any skin left.'

'I expect he's trying to get rid of the formalin smell.' She stood up and moved away from the dressing-table. Carless

151

picked up the evening gown from the bed and held it for her to step into, then went round to the back of her and began methodically to hook and button her up. She cast a single but burning glance of disapproval at his lordship as she passed. It didn't seem decent to her for a gentleman to watch his wife dress; but she'd not maided for a peeress before, so she supposed she'd have to get used to different ways. Her previous lady, though quite genteel and very rich, had only been the wife of a knight, and *he* had made his money through manufacturing. You'd never have caught Sir Arnold lounging about in his wife's bedroom pretending to wind his watch – let alone Lady Tocketts *talking* to him in her underthings. Well, she supposed, that was the aristocracy for you!

When the hooks were all done and Carless showed signs of lingering, Venetia dismissed her, asking her to come and tell her when Mr Oliver was ready.

As the door closed behind her, Overton put his watch away and puffed out his breath in mock relief. 'If looks could kill,' he murmured.

'She's rather strict, I agree. Obviously the Tocketts were people of superior sensibility.'

'Evidently. How do you find her, otherwise?'

'Oh, she's very skilled, and quick, and keeps everything tidy. I've no complaints, except that she's new, and I'd got used to my dear old Hopkins.'

'We shall have to mend our ways,' said Overton. 'You don't want to lose her, when maids are so hard to come by. Servants of all sorts, come to that. So many men have volunteered – do you know they were talking in the club yesterday about the possibility of getting *females* to serve in the dining-room?'

'*Ruat coelum!*' Venetia laughed. 'What is the world coming to?'

'My thoughts exactly. It's lucky quite a lot of the club servants are too elderly to join the army, or we should be inundated.'

Carless came in to say that Mr Oliver was on his way

downstairs. She gathered up Venetia's opera cloak, stood aside to let her employers go first, and fell in behind with Ash, his lordship's man. Oliver, the Overtons' younger son, who had followed his mother into the medical profession, was waiting by the door. Venetia thought he was looking extremely handsome in evening black-and-white. When the boys had been younger, Thomas had always outshone him in looks and presence, and Oliver had fallen back, as over-shadowed children often do, on clowning and humour to make himself loved. But with no Thomas nearby, he was not lessened by comparison; and, besides, at twenty-nine he had grown into better looks with maturity, his hair had darkened, and his humour had been softened by the weight and self-confidence that came from his profession. It was just a pity, she thought, being completely the mother about it, that he showed no sign of wanting to get married.

He seemed to have been having a discussion with Burton, the butler, and as Venetia came down the last flight he looked up at her and said, 'Dearest Mama, tell me it isn't true! Not only have I had to get myself up in evening fig, but Burton says I have to wear a flower in my button-hole.'

'I endeavoured to explain, my lady,' said Burton, anxiously, 'that it is quite customary at the opera. A gardenia – quite suitable. I have his lordship's here.'

'Oliver, darling, don't you think that Burton knows best?' Venetia said. She held out her hand for the flower and stepped close to her son to fasten it herself. 'We mustn't scandalise the servants,' she whispered. 'Your father's already sent Carless into fits.'

'I dread to think what you two have been doing up there,' Oliver said sternly, not bothering to lower his voice. 'I've been waiting here for ages for you.'

'You lie, you dog!' said Venetia. 'I know you've only just come down.'

Ash put in his lordship's gardenia and draped his cloak, and then Burton opened the door and they trooped out into the pleasant spring evening to the waiting motor-car.

Oliver took the backward seat, and as soon as they were

shut in together he said, 'Seriously, Mum, don't you think the flower is going too far?'

'Not at all, dear. It looks very nice.'

'I daren't think how much a forced hothouse gardenia costs in March.'

'You are not having to pay for it, however.'

'Heartless mother,' Oliver grumbled. 'She cares nothing for her child's suffering. It's bad enough having to go to the opera at all. Why can't Holkam have a dinner party like everyone else? What are we seeing, anyway?'

'*Lohengrin*,' Venetia said with malicious pleasure.

Oliver put his head in his hands. 'Not Wagner! Dear Lord!'

'How ever did we rear such an uncultured son?' Overton enquired.

'I'm not uncultured. I like opera. And, in fact, there's nothing wrong with Wagner that couldn't be cured by taking out three notes in every four.'

'Leave a guinea with the manager to have yourself called away to a medical emergency,' Overton suggested blandly.

'I'm fully intending to be needed at the War Office.'

'You shall not!' Venetia said at once. 'Behave yourselves, both of you! It's not often we are invited anywhere by Holkam and I won't have the family peace jeopardised.'

Overton made a face at his son. 'Oh dear. Now I've stymied myself. What happens if there's a genuine emergency?'

'Will there be?' Oliver asked.

'Oh, I think not. The fuss about the sinking of our ships in the Dardanelles has pretty well died down now. They were old ships anyway, and if the mines hadn't sunk them they'd be going for scrap – though you won't read *that* in the newspapers. The Easterners are disappointed, of course, but frankly it was only Churchill and Lloyd George who thought the navy could do it alone. Now they've got their new plan of peninsular landings to play with, and that will keep them quiet for a while.'

'It was bad luck hitting those mines,' Oliver said. 'I thought the minesweepers had cleared the passage before-hand?'

154

'They had, but that particular line of mines had been laid parallel with the shore, not across the narrows, so it was missed. Between you and me,' he added, leaning forward a little, 'the ships couldn't have gone on anyway. They'd used up all their ammunition by the end of the first day, and there was no more available, so they had to withdraw. But you won't read that in the papers either.'

'This shortage of ammunition is becoming quite a scandal,' Venetia said.

'Sir John French complained bitterly again after Neuve Chapelle,' said Overton. 'He telegraphed the War Council to say that he'd had to call off the offensive because of it.'

Venetia nodded. 'I heard unofficially – from Lady Lewis, whose son is a subaltern in the artillery – that some of the heavy guns were down to one round each, which they were told to keep in case the Germans attacked.'

Oliver laughed, but his father said, 'No, it's true. Fortunately there's no sign of the Germans doing anything but sitting tight and licking their wounds.'

'What does the War Council say about it?' Oliver asked.

'When Sir John complained, Kitchener wrote back and told him that the expenditure of shells in the first half of March had been profligate, and that he must use the strictest economy in future.'

'It doesn't sound like much of a way to fight a war,' said Oliver. 'But I suppose they must be pleased about the victory at Neuve Chapelle, at any rate?'

'I don't think they care much about it, to be frank,' said Overton. 'Their hearts and minds are all on the Dardanelles – that's where they expect the breakthrough. They keep talking about how Wellington attacked in Spain in order to defeat Napoleon. But the fact is that defeat in Spain had very little effect on Napoleon. It was a side-show to him, and until he was beaten on his own ground, he wasn't beaten at all. Still, there's no point in trying to tell the Easterners that.'

'So Sir John and his men can fight their hearts out, but the War Council won't care?'

'That's rather the case, I'm afraid,' Overton said sadly.

When they arrived at the Opera House, the Holkams were waiting for them in the ante-room of their box. Violet was looking ravishing in a gown of pale blue silk brocaded with gold thread, the bodice decorated with tiny pearls and crystal beads, and she was wearing the sapphires that had been her father's wedding present to her. Venetia embraced her, and offered her hand to Holkam, who bowed over it correctly. Venetia could never warm to her son-in-law. He was tall and handsome, and before marriage had been considered the most desirable *parti* in the country. But though everyone had said he was charming, Venetia had felt even then that he was somehow rather dull. And when he had offered for Violet, it had been discovered that the estate he was to inherit was far more encumbered than anyone had realised. But Violet had declared herself desperately in love, and neither parent was willing to break her heart, so the match went ahead.

Venetia could have forgiven Holkam for being dull and impoverished, but after the marriage he had got into a political argument with Overton over the Parliament Act, and taken such offence that he had banned Violet from seeing her parents. The division was eventually healed by the intercession of Emma's late father, Tommy Weston, and the families were on terms again; but Venetia could not quite, in the depths of her heart, forgive Holkam for the misery he had caused them.

However, she never allowed her coolness to show. She accepted a glass of champagne from him, and chatted lightly about any neutral topics she could think of. Holkam had inherited a rather old-fashioned attitude of mind from his father – who had been elderly when Holkam was born – so it was as well to tread carefully with him. He deeply disapproved, for instance, of women doctors, so she had to remember never to mention her profession.

Having done her duty, she could now have her pleasure, and turned to Violet to say, 'You look more radiant than ever. You're positively sparkling tonight, my love.'

'That's because I have exciting news,' said Violet.

Venetia took in the shining eyes and slightly flushed cheeks and said, 'You're expecting another child!'

Oliver laughed. 'How the grandmother's mind always jumps to that conclusion!'

Violet, however, blushed uncomfortably. 'No, of course I'm not. How could you think it? I would break that news to you at home, not in a public place like this.'

'I'm sorry,' said Venetia, abjectly, thinking her daughter sometimes seemed a lot older than her.

'It's not about me at all,' Violet said. 'It's Holkam – he's going to the Front!'

Now there were congratulations, and Holkam's hand was shaken all over again.

'He's been longing for it ever since the war began,' Violet said. 'I was so proud that he volunteered right away, but it was disappointing for us both that he was only sent to Horseguards.'

'I believe I have your influence to thank, sir,' Holkam said to Overton, with as much warmth as his nature, and his disapproval of his wife's parents, allowed. 'I believe you said a good word for me in certain quarters?'

'No – Papa, did you really?' Violet cried. 'How kind you are!'

Oliver, edging close to his mother, whispered into her ear, 'Uriah the Hittite?' and she rapped his hand hard with her closed fan.

'I knew it was what you wanted,' Overton said to his daughter, 'so I just dropped a word in Kitchener's ear. But Holkam's own qualities spoke for themselves. I had little to do with it.'

'I'm sure you had a lot to do with it,' Violet said warmly.

'I'm sure too,' said Oliver, but was careful to move out of range of his mother's fan. It had ebony sticks, and it *hurt*. 'When will you be going, Holkam?'

'Almost immediately,' he said. 'I expect to get my travel orders tomorrow. I can't tell you exactly where I'm going, of course, but I'll be joining Headquarters' staff.'

'I've bought him a beautiful morocco writing-case as a goodbye present,' Violet said. 'To show how proud of him I am.' She squeezed his arm and he smiled down at her.

'You can be sure I shall use it to write to you as often as I can,' he said.

'Don't forget to take out a good medical kit,' Oliver said. 'I can give you suggestions, if you're not sure what's best to take.'

Holkam took that idea coolly. 'Thank you, but at Horseguards I have all the expert advice I need. And, by the way, when do you go?'

It was meant as a barbed question, but the only person it hurt was Violet. She pressed her husband's arm again, but in entreaty this time rather than affection. 'Oliver isn't in uniform,' she said.

For his sister's sake Oliver swallowed many of the answers he might have made to the question, and instead said calmly and pleasantly, 'There is a need for medical men here at home, too – perhaps the more so since so many doctors have gone abroad. Though I dare say, if the war goes on much longer, I may find I have to go too. But at the moment I see my duty here – and believe me, I never want for occupation.'

Holkam bowed slightly in acknowledgement. Perhaps fortunately, they were interrupted at that moment by the arrival of Lord and Lady Damerel, and Lady Damerel's unmarried sister Daphne, who made up the party. They were fashionable people, friends of the Holkams, and they already knew the exciting news. Lord Damerel now engaged Holkam on exactly what clothes he should pack for his expedition, and what tailor he should patronise for his uniform, despite the fact that he had been in uniform already for months.

Lady Damerel was bubbling over with war resolve – a common reaction to the news of Neuve Chapelle. The heaviness of the casualties had not shaken the determination of the people back home – quite the opposite. A new wave of fervour had swept the country. Many men who had held back had now hurried to volunteer, and those who could not go and fight were seeking any other way in which they might 'do their bit'. Committees proliferated, appeals filled the personal columns of every paper, and collections were taken up on street corners and in drawing-rooms, in railway stations, outside football grounds and at factory gates. One could not even be sure of avoiding being approached in fashionable restaurants.

So it was not surprising that Lady Damerel launched into her latest excitement, which was the Committee for Providing Comforts to the Wounded. 'They need absolutely everything, poor things, and where is it to come from if *we* don't provide it? Imagine, a poor fellow brought to a hospital over there doesn't even have any pyjamas! Well, of course, they're always in uniform when they're wounded, aren't they? And they're taken straight to the aid post and then the hospital, so they don't have a chance to go back and get their things. Though I'm not sure,' she faltered, 'why their pyjamas are not sent on after them by their regiment, once it's known where they are.'

'Dear Lady Damerel,' said Oliver, managing to keep a straight face, 'men on active service don't have pyjamas.'

'Well, they must have them somewhere,' she said logically. 'Otherwise what do they sleep in?'

'Their uniforms. Perhaps when they're out of the line they might sleep in their underwear.'

Lady Damerel was shocked. 'But, dear me, surely . . . ?' She seemed quite thrown by this idea.

'Many of the lower classes don't *own* pyjamas,' Oliver went on ruthlessly.

She rallied bravely. 'All the more reason, then, to make a contribution to the fund. The wounded need so many things, not just pyjamas but dressing-gowns, hot-water bottles, brushes and combs, face flannels, tooth-powder and so on; and then all the other things like cigarettes and chocolate and books and playing-cards to help keep them cheerful. Lady Desborough wants to send out a gramophone to our own particular hospital, but I'm not sure that would be allowed, on account of disturbing the seriously ill patients.

159

I mean, supposing one of the poor fellows was dying,' she added impressively, her eyes wide, 'and someone was playing ragtime. It wouldn't really be suitable, would it?'

To stop Oliver playing with Lady Damerel as a cat plays with a mouse, Venetia stepped in and said, 'Your new fund sounds very worthy, and I shall be sure to make a contribution.'

'Oh, thank you, Lady Overton! I knew I could depend on you. And what are you busy with at the moment?'

Venetia knew that she did not mean her medical work, but what committees and funds she was connected with – the only aspect of the war that had real meaning for Lady Damerel. So she said, 'I am trying to raise the money for a mobile X-ray machine. My godson in the RFC was shot down and severely fractured his ankle, and the outcome for him was made much worse by the lack of X-ray equipment. He is still very lame and there is some doubt if he will ever be completely sound again. I want to send a mobile X-ray vehicle to the Front – indeed, I would like to see a whole fleet of them. But that, of course, will cost a great deal of money.'

'Dear me,' said Lady Damerel, 'that sounds even more worthy than my fund! I shall have to send you a cheque.'

'Thank you so much,' said Venetia gravely. 'But since I was going to send you a cheque for yours, they'll cancel each other out. Why don't we each put the money into our own?'

'Yes, of course, what a sensible idea,' said Lady Damerel. 'How clear-headed you are, dear Lady Overton.'

It was necessary for them to go into the box now, for the performance was about to begin. Lady Damerel took her seat looking rather thoughtful, for it had just occurred to her that Lady Overton would have been likely to send a much larger donation than the one Lady Damerel had been going to send to *her*, so the cancelling-out was not going to work in her favour. Oliver also knew it, and taking a seat between his mother and the very shy and rather dull Daphne (who, he knew with weary resignation, had been invited 'for' him) he whispered to the former, 'Most economical, Mother dear, but rather unscrupulous, don't you think?'

'You can always send her a donation yourself,' Venetia whispered back, as the curtain rose.

Lenny's battalion got its call to go overseas at last, and he arrived at Morland Place for his embarkation leave on Wednesday, the 24th of March.

'Polly will be so disappointed,' Henrietta said. 'If only it had been next week, she would have been home. Her school breaks up on Tuesday.'

'I can hear her now,' said Jessie. ' "*It's not fair!*" ' It was a pretty good imitation, though perhaps a trifle unkind. She had just come in to luncheon from a visit to Heworth Park. Young English officers were convalescent there now, as well as Belgian, and she had heard harrowing stories from them about the actions they had been in. Ransome, who would never walk again, had been telling her about Ypres.

'I'll be sorry to go without seeing her,' Lenny said. 'She's a swell kid.'

'Don't let her hear you calling her a kid,' Jessie advised.

'Oh, I didn't mean it like that. I meant, she's a real brick.'

'She'll make our lives miserable for having missed you,' Jessie said gloomily. 'It's a pity, really, they gave you leave at all.'

Lenny flushed a little. 'I'm sorry you feel like that,' he said. 'But I'd have hated to go without saying goodbye to you all, when you've been so kind to me. Morland Place is my second home.'

Jessie looked at him properly for the first time since she'd got in. 'Forgive me,' she said, 'I'm cross and tired today. Of course I'm glad you came to say goodbye. I just wish the army had asked us before making its plans.'

'I wonder,' Lenny said. 'Since Polly can't come here, do you think I could go there and see her? Take her out to tea or something?'

'It's a lovely idea,' Henrietta said. 'Of course, we'd have to ask permission from the headmistress.'

161

'There's the telephone,' Lenny said. 'Surely the school must have the telephone?'

'Oh, yes, they do. I could telephone now and see if it's possible.' She sounded doubtful, thinking that Lenny was not a brother but only a distant cousin. On the other hand, it was almost the end of term and of Polly's school life so she wouldn't be missing anything important.

'They'd never let Lenny take her out on his own,' Jessie said to her mother. 'She'd have to have a chaperon.'

'Well, of course, dear,' said Henrietta. 'I shouldn't dream of suggesting otherwise – and neither would Lenny, I'm sure. But one of the teachers, surely, would go?'

'Not for one girl, not for tea, not for a cousin,' Jessie said, with the sureness of having been a boarder herself.

'Or one of the school maids?'

Jessie shook her head. 'It would have to be a close relation, and a married woman into the bargain, or they'd never let her out.' She paused a moment, and sighed. 'I'll do it. I'll drive you there in my car.'

'Oh, Jessie, would you?' Lenny said. 'You really are a trump.'

'If Mother can get permission. No, don't thank me any more. Really, it's self-defence, pure and simple. I can't bear to think of what Polly will say if she misses you.'

It was about an hour and a half's drive to Ripon, so there was just time to have luncheon and to change into something more suitable before the car was brought round. Brach had been lurking near Jessie for the last hour, sensing something unusual afoot, and as soon as the car door was opened she dashed across and flung herself in so as not to be left behind.

'I wasn't going to take you,' Jessie said to Brach, who said she knew that already and resisted all attempts to haul her out by her collar. 'Get over into the back, then.' She walloped Brach's backside and the bitch scrambled and tumbled over onto the back seat. 'And don't slobber down my neck,' she added, seating herself. 'This is an expensive dress.'

'You look very smart,' Lenny said, taking his place beside

162

her. 'Are you sure you wouldn't like me to drive? I know how.'

'Quite sure, thank you. Just look on your side and tell me if I'm going to clear the mounting block.'

'Sure you are. Bags of room.'

When they had cleared the track and got out onto the proper road, she said, 'Have you told your family you're going overseas?'

'I wrote to them right off, but of course they won't get it for a week or more. I had a letter from Pa last week. He's still pretty annoyed with me for volunteering, because of losing my citizenship, but now he says he thinks I was right to follow my conscience, and that the war is the right thing in itself, because of the way the Germans behaved. So I guess he's softening up okay. And there was a note in the envelope from Granny. She says she likes the photograph I sent her of me in uniform and keeps it on her dressing-table. She's not mad at me a bit. Granny's a swell egg, all right.'

'But what will happen after the war, when you can't go back?'

'Oh, I'll think about that when the time comes,' he said, with the lightness of one having too much fun to worry about the future.

Polly was waiting for them in the hall when they reached the school, ready dressed in hat and gloves and looking remarkably pretty, Jessie thought. The school uniform was a navy-blue skirt and white blouse, which suited her fairness, and the boater with the ribbons in the school colours gave her a debonair look.

'Hello! There you are!' she cried, as soon as they appeared. 'I was afraid something would happen and you wouldn't come. I had my fingers crossed hard about punctures and engine failures and everything. Oh, and you brought Brach with you! What a topping idea! You darling doggie, come over here!'

'Don't let her jump up at you,' Jessie warned.

A middle-aged woman standing beside Polly called

attention to herself with a sharp 'hem', and Polly straightened up from rubbing Brach's ears and said, 'Oh, sorry – this is Miss Fernyhough, the school secretary. Miss Fernyhough, my cousin Mrs Morland – and this is Mr Manning.' She said it with such huge, proprietorial pride that Jessie wanted to laugh – but, indeed, any man in uniform would have looked impressive in this closed, all-female environment; and Lenny was tall, well set-up, and handsome enough in his way.

Miss Fernyhough shook hands with them both, and even she got a spot of pink in her cheeks when Lenny said warmly, 'So good of you to let Polly come out with us this way, ma'am. I really do appreciate it. I'd have hated to go off overseas and not say goodbye. She's like a sister to me.'

Jessie saw Polly's indignantly opened mouth and kicked her discreetly as the secretary said, 'I understand you volunteered while on holiday here.'

'That's right, ma'am. With my own family so far away, I count myself pretty much half an Englishman, and I couldn't ignore the call.'

'Can we go now, Miss Fernyhough?' Polly said, seeing more chit-chat rising to the surface, and added pathetically, 'We have so little time.'

'Yes, of course. Off you go. Please have her back no later than five o'clock, Mrs Morland.'

Polly hurried them out, across the yard and into the street, and once they were through the gate she flung her back against it, pretended to mop her brow and said, 'Phew! I thought we'd never escape. I was afraid you'd never stop talking to her.'

'We had to be polite,' Jessie said. 'Now, where's the best place for tea?'

'The Tudor Tea Rooms,' Polly said promptly. 'Everyone goes there when their parents come for a visit. It's a famous place, and they do ripping teas.'

She led the way, hardly able to stop herself breaking into a run. The school was in a quiet, rather monastic-looking side-street, but it was only a very short walk to the main

164

square, where the Tudor Tea Rooms occupied a prominent place. Because of Brach they got a very nice corner table by the window, where she could lie out of the way of being trodden on. The waitress brought menus, and Polly said happily, 'Now for tea! I can have *anything*, can't I?' She looked at Jessie with sudden anxiety. 'I mean, I know you're not a parent, but it counts the same, doesn't it? And when parents take girls out to tea, the rule is they can have anything they want.'

'You make me feel old and staid,' Jessie said. 'But far be it from me to offend a sacred tradition. Go ahead and order what you like. I think I've got enough money with me. If not, they'll just have to send a bill.'

'Oh, goody! Thanks, Jessie. Then I'll have the smoked haddock and poached egg to start, and then the sausages, and hot buttered toast – with Gentleman's Relish, because in school they won't let us have it even if our parents send it. And then – meringues.'

'Meringues?' Jessie queried.

'I told you this was a famous place. That's what it's famous for. Everyone who comes here has meringues. You pretty well *have* to.'

'I'll take your word for it,' said Jessie.

With the food safely ordered, Polly was then free to concentrate on Lenny. 'So when do you go?'

'On Friday morning.'

'Yes, of course, I should have worked that out. And where are you going? Which part of the Front, or haven't they told you?' Even before Lenny answered, she scanned his face sharply and said, 'Don't tell me you're *not* going to the Front?'

'Okay, I won't. But we're not,' he said.

'Oh, Len, what rotten luck! I can't bear it! I made sure *you*'d be going, after poor Frank only got sent to horrid old Malta!'

'I know,' Lenny said, 'and I was kind of disappointed myself, but where we're going is important too, and I reckon we'll get our chance of going to the Front later.'

'So, where are you going?'

'To guard the Suez Canal.'

When Turkey had entered the war on Germany's side, it had closed off the Dardanelles to Allied shipping, which denied Russia its only warm-water sea route, and threatened British oil interests in Mesopotamia; but perhaps the most serious danger was to the Suez Canal, which was Britain's precious trade route to India and the Far East. In February, the Turks had mounted an attack across the Sinai desert, intending to sink ships in the canal to block it. They had hoped to be aided by Egyptian nationalists who objected to British rule. But in the event the nationalists seemed not to mind the British as much as they'd thought, and the Turkish attack was decisively repelled.

'It's all Indian troops guarding the canal,' Lenny explained, 'and as they're about the last regular troops available, they want them in France, so we're being sent out to relieve them. But as I said, it's pretty important work. The nation's prosperity depends on keeping that trade route open, and we're the fellows to do it.' And he slapped his manly chest, a joking gesture, but not concealing from Jessie that he really meant it.

Polly was harder to convince. 'It doesn't sound like very much to me. There won't be anyone there for you to fight – not Germans, or anyone proper, only Turks and natives, who don't count.'

'Well, you never know. The Bosch might decide to open up another front there after all.'

Polly shook her head at that, and then said, 'Poor Lenny. But it isn't your fault. I know you'd go to France if you could.'

'We'll still have our chance,' Lenny said. 'The colonel said as much when he gave us a speech about Suez. He said that once the Kitchener mobs were ready, one of them would be sent to relieve us, and we'd go to France, because by then we'd be the better troops. So you see?'

'Well,' said Polly, doubtfully, 'as long as the war doesn't end too soon . . .'

166

The relays of food began to arrive, and Jessie and Lenny drank tea and ate dainty egg and cress sandwiches, while Polly put away quantities of her chosen savouries, as if she hadn't been fed for a week. Jessie watched in amazement, forgetting her own capacity at that age, but noting with envy how Polly never got red-faced or sticky, or appeared to have her mouth full, however much she ate – an extremely useful accomplishment in a society that still expected ladies to be above such worldliness as enjoying their food. Then the waitress cleared the decks and brought a vast plate of meringues. They were large and sandwiched with cream, and Jessie thought the staff had rather gone mad to be bringing a dozen. But Polly rose manfully to the challenge, and disposed of eight before sitting back with a sigh and admitting defeat.

'I simply can't manage another crumb,' she said blissfully. She cocked an eye at her elders. 'Don't you even want *one?*'

'I'm not very hungry,' Jessie said.

'Meringues aren't really my favourite thing,' said Lenny.

'You don't know what you're missing,' Polly said, privately thinking she would never be *that* old.

Jessie smiled to herself, and said, 'Would you like to take the other four back with you? I'm sure the waitress could find a bag for them.'

'Really? Oh, Jessie, you are a brick! The other girls in my room would *die* for one! They are simply superlative, you know.'

Jessie looked at the clock. 'I think we had better go. I don't want to get you into trouble by being late.'

'Oh, is it that time already? Beastly prep – I don't see why we have to do it, when we're leaving next week anyway. But they're *frightfully* strict. I shall be so glad to leave horrid old school.'

They walked her back and delivered her into the front hall, where she gave Jessie a great hug and said, 'Thank you for a *ripping* tea.' And then she turned to Lenny and her self-possession faltered. She gave him her hand but her eyes filled with tears as he kissed it gallantly. 'Take care of yourself,' she said waveringly.

'Don't worry about me. I'll be fine,' he said. 'I'll write to you, if your father says it's all right. And will you write to me? The other fellows will have letters from their sisters and mothers and such, and it'll be pretty dull not getting any letters when all the others are having them.'

'Of *course* I will,' Polly said, 'if Daddy says I may. And I'm sure it'll be all right – we are cousins, after all.' A bell sounded. 'That's prep. I have to go.' She looked once more at each of them, then took her lip under her teeth and turned and walked away, head high, and very dignified. She didn't look back.

'She's a great kid,' Lenny said softly to Jessie, as they went out to the car.

Jessie thought of the schoolgirl eating meringues one after the other as though she were inhaling them; and the young lady on her dignity not allowing herself to cry at the parting. Fourteen was such a funny age, caught between worlds. Lenny would probably find a very different girl when he came home on leave – and just now, Jessie found herself glad for Polly's sake that he was going to boring old Suez after all.

168

BOOK TWO

At The Front

The green and grey and purple day is barred with clouds
  of dun
From Ypres city smouldering before the setting sun.
Another hour will see it flower, lamentable sight,
A bush of burning roses underneath the night.

Charles Scott-Moncrieff, 'Domum'

BOOK TWO

smile as she said I am going off to Salisbury to buy
the basic requirements. What fun to be shopping for one's
own house. Mother bought me all my linen as a house-
warming gift, and sent it down by the same train as Molly
(the Antelope was not amused to have to find room for
all those boxes), and my rental rates are languishing pro
tem in a drawer. I shall spend nothing but on two things
from my bedroom at home, and the furniture (that Aunt
Marjorie left me, which will come by the carrier . . . .

Brach gave a great whining yawn, which made her squeal,
and new legs unfurled her tongue to lick her nose, she decided
that

CHAPTER EIGHT

Though it was only the end of March, it was warm enough
for Jessie to sit in the rose garden to read her letters. There
was one seat that caught the morning sun, and she took
possession of it, while Brach flopped down in the grass at
her feet and squeezed her amber eyes against the sunshine,
like a cat. The roses already had fat shoots, some green,
some a soft red, and others copper-beech purple; a lone
bumble bee had been tempted out by the warmth, and
pottered along the border looking for something to eat.

. . . situation, wonderful views, and perfect for walks for
Rug. As the estate is still in probate, it will take rather a
long time for the purchase to go through. But the agent
has come to an agreement with the executors that we
should rent it for the time being, with the rental to be set
off against the price. The advantage is that we can move
in straight away (and you can imagine, dear Jessie, how
I long for my own house!). Also, if we discover anything
nasty, like bad drains or a leaking roof, the estate will have
to put it right. However, it means we can't get on with
the improvements we plan, as it is not ours to improve.

I have got two local girls, recommended by a very fierce
wing-commander's wife (that is, the wife is fierce, not the
wing-co, who is rather a poppet!) to scrub the place from
top to bottom so that we can move in next week. Molly
has come to stay with me for a few weeks to help me

171

settle in, so she and I are going off to Salisbury to buy the basic requirements. What fun to be shopping for one's own home! Mother bought me all my linen as a house-warming gift, and sent it down by the same train as Molly (the Antelope was *not* amused to have to find room for all those boxes, and my nuptial naps are languishing pro tem in a disused stable!). I'm to have one or two things from my bedroom at home, and the furniture Great Aunt Marjorie left me, which will come by the carrier . . .

Brach gave a great whining yawn, which made her sneeze, and having unfurled her tongue to lick her nose, she decided to put it to good use and began licking her forepaws, more catlike than ever. Jessie reached down a hand to scratch the dog's head, and she tilted up her face and smiled at her mistress.

Jessie thought of Helen's excitement over her first married home, and remembered her own pleasure in Maystone Villa when she first moved in. It was nice that Helen had her sister Molly there to reinforce it. Jessie had enjoyed a visit from Emma Weston in the early days, when Emma's enthusiasm for her 'darling little house' had made her see it with fresh eyes and appreciate it all the more.

Her other letter was from Violet. She wrote about Holkam's going off to France, and how proud she was of him, and then about her various committees and societies. She described a number of social activities she had undertaken, and some improvements she was making to her houses. Then she went on:

Emma has had a horrid cold, and though she is over it now, it has left her rather pulled. She ought to get out of London and into the country for a rest, and I wondered whether she could come to Morland Place. I know your uncle said that she was welcome any time. Would Easter be suitable? I am going down to Brancaster for a few days to see the children, but then I have a round of country-house visits that I feel would be too strenuous for Emma, and not give her the quiet and rest

172

she needs. Do let me know if it will be convenient. If not, then of course I shall make other arrangements.

And now I have a request to make for myself. When I come back to Town in May and the Season begins, won't you come and stay with me? Now, Jessie, do, do! I long so much to see you, but I have so many engagements already that I have to stay in Town. But if you were here we could go to them together, and I promise to find a charming man or two to escort you in Ned's absence. I am sure you need a break from all your toils – and if that is not enough to persuade you, then do it for me, because I want my friend more than you can think.

There was a note included in the envelope from Emma herself.

Violet thinks I need country food and air, but though I'm not the least unwell – I'm as fit as a horse, as always – I should love to come and visit you at dear Morland Place, and see the dogs and horses and everyone and everything. It will set me up nicely before my dutiful visit to Uncle Bruce and Aunt Betty at Aberlarich after Easter – quite the wettest time of year in Scotland, so it will probably give me tuberculosis unless I am *absolutely* hale and hearty before I go. Oh dear, that sounds unkind! I love my aunt and uncle dearly, but I wish they hadn't chosen to live in a damp old castle dripping with moss and miles from anywhere. But go I must, and since it's quite plain that Violet doesn't want me, won't you take pity on a poor orphan, dear Jessie, and plead my case with Uncle Teddy, and Aunt Hen and Aunt Alice, to come for Easter?

Jessie laughed at Emma's style, and thought there would be no need at all of pleading. Uncle Teddy (he was no uncle of Emma's but had begged her to call him so) could never have too many visitors, and in any case he adored Emma and would have liked her to make her home there. Polly would be pleased, too – she'd had rather a crush on Emma last time she had visited.

As for Violet's invitation, Jessie was tempted to accept, not only because it was a long time since she had seen Violet, but because she was beginning to feel restless and wanting a change. Physically, she was quite well again after the miscarriage, and her energy had returned, though she still had periods of sadness. But the upheaval of the move from Maystone, at a time when she was still in a state of emotional turmoil, had left her feeling disjointed, out of her place, and – surprisingly – lonely. When Ned had been at Black Brow he had seemed much closer: there had always been the hope of a brief visit from there. But Ned in France was as remote from her as if he had never existed. And while Morland Place was very dear to her, she missed ordering her own household. That was a surprise to her, for she had always seen household matters as a chore that interrupted her other occupations. But now, with nothing to do at home, she felt something missing from her life. Her mother ran everything with practised efficiency, and any attempt by Jessie to help was gently but firmly turned aside by Henrietta herself, who had been doing it so long it hardly occurred to her that it was work. 'No, darling, don't trouble yourself. You need to rest,' was Mother's response. But rest was not what Jessie wanted – it only left her prey to her unhappy memories, and worries about Ned at the front, her childless state, and what the future after the war held for her. Besides, even if she had wanted solitude, it was almost impossible to find it with such a number of people under one roof. On the occasions when she actually *wanted* to read quietly, she had only to pick up a book to have someone appear, servant or family member, as though summoned by the action, to disturb her.

To be lonely and yet never alone was perhaps the hardest combination to bear. She thought wistfully of the comfort of Violet, her oldest friend; and her restlessness turned eagerly towards the excitements of London during the Season. If anything could scour away her sadness it must be that; and Violet of all people would never ask her about

174

babies or commiserate with her over her lost one. Violet hardly even mentioned her own children. She thought she would go.

'I must say, you don't look particularly ill,' Jessie said, as Emma stepped down from the train, wearing a smart jacket and skirt of French navy and a very dashing small hat with a single feather that pointed straight upwards like a finger raised for attention. Not that Emma needed to do anything to gain attention. Her smiling face was so pretty that people passing looked at her with pleasure, and a gentleman in the carriage fought silently with the porter for the privilege of handing down her two bags and a hat-box.

'I'm not ill, not at all,' Emma said. 'It was just Violet's way of getting rid of me. I've outstayed my welcome,' she sighed melodramatically. 'A poor orphan is a tiresome burden on everyone!' The sparkling eyes gave her away, and she couldn't stop herself breaking into smiles. 'But she's going to stay with the dullest set of people on earth, so I'm glad to be out of it. I have rather a lot of luggage, I'm afraid,' she added, as they walked towards the luggage compartment, with the porter and her maid, Spencer, following, 'because of going to Scotland afterwards. I've had to pack all my thickest things. Imagine going to Scotland just when everyone there with any sense is *leaving* it! Those two trunks are mine, but I have all I need for the present in the valise and the carpet bag. The trunks can just be stored while I'm at Morland Place – boring tweeds and stout boots and so on. "Not wanted on voyage", you know.'

'You're reckoning without Polly,' Jessie said. 'She'll want to examine every stitch, boring tweeds or not.'

'Dear Polly! Where is she? I quite thought she'd be here to meet me.'

'She's playing tennis at the Cornleighs'. The engagement was made before we knew which train you were coming on. She was terribly torn, but I told her she simply couldn't cancel because it would leave Eileen without a partner. But I think she was glad to be made to go because Seb Cornleigh

175

is home on leave and she rather fancies herself in love with him – though last week it was Richard Canthorpe she was sighing over, after she saw him coming out of Makepeace's, and the week before it was the Laycock boy – and that's not even counting Lenny.'

'It's the age,' said Emma. 'I was always in love with someone when I was fourteen or fifteen – a different one every week, and some of them *most* unsuitable. I remember a certain piano-tuner who used to come to our house . . . Where's Uncle Teddy? Doesn't he always like to meet trains?'

'He had to go over to Layerthorpe, to Ned's factory. You know that the Government requisitioned it? There's some sort of labour dispute, and Uncle Teddy's gone to try to sort it out.'

'You hear things like that all the time. I must say, the workers seem to be getting awfully uppish. I can't understand them. When you think of our men at the Front . . .'

They walked out of the station to where Jessie's Austin was waiting.

'So this is your new motor? How dashing of you to drive yourself, Jessie! I long to learn, though I haven't a hope that Uncle Bruce or Cousin Venetia would ever let me have one of my own. Would you teach me to drive? Is it difficult?'

'Not really,' Jessie said, directing the porter with the luggage and realising at the same time the disadvantage of a small vehicle after the Arno. 'I think the trunks will have to be sent on – they'll never go in. Could you see to it for me, Barnet?'

'O' course, Mrs Morland. No trouble at all. Why, thank you, ma'am.' He touched his cap as the silver changed hands. 'Right kind of you. Any news o' Mr Ned, if I might mek so bold to ask?'

'Nothing lately. He was in the fighting at Neuve Chapelle – perhaps you heard that?'

'Aye, ma'am. Mr Morland told us all about it. Proud as Punch o' Mr Ned, he is. Mr Lennard – in the ticket office, ma'am—?'

'Yes, I know him.'

'His son was at Neuve Chapelle. He was killed the second day.'

'Oh, I'm so sorry!'

'Terrible sad thing. He were only nineteen.' He shook his head. 'I'm glad Mr Ned came out all right.'

Spencer took her place in the back beside one of the valises, her own luggage and the hat-box, and Emma got in beside Jessie, thinking what fun it was to ride in the front of a motor-car.

Manoeuvring the Austin out of the station yard, Jessie was making a mental note to ask her mother if she knew about Lennard's son. Mrs Lennard had been a maid at Morland Place in her youth, and Henrietta liked to keep an eye on all past employees.

'You were saying,' Emma resumed, 'that driving isn't difficult?'

'No, not really. You only have to have the nerve. Driving horses is much trickier.'

'I can't do that, either. I must practise my riding, too, while I'm here,' Emma said. 'Don't you find men have kept all the really interesting ways of "doing one's bit" to themselves? Violet seems quite content with her committees, but don't you sometimes long to do something more useful? I wonder if Uncle Teddy will have time to go on with my shooting lessons. He said I was getting quite good at it last time.'

'What has learning to shoot to do with it? I hope you're not planning to cut off your hair and run away for a soldier?'

Emma laughed. 'I don't think I'm quite mad enough for that. And I do love my hair. But I like to learn new things.'

'Well, Uncle Teddy will be delighted to go on teaching you,' Jessie said. 'He wants everyone to learn to shoot, so that if the Germans invade and Morland Place is besieged, we can hold out as long as possible. He says we must "sell our lives dear". Mother says it's a terrible expression, and frightens the maids into fits. But she can hit a target four times out of five now.'

'There, you see! I knew there had to be a use for learning,' said Emma happily. 'Dear Uncle Teddy! What fun you all have.'

On Easter Monday, Morland Place held a fête, which Teddy had been planning for the last six weeks. It had seemed to him too long to wait until the usual race-week celebration to hold a party. In any case, several of York's leading ladies had been badgering him to do something for their various funds. He might have signed a cheque – indeed, he already had, several times – but that was dull work; and as for flag days, he felt, shrewdly, that people would dig deeper into their pockets if there were some sort of fun attached to the extortion.

Easter Sunday was cloudy, with intermittent short spats of rain, which did not bode well. But during the night the clouds blew away, Easter Monday dawned clear, and by nine o'clock it was evidently going to be a fine, warm spring day. By eleven the crowds were arriving.

Preparations were complete. It was a tribute to the affection and respect in which he was held by the York Commercials that Colonel Hound had lent the occasion a platoon, both to act as a working party and to help with the fair itself. They had improved the track from the road to Morland Place, filling several holes and cindering a few muddy places, and put up the signposts made by the estate carpenter to show the way, in case there should be anyone who did not yet know it. A field had been set aside, its gate removed, as a vehicle park, motors on one side, wagonettes and private carriages on the other where there was shade from the trees and water-troughs for the horses. Two of the Commercials undertook to direct traffic. The fête itself was held on the neighbouring field, which they had also helped to arrange, setting up the tents, roping off the arena, and stringing the gay bunting along the hedges and from tree to tree.

There was a gratifyingly large turnout, sign that most people in York had forgotten that old, awful business about the *Titanic* – or at least that they no longer blamed Teddy for surviving. There were dignitaries – the mayor and his lady and several councillors, Colonel and Mrs Basset, senior officers from Fulford, Lord and Lady Grey. There were leading manufacturers, like Kitson, Hewson, Canthorpe, Godson and Stead, with their families. Representatives of the professions came, like the Swanns, the Tweedys, the Dykes, the Laxtons, the Laycocks and the Havergills. And neighbouring landowners and gentry folk joined villagers, tenants and all the decent people of York and its surroundings who welcomed a good day out on the Morland estate – just like the old days, as many of them commented happily to each other.

There was plenty to entertain them. Many of the diversions that traditionally made their appearance at the August fair were there: the hoop-la, the coconut shy, the shooting booth and the bran tub. There was a fortune-teller, in a tent decorated with cut-out stars, moons and 'mystical' signs, with an exotic robe and a heavy veil to conceal the fact that Madame Zara was in fact Miss Peterkin from the telephone exchange (her occupation perhaps explaining her uncanny omniscience). There was a bowling alley with a docile and very clean piglet sitting in a pen nearby, wearing a ribbon round its neck and attracting a great deal of attention from little girls. There were fancy-work stalls and bric-à-brac stalls, a guess-the-weight competition with an enormous iced cake (donated by Mrs Chubb of Bootham Park), a toffee-apple stall and one selling home-made fudge and coconut ice. There were balloons and baby-clothes to buy, ribbons, buttons, wooden toys, watercolour paintings, quill boxes and silk tassels. There was a photographic booth, courtesy of Bacon's of York, which was doing a brisk trade, especially with anyone in uniform. There was a refreshment tent where the big teapots were out in force again, along with an array of cakes and sandwiches and pies, and a beer tent set up and run by the landlord of the Have Another.

But that was by no means all: in the roped-off arena a series of entertainments was staged. There was some dancing by the local morris side to warm things up, then the platoon of the York Commercials demonstrated some very smart and complex marching and counter-marching. The Fulford polo team performed a musical ride to the strains of the Light Cavalry overture, played on a gramophone – a very popular event, marred only slightly by an incident when a child's ball rolled by mistake into the area and two of the ponies hurled themselves instinctively at it. Then the Clifton Ladies' First Aid Group gave a demonstration of bandaging and splinting with volunteers from the crowd, and a group of schoolchildren performed some Greek dancing with scarves.

Finally, a group of FANYs, with the aid of some convalescent soldiers lent by Clifton Hospital, staged a vignette of a battlefield. Exploding fireworks made flashes and plenty of smoke, the soldiers lay about groaning, and the FANYs dashed in, first of all two on horseback with medical kits bumping behind in haversacks, and then two more driving a borrowed van on which a large red cross had been painted, to represent an ambulance. Amid more fireworks, thrown enthusiastically (and sometimes, in his excitement, authentically at random) by little Billy Pike, they lifted two of the men onto stretchers, loaded them into the van and drove bumpily away.

As a finale the event could hardly have been surpassed, and after much applause there was a buzz of conversation. Not all the comment was favourable: there were those who did not think women should drive motors, and others – many of them – who believed war was men's business and there was no place for women at the Front. A few condemned the FANYs' demonstration as unwomanly or even downright immodest. But many more were enthused and impressed, and when the collection tins came round afterwards they were pleased to drop something in towards buying the organisation more ambulances.

Finally the mayor made a short speech, thanking their gracious host (Uncle Teddy looking suitably modest and embarrassed) and hostess (Aunt Alice in a new hat looking exactly as she always looked) and urging everyone to spend freely and fill the collection boxes as everything was being

done for a good cause. Then the York Railway Workers' Brass
Band struck up, playing a mixture of popular and patriotic
tunes as everyone dispersed among the other attractions.

In the crowd, Jessie found, one's eye was always drawn
to anyone in uniform. There were York Commercials, soldiers
from other regiments on leave, or not yet gone to their
battalion, and convalescents from Clifton Hospital and
Rowntree's. They were surrounded, wherever they went, by
a little crowd of mothers, fathers, sisters, lovers and little
brothers, circling like faithful, adoring satellites. Some of the
Commercials were carrying round collection boxes, as were
various committee ladies, Boy Scouts, and members of the
Morland family. It really was not possible for anyone at the
fair to get through the whole afternoon without passing a
shaken tin. Even baby Harriet, pushed out in her peram-
bulator by Nanny Emma, had a donations box balanced
before her on the apron.

And Polly was everywhere, smiling, chatting and cajoling.
She had a new dress for the occasion, and looked ravishing
in white muslin with a pink sash and a straw hat decorated
with large pink and white daisies. Her own particular pride
was that though she would not be fifteen for another month,
the hem of the dress was only just above her ankle. Since
many of the more active ladies now wore their gowns clearing
the ground by a good two or even three inches, her muslin
could not be distinguished from a grown-up dress. Polly had
achieved this transition by importuning Alice, who had
passed on the request to Teddy; his pride in Polly's beauty
and his dislike of denying Alice anything had done the trick.
Alice was, in her quiet way, pleased to have another female
in the house who was interested in clothes. Neither Henrietta
nor Jessie seemed to care in the least what they wore, and
though Ethel paid lip-service to the idea of fashion, she was
always more interested in her children than anything else,
and Alice was not forceful enough to keep a conversation
on track when it kept wandering off into toddling, teething
and temper tantrums.

Polly had such a way with her that she kept having to go

back to the house to empty her tin. But even while collecting she managed to have a great deal of fun, and collected two new swains – James Peckitt, of Peckitt's Boots and Shoes, and Algy Kitson, the silversmith's son. They asked permission to walk round with Polly and Eileen Cornleigh, and James Peckitt presented the coconut he had knocked over to Polly, while Algy Kitson managed to win a box of pretty-coloured soap for her on the hoop-la stall. However, these young men, though agreeable in their way, were only seventeen and sixteen respectively, so they had no hope of competing in her heart with the glorious Seb Cornleigh in uniform, demonstrating his prowess at the shooting booth and winning a small goldfish in a bowl. This, however, he presented to his youngest sister, twelve-year-old Dodo – a sad waste of an opportunity, in Polly's view.

Jessie played her own part, walking about with Brach at her heels, carrying a collection tin for the Comforts for the Wounded fund and chatting to neighbours, tenants, former servants and Morland pensioners, answering questions about Ned and listening to stories of sons, grandsons, brothers and cousins who had gone, or were going, or were longing to go, to the war. Brach wandered off after a while, bored with this aimless walk, and Jessie stopped to talk to her maids Peggy and Susie, who were accompanied by a brace of large and silent young men with whom they were walking out. She asked them if they were happy at Morland Place.

'Oh, yes, ma'am, thank you. It's nice being in a big servants' hall for a change, and Mr Sawry's very fair.'

'Mrs Stark's cooking is better than mine, an' all,' Peggy said, with a grin. 'She doesn't have trouble with blancmange that won't set an' a chicken that's raw in the middle,' she added, referring to two notable failures in her short culinary history.

'And Miss Spencer, ma'am – Miss Weston's maid – she's quite brightened us all up with her London talk, all about life at Lady Holkam's,' said Susie. 'There's never a dull moment there, by her accounts.'

'Well, I'm glad you're not missing Maystone Villa,' Jessie said, feeling obscurely hurt that they didn't.

'Oh, we do miss it, ma'am,' said Peggy hastily. 'But it's a nice change here, and there's always something going on.' Her focus changed as she looked at someone over Jessie's shoulder. 'Does that young gentleman want to talk to you, ma'am?'

Jessie turned, and found herself face-to-face with a tall, handsome young man in Green Howards' uniform, who was smiling at her enquiringly. For a moment she could not place him, and then memory flooded back. She held out her hand with a warm smile.

'Mr Gresham! How nice to see you.' Erskine Gresham took her hand. She had met him in Scarborough, on that ill-fated vacation she had spent there with her mother in December which had coincided with the German bombardment. He had been home convalescing from a wound taken at Ypres. 'What are you doing here? I thought you said you were going back immediately after Christmas. Did your wound take a turn for the worse?' His left arm was in a sling, she noted.

'Oh, this is a new one,' he said, gesturing with it. 'I did go back after Christmas, but I was only there for a couple of weeks when I got injured again.'

'Shot?' Jessie asked anxiously.

'Nothing so romantic, I'm afraid,' Erskine said, with a rueful smile. 'Like a fool I slipped in the mud as I was walking past a transport wagon, and fell under the wheels.'

'Oh, good Lord! I'm so sorry.'

'I was lucky the ground was so soft,' he said cheerfully. 'I sank so far into the mud it only broke my arm. And it's a clean break, so it will soon heal. My uniform, however, was a complete loss.'

He wanted to make light of it, so she did not press her sympathy. 'So you're on convalescent leave again?'

'Yes, and I happened to be in York this morning when I saw a leaflet about the fête, so I thought I'd toddle along and pay my respects. I hope it's all right to come without an invitation?'

'Everyone's welcome,' she said, 'and friends most of all. I'm *very* glad to see you.'

He beamed. 'May I walk with you? I have a sound right arm I can offer you – wrong side, I know, but as people say when there's any little inconvenience these days, there *is* a war on.'

She laughed and slipped her hand through the crook of the arm he offered her. It felt solid and strong under the slight harshness of the cloth. It was so nice, she thought, to be on a man's arm again. 'How are your parents?' she asked. 'And your sister?'

'They're well, thank you. Annoyed with me for re-appearing so soon when they were wanting to boast about my being at the Front. And Rosie's still working on Father to let her go to Somerville. I fancy there's been some small softening recently. Perhaps he's realising what a pleasantly quiet life he could have if she was elsewhere.'

'Are things getting back to normal after the bombardment?'

'Everyone's keeping their spirits up, but the town still looks a ruin. There's scaffolding up at the back of our house. It's so hard to get workmen to come when everyone in Scarborough needs them – and so many of them had enlisted anyway. I'm afraid it's the same everywhere, and it will be years before the town is fully rebuilt. The government promised compensation money, but none of it has appeared yet. I suppose they have other things on their mind.' He looked at her hesitantly, and then said in a low voice, 'I was so very sorry to hear about – about your baby. You were so wonderfully brave that day, and it seems monstrous that you should have had to suffer in consequence.'

Jessie shook her head slightly, unable to answer as the images rushed into her head and the pain came back, as fresh as the first day. Gresham, looking at her face, squeezed her hand against his body for a moment in an instinctive desire to comfort her. 'It may,' she began, lost her voice and found it again, 'it may not have been anything to do with that. According to my doctor. How did you hear about it?'

'From Dr Wren. I hope I haven't upset you by mentioning it. I only wanted you to know I thought your actions magnificent. You were a true heroine that day.'

She turned her head a little away, and asked, in a determinedly bright voice, 'How is the dear doctor? And Mrs Wren? We so enjoyed meeting them.'

'Oh, they're just the same, dashing about their good works, always cheerful. I say, I don't know about you, but I'm starving, and here we are, fortuitously just by the refreshment tent. Will you let me fetch you something? I'm sure you must be hungry.'

'I am,' Jessie discovered. She pushed her painful thoughts hard away, as he had done with what must be his bitter disappointment at being injured again so soon. She smiled. 'I should love some tea.'

'Good! Here's a nice table, just big enough for two. You sit and guard it while I go into battle with the frenzied mob. May I bring you a selection of things to eat?'

'Certainly. Everything in there is good. Our own Mrs Stark made quite a lot of it – including her special marmalade cake. You might look out for that, if there's any left.'

'Just as you say.' He threw her a smart salute and went away into the tent. Brach found her again while she was waiting and, having greeted her passionately, flopped down under her chair, out of the way of all the passing boots. Judging by the press in the refreshment tent, everyone else was trying to secure tea at the same time and it would be a while before Gresham came back, but she was happy enough just to sit and rest her feet – she had been on them since early in the morning. She went off into a reverie, and was brought back from it by the cold touch of Brach's nose on her hand. The bitch had got up and was swinging her tail hesitantly, staring at a woman who had paused by the table and was regarding Jessie with interest.

She was a stranger to Jessie, middle-aged, small and slight but with an air of strength and capability about her. Her neat face was firm, her eyes noticing and quick; her greying fair hair was tidily suppressed under a no-nonsense hat. Her skin had a yellowish tan, as though she had been long in a hot climate, and she wore a grey costume with nothing about it that pretended to fashion or even femininity – and yet Jessie immediately found her attractive to look at, though she could not think why. She began to smile without realising it, and at once the woman came over to her.

'A very well-run fair, don't you think?' she said. 'I'm new to the area, but everyone told me I shouldn't miss it, and I'm glad I came. I gather that these Morlands are quite the benefactors. It's one of the strengths of England, don't you think, that our best families have such good consciences?'

Evidently she did not know that Jessie was a daughter of the house, and between understanding that this was a tribute to the modesty of her appearance (unlike Polly, she had not dressed up, but had put on one of her older workaday coats and skirts in case any physical labour was required of her) and wondering how best to introduce the fact, she did not answer quickly enough and the woman went on.

'This fund-raising is an excellent thing, and we could not get on without it, but I've been watching you walk about with your collecting tin – if you'll forgive me – and I have the feeling somehow that it's not enough for you. Don't you long to do something more practical? "Good works" in themselves don't feed that restless desire to be active, to see a result for one's labours, to escape the common bounds and *achieve* something.' She laughed pleasantly. 'Now, tell me I am quite wrong and have misread your character most impertinently!'

'No, no, you are right, on the whole,' said Jessie. 'But how did you know?'

'You remind me of myself when I was your age. When you were a child, did you rail against the unfairness of being a girl?' Jessie laughed and nodded. 'Did you long for adventure, and tell yourself stories in which you dressed as a boy and ran away to foreign parts?'

'Yes, I did,' Jessie said. 'You're quite right.' Instinctively she put her fingers up to the scar on her cheek, a gesture not missed by the woman.

'So did I,' she said. 'And was the scandal of my family and a great disappointment to my parents. I didn't dress myself as a boy, but I did eventually run away to foreign parts, in the only way a woman can, unless she marries – as a nurse.'

That accounted, Jessie thought, for the air of capability and the tanned skin. 'Did you not want to marry?' she found she had asked. It really was an odd conversation – she didn't even know who this woman was.

'I wanted to,' she said, 'but Fate decreed otherwise.' She glanced at Jessie's hands, which were gloveless – no wonder she didn't take her for gentry! 'But I see you are married.'

'I don't feel it,' Jessie said. 'My husband is at the Front, and I'm living with my family again.'

'You have children?'

'No,' Jessie said, and left it at that.

'Then I understand completely why you long for activity. A husband and children use up a woman's energy, but without them she finds herself at a loss for something to do.'

'I have plenty to do,' Jessie said with a smile, and was about to explain who she was and what occupied her hours.

But the woman said, 'Plenty to do, but not the sort of thing you want to do. Nothing that satisfies your urge to help win the war.'

'War is men's business,' Jessie said, intrigued.

'You can't go and fight, that's true – and the world would sink into barbarism if ever women did – but there is something worthwhile and important you can do here at home.'

'You mean nursing, I take it?'

'Indeed I do. We need women like you – active, sensible, intelligent women of good education. I hope you will forgive me for proselytising, but I make a point of recruiting wherever I go, whenever I see good material going to waste.'

'Not completely to waste,' Jessie laughed. It was impossible to be offended by this brisk, forthright woman, whose intentions were so obviously honourable. 'I have my First Aid certificates. And I visit at Heworth Park, and read to the convalescents.'

'Good enough,' said the woman, dismissively, 'but there are plenty of fine ladies to undertake that dainty sort of work. *You* could do so much more – real work, work that desperately needs to be done. Let me urge you to join a VAD, my dear, and undertake nursing training at my hospital. I think you would make an excellent nurse – and we shall need more nurses than you can imagine before this war is ended.'

'*Your* hospital?'

'Yes, mine. The cat is out of the bag now,' she said with a smile. 'My name is Kemble – Margaret Kemble – and I am the new matron of Clifton Hospital. I take up my duties there tomorrow. Might I know your name?'

Now Jessie felt a little awkward, the conversation having gone so far. 'I'm Jessie Morland – Mrs Ned Morland.'

Margaret Kemble's eyes widened. 'Not—?' She jerked her head towards the house.

Jessie nodded. 'He's my uncle, and my husband's father. I married my cousin, you see. And I'm living at Morland Place now, while my husband's in France.'

'I see.' The woman was silent a moment, surveying Jessie's face. 'Well, obviously I've been under a misapprehension, and I hope you will excuse me if I've said anything inappropriate.'

'But you haven't! Please, don't apologise. I've been very interested in everything you've said. I'm sorry I didn't tell you before who I was – though if I had, I might not have got to hear what you had to say.'

'Hmm. Thinking back, I can see it must have been hard to interrupt me. I was somewhat on my hobby-horse.' She smiled. 'I'm rather sorry you have turned out to be one of the landed gentry, because I was looking forward to recruiting you to the cause. But I dare say you have many more ways open to you to help the war effort than I was imagining.'

'Well . . .' said Jessie, thinking of them. Out of the corner of her eye she saw Erskine Gresham emerge from the tent with a tray in his hands. She turned her head towards him, and Miss Kemble looked too.

'Ah, I see your company has returned – and better company than me by a long mark. I mustn't keep you any longer.' She hesitated and then held out her hand, and Jessie shook it, finding it hard and dry and much like her own, though for different reasons. 'It's been a pleasure to meet you, Mrs Morland.' She dropped Jessie's hand, and as she turned away, said, with an air of mischief, 'I still think you would have made a fine nurse.'

Gresham came up and put the tray down on the table. 'I hope I didn't interrupt your conversation with your friend.'

'She wasn't a friend. I've never met her before.'

'Oh. I'm sorry. It looked as though you'd known each other for years.'

'I think that's just the sort of person she is,' Jessie said.

Gresham made friends with Brach and praised her beauty and intelligence extravagantly until Jessie began to laugh and begged him to stop. She inspected the selection of dainties he had acquired. 'Even some of the marmalade cake! I thought it would all be gone. You are a fine forager.'

'A necessary skill for a subaltern in our mess,' he said modestly. 'You can't imagine the stampede for the trough at feeding-time. I have elbow-shaped bruises all over my body.'

They chatted and laughed and she felt completely at ease with him, as though they, too, had been old friends; and for a while the background feeling of loneliness of the past months went away. They were still sitting over their empty plates and cups when Uncle Teddy came up to the table with Polly on his arm, and Jessie recollected herself, blushed with guilt and said, 'Oh, goodness, I should have been out collecting.'

Gresham stood up and took the blame manfully. 'It's all my fault. I've kept her talking for my own pleasure.'

'My uncle, Mr Morland,' Jessie introduced. 'This is

Erskine Gresham, Uncle. I met him in Scarborough when Mother and I dined with his parents – I'm sure I told you.'

'You did,' Teddy said, extending a cordial hand. 'Glad to meet you, my boy. Wounded?'

Gresham told the tale briefly, and then, since Polly's eyes were enormous and sparkling with annoyance at being left out, Jessie hastened to introduce them. They shook hands and Polly said, 'Are you coming to the dance this evening, Lieutenant Gresham? I do hope so, because we're very short of men. He can come, can't he, Papa?'

'Of course he can, puss. You will, won't you, Gresham? Where are you staying? Not going back to Scarborough tonight?'

'I was intending to. I only came to York for the day, and saw the notice of your fair by chance.'

'Send a telegram, and come,' Teddy said. 'Unless you had an engagement this evening?'

'No, sir, only family dinner. But I don't have any things with me.'

'Oh, no matter, no matter at all. It's quite informal – and the ladies will like to see you in uniform. Stay and dine with us, and join our little dance. My daughter will never forgive me if I let you slip away.'

Now Polly blushed, and tugged his arm in annoyance, and tried to stand on her fourteen-year-old dignity. Gresham said, 'I'd be delighted to accept, sir, and thank you very much. And perhaps Miss Polly will favour me with a dance?'

She grew lofty. 'I shall try to find one for you, Mr Gresham, but it won't be the first or second. I'm already engaged for those.'

He bowed solemnly, and she went off on her father's arm, satisfied that she had put him in his place. Gresham turned to Jessie. 'Are you also engaged already?'

She laughed. 'No, I'm completely at your service. I'm not popular like Polly.'

'I hope you didn't mind my asking her first,' he said anxiously.

'Don't be silly,' Jessie said. 'I know exactly why you did

it. Shall we walk a bit? People are beginning to leave, and I really ought to shake my tin a bit more, or I shall have a bad conscience.'

It was, as Uncle Teddy said, only an informal dance, and she was a married woman; but she couldn't help feeling pleased and a little proud that she would have a handsome man to dance the very first with, when men were in short supply and every other girl would want to dance with him. She ought probably to refuse him and make him take on one of the unmarried girls, but she didn't intend to. She had not been looking forward to the evening, and now she was. She was sure Uncle Teddy would seat him next to her at dinner, as well, so she would have someone interesting to talk to during the meal.

They walked off among the thinning crowds, and he insisted on carrying the tin for her, and suggested a number of increasingly ludicrous ploys for extracting money from the public, which made her laugh so much that in the end she gave it up and they simply walked about, talking, until it was time to go in.

Jessie enjoyed Emma's visit. It was pleasant to have a female of near her own age to do things with – Polly was still too much a child, despite her newly lowered hems. Emma was a good companion, bubbling over with energy and good humour, interested in everything. She had plenty to talk about, and Jessie felt the pull of the wider horizon, and felt her own orbit dull and limited in comparison.

They went riding, accompanied by Polly when she hadn't another engagement, with various dogs following at heel. 'This is what I miss in London,' Emma said. 'Open air and the big sky, the sense of space. I miss riding. Violet doesn't ride at all, so of course I don't.'

'She never was very interested in horses,' Jessie remembered. 'But I'm sure she wouldn't mind if you went without her.'

'Yes, but one can't ride alone, and none of our friends rides either. And then, only think, a hired riding-school horse, and Rotten Row! Though of course,' she added thoughtfully, 'there are sometimes very pretty young men home on leave riding in the Park. I wonder if I could persuade Angela Draycott – she used to be Angela Burnet, you know – to ride with me? It seems a shame to waste the opportunity. But,' she reminded herself, 'I shan't be there to worry about it.'

'Shan't you?' Jessie asked.

'I'm going up to Aberlarich, had you forgotten?'

'There's all the rest of the summer. I should have thought a little exercise, even in Hyde Park, would be good for you.'

'I don't know where I shall be spending the summer. Violet is being very vague about it. I might have to come back here if it turns out she doesn't want me.'

'You know you're always welcome. But I hope you'll be there when I visit, in May.'

Erskine Gresham came over twice while Emma was there. With his damaged arm he was not equal to riding, but on the first day, as the weather was still fine, Jessie drove him, Emma and Polly out on a picnic on the bank of the river opposite Beningbrough Hall. It did not seem to trouble him at all to be the only man with three females to entertain, and he amused them so well that even Polly ceased to mourn the lack of a larger party. Jessie very much admired his aplomb in suiting his chat to the different ages and characters of each of them, without ever seeming in any way artificial. She supposed, observing him in a moment when Polly occupied his attention, that he simply liked people. She thought he would make a very good officer.

It was raining the second day he came, and they stayed indoors and played parlour games until luncheon. Teddy was home for the meal, and he and Gresham had a serious and manly talk about the war. More credit for Erskine, Jessie thought. After lunch, in a stroke of genius, he proposed a visit to the cinematograph in York. Polly and Emma were wild for the treat and, after some discussion, Teddy agreed that Jessie would provide sufficient chaperonage for his precious girls (not that he had any doubts about Gresham,

192

but it would not do to Have People Talk), so the four went in Jessie's car. It was a delightful experience for the girls, something quite new for all of them. There were newsreels, showing Tommies in France: marching past the camera grinning cheerfully, waving from the top of a converted double-decker bus with its lower windows blocked in, sitting in trenches drinking tea and smoking cigarettes. There was also an exciting piece where they 'went over the top' in clouds of smoke – none of them, fortunately, was hit. There was a recruitment piece, with a magnificently moustached sergeant marching up and down and eventually halting and saluting the audience, and then pointing directly at them, saying, 'Your country needs YOU!' There was also a Charles Chaplin comedy piece, called *His Prehistoric Past*, a romantic drama called *The Lonely Heart*, and a comic piece about a dog stealing sausages from a butcher's shop. The butcher grabbed the end of the links and was pulled along behind him. A policeman grabbed the butcher, a lady grabbed the policeman, and so on until ten people were running through the streets, dragged in a wildly swerving chain and leaving devastation in their wake. Everyone in the audience laughed until they cried; and driving home afterwards, the Morland party voted it the best of the show, though Polly was torn between that and *The Lonely Heart*, which had made her cry. It was a splendid outing.

Emma had not forgotten her desire to learn to drive, and Jessie yielded to her pleas, after consulting with Uncle Teddy and her mother as to whether she ought to get permission first from any of Emma's guardians. Henrietta said thoughtfully that she didn't think that driving, as long as it was only on the estate and not in any public place, would be frowned upon by the Abradales. 'I know there are a lot of people who think it unwomanly, but having the skill is a different matter from exercising it.'

Uncle Teddy was very busy at that time, appearing in the house only on his way to or from some urgent appointment. He was only too glad for Jessie to cede to Emma's request, since he himself could not continue her shooting lessons, owing to lack of time. 'Such a pity, when I'd as good as promised, but I have to go to Leeds tomorrow, and then to Black Brow when I get back, and there's the railway committee meeting this afternoon. I haven't a spare moment this fortnight.'

So Jessie sat beside Emma in the Austin as they bumped slowly round a field, stalling frequently, and occasionally driving into hedges. She praised Emma's perseverance, and said that she would soon get the hang of it. In a small, ignoble corner of her mind she could not help being just a little glad that there was something she could do better than her talented *protégée*, and that she had learnt to do it so much more easily.

'It's harder than it looks,' Emma said, frowning but undaunted as Jessie grabbed the steering-wheel for the fourth time, to keep them from veering into the gate. 'This thing is so wilful and stupid. A horse wouldn't keep bumping into things – oh, bother!'

Jessie had rather expected Polly to want to learn too, once she saw Emma having lessons; but Polly had overheard Seb Cornleigh deplore the sight of a woman driving a car, and so was loftily superior to the whole process.

'Well,' said Emma, at the end of her last lesson, as Jessie took over the wheel to drive the car back to the house, 'I *shall* get the hang of it in the end. It's just that when I concentrate on steering, the engine stalls, and when I think about not stalling, the silly thing drives itself into something. I must say, I do admire you, Jessie, for doing it so easily.'

Jessie said, 'Thank you. But there's really no need for you to be able to drive. You're such an heiress you will always be able to afford a chauffeur – and besides, living mostly in London, you can always take a taxi-cab. I don't know, really, why you want to learn.'

'Oh,' said Emma vaguely, 'it might come in useful. Cousin Venetia's chauffeur,' she added, as if she had just thought of it, 'volunteered, you know.'

'You can't think she'd hire you in his place,' Jessie laughed, and Emma blushed and shook her head and said she didn't mean that.

When Emma departed the weather turned cold, wet and windy, and everyone felt an anticlimax. The house seemed dull without her, the rain ran down the windowpanes from a leaden sky, the children were fractious, three of the maids developed colds, and the kitchen range would not draw properly so Mrs Stark's Yorkshire pudding would not rise, the first time such a terrible thing had happened.

Polly flopped about the house like a puppet with some vital strings cut, bewailing the weather, which had caused tennis parties and a rather ambitious picnic boat trip on the river ('It *is* only April,' said Henrietta) to be cancelled. She mourned that there would never be any fun, ever again, until even the notoriously good-tempered Ethel snapped at her that if she had nothing to do she could always turn out her bureau drawers and find the needlework scissors she had borrowed from Ethel and never returned. Uncle Teddy was away in Manchester, or he would have made some diversion for her. Alice offered to take her morning-visiting, but as Alice's friends were – to everyone but her – the dullest people on earth, the offer had no attraction for a fourteen-year-old just out of school. Henrietta suggested she help her mark linen, which was even worse. Nanny Emma, muttering darkly about 'idle hands', reminded her that there was plenty of sewing in the common basket. Finally Jessie took pity on her and said she would drive her over to the Cornleighs' house, where no doubt she would find Eileen in an equal state of meteorological misery.

Jessie had been feeling the let-down of Emma's departure too, though she hid it better, being ten years Polly's senior. But having delivered Polly, in both senses of the word, she started off home with a sigh and a feeling of restlessness. With her husband, and so many others, at the Front, she felt she ought to be doing something more positive to help. Committees, as Emma had said, were all very well, but she had seen often enough how they were little more than opportunities to drink tea and gossip. Any of the older ladies could run them, and do her reading to convalescent officers. She was young, vigorous, and had practical skills. She could not go and fight, but there ought to be *something* she could do that would make a real difference.

As she drove slowly along the Clifton Road, peering through the rain, she passed the big bulk of the hospital on her right, and suddenly put on the brake. The Austin sat there, pulsing rhythmically from the turning of the engine and steaming gently from bonnet and exhaust, while Jessie stared wide-eyed at nothing, her mind working. Then, with a new determination, she released the brake, backed up a little, and turned in at the gate.

She had to wait a while before the matron could see her, but was assured that it was only because she was very busy. She *would* come, if Mrs Morland would wait. Jessie sat on a hard chair in the corridor outside Matron's room, smelling the strange, institutional reek of soap, polish and disinfectant, and feeling as though she were back at school and waiting to see the headmistress because of some misdemeanour. By the time the brisk, clicking footsteps along the corridor heralded Matron's arrival, she felt both humble and guilty.

Miss Kemble stopped in front of her and examined her with an expression of interest and satisfaction. 'I *thought* I should see you again,' she said. 'Come in.'

The matron's room was crowded, a mixture of parlour and office, with a desk and cupboards and such-like on one side, and a fireplace on the other, in which a brisk little coal fire was burning, cheering on this grey, damp day. Before it were two comfortable, shabby chairs, and on the floor a worn Turkey carpet in rich, warming shades of port and sherry. On the mantelpiece stood a host of photographs in frames, many of other girls and women in nursing uniform, but others of 'civilians', presumably relatives, or perhaps grateful patients.

Matron Kemble took one armchair, gestured Jessie to the

196

other, and said, 'Well, now! I'm very pleased to see you. My little talk at your uncle's fair had an effect on you after all? I thought it would. I *saw* you wanted to do more than walk about with a collection box.'

'I do. I have for some time,' Jessie said. 'But it's hard to find exactly *what*. That's why I've been visiting convalescent officers.'

'Quite. But there are people and to spare to do that. Every genteel lady in the country can fancy herself in such a romantic setting. What we don't have is enough ladies willing to do real *work*.' She smiled, albeit rather grimly, and went on, 'In the train on my way to York, I heard one young lady say to another that she would quite fancy doing Red Cross work, but not if it meant getting her hands dirty or having to clean things. And the other agreed. "Oh, no, dear," she said, "I don't think one would like that at all."'

Jessie laughed too, though a little uncomfortably, for she knew plenty of ladies like that. But in justice she said, 'The matron at Heworth would not let us do anything for the officers other than read to them and write their letters and arrange flowers.'

'Well, *I* will let you,' said Miss Kemble. 'Join a VAD and come and nurse at my hospital. You will make a good nurse. You have the qualities. I see them in you.'

Jessie said awkwardly, 'The difficulty is that I have a lot of other duties – serious duties,' she added hastily, as a frown developed on the matron's face, 'that I cannot set aside. I can't join a VAD because I can't commit all my time to it. That's why I came to see you. I hoped that you might be able to put me in the way of useful work that I could do, other than on a full-time basis.'

'How many days a week would you be willing to do?' the matron asked suspiciously.

'I could manage two or three,' Jessie said.

Miss Kemble's face cleared. 'Make it three, and I can help you.' Jessie nodded. 'You can come to me as an auxiliary nurse – and if, later on, you find you can give yourself to nursing for the whole time, either here or elsewhere, you will find your experience stands you in good stead. I have battle casualties here, desperately wounded men who need real nursing – and as the war goes on, there will be more and more of them, and a need for more and more nurses. We women cannot go and fight, but in making sure our men have the best of care, we can do our part in supporting them and helping to shorten the war.'

'That's just what I want!' Jessie exclaimed.

Miss Kemble beamed. 'Then I shall help you on the way. Three days a week – and I don't despair of reeling you in, my dear, and making a proper nurse of you at last. Tell me, what are these duties of yours that you cannot get out of?'

'I have a stable to run. I breed and break horses – mostly now for the army, but I've also been training ponies to farm work, since the army has taken all the heavy horses.'

Miss Kemble blinked at this reply, which she could hardly have expected, and Jessie thought she regarded her with perhaps a little more respect. 'Well,' she said, 'if you can handle horses, you can handle sick men. I *knew* there was something about you. I'm never wrong about people.'

CHAPTER NINE

As the taxi-cab turned into Ebury Street, Violet found herself leaning forward and gripping the strap so tightly her fingers hurt. She forced herself to relax. This was a part of London she had never visited. It was a respectable enough street, of quite nice-looking terraced houses, each having a wrought-iron balcony along the front of the first-floor drawing-room – Londony, but nice, she thought. Some were evidently family houses for the well-to-do middle classes, others were bachelor lodgings for the better-off. But a titled female had little to do with the middling sort of people who lived in areas like this. The poor and the working classes came more in her way.

The cab slowed as the driver looked at the house numbers, and the Pekingeses caught her excitement and began to bark. 'Oh, hush!' she told them. The cab stopped and she leant forward and said, 'Is this it?'

'That's the one, mum – that'n there.' The driver displayed no curiosity, but she felt he was wondering all the same. Yet better the anonymity of the taxi-cab than her own motor and the inevitable discussion among her servants.

'Thank you,' Violet said, sitting back. The driver took his cue, nipped out of his seat and came round to open the door for her.

'Oh, thank you very much, mum,' he said, as she waved away the change, unable to bear the thought of fiddling with coins. She reached in for the dogs, and walked across the pavement and up the shallow steps to the door, hearing the taxi move off behind her.

And there before the door she paused to try to calm herself. In her docile, obedient life she had never done anything secret before, and the sense of peril and faint, indeterminate guilt made it difficult to breathe.

When she was a girl, she had used to have a dream – one that recurred at regular, though widely spaced, intervals. In her dream she could fly, but had not the power to get off the ground: she needed height. So she climbed up to the top of the house and out onto the roof. And there, in her dream, she paused, looking down at the street, tiny and far below, knowing that if it turned out she could not fly after all, jumping off the roof would kill her. A pause of mingled excitement and terror – and then she jumped! For a terrifying, agonising second she fell like a stone; but then frantic swimming motions of her arms and legs began to work and she flew, laboriously at first, and then, gaining height, soaring gloriously. She had loved those dreams and woken from them feeling a tingling delight at the memory of the sensation.

Standing here before this smartly black-painted door was like the moment on the roof in her old dream, poised on the brink of something that was both exciting and dangerous. She could still turn round and go back, but once she knocked on that door, she would have jumped. She felt that her life was about to change in some fundamental way. It was foolish to feel like that. She was doing nothing so very out of the ordinary, after all; certainly nothing *wrong*. Still, she felt that something different lay ahead of her, and she did not know whether it was a future of the delight of flying; or whether this time she was going to crash to the stones.

She lifted the heavy iron door-knocker and let it fall, and the thud was like the knocking of Fate.

It had begun at a party given by the Verneys. Lord Verney, who had not long come into the title and the fortune, had married Laura Mellis, one of three famously beautiful sisters of an old Somerset family. All the Mellis family had the reputation of being brilliant. They were high-spirited, unconventional, notable riders to hounds, witty conversationalists, and – that most double-edged of compliments – *artistic*. The Mellises were not wealthy any more, but all three girls had made good marriages. Verney was a lively young man of no particular talent or calling, but being extremely good-natured, as well as very much in love with the lovely Laura, he was perfectly willing to indulge her artistic tastes. Their house in Grosvenor Square had become a haven for painters, poets, sculptors, musicians – and even the better-known and more respectable novelists and actors. Invitations to their parties were greatly prized among the younger titled set, though some of the older and more staid thought them perhaps a little *too* exotic: art, these critics said, was all very well in its place – which was in the gallery, concert hall and theatre – but one didn't necessarily want it in one's drawing-room. And, they added, it was most unfortunate but true, that those involved in the *production* of art so often seemed, well, a little *raffish*, wouldn't you say, dear?

The Verneys and Holkams knew of each other, but they were not in the same set. If Holkam had troubled to think about it he probably would have discovered in himself just such a faint prejudice against excessive interest in the arts. His interests were political, his friends were clubmen and fellow members of the House. Violet had her own set, of smart young married people, who, though they went to plays and concerts in the course of the Season, did not pretend to great sensibility, nor interest themselves in the creators of what they saw. They did not claim to be *clever*.

Yet it was to just such an exotic Verney *soirée* that Violet had gone with Emma in the week after Holkam left for France. They had been escorted by Freddie Copthall and the Tommy Draycotts. Verney and Freddie Copthall had been at Eton together, which was the connection. Laura Verney had come upon Freddie and Violet in Bond Street one day, and when Freddie had introduced the ladies to each other, Lady Verney had instantly invited them both to her evening party. Violet, faintly alarmed by what she had heard of the Verney set, and in dread of the sort of conversations she feared she might encounter there, excused herself. She was glad to be able to say that she was already engaged – in fact, to dine *en famille* with the Draycotts. Yet as soon as she expressed her regret, she began, unaccountably, to feel it. A Verney invitation *was* prized, after all, and she had a certain curiosity about the set-up. It was rather dull to have to say one had never been there, especially if it was true.

The energetic Lady Verney, however, had not accepted the excuse. She had said at once that she knew Angela Draycott very well and had been intending to ask them too. In the event, the Draycotts had no desire to miss a Verney occasion, and sent Violet a note asking if she would be willing, instead of taking family dinner with them, to go with them to the Verneys'. Emma, also invited, thought there was no comparison for interest and excitement, and begged Violet to accept. And so to Grosvenor Square they had all gone.

The guest of honour at the *soirée* was the portraitist, Octavian Laidislaw. Violet had never heard of him, though it seemed most of the people at the party had. He was new, exciting, talented, and definitely on the rise. He was being talked about and written about in the serious papers, and it was beginning to be quite something, to say that one had been painted by Laidislaw. Laura Verney had: it was the unveiling of her portrait that formed the centrepiece of the evening. It was a beautiful piece of work, Violet thought, though unlike what she was accustomed to seeing by way of portraits in country houses. Laidislaw's work was soft and flowing. Laura Verney in paint looked even more beautiful than in life. What was rather shocking was that she was reclining in her chair, rather than sitting up straight in it. Her whole pose was informal and relaxed: her elbow resting on the arm of the chair, her cheek resting on her fingertips; the faint smile on her lips; her eyes gazing out – at the painter, one had to suppose – with a look of . . . well, what was it? A look of – of – *intimacy*. Not the look a married woman gives anyone but her husband, Violet thought, fascinated, or an unmarried woman gives anyone at all. The image was so alive one could almost expect the painted Lady Verney to rise from her painted armchair and step out through the picture-frame – an alarming, if thrilling, thought.

She came back to the painting again and again, unable to take her eyes from it, feeling a shiver inside her at that expression in the subject's eyes, which made the portrait so arresting and yet seemed almost *too* real. It was disturbing, though she could not precisely say why.

'You like it?' said a voice at her ear. She jumped, and turned her head to see Laidislaw himself standing beside her, a glass of champagne in his hand. He looked directly into her eyes and she found she could not draw hers away. He was smiling, and the immediacy of his gaze made her feel oddly as though she had known him for years – though he had not, in fact, yet been introduced to her. It felt almost as if they were alone together, as two friends might be who were at ease with each other.

She said weakly, 'I don't know anything about art.'

His reaction was not what she might have expected. 'Thank God for that!' he said, his smile widening. He had 'Corsair' looks – sallow skin, very dark eyes, very white teeth, and black curly hair, worn rather long. He was striking to look at, especially in the black and white of evening dress – which seemed only just to contain his dangerousness, like a collar and lead on a tiger.

'I love the opinions of fresh minds,' he went on. 'I've heard enough of the stale phrases of the "experts", the ridiculous nonsense they parrot by way of expertise. A painting is not meant to be dissected and analysed, like some poor dead mouse in a laboratory! A painting is meant to be looked at, that's all. The idea that you have to "know" anything about "art" before looking is the lie of the charlatan who is wanting to take your money somehow by teaching you what you already know. Do you have to take lessons to know how to breathe, how to eat? Of course not. So eat with your eyes! Do you like it?'

'Yes,' she said. She had a strange feeling of vertigo, as though she were falling into his eyes, though without actually moving.

'But?' he asked. 'Go on.' He waited for her reply, but he smiled as though he knew exactly what she was about to say next.

It was more than she did. This was exactly one of those conversations she had been afraid of. But she had to say something. Her mouth opened and the words 'It disturbs me,' came out. She startled herself, but she seemed to have pleased the artist.

'Excellent!' he said. 'That's not a "but", by the way – it's an "and". Laura's beauty *is* disturbing. True beauty always is. Don't you think she looks almost *combustible?*'

Violet shook her head. 'She glows as if there's a light inside her, but it's not a hot light.' Then she blushed, feeling she had been drawn into talking nonsense. She knew nothing about such things – he had teased her out, and now would laugh at her.

But he cocked his head a little, looking at her differently, his smile no longer sardonic but almost tender. 'When are you going to sit for me?' he asked abruptly, as if it was something that had already been decided, and only the actual date was left to be arranged.

'I – I hadn't thought—' she began awkwardly.

'Then think now. I must have you,' he said. His look, and the words, scalded her, though he only meant as a subject; of course he only meant that. *Must have you to paint.* That was all.

At that moment, to Violet's relief and sharp disappointment, they were interrupted. Laura Verney placed a long white hand on Laidislaw's arm and said, 'I must take you away, Octavian, and introduce you to Étienne Vouguoy. He could be useful to your career. Violet, my dear, you will forgive me?'

Laidislaw turned his dark eyes on the subject of his latest

204

work and said, 'You have not yet presented me to your friend Violet.'

'Have I not? Dear me, how remiss. I am very sorry. Violet, may I present Octavian Laidislaw? Laidislaw, the Countess of Holkam.'

He bowed over her hand, his lips not quite touching it. 'I am delighted to make your acquaintance – and devastated that I am to be taken away from you so soon.'

'Nonsensical man,' Lady Verney said. 'Come with me at once.' She called to her husband. 'Verney, come and speak to Violet. Laidislaw has been unsettling her.'

She led the artist away, as Verney joined Violet in front of the portrait and said, 'It's a lovely piece of work, isn't it?'

Violet contemplated it again. 'Do *you* like it?' she asked.

He laughed. 'It *is* rather brave of me, as her husband, to admit it, but I do. It will cause a sensation at the exhibition – something like the scandal of Sargent's *Madame X*, perhaps; which will be all to the good as far as Laddie's career is concerned. You think me too indulgent, perhaps? But a husband can hardly be offended by his wife's being found to be beautiful, especially by the greatest new talent to emerge in fifty years. A true eye that reveals truth. And I thought in my uxorious arrogance that only I saw my wife's special quality!'

Violet had no idea what he was talking about, but she could see by his satisfied, almost complacent expression as he gazed at the portrait, that he did like it. 'She is very beautiful,' she said at last.

Verney looked down at her. 'Laddie talks a great deal. You mustn't mind him. He doesn't mean to be impertinent,' he said kindly.

'Oh – no!' she protested, and left it at that.

That night in bed, unable to sleep, she thought about it. She remembered Verney's expression as he gazed at the painting of his wife, and imagined Holkam gazing thus at a painting of her. 'The greatest new talent to emerge in fifty years', Verney had said. Holkam had spoken in the past of wanting a portrait of Violet, but they had never got further than that. Wouldn't he want the best, if he could have it? She had heard, at that party, of how many women – and their husbands – had asked Laidislaw to paint them, and been refused. He painted only those he chose himself. So a Laidislaw portrait was a desirable object in itself. After the party Emma had said excitedly that everyone wanted to sit for him, but it was impossible to 'get in'. It would make a wonderful present for Holkam, then, a wonderful surprise present. It could be there when he came home on leave, a gift for his birthday in June. And Laidislaw had asked her – *he* had asked *her*. She remembered the exact tone of his voice and the exact look in his eyes when he had said, 'When are you going to sit for me?'

Perhaps he hadn't meant it. Perhaps he had been teasing. Perhaps he had been drunk – there was certainly an oddness about the whole encounter that might be accounted for by an excess of champagne. But the idea had taken hold of her, and she could not rest until she had made the enquiry. The next day, shopping in Bond Street with her maid, she passed the gallery she had heard spoken of at the party. Before she could lose courage she left Sanders outside and made herself go in and ask, with as much studied indifference as she could manage, for Laidislaw's address. At home again afterwards, she wrote him a note.

You said you wished to paint me. I should like a portrait as a gift for my husband, who is at the Front. I wish it to be a surprise, therefore you will oblige me by telling no-one, as it would certainly get back to him if it were generally known. If you still want to paint me, let me know when you wish to come here.

His reply came back by the next post.

I do not come to you, you come to me. That is how I work. Come on Tuesday at half past ten in the morning.

206

Dress plainly. Come alone, and tell no-one, and secrecy will be assured. *I* shall not speak of it.

So here she was, trembling on his front doorstep. The door was opened by a short, stout woman with a hard face, a hard body and hard hands that looked as though they had got that way slapping kitchenmaids. The dogs, held in Violet's arms, stared at her with goggling eyes, snuffling. Souchong growled and she shook him a little to silence him.

'Mr Laidislaw,' Violet said, as firmly as her dry mouth would allow her.

The woman looked Violet over in a way she was not used to, raking her with her yellowish brown eyes, her mouth closed tight as a rat-trap. Violet thought she had dressed plainly that morning, but the woman summed up the hat with the veil, the fur, the pearls and the two little silky dogs with practised ease, and knew exactly what she was dealing with.

'Is he expecting you?' she demanded, not because she had any doubt, but to exercise her power. She saw Violet's eyes flinch before her own, and her mouth hardened still more in triumph.

'Oh! Yes. Indeed. Yes, he is,' Violet managed.

'You can go up, then,' said the woman. 'Fust floor.' Violet hesitated, unused to having to show herself in. The woman gestured her past, her eyes mocking. 'I gotter bad back. I can't be going up and down stairs all day announcin' visitors. Fust floor, door to your right. You can't miss it.'

Violet mounted the stairs, feeling the hard eyes on her back as though they were passing right through her clothes and burning her skin. At the top there was a landing and a door, as promised, to the right, bearing a metal holder. It was just like the sort you had on your bedroom door at a country-house party, which was somehow comforting. In it was a white card, neatly lettered in black ink, saying *O. Laidislaw.*

She raised her hand to knock on the door, and paused. She could still – just – turn round and go away, with no-one any the wiser; but once she knocked, she was committed to her course of action. Her hand was trembling in its lavender suede glove. Come plainly dressed, he had said, and the very fact that he had mentioned her clothes excited her strangely. Her gloves were new, from Paris, bought just before the war, but never worn until today. They were the most expensive she had ever owned – but one had to wear gloves, after all: it didn't mean anything.

And then, before she could knock, the door opened and he was there, smiling down at her with that intimate look of his, which had intrigued and excited and frightened her in equal measure when she had first met him.

'I saw you getting out of the cab,' he said.

'I'm sorry,' she said, with a vague gesture behind her, meant to excuse her coming unannounced to his door.

'No, *I'm* sorry,' he said, 'about Mrs Hudson. She's a beast, but most landladies are, aren't they? She disapproves of me, but when fame and wealth have transported me away from her sphere, she will remember me with a sentimental sigh and claim to have been like a mother to me. Do come in. This is my space and, such as it is, at your disposal.'

And still trembling, Violet entered.

Through the innocent white door into the tiger's lair: it seemed an ordinary drawing-room – wallpaper, carpet, tall, curtained windows, marble fireplace at one end, polished oval table and chairs at the other. Two Louis XV armchairs and a settle were grouped at the fireplace. One or two small fine tables of the same period here and there in the room bore delicate porcelains; there was a bronze group of Laocoon on the mantelpiece instead of a clock. The absence of the one and the presence of the other seemed somehow significant, but in her present state of disequilibrium she could not determine why.

All this she took in in an instant but it was driven out of her head by what was *not* ordinary: the centre of the room was empty except for a red velvet and gilt *chaise-longue* with its back to the window, and facing it an easel with a canvas set up on it, and a low, much scuffed and stained table bearing painting equipment – palette, jars of brushes, tubes of paint, rags, scraper, charcoal. Her heart began to beat faster again at the sight of these tools of his trade, with which he was going to do something extraordinary to her.

He was watching her with that disturbing smile. 'Put down those absurd dogs and take off your gloves and hat. I like the veil – a pleasant touch. Women should always go veiled like that in public places. It gives a tantalising hint of glories imperfectly concealed.'

She put the dogs down, and they sniffed at Laidislaw's trousers and shoes, and then trotted off to inspect the room. She stripped off her gloves and then, feeling it was another Rubicon, threw back her veil and unpinned her hat. One did not take off one's hat when morning-visiting; or, indeed, ever in a public place – which made this, well, something else. He took the hat and gloves from her and laid them carelessly on a small table by the door. 'And the fur,' he said, but when she unclasped it and gave it to him, he handled it quite differently, looking at it keenly and running it through his hands. 'Yes,' he said, 'I think we may be able to use this.' And he took it across the room and laid it over the back of the *chaise-longue*, his fingers lingering over it as he arranged it.

Now she stood before him dressed as if she were at home, feeling almost naked. She clasped her hands lightly in front of her, awaiting orders, the 'equipment' always beckoning at the corner of her eye. It was like a visit from the doctor, she thought, except that the doctor was always careful to look at you as if he didn't see you, while Laidislaw looked as though seeing you were the whole purpose of life.

'Come, sit down,' he said. He guided her to the *chaise-longue* where she perched on the edge and in the centre, upright and rigid, as little of her touching the red velvet as possible. He looked down at her carefully for a moment and then turned away, going to the fireside corner where there were decanters on a tray. 'Let me give you a glass of sherry,' he said, returning with it. 'I don't bite, you know. What are you afraid of?'

She took the glass and managed to sip a little without spilling. The warmth of it in her throat and stomach gave her a little courage. 'I don't know,' she said.

'You do,' he contradicted, shockingly. She met his eyes fleetingly, and looked away. 'You are afraid that I will expose what is hidden inside you – and yet that is exactly what you hope that I *will* do. That is why you came here. You want me to find you out. Isn't that the truth?' She didn't answer. 'Violet, look at me. Isn't that the truth?'

She looked up, startled by the use of her name. 'I don't know,' she said. 'You mustn't – mustn't call me that.'

'Violet?' He smiled, kindly now. 'You think it is improper? But what will happen here between us is something outside the world, apart from society, not subject to its rules. It is not improper, impertinent, or indecent. Nothing bad can happen here, and you must and shall believe that. I am going to paint you, and to paint you I must know you completely, to the very bones. I must understand you, assimilate you. There can be no barriers between us. You and I will become as one flesh and one mind, and that composite thing will exist for ever, here, on my canvas.'

He had begun to move as he spoke, and her eyes had followed him, walking back and forth in front of her, to his easel, back again. She *wanted* to look at him, only it made her feel breathless. She had never looked at anyone in that way before. Looking at people had always had something of geography about it. You had to know where they were standing so that you did not bump into them. You looked at them when they were speaking because it was polite. You looked when you were introduced so that you would be able to identify them again. But those were not the reasons she looked at Laidislaw. She was not yet sure what the reasons actually were, but it felt very different, and not at all comfortable.

Back before her, he dropped suddenly to his knees in front of her, and she moved her hands in a weak, warding-off movement, as though she might have said, 'Don't!' But in fact she didn't speak. She looked into his eyes, now very

210

close, much too close to hers. Their black, sparkling depths seemed to pull her in, and she felt that sensation of vertigo again.

'Violet,' he said, and she felt his breath on her face, warm and sweet. 'The name so perfectly suits you. Small, shy, half hidden, hardly seen – yet with a powerful and indestructible beauty that can grip a man's heart. "Flower in the crannied wall" – and when I hold you in my hand, I shall know God in man. I shall paint you, Violet, and those who have eyes shall see you. They will be few enough – but I would prefer it that way. It will be my best work – I can feel it already! The world will acclaim it, but only a blessed handful will ever see what I shall have put down – what *we* will have made together here.'

'We?' she enquired breathlessly, intoxicated by his nearness and his words.

'Yes. Both of us have work to do. It will be hard for you – the hardest task of your life, perhaps. Are you ready for it? Great deeds demand great sacrifice. Art is a hard master – but the rewards are great. I can give you the whole world.'

Why did those last words ring with her, as if she had heard them before? Being offered the whole world . . . She could not trace the reference in her mind.

'Are you ready?' he asked again. 'Do you want it as much as I want it?'

And she heard herself say, 'Yes.'

'Then we shall begin.' He reached out and took hold of her chin, turning it so that she was in profile to him. 'How you tremble,' he said softly. His other hand came up and he stroked the backs of his fingers down her cheek with a touch so light she hardly felt it – and yet it seared her.

'You mustn't,' she whispered, but he did not seem to hear her.

'Such skin,' he said wonderingly. 'Alabaster is coarse beside it – and cold. No words can describe it. Nacreous – luminous. Words cannot come near. But *I* shall paint it. Yes – you *shall* be translated!'

'You mustn't,' she whispered faintly, 'touch me.'

211

And, shockingly, he laughed. 'Touch you?' He sprang to his feet, releasing her so that she swayed and felt she might fall. 'My dear Violet, you have not yet understood what is going to happen here! I shall touch you in every way you can be touched, in ways you have not conceived of!' He walked away with a lithe movement to pick up a sketching-pad. 'But I have told you already, what happens here is out of the world, out of time, out of reach. You have entered a place of great danger, yet paradoxically you are quite safe. The door is locked, no-one can come in, nothing can get out. What happens here is a secret for ever. You have only to be what Nature intended you to be. You will understand in time. Now I must begin.'

He took up charcoal and began to draw. His eyes moved from his work to her and back with a gaze that was at once impersonal and intimate, so that she felt he was still touching the skin of her face, touching with his eyes as he had touched with his fingers. The sensation kept her body in a state of fluttering tension that was strangely pleasurable. She wanted it to go on for ever.

The dogs found a patch of sunshine on the carpet and curled up together, noses on paws, looking up sometimes without moving their heads, so that their curved cinnamon eyebrows rose as if in comment on what was happening.

The family were doubtful about the wisdom of Jessie's trying to do real nursing at Clifton Hospital.

'It's wounded Tommies they have there,' Ethel said. 'Not officers.'

'Tommies need nursing just as much as officers,' Jessie said.

'Yes, but not by you,' said Ethel. 'They're not of our class. You don't want to be mingling with the lower classes – labourers . . . common, rough people.'

Jessie was beginning to feel a little annoyed. 'I mingle with farm-workers and stablemen every day.'

'Yes, but those are people you've known all your life. And you don't have to see them in bed, and *do* things for them,'

212

Ethel pointed out. 'Touch them. You might have to *wash* them – think of that! And they're *men*. It's not like taking care of one of our own sick maids.'

'I think these poor fellows, who have risked everything for our sake at the Front, deserve the best of care.'

'Of course they do,' Henrietta said. 'And nursing is a noble calling. But I'm not sure you've thought about it quite carefully enough, darling. Nursing isn't just a matter of wiping someone's brow or holding his hand, you know. There are sights and smells and – and – *fluids* involved. There are activities you might be asked to perform that I don't think you would like.'

Alice spoke up. 'I couldn't do anything like that for my life, Jessie, but I accept that you may see things differently from me,' she said kindly. 'All the same, you can't do just anything you like in this world, without regard for what people think. And people don't think highly of nursing. Nurses are not drawn from our walk of life, and if you're looked down on for doing it, it will reflect on your family.'

Jessie knew what she was thinking: Teddy had only just regained his place in society, and Alice did not want anything to upset the new equilibrium. And she knew that most respectable families would be horrified if a daughter wanted to be a nurse. But she was not an innocent girl, she was a married woman; and she already did things far out of the ordinary, like running a stable. Besides, weren't they all involved together in a deadly struggle against the Hun? 'Things are different in wartime,' she said, with confidence now. 'People won't look down on me. They might wonder, like you, how I could want to, but it isn't something disgraceful.'

'No, of course not,' Henrietta said, rallying to her. 'Service to others can never be that. I was only afraid you hadn't realised what might be involved. If you're sure you want to do it, you have my blessing. But you'd better ask your uncle when he gets home.'

Teddy came home tired out from Manchester, but when Jessie asked him for a private talk he invited her straight

213

away to the steward's room and listened to her with courtesy. He shook his head. 'Nursing is not for girls of your class.'

'But I'm not a girl any more, and women of all classes are going into VAD work. *Titled* girls, even.'

'They do the sort of thing you're already doing – hospital visiting, and reading to convalescents. That's quite suitable. Why can't you satisfy yourself with it?'

'Could you be satisfied with less than you know you could do?' she asked.

He shifted uncomfortably. 'A woman has to be more careful. I don't know why you *want* to nurse, anyway. It's a nasty business. You should be glad you don't have to – that there are others willing to do it. What is so interesting in nursing?'

'Cousin Venetia might tell you,' Jessie said, thinking this the clinching argument.

But he said, 'Venetia's a doctor, and that's a profession. It confers a status. A nurse is little better than a domestic servant. And in any case, Venetia's an exceptional person. Just do your committees and hospital visiting. That and the horses are enough war work for you, Jess. That's all anyone expects of you.'

'Cousin Oliver's doctor-friend in London said, before the war even began, that people like me should train for nursing; and the matron of Clifton Hospital said that we will need more nurses than you can imagine before it's over. And with Ned at the Front, risking his life to keep us all safe here at home, I think we ought to do everything we can for the war effort, not just the easy, agreeable things, but the hard things too. *You*'ve never spared yourself, Uncle; and I have the same blood in my veins.'

Teddy opened his mouth to speak, and closed it again. He recognised the stubborn tilt of a chin when he saw it, and remembered that arguing with Jessie rarely had any effect. She always had to find out for herself – like the time she had ridden her father's stallion and almost killed herself. Explaining the possible consequences to her beforehand

214

would not have prevented her from trying. Well, now she had another bee in her bonnet. He suspected that she had no idea what nursing entailed, and that once she found out she would soon get tired of it. She had never tried to ride the stallion again – experience was the great teacher.

So he smiled and said, 'Well, you're of age, so you may do as you please. I applaud your spirit, and wish you well with it.'

Jessie, braced for argument, felt as though she had pushed at a locked door and had it swing open. She supposed the mention of Ned had done the trick. 'Oh. Well, thank you,' she said, and went away.

Teddy rubbed his eyes wearily, and settled down to read the day's mail, but with a small smile on his lips. She'd learn! And at least he didn't have to worry about Polly. Polly was far too dainty a girl, and hated to get her hands dirty. She looked up to Jessie, but she wouldn't copy her in this, at least.

Jessie had told Matron Kemble that she would be going to London for a month in May, and proposed waiting until she came back to begin; but Miss Kemble said that she would sooner have her begin straight away, even if only for a few weeks, and continue afterwards. Perhaps she thought Jessie might change her mind if she had time to think about it. Well, she would find out, Jessie thought. With everyone convinced she would fail, she was more determined than ever to succeed.

On her first day she was directed to Maitland Ward, one of the old wards in the main hospital block, which had been given over to wounded soldiers. The uniform, which she had bought the day before – or acquired, really, since Uncle Teddy said she needn't pay for it – in the section of Makepeace's dedicated to servants' uniforms and the like, felt stiff and strange, and the high, hard collar made her hold her head up in an unnatural manner. But she was proud of it, feeling that it made her belong in a way she never had when reading to convalescent officers.

215

She stepped in through the swing doors, and at the sight of those twenty-four beds, each with an unknown man lying in it, the realisation struck her of what she had undertaken and exactly why her family had thought she ought not to. Many eyes turned to look at her with interest, and entirely without deference. She felt exposed to them, at their mercy. They were strangers to her, and to them she was not Mrs Morland of Morland Place, but an unknown female to whom they might be impertinent without fear of reprisal. Furthermore, seeing the stripes of pyjama cotton above the folded-down sheet of the nearest bed, she became suddenly, violently aware of their bodies – male bodies, which at any moment she might have to look at or touch. Accidentally she met the eyes of the nearest owner of pyjamas. He grinned at her, and she felt a blush run violently up her face from under her tight collar, and hastily averted her gaze.

A small, white, definitely female figure came click-clicking rapidly up the centre of the ward towards her. Jessie fixed her eyes gratefully on it, and smiled in relief. It was a woman in her forties, small and wiry, with sandy, frizzy hair under her starched cap, pale green, protuberant eyes, and parched-looking skin. She did not return Jessie's smile – indeed, seemed incensed by it.

'What do you want, Nurse? Don't stand there grinning like an ape. Even if *you* haven't work to do, we have more than enough on this ward! I suppose you've brought a message. Deliver it, then, and get back to your own ward at once.'

Jessie, while thrilled to have been mistaken for a real nurse, was disconcerted to be spoken to so harshly. She had thought to be welcomed with open arms. 'I was told to report to Sister Morgan,' she said.

'*I* am Sister Morgan. And who are you?' She spoke rapidly, with a faint Welsh accent, which seemed to make all her words sharper along the edges than a Yorkshire person could have made them.

'I'm Jessie Morland,' said Jessie. 'Matron sent me to help.'

'Help?' The pale eyes doubted it as they looked Jessie up and down. 'VAD, are you?'

216

'No. I'm to be an auxiliary nurse.'

'*Sister*. You address me as Sister. And what use do you think you'll be? Have you got any experience?'

'No, but I can learn,' Jessie said, and added hastily, in response to the raised eyebrows, 'Sister. I have my First Aid and Home Nursing certificates.'

Sister Morgan rolled her eyes. 'God help us! And Matron sent you, did she? Two weeks in the place and she wants to turn us all upside-down. I haven't got time to run about after *ladies*!' She invested the word with infinite scorn. 'We've got badly wounded men here, in case you hadn't noticed. They don't need reading to, or their hands held, they need *nursing*.'

'You won't have to run after me, Sister,' Jessie said stiffly. 'I didn't expect to hold the men's hands. I'm here to help. I want to be useful. I'll do whatever you want me to.'

'On my ward,' Sister said sharply, 'you'll do as you're told, like everybody else.'

'Yes, Sister,' Jessie said, and managed to stop herself adding, 'of course.'

Sister Morgan stared at her a moment, her mind evidently working. 'So, you want to be useful do you?'

'Yes, Sister.'

'And you'll do whatever jobs I give you?'

'Yes, Sister.'

'Because I won't have argument. Anyone who works on my ward does exactly what I say, and no answering back.'

'I understand, Sister. It's what I expected.'

Sister Morgan grinned then. There was no mirth in it. 'Oh, it was, was it? Well, then—'

She turned towards a nurse who was scurrying past carrying a small tower of large metal objects. 'Nurse Dicks! Give those to Nurse Morland. She's the auxiliary nurse. Show her where the sluice is, tell her what to do. She can empty and scour them. Hurry up, Nurse, you haven't got all day.'

'Yes, Sister,' the nurse gasped, hesitated a moment, and passed the tower to Jessie. 'This way.' She scurried off, and

Jessie followed as fast as she could while balancing the tower. A terrible smell was assailing her nostrils, and she knew, now, what these objects were. She had never seen them in Heworth Park (the officers would conquer nature rather than send for a bedpan when there was a lady present), but she had known of their existence.

The little nurse turned to her in a doorway. 'This is the sluice. You empty them there, and then scrub them at the sink there. There's the brushes and the disinfectant. Then stack them over there. And leave everything tidy. Sister checks everything, and she goes mad if anything's out o' place.' She was small, dark, rather thin, had a very young-looking face, and a York accent. She was obviously poised to dash off again, but Jessie stopped her.

'Wait! What's your name?'

'Dicks. I'm the junior nurse.'

'What's your first name?'

She made a grimace. 'We don't use first names here. Lord, you're green! VAD, are you?'

'No.'

'Lucky for you. Sister hates VADs like poison. Well, if you're auxiliary that makes you junior to me, so I reckon t' bedpans'll be all yours from now on. Suits me!' She swung round. 'I've got to get on.'

Jessie managed to get in one more question. 'Does everyone always move as fast as this?'

Dicks rolled her eyes. 'Fast? This is a quiet time. You wait!' And she was gone.

Jessie faced her unpleasant task alone. There was no use beefing about it – everyone had warned her, and it was obvious that as the least experienced person on the ward she would be bound to be given the most menial tasks. She had wanted to be useful, and if this was the only way she could be useful at the moment, so be it. It was probably a test. When the sceptical sister saw she did the horrid jobs without complaining, she would be given more interesting things to do. She held her breath and began. Cleaning up excreta was not what she'd had in mind when

218

she had argued to be allowed to nurse, and a couple of times her throat rippled at the smell and sight of it; but she told herself firmly that it was no different from mucking out a loose box, and she had done that before, many times. Human droppings smelled much worse than horses', of course, and there was the embarrassing social aspect to it. But if she could do this for horses, how could she refuse to do it for wounded heroes? She should be proud to serve them. She tried to feel proud, and breathed through her mouth.

She had just about finished when another nurse stuck her head round the door – a taller, fair girl in her mid-twenties. She surveyed Jessie with cold eyes. 'Are you Morland? Lord, haven't you finished yet?'

'Yes, I've finished now. May I know your name?'

'"May I know your name?"' she mimicked. 'Posh, aren't we? It's Cameron – much good may it do you! You're to go and make the men's drinks and take them round.'

'Where—?' Jessie began.

'Kitchen, o' course. Dicks'll help you. Well, hurry up, then! You haven't got all day.'

She hurried. In the kitchen Dicks was fretting over a stove on which she was heating a giant kettle and a saucepan of milk simultaneously. There was a list of the bed numbers and the men's beverage preferences, but no names. She wondered if they called them by their number. There was tea, cocoa, hot milk, cold milk and Bovril. She tried to help but she simply didn't move quickly enough for Dicks and was always in her way. 'We'll never get done in time,' Dicks wailed, almost in tears.

'Why such a hurry?' Jessie asked helplessly.

'Because if we're late wi' drinks, the men'll still be at 'em when Cameron and Clarke do the temperatures, and then there'll be trouble. The readin's'll be wrong.'

'Oh dear, I see. Well, you can say it's my fault, that I slowed you down.'

Dicks gave her a strange look. 'Aye, I will an' all, don't you worry!' she said brusquely.

219

If Jessie had hoped for any *esprit de corps* among nurses, she was finding a harsher truth.

At the end of her first day, Jessie was exhausted. Her feet were on fire, her back ached, her head ached, her hands were sore and red, and her starched collar had rubbed a chafe round her neck, before it had wilted in the heat to malleability. She had spent most of the day in the sluice, emptying and washing bedpans, disposing of soiled dressings and unspeakable messes in kidney dishes, and cleaning the sluice room itself – this last, she was to understand, was entirely her responsibility, and if other nurses made a mess she was to clean it up or bear the lash of Sister's tongue.

She had also had to clean the kitchen and the lavatory, and had been exiled for some time in a store-cupboard, rolling bandages. She had hardly been in the ward itself at all – in fact, she felt there was a conspiracy to keep her away from the patients. The only time she had seen them was when she and Dicks took round their drinks, and handed out and collected their meal trays, and even then there was no time for any real contact. She did not know a single name, and had only a diffused and muddled impression of a succession of eyes, blue ones, brown ones, green ones, bloodshot ones; faces, brown or pale, smooth or lined, friendly, curious or remote with pain; bandages, casts and slings, and glimpsed horrors of mutilation; smell of blood, smell of pus, and disinfectant, and urine. Some had said, 'Hello! You're new. What's your name?' and one or two had made more personal remarks; and one with a broad Scottish accent, had asked if she fancied coming back 'the neet' and slipping into bed with him. She had been annoyed to feel herself blushing, especially as it made several of them laugh, and as she hadn't really been offended at all. Dicks had given her that look again, and said, 'You'll get used to it. It's as well some of 'em *are* cheeky, with what they've to put up with.'

'I don't mind it,' she had asserted.

'You do,' Dicks said. 'You're bloody soft, you are. Ooh,

pardon my French, your ladyship, I shoulda said *blinkin'*. What *are* you doing here – the likes of you?'

'I want to be useful,' Jessie said.

'Oh, aye. Well, you'll be that, all right, before Sister's through with you.'

That, she thought, was the hardest thing about her first day – that Dicks showed her no friendship, that none of the nurses showed the slightest kindness to her. The low point had come in the afternoon when she was toiling alone in the sluice. Sister had given her a heap of bloody bandages to wash. Her hands were sore and flinched from the hot water and washing soda, and she was dog-tired and close to tears. Uncle Teddy had been wrong, she thought, when he said she would be little better than a domestic servant. In fact she was far less than a domestic servant. Could it really be helping anyone for her to be doing this filthy toil? Surely her abilities could be better used in some other way? Much as she hated to admit the family had been right, perhaps she should accept defeat gracefully and give it up. *They* would not laugh at her for having been so stubborn and so wrong. Longing thoughts of home and its comforts got her through another five minutes. Suppose she just left now? No-one liked her or wanted her here, and if she was going to give up, why not sooner rather than later? What could they do to her, after all? They couldn't make her stay, or punish her.

And then she heard two nurses talking outside the sluice-room door, out of sight to her as she stood at the sink. She didn't yet know the other nurses well enough to recognise their voices, but there was no mistaking the Scottish burr of Beattie, the First Nurse, and she knew by now the harsh tones of the Senior Nurse, Clarke, who had told her off a number of times during the day.

'Sister's got a real down on this new girl,' Beattie said.

'Well, you know why,' said Clarke. 'She hates VADs. And this one's just like the rest – a right little madam, thinking she's better than us, with her lah-di-dah accent. Sister'll soon get her out – and good riddance.'

'Ach, no, it's a shame,' Beattie said mildly. 'We can do with all the pairs of hands we can get. And this one's all right. She's not complained yet, for all that Sister's giving her all the worst jobs.'

'Sister'll have her out by tonight – tomorrow at the latest,' Clarke said, with relish. 'She'll break her like a twig, you'll see. I think the end of this is blocked. I can't get it on.'

'Give it to me. You have to twist it a bit.' A breathing silence. 'Well, I still think it's a pity, all the same. What for are we making it too hard for people to help when they want to?'

'They don't want to help, that sort. They just want to swank about in the uniform giving themselves airs, while we do all the hard work. That's it – you've got it. Give it here again.'

'I don't know. I think we should give her a chance. She could make a good nurse, and we need nurses, wherever they come from. There's a war on, you know.'

'Oh, you're too soft for your own good, you are, Beattie! Always trying to see people's good side. You'll catch cold at it one day. I'll take any money you like that her ladyship doesn't stay the week.'

'I don't bet, but if I did, I'd bet she stays. Don't screw that too tight, or you'll break the thread. There, that'll do. Are you going to irrigate that belly in number two?'

'I thought you were going to do it. I've got number twelve's dressing to do yet.'

'Puir boy,' Beattie said, her accent strengthening with emotion. 'Dr Sanger said he's going to have to amputate again – take it off further up. And he's only a wee laddie – can't be more than eighteen. I've a brother at hame just his age. It's no' right. This rotten war!'

'I'll do the belly, you do the leg,' said Clarke, unmoved, and the two went away.

Jessie was shaken by what she had heard, that Sister Morgan was so determined to be rid of her, and that Clarke agreed with the plan. She had not expected to meet with such animosity: weren't they all supposed to be on the same

222

side? But then the Morland grit in her soul made itself felt. She could be determined too. She would not be ousted! She would show Sister who was the better woman. She would do all the rotten jobs until Sister was forced to admit she was worthy of her place. She was not going to slink away with her tail between her legs. She was going to make them wonder how they ever did without her!

Two things strengthened her resolve not to be beaten: one was Beattie's more liberal response. It gave her some hope if there was *someone* on the ward who was on her side. And the other thing was what Beattie had said about the boy in number twelve. It had been easy, while she toiled all day in the sluice, to forget what this was all about. It was not her feelings, or even Sister's, that mattered. It was the men, who had faced death for them, and suffered grievous injury. Whatever she did, even if she scrubbed bedpans for the rest of the war, it was not too great a sacrifice on her part. And if she was doing that, it released a more experienced nurse for other tasks, didn't it?

So she went home at last exhausted, almost falling asleep over the steering-wheel, but determined to carry on. When she got back to Morland Place, Sawry opened the door for her, gently eased off her coat, and told her that her mother had ordered cocoa to be kept hot for her in the kitchen. It was good to be home.

CHAPTER TEN

Jessie had a letter from Bertie, and read it in her bedroom with her burning feet up on a stack of pillows.

I am delighted that you are nursing, and hope the Ugly Sister soon realises your true worth and allows you to participate fully! I know you will not be deterred by hard work, but don't worry about the opposition you meet. Old attitudes die hard, but die they will and must as this war continues. Nursing is the most valuable thing a woman can do for those at the Front, and I honour you for it. It makes me feel closer to you, to know you are doing for those soldiers what I hope some other Angel would do for me if ever I should need it.

It seems we are to leave Plug Street soon. It has been rather a holiday to be here, mostly quiet, though Fritz sends over some hate now and then to remind us of our duty. The weather has been fine, and the woods themselves are surprisingly untouched. Everything is coming into leaf. Even the stumps of damaged trees are sprouting. Life is such a strong force, thank God! The woods belong to a rich merchant who stocked them for shooting, and we hear pheasant all the time, croaking away in the undergrowth. Fenniman and I talk wistfully about the delights of shooting, but somehow our appetite for killing is not what it was. The pheasants seem such handsome and harmless birds that even the prospect of eating them isn't enough to make us go after them. It has been a pleasant interlude here, and we are all sorry to go. We are to go back to our old place – you will know where I mean. This may be normal rotation, or it may mean that there is a bit of a 'wind-up' coming. I haven't heard anything for certain yet.

So Bertie was going back to Ypres, Jessie thought. She hoped he would be safe. It had been good to think of him in Plug Street Wood and out of danger, but the very name of Ypres was associated in the mind with the terrible fighting of the previous autumn. If there was to be a 'wind-up', she would need her exhausting work more than ever to keep her mind from useless worrying, in the anxious intervals between letters. It made her glow that Bertie approved so heartily of her nursing. And it was comforting that he understood so immediately that every soldier on the ward was the representative to her of her own loved ones. Thinking of this, and of Bertie, the mysterious Plug Street Wood, and the awful Ypres, the pain in her feet faded, and she fell asleep.

She had been two weeks at the hospital now, and was glad she had only 'signed up' for three days a week. She wasn't sure her body could have stood more. Sister Morgan continued to give all the most disagreeable and laborious tasks to her. It almost seemed that when there was any actual nursing to be done, she made sure Jessie was out of the way; as if she was determined to stop her learning anything of the skills that might make her a nurse rather than a skivvy. She would not even allow Jessie to feed those who could not manage for themselves – a job the nurses would willingly have left to her since it was so time-consuming.

Most of her day was spent in cleaning of one sort or another: the wards had to be dusted, floors swept, bedside lockers scoured, bed-wheels oiled; the bath in the patients' bathroom had to be scoured; the balcony where they were wheeled out to take the air had to be swept and the railings dusted. She toiled long hours in the sluice, and when not there was to be found in the kitchen, making tea and Bovril and cocoa for the men, boiling their breakfast eggs, cutting bread and butter, washing up the resultant crockery and cutlery, and cleaning the kitchen itself.

The only direct contact she had with the patients was when she took round their trays and collected them again, gave out and collected bedpans. But sometimes one would ask her to hand him something or fetch him something as she passed by, and would want to talk to her. She recognised that they were bored, in pain, and longed for diversion; but if she tried to chat, after only a few words Sister or Clarke or Cameron would appear like magic and send her away. 'You haven't time to stand there gossiping, Nurse!' At least by this snatched method she began to learn the patients' names, and to be able to put a face to a condition. She got the impression that some of the men felt sorry for her, and sided with her against Sister.

But Sister Morgan had the power of a dictator in the ward, and the fiat was that 'the VAD', as she called Jessie, should not be allowed to go near the patients. The VAD was to be confined to the sluice, unless there was a spillage, in which case it was 'Don't clean that up, Nurse – let the VAD do it.' Jessie learnt from Dicks that VADs did not usually remain long on Sister Morgan's ward: they soon flounced out or left in tears. Dicks was the nurse with whom she had most contact. She grew a little less hostile as time went on, especially as Jessie was doing the 'nasty' jobs that had previously been her portion. She talked to her a little, and told her things, though she never went so far as to be friendly. She gave the impression she thought Jessie was unbalanced. She said once, wonderingly, 'If I was rich like you, you'd never catch me bein' a nurse. I'd sit at home all day with me feet oop an' eat chocolates.'

'Don't you like nursing?' Jessie asked.

'Hate it. The hours are rotten, your feet hurt all t' time, Sister's a cow and Clarke's a bitch.'

They were making beds together, a task so congenial in Jessie's terms, Sister would not have allowed it had it not been Foxton's day off – Foxton being the next most junior.

'I just don't know what you're *doing* here,' Dicks said, tucking corners. Fortunately Jessie had learnt how to do that when helping her mother in childhood – though she was much slower than Dicks.

'I want to help,' Jessie said, for the hundredth time.

'Aye, well, Sister'll have you out before the end o' t' month,' Dicks said. 'Hurry up, can't you? We'll never get done.'

Jessie noticed that it had gone from 'before the end of the day' to 'before the end of the month', and it made her even more grimly determined to do her bit, and to do it here. She gritted her teeth and endured, and found a perverse satisfaction in taking the worst that Sister Morgan could throw at her without buckling. And the more Jessie stuck it out, the more Sister hated her. She gathered, from something she overheard, that a lady-visitor had told Sister that Auxiliary Nurse Morland was the niece of Mr Morland of Morland Place, and had explained who he was and what his importance was to the neighbourhood. The information had increased Sister's resentment: on that day she had been particularly spiteful to Jessie, as if she had been boasting of her connections and asking for favours on the strength of it.

Her hours, on her three days, were eight a.m. until one p.m., and five p.m. until nine p.m.; but she had to be on the ward a quarter of an hour before the morning shift, in order to stand in attendance as the night nurses handed over to the day nurses and the report was made; and at the end of the day she had to remain a quarter-hour while the process was reversed. She suspected the extra minutes were meant simply as a punishment by Sister Morgan, since she was not allowed to speak or ask questions and had been forbidden to touch any patient's chart or records. But she listened as hard as she could from her lowly position at the back and tried her best to understand the medical terms and the condition of the men in the anonymous beds.

The hours were long and the work hard, and when she went home in the middle of the day, she was sometimes too tired to eat anything, and had to lie on her bed with her feet propped up by pillows to try to cool them. Four hours off in the afternoon had seemed like a long break when she had been told about it, but in reality it was eaten up by the journey to and from the hospital, and by doing all the small tasks that had seemed to take no time at all when her time was all her own. She was lucky, she knew, to have Morland Place to come back to, to have her Austin to save her the walk to and from Clifton, to have servants to prepare her meals at odd times of the day and to do her washing and mending. She wondered how ordinary nurses from humbler backgrounds managed. To have to mend one's stockings oneself at half past nine in the evening, when every muscle ached, one's feet throbbed and one longed only for sleep must be the last straw.

But for all Sister Morgan could do, she gradually got to know the men on Maitland Ward, and then she knew that it was all worth while. They were either regulars or the first intake of volunteers, so they had all been, before wounding, in the prime of life and health: young men of good physique and fine muscular fitness. And because they were the cream of young manhood, they fought off pain and sickness and the debilitation of their wounds with a power to heal that was impressive. As she got to know them, Jessie admired them more and more for the cheerfulness with which they bore their suffering. It put her toils into perspective, and she began to believe in her heart, rather than merely with her intellect, that the things she did were not disagreeable or degrading because they were done for them.

So when at home her mother hinted that it was all too much for her, Ethel frowned, Alice shook her head, or Polly shuddered, 'I don't know how you *could*!'; when they asked her if she wouldn't give it up, she looked surprised and said, 'Oh, no!' And soon enough, as the days passed, they stopped asking.

* * *

They arrived in Ypres at night, a mild night under a clear sky, with a bright sliver of moon lying on its back like a native boat sailing the darkness. *Moon on her back, rain in her lap*, so said an old groom from his childhood in Bertie's memory; but he didn't believe it. There was no smell of rain in the air. The Germans were putting up flares all along their line, and the strange, greenish, flickering glow marked out the curve of the salient where the enemy had sat, since November, along the line of the ground they had won; a curve of eldritch fire to show where Bertie and his ragged companions had stopped them, with a desperate, heart-tearing effort, from overrunning the ancient town of Ypres.

Ypres itself was very much the worse for wear: the stout rampart walls, built by the military genius Vauban, still stood, but the handsome spires and towers, gables and pinnacles that had once reared above them had been battered away, shelled to ruin by the Germans: from the modestly high ground the enemy occupied across the low plain, anything above house-height stood up silhouetted against the sky and made a tempting target. Within the ramparts there were shells of houses, burnt-out buildings, rubble-filled gaps where once grand mansions had stood, craters in roads and squares; there were houses with holed roofs, missing chimneys, walls leaning crazily; houses where a whole side had been blown off, and the wallpaper and fireplaces and odd bits of furniture, unreachable on upper floors, were exposed pathetically as in an opened doll's house.

But the town was far from empty. Many inhabitants had fled back in the autumn, but others had stayed, either from defiance or because they had nowhere else to go. They lived makeshift in the remains of their own or other people's patched-up houses, retiring to the cellars at night for fear of bombardment, and creeping out in the daytime, risking the occasional daylight shell to do what they had to, to survive. The thousands of soldiers who passed through, going up to the line or down to rest, who worked at various headquarters in the town, who came out of sightseeing curiosity, or to visit the bars and restaurants – these were now the natives' means of earning a living.

The remaining citizens were a problem for the authorities, not least because the local water supplies were now hopelessly polluted. Typhoid had struck in January and was still raging, and the victims were stretching the already challenged medical facilities to the limit. Bertie's unit had all been vaccinated before they left Plug Street, and they had been warned not to drink water from any but an official military source. The town they had fought so hard to save last autumn was beginning to smell bad, Bertie discovered; but still, by moonlight, it had a crazy grandeur, with its torn and skeletal roof line seeming to tremble against the sky as the flash of flares and artillery came and went.

They were billeted for the night in a small textiles factory, partly ruined, the machinery long since gone. The men bedded down on the empty machine floor. Half the owner's house, which had been attached to it, still stood, and made the officers a little more comfortable in its remaining rooms. The weird night life of Ypres was in full swing, in the bars and restaurants that still flourished behind boarded-up windows and patched-up walls. They were named usually after the barmaid or proprietor – Julie's, or Jeanne's, or Duval's – but sometimes were known by their old name – Le Cathédrale, Le Moulin – or a new one the soldiers had bestowed – the Ritz, the Cat and Fiddle, the Dead Horse Saloon. Wine and beer could always be had, and food, variable and much of it from tinned sources, but still welcome as a change. By day there were still pâtisseries open, and souvenir shops, and lace shops, and market stalls in the square. In the undamaged villages on the far side of Ypres, bakers still baked and sent up their bread for breakfast, and farmers sent in eggs, meat and vegetables for the high price they could get in the shattered town.

Bertie was still with the remnant of his old battalion. The West Herts had been reduced by the end of the first Ypres battle to 108 men and three officers, and when they had gone down to rest, there had been talk about splitting them up and 'sowing' them among the new units coming out, to give some battle-experienced stiffening to the untried Terriers. But in the end they had been banded together with some other remnants to make a 'half-battalion', as it was known, until their own regiments could send out fresh battalions, which they could join. It meant that Bertie was still with his friends, Fenniman and Pennyfather, and the tough, weathered Tommies with whom he had gone through so much. The half-battalion was known as Frobisher's, after the commanding officer of the moment, a major of the Worcesters who had been made acting-colonel.

They had a whole day in their billet in the town before going up to the line; and after fatigues, the men made the most of it, sightseeing and shopping, poking around in the ruins in the hope of treasure or souvenirs, and – the crowning pleasure – eating in a café. An omelette and fried potatoes represented the giddy limit of hedonistic pleasure to most Tommies.

Bertie and Fenniman strolled off together and had luncheon in Madame Duval's, a café recommended by an engineer officer they met, who was billeted in the catacombs inside the rampart walls – 'the safest billet in Belgium,' as he said. At Duval's they had a fine feast of tinned pilchards, a ragout of mutton, cold beef and pickles, fresh bread, and a couple of bottles of red wine. Then, having followed up the rumour of cigars at a shop in a back-street (the rumour turned out to be only half true – there were cigars, but they had been 'rescued' from a flooded cellar and were spoilt beyond repair), they wandered until they found a quiet spot where they could sit and doze in the sun. It was the garden of one of the town's numerous convents. The building itself had been shattered – the nuns had been evacuated long before – and the high wall onto the street was no more, but they climbed over the rubble and found an untouched corner of lawn, daisy-spangled, with a gnarled, leaning apple tree. The outer walls, over which an espaliered peach rambled in the sun, sheltered it and magnified the heat. It was a beautiful, mild spring day, with a blue sky lightly fretted with

231

the whitest wisps of cloud, like blown swan's feathers. The intermittent sound of the guns was far off: nearby there was the chattering of jackdaws in a church tower, and the sound of sparrows bickering as they nested in the holes in the walls. It was all very peaceful.

'Sometimes,' Fenniman drawled, as he blew his cigarette smoke up through the branches, 'it's not such a bad old war.'

'I heard the oddest rumour,' Bertie said, propping his folded arm behind his head. 'I meant to tell you. After you turned in last night, I stepped outside for a last smoke, and some Highlanders came along. Camerons, I think they were. Their officer stopped for a chin, and he said they'd been given lunch by some French officers when they came up to the line to take over the sector from them.'

'What did they have?'

'Can't remember if he said. I think he mentioned coffee and brandy afterwards. But the point is, these French officers told the Cameron officers that when they were up in the northern sector of the salient a couple of weeks ago, they took a German prisoner who told them the Bosch were planning a big offensive, using poison gas.'

'Poison gas?' Fenniman said, startled out of his languor.

Bertie nodded. 'That's what the Cameron said. He said the Frogs told him the German had been quite chatty about it, quite specific: so many cylinders, such and such a size, buried in such a place, all filled with chlorine gas. Deadly poison. Said the Huns had all been issued with special respirators in preparation for the attack.'

Fenniman relaxed. 'Oh, it must be tosh. Even the Huns wouldn't do that – not use gas. There are limits.'

'Well,' said Bertie. They smoked in silence.

'Did the Frogs believe it?' Fenniman asked, after a while.

'Apparently their intelligence wallahs decided in the end it was all too easy and the German must have allowed himself to be caught, deliberately to sow the story. He knew exactly where the attack was going to happen, you see, so they decided it was a Bosch ruse to make us move everyone out of the danger zone so they could just walk over.'

'That seems more likely to me. They're a devious bunch of hounds,' Fenniman said. 'They'd say anything for a free ticket.'

'Hmm,' said Bertie. 'Curious, though.'

'Curious,' Fenniman agreed. He smoked on, but there was a frown between his brows.

At last Bertie ground out the stub of his cigarette in the earth. 'Not our business, anyway. Ours but to do or die. We've just time for a bit of a stroll before we have to get back. Fancy a walk up to the canal? I hear there's a place up there that has decent coffee.'

Lord Overton, coming in from the War Office, and finding his wife about to go and dress for a luncheon, said he would walk upstairs with her. 'The oddest thing has just come in on Reuter's,' he said. 'Apparently the German newspapers have been carrying a story that the British have used poison gas against them.'

Venetia looked startled. 'Surely not?'

'Of course we haven't. But it didn't stop the German press from making plenty of fuss about our wickedness and depravity. How we'd broken not only the rules of war, but the unwritten laws of civilisation itself. Paragraphs of the stuff – you can imagine.'

Venetia paused on the landing. 'I don't understand. Why would they publish a lie?'

'Why indeed?' said Overton, lightly, opening the door of her bedroom for her.

'Is it simply more of their vile propaganda?' Venetia asked, walking in. She began to unbutton her cuffs. 'Something to encourage their own people? It must be hard for them to maintain morale at home. As the aggressors, they can't make a moral case for the war.'

'Propaganda it most certainly is,' said Overton, closing the door behind him, 'but I wonder if there isn't something more specific behind it.' He sat down on a small gilded chair, which had never been intended for anything but decoration, or for having a pair of gloves dropped on it in passing,

233

and it creaked under him. 'You see, for months past we've had reports that the Germans are planning a gas attack. Not intelligence, precisely, just rumours. We've dismissed it as nonsense because we've always assumed they would never do anything so frightful. Poison gas is strictly forbidden by the Hague Convention, and the Germans signed up to that just as we did. But now this business in the German press would seem to confirm it.'

'You mean,' said Venetia, turning to him, 'that the only reason they would publish that particular lie would be to justify using gas themselves?'

'It's the only reason I can think of. They could call it retaliation then, you see. They wouldn't be blamed for doing it first.'

'But that's – *vile*!' she cried, unable to find a word adequate to her feelings.

'More vile than using the gas in the first place?'

'In a way, yes.'

He smiled a little. 'Well, perhaps. "Who steals my good name" and so on. But if they are planning a gas attack, it shows a certain desperation in their high command. It means they believe they can't break through by conventional methods.'

'Do you believe there will be a gas attack?'

'I didn't, until today. Now I think the rumours were probably true. And perhaps the only reason they haven't begun already is the weather.'

'The weather?'

'Well, the wind, at all events. I've been checking weather reports from the Front. Obviously with a gas attack it's important the stuff blows towards your enemy, not over your own men. And the wind's been steady from the south for weeks now. Exactly the wrong direction for the Germans.'

'So, then, it could come at any time – whenever the wind changes?'

Overton nodded. 'If I'm right.' He stood up. 'I'd better let you ring for Carless, or you'll be late.'

'*If* you're right?' Venetia pursued.

'Mine is not the majority opinion,' he said drily. Venetia looked at him with sympathy. To play Cassandra was not a comfortable thing. 'Where do you lunch?' he asked her.

'Claridges. With Kitty Sandown and Claudia Worsley. Kitty thinks she might be able to get Grey to talk to Lloyd George about my mobile X-ray units.'

'Then I definitely mustn't keep you.' He kissed her cheek, pressing her hands. 'I look forward to dining with you tonight, even if it is at the Mansion House. I don't see enough of you these days, my love.'

'For two pins . . .' Venetia smiled, laying her hands against his chest.

'Not if you hope to win over Lloyd George,' he replied, giving them back to her. 'He's the speaker tonight, and he'd notice two empty chairs.'

He headed for the door. As he opened it, Venetia said, with a troubled look, 'Gas, Beauty? Really?'

He looked back. 'Don't worry about it,' he advised. 'I may well be wrong.'

But he hardly ever is, she thought, as the door closed behind him.

Frobisher's force went up on the night of the 21st of April, marching through Wieltje and on up the Gravenstafel road. The road was so bad that it was slow going, and when daylight came they were still a mile short of Gravenstafel, and two miles from their destination. They were supposed to relieve a section where the British-held line joined the Canadian-held. But a change-over could not be undertaken in daylight, and fresh orders came that they were to remain where they were for the day, in a tiny, battered village, and go into the line the following night. The displeasure of the soldiers waiting to be relieved could be imagined; but Frobisher's were not too pleased with the situation either. Behind the line in the Canadian sector was an area known as Locality C, where the bodies of the casualties of last autumn were still lying unburied. The German line ran very close there, and it had been too dangerous to go out and

235

get them in. The smell reached Frobisher's quite clearly where they halted.

'I'd sooner risk old Fritz in daylight than spend a day smelling that,' grumbled Cooper, Bertie's servant. 'I thought we was shot of bloody Wipers when we moved out in Feb'ry. Now 'ere we are back again! They save all the rotten jobs for the half-battalions. You'd've thought we'd suffered enough already, but no . . .'

Cooper could carry on like that indefinitely once he got into his stride, and Bertie abandoned him and went out, thinking the smell outside was more tolerable than the monologue inside. It was another lovely day, mild, gentle, with a high blue sky and soft golden sunshine. The Germans were quiet all day, as if enjoying the weather as much as anyone. There were a few shells aimed at Ypres, and the occasional burst of machine-gun fire in the distance, but otherwise nothing disturbed the peace. The men, expert now at taking their ease where they found it, sat around in sheltered corners chatting, writing home, playing cards, or else stretched out asleep with their caps over their eyes.

In the afternoon Frobisher came across Bertie smoking and reading a book, and invited him to come with him for 'a spot of obbo'.

'I've had a look at what's left of the church tower. The stairs inside are intact, and the structure seems sound enough. I think it might be instructive to take a look at the lie of the land from up there. We shan't have another chance once we go into the line.'

'You don't think we'd be exposing ourselves to fire, sir?' Bertie asked.

'I don't think so – those trees over there screen the tower nicely, now the top of it's gone. As long as we're careful with the field-glasses, and don't go in for any of that heliographing stuff. But we'll be looking north and east, so we should be all right. What d'you say?'

'Thank you, sir, I'd like to come.'

'Jolly good,' said Frobisher, smiling. Discipline in these half-battalions of survivors was less rigid than in the army

236

in general, and officers tended to be aware that their juniors were junior only in name, rarely in experience or talent. Frobisher was only a year or two older than Bertie, and evidently liked him. His second-in-command was a grizzled veteran of near fifty with whom he had nothing in common, so he tended to confide in Bertie, and even rely on him, rather than on Major Truscott.

They made their way along the village street, keeping to the shadows of the buildings, and across the graveyard to the little church. It had been badly battered at some point, and the roof was gone. All that remained of the stained-glass windows was a few twisted strands of lead with jagged shards still sticking to the lower corners. Bertie reflected there could hardly be an intact pane of glass within twenty miles of Ypres. Inside the body of the church, there was nothing but a litter of rubble, shattered roof tiles and bits of burnt rafters: everything removable had been taken – even the pews would have been broken up for firewood. All this was obviously the result of shelling, and Bertie wondered whether Frobisher was right about this being a safe expedition; but after eight months of the war he had developed a certain fatalism. The Hun was quiet today, and provided they did not present an obvious target there was no reason to think he would waste a shell on them.

He followed Frobisher up the stone staircase that wound round inside the tower. The top of it had been blown off, down as far as the bell chamber. The single bell still hung from a solid rafter balanced across the truncated walls, and Bertie glanced up at it nervously, thinking it looked unsafe, its gaping mouth somehow threatening. But there was a hole in it through which the sunlight fell, and the clapper had gone, so it could not speak and give them away. Still, he didn't like walking under it, and made a detour to avoid it.

The bell chamber had unglazed louvred windows on four sides, but in all of them the wooden slats had been damaged, leaving holes they could look out of. The country lay quiet below them, dithering a little in the afternoon warmth, not a man or animal in sight. There were still trees and hedges around, still greenness to be seen: the place had not gone beyond saving yet. If both armies withdrew now, the scars would soon be covered over. To the north-west, about a mile away, was the village of St Julien, a strategic point Bertie remembered from the previous year. He pointed it out to Frobisher, who thanked him and said he knew he had been right to bring Bertie – he himself had not served in Ypres before. Bertie pointed out Mouse Trap Ridge, beyond St Julien, and Kitchener's Wood, where there was a British heavy-gun emplacement.

'I didn't think Kitchener had ever visited here,' said Frobisher.

'Oh, no, it's nothing to do with the Old Man. It's our lads' corruption of the French: Bois des Cuisiniers – Cooks' Wood.'

'I wonder if these places will ever get their real names back,' Frobisher said. He got out a rather tattered and much-drawn-upon map, and together they studied it and noted the reality of the places marked. From St Julien the road ran north-east towards Poelcapelle, where the Canadian section of the line ended and the French began. The French section of the line curved round westwards to Steenstraat, which was on the canal that ran northwards out of Ypres, and there the Belgians took it over.

'I heard,' said Bertie, 'that we – the British – were supposed to have taken over that section from the French. We were to have held the whole northern sector of the Front, so the French could withdraw and mount their campaign at Artois. But then the Twenty-ninth Division had to go to the Dardanelles, and there was no-one else to send, so the French are stuck with it.'

Frobisher didn't seem interested in matters of higher strategy. 'I sometimes wonder if we'll be here for the rest of our lives. We can't shift the Germans and they can't shift us.'

'We took Hill 60 from them,' Bertie reminded him. Only a few days ago a brilliant action had taken that important piece of high ground on the far south-eastern rim of the salient.

238

'Yes, of course,' Frobisher said, with an air of recollecting himself. 'I was being gloomy. Pay no attention.'

A soft little breeze had got up, and it was warm enough that afternoon for it to be welcome.

'Wind's changed direction,' Bertie remarked. It had swung right round to the north-east. He hoped that would not bring the rain back. He had seen enough of Belgian rain last autumn.

Some time later, Frobisher said, 'Well, I think I've seen all I want. How about a cup of tea? It's about time, I think.' He looked at his watch. 'Getting on for five.'

Bertie was about to accept the invitation and turn away from the window, when something caught his eye. He put his field-glasses up again. 'My God,' he breathed.

Frobisher turned back, alerted by the tone of his voice. 'What is it?' he said. He looked through his field-glasses too, and then said again, but with a different intonation, 'What *is* it?'

It was a strange greenish-yellow cloud, which seemed to rise from the ground just about where they knew the German line must be. As they watched, it came rolling with a horrible air of animation towards the Allied trenches.

'It's gas,' said Bertie. He felt cold and sick with the realisation.

'Gas?' Frobisher sounded incredulous.

'I heard rumours. A chap I met heard from some French officers there'd been talk of a gas attack. It's going straight towards the Canadians!'

'No, wait, it's veering – the Frogs are going to get it.' At that moment the Germans opened fire. The air, the stonework under their fingers, the slabs under their feet, trembled with the tremendous percussion of their heavy artillery. Out of the corner of his eye Bertie saw the mute bell rock a little. 'I must get on the blower, warn Headquarters,' Frobisher shouted above the din, running for the stairs. But Bertie could not drag his eyes away from the horror. If he had had any doubt that it was gas, it was soon vanquished. The heavy cloud rolled inexorably with the gentle breeze over the French-held line of trenches, which their Algerian troops had just taken over. On the right of their line, at the edge of the cloud, Bertie saw the soldiers come tumbling out of the trenches, running for their lives, scattering in panic, throwing away their rifles. He could not hear their cries from this distance, but he could see them claw at their throats and chests. From the centre and left of the French line no-one emerged; but as the cloud advanced he saw men get up from the reserve trenches, first one or two, then more, then all, and go running, desperately scrambling over the wounded earth and away from this hideous silent menace.

Bertie discovered he was swearing in a helpless stream, and his eyes were wet. 'They did it,' he said. 'The bastards did it. Oh, my God, they did it.'

He dragged the glasses from his face and himself from the window, wiping his eyes on his sleeve. He thought of the trenches from which no-one had emerged. They wouldn't have stood a chance, poor devils – choked to death in minutes. Dear God! This had changed everything. He crossed the room almost blindly, heading for the stairs and his duty. British guns had opened fire now from behind the Canadian line, answering the German shells, and the noise and vibration were intolerable up here. It seemed to be battering the very thoughts out of his head; he felt it like a pressure in the veins of his neck and temples. Now, though it had no clapper, the bell made a soft murmur – the sound waves caught inside it, agitating its metal curves, he supposed. A natural phenomenon. Yet he glanced at it fearfully. Its gaping mouth seemed to threaten to engulf him; its murmur was a gloating voice.

You have a bad dose of the horrors, he told himself, from what seemed like a vast distance. One foot in front of the other – that's right. He reached the stairs and ran down as if something loosed from Hell were after him.

Behind their battering artillery, the German infantry crept forward, preparing to fight the weakened foe for territory.

But there was no-one to fight. The whole French section had collapsed, and those few front-line soldiers who had not died, and the reserve troops behind them, were running for their lives from the yellow cloud. By nightfall a four-mile stretch of the line to the north-east of Ypres had changed from a convex curve to a deep concave. It was as if the German Army had taken a great bite out of the salient.

The Canadians, to the right of the bite, had spread out and were filling the gap on the new line, down as far as Kitchener's Wood. It was they who were largely responsible for stopping the Germans getting even further.

'God knows why the Bosch have halted,' Frobisher said, addressing his officers later. He looked shaken, but his voice was calm now that he had received orders, and there was something for him to do. Inaction was always harder to bear. 'They could have walked straight through and taken Ypres, and there's not a damned thing we could have done to stop them. But it appears they're digging in. It's a stroke of luck for us – gives us a little time to regroup. Our orders have just come through. We're to move up to St Julien.'

The Germans were still shelling, and the Canadians, who had managed to move their guns back, were replying. Here and there along the new line small outposts of Allied resistance were firing back, but the gaps in the line were enormous. It was imperative to get reserves up and into trenches before daylight came and the Germans discovered the situation. At the inmost part of the new concave line, they were only two miles from the walls of Ypres.

But getting reserves up was difficult, for the roads were choked with wounded and gassed soldiers trying to get back, and with fleeing, panicking civilians. A surprising number of Belgians had refused all along to leave their farms and cottages, whatever the danger of German shells. Despite its deserted appearance, the salient had been peopled with largely unseen peasants, clinging to their battered farmhouses, still trying to tend the fields and the cows, pigs and chickens that were all they had in the world. Now the gas had done what the shells could not: in the face of the silent

241

killer, they had taken to the roads with whatever posses-
sions they could grab. And as they and the first gassed
soldiers reached Ypres, the citizens there also took to flight,
further clogging the roads.

Frobisher's was one of the few reserve units near the line,
and they had received orders from General Alderson, in
command of the Canadian Division, to come to their aid.
The Canuks – as they were affectionately known – were now
covering an extra two miles of line, and were spread dangerously thin. As Bertie and his men groped and stumbled
through the darkness towards St Julien, the stink of the gas
was still in the air, a nauseatingly bitter tang that made their
noses and eyes burn. But that was hardly more than an
inconvenience; what must it have been like for the troops
who took the full brunt? They saw as they got closer. Dead
birds had fallen out of trees, dead cows lay in the fields,
dead chickens in the farmyards. Dead rats that had staggered out of barns and sheds lay in the road where they
had fallen in flight. The men exclaimed in low voices over
this new turn of events. Bertie stumbled on a dead cat, and
heard Cooper mutter, 'There you are, y'see. And what can
kill a cat?'

Nobody said anything when they began to come across
dead men. They lay sprawled, their hands clutching at their
throats, contorted with agony; discoloured faces with foam
on their lips. This was not warfare, Bertie thought. This was
plain evil. He saw on the faces of his men the same horror,
which quickly turned to a grim determination.

They halted outside St Julien, and the gas smell was
stronger than ever. Frobisher called his officers together and
they went up to the ruined farmhouse that was the temporary headquarters of the Canadian Division. General
Alderson had been inspecting his gun batteries at the time
of the gas attack, and so was one of the few senior officers
on the spot. They expected him to give orders for consoli-
dating the line and digging in, but the general had a bolder
plan.

'Gentlemen,' he said, 'there are four British guns in

242

Kitchener's Wood. The Germans have them now. I do not propose to leave them in the enjoyment of them.' They looked at him with interest. 'I hardly need to tell you the strategic importance of the wood. It stands on Mouse Trap Ridge, and gives protection to this village and a considerable area of the plain to the west. In the hands of the Germans, it would be a great nuisance. In the lee of the ridge, they would be able to assemble men and bring up guns with impunity, and from the wood they could sweep the whole approach to Ypres.'

His eyes moved round them. He was a tall, big-built, pleasant man, very popular with his men. With his small dark eyes, his bulbous nose and large moustaches, he looked in normal times like a friendly walrus. But there was nothing comical about him now: his expression was steely. 'Gentlemen,' he went on, 'we shall counter-attack. The Germans have halted and are digging in, which suggests they do not know how many men are facing them. If they discover how few we are, they will renew the attack, and Ypres will be lost. But a determined counter-attack, mounted without delay, will be the last thing they expect. It will make them think we are still here in force. A successful bluff will recapture the wood, restore the guns to us, and deeply unsettle the enemy. Above all, it will buy us time. Reserves are coming up to fill the gaps in the line but it is essential that we force the Hun onto the back foot before he realises those gaps exist.' He thumped his leather-gloved fist into his hand to emphasise the importance of the last words; but everyone in the room was nodding, fully apprised of the seriousness of the situation.

His voice became gentler. 'I will not conceal from you, gentlemen, what your own intelligence will tell you – that this will be something in the way of a sacrificial charge. I can give you no machine-gun or artillery support. Sheer courage and determination will win the ground and drive the enemy back. But the cost will be heavy.'

Bertie found himself, as one does in a moment of great tension, looking at something inconsequential. It was a section of the plaster on the farmhouse wall behind the general's shoulder. A piece had fallen out of it, revealing the ancient red brick behind, and from this red patch cracks radiated in all directions. The patch was roughly the shape of Ypres on a map, and the cracks might have represented the roads running out of it. How odd, he thought, that a random shell blast should have done precisely this damage. The thing that they were fighting for – Ypres – was impressed into the wall for them all to remember. But that was not what they were fighting for, really. It was the immediate objective, but the reality was something much greater and simpler. They were defending decency and freedom, the right of people to live in peace on their own lands. They were fighting for life.

He suddenly became acutely aware of everything around him – his own body, tired but strong, inside his clothes; the slight chafe of his uniform collar against the back of his neck; the smell of the farmhouse – dank, a hint of mildew, dirty sacks and damp plaster – and the metallic smell of water somewhere nearby; the background sounds – a telephone operator in the scullery next door talking low and urgently, the whine and crump of shells falling outside. A particularly loud crash made the ground under his boots shake, and a drift of plaster floated down from the low ceiling and dusted Alderson's hat, but no-one in the room flinched. He had a strange, fatalistic feeling that this room was the last he would ever see, and that that was why he was seeing it so clearly. But he was not afraid. He was almost exalted.

'We attack at midnight,' the general said.

It went with him, the exalted feeling, like a kind of joy, and communicated itself to his men. He never remembered what he said to them, but his language was not elevated. He told them in an ordinary voice the least and plainest facts about the situation and the objective; but all of them knew the reality – that here and now they were to perform deeds that would save Ypres from the enemy, or let it fall into his hands.

Bertie looked round the faces, so familiar to him now, most of them men who had been through other hells with him. Baugh, Binns, Cole, Cooper, 'Windy' Gale, 'Bill' Harper (nicknamed after the song), Heaton, Ives, 'Jack' Joseph (all his brothers were in the navy), Lorne, Mitchell, Petts . . . In that moment he loved them as he had never loved a woman; and they looked back at him, and caught his joy, and there was determination in their faces, and fierce excitement, but no fear.

When the whistle sounded they launched themselves into the darkness like men kicking off into unknown water. There were two fields to cross, and two hedges to pass through; the little sickle moon to see by, blurred with a fine, high mist. The Canucks they were supporting – the 10th Canadian and the 16th Canadian Scottish – were fine big men, proud of volunteering to help the Old Country, proud of their new country as of their old roots. They had not been many weeks in France, and this was their first real battle. Nothing was going to stop them. They were going to show what Canadians could do! And Frobisher's, the last of the regulars, the old army, would never let a volunteer get in front of them. Shoulder to shoulder they ran.

The firing started. Probably the Germans could not see them, but they hardly needed to. They could hear where the attack was coming from, and they simply sprayed the area with machine-gun fire, like firemen with a hose. Men fell, on every side they fell: some twisting, some flinging out their arms; some headlong like divers, skidding along the ground a little until they came to rest; some writhing and cursing – those were the ones who might live; some silently like logs, dead before the earth met them. The air was thick with death, with hot lead like a cloud of stinging insects, but infinitely more deadly. Bertie ran with his men, hardly feeling the tussocky earth under his feet. Another night he might have feared to stumble, but tonight he knew he would fly from tuft to tuft, until his bullet found him. 'Come on!' he yelled. 'West Herts! West Herts!' The words didn't matter. He was there to bring his men – those who survived – to the point, like the huntsman putting hounds into a wood. Get them to the point, and they would not need him any more. If he could survive that long – if God let him! He made no attempt to avoid the hail of death. It was pointless – there was too much of it; and he knew in any case that this was his last charge. So he ran straight, unflinching, and his men ran with him, buoyed by his heedlessness of death.

And then the firing was coming from point-blank range, they were at the woods, and the men in grey were in front of them, scrambling up from their positions. Bertie yelled and emptied his pistol into them. All the men had been instructed to make as much noise as possible, and his men, the survivors, went howling in, bayonets thrusting. There was a brief struggle, but the charge carried: the Germans fell back, flung away their arms, tried to run, and were cut down. Alderson had known, Bertie thought dazedly; the canny old fellow had known the Bosch could not stand a charge, a hand-to-hand fight. He grabbed up a discarded rifle and used its bayonet now his pistol was empty. There were dead Germans underfoot now, and they were pursuing the fleeing remnant through the wood. One grey man in front of him turned and Bertie caught a glimpse of his face, wide and white and gaping, before he ran him through – had he meant to fight or surrender? But there was no surrender here. The wood was full of plunging bodies, screaming oaths, the smashing of undergrowth and splintering of twigs, and the uncertain moonlight gave it all a strange, theatrical unreality.

They passed the four British guns, with dead men sprawled around them, but a simple glance could see that the Germans had already disabled them. A pity – but at least they were no use to the enemy. And now they were at the further end of the wood, and the last few live Germans were scrambling away into the darkness towards their comrades. Down the Allied line came the order to halt, there at the edge of the wood, and Bertie ordered his surviving men to start digging in.

And then he paused and drew breath for a moment, looked round, and realised that he was not dead, he had not been killed after all. It seemed a circumstance of great oddness to him, given that he had written off his life so calmly, but in the dreamlike euphoria of the moment it did not seem of much importance. A Canadian captain, a giant of a man who would have made two of Bertie, came up and clapped him on the back and shook his hand, grinning, and Bertie responded with a mad grin of his own, but he never knew what the man had said to him. Congratulations, expressions of fellow-feeling, no doubt, but the words were for ever lost in a kind of battle-deafness, which had made a singing silence inside Bertie's head.

CHAPTER ELEVEN

Hardly had they got themselves into their newly dug trenches than the Germans began to bombard the wood. Shells poured down: the air was filled with their screaming, clashing din, the ground trembled under continuous insult. The trees that provided partial cover were splintered, and now the explosions were smashing into the earthworks, blowing fountains of soil and stones into the air. It would not be long before they were destroyed, and the men would have to retreat. Risking a quick look over the top, Bertie could see that the Germans were digging themselves into a new position about two hundred yards in front of the wood. Since the Allies had no artillery, there was nothing they could do about it, and the enemy could pound them until they were forced back.

But that was reckoning without the Canadians. As they had chosen the bold option before, now again they preferred it to sitting down under fire. The 10th Canadian under Colonel Boyle led a daring assault to try to take the new German position before they should have finished digging in. Frobisher's were left with the 16th Canadian Scottish to hold the position at the edge of the wood.

The Germans put up withering fire, and at times it looked as though nothing could live under it. Scores of men fell; others crawled into cover and kept firing, getting forward by fits and starts as the opportunity allowed. Despite their heavy losses, somehow the 10th kept up the attack, keeping the Germans occupied and allowing the rest of force to hold on to the wood. But in the early hours of the morning it could be seen that more German troops were coming up, and the 10th's forward position was too exposed, in danger of being outflanked as well as overrun. The order came for the whole force to withdraw, leaving the wood they had taken at such price, and pull back to a line of old trenches on the other side, to dig in and wait for reinforcements.

Dawn was coming, but fortunately the morning was misty, which gave a little more time to the weary men as they laboured with entrenching tools to get themselves under cover before full daylight. And before daybreak on the 23rd of April, the first reinforcements arrived, in the form of Geddes' force. They were a mixture like Frobisher's – three and a half battalions of 'odds-and-ends' under the command of Colonel Geddes of the Buffs. There were Buffs, Leinsters, Middlesex, and Yorks and Lancasters among them; there was even a truncated company of Northumberland Fusiliers, numbering 120 men and two officers, who had been fighting at Hill 60 and got separated from their regiment. It was a small enough force, considering that its orders were not only to fill the gaps in the line held by the Canadians but also to extend it into what had been the French sector; to hold the Germans down and yet also to attack if at all possible and regain lost ground. But two thousand Canadians had just driven back an entire German division without artillery support. Miracles could happen.

As detachments of Geddes' force came into the line, Frobisher's were ordered to withdraw to St Julien to find the rest of their division. It was no easy matter to get out, for the trenches were under constant fire, and given the present fluid nature of the front, sniper fire could come from almost any direction. Tired and desperately hungry, they had to dash from cover to cover, sometimes scrambling along bent double in the shelter of a half-demolished hedge, sometimes crawling along a muddy road ditch. Bertie lost one of his men, Nichols, when he tried to ease his aching back by straightening up for a moment, and a sniper shot him through the back of the neck. But after two miles of hard going they got out of range of the enemy, and were able to form up in the road and at least walk upright like men.

Now at last they were able to take a roll-call and see who was missing. Casualties had not been as heavy as Bertie had expected: in all, about a third of their number was missing – killed, injured or captured. Bertie himself had lost a dozen men, including Lofty Small, a short, barrel-shaped man with a powerful tenor voice who had been the mainstay of their rest-period entertainments, and Timmy Binns and Billy Smith, who had been leading lights of the C Company football team back home in England, when C Company had still existed. About another dozen were sporting wounds, including Cooper, who seemed more surprised than upset – since he had come through so far without a scratch – to find the tip of his left ear missing and blood pouring down his neck. He had no idea when it had happened.

St Julien, when they neared it, was being shelled, and many of the houses on the side nearest the Germans were on fire. Headquarters had moved to another house further out of range, and it took a while to locate it; but there was a cottage being used as a dressing-station just where they had halted, and they were able to send their wounded in to get attention. The rest of the men fell out beside the road while Frobisher and Truscott went off to get their new orders. Before they returned, a water cart came by, and stopped to give the men a drink, which was more welcome to them even than food after the exertions of the night.

It was two hours before the senior officers returned, reflecting the difficulty of communication in the circumstances. All the telephone lines in the salient ran through Ypres, and the shells knocked them out faster than the signals engineers could mend them. After a day and night of mad activity, units were so scattered that it was hard for anyone to know where anyone else was. But Frobisher's own divisional commander, General Smith-Dorrien, had been walking back to Ypres from Hill 60 at the time of the gas attack, and had seen what had happened, and was therefore better informed than anyone except perhaps General Alderson. It was he who had dispatched Geddes' force to the rescue. His orders to Frobisher's were now to go back and join up with them; and the order from Colonel Geddes was to reinforce a section of the line to the left of St Julien. So away the weary men marched again.

It was a strange day. The Germans still seemed reluctant to advance, and the Allies' aim was to feed that reluctance by persuading them that a large force was facing them. So Frobisher's were sent into various ditches and firing positions where they had to fire a number of rounds; then move further along the line and fire again; then move again. Between them they had to occupy a section of the line three times too long for them, and make themselves seem like three times as many. Back and forth they went all day. Sometimes they were ordered to advance a little, firing hard, and then retire – anything to keep the enemy guessing.

Towards sundown they were moved to a new position, just vacated by some other troops, along the edge of a slight bank that led down to a stream, and there told to dig themselves a trench for the night. The sun was declining, the warm day fading to misty evening; there was distant shellfire – it had not ceased all day – and here and there, from nearer at hand, the brattle of rifle and machine-gun fire. It was not always possible to tell which side was firing. Along the edge of the stream was a row of willows, which had been beaten down and shattered by shell-fire, and Bertie sent a section of his men down there to pile up the debris and interlace branches to make a sort of hedge along the stream bank, as an alternative to barbed wire. It would give them just a little extra protection, slow the enemy down if they did decide to attack.

Pennyfather came up to him in the gloaming to report. He had a grimy bandage round one hand where he had taken a bullet graze in Kitchener's Wood. 'All done, sir. It won't stop them, but at least we'll hear them if they try to cross.' He paused and looked around, then back at Bertie. 'It seems quiet. Do you think they'll come?'

'I don't know,' Bertie said honestly. 'I don't know, now, where they are. How are the men getting on with the trenches?'

'Pretty well, sir. Almost finished. Is any food coming up?'

'I don't know that, either,' he said, with a faint smile, and Pennyfather nodded, with a rueful smile of his own.

In fact, they had moved about so much during the day that not only did Bertie not know where the Germans were, he hardly knew where he was, either. The men had not slept for a night and a day, and would not sleep this night, either. They were exhausted, hungry, thirsty, and though the day had been warm, the evening was turning chilly, so they would likely be cold in the night. They were short of ammunition, too. He hoped the brass remembered to send some up with dinner – if they remembered to send dinner. It was hard not to give in to the horrid feeling that no-one knew they were here, wherever here was.

All that day, St George's Day, the Germans had rained down shells, not only on the battlefield but on Ypres, to which they were considerably closer as a result of their advance. The city, which had still borne a semblance of its old self the day before, was being pulverised into utter ruin, and in the splintered ancient wood of rafters, floorboards and window-frames, fire bloomed like golden roses. The Cloth Hall and the Cathedral, the city's finest buildings, were in flames, along with hundreds of houses. Ypres burned. There was no-one to put the fires out. Most of the remaining residents had fled before the menace of gas, and the last few were huddled in cellars while their city was beaten flat around them.

All day the hard-pressed Allied troops went back and forth, fighting desperately to hold the line until reinforcements came up. The Canadians had performed miracles on the right, and on the left the Belgians had come to the aid of those French who had survived the gassing. There had been fierce fighting, and the line had been driven back dangerously, but they had managed to hold it at last at the canal. But the situation was desperate, and only the Germans' inexplicable failure to advance in a full-scale infantry assault had prevented their taking Ypres.

Early in the morning, Sir John French had been to visit his French counterpart, General Foch, to discuss the situation. French had his mind and his heart set on the joint offensive at Artois, which he had been planning with Marshal Joffre, and against which he had been carefully husbanding both men and ammunition. He had lost the 29th Division, his only spare troops, who were on their way to the Dardanelles, and to send anyone to the aid of Ypres would mean weakening the line elsewhere. The situation in Ypres was so desperate, and casualties had already been so high, that it seemed more sensible to withdraw altogether and let the town fall.

But General Foch was appalled at the idea. Ypres was the last corner of Belgium left in Allied hands, and the French frontier was only ten miles to the south of it. He argued earnestly and optimistically for a joint counter-attack. The ground lost could and would be won back. It *must* be won back – any other course was unthinkable. Sir John French was not immune to the argument – the defence of Belgium was the reason Britain had gone to war in the first place, and Ypres was almost the last barrier between the Germans and the Channel ports. It would not be well received at home for it to be abandoned. He reluctantly agreed to reinforce the Second Army, and as soon as Foch's reinforcements arrived, the attack would go in. Both agreed that it had better be done sooner rather than later, before the Germans, who were obviously digging in, made themselves impregnable.

The attack had been planned for three o'clock that afternoon, the 23rd; but the congestion on the roads all around Ypres was so bad that the fresh troops could not be got into position until well after four. Unfortunately the artillery barrage that had been planned for a quarter to three could not be postponed in time, and it did nothing but alert the enemy to the fact that an attack was coming. So when the assault went in at half past four, the men charged exposed across open ground towards a prepared enemy, and the losses were appalling. No new ground was taken; the survivors who crawled back after dark were a mere remnant of the fresh troops who had marched up, men who might otherwise have been used to strengthen the line.

Bertie and the men of Frobisher's knew nothing of the counter-attack until after dark, when food and ammunition were brought up to them, with the day's news.

Later, Bertie and Fenniman shared a cigarette in a ramshackle wooden dug-out, knocked together more as a shelter in case it rained, since it would provide about the same defence against shell-fire as a kitchen table.

'Damn and blast the bloody brass,' Fenniman said bitterly. 'What are they playing at? Those men could have relieved us. What was the point of throwing them away like that? Attacking in broad daylight without artillery!'

'It would have been better to pull back and consolidate a shorter line, in my view,' Bertie said. 'We can't hold the present salient with the number of men we've got.'

'What's the point of a smaller salient? Abandon bloody old Ypres altogether, that's what we should do,' said Fenniman.

Bertie smiled at him affectionately. 'Come on, Fen. You know you don't mean that. Have your moan by all means, but you know we can't let the Bosch have their own way without a fight.' He stared out into the darkness. 'I wonder what they're up to. Why haven't they attacked?'

'They will,' said Fenniman.

'Yes, but where?' said Bertie.

At three in the morning the Germans opened up a tremendous barrage against the Canadian part of the line in front of Locality C. The Canadians had only taken over the line from the French on the 17th, and had found the defences very poor, the trenches little more than a series of rifle pits, some connected and others not, with very poor sandbagging, no barbed wire, and no communication trenches. For the past week they had been labouring to improve matters; now the pounding bombardment ripped through the defences, inflicting terrible casualties. After an hour of shelling, the enemy released another gas cloud, and in the wake of it mounted the long-feared infantry assault.

Bertie had just made a round of his sentries when the barrage began, over to the east of them, but sounding horribly close. Every man at once roused up and took position along the parapet, though the area in front of them seemed quiet. Beyond the stream were scattered trees – not dense enough to be called a wood, and most of them damaged – and then open fields, lit by the misty moon, which was declining towards moonset. It was cold, and the men had no greatcoats. Some of them shivered as they faced the empty country, but Bertie knew it was not fear: they had all done this so many times before.

It was not long before Frobisher called the officers together. 'New orders,' he said. He was a man of swarthy complexion, and his chin and cheeks were dark with unshaven growth, while behind it his skin looked pale and waxy with tiredness, and his eyes were red-rimmed. Bertie supposed none of them looked any better.

His expression was grim. 'The Canadians are catching it again, poor devils. The triple-damned Huns have launched another gas attack on their eastern front, between the Poelcapelle road and Gravenstafel. You've all heard the bombardment. Now the German infantry is massing. We're to go and support the Canucks. Get your men together.'

'What about our position here, sir?' asked one of the captains.

'There's no-one to take it over from us. We have to abandon it. We're needed elsewhere.'

Word always spread like wildfire in such situations, and by the time Bertie got back to his men, they all knew everything he had to tell them.

'What about the gas, sir?' Ives asked.

'It may have dispersed by the time we get there. If it hasn't, tie something over your nose and mouth: handkerchief,

255

scarf – your field-bandage, if you've nothing else. It'll help a bit. Oh, and apparently it works better if it's wet.'

'Wet, sir?'

'Where'd we get water, sir?'

'My water bottle's been empty since yes'd'y afternoon.'

'Then find something else that's wet,' Bertie said, fixing them with a look.

Cooper translated with a grin: 'Piss on yer hankies, the captain means.'

Through the dark morning they marched towards the sounds of Hell. The barrage was still going on, presumably to prevent reserves coming up, and the sky was lit lurid, black and smoky orange, with brighter flashes as the guns barked. The noise was too great to hear much of the other sounds of battle. When they got onto the road, they saw Canadians and Highlanders coming down, wounded or gassed, the latter staggering and gasping, some with their field-bandage tied round their eyes. Sometimes they saw a man drop, foaming at the lips, clawing at his throat. It was worse, much worse, than the battle wounds they all understood.

They were under shell-fire now, screaming death that came out of the blank sky and blew men apart. Bertie saw one fall beside two of his men: Heaton's body below the waist simply disappeared, while Mitchell was blasted into nothing. Others of his men were wounded and had to be left behind, and those who could move joined forces with the Canadians and went hobbling and limping back, leaning on and leading the gas-blind.

Now they were past the worst of the shelling and could smell the gas, the vile and bitter, corrosive stink of it. It was nauseating, and made their eyes burn, and some started coughing and retching. The noise of battle was ahead of them on both sides, while in the centre there was a human silence where the gas had been thickest. No-one there was manning the front line. There were dead men lying everywhere, faces contorted and blue, sprawled amid the litter of battle, where they had staggered away from the poisonous cloud.

Now here were the reserve trenches, but there was no-one in them, alive or dead; they jumped over or scrambled through them, and went on, quickening their pace. The Canadians' front now formed a salient of its own, like an arrowhead, east-facing along the original line between Gravenstafel and the Poelcapelle road, then swinging sharply southwest towards St Julien where the French line had collapsed. The Germans were attacking all round the salient, trying to collapse the two sides together and fold up the defenders entirely. The Canadians, with the support of some Highlanders, were defending fiercely, but there was a gap in the eastern-facing line where the gas had been thickest and the Canadians had been killed or forced back.

Frobisher's came up to the line on the right of the gap, and joined the Canadians at the parapets, where they were holding off the German hordes, if only just. The West Kents settled in almost with a feeling of relief. This was battle as they understood it. They fired and reloaded and fired, the rapid fire for which they were famous, which had beaten the Bosch every time. The Canadians had machine-gun sections, too, which poured their deadly hail into the grey masses, and by the use of crossfire protected the gap in the line where their comrades had been gassed. The German numbers seemed immense, uncountable, and more were coming all the time, another springing up as if by black alchemy wherever one fell. They fell in huge numbers. Their losses were as great as those of the Allies when they had attacked frontally; but the Germans had far more men here, ten times as many as the defenders.

The gas was an added hazard, but on this side it had dispersed enough not to be lethal. It seemed to affect some men more than others, and there were those who, after a short time, fell out of the line, pale and choking, gasping for breath, retching helplessly. Others managed to fight on, suffering from burning eyes and throats, but finding that a wet handkerchief over the mouth did help. The breeze that had brought the gas rolling over was working in their favour now, rolling it away behind them. Those retreating, ironically, were worse off, for they were keeping pace with the cloud.

They fought on as the day broadened. There was no need any more to think: battle was joined, and they knew what to do without thinking. At about two in the afternoon news came through that the Germans had taken St Julien, and when Bertie heard, he thought briefly of their overnight position and wondered if the gap they had left had been instrumental in the fall. But they had been far more needed here. Without them, the line might not have held.

But more Germans came, and always more; and the enemy had a seemingly endless supply of ammunition. They shelled the whole salient and the town relentlessly all day, while the Allied batteries were desperately short of shells, and what they had were mostly for field guns. With these the gunners were able to help beat off the Germans' infantry attacks, but they could do nothing to knock out their big guns. For that, heavy artillery was needed – and the heavy artillery were almost out of ammunition.

By nightfall the Canadian line was still holding, but there were no more reserve troops to send in, and the position was untenable. The order came up to retire to a new line further back, shrinking the salient around Ypres, but giving them a chance to close up and consolidate. The weary, red-eyed men of Frobisher's staggered back with the Canadians, through the shell-pounded night. Ahead of them, Ypres burned: the whole town was ablaze, with golden flames leaping in the darkness, silhouetting windowless façades like frail black grids across a furnace. Bitter smoke flattened out sideways in the breeze. The shells went on falling, on the retreating men, on their positions, on farmhouses and woods and aid stations, on the wounded going down and reliefs going up, on the transports bringing up food and ammunition and the ambulances taking casualties back. The armies had abandoned Ypres, and the dressing stations had had to move as far back as Vlamertinghe to be safe, making the journey even longer for the wounded.

The surviving men of Frobisher's moved back through

the luridly lit darkness, through the madness of shells, past stinking shell-holes, dead horses, overturned limbers, past limping, bloodied men and stretcher-bearers and the countless dead, to their new position. They settled in for another night, searching the darkness in front of them with aching eyes, hoping for no attack, hoping for a meal to reach them, and ammunition, and, most longed-for of all, hot tea. The Germans pressed forward in the darkness, and shelled without pause, but the line around Ypres held. It held, and the burning city was still in Allied hands.

The news of the first gas attack horrified those at home. The newspaper leaders were full of furious indignation at this new 'frightfulness' of the Hun, but the official reports from the War Office emphasised that the Allies were holding on, that the Germans had been halted, and that counter-offensives were being mounted. There was no doubt in the public's mind that the Tommies were in a tight spot, but equally no doubt that they would fight their way out of it. There had been tight spots before, and always the Bosch had been sent packing. So it would be this time.

For those with someone in the Ypres theatre it was harder. Jessie was more glad than ever of her hospital work. She wanted to be tired out, too tired to think about what might have happened to Bertie. There was the gas, and there were the 'heavy casualties', and it would be days at least before she could hope to hear whether he had been a victim of either. She felt numb and dazed with anxiety, her heart a constant iron pain in her breast, which only the sleep of exhaustion could still for a while. At the hospital she worked harder than ever, jumped to undertake every job, no matter how unpleasant, so that there should be no moment unoccupied. She performed her tasks with a kind of humble gratitude, remembering Bertie's words, that whatever she did for these men, she did for him and his comrades at the Front. She prayed that if he was wounded, someone was looking after him properly; of the other possibility, that he lay already dead in some abandoned corner of the battlefield, she would not allow herself to think directly, though the possibility was there in the corner of her mind, impossible to ignore, impossible to contemplate.

On Sunday the 25th she was not working at the hospital, and her mother was so pleased to have her at home that she felt wearily glad to be giving her the pleasure, but the day was a trial to her. Uncle Teddy spoke the morning prayers in the chapel, but at breakfast he said that because of the situation in Ypres the whole family should go to church for the morning service. 'We ought to be seen there,' he said. 'We ought to lead the prayers. There are a lot of villagers who have people out there. It will comfort them to see us and speak to us.'

Jessie did not resist his decree, but the church was not a comforting place for her to be, with its memorials to the dead, its emphasis on the other world, into which so many in Flanders must already have passed. She knew that as a Christian she should not mourn a man who had made a good death fighting for what was right, but as a woman she could not be so objective. She stood and sat when the others stood and sat, she sang the hymns, she listened to the sermon. The vicar spoke eloquently of the courage and endurance of the British Army, of the need for equal fortitude at home, of his faith that they would come through this trial as all the trials before. Jessie listened, but the words meant nothing, were the merest empty platitudes. All the reality of the war now was Bertie, his warm body out there in the Ypres salient facing any number of hideous deaths; her mind could grip nothing else. And when the prayers were spoken, her own mind was blank. God knew what she wanted of Him. She could not make the words again.

At home, over the Sunday luncheon, words flowed back and forth like a tide above her head, not touching her. Teddy and Robbie discussed the war news in the Sunday newspapers, speculated on the unwritten detail, put forward their own strategies. Ethel and Alice discussed the continuing scandal of the 'Brides in the Bath' murders: a date had been set for the trial, and the details had been pushed by Ypres

260

and the gas attack from the front pages, but not entirely annihilated. Polly chattered to Henrietta about various tennis parties and outings she had been invited to or hoped to be invited to, and wondered in a hinting sort of way what presents she might receive for her birthday next month, and what kind of celebration Father might be thinking of making for her.

Only Henrietta looked at Jessie, silent before her barely touched plate, and knew what was going on inside her. She herself was worried about Bertie, her 'extra son', but the difference in their ages made it easier for her to bear. After luncheon she suggested Jessie go out riding, and neatly deflected Polly from asking to go with her, for which Jessie threw her a look of gratitude. And so Jessie took Hotspur out onto the moor and galloped until they were both tired, and the open air and the good companionship of the horse eased her ache a little. On the way home she stopped at Twelvetrees and became thoroughly absorbed in the training of a young horse who refused to lunge on the right rein. So the day passed. In the evening she made a determined attempt to keep her mind off by playing games with Polly and, after she had gone to bed, joining a round of cards with her mother, Ethel and Alice.

It worked pretty well until she was in bed, and then in the moments before sleep the quietness swirled back in, blowing away like dry, dead leaves the light occupations she had put into her mind, and revealing the adamant underneath: *Is he all right? When will I know? When will I hear?*

On Monday morning there was fresh trouble for her: a scribbled note came from Ned, to say that his battalion had been called for as reinforcements, and was on its way to Ypres.

Ned's battalion were down at rest when the change of orders came. Their billet was quite a good one, a series of wooden farm buildings, sound and dry, and they woke the first morning looking forward to enjoying the pleasant spring sunshine between fatigues. Letters and parcels caught up with them that first morning, so there was news from home to be absorbed, and the bounty of chocolate, cakes, biscuits, cigarettes and tinned delicacies to be shared out. The officers were as eager as the men for their mail. As welcome to them as chocolate and cigarettes was reading matter, and several of them were having books and magazines sent out by the people at home. Redwing of B Company received several editions of the *Boys Own Paper*, containing the latest episodes of the serial, *The Lighthouse at the End of the World*, by Jules Verne, which a number of them had been following. An elaborate rota for borrowing was already being worked out.

There was a rusty old water-tank, holed and empty, behind the farmyard, and some of the men were planning to line it with a tarpaulin and fill it with water so that everyone could have a much-needed bath. For many the height of their rest-time ambition was to find an *estaminet* in the nearby village where they could enjoy a glass of beer or a bottle of *vin rouge*; others were planning more ambitious activities. There was to be a football match, with the pick of the battalion's players organised into two teams, to be named the Frogs and the Rosbiffs – Lieutenant Redwing was their coach. Yet another group was planning a concert party, and Major Houseman, the acting CO, had agreed to let them off fatigues so that they could rehearse. During the day they took over the smallest barn – an old apple store – for their business, kept the door shut and had a patrol outside so that no-one could peep through the cracks.

The junior officers had their minds fixed on a splendid dinner that was planned for the evening. Flanders was famous for its asparagus, which had just come into season, and every market was loaded with it. They had all 'chipped in', and there was to be a feast of asparagus with melted butter, followed by roast chicken (Nugent was to scour the district for the chickens, price no object) with fried potatoes, and the best and ripest cheese that the market could provide, all accompanied by champagne and wine, which Vernon of B Company, who was privately wealthy and had

262

a motor with him at the front, was to drive into town to purchase.

It was a splendid feast, and everybody got very drunk. It was the first time since they were in action that they had been properly at rest, and now at last the memory of the friends they had lost came back to them. Toasts were drunk, the departed were spoken of in phrases increasingly extravagant as more bottles were emptied. The South Kents had all been together a long time, and they had been untried in battle before Neuve Chapelle. The remembering was harder for them, given the high spirits and high hopes with which they had come out to France. They had won glory, but there had been a price to pay. Almost half the battalion was gone.

When all the wine was finished, some staggered off to bed, some fell asleep where they sat, and the rest sat smoking in a rich, melancholy silence, staring at nothing. At last Vernon spoke up. 'Damnit, I'm getting damnably sober! This won't do. Won't do at all. There must be something left to drink.'

'Not a thing,' said Redwing, his particular friend, raising his head from his arms and demonstrating the emptiness of the nearest bottle by holding it up and inverting it. 'Drunk the lot, old bean.'

'Well, then,' Vernon said, struggling to his feet, 'got to do something about it. Got to go out. I know a place – jolly little place, not far. Couple of villages away. Very jolly. Who's coming? You'll come, won't you, Tommy, my Tommy?'

'Anything you say,' said Redwing, genially. 'Go anywhere, do anything. No expense spared.'

Vernon leaned over him tenderly. 'You're talking nonsense, Tommy old thing. Thought you ought to know.'

Redwing shook his head reproachfully. 'Must be drunk. Someone must've been giving me in-inebriating beverages.' He pulled himself up on Vernon's arm, and stood, swaying slightly and smiling around. 'Are we going?'

'We're going,' Vernon confirmed. 'Who else? Come on, you bores, don't sit there frowsting in your own vile juices!'

'I'll come,' said Smythe, of A Company.

'Me too,' said Paterson, getting to his feet. 'I may be drunk, but I'm not nearly drunk enough. I keep remembering – well, something.'

There was a murmur at that. They all kept remembering. Upjohn and Cyrilson got up to join the party, then Nugent scrambled to his feet. 'Jolly place, you say?'

'Very jolly,' Vernon said.

'Count me in, then. Jolliness is just what I want. Come on, Morland.'

Ned looked up. 'Was thinking of going to bed.'

'Oh, bosh! The night is young. Tell him he's got to come, Vernon.'

'Won't go without him,' Vernon said, with great and immediate sincerity. 'Essential he comes. Couldn't think of going without – er, what's his name?'

Everybody laughed, and Ned gave in and got up too. The laughter had not been against him, but had included him. He was enough one of them by now to be the butt of their humour, and it made him feel good. He had been something of an outsider most of his life, and this camaraderie was food for his soul, something he had lacked so long he had hardly been aware he wanted it. But he wanted it now. Knatchbull was dead, who had praised the fifty he had made in the Eton-Harrow match, and little Brown, and Singer with whom he'd shared a meal at Southampton and who had talked so fondly of his sisters back at home. But these fellows were alive and warm and full of laughter, and they wanted his company.

'I'm game,' he said.

'Come on, then, Game,' said Vernon, leading the way out. Laughing, they spilled out into the chilly night, and Ned found he had his arm linked through Nugent's.

The eight of them piled into Vernon's motor, then Redwing had to pile out again to swing the crank. But they were soon off, and the cold air must have sobered Vernon enough – or he had not been as drunk as he seemed – for he had no difficulty in keeping the vehicle straight, and seemed to know exactly where he was going. They sang a little as they roared along the French country lanes, and sometimes were answered by a farm dog, bursting into furious barking as they passed.

After about a quarter of an hour they came into another village, Loisené. It was far enough from the front not to have been shelled, but there were other signs of occupation – army vehicles parked beside the road, hand-written signs in English on some doors and in windows, a few soldiers in the streets here and there, and a sentry on duty outside the *mairie*, which was obviously someone's headquarters. Vernon drove through the village square and down a side-street, turned off down an even narrower street, and stopped outside a tall, narrow house. There were lights on inside, and the curtains were red, so they shone through in a warm glow. Ned was reminded of holding his hand up against the sun, when he was a child, to see the halo of blood round his fingers.

'Is this it?' Smythe demanded.

'This is it. Pile out, chaps,' said Vernon. He knocked long and vigorously on the front door, while the others crowded behind him, breathing down his neck. There was a sound of music and conversation inside. 'I hear girls!' Paterson whispered in awe.

'Girls? What are they?' said Cyrilson.

'You remember, old thing,' said Upjohn. 'Like chaps, but with more interesting bumps.'

The door opened a slit, and Vernon conducted a conversation with someone inside. His French was superb and Ned could not tell what he was saying. The door opened further. A middle-aged woman stood there in evening dress, her face painted, her hair elaborately dressed, jewellery glittering at her neck and ears. ''Ow many?' she asked.

'Eight of us,' Vernon said.

'Ver' well. *D'accord*.' The door was screened with a heavy blanket, so they could not see inside until she pulled it back and they stepped through. Not a bar or café, Ned saw, but a parlour, heavily decorated after the style of the last century,

265

with red flock wallpaper and crimson upholstery on the sofas and chairs. The lighting was low, from lamps set up on the tables round which the seats were grouped. Some were oil lamps and some had candles inside them, but all had red shades, so the light was blood-coloured: it was like being inside a womb, Ned thought. The air was hot and smoky, and smelled of paraffin and wax and cigarettes and bodies and a clash of cheap scents and face powders – rather a fug, in fact, but Ned breathed it in with enjoyment, because it was the essence of everything that was not the army, not war, not exclusively masculine. It smelt like life, and life was what he was after tonight – life and friendship, to drive away the memories of the dead.

Music was coming unevenly from a gramophone, but it seemed only there to take the edge off the silence, for no-one was listening to it. Half a dozen tables were occupied, by French and Belgian officers and one or two French civilians, talking to women who were all in evening dress. The low light winked off their sequins and jewellery, gleamed on white polished shoulders, touched the crowns of elaborate coiffures. Some of them looked round at the newcomers, and Ned saw Egyptian-painted eyes and red-painted mouths and suddenly realised where it was that Vernon had brought them. A cold splash of sobriety hit him. The woman – the *madame?* – was showing them to a big round table in the corner, next to another curtained doorway. She was chatting to Vernon, and Ned could not reach him to jog his sleeve. He managed to touch Redwing.

'Redwing,' he hissed urgently. 'I can't stay here. I must go. I'm a married man.'

Redwing glanced back, distracted, but only shook his head. Ned saw a bundle of notes pass from Vernon to the woman, which apparently impressed her with its thickness, for her face broke into a wide smile, and she began clicking her fingers for her staff, and urging the Kents into the chairs round the table. Waiters appeared with bottles and glasses on trays, and at the same time young women appeared from nowhere and sat down with the men. All this traffic made it impossible for Ned either to reach Vernon or to back away. He found himself sitting, willy-nilly, with girls either side of him – he could smell their sweat and their hair under the gale of scent that enveloped the table. Vernon was already in conversation with a young blonde girl beside him, and she was laughing extravagantly. Ned leant across the table and shouted at him. He looked up.

'I can't stay here.' Ned tried to whisper, out of courtesy to the females, but Vernon could not hear him over the noise, and he was obliged to shout. Redwing helped out and relayed his message, and Vernon laughed and shook his head.

'We're just having a few drinks, old chap,' Vernon bellowed back. 'That's all. Nothing for you to get the wind up about. Just a few more bottles of the good old *vin du pays*, and a nice girl or two to pour it for us. Innocent pleasures. Relax and enjoy yourself.'

The bottles were being plunked down on the table, cigarettes were being offered and lit. The girl sitting on his right got up and changed places with another, and his new companion poured out a glass and pushed it towards him with a hesitant little gesture. He looked at her, realised he was frowning, and relaxed his face into a smile. At once she smiled back. Under her *maquillage* she seemed very young – he would have thought her sixteen or seventeen at most. 'Thank you,' he said, and then remembered. '*Merci.*'

She poured herself a glass and lifted it to him in a toast. They clinked and drank.

Some conversation must be had. 'What's your name?' he asked.

'I am Céline,' she said. 'But I do not speak well the English. *Je m'excuse. Je suis désolée.*'

The rough red wine met his previous potations, joined hands and danced him round. 'I don't want you to be desolated,' he said. 'I want you to be happy.'

She laughed. She had very nice teeth, he noticed, and a sweet, plump young face, large dark eyes like a fawn's, and dark brown hair done up behind and crimped into curls at

267

the front. '*En effet, je suis très heureuse, surtout que vous parlez français!* What is your name?'

'Edward,' he said.

'Ah, Édouard, that is my favourite name,' she replied in French, and they continued in that language. 'Of all names in the world I like it the best!'

'I'm sure you say that to everyone.'

She opened her eyes wide, as if a little hurt. 'But no! It is true. I 'ave always like the name Édouard! Why should I lie to you?'

'I'm sorry,' he said, and she smiled, satisfied. She was very young, he thought, and unspoiled. He must not judge her by the surroundings. Girls must get on however they could in these times.

'And you are English officer,' she said next.

'A lieutenant.'

'Lefftenant. How droll it sounds! But nice. I like very much English officer, because always you are polite and kind, not like the French Army, who treat us like—' She reached after the right word.

'*Comme les meubles,*' he supplied. Like furniture.

'*Oui, ça va! Exactement!* It is very good that all you English officers speak French so nicely. England must be a nice place, because you are all so kind and nice to us. And you have come to save us from the *sales Boches.* We are all so grateful to you – you know?'

She had a sweet, soft voice, like a little dove cooing, and he had to lean closer to hear her as the noise of conversation rose. He offered her a cigarette and lit it for her, and was entranced by the way she took in the smoke and blew it upwards away from his face, and how she inspected the side of it with interest as if she wanted to remember the brand. At home he did not know any women who smoked. He pushed the pack towards her and told her to keep it – he had another in his pocket. She smiled ravishingly at him and thanked him, tucking it into her sequined bodice with a gesture that charmed him with its neatness. 'You're like a squirrel hiding away a nut,' he said in English.

'What is "squi-weel"?' she asked, floundering over the word.

He couldn't remember the French for squirrel, and had to try to describe it, with gestures, that finally had her laughing helplessly, and made him grin, too, at his helplessness.

'Oh, you are funny, Édouard.' She refilled his glass. 'I think I like you very much.'

'I like you too,' he said.

'Tell me about yourself,' she said. She put her plump elbows on the table, rested her pretty young face in her hands, and gave him her whole attention. So he began, awkwardly, because his French was barely up to it, and because it was not a thing he found easy in any case, to talk about himself. But she gave him her whole attention, nodding now and then, her soft eyes fixed on his face, seeming to want nothing more than to be with him and listen to him. It was balm to his soul. He had never had a woman treat him with such reverence. She was everything, he thought, that was desirable: soft, gentle, compliant, feminine – and admiring of him. He revelled in it after so long with nothing but men around him.

Someone turned up the gramophone, on which a woman was singing a sad love-song in French. He broke off, unable to compete with it. So Céline moved a little closer and sang along with it, in a little, husky voice, looking directly into Ned's eyes as she did. He drank more wine, and listened, as gradually she let her pretty head droop nearer to his, graceful as a flower. She smelled clean under the scent, and her hair was clean, and when at the end of the song she moved the last centimetre closer to him and presented him with her full red lips, he thought it no harm – only polite, really – to kiss them.

She sighed with apparent pleasure, and poured him more wine. Ned lifted the glass in a toast to her, and she clinked glasses with him, her eyes never leaving his over the rim as she drank. All around him the other fellows were drinking wine, smoking, and chatting with the other young ladies, roars of laughter punctuating their efforts to make themselves understood. Under the table, Céline's small, warm hand slipped onto his knee, and it seemed a gesture of pure kindness. He felt completely at home, warm, comfortable, and relaxed at last. He thought Vernon had been right about this place. It was very jolly.

Three days later the new orders came, in the morning, suddenly and urgently, and the South Kents had to pack up their kit, form up, and march out within the hour. Everyone was disappointed to be cheated of the pleasures they had planned for their rest period, but there was a buzz of excitement all the same as they wondered what was up and where they were going. Rumours sprang up from nowhere and a dozen different destinations were suggested. Quite a few people had drunk too much the night before, but in the general excitement and violent exertion, alcohol was sweated out and debility burned away, and in the dust raised by marching, the red eyes of a few went unnoticed.

They marched to Béthune, where they were put on a train that chugged its way slowly to Hazebrouck, the Forward Headquarters town, and from there they might have gone almost anywhere. But they were turned off the train and, after a wait, a fleet of red London buses arrived to take them up to Poperinghe. There was no doubt, then, that they were heading for Ypres. They had to march the last part from Poperinghe, and the sound of the continuous shelling came to them clearly.

The road was choked with soldiers going up, and civilians fleeing with their belongings in bundles and on carts; and on either side of the road and all along the railway tracks, people had fallen out and were lying abandoned in sleep, or sitting huddled in dazed exhaustion. Up ahead of them, Ypres was ablaze. They could see the flames leaping in the gathering dusk, the pall of black smoke hanging over the town as the shells continued to fall. They were halted for a while, turning into a field on the outskirts while they waited for the road to clear, and they had plenty of time to stare at the tortured town and wonder what they were walking into. The men fell silent and grave, their excitement turned to tension. Ned heard the man nearest him, Falmer, mutter, 'Blimey! How we going to get through that lot?'

They had to pass through the town to get up to the line, running the gauntlet of the shells. To minimise loss, the battalion was broken down into platoons and, leaving fifty-yard gaps between them, each made a run for it. Ned went at the front of his men, leading the way into the inferno. The noise was unbearable, not just the scream and thump of shells, but the roar of the flames, and the thunder of falling buildings. Ned could feel the scorching breath of the fire on his skin, saw the smoky flames lick upwards into the darkening sky, the sprays of red sparks leap like fountains of rubies when a beam collapsed. They picked their way through the rubble, skirted craters, watched nervously for collapsing walls, shielded their faces from clouds of brick dust and gouts of smoke, and all the while shells exploded and shrapnel flew only yards away.

It was full dark by the time they all got through, and miraculously there had only been two casualties. They were glad to be out of Ypres, though the way ahead was hardly less dangerous. Nowhere was safe from shells, but it felt better to be out of that desperate place and into the anonymity of the night and the open air. They formed up, and though there was no possibility of marching on the ruined and congested roads, they did their best to walk like soldiers on the road up to Wieltje.

On the Sunday morning, the 25th, there had been a counter-attack to try to retake St Julien. It was supposed to go in at three thirty in the morning but, like its predecessor, it had been postponed because the troops could not get into position in time, and just as before, the postponement order did not reach the artillery, so that their bombardment did nothing but warn the enemy that an attack was coming. Instead of an attack in the dark by fifteen battalions, there was an advance in broad daylight

271

by only five, and half of them fell to German machine-gun fire and field artillery.

The attack had been at the direct order of Sir John French, very much against the wishes of Sir Horace Smith-Dorrien, the commander of the Second Army. He had not been keen on the idea of the first counter-attack, doubting the ability of the French to do their part; and the costly failure that had ensued made the second attempt seem like madness to him. He had lost another two thousand men that morning, who would have been better employed strengthening the line and relieving the battle-weary, and on Sunday evening he drove to Hazebrouck to see the Commander-in-Chief and put his views to him.

There was an old line of well-built trenches, which made a smaller semi-circle round Ypres, from the road in front of Hill 60, around in front of Wieltje and just in behind Mouse Trap Ridge. It was so well fortified the Tommies had nick-named it the GHQ line, and it had been intended as a position to fall back to in the last resort. Smith-Dorrien now suggested that the Allies retreat to it, giving them a shorter line and smaller salient to defend. He also recommended withdrawing many of the troops at present on the ground, who in his view were doing nothing but confuse matters and provide the Germans with a target. With a shorter line they could man it with proper reserves and reliefs, and when the situation had stabilised they could mount a properly planned offensive and throw the enemy back.

The suggestion was received coolly by Sir John French. French had disliked him ever since Le Cateau, when Smith-Dorrien had resisted French's orders to retreat, and mounted instead a brilliant rearguard action that had saved the day. French had been chilly towards Smith-Dorrien ever since. Besides, he had promised General Foch that he would support him in the counter-attacks; and besides again, Smith-Dorrien's plan involved waiting until the situation in Ypres quietened down, and French could not afford to wait. He needed to get it settled quickly so that he could get on with the joint attack at Artois. So he told Smith-Dorrien that there would be no withdrawal: ground must be given up only in the most extreme circumstances. The French must be given their chance to counter-attack and redeem the situation.

Smith-Dorrien returned to his advanced report centre at Poperinghe to learn that the French were planning another offensive the next day, on the 26th, but with what he considered a quite inadequate force. It was to go in at two o'clock in the afternoon, when his reinforcements would have had no time to rest after their journey, and some would hardly have had time to reach the line at all. So sure was he that the plan spelled disaster that he telephoned to Hazebrouck Headquarters again, to beg Sir John to cancel the attack.

Perhaps if French had not already gone to bed, where he had to be woken to take the call, he might have listened with more patience. As it was, he was merely incensed by further argument from a subordinate, and told Smith-Dorrien curtly that the attack was to go ahead. It was his direct order.

At two p.m. exactly the South Kents went over the top. They had the French to the left and the Indians to the right, and the artillery had laid down a barrage for them to move in behind. But the German artillery were already firing back, and their bombardment outweighed the Allies' by two to one at least. There was fifteen hundred yards to cover, through air thick with flying metal, across a wide, flat valley floor, and the Allied troops were mown down like rye before the sickle. The Germans even had howitzers firing on them, and each one of their shells could blow an entire platoon to pieces. Clods and stones and bodies flew up into the air, huge shell-holes swallowed men like demon mouths. There was no thinking, almost no breathing, as the Kents ran towards the enemy position, eyes fixed ahead, minds numb to the comrades falling all around, to the bodies that carpeted the ground before and behind. Each man had given himself up to die. There was no chance to dodge or duck, no way to avoid death: it took you or it didn't.

Three-quarters of them fell; the remainder reached a position just behind the German wire, and there had to lie down and take what cover they could, firing when a target presented itself. Ned was among them. Death had not chosen him, and in dazed moments during the afternoon he wondered how it was that he had escaped when there had been so many bullets, so much shrapnel, as thick as rain in a summer storm. It must have been a matter of fractions of inches, thousands of times, yet they had all missed him – him and these few other survivors. He had got into a shell-hole with a dozen of his men, and now, as long as they kept their heads down, they were out of range of the machine-guns. In intervals between firing to keep the Germans occupied, he crawled round his men to supervise the tending of their wounds as best he could. Then there was nothing to do but hold on, and wait for darkness.

As dusk began to fall he sat with his back to the earth wall and took out of his pocket the photograph of Jessie he carried there always. He stroked it with his thumb, fixing his eyes in the growing gloom on her face. But she didn't seem real to him. The more he looked at her picture, the less he could call her living face to mind. Céline had more reality. He closed his eyes and her image bustled about behind his eyelids. He wanted to feel bad about that, waited for the guilt and shame to come – would have welcomed it, wanting to feel something, *anything*, about what had once been his life. But he was subsumed by the numbness of battle. His life back home was as detached from him as something he had read in a book; the images of Yorkshire his mind offered him as unconvincing as a theatre backdrop. The howling, trembling darkness, the grimed faces and white eyes of his men, the smell of mud and lyddite – those were the only reality. When it was full dark, they would try to crawl back and live, but the truth was they were all too tired to be afraid of dying, and that seemed to his weary, dazed mind to be all wrong.

That evening Smith-Dorrien wrote a long report to the Commander-in-Chief. The French attack had not taken

274

place. Apart from the battalion on the left before St Julien, none of them had advanced, leaving the British to take the brunt of the offensive. Losses had been heavy. The French proposed renewing the attack the next day, but Sir Horace made it clear that he saw no point in that, and said that he did not intend to co-operate unless the French could guarantee greater resources and more effective action. He gave a detailed explanation of the present situation, and repeated his advice that the British should pull back to the GHQ line.

The following day, even as the French attack was mounted and failed miserably to gain any ground, a telegram was sent to General Smith-Dorrien from GHQ, ordering him to hand over his command to his subordinate, General Sir Herbert Plumer. The telegram, contrary to usual practice, was not encoded, but sent *en clair*, so that anyone could read it: a deliberate humiliation to Smith-Dorrien from the Commander-in-Chief. His own men in the Second Army resented it quite as much as Smith-Dorrien himself – he was a popular and much-respected leader.

On the 28th Plumer sent his letter of acceptance to Sir John French, but in concise and forcible terms he gave his opinion that the present line could not be held, and that further attacks could not succeed and would only lead to expensive loss of life. He proposed that the British should withdraw to the GHQ line, and that this retirement should not be delayed. It was Smith-Dorrien's advice to the letter.

And by some miracle, the German bombardment petered out, and comparative quiet reigned over the tortured salient. Though he did not order the retirement, Sir John French did order the improvement and strengthening of the GHQ line, and every man not otherwise engaged was put to work digging trenches, filling sandbags, reeling out barbed wire, making communication trenches and gun positions. He also ordered the withdrawal of superfluous men and materials from the salient, and directed that the reinforcements coming up should be used to relieve the battle-weary troops.

Frobisher's force came down on the night of the 27th,

having been in the line for five days, in battle for a great deal of the time, and asleep for very little of it. By dawn they were behind Ypres and well on their way to Vlamertinghe; and when they reached their billets at last the men fell into exhausted sleep. Bertie kept himself awake for a little longer, to write a brief note to tell Jessie that he was all right.

CHAPTER TWELVE

On the 1st of May General Foch was ordered by Marshal Joffre to abandon his costly attempts to regain the ground lost in the Ypres salient, and with some relief Sir John French ordered the withdrawal of British troops to the GHQ line to begin that night. It had to be done stealthily and in stages so that the Germans should not get wind of it. On the night of the 3rd, the last position, the centre of the old salient at Racecourse Wood – in which Bertie had fought hand to hand with the Germans the autumn before – was quietly abandoned. A small rearguard covered the retreat by going up and down the line firing, to make it seem that the front was still occupied. When they, in their turn, retreated, the Germans thought that the cessation of fire meant the Allies were advancing, and they set up a tremendous barrage, shelling the empty trenches and machine-gunning the empty ground in front of them. It gave the weary troops some satisfaction to know that Fritz was wasting his substance on the desert air.

By morning everyone was back on the GHQ line, and the new front ran flat along the canal for two miles from Steenstraat, then curved outwards to cross the Poelcapelle road near Wieltje, made a loop outwards around the Hooge château, and then curved back south to Hill 60.

The respite did not last long. On the morning of the 4th German aeroplanes were out looking for their missing enemies, and it did not take them long to find them. The airmen dropped smoke bars over the side of their machines above the Allied trenches to mark their position. It was a beautiful early summer day, with a cloudless sky and not the slightest breeze, and the smoke bars hung motionless, giving the Germans all the information they needed to advance.

For many of those manning the trenches it was the first actual sight of the enemy they had ever had, and they stared in amazement as the hordes in grey came running down the slopes from the higher ground of the old front line, pouring like muddy water, spreading out and advancing towards a new position. Then the German artillery got the range of the GHQ line. They began to pound the defences and there was no more staring.

Frobisher's had been back in the line since the night of the 30th/1st, after three days of rest, and during the night of the 4th/5th they could hear the sounds of the Germans digging in, the scrape of shovel and the clink of entrenching tool, the faint sound of voices giving orders, the rattle and snick as barbed wire was rolled out. By morning, Bertie thought, they would have settled in and the lines would face each other just as before.

The army was enforcing an evacuation of the last few residents remaining in Ypres, and by six p.m. on the 8th the place was empty. All day the Germans had been subjecting the town to a renewed heavy barrage, the start of a new offensive, though little now remained standing for them to devastate. Orders came to the troops manning the trenches that they were to hold on at all costs, and not to call for reinforcements, for all the spare troops would be needed for the joint Allied offensive further south. The order came from General Sir Herbert Plumer, now commander of the whole Second Army: Smith-Dorrien had been ordered by Sir John French to return to England.

Matters were perilous enough in Flanders, but the Easterners' campaign to relieve the situation by attacking in the Dardanelles was not going to plan. The intention was to land troops on the tip of the Gallipoli peninsula. They would advance inland from there and secure the central heights, destroy the Turkish batteries, and thus open the Straits for the naval force to steam up and seize Constantinople.

It was a motley force that assembled in Egypt during March and early April, under the command of General Sir Ian Hamilton. Its main constituents were the British 29th Division, with the 1st Royal Naval Infantry Division; the French 1st Infantry Division; and the Australia and New Zealand Army Corps (who were known for brevity as the Anzacs). And there were odd contingents attached from various parts of the Empire, from the imposing 29th Indian Infantry Brigade down to the colourful Assyrian Jewish Refugee Mule Corps. But secrecy proved impossible in Alexandria, and long before the force set sail it was being openly reported in the newspapers exactly what it consisted of and where it was going.

Scanning the shore of the peninsula through field-glasses from the ships that carried them, army commanders could see that they were expected: there were streaks of new brown in the lush green, and the sparkle of barbed wire, where the Turks were digging in. They could also see that the terrain was much more difficult in reality than it had looked on the geographers' maps, which was all they had had access to before. The heights were steeper, the ravines narrower, deeper, more precipitous – a savage place of razor-edged ridges divided by chasms dense with impenetrable growth, a landscape where only a mountain-goat would move easily.

In the early morning on the 25th of April the attack went in. The French made a diversionary landing on the inner side of the peninsula, while the British landed on five separate beaches from the tip at Cape Helles up the Aegean coast. At three beaches the British got ashore without much difficulty, but at the other two there was heavy resistance, and the troops were cut down by a hail of fire from Turks well hidden on the higher ground.

The Anzacs were to have landed thirteen miles further

north, but they were swept past their assigned beach by strong currents, though they managed eventually to get ashore in a bay, which therefore became known as Anzac Cove. They pushed inland and managed to reach high ground, but there they met heavy Turkish opposition and were driven back down, almost to the beach.

Since then the forces had managed to advance only a few miles, and with heartbreaking effort and heavy losses. Though it was still only early summer, the heat was terrible, the dust almost unendurable. Water was a problem, for it had all to be brought in by boat, and the rations, bully beef and biscuit, jam and cheese, only increased the men's thirst. Burying the dead on the thin stony ground was difficult; digging latrines a constant, exhausting labour. Flies and other insect pests multiplied with every day; wounds went bad, and half of the men were down with dysentery. And still the Turks – for whom conditions could hardly have been much better – clung to their positions, and raked any advancing troops with machine-gun fire. By the end of the first week of May, the surviving soldiers were debilitated and disheartened, weakened by sickness, short of ammunition, and capable of doing nothing but holding on to their beachheads and waiting for reinforcements.

So matters on both fronts were a cause for concern, when on the 7th of May the news came that *Lusitania*, an unarmed passenger liner, had been sunk by a German U-boat off the coast of Ireland. She had maintained her regular passages between New York and Liverpool since the war began, relying on her speed to keep her safe, despite the warning from the German Embassy that any ship sailing the Atlantic under the British flag did so at her own risk. She left New York on the 1st of May, and at one twenty p.m. on the 7th she was torpedoed some ten miles off the Old Head of Kinsale, and sank within eighteen minutes. Further news coming in from the ships that had steamed to the rescue indicated that some twelve hundred people had perished, while only around seven hundred and fifty had been saved.

280

The news affected Teddy badly, bringing the memories of the sinking of *Titanic*, which were never far below the surface, surging up fresh and vivid in his mind. *Lusitania* and her sister ship, *Mauretania*, had been the largest and most luxurious ships in service before *Titanic* and her sister, *Olympic*, were launched. Indeed, it was precisely to challenge the Cunarders for the Atlantic run that the White Star giants had been designed and built. But the Cunarders had always been faster, and *Lusitania* held the Blue Riband in both directions, having made five record crossings. The destruction of the lovely ship, the speed of her sinking, and the terrible death-toll, all brought back that hideous night in 1912, and for days Teddy was silent and distressed, shut himself away in the steward's room and did not come to meals. Sleep was attended with horrible nightmares, and he took to sitting up and trying to read through the night, afraid to lie down and drop off.

Alice worried deeply about him, and at last begged Henrietta to speak to him.

'Why me, Alice dear? You're his wife. It's you who will comfort him best.'

'But you're his sister. You've known him all his life. I don't know how to reach him when he's like this. Remember back then, after it happened?' She shuddered at the memory. 'I couldn't do anything for him then, either.'

But even as they were discussing it, Polly had acted. She might sometimes behave in a flighty way, but she loved her father dearly. She went to the steward's room, paused a moment before the closed door, and then went in without knocking. 'Daddy?'

The spaniel, Muffy, lay dejectedly on the rug before the unlit fire, head on paws. He rolled his eyes up as Polly came in, and twitched the end of his feathery tail, but he was too miserable to get up. Teddy was sitting at his desk, his hands resting on its surface, his face set and grey with exhaustion and grief, staring blankly at nothing. He made no reaction to Polly's presence.

'Daddy, it's me,' she said anxiously. She crossed to his desk and stood directly in front of him. 'It's me. Polly.'

281

He raised his head slightly, his eyes focused on her; and he frowned. She had never had him look at her and frown in her whole life. Her eyes filled with tears. 'Don't be sad, Daddy,' she said. 'Please!'

Teddy shook his head, trying to shake away the thoughts that haunted him. He tried to smile at Polly – his precious girl, so beautiful, so bright and full of life – but he was locked away in that dark place where, in a still moment inside the madness, he had been offered the choice between life and death. He had watched so many husbands and wives say goodbye for ever on *Titanic*'s deck, watched the men step back calmly to accept their deaths, so that their wives would go quietly into the boats. He should have died with them. The thought of the twelve hundred souls who had just now perished in the foggy Irish waters brought fresh to his mind the terrible cries of the hundreds dying in the icy dark on the night *Titanic* sank, the night he had stepped into the lifeboat and left them behind. He felt his heart was breaking all over again.

'I should have died too,' he said, in a voice that cracked with unuse after his long silence. But in that moment – the moment that seemed to go on for ever because he relived it so often – in that moment he had chosen life and, with it, endless guilt. 'I should have let the boat go.'

A tear escaped onto Polly's cheek, and she dashed it away, and sniffed hard, not wanting to cry, because she needed to speak. 'Don't say that, Daddy, *please*. How could you want to be dead? We don't want you dead. We're *glad* you came back. Don't you want to be with us?'

'My darling,' he began, but said nothing more, unable to find the right words. Of *course* he wanted to be with them. Of course he did. But—

'If you love me, you *can't* wish you had died, and never come back, and made us all *miserable*.' On that last, treacherous word, her control broke and she let out a single sob before she caught herself back. 'You did the right thing, Daddy. No-one blames you. Anyone would have done the same.'

But they didn't, he thought wearily. That was the point.

They stepped back and let the boats go, and died like gentlemen. And she was wrong to say no-one blamed him. He blamed himself.

And yet – and yet . . . Life was good. Life was worth holding on to. He loved his children and his family and his home; he loved Yorkshire and England; he did good work, he was useful, and he truly believed his little piece of the world, at least, was a better place for his activities. The chance had been offered him to live – and would it not have been a sin to squander it, to have stepped back and let that place go empty, let his family mourn and his children grow up fatherless?

He should have died, but he had chosen to live – a choice that had not been given to those poor souls on *Lusitania*. A fresh surge of grief rushed through him at the thought of them, but he bore it and let it pass, gripping on to the thought of his family as a man holds on to a rock as a wave piles over him. He had chosen this life, and it was *good*.

Polly watched him anxiously, unable to know how his thoughts ran. But then she saw him smile – a frail, painful smile, but like the first gleam of sunlight through clouds.

'You're right,' he said. 'I am glad to be alive.'

'Oh, Daddy,' she said, and ran round the desk into his arms, and pressed against him, her damp cheek against his. He held her, and stroked her hair, then put her gently away. There were tears on his cheek, she saw, but she did not know if they were her own or his.

'Leave me now, sweetheart,' he said. 'It's all right,' he added, in answer to her look. 'I shall come very soon. Just give me a little while to compose myself. Go on, like a good girl.'

She left him, reluctant but obedient. He sat a while, staring into his mind. He had thought that he might cry a little and then feel better, but his sorrow had sunk back to its accustomed place, where he had grown used to living with it. It would never leave him, he knew, but it was part of the price he must pay for this extension of his life, and he paid it willingly, for the joy he had of Polly, Ned and little James, Alice, Henrietta, Jessie, all his family. He was blessed, perhaps uniquely blessed, and he must never forget that.

They would have special prayers in the chapel tonight, he thought, the whole household together, for the *Lusitania*. The dead must have their rites; but they must pray for the living as well, for the war to be over soon and their people to come safely home to them.

He stood up, straightened his jacket, and started for the door. Muffy looked up at the movement, and at the sight of his master's face knew that he had come back and was feeling better. He jumped up, tail waving, and smiled up at Teddy, hopeful.

'Come on, then.' Teddy said.

Muffy fell in gladly at his heels. Had he not been such an old dog, he would have frisked for joy.

The sinking of *Lusitania* brought furious protest from President Wilson of the United States, and provoked anti-German riots in many parts of England. In Liverpool, a city always especially sensitive to maritime matters, troops had to be called in after three days of rioting caused widespread destruction and showed no sign of ending. More details of the sinking came as the days passed. It seemed there had been two explosions before she turned over and sank, though the U-boat admitted to firing only one torpedo. The German Government issued a statement that the second explosion had been caused by the huge cargo of shells and rifle ammunition that *Lusitania* had been carrying, disguised as bales of fur and boxes of cheese; and claimed that as these goods were clearly contraband in time of war, the U-boat had been within its rights to attack the ship. The British and American governments fiercely denied there was any such cargo.

The US government was particularly incensed by the incident as 128 of those who perished had been American citizens. *Lusitania*, they said, was not in government service, and therefore the attack on her was 'contrary to international law and the conventions of all civilized nations'. Relations between the United States, which had been maintaining a neutral status since the beginning of the war, and Germany became very tense. The German government tried belatedly to mend matters by offering to end submarine sinkings if the blockade against them would allow food through. Grey, the British foreign secretary, recommended accepting the offer, but the Admiralty indignantly refused, and since public opinion had been hardened by the Germans' barbarism in sinking an unarmed passenger ship, the offer was rejected.

A letter from Henrietta to her daughter Lizzie in Flagstaff crossed with one from Lizzie to her. Lizzie, her husband Ashley and their three children had been on *Titanic* the night she foundered, but had all survived to take up their new life in Arizona. The boys, Martial and Rupert, were sixteen and fifteen now, both at high school, and Rose was six.

This terrible business brought it all back to me. I was glad the children were at school because for hours all I could do was sit and cry. The old memories I thought I'd packed away came jumping up as fresh as new paint, only a million times more frightful. Just writing about it makes me cry all over again. Those vile Germans! They aren't fit to share the world with decent people. I can tell you that there is great outrage here. A lot of people are saying we should go to war with Germany. Will it happen? That's government business, I guess. Americans prize their neutrality, but once attack them, and they 'get riled up', as our gardener, Silas, says. The children seem to be coping with it better than me. The boys were rather quiet for an hour or two, but they have so much else on their minds, these days, they soon bounced back.

Rupert is doing very well at sport. He has been chosen for his school teams in baseball and football. I'm afraid these occupy him much more than his lessons. ('Football' is not the sort English children play, but a sort of second cousin to rugby.) Mart is the intellectual one, as you know. He's showing quite a turn for

285

mathematics and engineering. He is building himself an engine at the moment, which he hopes to fit to his bicycle, if you please! I know he feels this new disaster in his quiet way. On the evening of the day the news came in, he said when I kissed him goodnight, 'Do you think they suffered much, Mum? They say drowning isn't bad. I guess it would be being afraid that hurt most.' Rose doesn't remember much about *Titanic* at all, and the news went right over her head in the excitement of getting a star for her reading at school.

Ashley is 'out in the woods' at the moment, looking at some logging prospects in the north of the state. He's been away two weeks already, and I do miss him so, especially now with this horrible thing happening. But I had a lovely letter from Aunt Ruth, and that was a comfort. She says she has fine letters from Lenny, with very droll accounts of army life and Egypt. Aunt Ruth is so wonderful for her age. She says she is mounting a campaign with her Congressman to have the law revoked that says American lads fighting in the British Army must lose their citizenship. It maddens her that Lenny should be punished for doing what she thinks is right. In the light of public feeling about *Lusitania*, I wouldn't be surprised if she succeeds. She has such determination and vigour, I'd back her against President Wilson any day!

Jessie missed the upsets at home because she had already left for London. She was not unhappy to be getting away from the hospital for a while. The work was very hard, and she was very tired; and though the exhaustion had served its purpose for her, she felt a break now would allow her to get her second wind. She had received Bertie's letter on the 30th of April, and one from Ned two days later, and with her immediate fears resolved she was in the right mood for a trip to London.

Violet, she thought, looked extremely well. She came to meet the train as before, with her little dogs under her arm. Her smart coat and dress of brown silk, pearls, light fur wrap, and fashionable hat – small, of brown velvet, and decorated with a gold-coloured hackle in a diamond holder – made her look every inch the Town lady. But there was a difference about her, Jessie thought – an extra sparkle in her eyes and more colour in her cheeks. She laughed with delight as she kissed Jessie, and seemed altogether more animated than the gentle, serene Violet of before.

'Have you heard from Holkam lately?' Jessie asked, trying to think what could have caused this effervescence, as they settled themselves into the motor.

'Not for a few days,' said Violet. 'Why do you ask? Oh, he isn't in any danger. He's at Headquarters with Sir John French. Such trouble Sir John's had with General Smith-Dorrien! He took away his command and then, he says, the man simply wouldn't resign! Holkam said there was no hinting him away, until Sir John gave him a direct order to go home.'

'Does Holkam like working for Sir John?'

'Oh, yes, he admires him very much. But between you and me, he says that Douglas Haig is the coming man. He says the government has no faith in French, and thinks he won't last beyond the year, unless he manages to get some great victory to his credit. So Holkam's been taking pains to make himself known to Haig, and be agreeable to him, ready for the change of command. How is Ned?'

'He's still at Ypres. His battalion had just gone down to rest when the fighting began again. He wrote to me that he's all right, not wounded or anything. Of course, he'll have to go back into the line, unless the Germans quieten down again.'

'It must be a worry for you.' Violet laid a hand over hers.

She nodded. 'All one can do is try to keep one's mind occupied until the next letter comes.'

'I shall do all I can to help you,' said Violet. 'I've lots of lovely things planned. Although,' she added, with an anxious look, 'there are one or two days when I shall have to leave you to your own resources for an hour or two.'

Jessie looked receptive, but Violet didn't elaborate, which was a little of a surprise. But of course she did not have to explain herself, even to Jessie. She smiled. 'That's all right. You don't have to nursemaid me every minute, Violet dear. In any case, I have some duty calls to make.'

The first duty visit Jessie made was to Maud, and was one she wanted to be done with. She hoped that Maud might be out, in which case Maud would have to make the return visit to her at Violet's house, which would mean a very short, formal call. She knocked on the door of the house in Pont Street and it was opened by a maid – the butler remained all the time in the country, at Beaumont Manor. Jessie asked if Lady Parke was at leisure.

'I'm not sure, madam,' the maid said, accepting the proffered card. 'I'll enquire for you.'

She admitted Jessie to the hall and went away upstairs. It would be an interesting situation, Jessie thought, if Maud was in but would not receive her. But the maid came back moments later to say that her ladyship had company but would be glad to see her and showed Jessie up to the drawing-room.

Maud greeted her coolly, but that was merely her way. She was a person without great enthusiasms. She had matured into a handsome woman, well-dressed without being in the forefront of fashion, with calm manners and a rather blank expression, so that Jessie always thought she looked like one of those illustrations in magazines of ladies' modes, where all the detail was in the gown. There was nothing to dislike about her, but Jessie had never quite forgiven her for rejecting her brother Jack, who had been desperately in love with her in his younger days. Of course, if he had married Maud he would never have met Helen, and Jessie loved Helen and thought her perfect for her brother, so it was illogical to blame Maud. But Jessie was as capable of being illogical as the next woman when it came to family. Besides, she could not help feeling there was something wrong with a person who could not love her darling Jackie.

And Maud had married Bertie. Jessie tried not to think

288

about that too often, for her feelings were too uncertain and too dangerous for her to want to probe them.

The 'company' turned out to be not only Maud's father Richard, who lived with her, but a stranger, too.

Richard greeted her warmly, shaking her hand in both his, and asked after her uncle. She said Uncle Teddy was very well, while remarking to herself that Richard Puddephat had aged a great deal since she last saw him. He was only a few years older than Uncle Teddy, but he looked ten, and thin and frail into the bargain. But he seemed cheerful and animated, which perhaps was something to do with the visitor, for he led her to him at once with the air of bestowing a great compliment.

'Do allow me to present a very dear friend, who is visiting from India, and has done us the honour of staying with us in our humble house while he conducts some business. This is Lord Manvers – John Manvers – Mrs Ned Morland.'

Jessie extended her hand to the man who had stood up, of course, as soon as she came in, revealing himself to be both unusually tall and very well-built. He towered over her, and her hand disappeared entirely in his, but, when she looked up at him, his smile was charming, and there was nothing at all threatening about him. She took him to be in his middle forties, but there was no thread of grey in his thick brown hair. His face was rather brown and weather-lined, as one would expect, but it was lean and firm, with strong, regular features – handsome, she would have said, but with the sort of handsomeness that comes from good character, pleasant temper and an affectionate heart. He was the sort of person, she thought, whom you would trust instantly – with his air of capability and his big, strong body – to take care of you in any situation.

'Mrs Morland,' he said. 'I'm delighted to meet you.' He smiled as if he really was.

'I hope I'm not intruding,' she said. 'You must have so much to say to your old friends.'

'Oh, we've got over that sort of thing by now,' he said. 'I arrived yesterday and I had a long session with Richard last night.'

289

'Won't you sit down?' Maud said. Jessie looked at her, and saw that she was gesturing her to a chair; but Manvers still had hold of Jessie's hand, and he sat on the settle, taking Jessie down with him to sit beside him. She couldn't help noticing that Maud's cheeks were a little pink, and wondered what in the last few moments could have upset her.

Richard took the chair Maud had meant for Jessie, and, sitting forward eagerly, explained, 'John is a horseman too, you know. He used to find horses in Ireland for me, when I was too busy to go over there. A great eye for a horse – and great hands too,' he added, with a laugh. Manvers opened and spread them for inspection, smiling. 'He can ride a horse and lead three others. Hold a wild stallion as if it were a newborn foal. But for all their size and strength, they're as gentle as a woman's. I'd trust any horse's mouth to him.'

'Father, you're embarrassing him,' Maud rebuked.

Manvers smiled at her. 'Embarrassed by praise? I think you have mistaken me for a modest man. I'm purring like a tea-kettle.'

Jessie laughed, but noted that Maud's blush had increased. Did she dislike being teased by this man? It was very gentle teasing. No, she wasn't upset – it was something else. She was looking at Manvers with more warmth than her cool eyes usually betrayed.

'And what do you do in India?' Jessie asked him.

'I farm,' he said. 'I have an estate where I grow wheat, millet and sugar – cash crops – and I breed horses, but that's more of a hobby.'

'Polo ponies?' Jessie asked with interest. 'Do you play?'

'Mrs Morland, you can't have looked at me properly,' he said. 'If I tried to mount a polo pony, my feet would touch the ground on either side and the poor thing would run out from under me. No, no, I breed racehorses. Though what effect this wretched war is going to have on the racing calendar we can't yet tell. So many of our best people away. Mind you, I'm in better case than if I *had* bred polo ponies.

That depends almost entirely on the army. I should be bankrupt already if I had gone that way.'

'The army took mine,' Jessie said. 'And my hunters. Of course, one has to do one's bit, but I don't imagine army life is kind to them.'

'You breed horses as well?' he asked, his eyes lighting up.

'I was just about to tell you so,' said Richard, and plunged into an explanation of the Morland-Puddephat-Parke connection, which led to a satisfying conversation about what Jessie did, what Lord Manvers did, and horses in general. From little hints dropped, Jessie gathered he had been quite a wild character in his youth, travelling the world in a gypsy manner until India finally captured his heart and he settled down. He was in England to interview his bank and rearrange finances, and also to buy some things he felt were better done here than in India. 'Like saddles, clothes, books and so on. I make a trip every couple of years. And I was hoping to buy some horses, but I'm afraid the army has them all.'

'Can't you get horses in India?' Jessie asked.

'Yes, but they're all so small. Not up to my size and weight. I breed my own saddle horses because I have to, and I'd hoped to find some new breeding stock while I was here. Well, I shall have to make do, it seems.'

'You might still find something in Ireland,' Richard said. 'It hasn't been denuded in the same way.'

Manvers opened his mouth to speak, but Maud broke in: 'You aren't going to Ireland, are you? I thought you were staying here for your whole visit.'

Manvers looked at her kindly. 'I hadn't thought of it until this moment. But I should be sorry to go away when I am made so welcome.'

Maud met his eyes, and a sort of confusion seemed to pass through her own. She turned to Jessie and said abruptly, 'But we haven't asked what brings you to London.'

'I – I'm staying with my cousin Violet,' Jessie said, surprised at the change of direction.

'Ah, yes, of course. One sees Lady Holkam everywhere, and she's never out of the illustrated papers. She's very active

291

in war work, I believe. My own branch of the Red Cross is very busy at the moment making gas masks. The War Office sent out instructions and we provided the gauze and cotton wool. We've sent off a hundred already to the Army Clothing Department, in Pimlico, and they sent a very kind letter back, saying our effort was outstanding.'

'You must be very proud,' Jessie said.

'Well, we like to think that we do our bit for the war effort. The War Office want half a million of them as a temporary measure, until they can manufacture something more substantial, so in view of the emergency, we gave up all our other activities to concentrate on it.'

She glanced at Manvers, who responded with a warm look and said, 'Nothing can be more important than protecting our brave soldiers from the gas. I've read about its terrible effects.' Maud was pleased by the comment.

'Have you heard from Bertie recently?' Jessie asked, realising that he had not been mentioned so far. It was a natural progression in her thoughts from the mention of the gas, but Maud looked surprised, and then her face became its usual cool blank.

'I had a letter yesterday,' she said, 'but it doesn't say much about the situation in France. He asked a lot of questions about the state of things at Beaumont, which I am quite unable to answer – questions about stock and milk yields and crops and so on. I sent it on to his agent, which I suppose must be what he meant me to do, for he really couldn't have expected me to know what he was talking about.' She sounded a little cross.

'Have you been at Beaumont recently?' Jessie asked.

'No, not since October, when my father and I had a small shooting party there. I prefer to live in London, and so does Father.'

'True, my love, but I should like Manvers to see it. My son-in-law has the makings of a fine herd of beef cattle down there. Are you interested in cattle, John?'

'I am indeed, and I should like to see them,' Manvers replied.

But this did not seem to suit Maud. 'There's nothing to look at in a herd of cattle, Father. And there's no need for us to go down. The agent handles everything.'

'But – don't you go down to see your little boy?' Jessie asked, puzzled.

Maud raised her eyebrows, and then said calmly, 'Oh, I understand you. You thought little Richard was at Beaumont? No, he lives here with us now. So much more convenient.'

'He's a splendid boy,' Richard said eagerly. 'Would you like to see him?'

'Oh, Father, our guests don't want to be bothered with a child,' Maud said. But Richard had already rung the bell, and when the parlour-maid appeared he gave the summons. In the interval that followed, in which there was inconsequential talk, Jessie observed the faces around her and concluded that the only person who really wanted the child brought down was Richard. Maud did not, for some reason, and was looking a little pink and vexed; Lord Manvers seemed either bored or uncomfortable; and Jessie was afraid of what she would feel on being presented for the first time with Bertie's son.

A nursery-maid in a much-frilled cap came in holding little Richard by the hand. He was three years old, a sturdy little boy in knickerbockers, fair-haired and blue-eyed and just a little solemn at being sent for so suddenly to meet strangers. Like most children he was an intriguing mixture of his parents in appearance, and as both mother and father were good-looking he seemed likely to grow up handsome. Jessie thought he had Bertie's eyes, and as his shyness wore off and he warmed into liveliness, she could see his father in him, not so much in his features as in his expressions, as though a faint ghost of Bertie lived behind the child's face and looked out now and then through the pliant flesh. It plucked at her heart in a way that was both agonising and delightful. Did Maud know how lucky she was? If only he could have been hers. When the child confided in her, 'My daddy's at the Front. I'm going to be a soldier too when I grow up,' she found there was a lump in her throat that prevented her from answering. Her lost baby – her failure to give Ned an heir – her convoluted feelings for Bertie – her worry for both – all churned painfully inside her.

The nursery visit did not last long. Maud sent the child away, and soon after that Jessie rose to take her leave. Richard parted with her fondly; Manvers towered over her hand and proclaimed himself delighted to have met her, with a crinkle of the eyes that conveyed sincerity; and Maud said she would walk downstairs with her, a great civility Jessie had not expected.

She soon discovered its purpose. When they were alone on the stairs, Maud said, 'I should have prevented my father from having my boy brought down. I'm sorry. I had forgotten for a moment about your miscarriage. I expect seeing little Richard brought back painful memories for you.'

Was that why she had looked unwilling? She had not thought Maud so sensitive. 'It was quite all right,' she said, struggling with her feelings. 'He's a lovely child.'

'He is,' said Maud, 'and that must make the contrast between your own unfortunate situation and my happy one all the stronger.' Jessie blinked at that, but Maud did not mean to be unkind, she thought: it was only that she was unimaginative. Maud went on, her eyes on the middle distance: 'Yes, I always think it's a comfort that, if anything should happen to Bertie, I would still have his son to remember him by. But you would have nothing at all, if Ned should be killed. It would be almost as though you had never been married. That would be so terrible for you, to be left with nothing. I do feel for you.'

It was all Jessie could do to say goodbye, shake hands, and hurry out of the house without letting tears get the better of her. Outside she almost scrambled into Violet's motor, heartily glad that her friend had insisted she take it, so that she did not have to deal with a cab just then. In its leathern seclusion she took a deep breath and composed herself. Surely Maud could not have meant to be unkind? No, no, it was just a little tactlessness. Anyway, she couldn't expect people to treat her with kid gloves for ever. But Jessie was glad all the same that it was over for another year. She could never be easy in Maud's presence.

Her second visit, on the next day that Violet was otherwise engaged, she undertook with considerable curiosity and far more expectation of pleasure. She had promised Frank that she would visit Maria Stanhope, and she set out one Tuesday late in the morning with the hope of being able to take her to luncheon. Since she didn't know beforehand what day Violet would be busy, she could not give any warning, but she knew Miss Stanhope always took sandwiches to work with her, so she was unlikely to be already engaged. She set off for Bloomsbury in a state of keen anticipation, wondering what the woman who had so dazzled her unsusceptible brother would be like. She had promised Frank that she would write to his beloved, but had not yet got round to it, which made her feel rather guilty. Well, she would put that right today – give her luncheon, thoroughly get to know her.

It was perhaps lucky that Violet had again insisted she take the motor, with its coat of arms on the side panel, for the gatekeeper sprang to attention and admitted her to the front yard and, on learning her destination, summoned a beadle to escort her up there. On the way up the stairs, the beadle, a solid, grizzled individual in dark livery, confided that Mr Benson, the librarian, wasn't much for visitors but he dared say he'd make an exception in her case.

From this Jessie gathered that Mr Benson was the dragon to be slain before she could reach the maiden, and made up her mind to charm him. The beadle presented her, then added something to the librarian in a voice too low for Jessie to make it out, but she guessed that it was something about her arriving in the Earl of Holkam's car.

Benson was a smallish, desiccated man in a dusty-looking suit with a heavy gold chain across the fob. He had stiff white eyebrows like an Airedale terrier, and faded blue eyes that looked at her severely over the top of half-moon spectacles. He seemed about to say something crushing to her, so she got her word in first, offering her hand with a warm smile so that he could not refuse to shake it without being rude.

'It's so kind of you to allow me to interrupt you. I know you must be tremendously busy. But, goodness, what a wonderful library! It must have taken years to assemble so many books. How proud you must be of it! Would you tell me something of its history?'

It seemed to be the right approach for, though not exactly chatty, Benson became moderately eloquent about his library and its origins. Jessie listened with her eyes fixed on his face and a look of admiration on hers. She had always got on well with elderly men, and had formed the opinion that they were generally crusty with women because they felt women took no interest in them; but flatter them with a request for their opinion or some story of their salad days, and they thawed. In the end it was with something almost approaching a twinkle that Benson interrupted himself to say, 'But I'm sure you didn't come here to learn the history of my library, Mrs Morland. Your brother could surely tell you anything you want to know in that respect.'

Jessie managed to dimple at him. 'You know who I am?'

'Of course. Mr Frank Compton's connection with the Morland family and the Holkams is well known. He has been a great addition to this university, and his absence in uniform is a loss to us all. Might I enquire if you have any news of him?'

'Only that he is in Malta, but fretting to get to the Front.'

'The impetuosity of youth,' Benson said, though not as if he really condemned it. Perhaps, Jessie thought, he wished he could go too.

'If you know who I am, I expect you have guessed my mission. With your kind approval, I would very much like to take Miss Stanhope to luncheon.'

He cooled a fraction. 'Miss Stanhope may do anything she pleases in her luncheon hour. It is not for me to dictate.

But her luncheon hour does not begin until one o'clock.' He drew out a fat gold hunter from the fob pocket and opened it. 'It is now five-and-twenty minutes before the hour.'

Jessie regrouped. 'Then I will not trespass any more on your valuable time, Mr Benson, but could I trouble you to convey a message to Miss Stanhope for me? That I should be honoured by her company at luncheon, and that I will wait for her in the motor in the forecourt.'

Benson bowed slightly in consent, and asked if she required a beadle to show her the way out.

So it was not in her own environment but in the college courtyard that Jessie first set eyes on Maria Stanhope. At a few minutes past one she came hurrying out and down the steps, looking about her with a frown. Jessie murmured a word to the chauffeur and he came round to open the door for Jessie to step out. Miss Stanhope saw her, and came across with an odd mixture of haste and reluctance. 'Mrs Morland?' she said doubtfully, her eyes going past Jessie to the coat of arms on the panel.

Jessie smiled. 'Yes, it is me. Don't worry about the motor – it's borrowed.'

Miss Stanhope smiled too, but not all the reserve left her face. She was smaller than Jessie, and looked up at her from under her brows, and with her brown eyes and thick curly brown hair she made Jessie think of a wary animal approaching an outstretched human hand. Would it caress or strike? Jessie thought her not pretty exactly, but certainly striking, with her dark eyes and pale skin – too pale for convention, the result of working long hours indoors, perhaps; and she was too thin, as well. But it gave her an air of delicacy, which, along with the strength of her features, made an intriguing combination. Her clothes, a dark blue jacket and skirt over a lighter blue blouse, were well kept, but out of fashion and probably much mended. The lapels of the jacket had that lighter, rubbed look along the edges from old age that nothing can disguise; the skirt had been neatly repaired where it had been ripped at some point near the hem; and the hat had been made over not once, she guessed, but many times. But the blouse was spotless and crisp, with beautiful pin-tucking down the front. It came to her in a flash of insight that Miss Stanhope wore a blue blouse rather than the conventional white because she took off her jacket in the library, and handling old books would be a grubby business.

All these things Jessie noticed and thought in a flash, and as she had been poor herself in her childhood she felt a sympathy with this young woman who had to make do and mend as the Comptons once had. It must have been worse for Miss Stanhope to bear, for Jessie had been a child and not much interested in her appearance. Miss Stanhope was a young woman who had to go out in the world, and probably suffered endless pinpricks of pitying or contemptuous looks from better-off young ladies, and the worse humiliation of seeing the eyes of young men slide over her as if she weren't there. What must she have thought when Frank suddenly noticed her?

'Do step in,' she said. 'I promised Frank I would come and see you if I came to London, so I hope you don't think it impertinent of me to descend on you like this and carry you off to luncheon, but I did so much want to meet you.'

'It's very kind of you,' Miss Stanhope said, 'but I only have an hour. I must be back by two o'clock or Mr Benson will be angry.'

'I understand that,' Jessie said. 'So shall we go? It's the benefit of having borrowed a motor than I can whisk you off so much more quickly.'

Miss Stanhope offered no more objections but stepped into the car. Jessie, who had been intending to lunch at the Ritz, as being a suitable environment for two unaccompanied ladies, changed her mind and told Dawson to take them instead to Selfridges, where the restaurant, she felt, would not seem so intimidating to her guest.

Miss Stanhope sat rather stiffly, and on the edge of her seat, holding on to the side strap, as though at any moment she might be ordered to leave. Jessie wondered what she

298

could do to put the young woman at ease, and decided that any more intimate conversation would have to wait until they were facing each other at a table. For now, she explained her own presence.

'Lady Holkam was my childhood friend – our mothers are cousins – and every now and then, when I have a fancy for a taste of luxury, she lets me come and stay with her. She is the kindest person, though her way of life and mine are so far apart. It's a particularly strong contrast this time because I've been nursing in a hospital for the last month, and nothing could be more different.'

She thought that neatly set out her credentials for being more on Miss Stanhope's side of the wealth divide than on the Holkams'. The last part certainly caught Miss Stanhope's attention, and she asked, 'You've been nursing? That must be very interesting. How did you come to do that?'

Since it was obvious that she was more comfortable listening than talking, Jessie told her about Matron Kemble and Sister Morgan and her hard and dirty work and made it sound light and amusing, with funny stories about her mishaps. But Miss Stanhope saw through that and said, 'I think what you are doing is very fine, and I honour you for it. So many people talk about "doing their bit" but never actually do anything that inconveniences them in the slightest.'

'My family all thought I was mad,' Jessie said with a smile. 'But my husband is at the Front, and I must say that it takes one's mind off wonderfully. I'm so tired at the end of the day that I don't have any trouble falling asleep. Ah, here we are.'

Selfridges was unusually busy, and when they reached the restaurant it seemed to be completely full. The reason was not far to seek – Ivor Novello was singing and accompanying himself on the piano. The restaurant manager explained that it was in aid of the relief of the wounded, and that a collection box would be brought round later; but apologised that the only table he had left was on the far side, well away from the piano and in what was evidently an unfavoured corner near the service doors.

Jessie didn't mind at all. Since she wanted to talk privately to Frank's young lady it was positively a benefit, and she accepted promptly. When they sat down and a stray sunbeam from the window lit Miss Stanhope's face, she noted that it was not only pale and thin but looked tired, and it came to her that the poor thing was probably hungry. So though she was not particularly hungry herself, she ordered heartily in the hope that Miss Stanhope would take that as licence to do likewise. It worked: Miss Stanhope said she would have the same. She refused wine, saying with a small smile that Mr Benson would be horrified if he smelt it on her breath, so Jessie ordered lemonade for them both.

'This restaurant does an excellent Italian vegetable soup,' Jessie said, to break the silence when the waiter had departed. 'It's one of their specialities.'

Miss Stanhope showed her character by saying at once, with a direct look, 'I'm sure you didn't bring me here to talk about the food. Please, won't you tell me what it is you wanted to say?'

From the shadow in her eyes she evidently thought it was going to be painful, and she was facing up to it rather than trying to run away. Jessie admired her for that. She smiled and said, 'Don't look so apprehensive. What can I have to say to you that would be so bad?'

'That you don't want me to see Frank – your brother – any more.'

'Why on earth should I do that?'

'Mrs Morland, please, don't toy with me. It must be as obvious to you as it is to me that I am not his social equal. It would be natural for his family to disapprove.'

'In the first place, Frank hasn't told anyone in the family but me. In the second place, he wouldn't listen to me if I tried to persuade him to give you up. And in the third place, I have no desire whatever to do so.' Miss Stanhope began to speak and Jessie went on quickly: 'As to your not being Frank's social equal, I think that's perfect nonsense, and you will oblige me by not talking in that vein any more.'

300

Miss Stanhope managed a tense smile, but said, 'You are very kind. But I have to tell you that there is no understanding between Mr Compton and me. We are – we are not engaged. In fact, marriage has never been spoken of.'

Jessie saw it all now. Miss Stanhope thought that Frank had gone away to the war and that she would never see him again. She thought his family had frightened him off declaring himself before he went, and that Jessie was here to put the final nail in the coffin of her hopes, in case she decided to pursue Frank when he returned. Impulsively she reached across the table and placed her hand on Miss Stanhope's.

'Oh, my dear!' she said. 'Frank loves you very much. He told me so in the most heartfelt terms. The only reason he didn't declare himself to you before he went away was that he thought it wasn't fair to you. I told him he was a fool and a villain, and that any girl would rather have the offer made and choose for herself whether it was fair or not – but men are odd creatures. Their ideas of nobility are different from ours. He said he didn't know how long he would be away or when he would be able to marry you if you accepted, and that it was unfair to make you tie yourself down, when you might meet someone else while you were waiting whom you liked more – or at any rate someone who had better prospects.'

'The idiot!' Miss Stanhope said fiercely, and Jessie laughed.

'Quite. Miss Stanhope – may I call you Maria? I know we've only just met, but as I hope one day that you will be my sister—'

'Of course,' she said, with a blush at the last words.

'And please will you call me Jessie?'

The soup arrived at that moment. Maria addressed hers with a barely controlled eagerness, which made Jessie sure she had been right about her being hungry, so she didn't bother her with conversation until their bowls were empty. A slight touch of colour now warmed the pale cheeks, and the dark eyes were brighter. As she laid down her spoon,

301

Maria said, 'Mrs Morland – Jessie, I mean – please tell me: did he really say he loved me?'

'Yes. And he said he couldn't imagine life without you. I hope you love him?'

'Oh, *yes*!'

'Well, that's a relief,' said Jessie. 'It could all have been very embarrassing otherwise.'

Maria laughed. 'Would you have walked out and left me to pay the bill?'

'Very likely. I am very fond of Frankie, you know.'

'I can't imagine how anyone could feel otherwise.'

'Well, there's my brother Robbie. I think he always regarded Frank with mystification. No-one understands quite what it is he does in the university. He tried to explain quanta to me once, but without much success. However, now he's "'listed for a soldier", Rob feels more comfortable with him. Frankie always loved to play at soldiers when he was a boy, so I think Rob believes the mathematical stuff was an aberration and that he's reverting to his true nature.'

'It must be wonderful to have a large family.'

'Well, it is, rather. It's especially nice to be the only girl. I used to lord it over them terribly when we were all little.' She talked about her childhood and Morland Place, breaking off when the cutlets arrived.

When the waiter had departed again, Maria said, a little shyly, 'Have you had a letter from Frank since he went to Malta?'

'Yes, just before I came to London. I brought it with me, so you can read it if you like, though it isn't very interesting, only about the journey there and settling in. But it reminded me that I had been very remiss about writing to *you*, as he asked me, so I thought I'd make amends by giving you luncheon.'

'He wanted you to write to me?'

'I told him if he got engaged to you he could write to you himself.' She looked at her companion's expression and added, in imitation, '*The idiot!*'

They both laughed. With food inside her and the apprehension removed, Maria Stanhope became a different person. She sparkled, entertaining Jessie with wide-ranging conversation, and in her animation looking so much beyond pretty that Jessie thought her really beautiful. It was no wonder dull old Frank had been captivated. The mystery was why Maria loved him, and since Jessie acquitted her of any mercenary motive, she decided it must be because Maria was extremely clever herself and therefore could appreciate Frank's brain as his stupid sister could not.

By the end of luncheon – after apple pie and custard sauce – Jessie felt they were friends. It was sad, she thought, that the lovers should be parted, and that their prospects were so distant. It might be years before the war ended, despite everyone's saying it could not go on beyond 1916, and then it might be years more before Frank earned enough to be able to afford an establishment. But if Jessie had learnt anything today, it was that there was no likelihood Maria Stanhope would meet anyone she liked more. She had given her heart, and her character was such that she would never be able to take it back again. Jessie determined to write a stiff letter to Frank on the subject of declaring himself and getting engaged as soon as he possibly could. Maria deserved to have that comfort, at least, while they were forced to remain apart.

The waiter returned to suggest coffee, and Maria seemed suddenly brought back to the present, and asked Jessie what the time was. It was a quarter past two. Her face paled at the news and only good manners prevented her from leaping to her feet. 'I must get back! I shall be in such trouble for being late. What will Mr Benson say?'

'The bill, please, at once,' Jessie said to the waiter, and to Maria, 'Please don't worry. I'll get you back as quickly as possible, and explain to Mr Benson that it was all my fault.'

Maria didn't look comforted. She evidently thought Jessie's influence with Mr Benson not worth the mention. 'What will I do if I lose my job?' she mourned, but in a quiet voice.

'He shan't dismiss you,' Jessie said firmly, though she knew, too, that she had no control over the matter. It brought the difficulty of Maria's situation into sharp focus. Jessie's family had been poor in her childhood – they had almost been homeless at one time – but since they had gone to live at Morland Place she had never had to worry about her next meal, or the roof over her head. Maria, she understood, was worried about precisely those things. While Jessie worked hard at the hospital because she wanted to, Maria went to work because she had to. She felt guilty that she had so lightly let her stay beyond her hour and not kept an eye on the time.

So when they got back to the college, she insisted on going up to the library with Maria, and approached Mr Benson with a frank apology.

'I am so very sorry. It is entirely my fault that Miss Stanhope is late. I was enjoying my conversation with her so much I forgot to look at the time. Please promise me you won't be angry with her. I shall never let such a thing happen again.'

Benson did not go so far as to soften his expression, but he did say, 'I hardly expected anything else when you took her away in your motor-car. A lady in your position cannot, of course, understand the discipline of regimented hours. But as I can see that Miss Stanhope could hardly *force* you to bring her back on time, I shall say nothing more about the matter – this time.'

'You are very kind,' Jessie said, offering her hand again, so that he could hardly avoid taking it. 'I feel very guilty, and I'm glad you have been so just as to pour your anger on me, not on her, for indeed she couldn't help it.'

'I think you are making game of me, Mrs Morland. You cannot think I would presume to express anger towards you.'

Jessie managed another dimple. 'You would be perfectly within your rights. But I'm glad to be spared. I do most truly apologise for disrupting your day.'

He could only say something gracious in the face of her

penitence, and Jessie took her leave, hoping she had done enough. If she were to meet Miss Stanhope again, she thought, she must make sure it was when her working day was done.

CHAPTER THIRTEEN

Where did Violet go? She never spoke about it, and in the absence of any such confidence it was impossible for Jessie to ask. It was a puzzle, because Violet had never kept any secrets from her. Logic intervened to remind her that if Violet *had* kept secrets, Jessie would not know about them; but Violet's nature had always been simple and straightforward, and it did not seem *like* her to do anything *sub rosa*. When Jessie met her just coming in after one of these absences, she had smiled and murmured something vague and gone straight upstairs, and she had seemed to Jessie to have a – a sort of *glow* about her, something that made her look more beautiful than ever. Whatever it was it had gone by the time she came downstairs again and she was just the same open, friendly, gentle, gloriously lovely Violet of old. Had she, perhaps, Jessie wondered, discovered some secret and unusually efficacious spa in London? But then it would not be like Violet to keep the knowledge to herself. She might not want everyone in London to know, but she would have told Jessie about it.

No, it was a mystery beyond solving, and Jessie obliged her mind, in courtesy, to drop the subject. In between, her London visit was all pleasure. Violet had determined that her friend should see all the best of the shows, plays, exhibitions and other highlights of the Season, and had the tickets bought and the parties arranged. She also had invitations to dinners, *soirées* and dances (she had so many, in

306

fact, that she had to – as Jessie described it – 'winnow them out', and accept only those she thought would most amuse her friend). And in between, there were shopping, morning-visits and luncheons with Violet's 'set'. As promised, she always had an escort arranged for Jessie – some attractive and amusing young man, generally in uniform – to give her his arm, attend to her wants at table, dance with her, or entertain her with light and lively talk as the occasion demanded.

Despite the heavy programme of jollity, there were still opportunities for the two of them just to sit and chat. One morning, when they were late rising after an evening party, a message was brought to Jessie with her tea asking if she would care to have her breakfast in her ladyship's room. She put on a wrapper and hurried along, and found Violet sitting up in bed in a froth of lace and silk, with a heap of mail and her two little dogs for company.

'I thought it would save trouble if we had trays this morning rather than setting the breakfast table,' Violet said. 'Emma's still asleep, so we can have a quiet coze, just by ourselves.' She looked at Jessie with almost naked longing.

Jessie laughed. 'What a lovely idea. It will be just like old times, when we came out together.'

Of course, in those days all their conversation had revolved around getting married, which was supposed to be the end of the journey and the beginning of all delight. She suspected that, in both their cases, marriage hadn't answered their girl-hood dreams. Violet claimed to be content with her husband, though she and Holkam seemed to lead quite separate lives. But Violet had always hated the physical side of marriage, so perhaps the separation was comfortable to her. And though Jessie had known Ned all her life, he was still alien in his maleness, and their frequent quarrels had stemmed from her failure to understand his mind, and his inability to understand hers. What it came down to, she thought, was that their marriages had left both of them lonely, and she wondered, in a moment of piercing sadness, whether it was always so.

But this morning it did seem a little like old times. A small table was set up to one side of the bed, and the maids brought in two breakfast trays. Fitzjames House breakfasts were always delicious, and over buttered eggs, crisp bacon and wonderful pink field mushrooms, with toast, butter and marmalade and lots of hot, aromatic coffee, the two young women talked and laughed – chattered, even – and the May sunshine outside the window was not warmer than the feeling of ease and affection inside. The sadnesses of their respective adulthoods faded away. Jessie forgot her dead babies, her aching failure to provide Ned with a child, the miserable sense of alienation from him when he had come to say goodbye to go overseas. Violet forgot that for a long time her beloved husband had forbidden her to see or even write to her parents; and that now that they had their three children and did not need to have sexual congress any more, Holkam kept company with brash young women with dyed hair and over-bright faces and clothes. He was discreet about it – she had only found out by accident – but it hurt her pride that he preferred them to her, the sort of females on whom the smell of cheap scent did not quite disguise the fact that they did not wash enough.

They could not always breakfast like that, because it would have been unfair to Emma, but now and then, after a very late evening, Violet would decree 'trays in the morning', and Jessie would be woken with the polite enquiry, and hurry along to Violet's lacy bower. It was a little secret extra treat for two old friends.

So all in all Jessie was having a lovely time in London. The only thing she missed was outdoor exercise. Violet did not ride and seldom walked – except the length of Bond Street, as she looked at the shops – and since they were almost always together, Jessie got no exercise either. She missed riding, the open moors, the smell of the unused air – so different from London's warm and laden effusions. But she enjoyed her dips into Violet's life enormously, and relished the ways in which it was so different from her own. Violet was a kind and generous companion and a dear friend, and after the miseries of the winter and the hard work she had put in at the hospital, it was lovely to relax and simply enjoy herself.

On the 9th of May there had been another battle in the vicinity of Neuve Chapelle, with the renewed intention of capturing Aubers Ridge. It had been a joint venture with the French under Joffre, and the British commanded by Sir Douglas Haig. The French had met with some success: they had prepared the way with a long and heavy bombardment, and had taken some important ground, before a lack of reserves, who were being held too far back, had forced them to halt and then retire.

The British bombardment had done little good. There was simply not enough of it to begin with; and then, shockingly, something like a third of the shells were 'duds' – the new word – which failed to explode on impact, while others did not properly fit the guns they were meant for. The barrage had had little effect on the heavily defended German trenches – had hardly even damaged the barbed wire. The infantry assault had followed, but it had gained no ground, and losses were heavy: eleven thousand men and four hundred and fifty officers had fallen that day, mown down by German machine-guns and artillery as they struggled to reach the ridge. When darkness fell and the survivors began to make their way back to safety, General Haig had ordered a renewed attack on the 10th. During the night the troops had attempted to regroup, but it had emerged the following morning that there were simply not enough shells and rifle ammunition for another assault, and it was cancelled.

Some days later the Overtons were dining at the Sandowns' house in Piccadilly. It was a large party, and the Asquiths were among the guests. The time came for the ladies to withdraw, and Venetia gave a secret backward glance at Overton, and a roll of the eyes, for she disliked the practice heartily. But, he told himself, there were several political wives present, so there might be a more interesting conversation than the usual servants-and-children; and the very presence of Margot Asquith promised that the talk would not flag. Venetia did not like her, and found her constant self-aggrandisement irritating ('I've only to mention someone in the public eye for her to say, "Oh, he's so fond of me – we're *such* friends"') but there was no doubt she had plenty to say on important topics and had as little patience as Venetia for the domestic.

The gentlemen began changing places at the dining-table, walking about to stretch their legs, forming and re-forming conversational groups. In all this movement it was easy enough for the prime minister to draw Overton, with a nod and a gesture, into the ante-room. Overton followed and closed the door behind him, shutting out the sounds of male voices and the smell of cigar smoke, and walked over to the small table where Asquith was leaning on his hands, looking at a report he had placed there.

'I'm sorry to take you away from your port and cigar,' he said. 'I shan't keep you long, but I wanted to consult you informally about something, and there's no privacy at Downing Street. Tell me, what do you make of this?'

Overton took it up and read it. It was a memorandum from Sir John French, in which he laid the blame for the failure at Aubers Ridge squarely on the shortage of muni-tions. He said he had repeatedly complained to the War Office about the shortage of shells, but without result. As evidence, he attached copies of correspondence between himself and the War Office on the subject.

'I imagine Sir John's state of mind is not news to you,' said Asquith, as Overton looked up from the papers, eyebrows raised.

'I'm aware there has been a current of hostility between him and Lord Kitchener for some time,' Overton agreed, 'ever since K visited him in France wearing full field-marshal's uniform – which was tactless on Sir John's own ground. And K dislikes and distrusts Sir John.'

Asquith moved a hand. He had no interest in gossip. It had been said of him that he shook off intrigue as a dog

310

shook off water. 'I was referring to his opinion about the shortage of ammunition.'

'As to that, we've all heard the rumblings,' Overton said. Rumours had been passing around drawing-rooms and clubs for some time now.

'Just so,' said Asquith. 'But Lord Kitchener assured me categorically that there *is* no shortage. He said the supply of shells was adequate, and I had no alternative but to accept his word. He is, after all, the secretary of state for war; and the prime minister,' he concluded wryly, 'is not sent copies of War Office correspondence.'

Overton knew that the War Office and the Admiralty liked to operate in secrecy, both from each other and from the government of the day. They claimed it was necessary in time of war, for reasons of national security. A soldier to his boots, Overton had always thought it folly to consult politicians about military strategy; but equally it was folly to keep them in complete ignorance of what was going on. He had some sympathy with the prime minister.

'Three weeks ago,' Asquith continued, his dry voice passionless, his dry face as disinterested as a lawyer's, 'I made a public speech in Newcastle, declaring there was no shortage of munitions, and that the rumours were all humbug. It was extensively reported in all the newspapers. And now *this*,' he gestured towards the papers, 'is to be the subject of a front-page story in *The Times* tomorrow.'

'*The Times*? Oh, good Lord!'

'You know what Northcliffe thinks of the government,' Asquith said. 'He will not fail to make the most sensational use of it. I shall be made to look a fool and a poltroon. More seriously, the confidence of the public may be shaken.'

'But how did Northcliffe get hold of it?' Overton asked.

Asquith explained. It seemed that the newspaper's military correspondent, Colonel Charles Repington, had tried to interview Sir Douglas Haig after the battle of Aubers Ridge. Haig brushed him off brusquely, too busy to talk to journalists, so Repington went instead to Sir John French. French was already seething because his repeated

311

complaints had been ignored. He had watched the battle from a church tower and was convinced that there had not been enough of a bombardment. He had husbanded every shell and round he could garner for this joint assault, leaving other parts of the line dangerously short, but it had not been nearly enough. The attack had failed – at great expense of his men's lives – for lack of ammunition.

And the last straw was that he had just received a direct order from Lord Kitchener to release twenty thousand rounds of his precious ammunition at once, to be sent to the Dardanelles! Repington had arrived just in time to see Sir John reach the end of his tether. In the wake of the Aubers Ridge failure, it was too much. The enemy had ammunition to waste, while his men were rationed to so many rounds per gun per day. How could he fight a war in those conditions? He had told Repington, and Repington was going to tell the world: British soldiers had died at Aubers Ridge because the army was short of shells.

'How did you come by these documents?' Overton asked. 'Surely Northcliffe would not risk your spoiling his "scoop"?'

'Sir John French asked Repington to hold off his story until tomorrow, while he sent three copies by hand to Lloyd George, Balfour and Bonar Law.'

The opposition, Overton thought: Balfour and Bonar Law of the official opposition, Lloyd George the enemy within – the man who wanted Asquith's job.

'Fortunately,' Asquith concluded, 'someone ensured that a copy also fell into my hands. The Cabinet leaks we all deplore have had their use in this case.'

It was always difficult to tell when Asquith was making a joke, so Overton forbore to smile. The situation was grave enough, in all conscience. 'This will explode like a bomb when it hits the streets tomorrow,' he said.

'It's an extremely unpleasant situation,' said Asquith, where another man would have cried, *It's the devil of a mess!* 'I foresee endless trouble.' And he looked, and sounded, as though he could hardly bear the thought of it: the lines had settled in his face since the turn of the year; his pale, level eyes were bistred. 'What I wanted to ask you,' he went on, drawing himself together, the veil descending again over his expression, 'was your opinion, as someone who knows both parties personally: is there really a shortage? French says there is. Kitchener says that French is too extravagant with shells. And he hints that he complains about a shortage in order to cover his own failures. Who is telling the truth? You may be sure that anything you say will go no further.'

Overton had guessed what was coming and had his answer ready. He had no wish to abuse either man, having affection and respect, in different ways, for both. But bigger things were at stake and the truth must be told. 'Lord Kitchener is used to wars on quite a different scale, fought in quite a different way. I don't think he can conceive how so much ammunition *can* be less than ample. He believes it must be enough, and so he says that it *is* enough. But the truth is that Sir John *has* been severely hampered by lack of munitions, of shells in particular. He has spoken to me about it, and I have heard the same from other senior men at the Front. There is no doubt about it.'

Asquith nodded, just one brusque movement. 'Then the matter is clear. Something must be done. Thank you, Lord Overton. We had better rejoin the company now, before we are missed.'

They had not been gone many minutes. When they returned to the dining-room, people were still changing seats, and there were groups standing here and there, deep in conversation, while a footman circulated the humidor and the butler set out the port. Talk was loud and cigar smoke was beginning to wreathe. Only Sandown himself cast Overton a glance over the shoulder of the man he was talking to, with a look of enquiry that said he had noted their absence, as a good host should. Asquith moved away and joined a group that was talking about horse-racing – perhaps, since he had no interest in the subject, it was a ploy to avoid talking about any political topic. Overton made his way down the room to join his host. Sandown was as deep as

313

the grave and a monument of tact, and he could rely on him not to mention the matter here or elsewhere.

Seeking refuge in his club the next day, he found his son Oliver there before him. He was surprised: Oliver had been put down for Brooks's as soon as he came of age, but he had never been very much of a clubman. Once he had started medical training he had been too busy, and now that he was a practising physician he used it rarely, though he always professed a fondness for the old place, and agreed that no man could be entirely without his club. His presence was soon explained. 'I thought I'd find you here,' he said. 'Come and have something. Tea? No, you look as though you need something stronger.' He led the way to two comfortable chairs in a secluded corner and ordered whisky for them both. 'You've seen the papers, I suppose?' he said, when they were settled.

'Yes. It's a damnable way for it to come to light. Asquith is furious – as far as he's ever furious about anything – because French went to the public over the government's head. Kitchener's outraged at the breach of military courtesy. And the opposition is going to make hay.'

'Is that what you've been discussing at the War Council today?' Oliver asked.

'Lord, no. It's not a War Council matter – though I daresay it contributed a little to the air of gloom. Not that there's any need to look for reasons. We have stalemate on the Western Front, and now the Eastern Front has proved a complete failure.'

The whiskies arrived, and Overton drank, frowning in thought, while his son made himself more comfortable, stretching out his legs and setting his glass on the broad leather arm of the chair. Oliver at twenty-seven looked very much like the Beauty Winchmore of the same age, with a handsome, good-humoured face, fine, athletic figure and thick brown hair, as glossy as a well-groomed horse. He dressed well, as a physician had to, but quietly, without the little dandy touches his father might have employed back

314

then, in a different age. He still lived 'at home', occupying a modest room on the second floor, because it seemed to him absurd to be paying out for a separate establishment when he was unmarried, and when he knew his parents both enjoyed having him there. His mother had been a great help to him in his career, and on the rare evenings when they were both at home and unengaged, they had lively conversations – and not infrequently lively, though affectionate, arguments.

He eyed his father now with sympathy. 'You never did think much of it as a plan, did you, Dad?'

'The Dardanelles? I never understood why they thought it would help. But if the infantry had gone in at the same time as the naval attack, there might have been some hope of taking Constantinople. As it is, we lost the element of surprise and the Turks were ready for us. They have the high ground, they're dug in, and frontal assault is just as hopeless as it is on the Western Front. We ought to cut our losses and get out, but mine was the only voice to advocate it. Everyone else said withdrawal was impossible. They're not willing to face the public and tell them that the great British Army had been defeated by a bunch of Turks.'

'Would you want to be the one to do it?'

'Better that than to throw away more lives. I've read the reports. The terrain is impossible, the climate is horrible, and sickness and disease are killing more than all the assaults put together. But they won't consider withdrawal, so there's no point in talking about it.'

'What *did* they consider?'

'Either to subject the Turks to a siege, which would mean a long-term commitment of men and arms, with no prospect of good news for the public for months or even years—'

'Not a politician's first choice,' said Oliver. 'Or?'

'Or to send in large numbers of reinforcements for an all-out attack, to bring matters to a conclusion. Desirable in political terms, but considering that we don't have enough men or ammunition to fight the war properly on the Western Front, hardly practicable.'

'So what did the Council decide in the end?'

'Oh,' said Overton, a touch wearily, 'to ask Sir Ian Hamilton what forces he would need to guarantee a successful attack and carry the peninsula.'

Oliver snorted. 'One would have thought they'd have asked him that before he started.'

'The problem was that he wasn't brought in until the naval attack had failed, by which time the situation was already lost.' He sipped and sighed. 'Fisher is very unhappy about it all. He was promised that if the sea attack failed, the navy would be withdrawn, and now it looks as though his ships will be tied up there for a long campaign.'

'What does he want to do with the navy, then?'

'Blockade Germany, tempt the German fleet to come out to fight, and then beat them so soundly they sue for peace. Fisher's spent his life building up the navy: he can't bear to think of his precious ships being frittered away in the east. And, of course, he hates Churchill. Mind you, I don't think Fisher would care to be dictated to by any landman – but especially not this one. He hates his ebullience, his dogmatism, his high-handedness. And Churchill *will* go over his head and consult the senior sea officers directly, which is tactless. Fisher said to me as we were leaving that he felt he would have to resign.'

'That would cause a crisis,' Oliver said. 'But perhaps we need one. No one can pretend the war is going well. Another whisky?'

'No, I'd better go home. I only called in for a moment to clear my head, but your mother will want to know what happened today. Are you engaged this evening? Oh, good, neither are we, so we can have a quiet family dinner for once.'

They walked to Manchester Square through the sweet mildness of a May late afternoon: the trees bursting with greenness, sparrows chirping madly from every gutter, shop windows full of the new season's fashions, the women all in light summer silks. It seemed mad and wrong that they should be at war, that a hundred miles away in France young men were being killed and maimed, their minds full of guns, gas, shells and death, when they should have been thinking about cricket and beer and long summer evenings of courtship.

The Holkam motor was parked outside the house, and upstairs they found Violet, Jessie and Emma sitting with Venetia in the drawing-room.

'What a delightful group,' said Overton, as he came into the room. 'All my favourite women together. I should like to have it captured in a photograph.'

'Papa, have you seen the newspapers?' Violet said at once. 'Isn't it terrible? We were out all day and everyone's talking about it. This is the first chance we've had to come and find out what's really going on.'

There was no avoiding going over it all again, but Overton had been restored by his club, his whisky and his walk, and explained with calm good humour. 'Mind you,' he added in conclusion, 'one has some sympathy with Kitchener. All his able officers have gone out to the Front, and he's left with a handful of poor old boys dug out of retirement, no use for anything but to tell him he's right, no matter what.'

'Get rid of him,' said Venetia. 'I've said it before.'

Overton smiled at her indulgently. 'My love, his birthday is coming up on the 24th of June, and the Kitchener's Birthday Recruitment Drive is in the last stages of planning. We've hundreds of posters printed, banners, bunting, special armbands, halls booked, speeches written. The whole nation will be involved. We can't throw him out now.'

'Well, something must be done.'

'Of course. We have to find some way to circumvent him. We can't run a modern war on the same lines as the eastern campaigns of his youth. But I'm afraid it will cause more of an upheaval than that. The government could fall.'

'Do you really think so?' Emma asked, seeming more pleased at the idea than troubled. Upheaval to her was always more interesting than the *status quo*.

'The government is a minority in the House of Commons,' Overton said. 'Without the Labour and National Party votes,

317

they would not be able to do business at all. The Conservatives are the biggest party, but they've been co-operating with the government since the war began for the good of the nation. However, if they withdraw that cooperation, which they might well do over this shells business, they could bring the government down.'

'But would they?' Oliver asked. 'Surely that wouldn't look good, with a war on. They might be accused of being un-patriotic.'

'True,' said Overton. 'But if they threaten it, Asquith will have to give them something to keep them quiet. And it all plays into Lloyd George's hands. He wants Asquith's job.'

'Perhaps he ought to have it,' Venetia said.

Overton looked his surprise at her. 'I thought you loathed him.'

'I don't like him. But, then, I don't much care for Asquith – and I've thought for some time that he just isn't suited to war. He's too much the lawyer. Calm, abstract discussions in club rooms are all very well for peacetime, but war isn't a polite, scholarly business. It's vulgar, bustling, noisy and energetic – all the things he hates.'

'And you think we need a bustling, energetic, vulgar man as leader?' Overton said, smiling.

'I think you could be right, Mum,' said Oliver, pleased with the idea. 'We need someone who will barge along and get things done, and not mind people's feelings.'

'But I'm not sure Lloyd George is the right man,' said Overton. 'His ambition may be boundless, but I'm not convinced of his abilities. He's rather a second-rater.'

'Perhaps,' said Jessie – tentatively, for she had never really thought about politics before – 'what's needed is a govern-ment of the best people, no matter what party they belong to, who will all work together to win the war.'

Lord Overton looked at her kindly. 'A coalition? They work for some countries, but we haven't a good record with them here. Our governments work on Cabinet loyalty and fellow-feeling. Without them, I'm afraid there would be rivalry, intrigue and attempted coups.'

'Even in wartime?' Jessie asked.

'Ambition doesn't die in wartime,' Oliver said. 'Men are quite capable of being patriotic and ambitious at the same time. And after all, if you're convinced that you're the best man to lead the nation, it would be positively unpatriotic *not* to try to seize the position.'

'I think you're roasting me,' Jessie said, smiling at him.

'Only a little,' he said, grinning back.

'I'll tell you one thing,' Overton said. 'Coalition or not, there'll have to be some consensus among our leaders in the next few months, because the shell shortage is not the only one. We're short of men, too, and sooner or later we are going to have to face the fact that voluntary enlistment won't provide enough.'

'Oh, my dear, not conscription!' Venetia exclaimed. It was a horrible idea, a foreign idea, to a nation that loved freedom.

'I'm afraid so,' Overton said gently. 'Even Kitchener admits we'll need a million and a half men in uniform by the end of the year, and no-one in either House seriously believes that number can be found without conscription.'

Oliver noticed at that point that two at least of the three young women in the room were becoming glazed with boredom, and took pity on them by changing the subject. 'What are you three up to tonight, Violet? Ball, rout or dinner?'

'None of those,' Violet said. 'We're going to the Palace.'

Venetia, whose mind had still been on conscription, started at that and said, 'But shouldn't you be going home to change? You know how early the King and Queen dine, and it would be terribly bad form to be late.'

Oliver grinned. 'No, Mother darling, I fancy our little Vi means the Palace Theatre.'

'That's right,' Violet agreed. 'We are going to see *The Passing Show*. I do so like Basil Hallam, don't you? And everyone says the songs are even better than last year's. Why don't you come with us, Oliver? I'm sure we can get another ticket. Do come.'

'Thank you, but no. I'm for a quiet dinner with the Aged

Ps, and early bed. My life is too hectic as it is. I don't think I could bear the excitement of hearing "I'm Gilbert the Filbert" sung by the Knut himself.' He turned to Jessie and said, 'By the way, talking of dining, I've been meaning to ask you if you would care to come with me to the Darroways' one evening – if "dine" is not too grand a term for it. Sometimes it more resembles feeding-time at the zoo, but that's part of the charm.'

'I'd love to,' Jessie said.

Venetia interposed: 'No, no, Oliver, we must invite them to dine here. I haven't seen Mark Darroway in an age, and I'd love to catch up with the dear fellow.'

Oliver looked pleased. 'Would you really? It would be a great compliment and I know they'd love it.'

'I owe him a great deal,' Venetia said. 'Now, when could we do it?' She thought. 'Oh dear, I did think that at my great age I might be spared being engaged for every moment of the Season! What about the twenty-second? We have something on then, but I'm sure I can get out of it. Beauty, is that all right with you? It's only Lady Dawnay's tableaux in aid of the Red Cross.'

'I'd be delighted to be spared them, my dear,' Overton said.

'I'm pretty sure I'm free,' said Oliver, 'or if I'm not I shall "chuck" whatever it is. And the Darroways will be sure to be. I have a standing invitation to dine with them any day. So that only leaves the girls.' He looked at Violet.

'Oh, are we all invited?' she said.

'It would be nice if you could come,' Venetia said. 'We haven't had dinner with you for so long, and the Darroways are excellent company, you know. You'd enjoy them. It would make a very nice little party.'

'The twenty-second?' Violet said, casting her mind through her diary, which she carried in her mind so perfectly she hardly needed to write it down at home. 'We have tickets for the play at Drury Lane, but I can change those. Freddie was coming with us – shall I ask him, Mama? Then with Oliver for Jessie, we'll only need someone for Emma to be even.'

Venetia smiled at her beautiful daughter, thinking that she didn't mind a whit whether they were even or not; but she said, 'I'll find someone, don't worry about it. And, I've just thought, shall I ask Olivia and Charlie?'

'Good idea,' said Overton. 'They'll give a little light relief to the non-medical members of the company, like me. The whole thing might descend into a prolonged post-mortem otherwise.'

'Don't be silly, darling,' said Venetia. 'There'll only be three doctors among us.'

'Oh, do ask them,' Violet said. 'I'd love to see Aunt Olivia. But would she come up to London just for a dinner?'

Venetia's sister had lived a quiet life with her husband in the country since they retired from Court service. They had a little house on the edge of the ducal estate that had been her and Venetia's childhood home, and was now in the possession of the distant cousin who had inherited the title. The present duke was a kindly man, who made Olivia welcome in his home and gave her the freedom of the grounds, and since she loved Ravendene so much, there was little to tempt her ever to travel.

'I'll invite them to stay for a few days,' said Venetia. 'Livy's sure to want some new clothes.' Olivia had always been the beauty of the family, and even in her sixties she loved to dress. 'Very well, I'll write a note to the Darroways, but we'll call it settled, shall we?'

The young women got up soon afterwards to take their leave. Under cover of the leave-takings, Oliver murmured to Jessie, 'I hope you don't object to the substitution? Manchester Square in all its glory for the cosy fug of Soho Square?'

'Not at all. It was nice of Cousin Venetia to think of it.'

'Oh, Mum's very human, you know. Comes of having to slum it while she was a medical student. That's when she met Darroway – he was her crammer.'

'Yes, I know. You told me.'

'So I did. It must be premature senility. Or perhaps the excitement of knowing that, in my dear sister's words, I am

321

"for" you.' He took her hand and bowed over it with a mocking smile. 'Oh, would that 'twere so! But alas, you are not free.'

'Now don't be an ass,' she said. 'You wouldn't say such things if I *were* free.'

'How can you say so?' he said indignantly.

'Because it's by *not* saying such things that you've managed to remain uncaptured to such a great age.'

'How she tramples on my heart! Well, in the absence of love, I'll accept a dinner-date.'

Violet saw Laidislaw's drawing-room in her mind as an enchanted cave, into which she stepped by magic, and where everything was transformed. Her times there were of strange, breathless pleasure. He gave her sherry or Madeira or Marsala, and small delightful things to eat – crystallised plums from Karlsbad, Italian ratafia biscuits, tiny, intriguing cakes, *langues-de-chat*, chocolate-covered cherries, little stars cut out of marzipan – and she sat in the sweet sunshine on the red velvet couch while he drew her obsessively, turning the page of his sketching-pad and beginning again as soon as he had finished.

And she talked. Never in her life had she talked so much. That first day, as she sat nervously stiff, feeling his eyes touching her in a way that seemed shockingly intimate, he had said, 'I cannot work in silence. You must tell me about yourself.'

'Tell you what?' she had enquired faintly.

'Everything. Tell me everything you remember about your life. Begin at the beginning.'

And so, stiltedly at first, but with increasing fluency, she had described her life to him. She had spoken of her parents: of her mother's drive and genius and greatness, and how humbly grateful she had always felt to be loved by such a woman; of her father's sweetness of disposition, and his charm, which made everyone love him. She spoke of her grandmother, the duchess, whom she just remembered, how grand she had been and at the same time how near and kind.

322

She spoke of her darling brothers, the visits to Yorkshire they had used to make in the summer, and the children at Morland Place – Jessie and her brothers and Ned – who had seemed to her such a wonderful, lively multitude. It was so good of them to let her join in their plays, when she was such a dull child, really, never with any interesting ideas, like Jessie. She talked of Jessie's exploits and their friendship, and how they had come out together, and what fun it had been.

With skilfully inserted questions he kept her talking while he drew and drew and drew her. She had never really spoken about herself before, and after the first awkwardness of feeling that it was wrong – that if it did not disgust him with her self-centredness, it must at least be boring him – she found a wonderful sense of release in it. It was as though something done up too tight, which had been pinching uncomfortably for years, had at last been loosened. The horrid red marks it must have left gradually faded, and whatever had been confined seemed to grow smooth and full and lovely inside her, so that it sometimes seemed she could feel it against her skin, but on the inside – a strange but delicious feeling.

By the time her narration came to her falling in love with Lord Brancaster, as he then was, and their subsequent relationship, she was so at ease with telling her story that she hardly hesitated. Laidislaw seemed to ask more questions about this, probing not for the mere facts of it but for her feelings and thoughts. It felt more perilous, in an exciting way, but she did not hesitate. She had got used to talking now, to his being there, to his listening to her and knowing things about her, just as she had had to get used to his touching her. At first when he had crossed the room with his impetuous step and rearranged a hand or arm, turned her head or tilted it with his fingers on her chin, pushed her gently to make her recline a little more or sit the other way round, she had almost flinched from him, and it had made her tremble violently with the feeling that this was an intimacy too far, and that she was as culpable in allowing it as he was in offering it.

But the almost fairytale atmosphere of her visits to this room gradually wore away any feeling of wrongdoing. He had said that what happened here was outside the world, and it felt exactly that. The tiny glasses of wine, the miniature sweetmeats added to the wonder, as did the continuing May sunshine, which crept into the room through muslin curtains and gilded everything with a soft, fuzzy radiance. She no longer noticed what she was telling him, how far into her private self she was delving in response to his questions. She was only aware of the wonderful sense of loosening inside her, and of a great, almost breathless happiness that made her want to tell him things, as being the only gift she had to give him in return for how he had made her feel.

She had almost forgotten the portrait. There seemed to be no need for a reason to be here, and it did not occur to her to wonder why he drew her over and over again in a sketching-pad, or why he had not approached the empty canvas that always stood on his easel during her visits.

But she arrived one day as usual, and when he had locked the door and helped her out of her hat, gloves and fur, he said quite abruptly, 'I think I am ready to begin.'

'Begin?' she asked vaguely, watching the dogs perform their usual searching trot about the room. 'Begin what?'

He smiled. 'Dear Violet! Begin the portrait, of course. Had you forgotten?'

She blushed a little. 'No – of course not.'

He laid a finger on her lips to silence her and said, 'No need to perjure yourself. It was my wish that you should forget. I had half forgotten it myself – or, at least, I wished that I could. I had no desire to rupture the golden membrane that had enclosed us these past weeks. But we are ready to move on to the next stage, and that, I promise you, will be delightful too.' Though he said *I promise you*, he regarded her with a slight question, as though he were not, in fact, quite sure of what he said. 'Are you ready?' he asked her softly. She looked up into his face. She had grown tolerably accustomed by now to his standing so close to her, but it

still made her feel breathless to look into his eyes sometimes, when they held a particular expression – the one they
held now.

'I'm ready,' she said.

'Do you trust me?' he asked next. His dark eyes searched
her, and she felt the loosened thing inside her move, as
though it had sighed.

'Yes,' she said.

Then he touched her. He touched her with his fingers as
so often he had touched her with his eyes, 'seeing' with
them. He drew them lightly over her brow and down her
nose, brushed them delicately across her cheekbones and
round the curve of her jaw to her chin; then traced, with a
touch like a feather, the outline of her lips.

'Such a mouth!' he said, in a voice as quiet as breathing.
'It is made for passion, yet it sleeps in innocence. You are
a sleep-walker in your own life, Violet. You move through it
so lightly, as innocent as a child in a white cotton nightgown holding her nurse's hand as she goes up to bed. You
are a dream of yourself, and in that dream nothing touches
you: you glide like a phantasm, never touching the ground,
and the firelight shows through you. But there is such power
in you, power you have never imagined. And fire – such fire
in here, waiting to be lit. I see fire and power in the lines
of this mouth, in these slumberous eyes. You have such beautiful eyelids, heavy and curved as the petals of a white rose.
I should like to see them brooding with desire. Lovely, lovely
Violet.'

She felt as though her bones were turning to water, everything inside her was warmly melting, the loosened thing was
yearning towards him. But she whispered, 'You mustn't,'
and could go no further.

He looked at her differently now, not the brooding,
disturbing look, but his more ordinary face, dark, sardonic,
gently mocking, yet so attractive in its knowingness. 'No, I
mustn't,' he said lightly, 'but I undoubtedly shall. And so
will you. Once the fire is lit, it will consume everything. But
first, the portrait. I cannot paint you in these things. It pains

325

me even to look at them. No, don't frown, they are perfectly adequate for their purpose in the outside world, but we are not *in* the outside world, dear Violet, and here, for me, you must wear something that matches the inside rather than the outside.'

'I don't understand,' she said.

'I wish you to change into something else. In my bedroom next door I have laid out something for you to wear. Please go and put it on.'

It was the measure of his spell over her that, though she felt a tight excitement of sin at the very idea of entering his bedroom, let alone changing her clothes there, she went without further comment through the door at the far end of the room. But just inside the door, before she had allowed herself to look at the room, she turned back to him, blushing again. 'I cannot,' she said. 'My maid dressed me this morning. I cannot undo my buttons.'

He did not laugh at her. He seemed, on the contrary, touched by her words. 'Then I shall undo them for you,' he said. 'Yes, and do them up again afterwards.' He walked across to her. 'Turn your back to me.' She obeyed, but as his hand touched the back of her neck she started, and trembled. 'Don't be afraid,' he said. 'You told me you trust me. No harm can come to you here – don't you believe it?'

And as his fingers began travelling downwards, skilfully flicking open the tiny pearl buttons that fastened her blouse from neck to waist, that liquid warmth ran through her again, and she relaxed, and said at last, 'Yes.'

Alone in his bedroom, with the door closed behind her, she dared to look about. She had never been in a man's bedroom before, and it interested her too much to feel any shame about it. There was a very large, modern bed with a walnut headboard, and a heavy counterpane of burgundy-coloured brocade. There was a large walnut wardrobe with a looking-glass in the door; a vast Georgian mahogany chest of drawers; a rosewood dressing-table; a leather sofa across the foot of the bed. There was a dark, ancient Turkey carpet

on the floor, and the curtains were of wine-red velvet, drawn
back, with the same muslin drapes covering the window.
Everything was dark and handsome and well polished, and
infinitely masculine. She drew a breath of satisfaction. Such
personal things as lay about were masculine too – a pair of
mahogany-backed hairbrushes, a clothes brush, a gold half-
hunter lying on top of the dresser. On the bedside table was
a small, heavy French carriage clock, a spectacles-case, and a
leather-bound book. She went over and picked it up, with
a sense of anticipation she could not account for. It was a
book of poetry by someone called Stéphane Mallarmé. She
turned a page or two, and discovered the poems were written
in French. The book had been well read, and fell open in
several favoured places. She read a line or two at one of the
sites.

> *Rien au réveil que vous n'ayez*
> *Envisagé de quelque moue*
> *Pire si le rire secoue*
> *Votre aile sur les oreillers*

The words were delicious and mysterious; the lack of
punctuation and the rhymes and internal rhymes making
it feel loose and lovely as if one could understand it almost
without reading it, as if the words could flow into one's
mind without effort of comprehension. *Nothing at waking
that you have not envisaged with a little pout, worse if laughter
shakes your wing on the pillows.* She saw at once a man
watching his beloved sleep, her hair like wings on the
pillow, wondering as she smiles in dream, longing for her
to wake and smile at him but determined not to disturb
her. The strange, somnambulant poetry was at one with
this place and all it was to her. She put the book down,
and took up the dress he had laid out for her. It was a
loose, flowing gown with wide, hanging sleeves, rather
William Morris-y, she thought. It was of peacock-blue silk,
with a motif of large white madonna lilies with green stems
on the front, while the back, which ran out to a slight

train, was patterned with peacock's eyes. She had never worn such a thing before, nor such colours – even in the brief fashion for 'Orientalism' a few years back. She put it on – it pulled over the head and hung loosely, except for a simple tie, which drew it in under the bust – and regarded herself in the looking-glass. Moments before she had avoided the mirror, afraid of the sight of herself standing in his bedroom; now she gazed without embarrassment, altered fundamentally by this out-of-the-ordinary garment.

She walked, a little self-consciously, back into the drawing-room. He turned to look at her, and she smiled nervously, waiting for his judgement.

'Yes,' he said. 'The colours are just right, just as I imagined. You must take off your shoes. You must be barefoot.' He waited while she sat and did this, then stood up again. Then he walked towards her. 'But not the hair,' he said. He reached a hand behind her and she felt his fingers searching out her pins. She made no protest as he drew them out and then, with both hands, loosened her hair and spread it over her shoulders, letting it tumble through them as a man might handle something very precious.

'Lovely, lovely,' he said. 'Now you are fit and ready for me, and we can begin work. Come, come.' He held out his hand and she placed hers in it and he led her to the sofa. A languorous warmth was over her, and she let him place her as he wished, handling her limbs and moving her head, drawing the long curls of her dark hair through his fingers and laying them just so, arranging the folds of the gown, drawing out one bare foot from under the hem, and caressing it into the position he wanted. Then with no more talk he went to the easel and, on the canvas itself this time, began to draw.

Violet reclined as he had placed her, utterly relaxed, at ease, unafraid. The touch of his eyes was a deep pleasure. She wanted nothing more than to be here, with him, like this, for ever. The world and its concerns were too far away for her to be able to hear the wash of them on the shore of this enchanted island. In this gown, her feet bare, her hair loosened, she was not Violet any more. She was simultaneously the dreamed-of and the dreamer; and she wanted never to wake.

CHAPTER FOURTEEN

Lord Fisher resigned on the 15th of May. There was uproar in the House of Commons, and little knots of men were seen everywhere in the Palace of Westminster and the major clubs, heads close together, mouths moving rapidly, hands waving, fingers jabbing urgently. The government had been ineffectual in conducting the war. The shells scandal was still filling the newspapers. Casualty lists continued to come in, and the losses this year had been terrible, for the gain of no ground. In the Dardanelles another stalemate was looming. Speeches were made in the Chamber attacking the government in the most virulent terms: 'scandalous neglect'; 'innumerable blunders'; 'seriously endangered the security of the country'; 'failure . . . chaos . . . hopelessness . . .'

'There's enough volatile gas circulating to blow both Houses sky high,' Overton said.

'Will the government fall?' Venetia asked.

'It's possible. I don't think that was Bonar Law's intention, but his Unionist backbenchers are growing frisky, and they won't stand for Fisher's resigning if Churchill stays. Everyone knows that the Dardanelles campaign was Churchill's idea, and the Unionists hate him because of his attitude to Ireland. They'll be hard for Law to control. But it's Lloyd George who is the unknown quantity.'

'Boundless ambition and no scruples,' Venetia said.

'And he's too fond of bypassing Parliament and going

330

straight to the newspapers. If he pools forces with Law, something's bound to happen.'

It happened on the 17th of May, when Bonar Law and Lloyd George together sought an audience of the prime minister.

'I met our friend Addison in the lobby,' Overton said. Christopher Addison was a physician turned politician: he had been a lecturer in anatomy at Charing Cross Hospital, and then in 1910 became the Liberal member for Hoxton. Both Overtons had known him for years. 'He told me what Lloyd George told him about it. It was a very short meeting, not more than a quarter of an hour. Apparently, Lloyd George meant to ambush Asquith, but Asquith saw it coming and had his answers ready.' Overton chuckled. 'I don't care for him much, but it has to be said that he's a canny creature at times. For all his air of *laissez-faire*, he can move nimbly when he needs to. Of course, Addison didn't quite put it like this, but it seems that Law and Lloyd George went blustering in to demand a coalition on the grounds of Asquith's abject failure, and Asquith got in first and quietly proposed it in the national interest, on the grounds that the Unionists had no administrative ability. I'd have enjoyed seeing Law's expression at that point.'

Venetia made an impatient gesture. 'What does it matter? He was forced to accept a coalition anyway.'

'But on his own terms,' Overton pointed out. 'He'll be at the head of it, and he'll have the disposition of the Cabinet. I think he won't mind a coalition, in any case. Given the Liberal minority in the House, things couldn't go on as they were. And it will give him the chance to solve his worst problem, by letting the Unionists push Kitchener out and take the blame for it.'

'The backbenchers won't like it,' Venetia mused. 'The Liberal government dissolved in fifteen minutes, without a by-your-leave? The Unionists cheated of their chance at power?'

'True. It's a strange situation – the front benches united against the back, if you like. But they can't complain for fear of looking unpatriotic.'

331

Over the next few days, the details of the new Cabinet became known. Churchill's head was one essential of the settlement, and he was given the Duchy of Lancaster, a humiliating demotion. 'I don't think he'll stick it long,' said Overton. 'If he's not moved up again soon, he may resign.'

'A good thing, too,' said Venetia. She had never forgiven him for his fierce opposition to the female franchise.

Balfour, Asquith's only Unionist friend, took Churchill's place at the Admiralty. As a gesture to Labour, one of their members, Arthur Henderson, was given Education, the first taste of Cabinet power for the party. But the Unionists insisted that Asquith's friend Haldane, the lord chancellor, had to go.

Overton was angry about it. 'They revived that disgusting nonsense in the *Daily Mail* about his having pro-German sympathies. He's the best minister of war we've ever had. Without his reforms we shouldn't have been able to mobilise as quickly as we did, and Germany would have walked over France unopposed. It's an outrage that they should push a fine statesman out for such a trumped-up reason.'

The Unionists also evaded the dismissal of Kitchener; but it hardly mattered, as his powers were dramatically reduced.

'There's going to be a Ministry of Munitions,' Overton explained to his wife. 'After all the fuss in the Northcliffe press, it was inevitable – and, of course, Lloyd George is to head it. Addison says he'll take over all the powers of the Ordnance Department as soon as he can wrest them from the War Office.'

'Well, perhaps he'll get things done, at least,' said Venetia. 'We can't keep sending our men to fight the Germans with their bare hands, for want of ammunition. What else?'

'Grey stays at the Foreign Office, and Reggie McKenna is to take the Exchequer – so, really, the Unionists haven't done very well out of it at all,' said Overton. 'Even Bonar Law only gets the Colonial Office.'

'Asquith seems to have come off pretty well, all things considered,' said Venetia.

'Yes,' said Overton, 'as long as he can hold the thing together. I don't think Law will give him any trouble. Lloyd George is the one he will have to watch – but munitions will keep him too busy to intrigue, at least for a few months.'

Venetia had no intention of inviting anyone 'for' Emma, for her dinner for the Darroways, but in deference to Violet's artistic feelings (and those of the servants, who liked things to be done properly), she did look around for a suitable man who would dine solo to make the numbers even. She decided to ask Christopher Addison, who she thought would be the ideal guest for several reasons. He was a physician, which fitted in with the medical flavour of the evening, and as parliamentary secretary to the Board of Education he had been studying the effects on health of poor housing, which was something Venetia had been interested in for some time. He also had novel ideas about wanting to establish a Ministry of Health, which she was not sure she agreed with, but would relish the chance to argue about. Furthermore, it had just emerged that his friend Lloyd George was to appoint him parliamentary secretary to the new Ministry of Munitions, which made him very much the man of the moment, who could tell them what was to be done to mend the crisis.

All seemed to be working in Venetia's favour when she discovered that his wife was in Scotland on a visit with the children, which meant he could dine *en garçon*. But then it emerged he had another engagement that evening, so he couldn't dine at all.

'Bother,' she said to Overton. 'I really wanted to talk to him about the spread of tuberculosis in the slums.'

'What a treat he's missed!' said Overton.

'Laugh at me if you please. But there's hardly any time left to find a replacement, and I shall be looked askance at by my own daughter for having odd numbers.'

'Your troubles are mine, my love,' he said, his eyes still laughing at her.

She had already been disappointed by a reply from her sister refusing the invitation because she was unwell.

'Nothing serious, darling,' Olivia had written, 'just a little digestive disorder, which makes travelling difficult. Quite embarrassing at my age, I must say, and tiresome too, when I should have liked nothing better than to come and see my dear old Sissy. But when I'm better I shall make a point of taking up the invitation and visiting you – or perhaps you might be dragged away from all your concerns and come and stay with us? I'm sure a break would do you good – and it would do *me* good to see you.'

Now Overton said, 'Why don't you ask Charlie Du Cane if he'll come alone?'

'He wouldn't leave Olivia if she's not well. And I'm not so desperate that I would take him away from her. I'll find someone – it's just that Addison would have been so perfect.'

Fate, which had spoiled her Addison plan, took a hand and presented her the same day with a very attractive alternative.

'It really is a coincidence,' she said to Overton as she showed him the letter. It was from a young second cousin of Charles Du Cane, who was a captain in the RAMC. He wrote that he had a short period of leave coming up, and begged the honour of presenting himself on the twenty-second to pay his respects.

Venetia had met Christopher Westhoven several times before, and liked him very much. His mother had died when he was fourteen, and his father, Lord Westhoven of Lutterworth, had married again almost immediately. He had meant to provide a mother for Christopher and his elder brother Roger; but the boys had not got on with their step-mother – a rather brittle young woman who had seemed to resent their presence in the house whenever they returned from school. The atmosphere had become so strained that even their father had noticed and, unable to be disloyal to either his wife or his children, did his best to keep them apart by arranging for the boys to spend most of their school holidays elsewhere, with friends and relatives. Olivia and Charlie had had them to stay several times, and had brought them to visit the Overtons when on pleasure-trips to London.

334

Venetia had particularly liked young Kit, shy and sensitive but with an eager intelligence, and an interest in medicine that she suspected she might have inspired, and was glad to encourage. Both boys were now at the Front. Roger had joined the Guards as soon as he left Oxford and was a major with Headquarters staff. He was Lord Westhoven now, his father having died just before the war broke out. Kit had volunteered in the earliest days of the war and was serving in Ypres. Neither was married, something Venetia attributed to the unhappy relationship with their stepmother. Plainly Kit did not wish to visit her while on leave. Venetia guessed that Captain Westhoven preferred to spend his short time in London rather than in a series of trains and taxis; but as the younger son he would not be too flush in the pocket, and hotels these days were expensive. She wrote back at once inviting him to stay at Manchester Square while he was on leave, and asking him to consider himself engaged for dinner on the 22nd. His reply was so prompt and eager, she felt she had interpreted the situation correctly.

'Well, that worked out very luckily,' she said, having read his reply to her husband.

'And he's a more suitable person for Emma than Addison, being nearer her age – not to say unmarried,' Overton said.

Venetia looked severe. 'You know I wasn't inviting Addison "for" Emma.'

'But don't you think it would be a good thing if she fell in love with young Westhoven anyway? I know you'd like to see her settled. We like him, he's a connection, and his family is very good.'

'I don't think he has any money,' Venetia said, neatly trapped into considering it. 'His brother has the title, of course.'

'But Emma has so much, she can do without a rich husband. And who knows what may happen to the brother in wartime? The Guards never hold back in battle.'

She realised belatedly she was being roasted. 'Oh, Beauty, what a dreadful thing to say! I am not going to match-make

335

for Emma, so you may stop leading me astray in that reprehensible manner.'

She found herself thinking about it even so, and cursed her husband's errant sense of humour several times in the days before the dinner party.

On the 22nd of May, early in the morning, half a battalion of Royal Scots Territorials was travelling by train southwards towards the Scottish border, *en route* for Liverpool and Gallipoli – the other two companies were following on another train two hours behind. The train picked up speed as it headed for Quintinshill, just outside Gretna, and at speed it crashed into a stationary train, with a noise that was heard six miles away. The impact was so great that the troop train was crushed to half its length, some carriages telescoped together, others rearing up and crashing down on top of those behind them, the whole mass thirty feet high and spread across both lines. Some men were thrown clear by the impact, others were struggling to free themselves or climb out through the windows – troop-train doors were always locked in transit – when only minutes after the initial impact a northbound express ploughed into the wreckage. The express was lit by gas lamps. The tanks under the carriages exploded and set fire to the splintered remains of all three trains.

Many who had miraculously escaped the first impact and were trying to free colleagues were killed by the second; some who had managed to scramble away up the embankments were struck by flaming debris from the explosions; many more were burned to death, trapped in the wreckage. The single local fire engine that arrived could do little but try to damp the fires where rescuers were working. Local villagers and a doctor rushed to the scene to do what they could, but it was two hours before an ambulance train could get there from Carlisle with more medical help.

The horrifying news was soon known all round the country, and the dinner party at Manchester Square began in a rather sombre mood. But there was a warmth of good

336

fellowship to break through the clouds. Venetia hadn't seen Mark Darroway in a while, and greeted him eagerly, giving him both hands and offering her cheek for his kiss. He was a year older than her, tall, thin and slightly stooped – like a grey heron, Jessie always thought – with bright dark eyes that held humour, intelligence and compassion in equal measure. Despite his considerable abilities he had never sought the higher planes of the medical profession, but gave his life to doctoring the poorest sort in the slums of Soho.

In their youth Venetia and Darroway had been as close as brother and sister – one of those occasional miraculous friendships that cross all barriers and unite people who might expect to be poles apart. Since that time their affection had never wavered, and was regarded with indulgence by their respective spouses, who could feel rather left out when the old friends talked medicine. Katherine Darroway was as round and plump and plushy as her husband was spare: a motherly creature, but with a good mind of her own, which she had dedicated to helping her husband in his work.

Jessie had always met them before on their own ground – their tall, shabby house in Soho Square. She thought, when they arrived, that they looked out of place in Venetia's drawing room. They were correctly dressed, but against the smart, well-kept black and white of Lord Overton, Oliver, and Freddie Copthall, Mark's tail coat showed the greenish tint of black suiting that is well worn and was cheap in the first place, while his cufflinks were unconvincingly brassy. Katherine's Parma-violet gown was an old one that had been let out, as betrayed by the difference in colour of the material that had been inside the seams. Its *décolletage* demanded a necklace, but as Katherine had no jewellery apart from her wedding and engagement rings, she had supplied the deficiency with a piece of velvet ribbon round the throat, which hardly answered. Venetia, who was as uninterested in clothes as it was possible to be, nevertheless had a maid, and was impeccably dressed in a rust-coloured silk gown, with pearls at throat and ears; while Violet was exquisite in dark blue silk and wearing her sapphires – her father's wedding present to her. Just for a moment, Jessie felt sorry for the Darroways; but they and the Overtons seemed so completely at ease with each other that she soon forgot all about it.

Captain Westhoven was the guest of honour. He had arrived just after luncheon, and Oliver whispered to Jessie that he had spent the whole afternoon in the bathroom, madly scrubbing. 'He was terrified he'd smell of the Front, or frighten us all by producing a louse at the wrong moment. Of course, he was deloused before he left Vlamertinghe, but they can be persistent little beggars.'

Jessie assumed he was teasing, and pinched his arm, hard. Westhoven turned out to be a lean, handsome man in his mid-twenties, with bright blue eyes, and very fair skin – a little weather-roughened at present, but still the sort that showed every blush. He had unruly fair hair, which, since he had a way of running his hands through it distractedly at moments of conversational passion, soon escaped its bonds of macassar and resumed its natural habit of sprouting and waving upwards and outwards, like a lion's mane. He was the sort of nice-looking, slightly shy young man that older women dote on, and it was soon plain to Jessie that both Venetia and Katherine Darroway had taken a shine to him. In the drawing-room before dinner, they were one either side of him and deep in conversation. Overton watched with amusement, and thought there was not much chance of Emma getting to know him.

At table, Westhoven was seated next to Venetia, and she had Darroway on the other side of her, so it was natural that the initial talk was medical. In response to Darroway's question, Westhoven said that he had volunteered for the RAMC as soon as war was declared.

'You're lucky to be a man,' Venetia said. 'Women are allowed to be doctors now – albeit somewhat grudgingly – but they are still not allowed to practise at the Front. Louisa Garrett and a group of female physicians offered their services to the War Office last August, and were told to go home and keep quiet.'

'It's an attitude that will have to change,' Darroway said, 'as the war goes on. There'll be no room for such niceness in the face of modern warfare.'

'Warfare has always been horrible,' Venetia said. 'It was war that finally convinced me I had to be a doctor.'

'How so, ma'am?' Westhoven asked.

'I was in Berlin with the crown princess's suite during the Franco-Prussian war. We visited the war hospitals, and they were so badly run and the medical staff such ignorant brutes, I knew I had to do something. My mother had nursed in the Crimea, but nursing wasn't enough for me. I knew I could be a better doctor than those Prussian butchers.' She turned to Darroway and smiled. 'If it hadn't been for you, I shouldn't have succeeded, of course.'

'You would have succeeded,' Darroway said. 'Your own determination would have carried you, with or without my help.'

'I can't imagine how difficult it must have been for you,' Westhoven said admiringly. 'I'm such a fool, I found it hard enough to pass the examinations, even without everyone's hand being against me.'

'It was hard,' Venetia reflected, 'and being separated from my family was the hardest thing of all. But I had to do it. The wounded soldiers in the Berlin hospital affected me so much – their endurance, their courage, even cheerfulness in the face of terrible affliction. I was fascinated – no, that's not the right word. Perhaps there isn't a right word for the combination of excitement and pity I felt, when I saw what the human body could endure and survive: its toughness and frailty, the *gallantry* of its healing processes. It's a wonder I have never lost. It's one of the reasons I continue with my research into tuberculosis: so many die from it, and it makes me frantic that I can't find the way to stop it. The human body can survive so much – sometimes, it seems, against all the odds – and yet TB can carry off a strong man in days.'

Westhoven was nodding. 'Yes, I know exactly what you mean. With the wounded, it's almost as if the body itself were a separate person, which decides to live or die without reference to the owner. Horrible though the wounds are, there is such a fascination to it.'

There was plenty of general conversation as the dinner progressed, about the political crisis, the shells scandal, the inexplicable shortage of string, and the rising prices in restaurants. The Darroways talked about the activities of a housing trust they were interested in, which aimed to improve some of the slums around Soho and St Giles. Violet and Freddie Copthall talked about the various shows and revues, and Westhoven responded with a description of *A Mother's Tears*, a sentimental piece played by a group of Suffolks to their battalion when they were out on rest. It had made such a sensation that their colonel had spoken to the adjutant-general, and it had been repeated before several other units in the area. Westhoven had caught a performance. 'There's talk now, if it stays quiet in Ypres, of having them take it on tour around the hospitals on the coast.'

'To cheer up the wounded?' Emma asked.

Westhoven smiled at her. 'Mostly, I suspect, to cheer up the staff.'

There was no withdrawal of the ladies. When the dessert was cleared and the port was brought on, Venetia said, 'You may smoke,' and the men lit up.

Darroway said to Westhoven, 'Tell us something about your work at the Front.'

Jessie thought he was looking very tired about the eyes, and wondered if he might prefer not to be the centre of attention; but Westhoven did not seem reluctant to talk.

'The difficulty is always the sudden influx of large numbers,' he said. 'Well, I suppose that's inevitable in war. However much you prepare before a battle, the moment comes when hundreds of men arrive at once, and you only have so many pairs of hands. I think all of us, from time to time, have a moment when our hearts quail and we wonder if we can cope with it all.'

Oliver and Darroway nodded at that. 'There was an explosion at a factory in Long Acre last week,' Oliver said. 'Dozens of badly burned and injured, and all needing attention at once.'

'Just so,' said Westhoven. 'Well, we deal with the worst cases first, take them into the operating room. The nurses have to look after the rest until we can get to them, and I must say they perform miracles. They clean and bandage wounds, give morphia for the pain and saline for the shock, splint fractures and do some of the suturing. And, of course, they reassure the men – that's terribly important when some of them are desperately wounded. The nurses carry so much of the burden, it's hard to remember they're supposed to be the weaker sex.'

'It's no surprise that women can achieve great things when they are given the chance,' said Katherine.

'Of course not,' said Westhoven, 'but the conditions there, and the sights and smells – the terrible wounds, the terrible numbers . . . Well, I suppose they're new to all of us. But I really think the nurses cope better than us. I've never seen one turn away, though I've seen some of the orderlies have to leave the room for a moment.'

'I've heard you're having a lot of trouble with tetanus now,' Venetia said.

'Yes, so many of these men come in after lying in the mud with open wounds for hours, waiting for the stretcher-bearers to get to them, and the soil around Ypres is heavily infected with the bacterium.'

'What is tetanus?' Emma asked.

'Lockjaw, dear,' Mrs Darroway answered kindly.

'I did know, but I'd forgotten,' Emma said. 'My uncle had a groom once who was bitten by a horse, who got it. But he got better.'

'It's treatable,' Westhoven said, 'and the sooner we can give them the anti-toxin the better their chances. Ideally we'd like to inject everyone as soon as they come in. But, of course, with such numbers all at once, it's hard for the nurses to get round everybody. The end stages can be horrible. We had a fellow last week who went into such severe spasm that he broke his own ribs.'

341

'What about the gas attacks?' Darroway asked. 'We've heard a lot about them from the military point of view, but nothing much from the medical.'

'I expect the government doesn't want the details to be widely known, for fear of affecting morale. But it will come out in the end. The nurses hate the gas far more than shells and bullets, because there's almost nothing to be done for the victims. They come in frothing at the mouth, in great pain, their chests distended, coughing and retching. As the effects progress, their lungs pretty well dissolve. Eventually they drown in their own blood and mucus.'

'You give them oxygen?' Venetia asked.

'When we have it. It helps those who are lightly affected, but it doesn't stop the progress of dissolution. You can see the advancing cyanosis. It's terrible to watch them fight for breath, knowing there's nothing you can do about it.'

'I've heard the gas causes blindness, too,' Oliver said.

'Yes, half the cases that come in are affected that way,' Westhoven said. 'The gas burns the conjunctivae, the eyelids swell and the eyes ooze pus. The only treatment we have is frequent bathing in bicarb solution, which seems to ease the pain and swelling a little. But most of the gas cases die anyway, from anoxia. I believe one or two have gone home, but how long they will survive is in question.'

'Lung damage is irreversible,' Venetia said. 'Lungs don't grow back.'

He turned to her. 'And the damn stuff is so pernicious. It hangs around for days. We've had men who've washed or shaved in water taken from shell-holes, who come in with burns to their faces. And it clings to their clothes and works through. We've found great water blisters on their skin when we undress them – when the blister bursts you can smell the chlorine in the serum. At the end of a session you find yourself feeling nauseous, with a raw throat and sore eyes, and that's just from what's coming off the victims' clothes and hair.'

'It sounds appalling,' Freddie Copthall said, looking a little pale from all this medical talk. 'I have to say I really

342

admire you. How you have the courage to face such horrors I can't imagine. I know I never could. Fighting is one thing, and I suppose we can all imagine ourselves finding the wherewithal in the heat of battle; but having to deal with the aftermath in cold blood . . .' He shook his head. 'Thank heaven there are fellows like you willing to do it, or what would happen to our soldiers?'

Jessie glanced involuntarily at Oliver, and he gave a grim little smile. 'Not up to your usual standard of tact, Freddie,' he said. 'Or are you deliberately trying to make me feel guilty for remaining here at home?'

'Oh, Lord!' Freddie groaned. 'What have I said? I didn't mean it like that at all.'

'I know what you meant,' Oliver said, 'and I agree with you. Westhoven's twice the man I am.'

Jessie could see he was teasing, but Westhoven looked embarrassed. The blood came visibly to his face, and in his dismay he seemed very young, like a schoolboy caught out in a bloomer. 'I shouldn't have gone on at such length about it,' he said apologetically. 'Especially not before ladies.'

'Nonsense. We asked you to tell us,' said Venetia.

'We're all grown-ups here,' Katherine said kindly. 'Even the "ladies". You haven't said anything you shouldn't.'

'I didn't mean any criticism of you, Winchmore,' Freddie said. 'Dash it, I'm still at home too.'

'Oliver stayed because someone had to,' Darroway said.

Westhoven, still a little pink, met Oliver's eyes earnestly. 'I hope you don't think I was – well, boasting, or anything. I'm not brave. When the casualties come in, one's too busy to think about funking, that's all.'

Now Oliver laughed. 'I think we'd better drop the subject before we get even more entangled in our efforts to condone me. I've always known I would have to go sooner or later, but I genuinely feel we need some doctors here at home as well.'

'Of course we do,' said Venetia. 'Accidents don't stop happening because we're at war. Your factory fire in Long Acre, for instance – and that terrible railway crash this morning.'

'I can't help thinking of the poor men trapped in the burning carriages,' Katherine said, with a shudder.

'I wish we could do more for burns victims,' Oliver said. 'There was a young airman came in to the Southport last week with bad burns to the hands and face. What does the future hold for him? What's the point of saving the poor fellow, when for the rest of his life he'll have to sit in a darkened room for fear of frightening people, and have his food cut up for him because his hands are useless claws? I wish we could find a way to reconstruct them.' He looked down at his own hands, by which he made his living, and then up at Westhoven's handsome face. 'Unlike lung tissue, we grow new skin all the time. If we could only find a way of directing and shaping it.'

Westhoven was plainly gripped by this suggestion. 'Reconstruction?' he said, staring at Oliver with interest. 'That would be a wonderful thing, if it were possible. And not just for burns – we see some terrible facial injuries from explosives coming in, too. Perhaps after the war you could make it a special study.'

'You might not have to wait until peacetime to see an advance,' said Darroway. 'Medical science always takes a leap forward during war, partly from necessity and partly because there are so many more cases to learn from and experiment on. It's the only good thing that ever comes out of conflict.'

'Although this time, perhaps, the women's cause might take a leap forward, too,' said Katherine. 'A lot of the former suffragettes are volunteering and doing very good work.'

Darroway looked at Jessie and smiled. 'I understand from Oliver that you've started nursing.'

'I remembered your telling me some time ago that it was the most important thing a woman could do if the war did come,' said Jessie. 'So I took my Red Cross certificates, and now I'm helping at a local hospital. But I wouldn't call what I do "nursing". The trained nurses don't much like volunteers, and the sister in particular likes to keep me in my place.'

'And what is your place?' Katherine asked.

'The sluice-room,' Jessie said, with a grin. 'I scrub and tidy and fetch and carry, but mostly I scrub – bedpans, mackintosh sheets, kidney dishes, baths, floors. If there were a National Certificate in scrubbing, I could pass with honours.'

Mark Darroway laughed, but Emma said indignantly, 'I do think it's shocking to abuse a willing volunteer like that. Can't you go over her head?'

Jessie shrugged. 'The work has to be done by someone. And by doing it I'm giving the trained nurses more time to do their job.'

'A noble sentiment,' said Darroway. 'But you are wasted on the menial. In my opinion you would make a fine nurse. You should come to London, join a VAD, and apply to nurse in a military hospital. You'd be trained properly then, to do real nursing.'

'My family would never hear of it,' Jessie smiled. 'They were horrified enough that I wanted to work in a local hospital. It would drive them to fits if I were to leave home into the bargain.'

Venetia thought this a good juncture to rise and take everyone into the drawing-room, where coffee was served, and the conversation broke up into smaller groups and diverse topics. She found herself on a sofa with Mark Darroway, deep in a do-you-remember sort of conversation, about their youthful days as medical students, the innocence of the world as it then was, and the changes that had come over it since. But as a good hostess, she still kept an eye on the rest of the company. Overton and Katherine Darroway were a conversational pair, as were Oliver and Jessie, chatting easily as old friends. The other four were talking together, though it looked as if Westhoven was doing most of the speaking, in response to questions Emma was putting. Venetia had shaken off Beauty's teasing suggestion, but she could not help thinking they made a nice couple, and that Westhoven's eyes were fixed on Emma's pretty face more often than on the other two. Freddie put in a comment of his own from time to time, and it was obvious that he was being droll, because often they all laughed. Only Violet, Venetia thought, was unusually quiet: she seemed perfectly happy, but detached, with a serene smile on her lovely countenance and a rather absent look, as if she were thinking about other things.

The evening came to an end, the visitors departed, and when Venetia returned to the drawing-room from seeing them off, she found Oliver pouring two more brandies for Westhoven and himself.

'A little nightcap, Mum?' he asked her. 'Father said to say he's gone up.'

'No, thank you, my dear. I'm going to bed too. It was a good gathering, don't you think?'

'Excellent, ma'am, and thank you very much,' said Westhoven.

'Very good,' said Oliver. 'A nice evening.' He handed the glass to Westhoven and answered his mother's look. 'We shan't be long.'

She smiled at him, thinking the measure in the glass portended a long conversation. Not just a 'nightcap', but pyjamas and dressing-gown too! 'Be as long as you like,' she said, 'but don't keep the servants up, will you, darling?'

'No, I won't. We'll look after ourselves.'

She left them settling into two armchairs drawn up to each other, brandies to hand and cigars newly lit, and thought how cosy they appeared together. She half wished she could stay up with them, but at her age her bed beckoned more strongly. It would be nice for Oliver if Westhoven became a friend. She sometimes worried that he seemed to have so few intimates, and wondered if living with his parents restricted him in any way. But it was his choice, after all. Still, Westhoven would be good for him, and she was glad she had asked him to stay. She thought of her own long chat with Mark Darroway, and smiled as she took herself off to bed. There was nothing like an old medical friend to talk to.

★　★　★

346

The full story of the Quintinshill disaster became known over the next few days. Quintinshill was a small station with one up line, one down line, and a passing loop. The two signalmen, Tinsley and Meakin, had made a friendly agreement about the change of shift: whoever was coming on for the day shift, which started at six o'clock, would catch the local train, which arrived at around six thirty. This gave him an extra half-hour in bed, besides making the journey much easier. Meanwhile the night-shift man would cover for him, logging the traffic movements on a piece of paper, to be transferred into the log book later so that it was in the right handwriting for the deception to be hidden.

It should have been a harmless subterfuge, as it had been on countless other occasions. The problem arose on the morning of the 22nd because the London to Glasgow express was late, and Meakin, who had had the night shift, had been forced to move a local down train onto the up line to allow it to go through. Normally the local would have been moved into the passing loop, but at the time the loop was already occupied by a coal train. Meakin handed over to Tinsley in the normal way at six thirty, passing him the piece of paper with the interim movements written out on it. Soon afterwards, while Tinsley was busy transferring the notes to the log, the next signal box down the line, at Kirtlebridge, rang through to offer the southbound troop train. Tinsley entirely forgot the stationary local train on the up line, still waiting to be told it could switch lines and proceed. He accepted the troop train.

The Quintinshill signal box was supplied with lever collars, which were supposed to be used to remind the signalmen not to clear a particular lever because of some obstruction on the line. But for some time the signalmen had not bothered with them. So there was nothing to warn Tinsley that he had forgotten something as he pulled the lever, and cleared the signal for the troop train to come through.

Two hundred and twenty-seven men died, and two hundred and forty-six were injured, some of them gravely.

347

There were terrible burn and crush injuries, and some men had to have limbs amputated to free them from the burning wreckage before the fire consumed them. It was the worst rail disaster of all time, and a devastating blow to Scotland and the army as a whole. Of the half-battalion of Royal Scots on the train, only sixty survived to roll-call the next day. The day after that, bruised, shaken and shocked, they embarked at Liverpool with the other two companies for the Dardanelles. The Terriers had been on local duties since the beginning of the war, guarding coastal defences, and had been longing, like all volunteers, to be going overseas to make a fight of it. The pity of their end, and the horror of it, filled the nation's minds.

Jessie was unable to give much of her attention to the disaster, because the news came, the day after the dinner party, that there was a renewed offensive in Ypres. Both Bertie and Ned were in the line. The action went on for two days; and it would be another two days after that before she could hope to hear from either of them. It made her realise at last what the war would mean for her, and for anyone with a man at the Front: just such regular periods of mental agony, relieved only temporarily by the news that he had come through this time, knowing always that there would be a next time, and a time after that – and how long could luck last? The process of strain and relief would only end when the war ended – or with the man's death.

She moved in a state of numbness through the days, feeling that life and even thought were suspended until the news came, for good or ill. She was grateful to Violet for remaining so serene through it all. Holkam being at Headquarters, the likelihood of his being killed or injured was much less – but Jessie had a strange feeling that Violet would not have exhibited the same anxiety as her, even had he been in the line. Perhaps she did not have the imagination to fret about what might happen to him, or perhaps it was a matter of temperament. Jessie knew it was not indifference. But at all events, it made things just a little easier

348

to bear, as though Violet were a rock to cling to, against a surging sea of dread.

Lord Overton kindly passed on to her the earliest news that the fighting had died down again, with the added comfort that intelligence suggested the Germans, too, had run out of men and ammunition at last, and that things would be quieter in Ypres for the time being. And then came a telegram from Ned – 'All well. Letter follows' – and then, at last, a letter from Bertie to say that he had come through with only a minor flesh wound.

After the strain of waiting, the relief of the news made Jessie more than willing to join in again with the pleasures of the Season, and on the evening of the day when she received Bertie's letter – a pathetically grubby piece of paper with scrawled pencil writing, which told of the exigencies under which it had been written – she went gladly with Violet and Emma to the Southport Hospital charity ball, danced every dance and was a lively companion to her partners. Oliver, who was one of them, remarked that he had never seen her looking prettier, and said that even Emma did not have more young men queuing for her hand.

'I feel as light as a feather tonight,' Jessie replied. 'Tomorrow I may be as heavy as lead, so you'd best take advantage while it lasts. It occurs to me, you see, that we are all living on the edge of disaster, not just the men at the Front.'

'War fever,' Oliver sighed. 'And I thought it was my stimulating company that was inspiring you tonight.'

'You're wasting your sighs on me. Go and breathe into the ear of an unmarried girl. There are lots here tonight. Look, there's a pretty one over there.'

'Antonia Blessingham?' He shuddered. 'A man-eater – and she laughs like a hyena. No, I'll stay with you, Mrs Morland, and be safe. You are infinitely soothing. If only you weren't married, you might soothe me all the time.'

'If you were any more soothed, you'd be comatose. Your mother told me how hard she had to work to make you come here tonight. For shame!'

'I was tired after a day's doctoring. Must you lecture me?'

'Not really. In fact we needn't talk at all,' Jessie said, suddenly feeling tired. 'Let's just go round in friendly silence. All this merry-making is wearing me out.'

'Aren't you enjoying your holiday?' he asked, sounding genuinely concerned.

'Oh, yes, very much. But in some ways, enjoying oneself is harder work than hard work. I'm almost looking forward to going home for a rest.'

He smiled. 'I know just what you mean.'

BOOK THREE

In Action

My share of fourscore years and ten
I'll gladly yield to any man,
And take no thought of 'where' or 'when',
Contented with my shorter span,
For I have learned what love may be,
And found a heart that understands,
And known a comrade's constancy,
And felt the grip of friendly hands.

Richard Molesworth Dennys, 'Better Far To Pass Away'

CHAPTER FIFTEEN

The Southport Hospital Ball was on the 30th of May; but the month had not delivered its last excitement yet. On the following night, there was a Zeppelin raid on London.

The airship, named after the German inventor Count Zeppelin, was an enormous, fish-shaped craft, five hundred feet long, able to carry a huge load of over four thousand pounds of bombs. The skin of the gas-bag was stretched over a rigid aluminium frame, and contained lateral fuel cells filled with hydrogen, which made the craft lighter than air and gave it its 'lift'. It carried two engines, which drove propellors for impulse and direction, so it was also known as a 'dirigible'. It could not reach any great speed – about fifty m.p.h. was its limit, and it more usually moved at around twenty m.p.h. – but it did not need to. From their hangars in occupied Belgium, the Zeppelins had only to climb in the late afternoon to a level where they found a favourable wind, cut their engines, and drift in silence across the water to England. Arriving in darkness, they dropped their bombs, then climbed to a greater height for safety and turned for home.

The first Zeppelin attack had happened on the night of the 19th of January, when two airships had crossed the North Sea to the Norfolk coast, where they had separated. By eight p.m. one of them had appeared over Great Yarmouth, dropped a bomb in an empty field, then drifted over the town, dropping more bombs. The explosions killed seventy-two-year-old Miss Martha Taylor, and a shoemaker, Samuel Smith, and injured thirteen others. The other Zeppelin dropped its bombs on King's Lynn, killing two more people.

The choice of targets was mysterious. Although Great Yarmouth had a port and could therefore just be considered a military target, it was of no strategic importance, and Lynn was nothing but a small market town. Experts said that dropping bombs from Zeppelins was easy, but hitting a target was near impossible; and that airships were susceptible to being blown off course by wind and weather. It was quite likely therefore that the targets had not been chosen, but were inadvertent. On the other hand, attacking harmless civilians might be the beginning of a new phase of warfare. After the business of the poison gas, who could doubt the Germans capable of it?

Since then, the east coast had been subjected to raids whenever there was a moonless night – because of their slow speed and large size, the Germans preferred the dark to give them the best chance of reaching their objective undetected. It made it all the more frightening to the helpless civilians, many of whom had barely got used to the idea of flight, and some of whom had never seen an aeroplane, to find the vast monster hanging in the air above them in defiance of nature, blocking out the sky. They were so enormous that they seemed to be right overhead even when they were several miles away – a phenomenon that meant more of them were reported than actually arrived.

On the 15th of April, Zeppelins bombed Lowestoft and Southwold, and on the 10th of May they dropped a hundred bombs on Southend. Reporting of earlier attacks had been restricted under the Defence of the Realm Act, to avoid causing widespread panic, but the raid on Southend could not be ignored. Three days later the King ordered the Kaiser, his son the Crown Prince, and all other German princes to be struck off the roll of Knights of the Garter. It was only a symbolic gesture – though the more striking because they were his own relatives – but it expressed a little of the outrage people were feeling at this new German 'frightfulness'.

Then came the raid of 31st of May. It was the first time London had been attacked. Even without moonlight, it was easy enough for a Zeppelin pilot to spot the Thames estuary, and follow the river into the heart of the capital. As the single airship drifted noiselessly in on the breeze, the first warning the defenders on the ground had was the gleam of the yellow-blue exhausts of its four engines, reflected on the taut underside of its gas-bag. By then it was too late.

That there *were* defenders at all was due to the foresight of the recently departed First Lord, Winston Churchill. Aerial defence of the nation had been in the hands of the Admiralty since August 1914, when virtually the entire Royal Flying Corps had left for France. Churchill had foreseen the Zeppelin attacks, and the necessity of defending at least London from them. He had flights of naval aeroplanes stationed at Eastchurch, Calshot and Hendon, and the few RFC machines that were available for home defence were stationed at Hounslow and Joyce Green. He had also arranged for landing grounds to be prepared in London parks, and had them provided with lighting systems so that they could operate at night. And he had created an Anti-Aircraft Corps for London, under the command of a Royal Navy captain – though because of the shortage of naval personnel it was manned entirely by volunteers, recruited from the university and the City.

But it was not easy to shoot down a Zeppelin. No-one had yet perfected high-angle gunnery, and the AA Corps had only ten guns, some of them of Boer War vintage. Even with searchlights, it was hard to find the targets in the dark sky, and because of the shape of the craft, even direct hits tended not to pierce the skin, but skid off it. And the airships were able to fly so high that more often than not the shots could not reach, but exploded well below them.

On the 31st of May, the home-defence aeroplanes took off, but because there was no advance warning of the raid, they were unable to get into position in time to stop it, or to climb high enough to attack the airship on its way home. The AA guns stuttered and the searchlights swept back and forth, but still the Zeppelin dropped ninety incendiary bombs and thirty grenades over the north-eastern suburbs of London, causing extensive fires, killing seven civilians and injuring another thirty-five. The defences accomplished nothing but to shower the London streets with shrapnel – to the delight of small boys the following day.

The anguish and fear the raid caused in the population was out of all proportion to the damage done or the fatalities caused.

'But that must be the purpose of them,' Jack said, as he and Helen read about it in the newspapers at breakfast the next day. 'It's naturally unsettling to have the enemy suddenly appear overhead when you thought he was in France.'

'And they come so silently,' Helen said. 'That's what I would find most unnerving. It gives the whole thing an almost supernatural feel.'

'You have too much imagination,' Jack said, stroking Rug's ears absently as the dog put his paws up on his master's knees, hoping for a little something from the table.

'Even so, I can't think how much it must cost the Germans to send the things. Can it really be worth their while? All in all, they haven't done very much damage.'

'How much would you like them to do?'

'You know I don't mean that,' Helen said, pouring more coffee. 'I'm trying to see it from the Germans' point of view. Why would they bother with them?'

'Well, I suppose it's a political weapon,' Jack said, absently putting his last corner of toast into Rug's mouth instead of his own. The dog retired under the table and crunched lustily. 'It makes the government look helpless, having the enemy appear right in the heart of the capital, as if they can just walk in when they want to. Particularly unnerving when we English haven't been invaded since 1066. And it creates fear and anxiety in the civilian population, which I suppose they think will sap the nation's morale. I must say, the newspapers are playing into the enemy's hands, with the fuss they're making.'

She looked across the table to see what he was reading and said, 'The *Daily News*? You can't expect any loyalty from *that* press.'

'What we really ought to be doing is taking the fight back to them. We should bomb the Zeppelin sheds in Belgium. There's no point in killing ants one by one – you have to take a kettle of boiling water and pour it down the nest hole.'

'How poetic,' Helen said. 'Why didn't Mr Churchill do that, I wonder?'

'As I understand it, he did have a plan, but never got round to implementing it.' He slipped a piece of sausage to Rug. Unfortunately it had mustard on it, as a violent volley of sneezes from under the table attested.

'Please don't feed the dog at the table,' Helen said. 'It teaches him bad manners.'

'Sorry. I didn't realise I was doing it,' said Jack. 'But I think Rug's manners are already formed. You can't teach an old dog new tricks.'

'As platitudes go, I've always thought that one particularly misinformed. Dogs are very nearly as adaptable as humans.'

'Yes, it ought to be, "You can't teach old cows new tricks." Now *there*'s an animal with a rigid frame of mind.'

Helen reverted to the subject. 'I suppose things will change a lot in the RNAS now that Churchill's gone.'

'I imagine so. Balfour's a much more traditional sort of man—'

'Everyone's more traditional than Churchill.'

'Quite – so it will be the old seadogs at the Admiralty who dictate RNAS policy from now on. And they're not likely to be interested in attacking Zeppelins. They'll want all their air power directed to anti-submarine duties.'

'Understandable,' Helen said. 'I remember their reaction when Hull and Scarborough were shelled last year – "the east coast must put up with it", or words to that effect.'

Jack swallowed the last of his sausage and put the newspaper aside. 'I'll tell you something else that's likely to change. Churchill really had no business taking on the air defence at home in the first place. I suppose he did it because he felt he'd do it better than anyone else. But the traditionalists at the Admiralty – and I met some of 'em when I was at Sopwith's – have never liked the idea of the navy being involved with air defence over land. I wouldn't be surprised if they press Asquith to hand that back to the army. They'll say they don't mind patrolling the sea, but once a hostile aircraft crosses the coast, it ought to be the army that brings it down.'

'Which means the RFC,' said Helen. 'But the RFC barely has enough aeroplanes for the offensive in France. How can it possibly provide a whole new force for home defence?'

'Well, it can't, obviously.' Jack moved restlessly as the old problem raised its head again. 'It's a nonsense having two separate air forces – and neither of them commanded by airmen. The duplication, the waste, the muddle – they're doing so much damage! The Admiralty gets the lion's share of the aeronautics budget and, thanks to Churchill, they can buy machines where they like. We have to struggle along with crumbs from the table, and everything has to go through the Royal Aircraft Factory, which stifles innovation like, like—'

'Wet cement?' Helen offered. She eyed her husband with sympathy. She knew how frustrated he felt, still unable to fly. The ankle that had been shattered when his aeroplane came down last autumn had seemed to be healing at last, then thrown another splinter of bone, which had set him back again, so he was ordered to put no weight on it. He must, she knew – though he did not talk about it – fear that he would never be sound enough to fly again. And on the design side, he was still unable to devise a working model for forward firing in an aeroplane. The single-seater aeroplane, with a machine-gun that could fire forwards and be operated by the pilot, would make all the difference in the world to the RFC's operations. At present you could only fire forwards from a 'pusher' aeroplane, because they had the engine and propellor behind; but only 'tractor' aeroplanes were fast enough and manoeuvrable enough to be worth developing as military craft. How to fire forwards without shooting away your own propellor? He pretty well knew how to do it in theory, but as in anything to do with the air – as he had learnt as a very young boy, before heavier-than-air flight had even been accomplished – it was putting the theory into practice that was the difficulty.

Seeing her companion had relapsed into frowning thought, Helen abandoned the conversation and returned to the newspaper, but her mind wandered too, to the more congenial subject of her house. Though the purchase had not gone through yet, they had decided to begin redecorating, and there was a great deal of new paper and paint about the ground floor – the disagreeable smell of new paint was just beginning to wear off. The owner's estate had seen to the drains and the plumbing, and there was scaffolding at present obscuring the front of the house as a man turned up intermittently to continue with repairs to the roof and repointing the chimneys. The irregularity of his appearances was a frustration to Helen, but apparently most of the building firm's employees had volunteered, and the remaining staff were spreading themselves thinly around the work on hand.

The kitchen was still dark, as they could not put in a new window until the house was theirs, but it had been scrubbed spotless, the walls white-painted, the range cleaned and put in order, and the chimney swept. The cook, an elderly local woman, was delighted with the stove. She said it worked a treat, and baked much better than those gas things, which dried food out to her mind, and weren't healthy, neither, for gas was gas whichever way you looked at it, and you didn't want it soaking into your food, it stood to reason. Helen had eaten gas-soaked food for most of her life, but she agreed earnestly with Mrs Binny for the sake of her light-as-air cakes and pastry.

Helen and Jack lived, for the moment, on the ground

floor, sleeping together in the small room and spending the rest of their time in the big one with the bay window. Their table, a gateleg, was set up in the bay, so that they could gaze out at the magnificent view as they ate. They had not entertained yet, so didn't need a separate dining-room, but Helen had plans for extending the house once it was theirs, putting the bathroom upstairs and building along that side so that the dining-room would have the view, too. And their present bedroom would make a delightful small sitting-room, or a study for Jack. Mrs Binny was using the other small downstairs room as her bedroom – more convenient, and she didn't like the look of them stairs, not with her legs. The housemaid, Aggie, came in daily, because she only lived down the road in the village, and they had a charwoman, Mrs Faulks, who came in twice a week. She did the heavy cleaning, and also – she was a treasure – helped out with the laundry. Helen had a pleasant way with servants, and was a good judge of character, and she felt settled already and quite happy with her two and a half. Once the house was theirs, of course – and if things should change – well, other arrangements would slot down happily into the structure she had set up. If she should find herself in the family way, for instance . . .

Aggie interrupted her daydream, coming in with the second post. Helen sorted the letters, passed Jack's over, and began to open hers.

Jack was roused from his contemplation of a bill by a small noise from his wife, and looked up to see that she was actually turning quite pink. 'What is it?' he asked. 'Helen? Are you really blushing? I don't believe it! What is it? Don't tell me I have a rival! I have to warn you that no amount of money will buy me off. You're stuck with me now, even if you have changed your mind.' She looked across at him, confused. 'Please put me out of my misery. Say *something*, even if it's only goodbye.'

'Oh, do hush!' she said, struggling with laughter. 'As if it could be that!'

'I'm relieved to hear it.'

'After the length of time you kept me waiting, I'm not likely to let you go.'

'Unhandsome of you to remind me of my stupidity, but we'll let it pass. What is it, then?'

'It's something rather exciting. I've had a letter—'

'I can see that.'

'But you keep interrupting me,' she protested. 'I've had the offer of a job.'

'Good Lord!' He stared. 'What do you want with a job? What sort of job? And why should it make you blush?'

'It was something I didn't tell you about because I wasn't sure how you'd feel about it, and I thought there was no point in upsetting you if it was impossible anyway. But now it seems – well, they'd like me to do it.'

'Do *what*?' Jack said. 'I shall be forced to strangle you if you don't tell me straight out what you've been up to, and then it won't be the Bride in the Bath splashed all over the newspapers, it will be the Bride at the Breakfast Table. *What job*?'

'Well, you see, everyone's so short of flyers, and it seemed an awful waste that I can fly and no-one's making use of it. I can't join the RFC, obviously—'

'I'm glad to hear you didn't contemplate it.'

'But I did think I could be useful, delivering aeroplanes from the factory to the bases. It seems such a waste of personnel to use a trained military airman to do that when a civilian could do it just as well.' She looked at her husband uncertainly, unable to read his face. 'You've always said I'm as good a flyer as any man—'

'Better than most,' said Jack.

'And I do so long to do something for the war effort. Well, this letter says they've accepted me. I'll get paid, too, which is a help, given how expensive the house is going to be. I hope you don't mind. I know how frustrated you feel, not being able to fly, and I do hope you won't think it tactless of me to want to fly when you can't, or – well – feel hurt, or – or that I'm undermining you or anything like that . . .'

361

Her explanation petered out in the face of Jack's silence. Had she wounded his male pride? Was he going to be Victorian about it and say no wife of *his* should have a job, even one as patriotic as this?

'After all,' she added, 'women of all sorts are joining VADs and doing things like nursing and driving and so on. So I thought—'

'Helen,' Jack said.

'Yes?'

'You're babbling, my love. Do you really think I'm such a dog-in-the-manger? I think it's a splendid idea. I only hope it doesn't take you away from me too often.'

'Oh, no, only once or twice a week at most,' she said, her voice lifting with relief. 'And only for the day. I might have to stay overnight once in a while, but with most trips I'll be able to get back the same day. Do you really not mind?'

'I'm furiously jealous,' he said, 'and utterly miserable that I still can't get up myself, but you are a splendid flyer and I'd be a rogue and a dog to want to deprive the country of your services. I love you for wanting to do it, and I love you for worrying about my feelings. You have my blessing – in so far as my blessing is important to you.'

'Of course it's important,' she said indignantly.

He grinned. 'But the fact that you didn't tell me about it suggests you weren't intending to ask my permission.'

'I didn't *really* think you'd try and stop me,' she confessed. 'I only didn't want you to be hurt, and I thought if they turned me down, then least said was soonest mended.'

'Come and kiss me,' he said, stretching out a hand. She came and sat on his lap and a satisfactory silence fell for a time. Aggie and Mrs Binny had had to grow used to coming upon the master and mistress 'behaving like newlyweds', as Mrs Binny put it. Aggie had told her she thought it was touching, and there was no harm in it. 'Better that than fighting like cat and dog, which my sister saw in her last place,' and Mrs Binny had said, 'Gentry oughtn't to do neither. But live and let live, I suppose. They'll grow out of it, I don't doubt.'

They were showing no signs of growing out of it yet, but this time they were not interrupted, so there was no harm done. When they stopped for breath, Jack said, 'I shall miss your services as a driver, though. How am I going to get about?'

'I asked the wing-co about that, and he said there was no reason why you shouldn't have an RFC driver. He was surprised you hadn't asked before,' said Helen.

Jack laughed. 'Now you've completely given yourself away. You considered every objection, didn't you? I half wish I had come the heavy, and told you you couldn't do it, just to see what your strategy was for overcoming my resistance.'

'You've just experienced it,' she said, and kissed him again.

'Ah, well, in that case, take it that I'm resisting a great deal, will you? Mmm. Anything else you'd like to do, that I could disapprove of? Don't be afraid to mention it, you know.'

But Helen was now laughing too much to carry on kissing him.

Jessie had a letter from Frank, which required another visit to Miss Stanhope. She decided that the best time to see her would be on Saturday when she had finished her half-day at work. 'I thought I would take her out to luncheon at a time when she can relax and enjoy it.'

'Do,' said Violet. 'I shan't be able to come with you because I have a fitting. It's a nuisance, but Roche can't put me in at any other time.'

'I'd like to come,' said Emma. 'May I? I'd like to meet Frank's beloved.'

Jessie smiled. 'That does sound strange.'

'Well, what else can I call her? Not his fiancée, because he's so idiotic about it.'

'Oh, I agree. I only meant that it's strange to think of Frankie *having* a beloved, when he was never interested in anything but equations and particles and so on.'

Jessie sent round a note, received a reply, and on the Saturday she and Emma went in a taxi-cab to Bloomsbury, picked up Miss Stanhope, who was waiting for them outside the college, and took her to the Ritz. She had decided now that Miss Stanhope's character was robust enough to withstand the splendour of it, and she knew Emma would like it better. Besides, Selfridges' restaurant on a Saturday would be disagreeably crowded.

She had telephoned in advance and asked for a table by the terrace windows, where they could look out over the Italian Garden and the park; and talking about the pleasant view got them over the first few awkward moments. Emma looked at Maria at first with wide-eyed interest, but as Maria returned the examination just as frankly, it soon passed. Maria was dressed much as before, except that the dark brown skirt and jacket were a degree less worn and shabby, and her blouse was white, with a rather nice cameo brooch at the throat. She wore a different hat, too, which looked freshly brushed and sported what was obviously a new feather. Forewarned, she had got herself up in her 'best', Jessie thought, touched. But it brought home to her again the difference in their circumstances. Though she herself had dressed plainly and had hinted to Emma that she should do the same, the difference between their respective clothes was obvious enough.

But it was impossible to feel sorry for Maria for very long, for she was not overcome by her surroundings, and seemed quite at ease. She looked around the pretty dining-room with appreciation, and said, 'This is the most luxurious place I've ever been in. It's very kind of you to bring me. I've passed it once or twice and wondered what it was like inside, but I never thought I'd ever eat here.'

Her unforced frankness put both her companions at ease. Emma said, 'I still feel rather excited about lunching here, myself. When my father was alive I was never allowed to eat anywhere except in private homes – and even now, Aunt Venetia is very particular about which restaurants I can go to. But no-one could object to the Ritz.'

'I should think not, indeed,' Maria laughed.

'Oh, no – I mean that it's quite respectable,' Emma said, and since that was hardly better, they all laughed.

Released from work and the worry of being late, Maria was in lively spirits, and the conversation bloomed between the three young women. Emma in particular seemed attracted to her, and they talked freely about a wide range of subjects, so that Jessie could see a friendship beginning.

The only time that Maria seemed in any way disturbed was when Emma's friends came over to the table to pay their respects. It was impossible for a popular girl like Emma to lunch in a place like the Ritz and not see someone she knew. John French and Tim Beaufort were rather bouncy young men, part of Emma's court. When introduced to Maria they bowed perfectly correctly and did not by so much as an eyebrow suggest she was in any way out of her place, but she responded coolly and withdrew from the subsequent conversation. Mr and Mrs George Westerham paused on their way to their table to say hello and ask if Emma had heard any news of Peter Hargrave. Edith Westerham asked if they were going to the Lanchesters' ball, and included Maria in the enquiry, which elicited only a brisk shake of the head. And then Tommy Draycott, who had married Emma's friend Angela Burnet, came over to say he and Angela were lunching with a party on the other side of the room, and invited them to join them. It was not, of course, for Maria to make the decision, but Jessie caught one glimpse of the distress in her eyes before she lowered them, and she said at once, 'Thank you, Tommy, but we are having rather a female sort of luncheon. Lots of secrets to exchange.'

'Of course. Excuse me,' Tommy said, perfectly agreeably, and took himself off. There was a moment's awkwardness at the table, when Jessie was afraid one of her companions would mention it – that Maria would apologise, or Emma would try to laugh the thing off, either of which would have been embarrassing – but then Emma began talking about a novel she was reading, and it emerged that Maria had just read it too, and the moment passed.

When they had finished luncheon, Jessie suggested they retire to the Palm Court so that she could show Maria

Frank's letter, which would not have been correct behaviour at the table. They settled in a secluded corner in the pretty room, where a pianist was quietly playing a selection of popular songs; the waiter brought coffee; and Jessie and Emma chatted while Maria read.

The letter had, of course, been written to Jessie, so she knew what it said.

Military life is much the same here as it was in England, except that the weather is nicer, which makes even our regular route marches along the coast road pleasant. Garrison duties are light, but the colonel keeps us busy all day, bringing us up to active duty standard, and every man is so eager to get to France that I believe they almost welcome the endless drills and lectures. One of the NCOs put everyone into a gloom the other day by saying that in peacetime it took three years to train a soldier to battle readiness, and you could see on every face the notion taking root that we would never get to the Front. But it emerged later that the powers-that-be expect us to be 'done to a turn' in only eight months, so that was all right!

My own circumstances have changed: a kind word and a hint from our colonel persuaded me to apply for a commission. I had not previously considered it because, not having gone to a public school, I was never in OTC, but it seems in these perilous times that is no longer considered an outright bar. So you may tell Mother, and those at home who may be impressed with such things, that I am now appointed a temporary second lieutenant. Training keeps me busier than ever. Battalion day starts with breakfast at 8 and parade at 8.30, and ends at 5.30. During that time I am with the platoon and share all the drills, route marches and manoeuvres, and take practical lessons from the sergeant-major on how and what to bellow on the parade ground. On top of that, I have to be up at the crack of dawn for two hours of officers' lectures before breakfast, with another two hours before dinner, and after dinner private study deep into the night.

I have to master signalling and map-reading, be au fait with specialist subjects like machine-gunnery and reconnaissance, and be able at the drop of a hat to lecture on any number of subjects, from the history of the regiment to personal hygiene on active service!

I was alarmed to discover that an officer has not only to command in battle, but feed, clothe and billet his platoon, attend to all their wants, and be responsible for their arms and equipment, from rifles to entrenching tools. There's so much to learn I can feel everything I ever knew about mathematics and physics being pushed out of my head to make room. The other day in the cook-house we were solemnly shown how to tell the difference between the carcases of a cat and a rabbit, so that we shall not be cozened by wily foreigners when provisioning our men. (The answer, you may like to know, lies in the number of ribs – otherwise they look remarkably similar when skinned, topped and tailed.)

Off duty, the men play football and cricket, and at weekends they can go into Valetta, where there are bars, cafés, a kinema, a theatre, and band recitals in the park. We officers are hardly ever at leisure, but when we can unstring the bow for an hour or two we like to make up sea-bathing parties. We take a picnic and Prendergast's gramophone and lie under the trees, listening to *La Traviata*, blowing a cloud and watching the stately procession of ships going past. There are plenty of cargo and troop ships, but the ones that disturb us are the hospital ships coming back from the Dardanelles. There are so many. What is happening out there? By our reckoning the casualties must be in the tens of thousands. Some of the sick have been brought here to the military hospital, and occasionally a shipful of the wounded will dock for a while on its way back to England. What news we hear is that things are not going well out east, and that reinforcements are badly needed in both theatres. It makes us more anxious than ever to be thought ready and sent to do our bit, but every new rumour of departure turns out to be false. How lucky Ned is to be in the thick of it already, and how proud of him you must be!

I hope you are enjoying your London stay and that you have been able to see something of Miss Stanhope. Please tell her that I think about her a great deal, and miss our times together more than I can express. I wish with all my heart things had been different so that I could have left matters in better order.

Jessie and Emma chatted quietly to give Maria the chance to read at her leisure. She lingered over the last three sentences, then discovered her handkerchief and discreetly blew her nose.

'Thank you,' she said, handing the letter back to Jessie. Their eyes met for a speaking moment, but there was nothing Jessie could say that had not already been said.

Emma broke the silence. 'It's such a pity that Jessie has to go back to Yorkshire so soon. I would so much like to have met you again, Miss Stanhope.'

'Does it depend on Mrs Morland, then?' Maria said. 'I should like to see you again, too. I think evenings would be difficult, but there are Saturday afternoons. Of course, my mother would insist on a chaperon in Town.'

'Lady Holkam is my chaperon,' Emma said, 'but I'm sometimes allowed to go out with just my maid, if it's to something like an exhibition or a gallery. Do you like that sort of thing? Would your mother allow it? Spencer is terribly respectable and strict.'

'I think she would,' Maria said gladly. 'And on Sundays sometimes I join a tennis party, at home in Wimbledon. Perhaps you would care to come out some time?' She said the last hesitantly, perhaps trying to imagine Emma in those surroundings.

But Emma said, 'Do you know, I've never played tennis. I should love to try.'

And the two girls smiled at each other. They were of an age, and though far apart in social position, they were united by a longing for friendship, which circumstances had thus far denied them.

★   ★   ★

Three days later, Violet had gone out alone again on one of her mysterious expeditions, and Jessie and Emma were idly discussing what to do with the day. Emma had been out late the night before, at the Lanchesters' ball, to which the Damerels had taken her, since neither Jessie nor Violet wanted to go. She was yawning and languid in consequence, while Jessie was fresh and restless, having gone with Violet to Manchester Square to enjoy a quiet evening, with the Overtons, Oliver, and Venetia's friend Lady Dawnay, of conversation and a few rubbers of bridge.

'Oh, I don't know what I want to do,' Emma said. 'I feel as if I've done everything already twice over!'

'Shocking,' said Jessie. 'Only nineteen and tired of the Season!'

'Not tired of it,' Emma stifled a yawn, 'only tired. And all the nicest men seem to be away. There wasn't anyone I like at the Lanchesters' last night.'

'Despite which you still danced every dance,' Jessie hazarded.

'Oh, well, it looks unkind to refuse. So what *shall* we do today?'

'The paintings at the New Gallery?'

'Oh, no. I want to do something *different*,' said Emma. 'Isn't there anything *you*'d like to do? After all, this is your last week.'

'What I'd really like is to go for a long walk, but I suppose that's out of the question, in London.'

Emma sat up straighter. 'I don't see why it should be. No-one can say it isn't respectable, only unusual. Yes, a walk would shake the cobwebs away. Shall we?'

Before Jessie could answer. Violet's butler, Varden, came in.

'Sir Percival Parke is below, with another gentleman, asking to see Mrs Morland,' he said, with a faint air of disapproval.

Jessie's heart bounded. Bertie! 'Show them up, please.'

'Neither gentleman has a card, madam,' Varden said, revealing the source of his irritation.

'I expect they've just come from the Front,' Jessie said. 'Please show them up at once.'

Varden inclined his head slightly and went away. Emma had brightened at the thought of visitors, and now she giggled. 'Does he think they are robbers impersonating gentlemen? They must be very bedraggled. Who is the other gentleman, I wonder?'

Swift, firm steps on the stair hustled Varden before them at an unbutlerish pace, and without waiting to be announced Bertie came in with another man just behind him.

'Jessie! I'm so glad I found you at home. I was afraid I'd have to search all over London.'

'Oh, Bertie!' Her eyes feasted on his face, while she took both his hands and felt a wonderful sense of connection to life, as though he were a cable through which power surged. He looked tired, too thin, his cheeks hollow, his hair greying at the temples and in a streak above his brow. He was in uniform, and it was shabby and worn, and there was a tear in the sleeve, which had been neatly mended. But the sight of him ravished her heart, and she wanted only to be crushed close to him and never let him go. Instead she reached up and kissed him – and was kissed in return – chastely on the cheek. He smelled of the familiar bay rum, an unfamiliar whiff of carbolic, and underneath them his own smell, the wheaten wholesomeness of his skin that made something kick in the base of her stomach, and brought a tumbling confusion of feelings that were like nostalgia: a memory of, and longing for, home.

'You're well?' she asked urgently. 'You're not wounded?'

'Only a scratch,' he said, gesturing at the mended tear. She could see the sleeve was bulkier there – there must be bandaging underneath. 'And you? You look well.'

He was devouring her with his eyes just as she was him. It had to stop, and the realisation came to both of them, so that they withdrew their hands smoothly at the same moment. Jessie turned to Emma to bring her forward.

'Emma, I don't think you've met my cousin Bertie, have you? Bertie, Emma Weston.'

370

They shook hands. Bertie smiled and said, 'We haven't actually met, but I've heard so much about you from Jessie.'

'Yes, she's talked about you, too.'

'And as I'm her cousin, you and I must be cousins of a sort, too.'

'I think we must be,' Emma said, displaying no dislike of the idea.

'May I present my friend Fenniman? Fen, my cousins Mrs Morland, and Miss Weston.'

He stepped forward, a tall, darkly handsome man, with a white scar running out from his thick black hair and down his weather-tanned forehead. He shook hands with Jessie, and when he turned to Emma he found her gazing at him with an intensity that seemed to give him pause, so that he took her hand and bowed over it a little, and then for a moment forgot to release it.

'Did it hurt?' she blurted out.

He smiled deprecatingly. 'Oh, this little thing? Not at all.' He touched the scar lightly. 'Nothing but a scratch. Now you should see Parke's arm – that's a sight worth pity!'

'How did it happen?' Emma asked, still staring.

'I really can't remember. It was during one of our quarrels with Fritz last autumn.'

'Fen and I have been through a few of those together,' Bertie said, and Jessie saw the affection in his eyes as he looked at the other man. 'In fact, we're almost the last survivors of our battalion, along with Pennyfather. He's dashed home to see his family. We, however, being footloose and family free, vowed to stay together and support each other, so we hurried along here in search of charm and beauty.'

'Family free?' Jessie queried. She hated having to do it, but she asked, 'Didn't you – go home?'

He met her eyes and for a moment there was a bleak, lost look that she understood only too well.

'I called at the house,' he said tonelessly, and she noted the differentiation between 'house' and 'home'. 'There was no-one there. It seems Richard has an old friend staying. They went to Ireland on business, and Maud and little

Richard went with them. The servants don't expect them back until Friday.'

'Ah,' said Jessie, trying to hide her relief.

Bertie went on, more cheerfully, 'And since Fen and I have only two days, there was no possibility of following them, so we decided to stay in London.'

'Only two days?' Emma said, with flattering dismay.

'I'm afraid so,' said Fenniman, smiling at her with devastating effect. 'But it's by way of a little extra, so it's a case of not looking gift horses in the mouth. We've been promised proper leave later in the summer, but at the moment they are reorganising our force. They didn't need us for a couple of days, and further considering that we're wounded, they sent us off to Blighty.'

'You're wounded too?' Emma said in tragic tones.

Fenniman grinned down at her. 'I should love to be able to say I merit such concern, Miss Weston, but it's just a scratch like Parke's, except that it's in the leg, not the arm.'

'Seventeen stitches,' Bertie said. 'Don't forget to mention that, Fen. Take all the sympathy you can get, old fellow – you'll get none from anyone in uniform.'

Jessie laughed. 'I can see you two really are friends.'

They all sat down, and Bertie asked diffidently, 'Have you heard from Ned lately?'

'Only a brief note, to say he was all right after the last attack. Do you see anything of him?'

'No, I haven't seen him at all.'

'But his battalion is in Ypres, too.'

'So I understand. There are a great many soldiers in Ypres. The salient may be very small now, but it's still big enough not to bump into people. He writes to you, I suppose?'

'Yes, but his letters never say very much – nothing at all about him, just what the battalion's doing. I thought if you'd seen him, you might know how he is really.'

'Keeping a stiff upper lip and not wearing his heart on his sleeve, I would take a wager,' said Bertie. 'He always was a good fellow.'

'Yes,' said Jessie. 'Always.' There was a brief but awkward

372

pause, and Jessie recollected her duty. 'But let me ring for refreshments. I imagine you would like something.'

'I don't think you should risk asking Violet's butler for anything,' Bertie said. 'He seemed to think we were not quite the thing.'

'You didn't have cards,' Jessie enlightened him.

'Ah, he's *that* sort of butler! Where is Violet, by the way?'

'Oh, she's out on private business. We are left to our own devices today.'

'And what were you going to do?'

'We were just thinking of a walk in the Park.'

'How novel! I didn't think ladies of high fashion ever walked.'

'We aren't ladies of high fashion,' Emma laughed. 'But it was Jessie's idea. I think she's missing Yorkshire.'

'When do you go back?' Bertie asked.

'On Saturday,' said Jessie.

'Leaving before Ascot week?'

'I shall have horses at home,' said Jessie. 'And I don't think my wardrobe could stand the strain of Ascot, anyway. Now, shall I ring for something?'

Bertie consulted Fenniman with a look, and said, 'No, don't. Will you allow us to escort you on your walk? I can't think of anything we'd like better. It's a beautiful day, and England is so green and untouched. May we?'

'Oh, yes, please,' said Emma, before Jessie could answer.

It was indeed a beautiful day, with that special clarity that only early June days in England have. The sky was high and blue, and the sunshine fell so pure through the lambent air it was almost heatless. The grass and the trees were so green the colour seemed to vibrate against the eye, and everything seemed to Jessie almost to be outlined, lifting away from its background as if it were more than three-dimensional. Had there ever been a bird so beautiful as a pigeon, with its iridescent green-gold neck, its garnet eyes and coral feet? Was there any tree so splendid as the London plane, tall as a cathedral, soaring like an anthem? Bertie's arm was under her fingers, his tall figure close to her, and her senses were so heightened, it was as if he emitted a radiation; as though she could feel the very breathing of his soul.

Fenniman had taken Emma on his arm, and they were walking a little ahead. Both men had automatically adjusted their stride to that of their companions, but Jessie and Bertie, without mentioning it, had instinctively slowed a little more, to let a space open between them and the other two.

'Are you really all right?' Bertie asked. 'I hated having to leave you in December. You looked so drawn and miserable.'

'You helped me a great deal,' Jessie said.

'But there's so much one can't say in a letter. I've wanted to ask you. I can see you are well physically, but what of the rest?' She didn't speak, and he said, 'Never mind, you needn't answer. I shouldn't have asked something so personal.'

'Oh, no, it isn't that. You can ask me anything. I was just thinking how to put it. I feel – hollow. Not all the time – I manage to forget it a lot of the time. But when I think of it, it's as though my baby really lived, and it comes along with me, a little sad ghost at my side – the sort you glimpse out of the corner of your eye, at home, at Morland Place, but when you turn to look at it directly, there's nothing there. Do you know that sort?'

'Yes, I know,' he said. His arm was pressing her fingers warmly against his side.

'But it never lived.' She was silent a moment. 'It was a boy. Dr Hasty didn't tell me, but Nanny Emma let it slip one day. And yet, you know, when I think about it, *really* think about it, I can't imagine myself the mother of a boy. The whole thing seems to be receding into the past at such a speed, it's like a fairy story, or something from history. Hardly real at all. My little ghost is only the ghost of a story-book person. Isn't that the saddest thing? I couldn't give him life, and now I can't even give him a past reality. There's just a hollow feeling sometimes, where he ought to be.'

There was silence for a moment, filled only with traffic

noises, and birdsong, the rustling of the trees, and the sound of Emma up ahead laughing at something Fenniman had said.

'I wish I could have been with you,' Bertie said quietly. 'I hated leaving you. This damned war . . .'

She drew back from the sadness. 'I wasn't all alone, you know. I was in the heart of my family.'

'Yes. And you had Brach.'

She laughed. 'Yes, what would I do without Brach?'

'You seem to be doing without her now.'

'Oh, I couldn't bring her here. Can you imagine my poor dog shut up in London? Do you know, this is the first time I've walked since I've been here, apart from crossing the pavement from the motor to someone's door. A great many doors, one way and another. Poor Brach would have gone mad.'

'She might have given you the excuse you needed to walk,' Bertie suggested.

'Oh, no! A footman would have taken her out for a five-minute sniff round the square, like Violet's Pekingeses.'

Bertie laughed. 'I can see how you've suffered.'

'I've had a lovely time: a lovely rest and a change. And I adore Violet.'

'Your Emma is a sweet girl, too.' They both looked at the other couple, drawing slowly ahead. Their heads were leaning more together all the time, and they talked and laughed constantly.

'She seems to be getting on very well with your friend,' Jessie said.

'Do you mind?'

'Not at all. He seems very nice, from the little I've seen of him. And you wouldn't have brought him if he hadn't been respectable.'

'He's the best of fellows. We've been through so much together. It makes a bond, like brotherhood but stronger.'

'You love him.'

Bertie smiled down at her. 'We chaps don't talk about loving each other. But I suppose that's what it is.'

'And he has no family?'

'He was an only child. His father was in the army. There's a small property somewhere in Hertfordshire, and I gather he has a private income.'

'You sound as though you're recommending him.'

'Well, he's devilish attractive to females, and I can see young Emma is quite smitten by his charms.'

'Wait until *he*'s smitten before you match-make,' Jessie suggested. 'These Byronic sorts tend to flit too rapidly from one female to another.'

'Now, how do you know that, my dear cousin? Has some Byronic sort been making love to you?'

'It's wartime, you know,' she said demurely. 'I've spent my whole time here dancing with handsome young men in uniform.'

'Damn their eyes!' said Bertie. 'But Fen's not like that. He's the best fellow that ever lived.'

'I'm glad to hear it. And I'm glad you have a friend over there. Are you going to be able to stay together? There was a plan once to split you up – you said in one of your letters.'

'No, I'm glad to say that idea's been dropped. They're bringing out a new battalion of West Herts, and we survivors are going to be absorbed into it. That's why we have this extra bit of leave. Our force is being redistributed, and while the dispositions are made, there's nothing for us to do over there.'

'And when you've been redistributed, what then?' Jessie asked, trying to sound unconcerned.

But he heard what she meant to keep from him. 'There's no sense in worrying,' he said. 'A war is what it is. And if anything happens—'

'It mustn't,' she said fiercely and low. 'I can't lose you. I *can't*.'

There had to be a silence now, for them to get back to their tenable positions. Then he said, lightly, cheerfully, 'Everything's quietened down around the salient. The intelligence wallahs say that the Germans have run short of men and ammunition, so they can't mount any more offensives

376

for the time being. Of course, they still shell us pretty regularly, but they won't be attacking, and neither will we. It'll be a case of sitting tight for some time – for weeks, certainly, perhaps even months.'

'And will you be staying in Ypres?'

'I don't know. They may want to put the new battalion in a quiet sector to begin with.'

'I thought you said Ypres was quiet now,' she accused him.

'Quie*ter*. And there are definite temptations in Ypres that the brass might want to keep impressionable young boys away from.'

'What sort of temptations?'

'The city itself is abandoned now, and it's prey to the new fad of "souveniring". There's everything to be picked up in the ruins – furniture, paintings, jewellery, silver, clothes, cellars full of fine wines.'

'Isn't that looting?' Jessie said, rather shocked.

'Yes, and it's strictly forbidden and heavily punished, which is why it might be best to keep young chaps away from it.'

She looked up at him. 'Your tone of voice suggests you've done some souveniring yourself.'

'There's a fine line to be drawn,' he admitted. 'We got a very nice stove for our dugout just before we left. It was lying under a heap of rubble in a ruined house, and if we hadn't taken it, the next shell would have smashed it to bits, so what was the point of leaving it? But I'd never let our men take valuables.'

'What about the fine wines?' she asked shrewdly.

He laughed. 'How well you know me! I have to say in my own defence I've never souvenired a wine cellar; but I have bought some exceptionally fine clarets at ridiculous prices from a fellow in Poperinghe. Well,' he shrugged, 'it was never going to be given back to its rightful owner. And for all I know, the fellow in Poperinghe may have *been* the owner.'

'But you didn't ask,' Jessie said. 'I can see the war is having a bad effect on your morals.'

377

'It has a bad effect on everything,' Bertie said, and looked around him like a man just waking up. 'You can't think how glorious it is to see trees in leaf, and grass that isn't cut up and churned to mud, and buildings with unbroken glass and roofs still on and no holes in the walls.' A carriage went by, with a pair of bays in harness. 'And well-fed horses,' he added. '*Live* horses, if it comes to that. There are dead ones lying everywhere around Ypres. No-one has time to bury them. I'm so sick of the sight of dead horses.'

She laid her free hand over his, and he gripped her fingers briefly and gratefully.

'I lost my last horse,' he said. 'They were stabled near the Menin Gate when we went into the line, and a shell dropped right onto the stable block and killed them all. He was only one I'd drawn from the battalion, but I'd got quite fond of him.' A pause, then, lightly, 'Good business for you, I suppose. How are things at Twelvetrees?'

'A nice crop of new foals early this year,' she said. 'And we've started backing the two-year-olds. The army will take them next January, I suppose.'

'What about the Bhutias?' he asked, and there was naked longing in his voice, for this talk of normal things, of the life left behind.

'I've got them out on the farms, replacing the work horses that were requisitioned. Don't worry, I've only lent them, and only to farmers I know will be good to them. Better they work than eat their heads off in a paddock. I kept back the mares with foal at foot, but I'm not breeding them again this year. There didn't seem any point.'

'No, you're right.'

They walked on, talking of horses and farming and home things. Fenniman and Emma were quite a long way ahead now, and evidently enjoying each other's company very much. Jessie was glad, both for them and because it left her alone with Bertie. They crossed over into Green Park, and half-way up the Queen's Walk the two ahead stopped and waited for Bertie and Jessie to catch up.

'I'm fearfully hungry,' Fenniman said. 'Do you think it

would be considered impertinent, Parke, if we were to ask these ladies to take luncheon with us?'

Emma, eager for the treat, jumped in first. 'Oh, no, not impertinent at all! It's considered frightfully patriotic to be seen lunching with a soldier in uniform. And it won't be improper because Jessie's a married woman.'

Jessie felt Bertie flinch from the word, from the thought; her own hand tightened involuntarily on his arm. They had managed to forget it as they walked and talked, because it felt so natural to be together, and there were no secrets and no barriers between them.

He said smoothly, 'In that case, may we have the honour of escorting you to the Ritz?'

'Not the Ritz,' Jessie said quickly. It was too public, too bright, too full of people who were likely to interrupt them, and she didn't want to be interrupted. 'Brown's would be better.'

'Brown's it shall be, then,' said Bertie. Emma didn't mind where it was, tucked her hand confidingly back under Fenniman's arm, and walked on. Jessie and Bertie followed, close behind now, and silent. Jessie could almost *feel* Bertie thinking, and she wondered if her own thoughts were screaming as loudly to him. They were so huge and uncontainable in her head that she could not believe he would not hear them.

Because the reminder that she was married had stripped all possible self-delusion from her, and she had to face the stark truth about Bertie, the thing she had always known underneath but had tried to suppress, to keep from herself as from everyone else. The first sight of him today in Violet's morning-room had told her in a blinding revelation. She loved him, utterly and for ever. Her affection for Ned was unchanged, but it had only ever been the sort of cousinly love one might have for a friend of one's childhood; and what she had thought, after their marriage, was love had been only physical passion. But Bertie she loved with every part of herself, mind and body and soul, and she always had, and she always would. He was a part of her; they were alike; his essence spoke to hers in a way that soothed and comforted and warmed and enlivened her as no-one and nothing else could do. He was the breath of life to her, and wherever he was in the world, she would turn to him, like a compass needle turning helplessly to the north, and long to go to him and be with him. He was her home, and to be apart from him was exile.

They walked in silence, her hand connecting her to him, her mind filled with the joy of being near him, her throat tight with tears. She loved him; but she was married, and so was he, and there was nothing to be done about it. They would never be together.

CHAPTER SIXTEEN

They had so little time, only two days, but they did not waste any of it. When they got back from luncheon they found Violet at home, and she greeted the visitors with warmth. She had known Bertie, too, in her childhood days, when she and her brothers had visited Yorkshire and played with the Compton children. She ordered tea and chatted graciously over the teacups, but she was absorbing the situation all the while. The three young women were engaged to dine that evening at the Tonbridges', and just as that restless moment arrived when the visitors felt they ought to offer to take their leave, Violet proposed that she should ask Lady Tonbridge if she could bring Bertie and Fenniman too.

'Oh, but it's far too late to disrupt her plans,' Bertie said. 'She'll have her table arranged. She won't want two strangers foisted on her at the last minute.'

Violet smiled. 'I can see you know nothing about the concerns of hostesses in wartime. To begin with, there are *never* enough men to go round. And in the second place, officers just back from the Front – and particularly from Ypres – are the highest prize one can boast. Lady Tonbridge will be thrilled to be able to offer her guests *two* on the same evening. The only question is whether you and Captain Fenniman want to be lionised in return for dinner. Perhaps you would rather dine quietly at your club.'

They hastened to assure her to the contrary, and she went away to telephone, coming back a few minutes later

381

to confirm that she had been right. Lady Tonbridge had been delighted, and had even praised Violet's generosity in being willing to share the officers with her. 'A lesser person would have kept them to herself. It's very handsome of you, Violet dear.'

So Jessie was able to be with Bertie for most of the evening. To be sure, she was not seated by him at dinner, and had very little opportunity to talk to him at the Tonbridges' house, but she was able to look at him and listen to him; and for her, every moment simply of being in his presence was precious. He and Fenniman answered all the questions patiently, making light, as soldiers do with civilians, of the hardships and dangers. One of the gentlemen at the table asked about the gas attacks. Jessie was reminded of the conversation at Venetia's dinner party and wondered if the answer would be as frank.

Bertie said, 'It was pretty bad at first, but the government was quick to react, and the first gauze gas masks started arriving at the beginning of May. The public were wonderful, I must say, the way they buckled down to making them. I think pretty well everyone has been issued with them now.'

'But are they effective?' someone else asked.

'Oh, yes,' Bertie said. 'Along with goggles, which nearly everyone has now, they work pretty well. A little awkward to wear, but that can't be helped. The horses have gas masks too, you know,' he added, knowing this would amuse.

'Oh, the poor horses!' Lady Tonbridge said. 'Of course, I hadn't thought, but they must suffer just like the men. How awful!'

'You'd think so, but in fact, ma'am, they don't seem as susceptible as us. I don't know why. Perhaps it's because by the time the gas reaches them, it has sunk below head height. Chlorine gas is very heavy. They're always kept quite far behind the line, you know. But we've adapted their nose-bags as gas masks, just to be on the safe side.'

The gentlemen around the table wanted to talk about the strategic situation, and Jessie noted how kindly both Bertie and Fenniman listened, allowing the gentlemen to tell them what *they* thought should be done – which was what they really wanted, even though they couched the introduction as a question. 'If I were Sir John,' they said, and, 'What Kitchener ought to consider,' and 'In Haig's place, I would . . .' And then at the end of their disquisition they would recollect themselves, and say hastily to the listening soldier in his worn uniform, 'Don't you agree?'

When the ladies withdrew, Emma murmured discontentedly to Jessie and Violet, 'I do so hate this silly custom. I'm so glad Aunt Venetia doesn't insist on it. Now I suppose the men will stay there all evening, and only come in when it's time to go.'

Jessie rather suspected she was right, given how much the gentlemen would all want to test their military theories on the newcomers; but perhaps Bertie and Fenniman had some influence, for they came in a remarkably short time. Violet, noticing how Fenniman immediately sought out Emma, murmured to Jessie, 'I think Emma is rather attracted to Captain Fenniman. What a pity they're here for such a short time.'

When Bertie entered, his eyes came straight to Jessie, but he was swiftly buttonholed by Lady Stanley, Admiral Stanley's wife, who performed a cutting-out exercise every bit as neat as any her husband had carried out in his midshipman days. She bore her prize off to a corner, where she was soon besieged by Mrs Danbury and Lady Sedgewick, who had not been quick enough off the mark to capture Captain Fenniman themselves, but didn't mean to leave it there. Jessie spent the rest of the evening with an old gentleman who was so tryingly deaf no-one else would converse with him. He was so pleased to have someone at last, he gripped her forearm with a claw-like hand to prevent her escape; but Jessie felt if she could not talk to Bertie, she did not mind what she did, and listened to him patiently, only allowing her eyes to stray now and then to where Bertie's head and shoulders rose above those of his companions. Whenever she looked at him, he was looking at her, and when their eyes met it was like a refreshing sip of water in the desert of polite society.

They were silent in the motor-car going home after-wards. Fenniman and Emma talked on, indefatigably. Violet looked out of the window in silent thought; and when the motor pulled up in front of St James's House, she said, 'I don't know, of course, Bertie, whether you and Captain Fenniman have plans for tomorrow, but if you have not, and if it would not bore you, would you care to spend the day with us?'

Bertie hardly needed to consult Fenniman: it was obvious where he would be happiest. 'We have no plans,' he said. 'We were thinking of asking if we might call on you.'

'Oh, then do come. Come up after breakfast,' said Violet. Emma's glad, grateful look was her reward.

The motor doors opened, and the officers got out to help the ladies down. They were staying at White's, Bertie's club, which was only a stroll away, round the corner in St James's Street. They escorted the ladies to the door and then made their bows.

'At eleven, then,' said Violet.

At breakfast, Violet revealed that she had cancelled all their engagements for the day. 'It was Mrs Hoover's Belgian Relief luncheon, and then the War Fund tea at Lady Skeffington's, but I thought it would be more pleasant for Bertie and Captain Fenniman to have a quiet day with us, rather than be surrounded by people, all asking them the same questions.'

'Yes, and Lady Skeffington is rather excitable,' Jessie said. 'She'd pounce on them in an embarrassing way.'

Violet smiled. 'I'm sure she'd already heard that we took them to the Tonbridges'. She sounded very sceptical when I excused myself.'

'What did you say?'

'Only that we wouldn't be able to come after all. Did you think I'd tell an untruth?'

'Not you, Violet dear. But what did you tell Mrs Hoover?'

'Oh, the truth. She was very gracious about it. She said it wasn't a formal luncheon, and all female, anyway, and that she didn't mind a bit. She said she perfectly understood, and that anyone with an officer home from the Front was automatically excused.'

'Well, I'm glad we have an excuse for getting out of those things,' Emma said. 'I wasn't looking forward to either of them – although I do like Mrs Hoover. She's so lively and natural, and always has interesting things to say. But everyone else would have been dull – and two funds in one day is rather much. I'd far sooner be with the men.'

Jessie saw that Emma had not realised the change of plans was for her benefit, and smiled inwardly. 'You needn't have a conscience,' she said. 'It can be your war work for today, to provide comfort for two lonely soldiers on leave.'

Bertie and Fenniman had to be at the station at seven o'clock that evening for their train. When they arrived at eleven, Violet had had time to think out her plans, and announced that she thought it would be nice for the gentlemen to escort them to the Japanese exhibition at the British Museum, and then to luncheon at Claridges. Jessie viewed these arrangements with indifference and supposed that Violet had devised them more or less at random. But when they got to the British Museum, she saw the point. The exhibition had been on long enough for there to be few people still going round, and those who were were not fashionables. Violet's set had already done it, talked about it, and forgotten it. These were the middling and academic sorts, who always waited until the entrance price came down; so there was no-one to recognise them. Walking about slowly and looking at things in glass cases was the perfect occupation for people who really only wanted to talk to each other. Fenniman and Emma walked together, and going round at their own pace were soon separated sufficiently for privacy, but still in sight, for decency's sake.

Sometimes Violet walked with Bertie and Jessie, and sometimes lingered behind them or went ahead, leaving them to their own devices. It was not, Jessie knew, that she was trying to afford her and Bertie the same space. Violet was strict in her notions, and would have been shocked at any thought of an illicit love between them. Jessie noted the

385

small smile that played around Violet's lips, and guessed that she was enjoying seeing the stubbornly heart-whole Emma so captivated by someone. Any seclusion granted to Jessie was purely accidental. But even when they had privacy, she and Bertie hardly conversed. After the long talk yesterday, they were content just to be together, walking in comfortable silence, or commenting mildly on the exhibits.

Over luncheon, Jessie saw the point of Claridges, too. It had always been a haunt for foreign royalty, and now was so full of displaced French and Belgian nobility and visiting Italian counts (Italy had just joined the war on the Allies' side) that there was no room for anyone who might interrupt them or ask them to join their party. The five of them had a most enjoyable meal, and even Violet – whose value in company was always rather to be charming, to listen and to put people at ease than to sparkle – became lively. The men dedicated themselves to entertaining, and afterwards Jessie always remembered it as being one of the most delightful occasions of her life, though she could never recall anything in particular that anyone had said.

Violet invited the officers back to the house for tea, and after tea asked Bertie if he would play the piano for them. He agreed readily, and asked Jessie to turn for him; and while he was playing Violet excused herself to the other two, saying she had letters to write, and slipped out, leaving them together on the sofa.

Jessie, beside Bertie on the long piano stool, now suddenly felt his closeness, and the imminence of his departure. It was already five o'clock. Soon he and Captain Fenniman would have to go back to White's to pack and prepare themselves. Since no-one was really listening any more, Bertie stopped playing the music in front of him and ran his hands over the keys idly, picking out, almost at random, bits of tunes interspersed with phrases and runs and arpeggios, so that they could converse. But nothing came to him, and all Jessie could think of to talk about was the war.

'How long do you think it will go on?' she asked at last. 'Will it be over by next year, as they say?'

'I hope so,' he said. 'We need more men, far more men. The first of the Kitchener units ought to be coming out this summer, and if we get enough munitions we should be able to mount a big offensive in the autumn and break through. One big break in the German line would make all the difference. Once we have them in retreat, we can roll them up in a matter of months. It could all be over by next summer. If only they hadn't opened up the second front!'

'In the Dardanelles, you mean?'

'Yes. It was a big mistake, in my view. If we had had the men and ammunition that were sent there, we might have broken through at Aubers Ridge. I suppose Hamilton might say he could have broken the Turks if he had had the men and ammunition we expended this spring. But either way, it was folly to divide our forces.'

'But we will win?' she asked, in a troubled tone.

'Oh, yes,' he said, matter-of-fact. 'We'll win all right. But they may break our hearts first.'

His hands moved as if without his volition, running from a ragtime tune, played at a poignantly sad pace, into the Moonlight Sonata, and after a few bars settled into the Chopin Berceuse in D flat, which he had played at Christmas when he had visited Morland Place. It was that which determined her to speak.

'When the fighting flared up again – on the twenty-second – and I had to wait to hear whether you and Ned were all right,' she began, 'it made me think about what the war will mean. While it goes on, there will never be a day free of anxiety. Every letter that comes only gives a few hours' relief, a new starting-point for the dread of the next action. You and your friend spoke lightly about it, last night at dinner, and I understand why, and honour you for it; but here, now, to me, you don't need to pretend.'

'I always said I would not,' he said. Behind them Emma laughed, and her voice rose for a few words – 'Oh, but I do think . . .' – before sinking again below hearing into her conversation with Fenniman.

387

'You may be killed,' Jessie said, with difficulty. 'I have to face the fact that it could happen.'

'Yes,' he said, quite seriously and calmly. 'It may happen. Battles favour the experienced, but shells and bullets don't ask who you are. I am a soldier, and the soldier's bargain is that he offers his life for the safety of his country and his people. I went willingly.'

'I know.'

The music faltered and fell apart into separate notes as he turned to look at her. 'I made the offer willingly, but I pray to God I come back.'

'Oh, Bertie,' she said. She bit her lip, but she had to go on. *Had* to. 'What we said – long ago – when we promised only to be cousins to each other—?'

'Yes,' he said. 'Well, it had to be. And I've tried to keep to it.'

'I know. I have too. But now, seeing you here for these two days, knowing what it means to go back—' She paused, and the music resumed. He was looking at the keys again, to release her, so that she need not say anything she would later regret. But she went on: 'I can't let you go, I can't let you face so much danger and uncertainty, without telling you. I would have no peace if I thought you didn't know, if you – if anything happened to you, and I had not told you.' She drew a shuddering sigh, and said, very quietly, 'I love you. Only you, always. I never loved anyone else. I've tried, I've really tried to be a good wife to Ned, and when the war's over I'll go on trying with all my strength. I thought, after I married, that I did love him, that it was all right, that it would be all right. But I see now that what I felt for him was only ever the same affection I had when he was just the cousin I grew up with. There was never anyone but you in my heart. I needed you to know that.'

'I love you, too,' he said, his voice as low as hers, and as sad. 'You know that. I think I always loved you, even when I didn't realise it. You are like a part of me, a piece of my soul, so that I'm not whole without you.'

She nodded, and tried to speak, but what came out was

only a rough breath with a sound like a sob. He played on, more loudly, to cover her if she should weep; but she was in control of herself again. 'Nothing can ever happen,' she said, and he barely caught the words. It was almost as if she were speaking to herself. 'There can only ever be this – being sometimes in the same room together. It's all we can hope for. But I needed you to know.'

'Yes,' he said. 'I'm glad you told me.'

She managed a crooked smile, though he was not looking at her. 'Promise me you'll try not to get killed. Promise me you'll try.'

'I will. I'll come home if I possibly can.'

She nodded and said no more. They could never be together, but knowing Bertie was in the world, that she might sometimes see him, meant everything to her. He finished the Chopin, then seemed to lose the will to go on playing. They sat in silence before the silent keys, until a few minutes later Violet came in, and they went to rejoin her and the others for the last little time they had; talking and smiling, watching Emma's eagerness, seeing her come to the realisation that the moment was ending and that, with Bertie, Fenniman would be going back to look death in the face. Something of adulthood came to her then: they saw it in her expression, and there was a beauty to it, as she tried to prevent it showing. But Jessie could not feel any pity for her. She loved where she might, and if he survived, there was hope at the end of it. And if he didn't survive – well, she would still have been ennobled by loving; better that than never loving at all.

It was time to go. Emma's eyes were dangerously bright, but Violet was as calm and charming as ever, Fenniman tried for lightness, and between them they got Emma through the moment. Bertie took Jessie's hand, lifted it to his lips, laid them on it. His eyes held hers a moment. Then he released her hand gently and said, 'Goodbye.'

She nodded, unable to speak.

And then the men were gone. It was Thursday evening, and Jessie was to go back to Yorkshire on Saturday morning.

389

She had enjoyed her stay with Violet, but she wished Friday away now. She was ready to go home.

Uncle Teddy was waiting at the station to meet her train. As usual he had judged exactly where her compartment would stop, and jumped forward to open the door for her and help her down. He enveloped her in a hug and said, 'I'm so glad you are home safe and sound. That dreadful Zeppelin raid! Those damned Germans go from bad to worse: gas, U-boats and now this.'

'The bombs didn't fall anywhere near us,' she assured him.

'But they might have. You have to think of that,' he said. He had a porter hovering at his elbow ready to deal with Jessie's luggage, and the ticket collector made a path for them through the barrier: Mr Edward Morland, whose father had done so much to bring the railway to York, would never have to wait in a queue.

'How is everyone?' Jessie asked. 'How's Mother?'

'Oh, she's fine. Baby Harriet had a cold, and James fell and cut his forehead. Nanny Emma scalded her hand making cocoa. Rob ran his bicycle down a rut and bent the wheel and had to push it all the way home. The bullocks broke out of their field through that weak place in the hedge, but we got them back before they did any damage. My poor old Muffy had a gumboil, of all things, and went off his feed. And we're cutting the hay next week.'

'Goodness! So much excitement in just four weeks.' They stepped out into the June sunshine.

'Oh, we're all muddling along all right. We missed you, though. I did especially. No-one else wants to play chess with me of an evening.'

'Robbie would, if you asked him.'

'He's too easy to beat.' He looked at her affectionately. 'Damned glad you came to live with us when Ned went away – best decision you could have made. Did you hear anything more from him?'

'No, but I saw Bertie in London.'

'Bertie! How so? How was the dear fellow?'

Talking about Bertie took them to the motor, where Simmons was waiting, his nice face creased with smiles, his grizzled hair showing under his cap. Jessie thought of the talk at the Overtons' about conscription, and was glad at least that, if it came, Simmons would not be called. She knew Uncle Teddy was very fond of him, and wouldn't care to have to find another chauffeur. She gave him her hand with a warm smile, and he shook it gingerly as if he was afraid he might break it, and said, 'Nice to have you back, ma'am.'

The drive didn't take long. There was Morland Place, its stones mellow in the sun, and she felt a great upsurge of love for it, and of gladness to be home. As the motor stopped, Brach reached them first. She put her paws up on the side window, and her great weight prevented Jessie from opening the door. In her frustration Brach began to sing, and lavishly licked the glass where she could see Jessie through it. Sawry was standing in the doorway to greet them, and sent one of the footmen, William, to haul the dog off so that Simmons could let Jessie out. As soon as she was upright she grinned at William and said, 'You can let her go,' and braced herself to receive a passionate hound full in the chest. 'Oh, you great fool! Don't wash my face.' The other dogs crowded round with interest, smiling and lashing their tails, always ready to join in any excitement.

Polly reached her second. 'Oh, I'm *glad* you're back! It's been awfully dull without you. No-one wants to ride with me and everyone says you won't today either because you'll be too tired, but it's only a train journey and you've been sitting down all the time, so I don't see how you *can* be tired. You aren't tired, are you?'

'Not especially,' Jessie said, laughing.

'Oh, good. I *knew* you'd want to go for a ride after lunch, with not having any horses in London. It must have been horrid! And lunch is extra special because of welcoming you back, but I promised not to say what we're having because Daddy wants it to be a surprise.'

Henrietta reached her next, and enfolded her in a silent, warm embrace. Then she stood back to look at her, her hands still on Jessie's shoulders, and said, 'I've missed you. I'd got used to having you back home again, and I missed you.'

'I missed you, too,' Jessie said. After a month's absence Jessie saw her mother with fresh eyes. She looked worn, as though life was just rubbing and rubbing away at her, so that you could almost see through her. Jessie felt suddenly guilty about her jaunt of pleasure, and vowed to try to take some of her Mother's domestic burden from her.

Luncheon was a triumphant feast of delicacies, prepared by Mrs Stark, and there was champagne.

'That's what I wasn't to tell you,' said Polly. 'Daddy says I can have some too.'

'Half a glass,' Teddy said sternly. 'To welcome home the wanderer.'

'I've only been gone a month,' Jessie protested.

'We were terribly worried by the Zeppelin raid. It was in all the newspapers,' Alice said.

'We were afraid it might upset you,' Ethel said bluntly. 'Bring back memories, you know.'

Ah, was that it? Oddly, Jessie had not given a thought to the bombardment of Scarborough in all the Zeppelin talk. Perhaps it was because she had tried to shut her mind to anything to do with the miscarriage.

It emerged over luncheon that Teddy had been extremely exercised about the whole episode. 'I'm making preparations,' he said. 'In case of bombing, we should be pretty stout and secure here – the walls are thick enough, and even if we took a direct hit, we wouldn't be touched down in the cellars. But if there's an invasion, I don't mean us to sit down under it. I'm organising the estate staff and the servants, every able-bodied person, into a militia,' Teddy went on.

'Family too,' Polly said happily. 'We have drills and marching and target practice. And digging – lots of digging. When we go out riding, I'll have to show you where all the trenches are, so you don't fall down them.'

'And after luncheon,' Teddy continued, 'I'll show you the preparations I've been making down in the cellars. Food stores, blankets, candles – everything we'll need to hold out in a siege.'

'What about water?' Jessie asked.

'Oh, that's not a difficulty. The old well shaft runs right through. It was only a matter of making a new access hole at cellar level and installing a hand winch. That well has never failed, even in the longest drought. We should be able to hold out for months.'

It seemed from what everyone said that the whole neighbourhood had been deeply affected by the Zeppelin raid on London, coming as it did in succession to the bombardment and the other east-coast raids. York felt vulnerable, and most households were making arrangements for withstanding bombs from the skies, if and when they came. The mayor was thinking of getting out a general leaflet of advice. 'It'll tell people to go down into the cellar, if they have one. And for small houses, under the staircase is the safest place,' Teddy said. 'The City Council is looking at a system of air-raid warnings. Factory hooters, bells, whatever makes a noise – and policemen on bicycles blowing whistles where there's nothing else. When the warning goes off, everyone has to take cover.' He looked pleased. 'The Bosch won't catch *us* napping.'

Perhaps the fact that the new Ministry of Munitions was taking over Ned's requisitioned factory, and was converting it for filling shells, was another element in the prevailing excitement. Munitions were all the news, and having them so close to the heart of York made the city feel it was in the centre of things.

'Once they're settled in,' Teddy said, 'I shall see if I can't get on terms with the manager, whoever he will be, and have him give me the instructions on how to make a few small bombs or hand grenades. They could make all the difference to our defences.'

'Those old Huns will be jolly sorry if they ever try invading Yorkshire,' Polly concluded, with satisfaction.

393

'We'll make 'em pay for gassing our soldiers and sinking the *Lusitania*,' Teddy agreed, and they smiled fiercely at each other, looking, in that instant, startlingly alike.

Hotspur was glad to see Jessie, and whickered and stamped his feet as she approached. He pushed his head hard against her, and nibbled at her hands and pockets. 'Cupboard love!' Jessie laughed, slipping him a carrot, and he nodded his head up and down as he crunched it as if agreeing with her, while she stroked his neck and rubbed behind his ears. It was so good to get into her riding habit again, after all her smart London clothes, and good beyond expression to get up on Hotspur and clatter out over the drawbridge and into the green fields.

Polly was riding Vesper. Before Jessie went to London, Teddy had talked to her about his desire to give Polly a proper grown-up lady's horse for her birthday present, now she was fifteen. The difficulty was in finding a suitable mount, since so many had been requisitioned by the army. He asked Jessie's advice, but it was not hard to fathom where he was tending, and she saved him from having to ask by offering Vesper. 'Do you think she'd be suitable?' he asked, but with tell-tale eagerness.

'She's very young and not schooled yet, but she's very gentle, and Polly's a good horsewoman. She ought to be able to manage her.'

'With help and advice,' Teddy said. 'The mare would need schooling on. Would you do that?'

'Of course,' Jessie said. She had always known she might lose Vesper, and better this than have her sent to the Front. There was every chance Forrester would leave the mare, if she was Polly's only horse.

'I'll pay you for her,' Teddy said, and on this was unshakeable – and since she was a present for Polly and he obviously wanted to spend money on his daughter, Jessie yielded. He also bought a new saddle and bridle for Vesper, and a smart blue stable-rug with her name embroidered on it in white.

Jessie rather wished now she had been at home for Polly's

birthday, so that she could have seen her face when she saw her present.

'Daddy made me shut my eyes and led me out into the great hall, and when I opened them, the door was open and there was Wickes outside holding her. She looked so gorgeous in her new saddle and bridle, with red, white and blue ribbons plaited in her mane. I wish you had been there. Though I suppose you must have known all about it, if Daddy bought her from you.'

'I did,' said Jessie. 'Though not about the ribbons.'

'It was a wonderful present,' said Polly. 'I do love her so.' And she leant down to caress the mare's neck.

'How do you find her to ride?'

'It was strange at first – she's so much bigger. And I can't dash about the way I did on Misty, because she's not schooled. Though Mama and Aunt Hen say I shouldn't dash any more anyway, now I'm grown-up. But I miss it, a bit,' she said wistfully.

'You could always ride Misty when you want to dash,' Jessie suggested.

'Well,' said Polly, doubtfully, 'probably I am too old for that now. But, Jessie, Daddy says you are going to school her for me, but the thing is, I'd really, really like to do it myself, so that she's completely mine. Do you think I could?'

'You could, with help,' Jessie said. 'But it takes a lot of work, and you have to keep at it, every day, not just when you feel like it. Are you willing to put that much work into it?'

'Yes, I am,' Polly said earnestly. 'I know you think I'm harum-scarum, but that was when I was fourteen. Now I'm fifteen, I'm different. I want to do it and I *will* work hard. I'm bored with messing around, actually. I want to do something serious – if you'll help me.'

'Of course I will,' Jessie said fondly, smiling at the serious frown on the familiar, pretty face. How long the new resolve would last she didn't know, but either with Polly's help or without, it would be a pleasant task, an interesting occupation for the summer, and something more to keep her mind busy and away from difficult thoughts.

When she went back to the hospital, it would be too much to say that Sister Morgan was glad to see her, but she did at least greet her with a grim nod before she snapped a string of orders at her. The loftier nurses, like Clarke, ignored her entirely, but Beattie gave her a smile as she passed, and Foxton and Dicks went so far as to say they had missed her.

'We had to do all the sluice-room work ourselves,' said Dicks.

'So we're glad you're back,' said Foxton. 'You can do all the bedpans and kidney bowls now.'

It was the best she could have hoped for, she supposed; but her absence had evidently caused a change of heart, for that first day she was ordered to feed the patient in bed seven. Ambrose had lost an arm and the other was extensively bandaged and splinted. As he had also lost quite a few teeth in the same explosion, feeding him was a slow and messy business, so it was something the nurses were glad to shrug off onto her. But it was contact with a patient, and therefore much more like proper nursing than anything she had been allowed to do before. She was thrilled with her 'promotion'. Despite his dental deficiencies, Ambrose liked to talk, and from him she learnt a great deal about the other patients. Some of those she had known before had gone and there were new faces in the ward. There were casualties from Ypres among them, and though she was not allowed near them, she was interested to discover anything about them she could.

The improvement in her status continued. Because she was so willing and cheerful, the men liked her, and the spirit on the ward lifted because she was there, which affected everyone. The trained nurses, finding no conceit or assumption of superiority in her, began to accept her. When Sister was absent or off the ward and Beattie was in charge, the First Nurse began routinely to give her other tasks, like feeding and bed-making, and sometimes paused on her busy round to teach Jessie a little about the men's conditions and their treatment.

One day, presumably at Beattie's command, Nurse Roberts, who had never minded Jessie as much as the others, allowed her to help with a blanket bath. Jessie was nervous, afraid that she might be clumsy and awkward, but even more afraid that she would be embarrassed. The only male body she had ever had to do with was Ned's, and she had hardly ever *seen* that – only in glimpses. It was not customary even for husbands and wives to be naked before each other; unmarried girls never saw anything of a man but his face and hands. Complete ignorance of the anatomy and functioning of the male body was the rule before marriage – it was not something that would have been talked about even between mother and daughter. Jessie had been lucky that Ned had been gentle; and that he had been both able and willing to give her pleasure. Because of that she did not regard bodies as threatening or loathsome. But, still, Ned's was the only one she knew, and this soldier was a complete stranger. She was afraid embarrassment might make her unable to do what was needed; or, worse, might offend this man who had already suffered so much.

But when it came to it, the soldier accepted her help so naturally, and with such simple dignity, that she felt no shame, only gratitude that she should be allowed to care for him. There was nothing in the lean, muscular body to disgust or frighten. The puckered stump, which was all that was left of his right arm, filled her only with the same practical pity that a lame horse would have done.

When the bath was finished, Roberts looked speculatively at Jessie and said, 'Would you like to give this patient a shave, Nurse? I've got all those dressings to do before Sister comes back.'

'I've never shaved a man before,' Jessie said.

The soldier smiled and said, 'I don't mind being practised on. I'll tell you what to do, Nurse, don't worry. Mine's a safety razor, so you can't do much harm.'

'I'll leave you to it, then, Nurse Morland,' said Roberts, hurrying away. As she had said to Beattie, she thought Sister's attitude unwise. The more Morland was taught to do, the more useful she would be. Some of the other nurses were worried that if VADs were trained in any way, they might take their jobs after the war; but it seemed to Roberts that the end of the war was too far off to worry about. They needed all the helping hands they could get right now.

Jessie arranged a dry towel across the soldier's chest, looked at the shaving equipment on the locker, and said, 'What do I do first?'

Her experience of the practical handling of horses helped her in the tasks she was gradually given; and the more she was allowed to do for the men the more she wanted to do. Though the pain of her feet and her aching back never went away, she was too busy and too interested to notice them much. Nursing – even at this lowest level – was the perfect way to wipe all other concerns from her mind; and in bed at night she slept like a log, too tired for dreams.

The crowning moment of her return came one day when she was on her hands and knees oiling bed-wheels. The lofty Cameron came scudding past and said, 'Nurse, when you've finished that, wash your hands and come and find me. I'm going to change number three's dressings, and I might as well show you how to lay out a dressing tray properly. And then you can hold it for me while I do him.'

Jessie only said, 'Yes, Nurse,' quite meekly, but her heart lifted. It was the best gift she could have been given, to be thought worthy of being shown something a nurse needed to know. The future suddenly seemed brighter. She was glad to be back.

Violet loved Jessie and had enjoyed her visit, but she, too, was glad it was over. It was a strain to conceal her visits to Ebury Street, especially from Jessie, from whom she had never had secrets. She was glad that Emma had gone away as well, leaving just after Jessie to go down to stay with the Protheroes, who had a house in Datchet, and were getting

398

up a house-party for Ascot. They had two girls around Emma's age, and had also invited the Draycotts and Westerhams, so she would have plenty of friends to share the fun. The Protheroes had invited Violet at the same time, but they were not really her set, and she had pleaded off, using her committees as an excuse.

Left alone, she continued with the sort of things she had always done, but she went about them in a dream. It was as if there were two worlds, the one she had hitherto thought of as real, and the magical kingdom Laidislaw had created for her in Ebury Street, where a single suite of rooms had become bigger on the inside than the whole world. That place, in all its fantastic strangeness, now seemed the real one. The rest of her life was the dream, conducted in a flat, crudely constructed simulacrum of London, which had all the permanence and solidity of a stage set. The people she met seemed dull and wooden, nothing had any colour or texture, and she could not rouse herself to interest in any of it. It was fortunate that she had been so well brought up, so thoroughly trained in her social life, that she was able to continue functioning without either thought or will, so that nobody noticed any difference.

The only person she could not deceive was her maid, Sanders, who had not only been with her since her first grown-up dinner, but knew perfectly well, when she came home from one of her secret expeditions, that her hair was not done as Sanders had done it in the morning. Sanders was too good a servant to say anything, but she looked worried, and Violet was upset and a little hurt that her maid should suppose she was doing anything wrong.

But, of course, it *was* wrong, which was why she had to keep it secret. The original plan had been harmless enough – simply to have a portrait done for Holkam's birthday – but things had gone far beyond that now. Yet she could not keep away. The logical part of her mind, still operating as if on a distant mountain-top, told her that it would be foolish to draw back before the painting was finished, and that as yet she had done nothing *actually* wrong. The rest of her was in a swoon of longing for the resumption of the warm and richly coloured Real Life of the artist's room.

On the first visit after her companions had gone away, it was Laidislaw who opened the street door to her, so quickly upon her ringing the bell that he must have been waiting for her in the hall.

'Where is Mrs Hudson?'

'Away, thank the Lord! She's gone to visit one of her sisters in Portsmouth, hard though it is to believe that an unnatural phenomenon like her could *have* a sister. She does not return until tomorrow, and since the upstairs tenant is abroad for the whole summer, we have the house to ourselves. What *shall* we do with our glorious freedom?'

Violet didn't answer, knowing by now which of his questions were rhetorical. He was leading the way upstairs, in any case, so she should have had to answer to his back.

'No need to lock the door today,' he said, as he closed it behind her – but he did lock it. 'I want you to feel safe,' he said, as she put down the dogs and turned to him. 'Particularly safe today, my lovely Violet. Do you feel safe?'

'Yes,' she said, and then, since he seemed to want something more, 'It is nice to think that there's no-one else in the house.'

He laughed. 'Good, good! You understand. And have all your little Emmas and Fannys and Pollys gone away now? Is your time your own at last? Are you expected home?'

'No. I'm not expected anywhere,' she said, and felt an obscure thrill of anticipation. What could it mean? What did she expect? She had no idea. He was helping her off with her hat, gloves, fur, jacket.

'Sit down,' he said. 'No, not there.' She had gone towards the *chaise-longue*. 'Not yet. Sit in that chair, by the fireplace. I am not ready to draw you yet.' He went through to the bedroom and returned with a tray on which a bottle of champagne sat in an ice bucket, flanked with two glasses. 'Something a little different today,' he said.

'Are we celebrating?' Violet said doubtfully. He seemed

400

in a more than usually elated mood; his eyes seemed almost to throw sparks.

'We are celebrating something that has not yet happened. Do you feel like the White Queen?' Violet had no idea which White Queen he was talking about, so she said nothing. He opened the bottle, poured, handed her the glass. 'In fact,' he went on, 'it happened in my mind even before this. But we will celebrate the actual moment when the pin flies open, if you please.' He raised the glass. 'To Art.'

She could safely drink to that. 'To Art,' she said obediently, and drank. Oddly, it turned out to be exactly what she wanted – cold, effervescent, refreshing. She sipped again, and said, with pleasure, 'I think this is the first time I've drunk champagne at this time of the morning.'

'Don't tell me so!' said Laidislaw. 'Did your husband never bring you champagne in bed? Not even on your honeymoon? Have you never breakfasted together on a terrace above a blue sea on champagne and sun-warmed peaches?' When she shook her head, laughing, he said severely, 'Your husband passes all understanding. What is he about? What *does* he think love means?'

'I don't know,' Violet said. 'I'm not sure if *I* know what it means. I thought I did, once – when I was very young. But I suppose that was just foolishness.'

'*Au contraire*, my fabulous jewel, children have a very clear idea of love. They love freely and innocently and with great appreciation. It is only growing up that clouds the radiance. It is the great power of art – that it teaches us to love again with the same purity. That is what my portrait of you will do.' He drained his glass and leapt to his feet, refilled both glasses, then walked up and down as he spoke, energy seeming to flow from him in waves. 'It will be my greatest and best work – I can feel it! People will look at it and see utter beauty. They will see absolute love. It will transform their sad little mundane souls, and they will go away from my painting better people, and love each other better and more wisely – which is to say with the purity of children.'

'You talk a great deal about love,' Violet said, a little

timidly. Watching him go back and forth was like trying to keep a flashing kingfisher in view. He seemed brilliant and jewel-coloured to her dazzled view – and somehow dangerous. She felt that if she touched him he would sear her fingers, that she might burst into flames from the contact. But the danger was part of the attraction. She thought of a child crawling, hand outstretched, towards a fire. You had to be taught not to try to seize its great, powerful, flickering beauty. Was that part of what he meant by children loving properly, and adults losing the ability? She was trying to think things she had never thought before, and it was hard. She felt so many thoughts that she had no words for, swimming just out of reach, like the shadows of great fish down in the deepest water. So it was that she said, 'You talk a great deal about love. Is it so very important?'

'Important?' He whirled round and flung himself to his knees before her. A wavelet of champagne leapt over the rim of his glass at the movement and splashed Violet's hand. Laidislaw drained his glass again and put it aside as if it were a distraction. 'Important? It is everything! Love – and art, which are the same thing. Without them we are dumb beasts of burden, toiling for ever in the mud, with our eyes cast downwards, never knowing the stars are there, just above us, if we would only lift our heads.' He seized her hand and licked off the champagne, and the touch shocked her, though the action, oddly, did not, for she saw it was part of the same thing, the desire to cast away all distractions to his train of thought. He held her hand up between them in both his, and unfolded her fingers one by one, gently, as one might unfurl a half-opened rose. 'Love and art,' he said. 'They fill me like a surging tide, and I must give them expression! I must try to bring them to those who have eyes to see, but never look. Oh, Violet, my lovely Violet, you are my source, my inspiration, my perfect vessel! I never saw anyone like you before. Perhaps I never shall again.'

'Like me? But I'm – quite ordinary,' she said.

He laughed at that, his eyes glowing as he looked at her.

402

'No, you are quite extraordinary, as I knew the moment I saw you. You have the power in you to throw off convention and soar to heights undreamt-of in our shackled age. You are white fire, contained in a white rose! A burning rose, burning but never consumed! And my love will carry your perfection into the world.'

'Your love?' she asked, in a breath of a voice. 'Do you – do you love me?'

'Love you? Yes! As no man has before, or will again – not because you do not deserve loving, but because you do not allow it. You have hidden yourself away from others, my lovely ancress. You have never allowed anyone else to see you and know you as I do. So my love will be unique – but my painting will show you to the world, and others in their thousands will gaze at it and weep because their own lives have held nothing so transcendent. But they will go away knowing such love and beauty exist, and they will strive for them as never before. That is what our love will achieve, my Violet.' He brought her hand to his lips and kissed each finger with an intensity and a reverence that made her quiver to the centre of her being.

'It's too much,' she whispered. 'All that – it's too much.'

'No, you mustn't be afraid!' he cried. 'Fear is the enemy of love. Fear kills art. It blights all it touches. Do not be afraid. Draw from my strength, trust me. Do you trust me?'

'Yes,' she said.

'Truly?'

'With my life,' she found herself saying.

'Your life? Oh, I shall have more than that!' he said, laughing. 'Do you love me?'

'Yes,' she said, and her voice was a mere husk.

'Say it! You must say it, or everything will wither and die. You must love me and trust me, and together we will make great art. Say it!'

'I love you,' she said. The words were hard to say yet, as if in their passage they had broken some barrier, once she had said them she felt suddenly light and free. She said again, in a stronger voice, 'I love you.'

He kissed her hand again, and got up, drawing her with him. 'Then we shall begin work,' he said.

He led her into his bedroom, and went behind her to undo her buttons. 'There is one more thing,' he said. 'You have given me your mind: in these weeks of talking you have told me things about yourself you never told anyone else.'

'Yes, I have,' she said. 'How did you know?'

'I know everything about you. I know from the tone of your voice exactly how deep you have gone for each revelation, and how difficult its passage. Yes, you have given me your mind, and a good deal of your soul. You have given me your love and your trust. But there is one thing you have not yet given me.'

He finished the buttons. He came round in front of her, and with delicate fingers began to draw her blouse down from her shoulders. She was surprised and nervous, for he had always left the room while she undressed and put on the robe, but oddly she was not shocked or afraid.

'You have not yet given me your body,' he said, holding her gaze. 'But you will.'

Her mouth dried. She could not look away from his bright gaze, but she gasped, 'I can't. I mustn't.'

He raised a forefinger and laid it softly on her lips. 'Never say *I can't*. All things are possible. Between us, all things. We can move the earth. Listen to me, and don't struggle like a caught butterfly, or you will tear your wings. Just as I could not paint the outside of you without knowing the inside, so I cannot paint you clothed without knowing the essential flesh underneath. I must see you and know you to publish the truth of you.'

'But it's – wrong,' she protested weakly.

He laughed. 'Wrong? We are making art here, the highest calling of man! The drive to create is God-given. We try in our poor shadowy way to be like Him, to re-create the glorious world He gave us. He made us naked and beautiful. I must see you as He saw you in his mind when he designed you. You must give me that, before we can begin on our great work.'

404

Mesmerised by his words, transfixed by his eyes and his voice, she stood, trembling lightly, while he undressed her. In her adult life, no-one but her maid had ever seen her naked, and then only in the safety of the bath, with the water to cover her. And yet what was there to be ashamed of in nakedness? It was how God had made them. Her mind felt as if it were splitting in two, the greater part, heavy with all the ideas ingrained through the twenty-four years of her life, ripping away from the new part, which was filled tight and yet light as a bubble with the new notions he had given her.

'Let us have done with these ugly clothes,' he said softly. Her blouse was gone, her skirt unbuttoned and fallen to the floor. She felt awkward in garments never meant to be seen: corset, shift, gartered stockings. 'The teguments with which you face the world are designed to hide your beauty – had you thought of that, my Violet? It's true! How could people carry on with their lives and the dull, grinding, necessary things they must do, if they were all the while blinded by your true beauty? It must be kept hidden, it must be kept only for us. We shall see and rejoice, for we are in the service of a greater force.'

He took off her stockings, rolling them down neatly: everything he did was neat and quiet and easy, as if he had had a great deal of practice. It was rather like being undressed by Sanders, except that, at the last, Sanders stood behind and held a dressing-gown between them, to shield Violet's nakedness from her eyes. But Laidislaw's eyes were the whole point. He touched her with them all the time, and as they came closer, with each removed garment, to her skin, she felt so faint and tremulous she was afraid she might either fall down, or burn up like paper. Then gently, tenderly, he drew her shift over her head and cast it aside, and she was utterly naked before him.

And he looked at her. He looked and looked until her stomach turned to water and her knees shook. 'You are more beautiful even than I imagined,' he said seriously. He went behind her and took out her pins and loosened her hair, and she felt obscurely glad of it, as if it might cover her in some way. 'My poor Violet,' he murmured into her ear, 'how you tremble. Are you cold?'

'No,' she managed to say. 'Not cold.'

'Come then,' he said. 'Come then and lie down for me and let me draw you.'

He led her to the bed and she lay down, and he spent some time arranging her, the angle of her head, the position of her limbs, the spread of her hair. Oddly, the longer this went on, the less afraid she became, because his face was grave and his regard detached, the way they were sometimes when he drew her, so that it seemed it was the artist looking at her, not the man. Well, after all, women had posed naked for artists throughout history, and no-one thought it wrong, so why should not she? As her fear subsided, something else grew up in its place, a languorous heat, a soft loosening of everything inside her, so that she seemed to be in the process of melting back into the counterpane.

When he had done with her he fetched his sketching-pad, and began to draw, rather in the old way – turning the page and beginning again as soon as he had finished one sketch – but not as feverishly. He seemed to be taking more time, working over lines and curves instead of merely putting them down and moving on.

He began to talk again, asking her questions and drawing her out; and soon she had forgotten that she was lying naked on a man's bed in rooms in Ebury Street. She was back in that magical land where all was safe and delightful, and nothing mattered, nothing could hurt, nothing could be wrong. She eased her languid limbs softly against the counterpane, and felt that she was beautiful.

CHAPTER SEVENTEEN

Aeroplanes were still rare enough over York for the arrival of one in a Morland field to bring people running from all directions. Teddy had prepared the level field in which the Easter fair had been held, by having the grass cut, and then taking the heavy roller, pulled by Mouse and Minna, up and down the middle several times. Jessie observed the preparations with interest, but told her uncle that she was sure it wasn't necessary to have the ground quite flat. 'After all, in France they have to land wherever they can. You know last year Jack said in his letters that they put down in all sorts of unsuitable places.'

'He also said how nice it was to land on the racecourse,' Teddy said. 'There's no point in making them land on a rough patch when we can do better.'

Jessie held her peace after that, perfectly well aware that Uncle Teddy was enjoying the whole thing. She suspected he rather wished they were going to arrive at night so that he could have the fun of devising a lighting system for the 'airstrip'. On the day, in the third week of June, he encouraged the whole household to go out to witness the arrival, so at the appointed time the house was abandoned to the kitchen cat dozing on the top of the cool oven, and such mice and spiders as dared to take advantage of the situation. Everyone else was out in the field, being ushered into suitable positions round the margins by Uncle Teddy, with Polly his willing helper. Standing by her mother, Jessie murmured, 'What, no band?' and Henrietta suppressed a smile. Jessie did not know that it was only through her intervention that Teddy had not got out the bunting and flags again, to dress the airfield. 'Think how it will embarrass them,' she had urged, and he had yielded, though with obvious reluctance. 'It's not every day we have a visit like this,' he had said – and it was true.

Everyone was chatting quietly while they waited, until someone said, 'Ssh! Listen!' in urgent tones, and they all fell quiet, to hear, far off, mingled with the gentle sounds of the countryside and an intermittently bellowing bull out at Huntsham, the buzzing noise of an aeroplane engine.

'They're coming!' Henrietta whispered to Jessie, and caught her hand to squeeze it in excitement. The noise grew louder, everyone turned in the same direction and craned their heads upwards, and then the machine appeared, small as a bird to begin with, but flying straight and level as a bird never did, rapidly growing until it came close enough to send all the pigeons clattering up in panic from the house roof. It circled the airfield twice, and it was now that other people started to arrive, running from all directions, stumbling on tussocks as they stared upwards in wonder, unable to let the phenomenon out of their sight. Children headed the field, scrambling over gates and through hedges; women held up their skirts and clutched their hairpins, men snatched off their caps rather than lose them. One of the men from the village had brought his shotgun, fearing it might be the start of a German invasion. But the tenants and estate workers all knew who it was: Teddy's pride had spread the word extensively.

People were cheering now and waving as the little aeroplane circled lower, lined itself up with the nicely mown strip, and put down with a small bounce. Even before it had come to a stop, everyone was surging forward, including the usual mob of dogs, some of whom did not know whether they were supposed to greet or attack the strange creature from the sky. But normal discipline asserted itself to allow the Family through first. And there were the two figures, in leather jackets, flying-helmets and goggles, waving to the crowds, and unfastening their straps. It was impossible at first to tell them apart, though of course they knew one was Helen and the other Jack.

It was a novel and exciting way to pay a family visit, and they were giving pleasure to a much wider circle than their own flesh and blood. Applause broke out as the engine was switched off, as though some great and daring feat had been performed. People were still running in from outlying fields and joining the throng; the rooks in the trees to the north of the field were making an outraged racket; small boys were filtering with the ease of water through a sieve to the front of the crowd where they could gawp at the wonder without interference. Teddy was ready for action. Helen had said in her telephone call that Jack would need assistance to get down from the machine, and he had two large and muscular men at hand to do that, and afterwards to mount guard on the aeroplane, to make sure the wondering public gazed but did not touch.

Helen stood up and pulled off her helmet and goggles, causing a fresh upsurge of comment from the crowd on the fact that she was a woman. Then she picked up the third passenger, who had not been noted, and lifted him out onto the wing, whence he could jump down by himself. Jessie laughed and reached out for him. 'It's Rug! Dear old Rug! Oh, Mother, he's got goggles too!'

'We had to have a pair made for him,' Helen called down. 'He will stare into the wind.' Jessie, who was nearest, carefully removed the goggles and Rug celebrated his arrival by shaking himself vigorously all over until his ears rattled, waved his tail in greeting, and then trotted off ceremoniously to wet the nearest wheel. The house dogs surged after him, and an extensive welcoming ceremony got under way.

Meanwhile, among the humans, Helen handed down Jack's stick, helped him to extricate himself from the cockpit, and handed him down to the waiting arms of the burly helpers. It all looked difficult and painful, but once on level ground and with his stick in his hand, Jack seemed much more nimble. He pulled off his helmet and goggles and was engulfed by his mother's arms. Helen jumped down neatly from the wing. Her appearance was still causing a sensation among the onlookers, for she was wearing bulky trousers and big flying boots just like a man, and the word was filtering round to those who did not know that it was she who had been driving the aeroplane, not her husband.

'It looks so much fun,' Jessie said, giving her a sisterly kiss.

'It is,' Helen said. 'You should learn.'

Jessie laughed. 'When would I ever have reason to use the skill?'

'Well, then, you must let me take you up for a pleasure trip later.'

'Thank you. I'd really like that,' said Jessie.

They left the aeroplane and its ring of admirers and walked back to the house. Sawry, who had been somewhere, discreetly, in the crowd, weeded out the house servants and drove them back to their duties, and as the family strolled they were continually overtaken by scuttling domestics, murmuring, 'Excuse me,' as they darted by to get to the drawbridge first.

'It was a wonderful idea of yours,' Teddy said, 'to come by aeroplane.'

'It's certainly brightened up the neighbourhood,' Henrietta laughed, happy with her hand resting lightly on her son's arm. 'They'll talk about this for weeks.'

'I've never seen an aeroplane before,' Ethel said, checking anxiously that all her children were accounted for.

Polly held firmly onto little James, who was walking crabbed with his head turned back over his shoulder. 'But I want to *look*!' he cried, in tragic tones.

'After lunch,' she whispered to him. 'You shall have a good look after lunch, when everyone else has gone away.'

'What sort of aeroplane is it?' Jessie asked, largely for James's sake, since she didn't really care herself.

'It's a BE2,' Helen said. 'An observation machine. The observer sits in front and makes notes on the enemy's troop dispositions, artillery, sometimes things like factories and railway lines. On the newer version, the BE2c, he also works the machine-gun, which would be mounted on his cockpit. But this one is one of the early, unarmed ones. It's a training machine now, which is why we were allowed to borrow it.'

'How clever of you to know all that stuff,' Jessie said.

'Never mind that,' said Teddy. 'How clever of her to be able to drive the thing!'

Helen smiled nonchalantly. 'Oh, it's easy. The BE is very stable. Anyone could fly it – that was what it was designed for.'

'But it's slow, and not very manoeuvrable,' Jack said. 'Because it's designed to fly level, it doesn't like turning.'

One of the servants wanted Henrietta, and she stopped to talk to her, releasing Jack's arm, so Jessie fell back and took it, in case he needed steadying. He smiled down at his sister. 'It's all right, I'm not going to fall over.'

'How bad is it?' she asked him bluntly. 'I hated seeing you having to be helped down from the aeroplane like that.'

'Oh, I'm a bit unhandy that way at the moment,' he said lightly, 'but it's getting better. After the last X-ray the sawbones said he thought there were no more bone fragments to come, and that I should be able to heal normally now.'

'And how long will it take?'

'A few months, no more,' he said, but she could see longing in his eyes, rather than assurance. 'Of course, it'll be very weak for a time. I shall have to do special exercises to strengthen it. But I ought to be able to fly by the end of the year.'

'And then? Will they let you go back?'

'They'll have to,' he said grimly. 'I'm needed out there.'

'But if you're not fit—'

'I shall make myself fit.'

Helen, walking with Teddy, glanced back a moment as though she had felt his emotion, though she was too far ahead to have heard his words.

'How does Helen feel about that?' Jessie asked quietly.

411

'There's a war on,' Jack said. 'Hadn't you noticed?'

'I noticed.'

His expression softened. 'Of course you did. Don't worry, Helen knows what's what, and she married me with her eyes open. She's a flyer too. She understands.'

It was only when they were all indoors and gathered together in the drawing-room that Helen announced her great news. With her arm through her husband's, she gathered the attention of the throng and said, 'Jack and I have something to tell you.' She caught Henrietta's eye and smiled. 'I expect you can guess what it is. We're going to have a little Compton.'

Jessie loved her brother so much she felt the surge of joy for him before the pang of her own loss. Everyone was exclaiming, kissing, shaking hands. Henrietta was crushed silently in Jack's arms; Alice was crying happily.

'Oh, this is great news! Great!' Teddy cried.

'When will it be?' Ethel asked.

'In January,' said Helen.

Jessie thought she looked a little stunned by the idea, as well as radiant. She reached her at last and kissed her. 'Congratulations. I'm so very happy for you both. Do you want a boy or a girl?'

'I want a boy and Jack wants a girl, so either will please somebody,' Helen said. Jessie moved back and let Alice take her place. Teddy was sending for champagne, Sawry was expressing his polite pleasure, and the level of talk had soared. Jessie felt suddenly outside the throng, set apart by the wall of sound. She looked from delighted face to delighted face, the bright eyes, moving mouths, flushed cheeks. Helen looked so strong and healthy and richly coloured, her feet planted firmly, part of the stream of life, deserving her place in the sun. Jessie felt empty and useless, with no life in her. She thought again of the little ghost that went beside her, always just out of sight – her lost child. And then something cold touched her hand and made her jump. It was Brach's nose, given to her for comfort. The hound gazed up at her earnestly, gold eyes shining in the

412

shadow. The ghost was gone, she was inside the sound again, part of the family. Normality. Sawry gave her a glass, and now Uncle Teddy was calling for a toast: well, you couldn't have anything more normal than that, she thought.

It was a lovely family day, full of warmth and talk and laughter. The children were allowed to stay down for luncheon, which made it a special occasion for them, even without the added excitement of the two strangers from the air. And as it was a Saturday, Rob came home and joined them, and there was a touching reunion between the brothers, who had not met for many months. 'If only Frank were here,' Henrietta said.

'How is he? Have you heard from him lately?' Jack asked.

'He's still in Malta, fretting to go to the Front.'

'He's a temporary second lieutenant now, and hoping to be gazetted in the autumn,' said Teddy, 'so when he does go, he'll go as an officer.'

'I suppose there's not much to do in Malta,' Helen said. 'It must be frustrating for him.'

'How well you understand men, my love,' Jack said, grinning at her across the table.

'He doesn't understand why they're kept there, when men are so badly needed at the Front,' Jessie said. 'They get a lot of the Gallipoli casualties at the base hospital there. They see the hospital ships coming in every day so they know how badly things are going. He feels they're being wasted.'

'You always talk about Frank being wasted,' Polly objected, 'but you never spare a thought for poor Lenny, stuck out in Egypt.'

'But he's guarding the Suez Canal,' Jessie said. 'At least he's doing something useful and important.'

'Well, he'd sooner be killing Germans,' Polly said, with certainty.

Jack laughed. 'So would we all! Even Helen wants to 'list as a soldier – don't you, darling?'

'Not now I'm doing something useful,' she said serenely. 'Of course, when you go back I may feel very different. I may want to do something more important than delivering aeroplanes. Perhaps then I'll cut my hair off and put on a false moustache and join you at the Front.'

'You'll have something more important to do than fight the Germans,' Henrietta said. 'You'll be looking after the next generation. I suppose you'll have to give up your job soon?'

'In September, probably,' Helen acknowledged. 'There's nothing particularly dangerous about it, but by then I shan't be able to reach the controls. And as for climbing up on the wing . . .' Everyone laughed at the image conjured up, though Alice looked a little uncomfortable at such frankness.

'Talking of being useful,' Jack said to Jessie, 'how is your nursing adventure? Are you still the Queen of the Sluice-room?'

'Empress,' Jessie said, 'at least. But they are letting me do some other things now. Not exactly saving lives, but they let me fetch things and hold things as well as scrub them, and sometimes they explain to me what they're doing and why.'

'It sounds fascinating,' Jack said, laughing. 'But good for you, for sticking it out! Someone has to do the horrid jobs too.'

'We'll all be needed, one way or another, if this war goes on much longer,' Teddy said.

'Bertie says if the big push this autumn can break through, they ought to be able to roll everything up by next summer,' Jessie offered.

'Well, that's something I can drink to,' said Teddy.

After luncheon, Helen took those who were interested to see the aeroplane, while Jack stayed behind with his foot up and chatted to his mother and brother. Jessie noticed how good Helen was with the children, talking to them very naturally and explaining things in a way they could understand. She lifted them up one by one to let them sit in the cockpit and described how things worked. Then she offered Jessie and Polly turns in going up.

414

Polly said at once, 'No, thank you. I'm sure it's a very nice aeroplane but I don't like the smell and I'm sure I should be sick.'

'I'd love a turn,' Jessie said.

'Ugh!' said Polly. 'Sooner you than me. I'll take the children back, then. I hope you don't end up in France.'

'We shan't go far,' Helen said, in valediction.

'Shall I need a coat?' Jessie asked.

'No, you'll be fine. It's a warm day and we won't be going very high or very fast. Do you want to hop up? Put your foot there and your hand there – that's right – and into the cockpit.' There were still a few people hanging around the machine, and the two men were still on guard. Helen asked one of them to clear the runway for her, and the other to swing the propeller. She took one wing and the man took the other and they swung the aeroplane round; then she hopped up into the cockpit, and moments later the engine burst into life and they taxied down the runway and turned. She tapped Jessie on the shoulder, mouthed, 'Ready?' and put up her thumb. Jessie nodded, a little nervously, and they were off.

The dashing along the bumpy grass path was exciting, but at the moment the wheels left the earth Jessie felt her stomach sink, and as they soared upwards all her insides seemed to be lurching about in a most unsettling fashion. She thought it would be dreadfully shaming – not to say inconvenient – actually to be sick, and concentrated on controlling herself; but quite soon fascination took over, and she forgot to worry about her stomach. To be up here, above the earth, with nothing holding them up, no pillar, no string, just empty air all around! She saw a pigeon fly past, on the same level as her eyes, and marvelled at it. The sky looked wonderfully blue and close, as if she could grab fistfuls of it; the warm air rushed past her, and the various wires and struts made a singing noise that might have been the song of angels, it was so strange and lovely and ethereal. She looked down and saw the fields and trees and streams and tracks of her home place, the country she had ridden and

415

walked over since she was a girl, laid out like a child's toy farm below her. At first she could not recognise anything, but then Helen turned the aeroplane slowly round and she saw the walls of York and was able instantly to orientate herself. There was the Mickle Gate, there was the station, with a clockwork train running into it, carrying a thread of toy smoke; there was the river – oh, and there was Water End, the back road she used to take from Clifton when she rode or drove to Morland Place. So that was the Clifton Road, there! And as they turned again, running parallel to the road, she looked down and could see her house – or what had been her house, anyway, dear Maystone Villa. The aeroplane began to turn again, and she saw the grey bulk of the hospital on her right, and the rows of extra huts that had been put up in the grounds. Then they crossed Clifton Ings and back over the river.

It was all so fascinating! Helen pottered the aeroplane along only about sixty or seventy feet up, so that Jessie could see and recognise everything down below. Sometimes they passed over people, who looked up and waved. Out over the North Field they startled a flock of sheep, who ran before them idiotically until a hedge stopped them, when they veered round and ran back the other way. And then there was Morland Place, looking ancient and solid and intriguingly different from this angle, something familiar made interestingly strange, and Jessie realised they were dropping lower, and that the landing field was ahead of them. She felt a sharp pang of disappointment that the trip was over. And she had quite forgotten to feel sick.

'That was wonderful!' she said to Helen, when they were both back on firm ground (though it did feel oddly spongy to her just at first, too spongy and too rigid at the same time).

'I'm glad you enjoyed it,' Helen said, looking pleased. 'You didn't feel sick?'

'Only just at first, but then it was too interesting. I understand now why you feel you have to fly. Jackie too. He used to tell me, but I never understood, not *really*. I used to think, It can't be so *very* wonderful. But it is.'

'I think so,' Helen said. 'When I'm up in an aeroplane, I feel as if nothing can ever vex me or bother me or worry me again. One is just happy up there.'

'It must be sad for you to think about giving it up. If it were for anything other than a baby . . .'

'Yes, it makes me understand all the better how Jack feels. But he'll be flying again soon. And I shan't be kept out of the sky for ever.'

'You'll fly again when you've had the baby?'

'Certainly – and go back to my job, if they'll have me. Why? Do you think it shocking?'

'Goodness, no! I envy you, that's all.'

'I think people's attitude to women is going to have to change as the war goes on,' Helen said.

The last of the crowds had gone away while they were up, and the two guardians with them, so they were alone as they walked back, except for Brach, who emerged from under a hedge and pranced along with them, glad to have her mistress back. 'I don't know how it can be after that enormous lunch,' Jessie said, 'but I'm hungry again.'

Helen laughed. 'It's funny, flying always makes me hungry too. I hope I don't get dreadfully fat, or Jack will stop loving me.'

'Nonsense. He'll never do that,' Jessie said.

When they walked back into the drawing-room, Jessie noted how her brother's eyes flew to Helen, the warmth in them, and the little, intimate smile they exchanged, and realised again that her own words had not just been form. Jack would never stop loving Helen, and she thought how wonderful it must be to share that sort of feeling with your own husband, the man you were licensed to love and live with. Of course, it would make it all the harder for them to part, if or when Jack did go back to the Front; but that was a price she thought would be worth paying for such daily bliss.

After Ypres had quietened down, the remnant of the Kents had moved back to Neuve Chapelle, where they had been

417

joined by three new companies sent out from England, bringing the battalion's numbers almost back up to normal. The line was quiet there, now: just the usual, regular 'hate' sent over by the Germans, and answered by their own guns, and the inevitable activities of the snipers.

Life fell into a routine, with each company spending a few days in the firing line, a few days in the support trenches, then going into reserve. When in reserve they did not remain in the trenches, but were billeted a good mile behind the line, in a state of readiness. After reserve, they would go out into billets well behind the Front, on training and fatigues. The army kept up this constant rotation so that no-one spent very long together in the trenches – in practice no more than ten days in the month, and rarely more than three or four days at a time – which in turn kept the men's morale up. When they were in billets they could bathe, get their uniforms deloused, eat fresh food, receive their mail, and – if they had the money – visit the *estaminets* for beer and egg-and-chips. French law forbade the sale of alcohol in the war zone, but even if they had known about the embargo, the local people would have shrugged and assumed it did not apply to them. To a Frenchman the law was the law, but business was sacred.

In the third week of June the Kents went into billets in Locon, a village near Hinges. The officers' billet was a middling-size post hotel on the main road to Béthune, and they had the former lounge bar as their smoking room. On the first evening, Ned found himself, for want of anything else to do, poring over a map of the area, which was framed under glass and hanging on the wall beside the fireplace. Idly he found Neuve Chapelle, then looked for Locon, and his finger tracing from one to the other went past a small place called Loisené.

At once the memory of Céline rushed into his head like hot blood, so that he was sure he was blushing. He had felt terrible guilt as he marched away with his men towards the battle at Ypres – guilt for having broken his marriage vows, betrayed Jessie, given himself to another woman against all the teachings of the Church and his own conscience. How could he have done it? And not just once – that he might have shrugged off eventually as a regrettable result of getting drunk. But he had gone back the next night, and the next. Only the sudden call to pack up and leave had brought him to his senses. Vernon had encouraged him, of course – he wanted to go back, and liked to have company in his carousing; but Ned could not put the blame on Vernon. He had known exactly what he was doing. He had tried to resist Vernon's persuasions, but Céline had burned brightly in his mind, calling him back, as irresistible as a flame to a moth. So loving, so gentle, so passionate, she had made him feel he was the only man in the world she had ever cared for. It was intoxicating.

And then they had marched away, and on the journey he had had leisure to think. It was wrong, what he had done, and there was no excuse for it. He groaned at the thought of it, vowed never to slip again, decided that the next time he saw Jessie he would make a full confession and ask her forgiveness. He was wretched with guilt. But then everything had changed. The battle, the terrible sights he had seen, the dangers he had faced, the death and blood and violence all around him had burned his mind clean. When he came out of it – a survivor against all the odds, with so many of his men dead, mutilated, blown to bits all around him – it seemed to put things into a different perspective. Yes, he had done wrong, but it was a small and unimportant wrong in the scheme of things, in this hell of fire and blood he found himself in. He had done no real harm; and with life so uncertain, the future on so short a lease, he could not go on condemning himself. It was over and done with, and the best thing was to forget it. With his return to Neuve Chapelle, there had been so much to do, settling the new men into his platoon and training them in trench lore, along with his usual multitude of tasks and worries, that it had been easy to put the whole thing out of his mind.

But now suddenly Céline had entered his thoughts again, and he could not get her out. He remembered her

419

sweetness, her soft, husky voice, her kindness, and how interested she was in everything he had to say. She had given herself to him without reserve, as no-one ever had before. Her attention had been balm to his soul, made him feel fully a man again where, since December, there had been something missing.

Sweet Céline! But he had been remiss. He had spent three nights with her, and then gone away without a word. Well, that was the army's fault, of course. But he had not written or made any enquiries to see if she was all right. He ought to remedy that. He ought at least to thank her, explain why he had disappeared, tell her why he could not see her again. Apart from any other consideration, it was the least politeness demanded. He consulted his watch. It was not late yet. He looked round for Vernon, and then went to find him.

He was outside, smoking and leaning on a gate.

'I say, Vernon!'

'Morland, old thing. Fine night, isn't it? I love this time of year, when it hardly gets dark at all. Makes you feel all things are possible.'

'Yes, it's very nice. Vernon, I was wondering – are you using your motor tonight?'

Vernon's eye gleamed. 'Something on?'

'Not really.' Ned tried to look casual. 'I thought I ought to look up that young lady – Céline. See if she's all right.'

'Young lady?' Vernon looked puzzled, and then his eyebrows shot up. 'Oh, you mean *that* young lady.' He grinned. 'Why, Morland, you sly dog! Thought you could sneak off without anyone knowing, did you?' Ned looked away, feeling uncomfortable at the teasing, and Vernon regarded him with amusement. 'You're a strange fellow. But I must say it's an incandescently good idea of yours! A little feminine company is just what I want, now I come to think of it. I was feeling a little restless. Hold hard while I fetch Redwing, and we'll go together.'

'Oh – look – I didn't really want to go in a party,' Ned said awkwardly.

Vernon clapped his shoulder. 'No party, just the three of

420

us, you, me and Redders. Quite right, we don't want the damned rabble – all those baying Smythes and Cyrilsons.'

'I'm not sure you understand,' Ned said. 'I just want to make sure she's all right. Have a talk with her. That's all.'

Vernon's expression was ripe. 'Exactly what I want,' he said solemnly. 'Nothing more. The three of us, and a nice quiet evening in Loisené, talking to three nice young ladies, making sure they're all right. What a man for the ideas you are, Morland old chum!'

Ned, feeling ruffled by Vernon's assumption that his motives were carnal, was silent on the journey. They rolled through the luminous dusk, with the wheels throwing up veils of dust on the stock-scented air. The moon had risen, and hung huge and champagne-coloured, almost transparent, like a great soap bubble floating in the pale green sky. Redwing began to sing after a while, in his pleasant tenor, and Vernon joined in the choruses. The tune was the sweetly sentimental 'Keep The Home Fires Burning', but the words were a mildly obscene version popular in the battalion. The contrast was comic, and Ned found himself smiling against his will. His annoyance faded away, and he felt only glad to be of their company, accepted – a friend.

The house in the side-street looked just the same, and Vernon's knock produced the same painted lady, who greeted him with kisses on both cheeks and a rapid burst of French.

'It's quiet tonight,' Vernon said to them, over his shoulder, 'so we're particularly welcome. I think we may get a free bottle of wine out of it.'

Inside there was the same smoke, the same creaky gramophone, the same lamps. All the windows were curtained against the light evening, so there was the same womb-like red darkness; but a door in the back wall stood open, and through it, at the other end of a narrow passage, another open door revealed a pearly oblong of light and greenness, through which, distantly, came the sound of a thrush calling. It was like a magic doorway to another world – an escape route, perhaps? Then Madame slammed the door shut, making the darkness complete.

Only a handful of men were there, drinking and talking. The other tables were empty and the girls were sitting around, smoking and looking bored. They brightened at the sight of the three Kent officers; and as several got up to come towards them, Ned saw Céline at last, sitting in a corner, reading a book by the feeble light of a candle-lamp. She looked up, too, and he thought she seemed tense and unhappy; then she saw him, her face lit, and she was up and across the room to him.

'Édouard! Édouard! Oh, I am glad to see you! It has been such a long time. I thought you 'ad forgotten me.'

She put her arms round his neck and laid her soft, painted lips against his, and the smell of her perfume and the sensation of her pliant body pressing against his roused Ned's blood and brought back all the old feelings he had vowed to put aside. He longed for the comfort of her in the ugly and brutal world he inhabited. He tried desperately to push his emotions down, and told himself again, sternly, that he was just there to talk to her.

Vernon and Redwing were laughing. 'Oy-oy,' said Vernon. 'That's the sort of French conversation I understand. Sophie, Mimi, Marie-Claire, my little angels, come and sit with us, entertain us! Madame – some wine here, please.'

They took a table and the girls clustered round them, wine was brought and cigarettes lighted. Ned would have gone with them, but Céline hung soft and heavy on his arm, and held him back. 'No, no,' she murmured, 'I must 'ave you to myself. I 'ave so much to say to you.'

'And I to you,' Ned said nervously. 'That's what I came for, to talk to you.'

'Ver' well, we shall talk,' she said, her voice like a cat's purr, as she drew him towards the curtained doorway that led to the stairs. 'We shall talk afterwards.'

'No, there's to be no "afterwards",' Ned said, trying to resist. 'I only came to talk.'

She smiled, pulling him relentlessly. 'Just as you say,' she said. 'No afterwards. Only talk. But we will talk in my room, yes? So that we can be private. Ah, dear Édouard, so 'andsome you are! *Si gentil!* I 'ave think about you very much, and 'ope you will come back. I 'ave readed the book you gave me – see, I 'ave it 'ere – and my English is much better. Do you not see 'ow I am saying English ver' well? We shall 'ave fine talking, *mon cher*, about books and many things. But first I 'ave somesing to give you.' The curtain was pulled aside, and she coaxed him through. 'Come, you will like very much. It is quiet here since a long time, and I am much rested.'

The curtain fell behind them.

Emma had enjoyed her stay at Oakley Grange, the Protheroes' house at Datchet. Irene and Florence Protheroe were pleasant girls, friendly and lively without pretence. There had been the daily visits to Ascot, with all the excitement of the racing and the interest of the crowds of the eminent and the elegantly dressed. There had been various other entertainments: picnics and river trips, tennis and croquet, dinners and dances. And there had been a constant coming and going of visitors to keep them lively.

At the end of the fortnight, when the main party broke up, Lady Ravenhill, who had been staying with her daughter Sybil, invited Emma and Irene Protheroe to come back with her for a week or two to Marcham Hall, near Abingdon. It was always a concern of mothers with unmarried daughters to secure them company during the summer months, when the Season was winding down. The Ravenhills had not taken a house in London this year, because of the war, and Lady Ravenhill confessed that she thought poor Sybil, who had come out the year before, was having rather a thin time of it. It would be a kindness if Emma and Irene would come and stay and keep her amused. Florence Protheroe was going to stay with the family of her particular friend in the Cotswolds, and Irene had been dreading the flatness that would inevitably follow the Ascot party, so she accepted eagerly and persuaded Emma, with a fervent glance, to say that she would come if Lady Holkam didn't mind. A telegram to Violet ascertained that she didn't mind at all, and the three girls went off happily together with Lady Ravenhill by train and motor to Marcham.

Marcham Hall was a red-brick Tudor mansion with a proliferation of small, rather dark rooms, diamond-paned windows, chimneys like sticks of barley-sugar, and beams in awkward places. In winter it was bleak and chilly, and the enormous fireplace in the great hall, which was the principal gathering area, burned up vast tree-trunks without giving back much in the way of heat. The Ravenhills were a hardy family, and since in the winter they spent most of their time out of doors, hunting or shooting, the internal lack of comfort did not much bother them. But in the summer months – at least, when the summer was warm and dry – Marcham Hall was a charming place, with terraced walks, sheltered lawns, walled gardens, a profusion of flower beds and nicely placed benches to take advantage of them. There was, in addition, a fine stretch of Berkshire to ride over, should the fancy take one, dogs in a variety of shapes and sizes to go for walks with, and the pretty town of Abingdon just two miles away.

If the stay with the Protheroes had been marred by anything, it was the shortage of gentlemen, but this was not a difficulty at Marcham Hall since the girls were only there to amuse each other and were not expecting parties. However, Sybil was not slow to mention, when they arrived, that there was a convalescent hospital in Abingdon where she and her mother were accustomed to visit the officers, a pleasant habit that had only been broken by the visit to Datchet.

'If you shouldn't mind it, we could all go,' Sybil said.

'You don't do nursing, do you?' Irene asked suspiciously.

'Oh, no, nothing like that. Just talk to them and read to them, and run errands – change their library books or buy their cigarettes and postage stamps for them. That sort of thing. They're very nice fellows – and one ought to do one's bit,' she added, recollecting it.

'Well, I don't mind a bit,' said Emma. 'I should like to be able to help in some way.'

'I don't mind if it's just talking and reading,' Irene said, more doubtfully. 'As long as they're not terribly hurt. I can't bear the sight of blood.'

'No, there won't be any of that,' said Sybil.

They went up to the hospital on two afternoons a week. Irene found there were no grisly wounds on view to upset her. Some of the officers, to be sure, had been seriously hurt, but it was easy enough for her to leave those with a missing arm or leg or a heavily bandaged head to the other two, and spend her time chatting to someone whose injuries did not make her feel faint.

It was clear to Emma that Sybil had been doing sterling work here for some time, for she was well known not only to the patients but to the nurses. They treated her with a friendly deference, which was a tribute partly to her own frank and nonsense-free character, and partly to Lady Ravenhill's generosity to the hospital. Emma did her best to fit in. She did not want to be thought one of those girls who visited convalescent officers for their own amusement – though it *was* often very amusing. Most of the officers were at that stage of mending where boredom was more of a trial to them than pain, and the arrival of three pretty girls raised their spirits and brought out the best of their wit and conversation.

Sybil seemed to be developing a friendship with a Lieutenant Weedon, who was tied to his bed with a serious fracture of the leg but who, being a country boy, shared many of the same interests as her. They talked long and wistfully about hunting, horses, dogs, and the joys of country living. He was also an amateur ornithologist, and was trying to interest her, by means of books that she acquired for him, in birds of the non-edible sort.

Irene managed to flirt discreetly with several young men at once, especially those who were a little more mobile and were able to sit out on the terrace in the afternoons. Emma made herself generally useful. As Sybil had said, it was mostly chatting and running little errands – down to the nearest shop for cigarettes, chocolate and reading matter, or occasionally razor blades, toothpaste and other homely necessities. But though the young men flirted with her, and she responded, she did not feel herself in danger from any of them. A certain tall, dark man with a pale scar down his sunburnt brow beckoned always from the back of her memory, making those present pale in comparison.

There was one officer who lay in his bed in the corner and spoke to nobody, never asked for anything, and never met her eye as she passed. His leg was in plaster up to the thigh, strung up on counter-weights, and there was a new, pink scar running up his forehead into his hair, which reminded her, poignantly, of Captain Fenniman's. For that reason, perhaps, she felt rather tender towards Lieutenant Crathie, and worried that no-one talked to him or tried to amuse him. She asked once or twice, from the foot of his bed, if there was anything he wanted, but he never answered her; and if she persisted, he turned his head away towards the wall and closed his eyes.

One afternoon one of the officers had received a fine cake from his mother by post, and waited until the young ladies arrived to have them cut it up and hand it round.

'Didn't want to bother the nurses with it,' said Johnson to Emma. 'See everyone gets a piece, will you? There's a cherub.' It would not normally have been proper for a man to call a young lady a cherub on so slight an acquaintance, but considerable latitude was given to wounded heroes. When everyone else had a piece, Emma went up to Crathie's bed with the last slice on a plate.

'Would you like a piece of cake?' No answer. 'It's Lieutenant Johnson's birthday, you see, and his mother sent it. It looks awfully good.'

Crathie turned his face away, staring at the wall. Emma felt so sorry for him, she stepped a little closer. 'Is there anything I can get for you? Would you like some water, or a cup of tea?' Still he did not answer. 'Are you in pain? Shall I fetch the nurse?'

426

He muttered something, his face still turned away. Emma leant over him a little. 'I'm sorry, I didn't hear that. Please, won't you tell me if there's something I can do for you?'

'Leave me alone,' he said, in a low growl, which this time she did catch. 'Just leave me alone.'

'I'm sorry,' Emma began.

But Crathie rolled his head back on the pillow, glaring at her, and in the same movement lashed out with his arm, knocking the plate from her hand and sending it crashing to the floor. 'Get away from me! Leave me alone!'

Emma jerked back her head, startled, and he stared up at her with the pitiful ferocity of a trapped and wounded fox. 'What are you staring at?' he cried. 'Don't stare at me! I won't stand it! Go away! *Go away!*'

'I'm so sorry,' Emma said, backing away. She trod on a half of the broken plate and it snapped under her weight with a sharp crack. At the sound Crathie gave a shriek, and flung his arm over his face.

'*No more!*' he cried. '*No more! I can't stand any more!*' He tried to fling himself over in bed, but with his leg strung up he could not move, only set it swinging, which made him scream thinly with pain. But a nurse had come hurrying, with Sister behind her, and between them they restrained the man, who was sobbing now, and adjusted his leg. Another nurse arrived and they drew the screens round the bed while the first nurse scurried off for morphine.

Emma mutely cleared up the broken plate and cake, tears stinging her eyes. When she straightened, Lieutenant Kent, in the next bed, smiled kindly and said, 'Don't worry, Miss Weston. You didn't do anything wrong. It's shell-shock.'

Emma had never heard the term. 'I didn't mean to upset him,' she said. 'I just thought I could cheer him up a little.'

Kent shook his head. 'Not your fault. It's just that poor old Crathie's nerves are shot to blazes. He went through a frightful bombardment. Can't stand sudden noises. Reminds him of the Front.'

'Oh dear, I'm sorry,' Emma said contritely.

'And the poor chap's in a lot of pain. They don't know if they're going to be able to save his leg.'

'Oh, how awful!'

Kent nodded, and became, in his elliptical way, expansive. 'His entire platoon was wiped out at Hill 60, you know. Rather got him down. That and the whiz-bangs. Awful noise – can really sap the old spirit if you're the nervy type. Has nightmares about it. Wakes us up most nights, screaming. So it wasn't anything you did.'

Emma took what comfort she could from that, but it was the first time she had come up against the mental effects the war could have, and it made her realise a little more keenly what the men of her acquaintance were facing at the Front. Bad enough to think of them being killed, or coming back injured, like these fellows – minus a leg, perhaps – or worse. She shuddered at the thought. But what if they – if *he* – came back with his mind irrevocably damaged? That would be worse, wouldn't it? They could make artificial legs now, really good ones, she had heard. But they could not replace a shattered mind.

During their more leisured moments, sitting on a bench on a sunny terrace at Marcham Hall, or walking the less energetic dogs through the park, it was natural for the girls to exchange confidences. Officers being somewhat on their minds, and Captain Fenniman in particular on Emma's, she mentioned his London visit and the time she had spent with him. The others were at once eager to know all about him, and Emma was not unwilling to tell.

'And are you in love with him?' Irene asked directly.

Emma was taken off balance by the question. 'I – I really don't know. I liked him awfully. But I've only just met him, and we only had two days together.'

'Two days can be quite enough,' said Irene. 'My mother said she knew the first time she danced with Daddy that he was the one for her.'

'But she knew him already,' Sybil objected. 'He was her brother's friend. I know,' she explained to Emma, 'because they and my uncle Bob were all at school together. So even

428

if she didn't think about him before, she knew who he was and where he came from.'

'I don't really know anything much about Captain Fenniman,' Emma admitted. 'Except that he was very nice, and we talked and talked, which was bliss.'

'You're so lucky,' Irene said. 'All the young men my parents think are suitable are completely tongue-tied. I wonder if that means your captain *isn't* suitable? Perhaps being good at talking is something only unsuitable men are.'

Emma laughed, and said, 'I hope not. But in any case, I don't know when I'll see him again, or even if I ever *will* see him again. So there's not much point in my being in love with him, even if I thought I was – which I don't, quite, yet.'

'Just as well not to get too attached,' Sybil said approvingly.

'I shan't, not now,' Emma said. 'It's just something nice to think about, you know.'

'In bed, at night – yes, I know,' Sybil said. Was there a girl alive who did not have someone she thought about in that delicious time before going to sleep?

Irene sighed. 'The way things are going, thinking is all any of us are likely to have. Mama couldn't get *anyone* interesting for our Ascot party – everyone's away in the army. I wish this old war was over. The only way we see nice men now is when they're wounded.'

Emma thought of poor Crathie, and shivered, imagining for a fleeting moment that it was Fenniman in the same state. No, she couldn't bear the thought. Am I in love with him? she wondered. She thought, on the whole, not. Not yet. But he was the nicest and most interesting man she had ever met, and if they did meet again when the war was over – well, who knew?

CHAPTER EIGHTEEN

Violet and Octavian Laidislaw became lovers at the end of
June, on the day that he finally began painting the portrait.
All his preparations were over, the hundreds of drawings he
had made put aside. Now they had come to the real thing,
the consummation of all that had been said and done
between them. Violet, dressed in the richly coloured gown,
was arranged on the *chaise-longue*, her hair loose. The blank
canvas was on its easel, his palette, brushes, tools, rags and
pots on the little table beside it. He stood for a moment,
looking at her, as though he hesitated to plunge in. Gazing
back at him – in his shirtsleeves, his cuffs rolled up showing
his strong forearms, his hair already ruffled – she smiled
softly with pleasure at the sight of him.

As if that had been the sign he waited for, he seized a
brush and began. He did not work steadily, but with quick,
darting movements and long pauses: painting, then stopping to stand back and consider, to look at her again, then
springing back into his work. He made her think of a kingfisher, brilliant and powerful, plunging fearlessly into the
water that was its other element, passing between air and
river with a scatter of golden light and silver water, at home
in either, neither clinging to him.

Sometimes he walked up and down the room, as though
in a fever of composition – as though the movement of his
hand holding the brush was not sufficient to vent the wild
energy pent up inside him. He did not speak to her while

he painted, though his eyes when he looked at her were so wild and bright she half expected them to emit sparks. She did not speak either, but watched him in silence, reclining against a heap of cushions, utterly still, weighted by the burden of her beauty. She was enraptured, saturated by the joy of looking at him. She was in love with him, she knew that now. All he had taken from her over the weeks – her memories and thoughts, the yielding up of her fears and the breaking of her tabus – had brought her to this place where she was as free as a bird in the air, and loved him as easily as a bird sings.

She had no idea how much time passed. Quite abruptly he stopped, his hand falling to his side as though he were suddenly exhausted.

'It is enough for today,' he said.

She stirred almost painfully, not wanting it to be over. 'May I see?' she said.

He laughed, showing his teeth. 'See? No! I never show my work. Not until it is finished.' He flung down his palette and stuffed his brush carelessly into the pot with the others. 'You may move now. Let me help you – you must be stiff.'

'Stiff? No. I could lie here all day,' she said.

He came to her and knelt before her, lifting one of her hands and chafing it gently as though it were cold. 'You are a wonderful subject. How still you lie! And yet all the time breathing out beauty and passion. You make it so easy for me. To paint you is like swimming in a buoyant stream – I am carried along effortlessly.'

'It didn't look effortless,' she said, smiling. 'And now you look tired.' Greatly daring, she reached out her free hand and brushed the hair gently back from his brow. It was the first time she had touched him, and he made one of his kingfisher movements, caught that hand, too, and brought both to his mouth, kissing them fervently.

'Lovely Violet,' he said. 'We have made such a good start today, we deserve every pleasure in reward. Come, come with me. Can you rise up, poor muse, from your couch?'

He helped her up, and then drew her by one hand into

431

the bedroom. Earlier he had partly drawn the curtains against the glare of the summer sun, and it was dim and cool in there. He led her to the bed and there paused, looking at her gravely. He cupped her face in his hands and said softly, 'Is it what you want? Tell me.'

'Yes,' she whispered. It was the moment of no return – and yet it did not feel like a transition. Everything between them seemed part of the same, a journey on which they had embarked together, the end of which was not yet in view.

'So be it, then,' he said, and drew off the gown. She lay down without fear, because the action was not new to her now; but this time he did not draw her. He pulled off his shirt, and she saw the smooth, bare skin of his chest and arms for the first time, and a longing came over her to touch it, to run her hands over it. In a piercing moment she imagined how it would feel: velvet over steel; cool, with burning heat underneath. Her body yearned for his; she felt heavy with wanting, yet her nerves tingled with expectation. He sat on the edge of the bed and looked enquiringly down into her face, and she did what she had longed to do – ran both hands along his forearms and up his chest. As if that had answered his enquiry, he leant down and kissed her.

It was as though she had never been kissed before. Sensation seemed to explode inside her. She kissed him in passion, her hands clinging to him, pulling him closer. His hands were on her body, and where they touched they left a fire-trail of delight. He released himself, and she ached with loss, but it was only to remove the rest of his garments, and then he was stretched beside her, his cool-burning skin touching hers. *I love you!* she cried out, in her mind, but her lips made no sound but a little gasp before they were covered again by his.

The strange, ungainly thing she had done with her husband was no precedent for this: she had lain with him in duty and distaste, and found the transaction shameful and unpleasant. It had been an agricultural necessity, and she had been glad when the need for it had ceased. This was not the same act. It was something beautiful and imperative, ordained of the

432

gods. Laidislaw's touch lit her to flame, and she wanted to be closer and ever closer to him, to hold him and have him and be him, to be one thing with him. She burned for him, and when he entered her, she was consumed by flame, and reborn.

He did not speak her name, nor she his. They strove together in silence, but for their gasping breaths; but at the end he made a small cry of accomplishment that pierced her with a terrible tenderness. Afterwards they lay a long time in silence, holding each other. Violet drifted, her eyes closed, on a sea of bliss. Then he pushed himself up on one elbow and looked down at her, moving a strand of hair from her damp face with a gentle finger.

'I was right about you,' he said. 'I knew there was fire at the heart of my rose.' He smiled tenderly at her. 'Did you know it was there? No, I don't think you had the least idea, my Violet. What can he have been about, your husband? But I'm glad he never touched you in that way. I'm glad you kept it for me.'

'I never – loved – with him, like this,' she said haltingly, for she had no language for this new experience, the sensations of her nerves and mind and emotions, all thrumming in blissful unison. 'I don't think—' She paused, unsure whether it would be disloyal or not.

'You don't think?' he prompted her gently.

'I don't think he could be like that with me – the way you are. He didn't like me in that way.'

'Poor fellow,' said Laidislaw, and his voice was not contemptuous, but full of real pity.

Yes, she thought, surprised by the idea, Holkam was a poor fellow. He could not give and receive pleasure with her in this way. In her ignorance she had thought that no woman could find it other than distasteful. What a fool she had been! She knew now what it could be with the right person. She *understood*, now, what all the plays and poems and stories of love had been about.

It was a strange time to be thinking about her husband, but it comforted her to remember his proclivities: it removed

433

any last lingering sense of guilt. Physically, they had gone their separate ways once the children were born, and the pleasure he had sought with the highly painted ladies of the night had released her. She had never begrudged him that release, and now more than ever she was glad of it. Perhaps in France – *probably* in France, given what she had overheard in whispered conversations about army officers – he was enjoying himself with a series of *mademoiselles*. She hoped they could make him happy. But he could not love them, nor they him, as she and Laidislaw loved; he could not know this rapture. And so she could agree with her lover (*her lover!*) that he was a 'poor fellow'.

Laidislaw ran a finger softly over the contours of her face, following it with his eyes. 'We have done well today,' he said. 'Are you happy?'

'Very,' she said. 'Are you?'

'Utterly content,' he said. 'I could sleep now, except that I don't want to stop looking at you.'

'No-one ever looked at me as you do,' she said.

'Didn't I tell you so? And no-one made love to you as I have.'

'Didn't I tell you so?' she said, finding wit in herself, where it had never been before.

He laughed softly. 'Tomorrow?' he said. 'Can you come again tomorrow? I want to go on as soon as possible, while the inspiration is on me.'

'Yes, tomorrow.' She thought what a round, delicious, satisfying word it was. She had engagements, but she would cancel them. 'Tomorrow,' she said, and offered up her mouth for kissing again.

Away from him, she found an amazing new ability in herself to dissemble. She behaved in front of the rest of the world as though nothing had happened. She fulfilled her evening engagements and spoke to friends and directed servants like the Violet of old, though perhaps with a glow about her skin and eyes that the more discerning might have noticed. The Violet of old now seemed to her a separate creature:

something over and done with, resembling her but without life, like the cast skin of a snake. She would never be that Violet again. She *knew* things now, which had changed her for ever.

She was more than ever glad that Emma was away, so that there were no awkward excuses to be made. She could cancel engagements over the telephone, pleading a variety of excuses, but she was Emma's chaperon, and would have had to find alternatives for her, and give far better and more detailed explanations. When Emma came back she would have to find a way round the problem, but just now she was glad not to have to. She did not want anything to disturb her thoughts of Laidislaw.

She went to him the following morning – flew to him, perhaps, was nearer the truth. She did not know how he would greet her: would he be the painter or the lover? She put on her former-Violet face for Mrs Hudson, who looked at her as knowingly as if she had witnessed everything – but she had always looked at her like that. Violet refused to be upset. Laidislaw opened his door at her knock, but greeted her just as always, with the pleasant good morning, and helped her to shed her hat, gloves and dogs. She could sense that he was restless. 'Shall we begin at once?' he said, and she nodded obediently. Her eye strayed to the canvas on the easel as she passed, but it was covered with paper. In the bedroom he unhooked her, but went away and left her to change into the loose gown alone. If she felt a moment's disappointment, it was drowned with the fluttery feelings of mixed memory and anticipation as she glanced at the bed. It looked like nothing more than a bed this morning, but *she* knew that it was the fiery chariot on which she and her Apollo had ridden the skies.

When she returned to the other room, he was waiting impatiently to begin, and there was no conversation. He arranged her on the *chaise-longue* almost as if he could not bear the delay of it, and then leapt to his easel and flicked off the paper. He seized his palette and brush and began his eager painting, looking at her and at the canvas like a starving man at a banquet. He painted as if in a trance,

435

without speech; and when he finally flung down his brush, he seized her hand and almost ran with her to the bedroom. She had been so roused by watching him, and by the excitement he gave off, like a tangible heat, that her longing was a torment. They pulled off their clothes and fell together in passion; and it seemed even more wonderful than the day before, to a degree she would not have thought possible. Afterwards he lay propped on one elbow watching her face, and they talked.

They talked, as lovers do, of each other, and of the small past they shared, which seemed just then to encompass the whole world – or all of it that mattered. And he took up the book that lay by his bedside and read to her, more of the strange, voluptuous poetry of Mallarmé.

> *Si tu veux nous nous aimerons*
> *Avec tes lèvres, sans le dire.*

If you wish it, we shall love each other with your lips, without speaking of it. His voice caressed her, the words like liquid velvet, like the touch of his eyes on her skin, stroking her to an exquisite pleasure.

> *Muet, muet entre les ronds,*
> *Sylphe dans la pourpre d'empire,*
> *Un baiser flambant se déchire*
> *Jusqu'aux pointes des ailerons.*
> *Si tu veux, nous nous aimerons.*

It was her: she was the sylph in imperial purple – she saw herself in his eyes, soft white curves against the rich purple of the counterpane. *A kiss of flame tears right to the tip of its wings.* She understood. Flame, rose, wings, she saw them all, she was them. When the poem was done, she kissed him, long and deeply, as she had never kissed a man. *If you wish it, we shall love each other.* Oh, but she did wish it, she did!

She could not go to him every day. She had engagements she could not break, and others that, with her well-developed sense of social responsibility, she would not. But to be away from him was torment, and she thought about him all the time. A rich internal life of images and sounds played itself in her mind while she smiled and nodded and listened and talked polite small-talk. She laughed to herself when she thought of the Violet these people saw, the Countess of Holkam, so smart, so proper – a little dull, perhaps, but always to be relied on to do and say the right thing. How little they knew! Poor simple Freddie, her former constant companion, knew that something was different about her, but could not tell what. He looked at her, bewildered, like a dog trying to understand, and could only say, helplessly, 'You are very gay these days. Has something happened?'

And she smiled, her usual, calm, unemphatic smile, and said, 'No, nothing in particular.'

Sanders knew. She would not, never would, say anything, but she looked at her mistress with knowledge, and her hands, as they dressed and undressed her, said, *Oh, be careful! Be careful, my lady!* Once, when she was going out, she met her maid's eyes, and on an impulse reached out and pressed her hand. 'Don't worry,' she said. 'Be happy for me.' Sanders did not reply, only shook her head minutely, and smiled a troubled smile.

Sometimes when she went to him, he did not paint. If they had been apart a few days, they could not restrain themselves any longer, but flew together in love, like flame and salamander. And sometimes he would greet her in a kind of lassitude, and say, 'I cannot paint today. My wells are dry. Come and be my oasis.' Then they would make love, slow and languorous. Afterwards, sometimes they talked and sometimes were quiet but, in either case, the communion between them seemed continuous, like an unbroken stream that runs now darkly underground, and then sparkling on the surface.

She had never known such happiness. She drifted in a dream of bliss, which seemed perfectly defined by the strange, diffused and beautiful words of the poet that he murmured to her. Sometimes when he spoke love to her,

437

she hardly knew if it were English or French, his own words
or a poem.

O si chère de loin et proche et blanche, si
Delicieusement toi—

Dear and far off and near and white and so deliciously
herself, she lived the dream in his arms, and knew herself
uniquely beautiful and uniquely loved. She had no thought
about what might happen afterwards. There was no afterwards, no other time, no other place than this.

The Brides in the Bath trial reached its climax on the 1st of
July when Smith was found guilty of the murder of Bessie
Williams, Alice Smith and Margaret Lloyd, and was sentenced
to death. The trial had been going on since the 21st of June
in the Old Bailey, and while its sensational revelations had
gripped a certain section of the nation, it had nevertheless
had to fight for space in the newspapers with news of further
Zeppelin raids, and of industrial unrest up and down the
country.

Comment on the latter filled outraged leader columns,
and spluttered all over the letters page. Workers were casti-
gated for their lack of patriotism in striking at such a time.
Some believed that industrialists were making too much
money out of the war – 'profiteering', as it was known. They
refused to work overtime, or give up cherished but ineffi-
cient work practices, even for the sake of the war effort,
when they believed it would be helping to line their
employers' pockets. Other workers were outraged by the
entry of women into what had previously been male
preserves. Huge numbers of industrial hands had volunteered for the armed forces, and someone had to take over
their jobs; but women were rarely union members, and cared
nothing about ancient traditions and craft practices. This
'dilution', as it was called, of the workplace was fiercely
resisted by the unions, and they went on strike to enforce
the closed shop.

The union leaders earlier that year had signed an agreement with the Treasury to accept dilution, but their members were not behind them, and the government was left with the choice of either confrontation or conciliation. In July the dilution agreement was given the force of law: it was henceforth illegal to strike or otherwise to resist dilution. But the Cabinet was loath to use the law, for fear of making things worse.

'All in all,' Venetia said to Lord Overton, 'I am quite glad to be leaving the country for a little while. Everything seems to have become very gloomy of late.'

'You need a holiday, my love,' said Overton.

'I'm not sure it will be that,' Venetia said wryly. 'But it will be a change, at least.'

They were going to the Anglo-French Conference in Calais, which was due to begin on the 6th of July. Overton was going as Kitchener's aide; and K had, rather shyly, asked if Venetia would come too. 'I may very likely have to host a dinner, and in that case I shall need a hostess,' the old soldier said. 'I would be honoured if Lady Overton would consent to act for me.'

Venetia had been both flattered and perplexed. Kitchener notoriously had no time for women, but she had had dealings with him during the Boer War and he had treated her very fairly and civilly, and had taken something of a liking to her. But she had said so many cross and critical things to her husband over recent months about Kitchener's weaknesses that she felt guilty at accepting the implied compliment. She decided in the end that it was a compliment to Beauty rather than her, and that for her it would simply be a burdensome task.

But it would be interesting to see for herself something of what was happening in France. They travelled in great comfort. The crossing was smooth and seemed to take no time at all. Calais was, unsurprisingly, full of soldiers, and looked dirtier and shabbier than Venetia remembered it, though whether the one had anything to do with the other she could not say. The docks were crammed with shipping, and many of the vessels were hospital ships, for this was one of the main routes for the wounded home to England. There seemed to be wounded soldiers everywhere in the port area, lying on stretchers on the docksides, limping in bedraggled-looking column up gangplanks, sitting slumped against walls waiting to be told where to go. The sheer number surprised Venetia, for this was a quiet time all along the Front. What it must be like during a big push she could not imagine.

The professional part of her ached to go and help, and as if he had felt it, Overton closed his arm more tightly on her hand as they walked with the others into the Customs shed. They were wafted through effortlessly on a diplomatic zephyr, and shown to a fleet of highly polished motors waiting outside to take them to their hotel. It was just what Venetia would have expected of a French grand hotel: long on architectural flourish and short on plumbing. But their room was enormous, even quite sumptuous, and one quickly ceased to notice the faint smell of drains and mice.

The purpose of the conference was to discuss, in the light of the present stalemate, the future direction of the war. In Gallipoli, the troops were still clinging to the rocky edges of the peninsula while the Turks held the high ground. The British force had just been increased – with great difficulty and contrivance – to twelve divisions, while the Turks had fifteen, and the two lines of trenches faced each other just as they did in France, without anyone's knowing how a breakthrough could be made. The French had little interest in the eastern theatre, and wanted all efforts to be concentrated on freeing the homeland from the German invader. But Kitchener, with his long associations with the east, feared for British prestige if the Dardanelles expedition failed; and the British government wanted action on the Western Front postponed until the Gallipoli situation was resolved.

The conference went unexpectedly smoothly, given the opposing views of the two Allied nations. Overton was surprised and impressed with Kitchener's fluent French, which he spoke so well that sometimes only the French delegates could follow him. Perhaps his facility in the language surprised the French ministers, too, for they agreed with very little argument to everything he proposed. There would be no fresh offensive on the Western Front until the following year, when the new 'Kitchener Armies' should be ready; and the Eastern Front was not to be given up.

Dinner that night, hosted by Kitchener and with General Joffre as guest of honour, avoided all talk of war and politics, and was thus very comfortable and enjoyable to all. The food and wine were excellent, and the conversation around the table urbane and witty. As hostess, Venetia had Joseph Jacques Césaire Joffre as her dinner companion, and found him charming. He was much of an age with her, but looked older, though his considerable *embonpoint*, white hair and moustache did not conceal that he had been a very handsome man, and he still expected to be able to amuse a lady with the best of them. They talked of wine and horses and books, of their respective childhoods, and Joffre was interested to hear of Venetia's visit to Berlin in the seventies.

'We could see then what the Germans were about,' he said, when she described the military parades that had taken up so much public time. 'One can't say we were not warned. It was a pity the German states were ever allowed to unify.'

'It's a pity they unified under Prussian domination,' Venetia amended.

'But it could never have been any other way,' Joffre said. 'The Prussians would never have accepted rule by any other state. Conquest and glory, that's what they always wanted. It's there in every German, from Roman times onward. Cut open a German uniform, and that's what you'll find inside: Prussian lust for conquest and glory.' And then he seemed to realise that they had strayed onto temporarily forbidden ground, and turned the conversation lightly to the subject of music.

But the apparent agreement between the Allies was an illusion. Kitchener and Joffre had private talks away from the table while walking in the hotel grounds. Kitchener wanted his *protégé*, Sir Ian Hamilton, the commander in the Dardanelles, to make a further attack in August, which would require French support. Joffre had no faith in a renewed offensive in the east, but promised not to oppose the plan, if Kitchener would support a joint assault on the Western Front in the autumn. Kitchener agreed to an offensive in September, and even agreed that the choice of objective and date should be Joffre's. To Overton, who had attended him on the walk, Kitchener said afterwards, 'It is not what I would have wished, but we must make war as we have to, and not as we would like to.'

Afterwards, freed from their diplomatic duties, Venetia and Overton 'did a little gallivanting', as Beauty put it – though they did not gallivant far. Their own motor had been brought across by their chauffeur, and collected them from the hotel to motor on to St Omer, where they were to meet Madame Curie. Venetia had wanted to visit her in Paris, at the Radium Institute on the rue Pierre-Curie, a road in the Latin quarter that had been renamed in honour of her late husband when the building had been completed the previous August. But as it happened, she was to be in St Omer at the same time they were in Calais, which saved a journey.

Venetia had met Marie Curie through her friendship with Hertha Ayrton, the physicist, who had been a prominent member of the Women's Movement in earlier days, before the militant suffragettes had all but taken it over. Since then they had corresponded from time to time. Venetia had long had the idea that radium might have some effect on tuberculosis, which was her main research interest.

On this occasion, however, she wanted to talk to the younger woman about mobile X-ray machines. Marie Curie had managed, through her high degree of influence with the French government, to persuade them to appoint her Director of Red Cross Radiology and provide her with some funds, and she had adapted and fitted out the first X-ray ambulance.

'I felt from the first that the treatment of battle injuries would benefit from the use of X-rays – not just fractures, but to find the exact location of a bullet, for instance, before trying to remove it,' she told Venetia.

'Of course,' Venetia said. 'Much better than cutting down blind, especially if it were near some vital organ.'

'Exactly. So last August and September I gathered together all the apparatus I could find in the laboratories and stores, and set up radiology stations around Paris, operated by volunteer helpers – I gave them the training necessary. They did great service during the Marne campaign. But I saw at once they could not satisfy the needs of all the hospitals in the Paris region. What was needed was a mobile X-ray machine – a radiologic car, that could take the service to the patients.'

'Did you have it specially built?' asked Venetia.

'No, it was simply an ordinary touring-car. I had the body adapted, and equipped it with a complete radiologic apparatus.'

'What did you do about the electric current needed to generate the X-rays?'

'A simple dynamo, harnessed to the motor engine. It was a great success. Most of the hospitals were caring for badly wounded men who could not be moved to safer places further off – you understand, at that time we were expecting almost from day to day that the Germans might take Paris.'

'It must have been a terrible strain.'

She shrugged that away. 'Then, when things settled down, I saw how useful such a radiologic car would be in the battle zone itself, so in October Irène and I drove it to the Front.'

'Your daughter is very young, still,' Venetia commented.

'Yes, only seventeen, but mature for her age. She coped very well with the experience. And now I have a second car completed, which I have brought here to St Omer to demonstrate to some wealthy French families, in the hope of raising more funds. I have plans for twenty mobile units, if I can collect enough money.'

'I know what a difference they could make,' Venetia said. 'I am trying to get up my first X-ray car, and hoping it will be the first of many but, unlike you, I have no official title or government funding.'

Madame Curie smiled. 'You must wheedle, wheedle! The rich will give if you flatter them. Everyone likes to think she is individually important – and, yes, it is usually the women who give. And those who will not give money will sometimes give a motor-car – particularly now when petrol is so expensive. I have an engineering company that will convert them for a small charge, and manufacturers who will donate the equipment. The greatest difficulty is to find the assistants.'

'Is that why you went back to Paris?'

'Oh, I did not mean to run a mobile unit myself for the whole war. I am more useful in Paris, overseeing the scheme. And I had to set up the training courses. So many men are under arms, it is hard to find the right candidates. I think,' she added, with an amused look, 'that I must begin recruiting females. Will it incense the men, I wonder?'

'Did it incense them when you and Irène appeared at the Front?'

'Not a great deal, but then, I am known to be a hopeless case when it comes to feminine propriety.'

Venetia laughed. 'I have that reputation, too. I must say I hadn't yet thought as far as who would operate the machines – I haven't even acquired my first vehicle – but now I think of it, it will probably have to be women. The men don't like females at the Front, but they'll have to get used to it if the war goes on much longer.'

'I think it certainly will,' said Madame Curie. 'And so, my dear Madame, would you like to come and see how I arrange the interior? The vehicle is in the yard to the rear, if it will interest you to see it.'

'It will interest me very much,' Venetia said.

Primed with useful information and suggestions, and with her determination refuelled, Venetia left St Omer with Lord Overton. They were going to pay a visit to the Front at Ypres, partly for their own interest, and partly at the request

444

of Lord and Lady Dawnay, who had asked them to mark the grave of their elder son, Arthur, who had been killed there in the spring. They had given the Overtons a wooden cross for the purpose, which had been travelling with their luggage like a grim *memento mori*.

They motored to Hazebrouck where they met Major Greaves, the second-in-command of Dawnay's regiment. They lunched with him in a rather dirty hotel, where the food, however, was quite good: soup, roast beef and potatoes, and a coffee-flavoured blancmange, all evidently acceptable to the major, who ate as though he had lately been on much worse commons.

Afterwards they drove on towards Poperinghe, nicknamed Pops by the soldiery. It was a town through which almost everyone passed at some time, the railhead nearest the Front at Ypres, and the place many of them spent their rest time. As they approached, the ravages of war could be seen. The fields were pocked with shell-holes so that they looked like giants' solitaire boards. Trees had been blasted, houses were gutted and ruined, and the civilian population had obviously long since left. They passed a dead horse, lying in a roadside ditch, its poor hoofs pathetically in the air. And now they could hear the sound of the guns booming away.

'Is an attack taking place?' Venetia asked, a little nervously, for they sounded very loud and near.

Major Greaves raised his eyebrows. 'An attack? Oh, no. That's just old Fritz sending over some hate. It's a quiet time just now.'

'If that's quiet, I shouldn't like to be here when it's noisy,' Venetia said.

'I'm sure you wouldn't,' said Greaves. 'During a bombardment it feels as if all the blood is being driven out of your head. It's hard to think, let alone speak.'

He guided them to the cemetery, which was the extended graveyard of a part-ruined church. The walls still stood, though in a damaged state, but the roof had been blasted off and every window blown out – there were shards of stained glass and twisted strips of lead scattered about

445

among the graves, along with lumps of shrapnel. Descending from the car, Venetia stood for a moment, and then reached for Overton's arm for comfort. Nothing could have expressed the reality of war more vividly than the sad and crowded graveyard, the plots dug so close together there was only a strip the width of a human foot between them. Wooden crosses had been pushed into the ground at the head of the new graves, but many of them were merely two bits of rough timber nailed together, while some graves were marked only by a broken piece of a crate stuck upright with a name and date written on it in pencil. On some crosses forage caps had been hung; from one dangled an officer's pistol holster, empty. So many lost lives, each one an individual who was the centre of his own universe, leaving behind friends and families whose tears would never wet the grass now beginning to grow over his narrow resting-place.

At the edge of the cemetery there was a detachment of four soldiers in shirtsleeves and braces adding to a row of fresh graves, one of each pair down in the earth digging, the other resting. Each had his cap off and a cigarette between his lips; the resting men leant on their spades, watching the flying earth with blank eyes. Major Greaves approached them and borrowed a spade, then led the way to a grave marked with a piece of batten. The pencil writing was almost washed away, and Greaves had to squat and peer closely to be sure it was the right plot. Then he pulled out the rough marker, put the end of the cross into the hole, and said, 'Would you be so kind to hold it steady, my lord, while I knock it in?'

It was soon done, and Greaves stepped back while they all looked solemnly at the beautifully polished piece of hardwood, with the letters cut deeply and painted black to stand out: name, rank and regiment, and the dates that marked the beginning and end of a life: 1891–1915. He had been only twenty-five when he was cut down. *Fell*, that was the word, Venetia thought. When you saw these hundreds of graves huddled together, shoulder to shoulder and head to foot, and more being dug all the time, the word *fell* seemed appropriate. It was like the felling of a whole forest.

Three enormous explosions in quick succession shook the ground under her feet and she started in alarm. But Greaves did not move, and Overton only looked at her and shook his head. 'Not coming in this direction,' he said. She supposed men – or, at least, soldiers – had some instinct about these things.

Venetia had asked to see a front-line medical facility, and Greaves now conducted them to an advanced dressing station, of which there were normally two per brigade, set up out of the range of enemy fire. These were mobile units, but in the present quiet period they were settled in their positions. The purpose of the ADS was to receive the wounded from the regimental aid posts, which were well up just behind the reserve line, and give them such treatment as would make them stable enough to be taken back to the divisional casualty clearing station. It was probably in time of battle the most hectic of the stages between the action and the hospital, and even now when they arrived it gave the impression of intense busyness.

'There are always casualties, even in quiet periods,' Greaves said. 'As you can hear, the Germans go on sending over shells to keep us on our toes, and the snipers never rest.'

As well as shrapnel and bullet wounds, Venetia saw a Tommy with crush injuries where a stack of boxes had fallen on him, a man with two broken legs who had been hit by a lorry that rolled forward when its brake was not properly set, and a grey-faced, shivering cook who had slashed his own arm by accident while preparing meat for the evening's stew.

The nurses looked at Venetia rather aloofly, resenting, she guessed, yet another well-dressed lady 'sightseeing' in their station. But the doctors seemed, flatteringly, to know exactly who she was, and welcomed her frankly and respectfully, after which the nurses warmed a little – though that might have been because of Overton's charm, which he lavished on them while Venetia got closer to the wounded and watched their treatment and discussed it with the doctors. They seemed very young to her, and were obviously skilled and efficient, in stark contrast to what she had seen in Berlin during the Franco-Prussian war, and even sometimes in South Africa during the Boer War. But these young men, she reminded herself, would be volunteers from civilian medicine. She felt confident, in any case, that the wounded would receive the best of care, even when there was a 'flap' on.

Eventually Greaves had to remind her of the time, so fascinating she found it, and she shook hands all round and thanked everyone for their courtesy. Outside in the early-evening sunlight as they walked towards the motor, Venetia saw a familiar figure approaching. For an instant she could not place him, but as he saw her and began to smile, she realised it was Kit Westhoven. 'What are you doing here?' she asked, shaking his hand.

'This is my ADS,' he said, gesturing towards it. 'I'm on night duty. I was just going on.'

'A little early, isn't it?' Overton asked.

'Yes, sir, but Hawes wants to get off early today so I said I'd cover for him.' He looked deprecatingly at Major Greaves. 'You won't report us, sir?'

Greaves waved a hand. 'Not my business. In any case, you doctors are something of a rule unto yourselves, aren't you?'

Venetia chatted to Westhoven for a few moments, and then he asked, shyly and eagerly, 'How is your son – Dr Winchmore – Oliver?'

'He's very well, thank you. Busy, of course.'

'Of course. I did so enjoy meeting him when I stayed with you in London.'

'I'm sure he felt the same,' Venetia said. 'He has mentioned it several times.'

'Has he? He's spoken about me?'

'Yes,' said Venetia, amused. 'And the next time you have leave, you must come and stay with us again. I know Oliver would like to show you his work – and you might be interested in my research, too.'

'Thank you. You're very kind, and I should like that,' he said, and then added shyly, 'I wonder, do you think it would be all right if I wrote to him – to Oliver? There were some things we were discussing, to do with field surgery, and I'd like to send him some notes I made about one or two interesting cases.'

'Of course,' Venetia said. 'I'm sure he'd be delighted to hear from you. I'd offer to take a letter for you but we're leaving now for Hazebrouck.'

'There's no need to trouble you,' Westhoven said. 'The post is very good from here.'

They chatted a little longer, then said goodbye and walked on to the motor, and as Overton opened the door for her she murmured, 'What a sweet boy, to ask if he might write to Oliver! He must have had good manners beaten into him, to think it was necessary to ask.'

'He'll make somebody a charming son-in-law one day,' Overton smiled.

CHAPTER NINETEEN

Violet's idyll was abruptly interrupted at the end of July when she received a telegram from Holkam, saying that he was coming home on leave.

From Marcham Hall, Emma had gone with Sybil Ravenhill straight to the Damerels' country-house party in Hampshire, and in August she was expected in Scotland, with only a one-day stop in London on the way to collect clothes, so Violet had looked forward to an uninterrupted summer of bliss. She hurried to Ebury Street to tell Laidislaw.

'While he is here I shall not be able to come to you, but also I wanted to warn you not to send me any notes at home.'

'How long will it be?' he asked.

'Only a week,' she said. 'I don't think I could bear to be away from you for longer.'

'A week is an age!' he exclaimed. 'An aeon. And the painting is not finished.'

Her hand flew to her mouth. 'The painting! I had forgotten, it was meant to be his birthday present. I was going to give it to him as soon as he came on leave. I suppose it must wait until the next leave, now.'

He laughed. 'Longer, much longer! In fact, I don't know that you will ever be able to give it to him.'

'What do you mean? I ordered it for him.'

'Ordered it? Like a hamper from Fortnum's? My darling,

450

what we have done together here has gone far beyond that. Your portrait is divinely inspired. It is my masterpiece. It belongs to the world!'

Violet looked puzzled. 'You mean you want to exhibit it?'

'Yes, my love!'

'I'm not sure Holkam would like that.'

Laidislaw was on a flight, and paced the floor excitedly. 'It's too late for the Royal Academy summer exhibition now, but there's the National Portrait Exhibition in October. It's not too late to enter it for that. They know me, they won't want to inspect it first, so I can keep it secret until opening day, and then unveil it for everyone to see. It will cause a sensation! The newspapers and the illustrateds will be at my feet! And the best of the exhibition goes afterwards to New York – think of that! The world will know my name – and yours.'

'But I thought—' Violet began anxiously.

He cupped her face in his hands. 'Don't frown, my rose. It spoils your lovely face. You can't think I could allow my masterpiece to hang for ever on a wall in a dusty old house where no-one will see it?'

'That's what it was painted for.'

'No, it was painted for love! For life! For genius! It is the best thing I have ever done. It shall be fêted for all time; it shall be the new *Giaconda*. Don't fret, my love. You can find something else to buy for your husband, something more suited to his temperament. Something wooden, perhaps!'

'Oh, don't joke!'

'*Mon âme*, he would not have loved our painting as we love it. A man who is blind and deaf to your miraculous beauty does not deserve to see it, let alone to own it.'

He kissed her, and any argument died on her lips as she took fire from him. They fled to his crimson bed and lost themselves in a tangle of limbs, caresses and soft murmurs.

Afterwards, when she lay limp against his chest, his hand playing with her hair, she said, 'How shall I get through a week without seeing you?'

'It will be worse for me, knowing you are with him.' He kissed her brow. 'Promise me you will not lie with him.'

'Oh, no! Never, never again!' she cried, shocked at the thought. 'Don't be afraid. He would never ask. You know – I have told you – he doesn't care for me in that way.'

'It will be hard to keep away, knowing where you are. How shall I stop myself coming to beat on your door and demand you come back to me?'

'You mustn't do that,' she said seriously, pressing against him. 'It would ruin everything. We must keep our secret.'

'Yes, for now I suppose we must. Well, then, I shall go away,' he said. 'Out of Town, away from temptation. I shall go to the Arbuthnots at Aston Magna. I had an invitation from them yesterday, and the Verneys will be there, and some other agreeable souls. So you won't need to worry about me, my rose. I shall be among friends.'

Violet felt oddly hurt and jealous at the thought of 'friends' enjoying him when she could not. 'When he's gone, you'll come back?'

'Did you think anything would keep me from you?'

'I'll send a note as soon as he goes back to France.'

'And then we'll finish our great work. There is not much left to do. A few days will be enough.'

She pushed herself up a little, so that she could look into his face. 'And what then? What will happen to us?'

'Say my name. You never use my name,' he said. He ran a finger down her brow and the line of her nose to her lips.

'Octavian, then,' she said, thinking what a beautiful name it was, and how it suited him. His finger ran across her lips and she caught it and bit it gently; he laughed and pulled her down to him, and passion flared up again between them, so she forgot what she had asked him. Questions and answers alike were forgotten.

It was easier than Violet had expected to behave normally when Lord Holkam came home. Their life together had been conducted on such formal and ordered lines that it was the most natural thing in the world to fall back into the pattern. She met him at the station, and though there were hundreds of soldiers disembarking from the train, she saw him at once, climbing down from a first-class carriage with his old valise in his hand.

He seemed interestingly a stranger in his uniform; and very handsome. He had been the most sought-after bachelor in London when she came out, but he had chosen her. Violet had a large dowry, which for him had overcome the disadvantage of the faint whiff of scandal that hung about her mother. Venetia, to add to the enormity of being a lady-doctor and a suffragist, had blazed like a meteor through the social columns of the newspapers when she had jilted Lord Overton practically at the altar; and then again, years later, when she had married him after all. In Holkam's eyes – an attitude learnt from his father – a gentleman should never be in the newspapers for anything but a speech in the House or a military exploit; a lady should never be there at all.

Handsome and charming, Holkam had set to work on Violet, and she had fallen in love with him. How could she have done otherwise, utterly innocent as she was, and very young for her age? Other girls were much more sly and arch, but she had never understood what they meant when they whispered and giggled with their heads together. All Violet had ever wanted was to fall in love, marry and have children. A simple ambition anyone might have thought the easiest in the world to fulfil. It had seemed to go well at first. She had fallen in love with Holkam, and he had offered for her. Prince Charming had chosen *her*.

For the dizzy time between his proposal and the marriage she had lived in blissful anticipation of the happy-ever-after that was bound to come. Her wedding in the Abbey had been beautiful, the culmination of a fairy tale; and then she and her new husband had gone off on their honeymoon to France and Italy. On their first night together, when she discovered what marriage really meant, the bubble had burst. She had hated that thing he did to her, so much that she had been forced to shut it away in another compartment of her mind and simply never think of it. During the

453

daytime she loved him, admired him, enjoyed his company. She was delighted with him as a husband. It was only those brief and squalid episodes in bed that she loathed. Once she conceived, the visits from his bedroom to hers stopped, and there was nothing to mar their calm and comfortable life together, until the time came for the next child to be conceived. When she had three children, the night sorties stopped altogether, and she had thought herself completely happy.

Tall and handsome, he came striding towards the barrier in his glamorous uniform; and raising her cheek for his chaste kiss, she felt again the pleasure she had in him as a husband, the well-bred and personable man who knew something about every topic and was popular at every hostess's dinner table. They were what they had always been to each other. He chatted to her as they walked to the motor, and she smiled and responded, took his hand as he helped her up into the warm leather interior, and felt as if he had never been away.

Laidislaw glowed and fluttered like a burning bush in a corner of her mind: she was aware of it but did not look at it. The wild passion she had shared with him seemed something quite separate, as if it had happened to another person, not to her – not to the Countess of Holkam, who sat calmly saying, 'I see,' and 'Indeed!' and 'How interesting,' to her lord as they drove down the Mall. Well, perhaps after all she *was* another person, that lissom creature who had done such wild, abandoned things on the crimson-draped bed, winding naked limbs about naked limbs, in a tangle of loose hair and seeking lips and murmured words. It could not, after all, *possibly* be the Violet who was married to Lord Holkam. That Violet had always lived a calm, controlled life in the dry place far above the tide-line, where the ebb and flow of passion could not reach. And so she smiled at Holkam, and nodded, and chatted, and felt perfectly comfortable. *This* was real life.

It was not hard to pass the time with him. She had told people he was coming back, so they were much engaged.

Everyone wanted to dine them, and those too late to claim a dinner asked instead to lunch them. Violet did not leave her room in the morning until after he had left the house to walk off to his business engagements. They met at luncheon, went afterwards to a different group of friends for tea, and when they got home had only just time to bathe and dress for dinner. She was never alone with him, except in the motor, and for the few moments when they walked upstairs together, to part on the first floor and go to their separate rooms.

She found she enjoyed having him home, having her proper husband's arm to enter a room on, being part of a couple who were invited everywhere, known everywhere. She liked his conversation, so much weightier than Freddie Copthall's, so satisfyingly full of references she did not understand, which made her feel connected to a wider and more important world. She enjoyed being his wife again so much that she had no difficulty in shutting out the thoughts and memories she had feared would haunt and trip her. She thought about the portrait only once, when she gave him the birthday present she had bought for him in its place: a new leather valise with a matching dressing-case whose fittings were expensively of silver and tortoiseshell. He thanked her warmly, examined it with flattering interest and pronounced it the finest he had seen; and a small, cool voice in the furthest part of her mind had said, 'No, it would never have done to give him the portrait. Laidislaw was right. He simply would not see it.'

The days of his leave fled away. On the last evening they returned late from dinner at Lord and Lady Yearmouth's, and when she had given her wrap and gloves to Sanders and was turning towards the stairs, Holkam said, 'Are you very tired, my dear?'

She paused, and looked at him. He smiled invitingly. 'No, not very,' she said.

'Then come and talk to me for a little. I don't seem to have had a moment alone with you. Come into the library.'

She followed him obediently. In the library, sandwiches

and whisky were left ready, as they always were when they went out in the evening. It was so late, she found herself hungry again, and when he offered her something, she accepted a glass of sherry and took one or two of the small *foie-gras* triangles. He helped himself and sat too, leaning back and crossing his ankles easily, and looking at her without speaking at first. Then he said, 'This leave has flown away. It seems like yesterday that I arrived; and tomorrow I must go back.'

'Yes, it has gone quickly,' she said.

'And you'll be alone again. What do you do with yourself all the time when I'm away?'

'Oh, the usual things,' she said vaguely, knowing that he did not really want to know. He had said many times that he could not conceive how 'you females' managed to get through the day.

'I don't know when I shall be able to come again,' he said. 'Perhaps at Christmas, if things are quiet.'

'I hope so,' she said.

'Things are not what I expected out there,' he said, frowning. 'Before I went, I could not understand why we had not dealt with the enemy already. I thought it must be a simple case of mismanagement. Now I see things are more complicated. Oh, we *will* win, there's no doubt about that. But sometimes when I'm riding along near the line I look about me and – it's like the strangest dream. Not like war at all – nothing like any war I've read about. No movement, no strategy. How can you outmanoeuvre an enemy who never moves, whom you cannot even see? At times like that I wonder *how* we will win, what we can do that we haven't already done. Thank God I'm not a general. I should hate to be the one who has to answer that question, and answer to the country for the consequences.'

He talked on, and Violet nodded, having no clear idea what he meant by any of it. Her hunger assuaged, she was beginning to feel sleepy. She hoped he would stop soon so that she could go to bed, and swallowed a yawn that crept up on her.

456

But he saw the tell-tale flare of her nostrils, and he stopped talking, and smiled. 'Dear Violet,' he said. 'I always knew you would be the perfect wife. I chose well. Out of all the females in the *ton*, you were the only one I could rely on always to conduct herself properly. I'm very fond of you, you know.'

'And I am, of you,' she answered obediently.

'I'd forgotten,' he added softly, looking at her intently, 'how very beautiful you are. More beautiful even than when I first saw you.' She lowered her eyelashes, not knowing what to say, and he stood up and came over to her, lifted her hand to his lips and kissed it. The action disturbed her: it was not like him. She disliked the touch of him very much, and struggled to conceal it.

Perhaps he felt the small turmoil that went through her. He squeezed her hand and gave it back to her. 'Go on up to bed, my dear,' he said. 'I shall not be long after you.'

He did not kiss her goodnight, but she thought nothing of that as she made her escape, longing now for her bed. Sanders was waiting up for her, and she had the maid undo all her hooks and buttons, then told her she could go off. 'I'll manage the rest,' she said.

'Yes, my lady. Thank you, my lady,' Sanders said; but she gave Violet an odd look as she left, which Violet could not interpret. It seemed to have a question in it, and perhaps something of a warning.

Violet finished undressing, put on her nightgown and got into bed, aching for sleep; but as soon as she laid her head on the pillow she was wide awake. She was afraid of her thoughts if she stayed wakeful. She remembered how her nurse had said to her, when she was a little girl, that if you can't sleep, you should lie quite still and count in your head, and sleep would come when you didn't expect it. She had got to eight hundred and forty-six when the door of her bedroom opened, and every cell in her body seemed to contract with fear.

It was Holkam. He crossed the room and sat on the edge of the bed. She could smell his eau-de-Cologne – he had shaved again. My God, she thought, my God.

457

'It's been a long time,' he said softly. 'You looked so beautiful tonight – so beautiful. I am very proud of my lovely wife, you know. Dear Violet. Dear wife.' He slipped off his dressing-gown and got in beside her.

It did not last long. When it was over he sniffed once or twice, cleared his throat, kissed her cheek and said, 'Thank you, my dear,' then went away.

Violet remembered how once she had seen a swan shot by accident. It had passed over her, sleek and strong, rowing the air with its great wings; then there had been a crack of gunshot and it had tumbled like a stone to earth, bloodied and broken, graceful and free no more.

With Laidislaw she had flown; but Holkam had reminded her of what a base and joyless thing it could be. She turned on her side and wept, biting her forearm so that her sobs should not be heard.

The new offensive in the Dardanelles in August was meant to break the deadlock there, by making a new landing further up the Aegean coast of the peninsula. One of the problems of the campaign had been the difficulty of landing sufficient troops on the narrow rocky ledge around the coast for an all-out assault. A fresh landing would provide a foothold for extra troops, who could then join up with the Anzac forces and storm the heights. For the purpose, Kitchener scraped together three New Army divisions and two Territorial, which together made up the new IX Corps. Sir Ian Hamilton, in overall command of the Mediterranean force, asked for Byng or Rawlinson to be transferred from France to command it, but Kitchener would not weaken the Western Front by taking away experienced commanders. Of the generals available, the highest in the Army List was Sir Frederick Stopford. At sixty-one, he had never commanded men in battle and, indeed, had seen little action himself, but Kitchener insisted that proper military procedure was to give the command to the most senior man.

The plan was to land the new force at Sulva Bay on the 6th of August, after diversionary attacks at Cape Helles and

Anzac Bay, and for it to take the ring of hills surrounding the Sulva plain. The diversions worked, and the hills at Sulva were not entrenched and only lightly defended; but Stopford was convinced that no attack on the hills could succeed without artillery and decided instead to consolidate the plain. A great opportunity was lost. Stopford, moreover, remained on the ship, declining to go ashore, and compromising the chain of command. Muddle and disarray were the result, and by the time Hamilton, worried by the reported lack of advance, came to see for himself what was going on, the Turks had discovered the ruse and had scrambled back into position. The 32nd Brigade, ordered by Hamilton to advance, met heavy resistance and was virtually wiped out.

By the 15th of August Kitchener had yielded to Hamilton's urgent pleas, recalled Stopford and sent out Byng to replace him. But by then the Turks were dug in on the high ground, and attempts to shift them were repulsed with heavy losses. The situation at Sulva settled down into the same stalemate as existed at Anzac and Helles.

General Joffre had kept the bargain struck with Kitchener, and allowed the new offensive in the Dardanelles to take place. Now he called in his half of the favour. The British were to mount an attack on the German line at a date of his choosing in September. The place he had picked for the assault was a coal-mining district near Lens, centred on a village called Loos.

Holkam had been gone a week, and there was no word from Laidislaw. Violet's notes to him at Ebury Street went unanswered. She needed him desperately. She needed to expunge the memory of her husband's intrusion. She needed to make love with Laidislaw in passionate abandon, to have things made right again – for they were very wrong now. She felt unclean, and only Laidislaw could wash away the ugliness that was congress with Holkam.

She could not concentrate on any of her activities. She cancelled engagements, was not at home to callers, was frequently found not to have been listening when people talked to her. If it had been anyone else, they said to themselves, they would have diagnosed a bad case of love – but Violet Holkam was not the sort for an affair. Older friends assumed she was missing and worried for her husband, and said comforting things about duty and everyone being in the same boat. Violet didn't hear them. Her ears were attuned to a different source.

And then the note came: he was home, he wanted her at once. She flew to him, and they met and coupled in the frenzy of a fortnight's drought. Laidislaw was stunned, enchanted, captured all over again. He had never known a woman who could love in such an abandoned way. In truth, his sexual experience had not been great. He had loved many times, but his passions had been intellectual. Until Violet, he had never met a woman whose physical beauty was matched by her purity of spirit, who had such inner fire. All femalekind seemed insipid to him now, compared with her.

'Why were you so long from me?' she cried.

'It was hard to get away,' was all he said. 'They wanted me to stay longer, but I could not bear to.'

'I needed you so much,' she said; and decided in that moment not to tell him what had happened with Holkam. She did not want to poison his mind with the knowledge she hated so much in herself.

'I needed you, too,' he said. 'I found it quite hard to be polite to people when all I wanted was to rush away and be with you.'

She laughed, but she did not quite believe him. He was a social creature, and she thought that, however much he had missed her, he had still enjoyed himself. But she did not mind it. He was here now, and that was all that mattered.

In two visits he had finished the picture; but he would not show it to her.

'But, Octavian, it is my portrait. I ordered it, and I will be paying for it.'

He shook his head. 'No, my love. I told you, things have

gone beyond that now. As for paying for it, you shall not! I would not taint our love by taking money from you.'

'But, then, how will you manage? You must have money from somewhere.' She knew his private resources were not large.

'Don't worry about me,' he said, caressing her. 'I shan't want. The exhibition in October carries a large prize, and I shall certainly win it. And the same in New York.'

She turned her mouth for his kisses, and when they paused for breath she said, 'If you exhibit it, I shall see it then, so why not now?'

'Because I want it to burst upon the world. No-one shall see it until then. Not even you, my dearest love.'

He was a showman at heart, she thought. However much she pleaded, he would not budge, only laughed and changed the subject. So she accepted she would have to wait.

Lady Verney was worried. She had been pleased to see Laidislaw at Aston Magna, and found him in high spirits. Indeed, she had hardly ever seen him in anything else, but he seemed particularly illuminated and restless. He was the life and soul of the house-party, was always to be found at the centre of an admiring group, and drank late into the night with whoever happened to be still up. Often it was 'Tubby' Arbuthnot, who was hoping to persuade him to paint a portrait of his wife. Lady Verney was pretty sure Laddie never would, for as dear a person as Maggie Arbuthnot was, she had a long and toothy face and a large nose, and Laddie was not at the stage of his career or his life when he would set himself to find the beauty in everyone.

But as the week went on, she began to wonder what it was that Laddie was up to. She had not seen him for a while but, more mysteriously, she had not heard anything about his work since he had finished her portrait. Anyone whom Laidislaw was painting was unlikely to be reticent about it: it was something to boast about, and no-one in her circle had said a thing. No-one in any circle, for that matter. So being, as she fancied, one of his closer friends, she asked

461

him what he was doing these days. To her surprise, he would
not tell her.

'But you are working?' she said.

'Oh, yes,' he said, with a bright look in his eyes. 'I'm
certainly working.'

'Then what is it? Come, Laddie, why won't you tell me?'

'No, no, you shan't get it out of me,' he laughed. 'It's a
secret. You'll see.'

'A portrait?'

'A secret!'

She could not leave it at that. Several times during the
week she asked him, and he still refused to tell her. At last
he admitted that he was working on a portrait, but would
not name the sitter; and that was when she began to wonder.
She knew how intimate, even sensual, an experience it was
sitting for him. Was it possible that matters had got out of
hand, and that he was having an affair with his subject?
Nothing, on reflection, was more likely; and since his subject
was almost bound to be a married woman (what single
woman would have the resources and the freedom to sit, or
would risk her reputation by doing so?), the need for secrecy
was evident.

But, she thought with exasperation, does he not realise
that it must come out at last? When the husband saw the
painting, he would know his wife had been sitting. Well,
well, she supposed it might be laughed off as having been
meant as a surprise for the husband – which he would have
to pay for, naturally. If he was a genial, accommodating sort
of husband, he might not mind – would probably be flattered that the great Laidislaw had chosen his wife as a
subject. But a jealous, suspicious sort of husband might
wonder if there had been more than sitting going on – and
she was not convinced that Laddie would know the difference between the two, or even care if he did know.

Who *was* it? She ran her mind over the various women
of her acquaintance who were attractive enough to qualify
as sitters for him, but she could not believe that any of *them*
could have kept the secret from her. She discussed it with

her husband, and he laughed at her and said she was making too much of it. 'In any case, it's not our business. Laddie's a grown man and he'll take care of himself.'

'I'm not sure he's capable of it,' she said. 'He doesn't behave like a grown man most of the time.'

'Oh, well, he's an artist,' said Verney dismissively. 'Everyone makes allowance for the artistic temperament. He's a genius in his field, one gives him that – but he isn't the very brightest upstairs, darling. We can't claim that for him, much as we love him – though his poetic eloquence disguises the fact somewhat.'

'I know,' said Laura Verney, 'but that's what worries me. Laddie's a perfect poppet, but he's like a child when it comes to common sense and worldly wisdom. He's a dreamer of dreams, and I'm afraid he'll get himself into trouble.'

'Well, if he won't confide in you, there's nothing you can do,' said Verney, and she was obliged to leave it at that.

At the end of the week she and her husband went back to London to close up the house before going down to stay with her family in Somerset. Laidislaw was staying on at Aston. In London, Lady Verney was inveigled into attending a charity tableau, where Violet Holkam was also present. Laura waved across the room to her, but she did not respond.

'She doesn't see me,' she said to her companion, Jane Gresham.

'Who? Oh, you mean Lady Holkam? My dear, she doesn't see anyone! She's so amazingly absent-minded these days. I said so to Eva Preston yesterday, and she said perhaps she was missing her husband, because he's just been home on leave, you know, but I said, "No, my dear," because indeed she's been like it all summer. Head in the air and *such* a look on her face: you know the sort of thing, half here and half there. And always cancelling. She chucked Mrs Hoover – do you believe me? – though she's always spoken so highly of her. If it were anyone else,' Mrs Gresham lowered her voice, 'you might think she was in love, but that's one thing you can't suspect in her case. She's always been such a perfect *stick*, my dear, for all that she's young and so beautiful.'

Lady Verney managed to turn the conversation and keep it going in a new direction, but she was in a state of shock. She was remembering her unveiling party, and how she had interrupted Laddie talking to Violet, the intensity of the way he was looking at her, her blushing discomposure. *Oh, no, Laddie, not her, not Violet Holkam!* She was, it was true, the most beautiful woman in London, but not in the least worldly wise – indeed, as much a child as Laddie himself. It would be a disastrous combination. And of all people, Violet was married to Holkam, who was, in Laura's opinion, a stuffed shirt and a brute. If Laddie really was having an *affaire* with Violet, it could mean trouble. She would have to see him and warn him.

She sent round a note to his lodgings and, receiving no reply, went there in person. It was almost a week since she had come back from Aston Magna, and she had expected him to be back by now. But the knocker was off the door, so presumably neither he nor the upstairs tenant was back yet. While she hesitated, a man came out of the door of Mrs Hudson's quarters in the semi-basement, and looked up at her enquiringly. He was in a collarless shirt, and trousers held up with braces, and looked unshaven and gummy-eyed, as though he had only just woken up.

'Good morning,' she called. 'Is Mrs Hudson at home?'

He rubbed his hand over his whiskery chin. 'No, mum,' he replied. 'She's gone over 'er sister's, the one in Worthing. She wunt be back for a week. I'm lookin' after the 'ouse for 'er.'

Laura thought rapidly. 'I see. Well, I wonder if I could trouble you to let me in? When I was visiting Mr Laidislaw recently, I think I lost a bracelet. The fastening was weak and I'm afraid it must have fallen off. I can't think where else it could be, and I've looked everywhere I can think of. I'm an old friend of Mr Laidislaw's, and I'm sure he wouldn't mind if I quickly looked in his rooms.'

She hardly needed to have found an excuse. The man was perfectly willing to let her in – would have done so simply for the asking, she thought. As he conducted her upstairs she could smell the beer on his breath. He opened

464

Laddie's door and let her in, and leant on the door-jamb, staring into space. She might have rifled the place, she thought, for all he cared. She made pretence of looking about the floor, but her eyes went at once to the easel, where there was a painting, lightly covered by a sheet of tissue. She glanced back warily, but the man was picking his teeth with a finger and examining the results, his head half turned away from her. He clearly did not care what she did – unlike the sour, sharp-eyed Mrs H.

She lifted back the paper and looked at the painting, and her scalp lifted with shock. It was Violet Holkam, all right. The painting was brilliant – brilliant! Violet lived and glowed within the unframed margins, so that it was hard to believe mere brush-strokes and inanimate pigment could have produced this miracle of three-dimensional, vibrant reality. But it was not just Violet's beauty that was celebrated. She reclined, languorously, on the *chaise-longue* in a flowing pre-Raphaelite robe, gazing into the observer's eyes with an expression so voluptuous it was almost indecent. No-one looking at it could doubt that she and the painter were lovers. A slumberous passion invested the exquisite features, the lips half parted, the eyes yearning. One hand lay softly on her belly; the upper curves of her breasts suggested she was wearing nothing under the *déshabille*.

Laura did not think Holkam a sensitive man – far from it – but surely even he, if he saw this painting, would know what was what, especially as the sittings had been secret. And what, then, would happen to Violet? Holkam was the greatest stickler in London. He had even disapproved of his mother-in-law for being a *doctor*, for heaven's sake! How much more would he disapprove of his wife's being the mistress of a penniless artist? Ruin would face Violet – but he would take his revenge on Laidislaw too; and he had the power to hound Laddie out of society.

She covered the portrait – lingeringly: it was a magnificent piece of work – and turned back to the caretaker.

'I can't see it,' she said. 'I'll just write a note for Mr

Laidislaw, in case he has found it and put it away for me.'

She knew where Laddie kept pen and paper. She found her hands were shaking as she wrote, telling him to contact her *at once* on his return, without *fail*, on a matter of the most *extreme urgency*.

Jessie took Bertie's letter with her to the hospital, and stopped the car at the side of the road to read it. He wrote that the new battalion of West Herts had arrived from England.

. . . fresh-faced boys and, like all volunteers, eager for a scrap. We do a lot of marching, digging and drilling, much to their dismay. They thought all that was behind them when they embarked! They are growing fitter, but as to battle-preparedness, there is little we can do. The rumour is that there is a big push coming next month, and with raw troops all you can hope for is that their native grit will get them through. There is a chance that my boys will not be in it, having so recently arrived. Someone has to man the rest of the line, after all. Of course, they will hope to be in the thick of it. But I'd like to have longer with them under the everyday fire of a quiet section before they are pitched into full battle.

It is quiet all along the line at the moment. The weather is changeable, plenty of thunderstorms, but warm and with sunny spells. Even fatigues and route-marches seem less of a chore when the sun shines, and summer evenings in the green of the countryside are pleasant. We are billeted at a farm near Merville. The men help with the harvest, which they enjoy for a change – especially as there are none but females left on the land! There is usually a jug of local cider for reward at the end of a day in the fields – most welcome, since they spent all their money in the first few days, so visits to *estaminets* are out until next pay day.

We have gas drills every day as we've had new gas-masks issued. They're much better than the old sort – glass goggles with a breathing-tube attached. It

466

takes practice to breathe in through the nose and out through the mouth, and the valves make strange noises, some of them very vulgar indeed, much to our lads' delight! Gas drill tends to end in helpless hilarity. Long may the objects be a source of amusement.

When it's our turn in the trenches, the men are fascinated by the trenches opposite, and line up for the periscope in the hope of spying a German. They never do, of course, which causes intense speculation about what is going on over there. Are they lounging and smoking like us, or preparing that very moment to attack? Above all, how many of them are there – a thousand, a hundred or only ten? Fenniman opines that all the Germans have gone on holiday, leaving only a caretaker and his wife – the caretaker does the firing, while his wife sends up the flares! He speaks often of Emma, by the way. If it seems appropriate, would you convey to her his – what would be the right word? Love is too forward, respects too cool. Perhaps you might say he thinks of her – that is undoubtedly true.

And I think often of you, and of all at home, wishing with all my heart I might see you soon. Sometimes in the evening, leaning on a gate and smoking, watching the bats flicker by in the twilight, I imagine I am home. I tease myself with the thought that those I love are near by, in the house just behind me, and that at the end of the cigarette I shall turn and go in to them. That peaceful joy seems far away in daylight, but at dusk it comes closer, so that sometimes I can smell and feel and taste it, no more than a breath away.

The letter sat in her pocket all day as she toiled in the sluice and hurried back and forth on the ward with trays and bedpans. Already she knew most of it by heart. His strong black hand printed itself on her mind's background like the pattern of a familiar landscape, so that she knew it almost without reading it.

His letters were written for public consumption, of course,

for he knew that everyone at Morland Place would want to read them, so there could be nothing in them that was personal for Jessie – except that last paragraph. She knew how to interpret it. It warmed her heart, even while it made her want to weep, for the time he spoke of was infinitely far away, not just at the end of the war, but only to be found in dream, or perhaps at the end of their lives. Would they be allowed to be together in the after-life? She could not believe they would be kept apart through all eternity, only because each of them had made an unwise marriage. They had done their best in the circumstances. Surely God would have pity on them? But even that distant hope was small comfort now. She wanted to be with him in flesh and blood, here in this life – to cleave to him and know him and love him through whatever earthly years they were allowed. She was not saintly enough to love only with the spirit – and perhaps the torment she felt was the punishment for that weakness. Well, if it was, she embraced it. She would rather love him and suffer than have that love expunged from her mind. In the moments before sleep she allowed herself to imagine that she was standing by him at the gate, in the dusk, watching the bats flicker past, smelling the green, damp odours of the earth; not speaking, not touching, but simply being near each other. It was all she allowed herself to long for.

The weather was fine and the harvest was abundant, and Jessie took time from her other tasks to go and help with it. She loved harvest-time, working in the hot fields, seeing the golden forest come whispering down yard by yard, the ballet of the scythes. In the yard at Woodhouse the threshing machine stood, rattling and shuddering and stinking as it separated grain from straw; but out in the fields all was peaceful, as it had been for generations, time out of mind. The women with their skirts tucked up went behind the scythe men, gathering the fallen stems together into sheaves, the men followed them and bound and stooked, and the children gleaned into cupped aprons and cotton bags.

468

Around the margins of the field, farm cats hunted the disturbed mice, drawn from their barns by this once-a-year bounty. The labourers' dogs, lying in the green shade of the hedges, sides panting and frilled tongues dripping, watched the mad activity scornfully; but even they emerged from time to time to sprint after a jinking rabbit, which had dashed too close for their pride to ignore.

In the fields that had been cut earlier, the stooked corn baked in the sunshine, the sheaves steady on their broad bases, feathery heads drooping, and geese gorged themselves on fallen grains. The corn had dried so quickly in the fine weather that in the first fields to have gone under the scythe, the carts were already gathering. Pulled by Jessie's ponies this year, or by mules given by the army as compensation, they trundled slowly along the rows as the men threw the sheaves up, and then bore them off to the threshing machine.

'One day,' Uncle Teddy said, when he came out one August noon to check progress and found Jessie leading Mouse and Minna, who were pulling a cart half full of sheaves, 'one day all this will be done by machine – every process!'

'What a horrible thought,' Jessie said, stopping the ponies and taking out her handkerchief to dry her neck. 'No more horses? Farming wouldn't be farming without them.'

It was very hot today, and the corn dust stuck to her damp skin. She had lent Mouse and Minna for the harvest, and to keep the flies off their eyes she had tucked sprays of bracken under their crown-pieces, to hang down over their faces. Their lovely eyes glowed through the green shade as they watched her, and she rubbed their muzzles for them, knowing how itchy they must be. Brach had started out the day with her, but had disappeared long since to find somewhere cool to flop down.

'Machinery is more efficient,' Teddy said, screwing up his eyes to stare away across the fields.

'All stink and racket!'

'We'd get all this done in a tenth of the time.'

'But what would you do with the time you saved?' she laughed.

469

He smiled at her. 'Are you having a nice time? Your mother always used to help with the harvests, you know. You remind me of her, standing there with your sleeves rolled up.' He reached out and pulled a loose strand of hair away from her forehead and tucked it behind her ear for her. 'Don't get burned, will you?'

'No, I shall hand over when I get to the end of the row. I'm ready for a rest and a drink of something cold.'

She watched him walk away, his riding boots brushing through the dusty stubble, to where a labourer was holding Warrior for him over by the hedge. Her heart was filled with affection for him. Even on this hot day, he was properly attired in broadcloth, breeches and boots, immaculate neckcloth and nicely brushed hat. He would never let standards slip; and he had always been something of a dandy. The sky would fall – and there would be machines doing all the farm work, she thought, with a smile – before Mr Edward Morland of Morland Place looked anything less than the Master.

The gatherers had been waiting politely, but they were ready to move on, so she clicked to the ponies and led them on down the row. At the end, the cart was full, and the man who had been catching, up on the load, climbed into the driving seat, took the reins from her, and drove off towards the field gate and the track to Woodhouse.

She was in one of Huntsham's fields, so she thought she would seek the coolness of Harewood Whin, which was nearby, and one of her favourite places, where the Smawith brook ran along the edge of it. As she passed along the hedge Brach appeared from nowhere and joined her, and they plodded along together in the heat; until suddenly Brach stopped and threw her head up, staring into the distance. She began to sing.

'What is it, girl?' Jessie asked her; but she had gone, bounding from standstill to leaping motion, racing down the hedge as though she was on springs. A soldier was standing at the bottom of the field, at the corner where the home path joined it, his jacket slung across his shoulder, his head bare, waiting for her. Jessie hastened her step, as Brach reached him and greeted him extravagantly, and he dropped his jacket on the baked earth to leave both hands free to return the compliment.

'I thought you weren't due until tomorrow,' Jessie said, coming up to him.

He caressed Brach's head, shoved up under his hands, but his eyes were on Jessie. His face was screwed up against the brightness, which made him look as though he were smiling, but she didn't think he was. He was very brown, and his hair and eyebrows were bleached by the sun. His forearms – he had rolled up his sleeves – were lean and muscled and he looked very hard and fit. She felt a little afraid of him. She could not see him as her husband, whose body she had once delighted in. She tried to see him as dear old Ned, whom she had grown up with, but he didn't look like that Ned, either. He was completely a stranger now.

'I wasn't,' he said. His voice was as without inflexion as his face. There was nothing there for her, no love, no gladness to be back, no sadness either. He was a man she had met at the field corner, on his way somewhere. 'I wasn't, but I had the chance of a lift to Calais, instead of taking the train, so I was able to get an earlier crossing, and come up on the milk train.'

'Was it a good journey?' she asked politely, as one asks of travellers.

'Yes. Actually, I slept most of the way.' He seemed to tire of the subject. 'Where were you going?'

'Just for a walk,' she said. 'To the Whin – you know, my place by the brook with the fallen tree.'

He nodded minutely, though there was no recognition in his face. 'May I walk with you? I want to talk to you.'

'Of course,' she said. She hesitated a moment, but he did not take the initiative, so she walked past him through the open field gate, and he fell in beside her, with Brach still romping about him, trying to gain his attention, licking his hand and pawing his arm.

471

'Get down,' he said, looking down at the hound. She desisted, and went round to the other side to walk beside Jessie, as though her feelings were hurt.

They walked down the narrow path between hedges. The deep ruts of the winter had dried and the crests were breaking away now, wearing down almost to smoothness, disguised by the springing summer grass. The honeysuckle was finished, but the wild roses still bloomed in the hedge, and the first blackberries were ripening. Ned plucked one and put it into his mouth. 'They're early,' he said.

'It's been a hot summer,' she said.

And then they walked in silence. At the Whin, Brach left them and darted into the undergrowth, hunting for anything that would move. It was cool under the trees, so cool that it made Jessie's hot arms start to gooseflesh for a moment, but it was also somehow stuffy. It was silent – no birdsong, no wind moving in the trees – and little grey-brown flies came up out of the bracken and settled on their bare skin, and had to be brushed away. On the winding path they could not walk side by side. He stopped and let her go ahead, so she walked quickly towards her special place, anxious now to have it done with, whatever was coming. It was so uncomfortable to be with him and not know him, not be able to speak to him; and her mind was heavy with guilt, with the burden of the feelings she had for someone else, feelings she could not help, yet which were still her fault, her grievous fault.

Brach was at the stream before them: they could hear her lapping before they came in sight – great cold clopping laps that made you feel hot and thirsty just at the sound of them. The old tree trunk, soft with emerald moss like green velvet upholstery, seemed welcomingly familiar, and she sat down on it, and unconsciously sighed.

Ned, following her, heard the sigh, and was piercingly reminded of the last night he had been with her, of her sigh when he had finished making love to her. And in that moment he knew he could not tell her what he had come here with her to say. He had meant to tell her about Céline,

472

to make a clean breast of it, to admit his fault and beg her forgiveness. The awkwardness and guilt and shame of telling her would be his punishment; he would see her disappointment with him in her eyes. Perhaps she would be angry, too. But that would be his penance, and at the end there would be absolution. In telling her he would be purged clean, and they would be able to begin again, with a clean page turned, the past in the past and gone.

But he heard the sigh. He had been going to sit down beside her and take her hand, but instead he stood in front of her, looking down, searching her face. In the dappled, green-gold shade of the wood's edge she looked very beautiful. She was still she, and he had always thought her beautiful, even though her cheeks were golden with the sun instead of white as a lady's should be, and there were a few freckles across her nose. She had never cared for such things. It struck him suddenly that she should have been a man. He remembered how as a child she had railed against the unfairness of being a girl. Perhaps that was always what had been wrong with her. He remembered how she had scorned dancing and romancing when he had been courting her, preferring always to go for a ride. He remembered, after they were married, how often they had quarrelled, because she would not accept his authority over her. And she did manly things, like driving a motor and running her own business. It came to him then that she did not like being a woman. Perhaps – the thought had to be approached cautiously – that was why she could not bear him a child.

And yet they had been happy at first. He remembered it as a true thing; he was not mistaken. She had been happy, and he had pleased her in bed. His body shuddered involuntarily at the memory of their physical love. When had it changed? He didn't know. He couldn't tell. He only knew it was different now.

Céline had shown him that the things he had always admired about Jessie – her strength, her determination, her independence, her defence of her own opinion – were the very things that made her unsuitable as a wife. He wanted

473

a wife who would look up to him, defer to him, be protected and guided by him; a soft little thing he could cherish and shelter in his arms. Jessie was like a wild, unbroken horse: you would always love it for its beauty and untamed grace, but you could not put a saddle on it, nor harness it to your cart.

Jessie looked up at him patiently, waiting for him to begin. He had come here with her to tell her, to purge his soul of his sin. But he thought of Céline, her softness, her femininity, her absolute trust of him, her interest in everything about him, and he knew he could not betray her. He could not tell Jessie anything about her, because that would be to put her in Jessie's power. And – it came to him suddenly – he could not repent of Céline, because when he went back to France, *he would be going back to her*. He had not meant to when he came home to Morland Place. Almost he did not mean to now, even now. But somewhere deep inside him he knew that he would; that half reluctantly, wholly guiltily, however little he intended it, he would go and seek her out as soon as ever he could.

And in that case, what could he say to his wife? *His wife!* Guilt, ambivalence, longing, pity – they surged about inside him, and kept him silent.

At last Jessie said, 'Well? You wanted to talk to me? What about?'

He thought she looked at him coolly, not like someone in love. Perhaps she had been feeling doubts too. There was only one way to find out. He took a long breath, and said, 'Jess, do you ever think that we shouldn't have married each other?'

Her insides jumped as though she had touched a live wire. Could he read her thoughts? Had he discovered her guilty mind? 'I don't know what you mean,' she said faintly.

He plunged on, since he had to: 'We were always friends – before we married, I mean. We loved each other as cousins. Perhaps we should have stayed cousins and friends and not tried to – to make it something else.'

She stared at him, trying to read his face – but Ned had never had the most expressive of countenances. No, she thought, he could not know her heart; but perhaps he had detected some withdrawal in her. If so, she must reassure him. She could not, would not hurt him. They were married; after the war they would have to live together and find a way to be happy. Her secret must always remain her secret. And, more immediately, he was going back to France soon, to risk his life for her and all she held dear. He must go with confidence, believing in her wholehearted love. He deserved that. He deserved her loyalty.

But what to say? She said slowly, to give herself time, 'I think – I think that friendship ought to be at the foundation of every marriage.'

'But you don't think that perhaps – perhaps we knew each other too well?'

'You think it would be better if there were a mystery?' She was perplexed. It seemed such an odd thing to say.

He thought of Céline. Yes, some mystery, the secret dark glitter of feminine magic, to keep the heart on its toes. There had never been that between them. Jessie was almost wholly without feminine wiles. Yet that was what he had admired about her, in those years before their marriage – that she was straight and true. But he could not express any of this.

'I'm sorry,' Jessie said into his silence. It was all she could think of to say.

'No, don't be sorry. I didn't mean you to—' He paused, lost on an unmarked track among his thoughts.

'If I've been – if I've seemed different to you,' she went on, 'since the baby—' She swallowed. 'It was hard for me. I know it was hard for you, too, but – well, I'll get over it, I suppose, in time. I'm sorry if I've made you feel I didn't – love you enough.'

He was stricken. Like a dolt, a blind, blockheaded fool, he had forgotten for the moment how much she must be grieving for the baby. Pity seared him. He must never let her think his love had changed. She must never know about Céline. He was going away soon, and all he could do for her was to leave her with the assurance of his absolute love. She deserved that of him.

'I'm sorry,' he said. 'I shouldn't have spoken like that. I'm an unfeeling brute. I know you love me – and I love you, too. It's the war, and being away, and everything being strange and different and – oh, unnatural! It isn't a natural life at the Front.'

'No, I imagine not.'

'Please forget what I said. It was stupid of me. It was just idiotic war thoughts. I'm all right now. I'm over it.'

'Over it?' she said. She felt stupid, as though she'd been too long in the sun. Why precisely had he come here with her? Was it really for this vague, undirected talk? 'Was that what you wanted to say to me?' she said at last, when it seemed he would not say any more.

'Well,' he said, and looked away across the fields, out of the shade into the sunlight, 'I suppose so.'

She looked down at her hands. 'Everything's different because of the war,' she said, in a low voice. 'Everything's strange. When it's over—'

His gaze came back to her. He tried to smile, but it was painful and incomplete. He sat down and took her hand, and she turned her face to look at his, close to hers in the green shade. She could see every line and little hair, the sheen of moisture on his cheekbone, the tiny points of fair bristles coming through on his chin from this morning's shave. He was utterly familiar to her, and she did not know him at all.

'Yes, when the war's over and everything gets back to normal, it will be all right,' he said, pressing her hand. 'We'll begin again, and do everything properly. There'll be babies – lots of them. We'll be happy. I promise you.' But even as he said it, the end of the war seemed far off, minute in the distance, and he could not believe in it, or in that mythical country on the far side of it to which he supposed he would one day return. And because he knew his voice lacked conviction, he said again, shaking her hand a little, like a child trying to gain attention, 'I promise you.'

'Yes,' she said.

'Everything will be all right,' he said.

476

'Yes,' she said again; and then, because he was her husband, and she loved him, and she would be spending the rest of her life with him, she smiled, to please him, and saw some of the tension go out of his face. She smiled more. 'Everything will be all right,' she said.

CHAPTER TWENTY

It was several days after his return to London before Laidislaw found the time to answer Lady Verney's note. The day came when Emma Weston was in London on her way to Scotland and Violet was unable to see him, so, having nothing better to do, he trotted off to Grosvenor Square. Closing up was well advanced, and he was shown into a ghost-room, dim with the blinds half drawn, where the furniture was covered and mirrors, paintings and ornaments were all bagged in holland. Laura – ghostly herself in a grey dress – was watching her horologist removing the pendulums from various clocks.

'Laddie!' she cried. She waved a hand at the clock-man, who bowed and removed himself. 'Laddie, where have you been? Surely not at Aston all this time? I left the note for you days ago.'

'Most obliging of you,' he said, smiling. 'And how did you manage to get in?'

'The caretaker let me in,' she said.

'Hmm. Pity Mrs Hudson had to go away – a fellow is entitled to his privacy at home, one would have thought. Well, here I am, at all events. What did you want me for?'

She regarded him curiously. There was no consciousness in his face, no wariness of guilt. He seemed calm and pleased with himself, that was all. 'I saw the picture,' she said abruptly.

He shook his head indulgently. 'So I supposed. There

478

never was a female who could deny her curiosity. Think of Bluebeard's wife! But since you have looked – what did you think of it?'

'It's brilliant,' she said, 'but that's not the point.'

'Isn't it?'

'No. What I want to know is – what is Violet Holkam to you?'

He grinned. 'Darling Laura, is that really your business?'

'My God,' she breathed, 'you *are* having an *affaire*. I didn't want to believe it. How could you be so wantonly foolish?'

His smile faded. 'It isn't an *affaire*, and it isn't foolish. We are in love with each other – if it's any business of yours.'

'Laddie, dear,' Laura said gently, 'you know how fond of you I am. And I know how soft-hearted you are. But Violet Holkam, of all people! She isn't one of your hardened flirts, you know: she's as innocent as a new lamb.'

'*I* know that. It's one of the things I love about her.'

'*She*'s as innocent as a baby; and *you*, my dear, are not as worldly wise as you think you are. The combination could spell ruin for you both – especially as her husband is the greatest stickler in nature.'

Laidislaw waved all that away. 'He has had his three children of her, and they go their separate ways. He has mistresses – if that's what one calls women of the sort he seems to prefer. He won't object.'

'Oh, Laddie, Laddie!' Laura said sadly. 'I told you you weren't up to the rig. A man like that does not take it lightly if his property goes missing. What *he* does is not to govern what *she* does. Caesar's wife, my dear! He might possibly ignore a light flirtation, if it was discreetly carried on – but a full-blown *affaire*, thrust blatantly under his nose—'

'Nose, nonsense. Why should he ever find out?'

'He'll know the instant he sees the painting.'

'Well, perhaps he won't see it. He's in France now, and by the time he comes back, the exhibition will be over and the painting will be on its way to America.'

'What do you mean? What exhibition?' she asked, alarmed.

479

'The National Portrait Exhibition, in October. That's where I shall unveil it. It will win – I am quite confident. And the best of the exhibition goes afterwards to the Rothschild Gallery in New York, where it will win again.'

'You can't mean it? You can't mean you are going to put the painting on public display?'

'Why not?' he said, sounding annoyed now. 'It is the best thing I have ever done. You said yourself it was brilliant. It is my masterpiece, and I want the world to see it.'

She put her head in her hands. 'You innocent! You dear fool! Don't you see? If it goes in an exhibition *everyone* will know what you and Violet are to each other. It will be in all the papers. There is no surer way of telling Holkam than that – and no better way to make him rage! Not a discreet dalliance, but his wife's betrayal public knowledge, his private concerns spread all over the gossip pages. He is not the sort of man to wear horns gracefully – especially in the full glare of publicity.'

'Oh, he'll never know! Why would he read the art reviews? I'm sure he is the completest Philistine.'

'Even if he didn't see it in the papers, someone would tell him. People love to make mischief. Laddie, you can't do it. No-one must ever see the painting.'

His eyes opened wide. 'You cannot mean that!'

'If people see the picture they'll guess the truth, and then you'll be ruined. Holkam will see to it. And Violet will be ruined – and surely you can't want that?'

'Of course not, but that won't happen. You're making a fuss about nothing. The painting will be celebrated as a painting, that's all. Why should people think anything, except that she is a beautiful woman and I am the world's most brilliant painter?'

'It's all there to be seen in the portrait.'

'By you, perhaps, because you know me – and her – and you're a very sensitive person. But the rest of the world won't know. They will only see my genius. Don't worry, Laura dear. I wouldn't do anything to upset Violet. I *love* her, I tell you.'

'Please, Laddie, listen to me. You mustn't exhibit it.'

He laughed. 'You can't really think I'm going to lock my best painting in a cupboard for ever, and never let anyone see it? Don't *worry* so. Everything will be all right.'

He was not to be moved, and soon he kissed her cheek consolingly and strolled off, amused, looking forward to telling Violet about it when he saw her again.

Laura Verney stood silent and unmoving for some time after he had left, furiously pondering what was best to be done. *Was* she overreacting? Would others not see what she had seen in the portrait? She supposed it was possible, though she did not think so. But at least, she thought, Violet ought to be warned, so that she could make up her own mind. Violet was very innocent, and probably would not think of it for herself. Should she write her a note? But notes had a tendency to fall into the wrong hands. No, better she went to see her in person.

She wrote to Violet, asking if she could come to see her on such a day at such a time, to discuss something of importance. If the day or time were inconvenient, would Violet kindly indicate another date at the earliest possible moment, as the matter was of some urgency.

She received a reply by the next post. Violet thanked her for her note. She believed she knew what Laura wanted to discuss as their mutual friend had spoken to her about it. She thanked her for her concern, but was sure there was nothing at all to worry about, and depended on Laura's discretion to discuss the matter no further.

Fuming, Laura showed the letter to Verney. 'What do you think about that?'

Verney read it through. 'Very poorly expressed. She means "common friend" not "mutual friend". Mutuality can only refer to actions, not objects.'

'Darling, how can you think I wanted you to criticise her grammar?'

He handed the letter back and patted her hand. 'I think you are worrying too much, my love. It seems to me most unlikely that the world will see in the picture what you see

481

in it. People don't have your keen eye, and they don't know the characters involved.'

'That's what Laddie said.'

'Even Laddie can be right sometimes.'

'*You* haven't seen the picture!'

'Well, in any case, darling, there's nothing you can do about it. You've done all you can by warning them. If they choose to ignore your advice, you are not to blame for the consequences.'

'I don't want to be in the clear,' Laura told him. 'I want there to *be* no consequences for me not to be to blame for.'

He grinned. 'You wouldn't like a critique of *that* piece of grammar, would you?'

'It expressed exactly what I meant,' she said, with dignity.

'Forget about it. I'm sure you are overreacting. No-one will think a thing about it.' He slipped an arm around her waist. '*We* are going down to the country – think of that! Just you and me in a charming house, roses round the door, no guests for a whole week. I shall have you to myself at last.' He kissed her, with an air of promise. 'What's the first thing you mean to do when we get there?'

'Take off my corsets,' she said, and then laughed as he opened his eyes wide in pretended shock.

The weeks after Ned went back to France were strangely restful and domestic – not like war at all, he often found himself thinking. The battalion was still at the Front in the area of Neuve Chapelle, still following the normal 'quiet time' routine: three days in the first-line trenches, three in support, three days in reserve, and then out to rest at Locon. When he arrived his platoon was just going into the firing-line, so it was ten days before he could go and see Céline: ten days during which he could think seriously about her and about his situation; about Jessie, his marriage, and their future together. He and Jessie had parted fondly, and he had determined on the long and tedious journey that he would not see Céline again. After a week at Morland Place she had begun to seem unreal to him, and his feelings of

482

guilt for having broken his marriage vow had been stronger than his remembered affection. But she had been good to him, and was undoubtedly fond of him, and it would be the action of a cad to drop her without explanation. So he decided he would write to her when he got back to France, and tell her kindly and gently why he would not be coming to visit.

During the quiet nights in the line, sitting in the dugout between his rounds of the sentries, he sometimes got out pencil and paper and sat with them resting on the top of an upturned crate, by the uncertain light of a candle stuck into a bottle, thinking what to write. But words never had been his strong point. By the time they were marching back to Locon, he still had not written the letter. He had fallen back into the life of the soldier, and it fitted him like a comfortable pair of shoes: Morland Place now seemed far away; that day at Harewood Whin like a dream from another life. Here in the Tommy-infested countryside near Neuve Chapelle, Céline seemed much more real to him. He thought of her wistfully, and with longing. It would be better to go and see her, he decided, and tell her in person. It was only good manners. She deserved no less.

Two days later, she and another girl, Christine, were installed in Locon in a cottage that had been abandoned by its owners since the winter, under the keeping of Vernon and Ned. Céline had been more than willing to dedicate herself exclusively to him: she had wept tears of happiness at the idea. Matters had been amicably settled with Madame, who was not one to stand in a good girl's way. But Ned had not been happy to have her live alone, when he would not be able to visit her for ten days in each month: he had been afraid that she would be lonely, and a little worried that something might happen to her, with so many soldiers passing through all the time. Vernon, who had come with him to Loisené, said the matter was simply adjusted: he would be happy to have an exclusive girl himself, and have her closer at hand. Céline's best friend at Madame's establishment was Christine, a few years older than her, extremely pragmatic and sensible, and also one of Vernon's favourites.

Chattering excitedly, the girls packed their few things, kissed everybody in sight, shed a few happy tears, and climbed into Vernon's motor-car. They drove to Hinges first to do a little shopping – food, mostly, but also some new sheets and towels, soap and one or two other domestic necessities. The girls were almost beside themselves with excitement about the whole adventure. Neither had ever had a home of her own before. Christine had left her poor and crowded rural home some years before, when her father proposed to marry her off to an elderly man in the next village. She had been fending for herself since then, not doing very well until she had come upon Madame's establishment. Céline had been sent by her widowed father to live with an aunt when he went away to the war, but she hated the aunt – who had not wanted her and treated her badly – so much that she had run away and ended up at Madame's *faute de mieux*. To them the abandoned cottage was luxurious, and the pleasure of choosing things for their home an unknown indulgence. They chattered and laughed in delight all the afternoon, and since Vernon's French was better than their English, most of the conversation was in that language. Ned thought he had better become more proficient or he would be left out.

Neither girl was afraid of hard work, and between them they scoured the cottage, cleaned the windows, polished the old, worn furniture, and brought in such little touches as they could find to make it homelike – flowers on windowsills, scraps of ribbon to tie back the curtains. Vernon and Ned visited as often as they could get away – Ned more often than his friend. He thought that for Vernon Christine was a convenience he might shed as soon as it ceased to amuse him; but Ned felt a real sensation of warmth and happiness when he ducked through that low, narrow front door and Céline ran to greet him. She had cooked for her father after her mother died, and was quite skilled at it. She liked to cook for 'Édouard' and '*l'ami*', as she called Vernon, and have them sigh with satisfaction. After dinner she and Ned would stroll in the dusk, or sit by the lamplight. He would fill his pipe and she would hasten to light it for him. It made him laugh to see how gravely and carefully she performed the silly little task. They read, or talked, or sometimes he read aloud to her. On those cosy domestic evenings, if Vernon did not come to see her, Christine would take herself away and leave them alone. So it felt like home to Ned: so small and close and cosy and simple; no servants, just one man and one woman – and a cat that had hastened to adopt the girls as soon as they moved in. It seemed to him in those days that that was what life should be about: simple domestic pleasures. That was worth fighting for.

Céline's desire to learn English had only been skin-deep, expressed merely to flatter the English officer; so when Ned said he wanted to improve his French and asked that they should always speak that language together, she made no objection. It surprised him how quickly he came on: talking a language in real life was quite different from those dull lessons at school with M'sieur. His grounding in grammar had been sound, and the vocabulary and the idiom soon grafted themselves on and made him more fluent. She praised him extravagantly, and rewarded him with kisses, which generally led to the tiny bedroom with the sloping ceiling, the grand iron bedstead and the rag rug on the floor.

Coming 'home' to Céline from his soldier's duties was like coming home from work, back in that other world, which seemed so far off now, so unreal. The cottage and the woman made a little shard of stability in the uncertain world of war, and the weeks seemed long and the summer evenings endless, though they were beginning to draw in now. It felt to Ned as though it would never end, and he shut his mind to the future.

But perhaps it was inevitable that Céline could not quite do the same. One evening when it was raining they sat after dinner in the parlour, and the air felt so damp and chilly that Céline lit the fire. Vernon was with Christine in her bedroom: murmurs and occasional sounds of laughter emerged from behind the closed door, and sometimes hearty thumpings brought a fine dust of plaster down from the ceiling. Ned read aloud while Céline sewed, mending a tear in a blouse with tiny stitches, correcting his pronunciation now and then. He was reading *La Porte Étroite* by André Gide, a newish book lent to him by Vernon, who read things like that for pleasure.

And suddenly, as he paused to turn a page, she said, 'Édouard, what will happen to us?'

He looked up. 'To us?'

'Well, to me, then. I suppose you will not be here for ever. The army may take you away to a different part of the Front.'

'I will always look after you,' he said. 'And I will always come back.'

'The war will end one day. Then, I suppose, you will go home to England.'

'I suppose so,' he said uncomfortably.

'To your wife.'

'Céline—'

She lifted her hands. 'Oh, I understand. You were candid with me, you told me you were married. I cannot say I have been deceived. But I love you, Édouard, and I wish to stay with you always. I cannot imagine what it will be like to be without you.' He said nothing, unable to think of anything appropriate. 'When the war is over, and you go back to England, could I come too?' She looked at him earnestly. 'I would not make any difficulty for you. I would be quiet and discreet, but perhaps then you could still come and see me sometimes. When you were at liberty. Could I come with you and find a little place to hide away, do you think? A little mouse's hole somewhere near you, so you could come sometimes?'

He put the book down and held out his hands, and she slipped from her seat and knelt before him. What could he say to her? His tongue was still unready in French, when it came to the subtleties of this kind of conversation – not that he would have been a great deal better in English. He cared very much for Céline, and he did not want to hurt her. The situation was what it was. Above all, what could he say to her that was true?

'The end of the war is a long time off,' he said. 'We should not worry about it.'

'I hear people saying it will end next year,' she said.

'Next year seems a long time off to me,' he said helplessly.

She looked up, her eyes filled with tears. 'Then I cannot come? I must stay here, in France all alone?'

He could not bear her tears. He wiped them away gently with his thumb, then lifted her face to his to kiss her tenderly on the forehead and lips. 'You can come to England,' he said. 'I will find a place for you somewhere. I promise I will always look after you.'

She seemed satisfied with that, and smiled; put her soft arms round his neck and kissed him. He drew her up onto his lap, and wrapped in each other's arms they watched the fire crackle and leap up the chimney.

It came as a shock to Ned, though perhaps not to Céline, when orders came on the 15th of September for the battalion to move the next day. He had put unpleasant thoughts out of his head with great success, and was upset to be reminded so abruptly that there was a war on. As soon as he could get away he hurried to the cottage, and found both girls waiting, their arms folded round themselves, as women stand when trouble threatens, as if to keep out the cold.

'We know,' said Christine. 'You are moving away.'

'Yes,' said Ned. 'I can't tell you where, of course—'

'Oh, but we know,' said Céline. 'You are going to Vermelles. There is to be a battle around Loos-en-Gohelle.'

'How can you know that?' Ned said, astonished.

Christine shrugged. 'One knows certain things. In this village, nothing remains secret for long.'

'You must not talk about it,' he said urgently. Troop movements had to be kept secret, for fear of word filtering through to the Bosch. 'You must not tell anyone.'

'But all the world knows,' Christine said indifferently.

'The important thing is this,' Céline interrupted excitedly, 'that Vermelles is only about fifteen kilometres away. So though they have moved you, they have not moved you far. You will still be near us. You can still come to see me.'

'It's true, it isn't very far away,' he said. He stepped close and looked down at her, and she unwound her arms and slipped them round his waist. Christine watched them a moment, then moved away to give them privacy. 'But there is going to be a battle. I shan't be able to come for a long time, not until afterwards. We will have many things to do before the battle, and we will not have any leisure.'

'The battle will be on the twenty-fifth,' she said. 'Ten days from now.'

'How can you know that?'

She shrugged. 'So, when will you come?'

'As soon afterwards as I can. Two or three days, perhaps.'

'Then we shall be apart for a fortnight only. That is bad, but not too bad. And, Édouard, I was thinking – if the army moves you further away, I could move too. One place is like another to me. Christine and I could come and find another cottage.'

'Of course you could,' he said. 'Why didn't I think of that?'

'Oh, you are a man,' she laughed. 'You do not think of domestic things.'

'I must go,' he said, beginning to detach himself.

'But no! You must come upstairs first. We must say goodbye properly.' And she pressed herself against him, looking up ardently into his eyes.

He was gentle, but firm. He unpicked her hands and gave them back to her. 'No, love, I can't. I have to get back. I have a thousand things to do.' He reached into his pocket. 'Here is some money for food, to keep you for a while. It's not much, but it's all I can manage. I'm not a rich man, you know. Perhaps,' he essayed a little joke, to make the parting easier, 'perhaps you would rather choose another officer, a rich one?'

She shook her head, unsmiling. 'I want only you, Édouard.'

He kissed her forehead gently. 'I'm glad. Wait for me here, then, and I'll come back for you after the battle.'

'You are very good to me,' she said, her eyes filling. 'Thank you, dear Édouard.'

'Oh, Lord, don't cry,' he said in English.

She sniffed bravely. 'No, I won't cry.' She reverted to French without realising it. 'When one hears the battle is over, I will stand at the door, just here, and wait for you every hour until you come through that gate again.'

'You'll catch cold,' he said, with a smile.

'I never catch cold,' she said. 'I am strong.' She reached up and kissed him. '*Au revoir, mon âme. À ton retour.*'

'*Je reviens,*' he said, and went away.

The preparations for the battle were lengthy and painstaking. This was the battle that would break the Germans and put them on the run; it would mark the beginning of the end of the war, so nothing was to be left to chance.

The sector of the Front from Aubers Ridge to Lens was quiet, with nothing but the occasional bursts of machine-gun fire exchanged across no man's land to let the enemy know you were still there, and the ever-present danger from snipers. It was what would have been called a 'cushy billet', except for the digging. It was already going on when the Kents arrived, and they were thrown straight into it. Twelve thousand yards of new trench were dug in the days before the battle: assembly trenches behind the line, jumping-off trenches in front of the line, communication trenches linking everything to everything else, and listening saps run out into no man's land.

All the digging had to be done at night, because in daytime the Germans had observation balloons up. Even so, it was impossible to hide the results of all this activity from the enemy. The ground was chalky, and the new trenches showed up as long lines of white, gleaming in the sunshine against the brown and green of the undisturbed earth. There was no way to disguise them.

On the first night when Ned marched his platoon out to dig, everyone was very nervous. Their job, as had been explained to him, was to extend a jumping-off trench that had been started the day before by another battalion; and, as Ned reckoned to himself, since the trench was at present a dead-end, the Germans must know that someone would be coming up to finish the work, and would have had all day to get the range of it. He only hoped that his men would not have worked that out too. Whether they had or not, they knew that they were going out into no man's land, to a place well in front of the line, where even patrols crawled on their bellies and were careful to make no sound. He hardly had to remind them about being quiet, but he did warn them to be careful not to let their tools clink against each other or against anything else.

It was a warm, still night – the sort, he thought unhappily, on which sounds travel for miles – as he led his men in single file and almost on tiptoe down the sap that had been dug out towards the enemy. At the sap head they emerged and spread out along the line laid out in white tape by the Royal Engineers. Ned had never felt so exposed in his life – not even in battle. He and his men were simply standing up in the middle of an open space with no cover of any sort, right in front of the German line – and the Germans must know they were there. The slightest sound would tell the enemy they had arrived. It told the whole story that his orders were to carry on digging, no matter how heavy casualties were.

The platoon was divided into pairs, a pickman and a shoveller. Each pair was to dig a hole straight down as quickly as possible to give them shelter, and when the holes were the right depth, they would be joined together to form the trench with its bays and traverses. Ned saw the pairs disposed the right distances apart and whispered the order to begin. The pickmen began to swing, while the shovellers lay flat with the blade of the shovel upright beside their heads in case of fire. The sound of the picks thumping into the chalky earth seemed horribly loud: as well shout through

490

a megaphone, 'Open fire, we're here!' When the time came to swap over, the pickmen flung themselves down as though bullets were whistling over their heads, and the shovellers dug like men possessed.

And then a Very flare went up from the German line. The whole scene was bathed in ghostly grey-green light. Ned saw his men stretching away down the line, each like a cut-out against the depthless horizon, outlined in black. Ned saw his own shadow sharp-cut against the ground, and knew he was as marked out as they were. Every hair on his body seemed to stand on end. It was like finding himself naked in a spotlight on stage in front of a vast audience. In that moment his stretched imagination almost heard the rattle of gunfire, and felt the impact of the bullets striking his flesh. But the light died away, and nothing had happened.

He went down the line encouraging his men – not that they needed much encouragement. He had never seen men dig so fast. In what seemed an impossibly short time they were knee deep in their holes. Another flare went up. Now, surely, the firing would come? Ned waited with every nerve on edge. The men at least had work to do: he had only to stand there at the mercy of his imagination. But the light faded and no firing came. It was the most extraordinary thing. What was Fritz up to? The holes were getting deeper, at every moment offering more cover. Was it possible that despite the flares they had not been spotted?

The answer came after two hours when, without warning, a salvo of shells came over. They landed just beyond the line of digging men, exploding a few feet away and splattering earth, stones and shards of metal over them. It was obvious the gunners had the range of them. The Kents were experienced enough now to fling themselves flat at the first sound of a shell, and no-one was hurt. Ned found himself with his face to the earth and his hands gripping grass without any awareness of how he had got there – so automatic were his reactions. Another flight of shells screamed over and crumped into the earth. Ned pulled his head down tighter. A piece of shrapnel went

491

whickering over his head, and something heavy hit his hand and began to burn. He snatched his hand back and took a look. It was a piece of shrapnel the size of a page of a book. It had landed flat on the back of his hand, and it was the heat he had felt. If it had landed edge-on, it would have cut his hand off.

It was quiet again. Ned got up cautiously, and saw his men already lifting their heads. The holes they had dug were deep enough now to give them some shelter, except from a direct hit. But the shelling proved the Germans had the range of them. Now surely the machine-guns would start: they would strafe them as they stood up to dig. But again nothing happened. The flares went up at regular intervals, and from time to time a few rounds of shells came over, but otherwise the Germans seemed to ignore them. It was beyond comprehension, Ned thought, but from their point of view it was a miracle. When his watch told him their stint was over, and he called the men to return to the sap, they all came back, unharmed except for one or two cuts and grazes and a crop of blisters. To have raised blisters on hands so horny was proof of how fast and furiously they had worked.

They filed out of the trenches, formed up on the safe ground beyond, and marched back to their billets. It had started raining during the last hour of their stint, and the chalky soil had turned slimy. The men were coated with it, clogged and smeared; they were weary from the long hours of hard, physical labour, with the added strain of nerves from having to work under the eyes of the Germans. Marching through the darkness, now was the time when morale might sink, when the men might begin to feel 'fed up', as the saying was, especially as they must know there were many nights more of the same to go through. But Ned noted they were all holding themselves like soldiers, and when he spoke to anyone he got a cheerful response.

'Pretty hard work tonight,' he said to Acres.

'Yessir.'

'And more digging to come, I'm afraid.'

492

'Don't you worry, sir. We're used to it now. It all helps us beat the Bosch an' kill the Kaiser.'

What men they were, he thought, with pride. 'Long lie-in tomorrow,' he said.

'Yessir. Looking forward to it, sir,' said Acres.

There was a treat for them all when they woke late the next morning. They were billeted in the outskirts of Nœux-les-Mines, which was, as the name suggested, a mining village. The men were filthy from their night's labours, all of them grey-haired and grey-faced from the slimy chalk. When they were marched off to the pithead baths at the nearest mine, they could hardly believe their luck. There were proper showers and plentiful hot water – as much as they wanted. It was possible, Ned reflected, that at that moment they would not have swapped that blessed hot water even for a similar quantity of beer.

There was a good hot meal for them at midday, and since they were to be digging again that night they were let off all fatigues and had the afternoon to loll about or otherwise enjoy themselves. Some of them got up a knock-about football game; for others, greasy packs of cards came out, or comic papers, sent from home and passed round until they were frayed and fragile, or paper and pencil to write home. Others again had their portable hobbies – drawing, wood-carving, toy-making; some liked just to talk and smoke; and there were always those who reckoned, if the army didn't need you for an hour or two, the best thing to do was sleep.

It did not escape the notice of even the dullest Kent that there were preparations going on that involved gas. The heavy, unwieldy cylinders were brought in by train to the railhead at Béthune, and were moved by wagon to dumps behind the line; but then they had to be carried by hand after dark from the dumps into the forward trenches. Each cylinder took two men to carry it, and even then they could only move slowly, with frequent rests. It took most of the night for a pair of men to move one cylinder into position, so most battalions had their turn at the thankless labour during the preparation time. The mood among the men regarding the gas was quietly gloating. The bloody Bosch had started it, breaking the rules of decency by using the stuff at Ypres. Well, the British weren't going to be mugs about it. If Fritz wanted to fight dirty, he'd get a dose of his own medicine, and see how he liked that!

Other, more delicate preparations were undertaken by specialist teams – the laying of mines under the German lines. Welsh miners did the actual digging, though any skinny, undersized lad in any battalion might be seconded to wriggle behind them, passing back the excavated earth, before the engineers went in to lay the fuses.

All battalions were taken in turn by Company to see a scale model of the battlefield that had been laid out in a field, and was large enough for them to walk round. The top brass, Ned reflected, were leaving nothing to chance. Not only were the officers to be lectured with maps and plans and diagrams, but the men themselves were to go into battle knowing exactly what they were to do and where. The scale model, he found, impressed the men, and gave them confidence. They talked about it afterwards, and doubted the poor old German soldier was ever told anything in advance by his officers. Dumb as cattle, that's what German soldiers were, prodded into position in beastly ignorance. No wonder they broke and ran as soon as you got near them. The coming battle was as good as won. It would be hard work, but they were the men for that. And this time next year the war would be over, and they'd be back home in the various bosoms, family and otherwise, they had left behind.

Bertie wrote:

My dear Jessie, and all at home,

Just a note to let you know we have been moved to another part of the line. I can't tell you where, of course, but it wasn't a very long march, and we are now billeted about ten miles behind the Front. My lads were all

494

terribly excited by the move, and fervently hope that
we will soon be getting to grips with the enemy. We
spend our time drilling, practising and route marching
just as before, but they, of course, envisage themselves
in the heart of the battle, killing the Hun right and left
with blood-curdling yells! We are billeted in a mining
village, so not very pretty, but we officers have a
comfortable house and the men are in three big barns.
There is a duck-pond they make use of when off duty
– the ducks have long since flown, or been eaten! We
are only a mile or two from the Headquarters village,
and when we passed through it on our way here, I saw
Violet's husband, looking very prosperous, riding in a
large motor with the Army Commander. He passed in
a cloud of dust and didn't see me. He and the Old
Man looked very thick. I also think I saw Ned, though
it was rather far off and in twilight, but it was certainly
men of his regiment, marching back off night fatigues.
He looked well, as far as I could tell – if it was him.
There's not much more to say, but I hope to write
more in a day or two. At all events you know we will
do all we can to make you proud. Fen sends his warmest
regards to young Miss Emma, and hopes to see her
when we're next on leave. I hope she hasn't forgotten
him by then. He remains faithful.

Your loving cousin,
Bertie

Jessie knew by now the frustrations of letters from the
Front that had to be written to pass through the censor –
not only the official one, but the unofficial one of the family.
But she knew what he was telling her. It was no more than
rumour to the general public that there was to be a big
push, but those with the right contacts had received sufficient hints to be fairly sure it was coming, that it would be
soon, and that it would be in the Lens area. Now Bertie
was more or less confirming the location with his mention
of a mining village not a very long way from Merville; and,

moreover, was telling her that Ned was to be in it too. Ned's most recent letter had said only that they had moved, and that they were in a quiet part of the line.

What else could she glean? She knew from Violet that Lord Holkam had been trying to ingratiate himself with General Haig, so perhaps that was the commander Bertie had seen him with. Haig was commander of the First Army, while Bertie's battalion had been in the Second. If they had been moved up as reinforcements, it suggested a very big offensive indeed. But if they were ten miles behind the line, they were probably only the reserve troops, so perhaps they might not be called on – they were, after all, newly arrived in France and very green. But Ned was also there. His battalion was not so newly arrived, and some had been in action already. Would they be part of the main action? She felt a cold emptiness in her stomach at the thought of it.

The last bit of the letter – *I hope she hasn't forgotten him* and *he remains faithful* – referred, she knew, not only to Captain Fenniman but to Bertie. He was sending his love to her in a discreet way. She wished censorship did not prevent his telling her the details of the coming action. She would have felt much better about it all if she had known where exactly, and what exactly, and when exactly; if she could have got out a map and pored, if she could have drawn plans and diagrams, as she had when he was fighting in South Africa. This bland un-information was like having a soft black bag over one's head, muffling everything. She wanted to snatch it off and *see*.

She showed the letter to the family and they discussed it extensively, agreeing with her that he was telling them there was a big push coming soon, and that he and Ned would both be in it.

'It's like the dear boy to find a way to let us know,' said Henrietta.

Uncle Teddy got out a map and pointed out the likely places for Headquarters to be set up, and where that meant Ned and Bertie might be billeted. 'He says he hopes to write more in a day or two. That must mean the battle is imminent. A day or two. And this letter has been two days coming.'

'So it could be tomorrow,' Jessie said nervously.

'It could be happening right this minute,' Teddy said. 'We wouldn't know until afterwards.'

Jessie and Henrietta exchanged a look, and both seemed a little pale. Love made you hatefully selfish. *Let it be someone else's 'dear boy' who got hurt, who got killed. Not mine. Please not mine.*

'I shall never get used to this,' Jessie said.

There were to be two diversionary attacks, one at Aubers Ridge, and one at Ypres.

'At least we won't be involved in that,' Fenniman said. 'I've seen enough of bloody old Ypres.'

It was not just the location Bertie was glad to be spared: rumour had it that the order to the troops in the subsidiary actions was that they were to convince the Germans at all costs that theirs was the main assault. Therefore no attempt would be made to conceal their preparations from the enemy, and they were to attack and keep attacking *regardless of the level of casualties*. They were to be sacrificial lambs, in fact, Bertie thought.

Though the West Herts were billeted well behind the line, and were in the reserve under Sir John French for the coming action, they had been involved in the preparations since they had marched up. They had been labouring each night carrying up supplies and ammunition from dumps into the front lines. Bertie had seen gun positions being constructed too, and noted that they were much closer to the line than in previous battles. The generals wanted to be sure that the opening bombardment did its job. In places, the guns were no more than sixty yards from the German front line.

The bombardment started on Tuesday, the 21st of September. It was the heaviest of the war so far, and the men were thrilled with it. They slapped each other's backs with glee at the thought of old Fritz having to sit down under that lot, and told each other they wished their dad or their brother Joe back home could be here to hear it. They had no doubt it was softening up the enemy very nicely, as well as cutting through his wire and knocking his trenches to bits. The clashing, smashing noise was appalling, and went on all day without remission, and with very little reply from the Germans. It was like the sound of railway engines crashing into each other, Bertie thought: hundreds of titanic train crashes in the sky. There was a mighty thunderstorm on the Wednesday night, and the sound of it was like mouse-applause by comparison.

Everyone knew, now, that the battle was to be on the 25th, and on the 24th there were no more fatigues, just a day to get ready. That meant lots of inspections: feet, rifles, general kit. Letters home were scribbled, and 'green envelopes' handed out to those who wanted them: they could be sent uncensored, giving the men a chance to get personal messages and last requests away, and instructions about distributing their effects. Packs and greatcoats were handed in, extra ammunition distributed. The men had a good big stew at dinner-time, and the cooks had even managed to make a pudding, with stewed pears, which put everyone in a very good mood. In the evening there were sing-songs, though no camp fire to gather round, but the men made do with lamps. In various corners gambling schools were set up and business was brisk: it was thought to be bad luck, among the Tommies, to go into battle with money in your pocket.

The officers packed up their personal belongings and wrote their last letters home. During the afternoon Bertie and Fenniman went off in a borrowed motor to forage for delicacies for their respective officers' mess baskets, whose resources were at a lowish ebb after the march and the night fatigues. They hunted through all the shops in the area, though they avoided Hinges, which was the Headquarters village: it was not wise to poach on top-brass territory. They managed to find tins of sardines – always useful – and of peas. There were fresh apples and pears in plenty, and local cheeses. They bought biscuits, the strange, rather dry yellow cake the French seemed so fond of, ripe figs, some jars of honey, and a couple of dozen bottles of the local red wine – *vin très ordinaire*, as they called it. And finally, following the hint of a motherly woman in the café where they stopped to refresh themselves, before going back, with coffee and Cognac, they tracked down an almost whole ham, which they agreed to buy between them and share.

So the officers had a good meal that evening, and after their own sing-song, round the cottage piano in the house they were all squeezed into, they settled down at last to sleep, to the rumbling of another thunderstorm trying rather feebly to mimic the guns, and to the sound of torrential rain hammering on the roof slopes and rushing and gurgling down the gutters. Bertie thought of the poor devils who would be moving up to form the first wave, and would have to spend much of the night crouched uncomfortably in a trench under this downpour, and felt very sorry for them. But he didn't let it disturb him for long. There is so much luck in a soldier's life, both good and bad. When you were having the good, you couldn't spare too much thought for those having the bad. It would be your turn soon enough.

CHAPTER TWENTY-ONE

During the night six divisions of infantry had to move into position in the assembly trenches, in an area with few roads – and what there were, narrow and unsuited to heavy traffic. Movement was wearyingly slow, with frequent long and usually unexplained stops. The Kents did not get into position until after three in the morning, having shuffled along cobbled roads in the rain and stumbled across country through mud for eight hours. Given the general degree of fed-upness prevailing over their slow progress, Ned mentioned to his men that those who had got into position first had had to squat all night in a trench that was slowly filling with water. There was nothing like the misfortune of others to cheer up the average Tommy.

Ned sent his sergeant along the line to check the equipment of each man in his platoon once more, to make sure nothing had been lost – or jettisoned – on the journey. Each man carried, as well as his rifle, two extra bandoliers of ammunition and, instead of the pack, a haversack containing two days' rations, with an entrenching tool pushed down behind it. Gas masks were worn in the ready, rolled-up position. The winds had not been wholly favourable for a gas attack – very light, and tending to veer about between the south and the south-west – so General Haig would have to decide at the last minute whether to go ahead with it.

Just before dawn the colonel gave the 'up spirits' order, and two sergeants went along the top of the trench with a rum jar and a tin mug, giving each man a tot of neat rum to warm him up. The army allowed a ration of a tot a day per man, when the commanding officer thought the weather inclement. Fortunately, most colonels reckoned the weather was always inclement. But rumour travelled like wildfire along the trenches that morning that the colonel of the Camerons, who had religious convictions, had declared that if his men were going to meet their Maker that day they should not meet Him with liquor on their breath. He had ordered the precious stuff poured away, and the Camerons hadn't tasted a single drop. The horrifying story made the Kents feel so much better about their own circumstances that they were quite cheerful as they sat in the mud in the dark, listening to the British guns making the night tremble.

The battle was to be fought along a front of about four miles, from Auchy in the north to the outskirts of Lens in the south. The German and British lines were very close to each other, in places no more than sixty yards apart. The battlefield itself was a mixture of farmland – untended now since the summer of 1914 and run raggedly to seed – and coal workings. There were quarries and chalk pits here and there, and the pits' slag heaps, which were described on the maps either as *fosses* or *crassiers*, were like strange-shaped hills and ridges, as big as natural features, and plain to the naked eye.

On the British side, the village of Vermelles sat in the centre behind the line, with narrow country roads radiating from it like the spokes of half a wheel, across the German trenches to Auchy in the north, to Hulluch in the centre, and through Loos to Lens in the south. The main Béthune to Lens road ran parallel to the latter, bypassing Loos; and where each of these crossed the German line, the enemy had constructed a mighty redoubt, named on maps the Lens Road Redoubt, and the Loos Road Redoubt.

In the centre of the German line was a feature marked Lone Tree; in the north was the Hohenzollern Redoubt; and behind the Germans, the view was defined by a north-south ridge that carried the Lens to La Bassée road. But the most noticeable feature of the whole battlefield was in the south just beyond the village of Loos. Here the superstructure of some pit workings rose clear of the buildings, etched stark and black against the sky: twin pylons linked by a long iron walkway, the whole thing looking so familiar to anyone who had ever been to London that it had been named Tower Bridge.

The plan was to let out the gas at five fifty a.m., and for the infantry attack to go in at six thirty: it was important to allow forty minutes, because the Germans' gas masks were effective for thirty minutes, after which they had to be retreated with the neutralising chemicals. But at five fifty the wind was still light and variable. In some places the gas could be seen to drift over the German line and dip into the trenches; in other places it veered back towards the British line. Where this happened the gas officers ordered the vents closed and used smoke candles instead.

And at six thirty, whistles blew all up and down the line, and the first wave went over.

The Kents were in the second wave, behind the Camerons, on the right wing. On their right, the gas had rolled back and engulfed the 47th Division just as the whistles sounded. Smoke and gas obscured the view entirely, and the King's Own had to go over blind, encouraged by the wail of bagpipes: some doughty piper must have pulled off his gas mask at the peril of his own life to play the defiant music.

'Mad buggers, the Jocks,' Ned heard his sergeant, Wibley, mutter. Into the white veil, pierced with orange flashes, the King's disappeared to where the stammer of machine-guns told them the Germans were waiting.

In front of the Kents, things were easier. The wind was stronger, and blowing in the right direction; and the artillery had done its work in silencing the two redoubts. The Camerons went howling over at exactly six thirty, and Ned gave the order that sent his men scrambling forward into the trenches they had vacated. The trenches were deeply mired where the rain that had fallen during the night had been churned in by the passage of feet into the consistency of thick porage. They settled in, waiting for the signal, tension running like silver threads, binding them all together in this mad adventure. Ned looked down the line and saw every face set, not with fear but with grim determination. He thought of the Camerons going over without their tot of spirits, thought how wild that must have made them, and he grinned to himself. There was no excuse for the Kents not to do well!

'Ready, lads. Any minute now. We'll take anything the Jocks have left us,' he called. One or two of them looked round and grinned at him. His servant, Daltry, was at his elbow, so close he could hear his breathing, whistling at his ear. The signal came down the line. Ned blew his whistle, shouted, 'Come on!' and went up the ladder.

They ran out into no man's land. There were dead men lying sprawled on every side. A few steps from the parapet, Ned almost stepped on a Cameron who was lying flung on his back, face to the sky, a glistening red crater where the middle of his body should be, the edges of it still smoking. The Germans must be using small bombs. He jumped over the Jock without breaking stride. Beside him, one of his men, Kipps, was yelling like a madman; to the other side, Skinner fell like a stone, most of his head missing, and Ned hadn't even heard the explosion. He shouted, 'Come on!' again, and ran on towards the guns.

On the far left wing, in front of Auchy, the gas had blown back over the British line and, combined with heavy German shelling and machine-gun fire, had prevented any advance. To the right of that, the gas had gone forward, and the troops had successfully stormed the Hohenzollern Redoubt and reached the slag-heap beyond, where they were holding on, awaiting reinforcements; but to their right again, across the centre of the line, before Hulluch and at Lone Tree, the British were pinned down. The artillery barrage had failed, even after three days, to cut the wire, and the first wave had come up against it and been cut down. Unable to get forward, they had been sitting ducks for the German machine-gun and shell-fire. Whole companies had been wiped out.

But on the far right wing, though the reversal of the gas cloud had hampered the 47th Division so severely they had been beaten back with heavy casualties, the second wave had gone in, and the 47th had rallied and taken the German front line, the Double Crassier, and had reached the outskirts of Loos. Here they had been ordered to dig in and form a defensive flank for the centre. The plan was for the far left wing to do the same, and eventually for the two wings to swing inwards, like hinges. The left wing, however, had failed to break the German line at all, so there was no question of further manoeuvre from them.

The greatest success was on the centre right, where the 15th Division had been lucky with the gas, which had blown straight at the Germans. The Camerons, in the first wave, had attacked with such wild ferocity they had carried the front and the support German lines, before the second wave – in which the Kents were fighting – had even left the trenches. The attack went forward in fine style, hunting the fleeing Germans through the village of Loos and out the other side, and on up Hill 70, part of the ridge along which the Lens to La Bassée road ran. By nine in the morning, the Camerons had overrun the redoubt there, taken the hill, and were chasing the Germans down the other side.

But in the confusion of battle, things began to go wrong. The divisions that reached the ridge were intended to go straight over it on a wide front, and down the other side to attack the German defensive second line, which ran between the village of Hulluch and the Cité St Auguste. Despite its grand name, the latter was no more than a huddle of mine workings and pitmen's cottages, which the Germans had incorporated into their defences.

But the Germans fleeing over Hill 70 had not run eastwards, but southwards; not towards the Cité St Auguste but towards the Cité St Laurent, which was part of the suburbs of Lens, and very heavily fortified and invested by the enemy.

The Camerons, their blood up, raced after them, and the units that should have been alongside, veered and went after them. The whole attack had swung south in a disastrous direction; and the officers were unaware of the mistake. All the landmarks they were familiar with were now behind them, and with the unknown before them, the change of direction was not apparent to them. They sent back signals to Headquarters to say they were advancing on Cité St Auguste according to plan.

The Germans at St Laurent held fire until the men were only two hundred yards away, then opened up. The Camerons were on bare open ground; there was no shelter of any sort. They were cut down by every sort of fire, and those who survived could only lie down flat, press themselves into the earth, and pray. They waited for the artillery bombardment that should have supported the second phase of the attack, which would give them relief and, if it did not allow them to advance, would at least cover their retreat. But the signal had gone back that they were advancing on St Auguste, and when the barrage began, that was where the guns were aimed.

When the Kents reached Hill 70, there were fewer of them than before: their dead were scattered among the tartan tide of the fallen that marked the Camerons' passage from the British front line across no man's land, through Loos and up the hill. It was their fortune that they arrived on the hill shortly after Colonel Sandilands, the Camerons' commanding officer. With the benefit of field-glasses and a calmer frame of mind, he saw that his men were going the wrong way, and managed to halt the suicidal charge of those who were following.

There were men from nine different battalions on Hill 70 now, and very few officers. When Ned paused to take stock, he found he had about fifteen of his own platoon with him, along with Sergeant Wibley, who was wounded, though not seriously: shrapnel had shredded his left sleeve and he had a long, deep cut from wrist to elbow and several shallower cuts on his upper arm. But he had wound his field-bandage round the deep cut, and the other cuts had already caked, and he said they weren't troubling him. The rest of the Kents were considerably mixed up with other uniforms, but they had already started sorting themselves out and rallying to their comrades. A scan of the immediate area suggested there were around a hundred and fifty of them in all; but Ned could not see any other officers.

He left Wibley in charge and went to make himself known to Colonel Sandilands. He gave a brief report on what forces he believed were left. Sandilands listened, and seemed unsurprised by anything Ned had to tell him.

'The only officer, hey? You must take charge, then,' he told him. 'Until and unless a more senior officer makes his appearance, you will command the surviving men of your battalion. We are going to dig in here, on the reverse side of the hill, until reinforcements arrive and we can renew the attack.' He told Ned briefly how the Camerons had charged in the wrong direction. 'We can expect a counter-attack from the enemy – they're massing in Lens even now – but we will do our damnedest to hang on here. We will not lightly give up what my men have purchased so dearly.'

He pointed out where Ned should dispose his men and told him to start them digging in. Ned said, 'Yes, sir,' and turned away. The weight of responsibility settled heavily on him. From lieutenant this morning to 'colonel' of the Kents before lunchtime, a counter-attack expected, and he was not even a proper soldier, only a volunteer. He prayed briefly but fervently that some other officer would turn up to take the burden from him. But then he thought that Sandilands had a much harder task. The muddle on the hill was considerable, and he had to sort it out and try to hold the position with what Ned calculated was no more than a thousand men – the strength of a single battalion. And meanwhile his own men, the Camerons, were lying out under fire before Cité St Laurent, their numbers shrinking all the time. For them Sandilands could do nothing. His heart, Ned thought, must be breaking.

* * * *

506

At Headquarters in Hinges, Sir Douglas Haig received the news that the first part of the attack had been successful: the German line had been broken, Loos had been taken, and the troops were pressing forward at considerable pace. It was necessary now to bring up the reserves, pour more and more men through the gap, and give the advance the impetus to drive the Germans out of their second line of defence. He sent an urgent request to Sir John French that the reserves should be put into the line at once.

Sir John was reluctant to do so. The reserve was very small, only three divisions, and they were the last spare men he had. Moreover, they were raw troops just out from England and their officers had no battle experience. He doubted they would be able to achieve much, and might even be a hindrance on the battlefield, merely adding to confusion and being wastefully cut down for no purpose. He had promised the commanders of the three divisions that they would not be sent in until and unless the Germans were absolutely smashed and on the run. They could join in pursuing a rout, but they would not be committed to a full battle.

But Haig's message did say that the enemy line had been broken and that his army was advancing at speed, which was pretty much the sort of circumstances French had agreed on, so at half past ten he gave the order.

It took a long time to reach all the scattered battalions, spread out behind the line in billets and bivouacs. Bertie's battalion received it at around eleven, but there were others further away than the West Herts. They formed up and marched out, but the journey to the Front was frustratingly slow. It had been hard enough for the first-wave troops to get into position because of the weight of traffic, but it was even worse now. The roads were so narrow that the men could only walk four abreast, and they were constantly having to break rank and squeeze to the side to let transport through. Supply wagons, ammunition wagons, messengers' motor-bicycles, staff cars and countless ambulances all helped to choke the roads and held up the reserves; and when they had to leave the roads and go across country it was no better. A night and half a day of rain and the passage of so many feet, wheels and hoofs had turned every field in the vicinity into a boot-clutching, exhausting morass of mud.

As the West Herts neared Vermelles, they could hear the guns pounding away, which cheered the men somewhat, as did the sight of gangs of German prisoners being escorted back – though the latter were somewhat balanced by the huge number of walking wounded dragging wearily by. It was late afternoon now: it had taken them six hours to cover six miles.

They were turned into a field behind the village and waited there for specific orders. They were long in coming. The men huddled together, muttering, and starting whenever a German shell crashed anywhere near. They'd had nothing since breakfast, so Bertie told his men to take the opportunity to eat something out of their battle rations. If they were to go into action soon, he thought, better they did so with some food inside them. It was only bully and biscuit, washed down with water, but it was better than an empty stomach.

At last their new colonel, Webster, appeared, and called the company commanders together. 'I have our orders, but I'm afraid they're pretty vague,' he said. 'Even Division admits it doesn't know quite what's going on out there, so we shall have to adapt to circumstances as we find them. We're to advance on Hill 70. This is it – here. And we're here.' He had opened out a map and with two of them holding the edges he pointed out the features marked on it. 'This is Loos – it seems we took that this morning. This is Lens – Fritz has that and it's heavily defended. Now, I don't know what we're going to find when we get to Hill 70. The fifteenth Division took it this morning but nobody knows if they still have it. So our orders are these: if the Germans hold the hill, we attack. If our chaps have it, we support them. And if there's no-one there, we dig in and wait for further orders.'

The captains started away back to their companies. Fenniman fell in beside Bertie for a time. 'Short and sweet,' he said. He looked around in the fading light, further obscured by smoke. It would be getting dark soon. 'Pleasant way to spend the evening. I love these little *soirées* of ours, don't you?'

'Keep a dance for me, you saucy wench,' Bertie responded, with a grin.

'On a serious note, how do we find this blasted hill?'

'Follow the road, I suppose,' said Bertie. 'What else can we do?'

'Do you mean the road that's being shelled by the Germans even as we speak?'

'The very same.'

'Ah, me. A short life and a merry.'

'It'll be a full moon tonight,' Bertie reminded him.

'Helpful for finding one's way,' Fenniman admitted, 'but also helpful for any unfriendly chaps trying to spot us, the better to blow off our heads.'

'Think of Ypres,' Bertie said persuasively. 'Things could be a lot worse.'

They were nearing the men now, and they could see how the short rest and the bite to eat had restored them. They looked excited at the prospect of action. Bertie noted a couple of them examining the Mills bombs they'd been issued with, grinning as though they were new toys they'd got from under the Christmas tree. He pointed it out to Fenniman.

'Silly devils,' Fenniman snorted, but with affection.

'War is softening you, Fen, old man,' said Bertie. 'When I first met you at Sandridge, you were so superior you hardly noticed ordinary mortals existed.'

'God, dear old Sandridge! How far away it all seems!' He looked suddenly bleak. 'Not many of us left. There's the Col gone – good old Abernethy. He was a decent sort.' The colonel had died of his wounds back in England during the winter. 'And Penkers – first-rate adj. The whole blessed battalion that marched out with us, bar a few friendly faces.'

'But we're still here, old man, bright and beautiful. Never forget that.'

'How do you stay so blasted cheerful?' Fenniman asked him suspiciously.

'I'll tell you my secret after the war,' Bertie promised, and went to his men.

The Germans counter-attacked from Lens just after noon. The few remaining Camerons lying out between Lens and the hill scrambled away and fled before them, but most were either killed or captured as the Germans overran them. On the hill, in the hastily dug trenches, the mixed force held on and fought off the attack, but was gradually pushed back, out of the trenches and then out of the redoubt they had held since nine that morning. But, in between the German salvos, they could hear, further off to the south, the sound of French guns: Joffre's attack was going in at last at Vimy Ridge. The sound was a welcome relief, for now the Germans were under attack on two fronts. It soon became apparent that they must have sent their reserves to strengthen the line against the French, rather than use them at Loos, for there was no general assault from the second defensive line. The British survivors were pushed back off the hill, but were able to hold on to the high ground to the north of it: they were not overcome. Now if they could stand fast until re-inforcements arrived, they could still push forward. And soon it would be night, and they might hope for a little respite.

The West Herts were at last marching up the road towards Loos. It must have come as a terrible shock to the lads just out of England to see for the first time what battle was really like. The noise was terrible, for the Germans were shelling the road and the whole area relentlessly, and the bombs burst with a terrible crash, sending lethal shrapnel whirling among them. The first time a man was hit and fell, there was a little flurry of those nearest him, whose instinct was to stop and help him. But the NCOs were on hand to drive them on, with 'Leave him. You can't help him,' and 'No breaking ranks, there!'

Bertie called, 'Steady, lads, steady. Eyes ahead.' The fours

510

re-formed and marched on. Bertie had spread his few seasoned soldiers about his company, and they adding a bracing of indifference to fire – real or assumed from pride, it didn't matter which.

It wasn't only the noise and explosions and the whirling shrapnel that were upsetting: all along the road, on both sides and sometimes even underfoot, there were dead men and dead officers; and dying ones too; and dead and dying horses. But after the first few horrified stares, the first involuntary flinching at the sight of the blood and spilled intestines and terrible wounds, the men kept their eyes front and marched on.

'That's my lads!' Bertie called out to them, proud of their steadiness. The traditions of the regiment, and their determination to stand well in each other's eyes, braced them against the terrible realities. 'You'll get your chance at the Bosch soon enough. We'll show 'em what West Herts men can do!' And the men held their heads up a little more, and set their faces as grimly as they could. Even little Langley, who was certainly under age, and had begun weeping with pity at the first pair of dead horses, stuck his nose in the air and stamped his feet down belligerently in an attempt to stop the tears seeping out from his eyes.

When they reached Loos they were stopped by a staff officer who gave them fresh orders: that they were to hold the village itself. There were dead lying everywhere – large numbers of Scots; and Bertie saw some Kents, too, and wondered briefly and pointlessly about Ned. They had been through here some time this morning; God only knew where they were now. The dead also included a cheering number of Germans; but there were one or two civilians, too, who must have been hiding in cellars all this time. The village was much the worse for wear. Shells were falling on it all the time, knocking great chunks out of buildings, as easily as if they were fruit cake, and sending the debris crashing among them, some buildings rumbling down entirely. The West Herts got themselves spread out and into position, to hold the village against the attacking Germans who had come down the road from Lens and were setting themselves up across the road to retake Loos. Firing at the enemy at last was the best settling medicine for the men. It made them feel like soldiers rather than helpless victims, and though they got barely a glimpse of the enemy, they rattled away steadily and looked more comfortable.

Darkness came on, but then the rain stopped, the sky began to clear, and a vast yellow moon came sailing out into the clear dark water between the cloud islands. The shelling, which had slackened off for a while, intensified again in the bright moonlight, and eventually became intolerable. The West Herts were forced to pull back and leave the village before they were all buried or blasted to bits.

In the early hours of the morning a new line was forming just the other side of the village, and Bertie's company were given a field and told to dig in and hold it. And there, under the bright moonlight, they stayed. Bertie ate a few mouthfuls of ration bully and biscuit brought to him by Cooper, and took a welcome gulp of whisky from his flask – though he would have traded it gladly for a cup of tea. He went along his line, checked with his NCOs and subalterns, scribbled his notes, and then lay down in the driest place he could find under a hedge and tried to sleep for an hour. As an experienced soldier, he could usually drop off anywhere, but perhaps the moon disturbed him. At all events, he lay wakeful, looking at its bright light through the mesh of branches, and listening to the booming of the guns. It was good, he thought, that they were in action at last. Things had gone well today, by all accounts, and tomorrow they should be able to press home the attack and put the Germans to flight. He longed for home, but home could only come with victory; therefore it was good that he was in action again.

When dawn began to break on Sunday the 26th, the clouds had come back, and a fine drizzle was falling, so fine it was almost like mist. Ned turned his face up into it and tried to collect enough on his tongue to assuage his thirst. There was a little water left in his bottle, but he wanted to save it as long as possible, not knowing when there would be any more. No food had come up the night before – he doubted that anyone even knew where they were, and if they did, the chances of reaching them were minuscule – but most of the men still had the remains of their battle rations, and without being asked they shared what they had among those who had lost them.

During the previous afternoon, as they had been pushed off the hill, a certain amount of reorganisation had happened. Some more troops had come up, and the unplanned bunching that had gone on in the first heady charge had been rectified, pushing the men northwards across a wider front. Now the surviving Kents were dug in across a field, on the eastern side of the Lens to La Bassée road, and to the north of a strip of plantation, called Bois Hugo on the maps. The west end of the wood came up to the road; the east end reached almost to the German defensive second line. Ned felt nervous of that. It would be all too easy for the Huns to slip into the wood and creep along it, outflanking them. He ordered a strict watch to be kept, and positioned his last remaining machine-gun on that side.

He was still in charge. No other officers had appeared. The whole of the previous day now seemed completely dreamlike – a mad, distorted dream of the sort one might have while in a fever. Had he really been there, done those things, witnessed those scenes? It all seemed impossible. He remembered the battle at Neuve Chapelle better: at least there had been some sense to it. Now he had only a hazy idea of where he was – he had been *told* the trees to his right were Bois Hugo, but they might just as well not have been – and no idea at all what would happen in the hours to come.

During the night a battalion of Northamptons had come up on the left of him and dug themselves in, which had been a comforting thought. But at first light he sent out a patrol, who came back with the news that the Northamptons had gone.

'I think they've pulled back, sir,' said Blean, whom he had made acting corporal. 'We saw some movement on the other side o' the road, but we didn't like to get closer, case they thought we was the Bosch, sir, and fired at us. But there's no-one out to the left of us, no-one at all.'

Ned nodded, as if it wasn't of much importance. He knew everything depended on the men's feeling confident. But it seemed as though his small force was 'up in the air', on the wrong side of the road and hundreds of yards in front of the new line.

At Hinges, Headquarters staff had worked all night trying to make sense of the reports that had come in, and to plot on the map where the troops actually were. Though there were one or two worrying gaps, everyone had got forward, and now on the left wing the British line ran close to the German defensive second line, wavering back and forth over the Lens to La Bassée road. In the centre it made a curve, running along the road as far as Chalet Wood, then bending round in front of Loos; and on the right wing there was a very stout section of line around the Double Crassier. Once the reserves had been got up, plugged the gaps between the three sections, and re-inforced the weak places, the whole front could renew the assault, take the German defensive second line, and put them to flight. But first, and most importantly, Hill 70 had to be retaken.

Orders began to filter slowly through to the units in the field. The bombardment was to resume at eight o'clock, then Hill 70 was to be taken, and then the whole front was to advance. Messengers did their best, but it was hard to know where anyone was. Some of the reserve had not reached the battlefield until after dark, and had had to struggle across a strange country with no landmarks, over roads that were barely tracks, clogged with a mass of other movements. It was something of a miracle if they got to the right place by morning. As for the units that had been in the field the day before, the runners could do no more than go to their last reported site, and if they weren't there, ask if anyone had seen them.

Orders reached the West Herts as they waited in their shallow trenches across the field beside Loos. The village was little more than a jumble of debris now, and Tower Bridge had taken a pounding from the shells during the night, so that it looked frayed and frail, loose girders and iron rods dangling and swaying in the breeze that drove the fine, soaking drizzle in sheets across the view. Colonel Webster called his officers together and told them they were to attack Hill 70 that morning. 'The remnant of the fifteenth Division should be there, but their commander has said they aren't fit to renew the attack. So we're going in. We follow the Northumberlands and the East Yorks.' The map was consulted again, but it was hard to make any sense of it in relation to the featureless and ruined terrain that was all they could glimpse through the rain. There were tracks on the ground that weren't marked on the map, and tracks on the map there was no hope of distinguishing on the ground. 'All we know,' said Webster apologetically, 'is that the hill is in *that* direction. I dare say it will become apparent when we see it. In any case, we shall have the other two battalions in front of us. Do your best, gentlemen. It is essential we take that hill.'

The officers went back to their men to pass on the orders; and as they were walking back, the bombardment started. It was eight o'clock.

All over England, the newspapers arrived on Sunday morning with thick black headlines screaming, 'REAL VICTORY AT LAST!'

At Morland Place, when Jessie came down to breakfast Uncle Teddy lowered the paper he had been devouring, beamed at her and cried, 'They've been fighting at Loos!' Her heart lurched at the word, and she came faltering towards the table.

He went back to the paper and read triumphantly, '"German line pierced in two places," it says here. Two

515

places! We took twenty thousand unwounded prisoners and thirty-three guns! "The British have advanced two and a half miles on a five-mile front south of La Bassée." We said that was where it was going to come off, didn't we? By Jove, this is first rate!'

Jessie helped herself to coffee and sat down, listening in silence as Teddy read out bits from the paper. The official communiqué from St Omer naturally did not give much detail, but the newspaper passed on what there was and speculated generously about what it meant and what the implications might be. The known facts, Jessie thought, trying to get a grip through the numbness of her mind, seemed to be that the German front line had been broken, the reserves were being brought up, and that the generals believed they would smash the second line today.

There was a great deal of conversation on the subject as each person in succession came down to breakfast, and the meal extended itself dangerously close to church-time. The map was got out and spread across the toast crumbs to be pored over and stabbed at, with 'There – that's where they'll be making a stand,' and 'I believe it must mean *here*.'

But Jessie could not join in the excited talk, and her family kindly left her alone to her thoughts. They were fighting yesterday, she thought, and they'll be fighting again today. The contemplation of a battle to come some time in the future was different from the sure and certain knowledge of a battle in the real, actual present. *They might be dead already*, came the hateful thought. She tried to shake it away, but it was the truth, wasn't it? Her husband and the man she loved: their frail human flesh had been exposed to flying shrapnel and machine-gun bullets, to gas and explosives. How could flesh withstand such things? They might even now be dead and stiffening out on some bleak and nameless field. She had no way of knowing. She must simply wait until word came, one way or the other. Her brain felt swollen and stiff; it was hard to pass thoughts through it, like trying to swallow with a sore throat. Alive or dead? She tried to remember the last thing she had said to each of them, because, if they were dead, it would be the last thing she would ever say to them. Why had she not made more of it when they were there? Looked at them, listened to them, appreciated them more – sucked every last drop out of the moment while it lasted? The truth was that you couldn't live like that: the part of your brain that knew what the future might bring could not hold sway for very long at a time. You would go mad if it did: your reason would snap like a rotten twig and leave you gibbering. But knowing that didn't make any difference.

How many had been killed? The newspapers had no figures. She wanted to know the bloody total, so that she could guess what the odds were for her own two. It was chance, Bertie had told her more than once; purely chance whether the bullet hit you or the man next to you. But the larger the casualty figures, the likelier it was that—

She made a strange moaning sound in her throat and shocked herself, put her hands to her face and looked round. No-one had noticed, except Henrietta, who had just got up to fetch herself more coffee. She paused by Jessie and laid a hand gently on her shoulder, and Jessie covered it with her own.

'We just have to wait,' Henrietta said, low, so that only Jessie heard it. 'Wait and pray.'

But how can I pray? Jessie thought. How can I say to God, 'Let it be someone else, not him?'

Her mother's touch had comforted her, just a little. But still she felt that she would be waiting all alone, in an ice-bound black place, for the eternity that would have to pass before news came – one way or the other. *Let them be all right*, she cried inwardly, and it was not so much a prayer as an invocation to older, darker gods, whose power was in the rocks and in the earth's fire. She could not ask the Christian God of reason, for she had no reason to offer in return.

The barrage lasted an hour, and was lifted at nine o'clock for the attack to go in. At nine o'clock the men in the trenches before Hill 70 scrambled over the top and went running up the slope towards the Germans, cheering madly. The Germans did not respond until the British troops were almost upon them, and then they opened up. Machine-gun fire like metal hail swept back and forth across the masses, and men stumbled, men fell, hundreds of them. It was 'dead ground'. The survivors flung themselves flat, and then began to crawl, trying to get back to the safety of the trenches.

The West Herts arrived in time to form part of the second wave. Bertie took his men over at about half past nine, and they ran like eager dogs with him, mouths wide with the excitement. The guns opened up again.

There were Northumberlands mixed up with Bertie's men, and he thought for a moment of how at the races riderless horses will keep going with the others, rather than be alone. The man in front of him – no more than a boy, really – lost the side of his head in a spray of bone and blood, and fell sideways into Bertie's path, making him lurch to the right and almost fall. He felt a vicious bang on his head, and putting his hand up, brought it away covered in blood. It was only a scalp wound, but it bled freely, and he had to get his handkerchief out to wipe his face, and then tie it round his brow to stop the blood dripping into his eyes. He reflected that if the soldier had not tripped him, the bullet would have got him smack through the forehead and killed him. Chance, just mad chance.

Despite their losses, they were able to reach the German trenches this time, and jumped down with screams of maddened triumph to stab and batter the grey men down. More troops were coming up behind them, and Bertie yelled to his men and waved them forward. They swung the ladders across and scrabbled up the parados as the new wave jumped down from the parados.

Out in the open again, Germans fleeing before them, and up ahead Hill 70 Redoubt. More trenches round its base, and machine-gun slits in all four sides, commanding the whole hill. How in hell had the Camerons taken it that morning? It was impregnable. They lay down and fired, got up and stumbled forward a little, lay down again. But their numbers were shrinking, and even these untried boys must be able to see that the redoubt could not be taken this way. The next time they dropped down, some began to crawl back. The next wave coming behind them were also green troops, and seeing more and more of the West Herts wriggling their way back, they wavered, then began to turn round. Soon they were all in retreat, back to the blessed safety of the trenches they had taken, where to crouch in the mud among the dead and mutilated seemed like blessed sanity after the hell of German strafing.

Ned and his men had been forgotten – or possibly, he thought, not having heard from them for so long, the top brass thought they were all dead. It occurred to him that he ought to send word back. As a lieutenant, it had not previously been his duty to report to HQ but, now he was the 'colonel', he realised belatedly that he ought to tell someone where he was. He sent for Blean, who had been his runner before, and scribbled a note on a page torn out of his notebook. 'Take that to Headquarters, wait and bring back fresh orders.'

'But how will I find Headquarters, sir?' he asked helplessly.

'*I* don't know, man,' Ned snapped, then pulled himself together and said more gently, 'Keep going in that direction, and then ask someone. Do your best, and use your wits. I've written our position – as far as I know it – on the paper. Come back here when you have something to bring.'

Blean went away; and shortly afterwards the Germans appeared, running up the slope through the misty rain, grey against grey. His men were ready. He hardly had to order them to fire. The Germans were taken by surprise, obviously not having realised there were men so far forward. Many died; others fell prone and started firing back. Over to the left, they jumped down into the trenches vacated by the Northumberlands during the night; but they did not stay there. They might have outflanked and surrounded the

Kents, but their orders must have been to attack the line on the other side of the road, for they soon climbed out and ran on.

The Germans in front of them went on firing, but they were in an exposed position, and eventually they started to fall back. It was only a temporary respite. More came up the slope, another wave sweeping towards them. Ned put extra men at the left end of the trench to protect their flank, and the Kents fired and reloaded steadily, thinning the German ranks considerably. This was what they knew. Even the youngsters were steadied by it: it much more resembled the training they had done back home than anything else they had experienced so far.

But Ned knew their position was not tenable. The enemy was behind them now as well, though they did not seem to be bothering about them yet. But sooner or later they would be outflanked and surrounded, and then either they would be slaughtered or they would have to surrender. He did not want to die, and he did not want to spend the rest of the war rotting in a German gaol. But what to do? What orders to give, and when? How to choose the right moment? He wished there were someone else! He was just a lieutenant – he couldn't make those sorts of decisions.

He shook himself. He *must* decide. All these men depended on him – and there were fewer of them all the time.

'Sir,' Daltry said warningly, at his ear. Ned turned to look. There were men in grey filtering through the trees of Bois Hugo. Ned's stomach chilled at the sight. Now they were on three sides of them.

Sergeant Wibley was there too. 'Maybe we ought to fall back, sir,' he said tentatively.

Bless him for making it look like Ned's decision! 'What do you suggest, Sergeant?' he said, as calmly as he could. It came out as a languid drawl. Good!

'Through the end of the wood, sir, while we can,' Wibley said quickly, gesturing. 'Can't go left, and we don't know what's behind us now. Through the wood before Fritz gets

520

up this far, and back to Hill 70. That's where everybody was, last time we saw 'em, and there's been sounds of fighting from that direction.'

'Good plan. Start getting the men away at once. You lead them, Wibley, and I'll take the rearguard. We'll keep the machine-gun and cover you.'

Wibley met his eyes. The rearguard's was the most dangerous position and they both knew it. 'Let me take the rearguard, sir,' he urged.

Ned shook his head, turning a little away so that the men would not hear what he said. 'You're more experienced than me. You've a better chance of getting the men away safely.' Wibley opened his mouth to protest further, and Ned said quietly but firmly, 'That's my order, Sergeant.'

Wibley shut his mouth again. He was too good a soldier to argue with an officer in the presence of so many other ranks. 'Yessir,' he said.

At eleven o'clock the Germans began bombarding the western slope of Hill 70, which they had not been able to do before, for fear of hitting their own men. But as the shells began to fall, the remnant of the attacking forces, pinned down in their trenches before the Hill 70 Redoubt, knew there could be no further hope of taking it. The hill was lost; but the rest of the plan might still be implemented. The idea had been to take the hill then link up with the troops on the left and sweep down from the ridge onto the German second line.

Messages went back and forth between the commanders in the field, and action was agreed. Troops were redistributed carefully to stiffen the line. The West Herts were taken out of their trench on the hill and moved north to a place on the line between Chalet Wood and Bois Hugo. There was firing coming from away on their left, where other troops were already engaged with the Germans. Bertie went down his line, checking on his men. On reaching the end of his section, he found the next men in line were in the uniform of the South Kents. A quick, startled glance told him there

521

were not many of them – perhaps a hundred, no more. Either they were lost, or they had taken heavy casualties.

'Where's your commanding officer?' he asked the nearest man.

'Dunno, sir,' he answered stupidly.

The man next to him, who seemed a little less dazed, said, 'All our officers was killed, sir, on the 'ill. There's only Mr Morland left.'

'Lieutenant Morland? Where is he?' Bertie asked eagerly. What a piece of luck! By God, what a piece of luck! He longed to shake Ned's hand.

'Back there, sir,' the man said, gesturing vaguely towards Bois Hugo. 'We was in the air, sir, and gettin' outflanked as well. So we had to make a run for it, sir, through the woods, and Mr Morland, 'e stopped be'ind, sir, with the rearguard, so's we could get away. I ain't seen 'im since.'

Bertie could not stay and talk longer, for his own duties were calling him. He scanned across the men's heads again, but could not see Ned; still, he might be there, even so. One man looked much like another when he was covered with mud and his face was streaked and grimed from battle. And they all wore the same caps. He might still be there. Bertie certainly hoped he was.

The fighting went on all day, all the way along the new line. Sometimes the line surged one way, sometimes the other. The Germans were beaten back and pursued by the British, leaping out of their trenches and running down almost to the German second line; but then the Germans would rally and the British would be beaten back. Neither side could quite overcome the other.

Ned had seen the last of his men away through the wood. With his rearguard party of ten and the machine-gun, he held the end of the trench, gradually falling back. They had accounted for a lot of Germans, but their numbers were shrinking. Tedder had been killed, and Dutton; and Field had fallen, shot in the chest, he thought, for he lay gasping like a landed fish, his eyes wide, his lips drawn back and bloody. They could not hold out for much longer without being overrun.

Finally Ned gave the order for the surviving few to make a run for it, staying himself to the last with Acres to cover them with the machine-gun, and if possible to get it away – it was too heavy for one man to carry at the run. The men scrambled out of the trench and ran towards the wood, while Ned and Acres laid a burst of fire to distract the enemy. But there were too many Germans – too much German fire. Ned saw Winfield and Falmer go down. Eastry fell, but then got up and staggered on, and Falmer crawled on, dragging a leg. The other three were already into the trees. He and Acres clambered out, carrying the machine-gun between them.

And then a shell landed somewhere near, with a *crump* that made the ground lift under his feet, and sent him flying in a graceful arc, to hit the ground some distance away. His landing cracked his head dizzyingly and knocked the breath out of him, but urgency made him flail over onto his front and look around. There seemed to be firing coming from every direction, but some of it was ricochets off the trees. Daltry, flat on his front, came wriggling back towards him.

From a shell-hole a little way off Ned could hear Acres moaning.

'Sir, sir, are you hurt?' Daltry cried, reaching Ned with his hands.

Yes, he was, he realised now. Turning himself over had been possible only in the first moments of numbness. Now pain was coming, raging like a tidal wave into his body. His legs felt both cold and hot. Broken? he wondered. Ribs broken – he discovered that as he tried to reach down and touch his legs, and the pain stabbed his side. He seemed to have no trousers on. He remembered Sergeant Wibley's sleeve and guessed that his trouser legs had been ripped to shreds by the blast. His legs were wet with blood. He was lucky they were still there. Most of his tunic had gone, too. The blast had blown him out of his clothes.

'I can't go on,' he said to Daltry. 'Get yourself away and join the others.'

'No, sir! No, sir! I can't leave you.'

'You can send someone back for me when it's over.'

'I won't leave you here!'

'Private Daltry, you will obey orders,' Ned croaked, in as close an approximation of an officer's bark as he could manage.

Daltry got onto his hands and knees. He was weeping. They had been together a long time, and the bond between a gentleman and his man was strong. 'I'll come back for you,' he said.

'Go,' Ned said. 'For God's sake, run!'

Daltry scrambled up and ran stumbling away. Shells and bullets were still flying. Ned watched until Daltry was safely in the trees, and then contemplated the shell-hole where Acres was hidden. If he could get into it, he thought, it would give him some shelter. It was received wisdom that shells don't fall in the same place twice. Whether it was true or not, he didn't know. But he hadn't long. The Germans would be coming soon. God only knew why they hadn't already.

It was not many paces – an uninjured man would have jumped into it in a second – but for Ned it was a passage of agony that seemed to last minutes, and ended with such pain as he slipped over the side of the shell-hole that he could not help screaming.

Acres was lying sprawled on his back, moaning; his foot was gone. Ned could not move again, even to go and help him – he was greying out with pain – but he saw that Acres had the machine-gun with him: either he had kept hold of it, or it had fallen into the hole with him by chance.

He must have lost consciousness then, though he thought it was only for a moment; he roused to hear the sound of the Germans advancing. It was just possible that they might escape notice, lying there in the hole. He glared across at Acres, who was still moaning, and hissed, 'Acres! Shut up, man! They're coming! Shut up!'

Acres opened his eyes and looked across at Ned with the expression of a hurt child. 'Me foot,' he moaned. 'Buggers 've got me foot.'

'*Be quiet!*' He could hear the thumping feet and the German voices shouting, and there were rifle shots flying overhead.

Acres said something else, and then his face became fixed with amazement. He was staring at a German officer who had appeared at the lip of the hole.

'Bloody Bosch!' he shouted, and struggled to sit up, reaching automatically for the machine-gun. He tried to swing it round to aim it, but in the confines of the hole he got the muzzle caught in the earth wall and couldn't free it in time. The German officer was quicker. He snatched out his pistol and shot Acres in the chest, and then jumped over the hole and ran on.

Ned lay immobile in shock. The officer hadn't even looked at him. Acres had saved his life, at the cost of his own.

The waves of German infantry thundered past, and no-one else even glanced into his hole. Ned's head was beginning to swim, and his grip on consciousness was lapsing. The shell blast must have concussed him, he thought vaguely, and he was losing blood from his many cuts. He drifted away.

Nightfall came, and the British had failed to take the German defensive second line, despite ferocious fighting and heavy losses. The troops furthest forward had been forced to fall back, but the gaps had at least been filled in, and the line now ran in a strong salient from the Hohenzollern Redoubt up to the Lens to La Bassée road before Hulluch, along the line of the road as far as Bois Hugo, and then performing a double bend round the wrong side of Hill 70 and the right side of Loos to the Double Crassier. At its deepest point, the salient was a little over a mile from the original front line. Ground had been gained – not much, it was true, but the Germans had been beaten, their line broken, and just a little more luck, or a few extra men, might have done it.

525

In the dark, the wounded started to come back, and the men settled in to hold the trenches and to hope that hot food would be coming up soon. Bertie and his men were in a trench that ran along the edge of Chalkpit Wood, which at least gave them a little shelter from the wind. They had fought hard that day, and many of them had fallen. Those who were left were exhausted, but not unhappy. A dreamlike quiet was over them. Bertie knew they were not yet ready to mourn their friends, or even to think about them. At the moment they only knew they had done well, had done their duty, had fought and not run away. They had something to be proud of. They were not just men now, they were soldiers. *Blooded*, Bertie thought, with an inner smile.

He didn't think the action would be resumed tomorrow. Their side was simply not up to it, and he knew there were no more reserves. What condition the Germans were in he could not know, but he thought they had given them a good beating, and doubted they would want to come out and take them on again. But if they did attack – well, it was easier to defend in trench warfare than to attack. Let 'em come – they wouldn't get past.

Cooper sidled up to him with a flask. It wasn't his – that had been emptied some time back, when he had gone round the nearest wounded and given them each a mouthful to keep them going.

'What's this?' he asked.

'Captain Fenniman's compliments, sir,' Cooper said blandly, 'and if you'd be so kind, to drink a toast to a young lady.'

'Is he all right?' Bertie asked.

'Not a scratch, sir,' said Cooper.

Bertie felt himself lightened of a worry he had not yet had a chance to notice. Fen had come through. Thank God! He drank from the flask with a silent toast to Miss Weston, in accordance with orders, and handed the flask back to Cooper. 'Thank Captain Fenniman for me, and tell him I'll buy him dinner in Piccadilly next leave.'

'Yessir.'

Cooper went off; and Bertie thought inevitably of Ned. Did he make it? Or had he already gone west when he spoke to that Kent? He thought of Jessie, and wondered how much she would mind if it were bad news. She was awfully fond of old Ned. Well, everyone was. He was such a nice fellow. He hoped to God he was all right.

Cooper, who had not gone very far, came back. 'Just heard, sir – grub's on the way. Ten minutes or so. 'Ot stew, sir, so they say. And tea.'

'Tea? Thank God,' said Bertie.

The Germans were shelling again, pounding the area between the two lines, searching in the dark for the trenches of the enemy who had plagued them all day. They had plenty of shells to waste, and perhaps it relieved their feelings a little over that lost mile of land.

The sound woke Ned from a doze, and for a moment he did not know where he was. It was dark, and raining again. The rain told him he was out of doors, not in his cot in some billet or other. His head hurt unbelievably much, so that at first he did not feel any other pains. He had only the vaguest memory of what had happened. He remembered a German officer with a pistol: had he shot him? What had happened to his legs?

He was lying against the edge of a shell crater, his head just below the rim, his legs stretched out before him. There was mud and blood all over them. He remembered then that before it had got dark he had had a look at them. They were pretty cut about, and he didn't know if they were broken or only badly bruised. There was one deep cut that would not stop bleeding. He ought to have had a field-bandage about him somewhere, but most of his tunic had gone, so presumably the bandage had gone with it. In any case, he didn't seem to be able to move his body – or, at least, not without pain. After some thought he had gouged out a palmful of wet mud from beside him and thrown it onto the cut. Even such a jarring had woken his leg to agony;

527

but after a few handfuls the mud bandage had worked, and the bleeding had stopped. He wasn't sure, now, if he could move again. He didn't feel inclined to try.

If only his head did not hurt so much. On the other side of the shell-hole, he saw now, there was a man lying, minus a foot, the breast of his uniform bloody, a surprised look on his face. Ned felt he ought to know his name, but his head hurt too much. Was the man dead? Yes, he thought so. He wished he had closed his eyes when he'd died. He looked awfully as though he was going to say something.

A German with a pistol – he remembered that. There had been others. Yes, he remembered now, Germans everywhere. The fighting had raged back and forth around him. But no-one else had even looked down into the shell-hole. And eventually it started to grow dark and he had drifted into unconsciousness.

Now the guns had woken him. He couldn't tell which direction they were firing from, but he guessed it would be the Germans. It always was the Germans. They had so many shells, so much ammunition, they never had to worry about wasting it. He looked across at the man on the other side of the hole, and the man stared back at him. 'How are you feeling?' Ned asked him. He didn't answer. Perhaps he didn't speak English. *'Comment allez vous?'* he asked. The man said nothing.

Then he noticed something. Shouldn't there have been a machine-gun? He was sure there had been one before. He stared, looked all round the small crater, but there was nowhere a machine-gun could be hidden, even if anyone had wanted to hide it. There definitely had been one, he thought, working it out painfully against the reluctance of his mind to grip. It must have been taken – which meant someone had been here. While he was asleep. Presumably they thought he was dead too, like that poor devil, whatever his name was. What luck that he had been asleep, or the German might have shot him.

And then the rolling rocks of pain in his head parted for a moment, and a terrible clarity came upon him; and with

528

it, a terrible thought. Perhaps it had not been a German. Perhaps it had been a British soldier who had come, looked in the trench, seen two dead men, taken the machine-gun and gone away. Someone from his own side. Oh, God, God! They had thought him dead and he had missed them, missed his one chance to be rescued. Now they would never come back. The thought of them leaving him behind for dead filled him with despair. He found himself weeping, helpless, infant tears. Lost, abandoned, alone, he wept.

The tears stopped at last, and he drifted, in and out of the black pain of consciousness. He woke to a heavy sound. The shelling was coming closer. He could feel the ground trembling with each percussion. Old Fritz sending over some hate. He didn't want to think about that. He turned his mind away in search of comfort, away from guns and death and darkness, and there was . . . there was . . . yes, a woman. His woman. Ah, that was better! He almost smiled. Céline – her name was Céline. He saw her at a cottage gate, looking down the lane, waiting for news. She was waiting for him. 'And what do you think about *that*, old man?' he boasted to the man opposite. The man opened his eyes very wide: shocking, he thought it. '*Mais elle est tres belle,*' Ned told him, '*et petite, et douce. Gentille, enfin. La petite Céline.*' And he had said to her, *Je reviens.* Well, he *would* come back. He had promised, so he would. 'So you can stare all you like, but you won't change my mind.'

Oh, he was forgetting, the man didn't speak English. No-one spoke English. Those shells certainly didn't. They said *woof* and *crump* in a language all their own.

Closer now. And was it getting darker? He couldn't see the man opposite so clearly now. He tried to shake his head to clear his vision, but it hurt too much – black lumps of pain rolling around inside. He let it be still, his head, everything. Too weak to move anything now, anyway. Just lie still. Someone would come. Someone would, wouldn't they?

Fritz was laying down a pattern. He remembered it had been like that once before. At . . . at . . . at Neuve Chapelle.

That was the name. He must be at Neuve Chapelle. A pretty French name. The sky above him was a beautiful blue, and the sun was shining, and Céline beside him shone with it as though outlined in white radiance. There was a skylark up there, singing and singing as though the world were not ending all around it. He watched it fluttering against the blue sky, throbbing with song, as he explained to Céline how Fritz was dropping his shells along the line, each one ten yards further along. It was a pattern.

'But then,' she said in French, looking at him directly, such a clear, firm look, like an angel getting the facts straight before putting them in the ledger, 'but then, the next shell will hit us, will it not?'

'Not the next shell,' he explained clearly, 'but the one after next. You see?' The next one landed about ten yards away, but directly in line. He was spattered with soil and stones and a few sods from the explosion. 'And now the next will land right here, right where we are.'

'I see,' said Céline. 'Yes, that is very clear.'

Clear, like the clear blue sky. Yes, here it comes, he said. He stared up at the blue, and the tiny black speck of the skylark – or, no, perhaps it wasn't the skylark any more. It was something bigger and blacker and it was coming closer all the time. He could hear it screaming through the air, hurtling black like a locomotive, like a great black boulder. It's coming, he said. *Il arrive, Céline.* It's coming! IT'S COMING!

sphere

To buy any of our books and to find out more about Sphere and Little, Brown Book Group, our authors and titles, as well as events and book clubs, visit our website

www.littlebrown.co.uk

and follow us on Twitter

@BingetheBooks
@TheCrimeVault
@LittleBrownUK

To order any Sphere titles p & p free in the UK please contact our mail order supplier on:

+44 (0)1832 737525

Customers not based in the UK should contact the same number for appropriate postage and packing costs.

sphere

To buy any of our books and to find out
more about Sphere and Little, Brown Book Group,
our authors and titles, as well as events and
book clubs, visit our website

www.littlebrown.co.uk

and follow us on Twitter

@BtweentheSheets
@TheCrimeVault
@LittleBrownUK

To order any Sphere titles p & p free in the UK,
please contact our mail order supplier on:

+ 44 (0)1832 737525

Customers not based in the UK should contact
the same number for appropriate postage
and packing costs.